Small Fry

~~~

By
K.R. Smith
~~~

'Small Fry' is registered
in the Cataloguing-in-Publication (CiP)
under the Australian Copyright Act 1968.

isabeldesequera@gmail.com

neendoesbc@hotmail.com

ISBN: **978-0-646-93285-9**

Circulate Series by K.R. Smith
'Circulate' 1st ed. copyright © 2005

~ Acknowledgments ~

Thank you Nina Ackerman and Isabel de Sequera for your help in producing another cover for the Circulate Series. Thanks Neen for letting me pilfer another one of your fantastic photos and Iz for the glorious graphics. Muchas gracias to you both for your contribution and support.

I'd also like to thank my beta readers Hazel Yates and Jan Smith. Thank you for your feedback and most of all, for your help. I tried to turn gibberish into English and I couldn't have done it without your input.

Cheers Karen Thoms and Neralie Want for answering my questions about motherhood. From birthing, to breastfeeding, to pondering with Karen how to feed fresh kill to a baby born with sharp teeth; to Neralie lending me a stack of baby books. Thanks guys for helping the writer whose only maternal instincts involve keeping cats, rats, or sea monkeys.

~ Contents ~

~~~~~~~~

"The most dangerous animal is a mother protecting her young."

(Picard to Troi, Star Trek: The Next Generation)

~~~~~~~~

~ 1 ~

3rd November 2363

We sat at the dining table in a tense manner, nursing our coffees. Declan sat on one side as I sat on the other. Our legs jiggled nervously and I think together we stared into our beverages, rather than consumed them.

A thick silence filled the living room, as I sensed my husband was trying not to look at his wife whom he inadvertently impregnated.

Normally, a married couple may celebrate this sort of thing? But not when they were a 300 year old European Werewolf, who just had his elderly body reversed to his twenties by his 297 year old wife, who was called the Last Circulator. Now the said European Werewolf was a Circulator too, it put a new spin on things.

Not only was I a Circulator but I was the tribe's first female Lokoti Werewolf. We've been mates for 273 years and where he had aged slowly, I did not. He got to show off a youthful wife however, the drawback was that I couldn't breed. With my bio-electromagnetic field in temporal flux, it not only stopped me from aging but also reproducing.

Now that I've turned my elderly husband into a Circulator too; his sperm matched my eggs bio-electromagnetic frequency and then... ta daa!

"B...you're pregnant." Declan uttered in astonishment.

He immediately smelled the change in my hormones the morning after celebrating his transformation.

I growled in frustration, as I rubbed my face from stress which caused my long, dark hair to flop over my dark blue eyes. This made my mate look up sharply, with his bright blue eyes wide with concern. His previous white hair was back to his youthful, dark blonde colour and it looked particularly spiky this morning.

How could I have been so stupid? I knew the reason why I couldn't breed was because of the whole temporal flux/bio-electromagnetic frequency thing! Why didn't it 'click' inside my mind, before my newly-youthful husband, pounced on his always-youthful wife to celebrate his change?

I guess Declan decided to take affirmative action, or try to get a grip on our situation.

He took a deep breath before he spoke, "OK, so you're pregnant."

I gave him an unimpressed look for stating the obvious.

"Shut up." He smirked at my expression. "But let's come up with a plan of attack, instead of sitting here in shock like a bomb's gone off."

"What plan of attack?" I said unhappily. "We're not planning a battle against a coven of European Vampires."

"You're 24 hours pregnant, B." He frowned. "24 hours means it's still just a bunch of cells inside of you." I gave him a peculiar look, wondering what he was trying to say? He went on, "Remember our first time together?"

"It may have been 279 years ago Dec, but yeah. I still remember our first time." I said dryly.

"Right." He cleared his throat. "Then do you remember what happened right after it? What I did to you?"

Abruptly I straightened, as if he had thrown a glass of icy water my way. "No, you don't mean...?"

"I'm 300 years old and yesterday I nearly died of old age! You turned me into a Circulator, so we could evolve to the space time continuum together. You and me having a baby, would be like an elderly human couple having kids at the age of 70!"

"But we don't have bodies of 70 year old humans!" I objected. "We're both physically in our twenties!"

"Two days ago, my joints would hurt just from going up the stairs! Two days ago, I was on pain medication for arthritis! You may have reversed my biological clock B, but I have an old soul. My mind still feels like it's an old man!"

"So what are you saying, Declan? That you don't want to have this thing? This child? This baby?" I asked offended.

"B, we're supposed to be evolving to the space time continuum, the way an elderly human packs up and moves to Florida for retirement!" He said indignantly. "I mean, can we take this thing with us to the space time continuum? We're supposed to turn into beings of light, so what's going to happen to the child inside you?"

I let out another growl as I rubbed my face again. I think this made my husband feel bad, as he stood up to move to the chair which was right beside mine. He rubbed my back as he spoke in a sympathetic voice.

"I know you used to want kids, especially since you couldn't have any. But I haven't heard you talk about babies for over fifty years, so I thought you finally grew out of it. With this happening to us now, it's like winning the lottery when we're already millionaires."

I buried my face in my hands and groaned back, "I don't know Declan. I really, really don't know."

"It's less than 24 hours, B." He cajoled. "All we're doing is stopping a bunch of cells. OK, look at it this way, you don't feel bad when you pull out a weed from amongst your daffodils do you? It's the same thing."

What did he just say?

I turned to look on in shock at what he was suggesting, "...huh?"

"Look, just think about that afternoon in the woods the first time we had sex." He tried to shrug it off. "You didn't mind then, did you?"

"Yeah, but you said it would stop me from getting pregnant! You didn't say it would end pregnancy!" I pulled away from his touch.

"What I'd do would be exactly the same thing." Declan said seriously. "I have to do this now or it won't work."

"And then what? I'll have to have an abortion the 'human' way?" I asked snidely.

"Yes."

"Declan!" I stood up in disgust. "Why are you so eager to kill this thing?!"

"B!" He stood up too, but in alarm. "Think about this!"

"I AM thinking about this! It's a bit hard to think about anything else!" I snapped back.

"B, please," his eyes watered, "you're carrying another European Werewolf in there." Then his eyes momentarily lowered to my abdomen. "And I swore I would be the last."

Warily, I took a step back from him, now seeing the light. "Is that your real reason why you don't want the baby, Declan?"

"Yes." He admitted. "I mean, think about our discussion all those years ago when Nairn tried to help us to get pregnant. Remember how I said that we should try for a girl, because a boy would be harder to train? What if it's a boy in there, B? There is no way we can take a new-born male European Werewolf into the space time continuum with us. It'd be like letting loose a demon inside of an unprepared heaven."

"Why are you so adamant that you want a girl?" I wondered aloud.

"Because they're not as strong as males!" He flared. "Female European Werewolves aren't as strong as males, just as female Lokoti Werewolves aren't as strong as their male counterparts! Besides, I don't trust other European Werewolves! A son of mine would sooner knock his Lokoti Werewolf mother out of the way, to attack the human she was trying to protect!"

"But you were a young male European Werewolf and you didn't hurt your mother..." I began to argue back, but his guilty expression stopped me.

"Once."

"What was that?" I thought I had misheard.

Declan's face paled, "Once I did when I was three years old, when the full moon triggered my first change. Luckily, your Dad, Grandpa and Grandfather were there. Your Dad caught my Mom before she hit the wall and your Grandfather caught me before I smashed through the locked front door. I would have made a run at a human, but the male Lokoti Werewolves were able to stop me."

At first I was startled into silence but then I tried to console.

"But Declan," I began, "it was your first change and you were only three years old. You had to be trained."

"I know, but it took years for my training to come into effect." He reminded. "Your Dad caught my Mom. But from the force I used when I threw her out of the way, I could have harmed Derik whom she was pregnant with at the time. Your Dad never trusted me because of it, which was why he hated the idea of you ending up with me."

At first I found it hard to imagine a three year old boy, throwing his mother against a wall when she tried to restrain him. But then I could, if the three year old was in his European Werewolf body. Since they expanded so much with supernatural muscle, he was probably as tall as an adult human, let alone stronger than one. Is this why he's so afraid of creating anymore European Werewolves, even as children?

"Hang on," I shook my head in disagreement, "don't forget that our baby will be half Lokoti Werewolf as well, like its mother."

"And what if it's also a Circulator, like its mother?" He arched a wary eyebrow. "Then it could have my strength and your speed! Just imagine if it snuck out of the house by instantaneously phasing, to go snacking on human that way. A Circulator – slash – European Werewolf; we could be creating an almost unstoppable murderer!"

"Declan!" I walked up to hold his head in my hands, to force him to look into my eyes. "I just did create a Circulator – slash – European Werewolf! And I have faith in YOU! Just as I have faith that we could train our child to respect life."

"B, you're not listening to me." He put my hands over his heart. "When I first turned at the age of three, the bloodlust almost ate me inside out! Night after night, your Grandfather sat with me. I tried so hard not to hunt human, for the sake of my Mom and my little brother. But just as much as I loved my family; sometimes when the pain got so bad, I would even crave THEM!"

I shook my head again, "I don't believe you."

"That first year that I changed, there was a reason why your Grandfather stayed with me night after night, to train me. Sometimes I'd stand in Derik's room and watch him sleep in his cot. At first I'd look on my little brother with love, but then my stomach would rumble, my mouth would water and the bloodlust would be saying, 'do it, feed your hunger! He'd taste so good and he'd take the pain away.' Then my Mom would come into the room and stroke my hair, thinking that I was acting all brotherly? Her soft hands smelled like the tenderest steak you've ever tasted in your life."

"Declan!" I cried out in alarm, as I pulled my hands back sharply.

"THIS is why I don't want to risk a son ever thinking that way about you!" He grabbed hold of my arms. "I may have fought the bloodlust to protect my loved ones, but I WILL NOT abide another threat to come along and destroy everything!"

"So what are you saying? That your son will want to eat me?" I asked, hurt. "Do you want to eat me Declan, like you wanted to eat your mother and brother?"

Suddenly he pulled me close, "I've always wanted you, B. You've always smelled delicious to me, especially with your Lokoti Werewolf pheromones. Then coupled with your aura as a Circulator, it's like making love to an angel. That's what you're like to me. You smell delicious, but I want to look on you, smell you and possess you forever. If a child of mine ever looked at you wrong? Then that would be the very last thing that young European Werewolf would ever do."

My eyes watered as I tried again to reach him, by cupping his face and looking into his watery blue eyes.

"Declan. Please. Stop." I pleaded. "Just listen to me! This child will be half Lokoti Werewolf too! My breed doesn't crave human family members nor members of the tribe. This child will be half you and me, and I firmly believe that it will be the amalgamation of the best of the both of us."

He sighed wearily and even in human form, his body could harden if he didn't want to listen. Usually he would hear me out, so why wasn't he now?

"You don't think that I'm listening to you? Why won't you hear me?" He argued. "B, turn off the stars in your eyes and wake up and smell the coffee! I WAS a young European Werewolf! I KNOW what young European Werewolves are like! Think about the SSIT Report on Different Breeds of Werewolves; it was noted that European Werewolf children have rarely been sighted. Think about why...did they run away from their parents to start hunting solo? Or did the monstrous parents annihilate the little devil, if the child either turned on them or they were too hard to control? Our child wouldn't turn after the age of ten like a Lokoti Werewolf does, but it will be born immediately as a Werewolf. Humans term toddlers going through the 'terrible twos' and in our case, it would be literally!"

My husband's pessimism was seriously scaring me. I pulled out of his arms which didn't want to let me go. When I took a step back, they tried to reclaim their hold so I took several more away.

Tearfully, I shook my head as I gave him a betrayed look, "No Declan."

"C'mon, just give me ten minutes and it'll all be over." His hand reached out.

I jumped backwards in fright! Who was this baby-killing monster? This can't be my loving mate for the past 273 years...!

As my form of protest, I turned towards the front door when suddenly, he moved in the speed of light, to block my path!

What the...?! We both froze in shock. Just then, he looked just like I did when I engaged my light speed reflexes; a bright blur.

Declan's been a Circulator just over 24 hours and he can already move in light speed? This unnerved me, at how his European Werewolf genes had leapt onto the Circulator bandwagon and were going for the reigns! It even gave him pause, as he looked from me to the door he was now standing in front of.

"Woah, I'm gonna have to get used to that." His eyebrows arose, before he turned back my way. "B, let's talk about this."

"I've tried to talk about it! You just want to kill it!" My voice went shrill.

"IT! That's right B, it's an IT!" He raised his voice.

"It's an IT until I know if IT'S a boy or a girl!" I said adamantly.

The monster's eyes narrowed, "There's no way in hell that thing is going to stay in you that long for you to find out."

"WHAT?!" I roared, as my dark blue eyes flashed their glowing turquoise colour.

Declan's blue eyes turned glowing green as he fixed his dangerous gaze on my abdomen, "Just ten minutes B and it will all be over."

He was really starting to frighten me and I mean seriously. I turned to march towards the back door, when again a bright blur sped past to block my path. This time when he skidded to a stop, neither of us looked surprised but only determined.

My mate held up his hands in a 'stop' gesture. "Let's just review the facts here, there's something else you haven't considered yet."

"Oh yeah and what's that?" I crossed my arms defensively.

"What happens to the mother with a European Werewolf growing inside of her?" His eyes drilled into mine.

I felt a pang of fear at his point, but I tried to cover it up by looking away.

"Fact one," he started to count on his left hand, "you're a female Lokoti Werewolf so you're forty times stronger than a human, but European Werewolves are a hundred times stronger. With that thing's strength, can you imagine what it's going to be like when it kicks? Fact two, you're gonna have something in there with claws! It could tear itself out of you if it wanted to! This also brings us to fact three; the change."

"Change? What change?" I huffed. "You already said it's immediately going to be a European Werewolf."

"What if the foetus changes into its supernatural shape while it's inside you? It could go from this..." he cupped his hands together to demonstrate, before dramatically widening them, "...to this in a matter of seconds."

Horrified, I backed away with bulging eyes as my mouth fell open...!

The father of my child looked on with a pained expression, "What's going to happen to the mother then? A female European Werewolf could cope with her greater strength, but what about a female Lokoti Werewolf?"

I shook my head in a maddening way, unable to cope with the apocalyptic picture he was painting.

He rushed forward to grab hold of my arms to plead, "C'mon B, let me do this! In ten minutes it will all be over, I promise! Just give me ten minutes!"

"No, Declan! No!" I squealed, terrified.

"If you still want a baby after all these years, then I'll go out and I'll find you one! I'll bring you back a human baby! But let's have a human baby, c'mon B!"

"No!" I started to cry as I tried to pull away.

My husband tearfully refused to let me go, "I mean it! I'll do it today, B! I'll find you a human baby and bring it back to you! But I'd do it as soon as I got rid of that thing inside you!"

"Stop it, Declan!" I tried harder to escape, but his grip was iron-clad.

"B, as soon as I do what I have to; we'll phase through time to when there are plenty of orphans. You can pick any human baby you want!"

Tears were streaming down both our faces now. We were at an impasse, I wanted to have this child and the father wanted to destroy it, because he was afraid it would destroy the mother. I was desperate for it to live, and he was turning desperate for it not to.

Knock, knock, knock!

Right at that moment, Ki opened our front door. "Er, hello?"

Normally, the tribe's Medicine Man didn't help himself to walking into people's homes, but our yelling must have prompted him. He looked on in concern at the scene he had stumbled into, of Declan gripping onto my arms as I was trying to squirm out of his grasp. I could tell he disapproved, as he frowned upon the sight of the bigger male preventing the smaller female's escape.

Ki spoke calmly, "Uncle Declan, can you please let go of Aunt B and maybe we can sit down and talk about what seems to be the trouble?"

He was carrying his 'medicine bundle' which was an old, black, leather doctor's bag which indicated he had come by to do a check-up.

"Scan her!" Declan barked out, as he didn't look away from my direction.

"What?" He blinked.

"SCAN HER!"

"OK, Uncle Dec." Our fellow Lokoti Werewolf, put up his hands in a surrender gesture. "Let's just remain calm, shall we?"

Slowly, he lowered his medicine bundle to the floor, as if he were wary of making any sudden moves around the volatile European Werewolf. Next, he opened his doctor's bag and pulled out his hand-held medical scanner. Then he returned to his feet and held up the technology, to show Declan.

"Scan her, Ki!" His Second in the pack, ordered.

Tearfully, I glared at my husband, "This isn't going to solve anything!"

"If you don't believe me B, let's get a medical opinion!" He retorted.

Ki looked from me to my husband, before he turned on the scanner and waved it in my direction.

"Well?" Declan looked his way, but he didn't let go of my arms.

"Aunt B is healthy and there's nothing to report..." Ki read off the screen, "...oh, hang on."

There was a pause, as we watched the Medicine Man blink then blink again, as if he didn't believe the results. He even waved the scanner over me again, to double check. We watched him go completely still for a minute, before he raised his other hand to rub his jaw to show his confusion.

"Well?" Declan repeated.

"Um, according to this..." Ki began.

"B's pregnant!" He finished impatiently.

"...from the elevated hormones in Aunt B's system, the scanner is saying that she's pregnant." Ki continued. "But from scanning the fertilized egg in the abdominal area, it looks like conception occurred just 24 hours ago."

"24 hours?!" We exclaimed in further surprise, before staring at the other.

"Then that means..." I began.

"...that I knocked you up on our first go." My husband finished.

"First go?" Ki lowered the scanner to look on the pair of us. "This was yesterday, after Uncle Dec nearly died of old age? How many goes were there?" When we passed him an unimpressed look, he finished with, "Never mind, you don't have to answer that."

"Our first go?" I raised my eyebrows at my European Werewolf mate. "Boy, there's everything about your kind that's strong, isn't there?"

"My argument exactly," he seethed, "which is why we have to nip this thing in the bud."

"With no pun intended?" I said snidely.

"Just remember that right now they're just cells, B." He spoke coldly. "Like I said, in ten minutes it'll all be over."

"Then what, Declan? What happens the next time we have sex? You heard the Medicine Man, you knocked me up the first go! I'll just get pregnant again since birth control doesn't work on our kind."

"Birth control for humans maybe." His voice turned icy. "But my kind has its own methods, one of them I'm trying to use now."

"What?!" I spluttered out in disgust. "So you want to do THIS all the time?!"

"What choice do I have?" He whined, like he was in physical pain.

"That's not birth control! That's genocide!" I cried out indignantly.

"What choice do we have?!" He raised his voice once more. "It's either them or you! You'll die if you have this thing!"

However, we were interrupted again by our Medicine Man, who was still stumped by the fact I was pregnant in the first place.

"Hang on here, people." Ki put up his hand. "Let me just get something straight... Uncle Declan nearly dies of old age and is turned into a Circulator by his mate who's another Circulator. You celebrate and Uncle Declan as a youthful European Werewolf again, impregnates his barren wife from the first round, which I assume there were many rounds. Now, have I got this right?"

"Yes!" He snapped bad-temperedly. "B's eggs are in temporal flux! B turned me into a Circulator by putting me into temporal flux! My swimmers are now in temporal flux! Do you get the picture, or do we have to draw you a frickin' diagram?!"

“Aaahhh....! Right! Got it!” Ki finally came on board. Then he tried to keep his casual demeanor as he turned back to my husband. “So um, Uncle Dec, how about you let go of Aunt B while we talk some more on this.”

But my mate growled back, “If I let go of her, she’ll go bolting out the door!”

I looked Ki's way for help. “He wants to kill it!”

“How about we all sit down and talk about this calmly -" The Medicine Man began to counsel.

“B’s carrying a baby European Werewolf inside of her, Ki!” My husband yelled. “Something that can claw her insides, or expand and squash every single organ in her body! Then if it's born, it can run in the speed of light since it has two Circulators for parents!”

“Oh.” His face fell, thanks to my husband’s description.

“But our baby will be half Lokoti Werewolf too!” I repeated. “Ki, tell him it will be half of me too!”

“Why yes it would be, but the question is what genetic traits would be inherent in the fetus?” He thought aloud.

“We can’t wait to find out!” Declan demanded. “We have to get rid of it now!”

“We have to do no such thing!” I shouted back.

Again, I tried to escape from the monster’s clutches, when he used his greater strength to pull me into a tight embrace.

“B please, don’t fight me on this!" He desperately held on. "Your life is in danger!”

“No it’s not!” I uselessly pushed against his chest. “It isn't, Declan!”

“You don’t know what you’re talking about!” He wore a helpless expression.

“Yes I do!” I fired up. “I'm not getting one of my ominous feelings, I have as a Circulator. I don’t have alarm bells going off inside of my head! If this was bad, then I’d have a vision to warn me!”

Our Medicine Man couldn’t stand watching our fight any longer. He crossed over to try to release me, by putting his hand on Declan's larger arm as he gave him a pointed look. This made my mate pause.

“Let’s just hear her out, please?” Ki spoke gravely. “Let her go, Uncle.”

“Fine!” He snapped. “But B, if you try anything stupid like running out those doors? You’ll see that I’m just as fast as you.”

“Oh yeah?” I fired back. “Do you think that’s all Circulators can do, just run really fast?”

Abruptly his arms tightened about me, as he growled in my ear, “Just you try it!”

“OK, I will!” I snarled back.

I tried to instantaneously phase from his grasp, but oddly I couldn’t.

Huh, what? That's strange. I tried again, but it didn't work. I should have disappeared in a bright flash of light from my house in Alaska, to reappear in Circulate HQ on Taurus Six. So why didn't I?

Next, I tried to put myself into phase, so I could slip from his hold but that didn't work either. My biological body wasn't turning into one made of light. What's going on here?

When I looked back over my shoulder at Declan whom was hugging me from behind; his eyes were squeezed shut and it looked like he was muttering something. It was like he was concentrating against me, but how?

"What are you doing?!" I cried out in alarm. "Stop it!"

I closed my eyes too, so I could concentrate harder when I felt something happen... I felt the usual warm and tingling sensation, but it wasn't enough. My skin momentarily glowed, but my biological body didn't dissolve into light.

Ki caught the look of panic on my face, which made him raise his medical scanner to see what was going on.

Whatever it was my mate was muttering became louder. I started to work out he was chanting the same thing over and over again. When I heard the words, I couldn't believe the simplistic mode he was somehow using, to stop me from going into phase!

"Stay with me stay with me stay with me stay with me stay with me stay with me stay with me stay with me stay with me ..."

Our Medicine Man lowered his scanner, to say in a surprised voice, "Somehow Uncle Declan is using his aura to affect your aura."

"What?!" My eyes nearly popped out of my head!

"He's using his bio-electromagnetic field to disrupt your bio-electromagnetic field." He reported. "I can see from the readings that you're trying to go into phase, by the electrical activity in your brain as well as along your central nerve system, increasing. However, so has Uncle Declan's but instead of going into phase, he's putting you out of phase."

I blanched over the kind of monster I had created. How is Declan learning his abilities as a Circulator so fast? This can't be right, nor can it be natural! This was so supernatural, it wasn't funny!

"Stay with me stay with me stay with me stay with me stay with me stay with me stay with me stay with me stay with me..." He continued.

"Stop it Declan!" I cried out helplessly.

"I will if you will." He replied amidst his chanting, whilst keeping his eyes closed.

Wait, I think this has happened before...to another Circulator. I wracked my brain as I tried to remember some instruction of what to do. I recalled that the Circulator escaped from the other Circulator doing this, by ending the bodily contact. This would only work if he was holding onto me, so our bio-electromagnetic fields were touching. He can't stop me from going into phase if he wasn't.

I decided to warn him first, "I can fight you off, even if it's just long enough to go into phase. But I would hurt you to make you let go of me. Once I go into phase and escape, who says I'll come back?"

Although I couldn't see his face properly as he was standing directly behind, I heard the hurt in his voice.

"I know you can B...but look at where I'm standing, with the back of your neck near my mouth. If I thought I was about to lose my grip, I'd bite you where I did when I made you unconscious, all those years ago. If it means knocking you out and then doing what I have to do, to end this pregnancy? Remember the first night you changed, let alone every other time I did what needed to be done, for the safety of my mate."

My heart raced, as I let out a helpless cry because I was scared to death for my child!

"Uncle Declan, please." Ki spoke forcefully. "If you don't release your hold on Aunt B, I'll have to call on our First to intervene."

That made him hesitate, as he knew what this meant... if Caesar was called here then Declan as his Second would have to obey. If my mate didn't, he'd have fourteen male Lokoti Werewolves, ready to fight the dissenter, as well as the threat to their first female Lokoti Werewolf.

I sensed his European Werewolf bloodlust almost throw back its head and roar out its battle cry! His bloodlust would find this kind of challenge fun! But it was his heart which stayed his murderous desires. He had spent the last 168 years as Second, he would be turning on his own men, let alone hurting his wife by fighting her people.

Finally, I felt Declan's hands release my arms then I was free...

I turned around to look dismayed on my mate for nearly harming his wife and child, as he tearfully gazed back.

"Tell me again you don't have a bad feeling about this?" He rasped out, as if he were having difficulty breathing. "Tell me how you're gonna live through this?"

"As Aunt B said, this child will be part Lokoti Werewolf too." Ki reminded. "Maybe this baby will be exactly half and half? I'll keep a close eye on Aunt B, I promise. You two won't be alone, no Lokoti Werewolf ever stands alone. You know this yourself, Uncle."

But Declan didn't seem to hear, he was to busy staring at his mate.

"Tell me B, what can you 'see'? Tell me what you 'see' in ours and the baby's future." He pleaded.

Next, he watched me turn to walk into the shadowy kitchen. The whole house darkened in fact, as the sun was taken away from the grey clouds which were heavy with snow. As if I were in a trance, I wandered over to the kitchen sink to stare out the window at my garden.

The grass was still short as the cold weather stagnated its growth. I saw the bare branches of our Jacaranda Tree bend in the strong wind. Then I stared at my withered garden plots, which were waiting to be buried under the thick snow of a long winter.

Our small, two bedroom, two story, brown wooden cottage with its stone chimney; sat on top of a hill in the community centre inside the vast Lokoti National Park, in the Alaska Range. Our home was normally cosy with life, love, cooking and company. We had family, tribe and pack whom we intermingled or hunted with. Our life could be called 'quiet' by some, but when you had to hide your supernatural state, where and how we lived was ideal.

The signs of winter coming, also represented signs of something else to come. Our home would be changed forever, as would be the people inside it. As if to confirm this, I saw a snowflake fly past on the icy wind.

I wasn't experiencing any visions whilst I stared hypnotically at life outside. Similar to my bad feelings which warned of danger, I felt several new sensations. They didn't fill me with a sense of dread, instead they filled me with a sense of purpose.

"Our daughter isn't going to be a Circulator." I spoke quietly, almost unsure of my own words. "She's going to be the eldest of three sisters and none of them will be 'Light People'. I am the last Circulator to be born."

Suddenly, the window rattled loudly from a gust of wind, as my Jacaranda Tree bent back and forth. I watched the snowflakes begin to fall thick and fast, but from the gale they fell in a sloping pattern. I watched the many white dots cover the grass.

"The timeline has to make adjustments to Declan's altered state of being." I said softly. "Because their mother changed their father, our daughters will be born, but not as Circulators."

Then I felt my mate come to stand beside at the sink, as his greater body heat radiated outwards.

"Daughters?" He asked hopeful. "No boys?"

A tear slipped down my cheek, as his relief didn't bring me happiness, but disappointment.

"And what would you have done if it was a son?" I challenged.

"If we had a son who was half Lokoti Werewolf but wasn't a Circulator? I would do exactly what I'm going to do now." He said firmly.

"And what's that?"

"Give his mother a kiss and a cuddle and help her raise the little troublemaker." He emitted a small smile.

"After everything that's happened today, what makes you think I want you for the job?" I took a step away.

Declan grinned like an idiot – a tearful idiot – but an idiot nonetheless.

"Since you said 'daughters' and not 'daughter', it means I'm let out of the doghouse sometime." He tried to joke.

"Lucky me." I said flatly, as I turned back towards the window.

Just then he laughed loudly as he leant on the kitchen sink. He seemed to be laughing in pure relief! He was guffawing like a man who had just been granted parole in the face of a death sentence.

He wiped his eyes on the back of his hands, “I can almost picture her now. She’s going to be tall and she’s going to make all of the boys work hard, by beating them in school and in sport.”

"Why do you say that?"

Declan continued, “She’s going to be half of you and half of me. I’m gonna teach her how to repair her hover-car if it breaks down. You’re gonna teach her soccer and help her with her homework. When she's not studying with you, she’ll be in the kitchen helping me cook.”

“Maybe we shouldn’t be placing all these expectations on her yet.” I said warily. “I mean, your last expectation was that she was going to kill her mother!”

I thought these words would have wounded him, but they did the exact opposite. Instead, Declan stood closely to smile down as his large hands moved to sit on my hips. His bright blue eyes fixated on my dark blue ones, before he lowered his face to gently bump foreheads. His spiky, dark blonde hair mixed in with my long, black layers.

“B, ever since I was 14 years old, I've been trained not to think of myself as a father.” He confessed with his eyes closed. “It was the age when the Lokoti Werewolves told me that I could never take a human woman for a mate, for risk of harming her or turning her. I thought if they’re scared of me changing her, then they probably wouldn’t want me to have kids that were like me, either."

That gave me pause, as his words and the emotion behind them hurt my heart. I watched him speak with his eyes closed as I felt his hot breath on my face. Although I was still furious with him, I didn't pull out of our embrace.

He continued, "I fell in love with you when I was 17 years old but remember, I had to wait until I was nearly 21 until I could have you, when you changed at the age of 18. Then you were married off to Grant and I had to wait five years before we were reunited. This only compounded the idea that the pack thought the risk of me breeding with you was far too great. Then it came out you were so-called barren and you couldn’t give Grant kids? I thought, 'she was meant to be mine all along!' Then for 273 years, I got to enjoy the marriage bed, without worrying the world about what the marriage could produce. Now a baby makes three? I’m sorry I didn’t run out and buy a bottle of champagne and a cigar. For nearly 300 years I was taught and self-taught that I wasn’t father material, because I could plant rotten seed.”

My eyes widened in further alarm, as I never knew his self-hatred was buried so deep, it was thoroughly rooted in his psyche.

“Declan, I would breed with you any day of the week and twice on Sunday.” I said strongly. “Why the hell do you think I threatened to hurt you, when you threatened to hurt the baby? I know the seed is as good as the man.”

My husband desperately peered into my eyes, “Say that again.”

I cupped his face, “I know the seed is as good as the man.”

“Say it again?”

“We’re going to have an awesome child, who’s going to be like her awesome father.”

"Say it again?"

"I don't want to procreate with anyone but you."

"Say it again?"

"Declan, I'm hungry." I whinged, as I changed the subject.

"Right! Food!" He instantly stood to attention. "Well B, you're a pregnant woman who's mated to the right guy for that. I'll keep you so full that you'll never get any of those renown cravings pregnant women have. Ki, would you like some brunch?"

However, when we turned to look outside the kitchen, our Medicine Man was no longer standing in our living area.

"Ki?" I called, but there was no answer.

We exchanged surprised glances before we departed the room to find our medical practitioner, his scanner and his medicine bundle, were gone.

"Oh." I said taken aback. "I guess he thought the emergency was over."

"That and I think he's gone to Caesar to have a talk about us." He frowned.

"Why?" I asked in alarm. "You did let go, eventually."

"Well B, let me put it this way," he casually leaned against the wall. "The tribe's first female Lokoti Werewolf turns the last European Werewolf who is her mate, into another Circulator. For over 250 years, everyone thinks she's barren and then bingo! Her handsome husband does the 'manly thing' by knocking her up. Our baby will be the world's first half Lokoti and half European Werewolf."

I smiled on his dry sense of humor, "I like your little explanations, they're like little stories in themselves."

"Thanks." He chuckled back. "So, what does the pregnant woman crave; bacon and eggs, or sausages and eggs, or even pancakes?"

"Um, how about all of the above?" I shrugged.

"I love my wife!" He guffawed. "Man, are we going to have fun over the next nine months."

"Man, are we going to have an interesting next ninety years." I corrected.

Declan pulled back to give an incredulous look, "Ninety years?!"

"There's kids and then there's grandkids." I reminded.

"Oh yeah." He frowned as he returned to the kitchen to cook. "By the time we make it to the space time continuum; we really will be like a pair of 70 year old humans, moving to Florida to retire."

"Yup." I moved to sit up on the bench to talk, while he made breakfast. "In a couple of years, you could have a daughter sitting here instead of me."

He passed a funny look as he passed me the ingredients from the fridge. "Why? Where will you be?"

“I don’t know, away lecturing or writing my papers?” I shrugged again.

“So because I’m the cook, I’m gonna turn into the 'house husband'?” He raised his eyebrows unimpressed.

“Well, you are retired.” I reminded.

“Hmm.” He frowned as he paused in his food preparation. “I guess you're right. After working at the Garage for over 250 years, I’m in no hurry to return. Our ‘rug rat’ is going to need money for food.”

“The way you constantly shove food down my throat, I doubt our kid will ever go hungry." I said dryly. "It’s a good thing we’re having Werewolf young. With their supernatural metabolism, we won’t have to worry about our child becoming obese.”

Out of the blue, Declan picked me up off the bench and swung me around in his arms!

“Damn straight!” He merrily laughed. “I’m going to be a father! Ladies and Gentlemen, I finally knocked up Bianca Sabre! I knocked up the unknockable woman! And she WANTS my child!”

At first I squealed in fright then in laughter, "We’re going to have a baby!”

“We’re going to have a baby!" He chanted. "We’re going to have a baby!”

“Declan!” I cupped his face. “Do you know how good it feels when I get to give the man I love, a child?”

He gently returned me to my feet before leaning in closely.

“About as good as it does for me, to know that I’ve finally given you the one thing that you always wanted?” He tenderly rubbed his nose against mine.

“I've always wanted you and I have that.” I stroked his cheek. “And now baby makes three!”

“Baby makes three.” He hugged me tightly. “My baby B and I are having a baby girl!”

“A one-of-a-kind, just like her parents.” I sighed happily.

“A beautiful girl, just like her beautiful mother.” He mumbled as his lips smothered mine.

I allowed this kiss although a part of me was still on guard. There was a tiny part of my brain that was murmuring, ‘careful’. My instincts didn’t entirely trust his turn around, all because his progeny would be female.

“Man, I feel like an idiot.” He shook his head at himself.

“Why?” I looked on closely.

“We could have done this ages ago!” He sounded annoyed with himself. “Just imagine what it could have been like, if this happened 273 years before. We could have started a family then, if I let you turn me into a Circulator sooner. My Mom would have been thrilled for us, if she were here. I wish I could have seen my human mother hold my daughter, before she died of old age.”

I felt a strong sense of longing inside of him as he pictured this. Then he let go of his wife to continue with cooking. I leaned against the kitchen bench as I watched and listened.

“Derik got to have the happy family life, with the wife and kids. He gave my Mom two grandchildren, whom she loved to death. I just wish that I could have done the same. I wish that the pack hadn’t feared the idea of me creating more European Werewolves, in the forms of children. I wish that your father trusted me enough to take care of you.”

This made my chest ache as I felt these old wounds of his, never healed. His expression was more than wistful, it was a mask of pain. He momentarily looked away from the food to meet my waiting gaze.

He recanted bitterly, “I remember the meeting the pack had with the Council of Tribal Elders, like it was only yesterday. They met to talk about the tribe’s first female Lokoti Werewolf, who was also a Circulator. Your Dad was beside himself with worry, he was scared that you might escape with your greater speed and kill a human. Then it was a Tribal Elder that came up with the idea of mating you to another Werewolf, who could stop you from craving human as well as help your training. Then everyone immediately looked at Grant, like I was invisible or something. Nobody glanced my way, much less thought of me as a possible suitor. When I spoke up by reminding everyone that it had been me who had stopped you from crossing the border of Lokoti land? Your Dad put a stop to it immediately. Hunter Wisetail walked over to stand beside his best friend Ian Elm and his brother Grant, and said that a female Lokoti Werewolf should be mated to a male Lokoti Werewolf. Of course the Tribal Elders all liked the sound of that.”

I heard the jealousy in Declan’s voice which never faded, even after 279 years.

“You mean Grant wasn’t asked?” I frowned. “When I first found out about the arranged marriage, he told me he had been asked.”

“Yeah he was formally asked at the meeting by the Tribal Elders. But with your aura and your pheromones, they may as well as have announced that he'd won the lottery!” He snorted. “I’m sure my feelings for you were suspected, even if they weren’t spoken of. Finn and your Grandfather made mention of them, just a couple of times. But they both knew I had to keep my distance before your change.”

I watched him slap the bacon bad-temperedly into the frying pan which instantly began to sizzle, before he threw in a couple of hashbrowns too.

“Finn and Grandfather knew?” I echoed in surprise.

Back then I thought our forbidden love had been a secret?

“At dinner at your grandparents house one night, when I was eighteen and you would have been fifteen years old; you walked off angry after one of our fights. Your Grandfather caught the expression on my face and gave me a close look. He asked, 'enjoying those sparks, Declan?' That was the only thing he ever said about it, as he probably thought I was just attracted to your aura.” He explained.

Declan cracked several eggs in a glass bowl and proceeded to beat them so hard, the whisk made a squealing sound against the sides. I watched him add the other ingredients for pancakes, as he prepared them from memory. He was such an old hand at this, he continued to cook as he talked.

"When it was just me and Finn working at the Garage; we would be leaning over a vehicle and he'd say as casual as can be, 'So Declan, do you like soccer?' I wouldn't look up as I'd be in the middle of something and I'd reply, 'Yeah I like it fine.' Then Finn would say, 'I was wondering why you kept watching the other kids play. Here I was thinking it could be over a girl instead, who just happened to be running around the field with your little brother.' In surprise, I dropped the wrench into the motor and hit my head on the hood!"

I cracked up laughing, as I could very well imagine the late Finn with his cheeky sense of humor, bringing it up like that.

My husband chuckled, "He'd only talk about it when we were alone. Sometimes in summer, during the long daylight hours when the bloodlust was making me restless, we would stay up until midnight repairing engines. It was when we talked the most. He'd sneakily bring you up by suddenly asking, 'So how's your spectator sport going?' We'd talk about you in the third person without actually saying your name. We always referred to you as 'that girl who liked playing soccer'."

I felt myself blush, as I hopped back up onto the bench to sit and listen. He finished off the pancake mix and left it on the bench. Then I watched him pull out another frying pan from one of the cupboards, to cook it in.

He went on, "When the truth came out about us and we first moved in together? Finn gave me an early mark every day for two months, so I could come home to you sooner. When I felt embarrassed at the favouritism he was showing, he said in front of the whole crew, 'You've done the hard work, Declan. Now it's time to enjoy the fruits of your labours'."

"Finn said that?" I asked, touched.

"Finn, my Mom and your Mom then your grandparents, seemed like the only people who didn't have a problem with our coupling." He said in irritation. "I felt your Dad and Ian's uneasiness for years. Your father never trusted me with you. If you had become pregnant by me at that time, your father would have had the same reservations that I spoke of; what carrying a European Werewolf could do to you."

"A half European and half Lokoti Werewolf." I corrected him again.

At that moment, Declan stopped what he was doing to lean in close.

"B, I'm gonna watch you like a hawk. I'm gonna be stuck to your side 24/7. I'm gonna be worse than superglue! Because as much as I'm hyped about the chance to play 'happy family' with a wife and kid? If this pregnancy turns dangerous for you in anyway -"

However, I interrupted him by dipping my finger into the raw pancake mix and smearing it across his cheek!

"There." I said simply. "I'm just preparing you for what it's going to be like feeding our baby."

"Well, if she's anything like her feisty mother, the food is going to hit the wall!" My mate guffawed about another incident in our past.

Then he dipped his finger into the mix, before he slowly ran it down my neck to my collar bone. Next, he leaned in to slowly lick it off with his hot tongue which made my stomach melt. He wasn't in a hurry to pull away either, in fact he pulled me closer as he turned really amorous.

"Um, Declan?" I opened my eyes when I noticed a new smell. "Your bacon is burning."

"B, you have no idea...!"

I tittered as I felt his sharpening teeth, bite harder into the soft tissue of my neck. But it was a combination of hunger and wariness, which made me push him off.

"We've hardly eaten in two days, between you nearly dying of old age then trying to end my pregnancy." I said indignantly. "I'm STARVED!"

Reluctantly, he pulled away whilst passing me a long look, before returning his attention to the stove.

*****

~ 2 ~

For the rest of the day I tried to keep a safe distance from my husband.

After brunch, Declan helped with cleaning up and I practically danced around him. I swung wide and did my best not to bump into his great build, which earned a peculiar look. Later in the day, when he was coming up the stairs whilst I was going down; I squeezed against the banister, so we wouldn't touch.

Then in the afternoon, I was reading a book on the couch when he came to sit beside and immediately I stood up.

"Um, I have to speak to my PA about something." I said lamely, before I hastily left for upstairs.

"Aw, c'mon!" He rolled his eyes. "You can come up with a better excuse than that!"

However, I ignored him as I continued to the bedroom.

Next, I overheard him mutter, "Oh yeah, this together forever business is turning out just peachy."

I stopped at the top of the stairs to turn around and say, "Excuse me while I call my PA to discuss the time table for my next series of lectures, to earn money for my child whom I'd love, whether it was a girl or not."

Declan didn't have a response to that, so I continued on my way.

Over the next hour, I laid on my bed conversing with my PA over the speaker on my mobile phone. I hardly ever used the video-phone feature, because I preferred people not to see my appearance. Especially since my latest academic identity was meant to be an older woman and I'd have to manipulate my appearance. However, as I organized my schedule with her, I had my laptop turned on.

Whilst we were planning my schedule, I'd say 'yay' or 'nay,' to the series of academic engagements she offered.

"You've been invited to a lunch at Cambridge University on 1st February next year." Aneet continued. "In attendance, will be several speakers on Ancient History in the Mediterranean."

"Ancient History in the Mediterranean?" I echoed. "I don't teach that topic."

"It's not a topic, it's a field." She said. "With all your papers on Rome, Greece, Egypt, Mesopotamia and Babylon, you do fall into that category."

"Oh, I see your point." I conceded. "But who else is going to be at this shindig?"

"Dr. Fielding, Dr. Golding, Dr. Jordan, Dr. Thewak and Dr. Humphries are just some of the many..." she prattled off, "...I think this is going to be some kind of symposium to honour past historians."

This made me pause, "Which past historians?"

"I think they're going to be honouring archaeologists and professors such as Dr. Jasmine Aviv, Dr. Jason Garret, Dr. Bianca Sabre, Dr. Bianca Wisetail and Dr. Ash Marzuq." She read out. "That's what it says on the invitation, anyways."

My face flushed when two of my past identities were read out.

"Um, can we please put the 1st February on the back burner?"

"Instead of clicking 'accept' or 'decline', would you like me to hit 'tentative'?" She asked.

"Yep." I agreed. "Now, what's next?"

"Aside from your papers, there's not much else. It's quite a few lunches in the next six months, but not many symposiums." She speculated.

"I'm not really interested in lunches." I sighed reluctantly. "All it is, is a bunch of academics who are normally bitchy to each other; hide their knives to stab you in the back with, to be friendly face to face."

"Would you like to decline the academic lunches and charity dinners and just stick to the lectures, Dr. Baker?" She offered, using my latest pseudonym.

"Yeah that'd be a good idea, Aneet." I decided. "So how are we looking so far, one lecture per month?"

"Yes except for March, when you have two lectures." She reported. "You have the one at the University of Technology Sydney and the other at Columbia."

Suddenly Declan's voice interrupted, which gave me a fright.

"March?"

My head turned sharply, to find my husband standing in the doorway, listening in. Then he came into the room to talk directly to my mobile phone.

"Sorry Aneet, in March B will be five months pregnant, which means she'll tire easily. I don't want her travelling around to do two lectures a month." He ordered.

She sounded surprised to hear his voice. "Oh er, Mr. Baker?"

"No, it's Mr. Sabre." He corrected sharply.

"Yes Mr. Sabre." She fumbled out. But he made her so nervous, she mispronounced his surname. Instead of saying *Sar-bra* it sounded like she said, *Say-ber*. "Er, did you just say that Dr. Baker would be pregnant? I mean um, is pregnant?"

I could hear the shock in my secretary's voice, as clear as a bell. She had been my Personal Assistant for the past thirty years, and through two pseudonyms. Although Aneet worked for me, she would also act as my liaison with the multinational company Hodge Endeavor, which was under Circulate control. This meant they would also hear of this. On my first day of being pregnant, the news of my 'happy condition' was being broadcasted.

The Circulate Mainframe, all the way at Circulate Headquarters on Taurus Six, monitored mine and humanities' timeline. It sent instructions via email and text messages, to myself or the Board of Hodge Endeavour. All I had to do, was turn up at the odd Board Meeting when an important decision was required. It ensured the company invested wisely and that I retained control for financial security. The powerful company's political connections, were also ideal in protecting the Circulate's and the Lokoti's anonymity.

Declan continued, "From January onwards, I don't want her doing more than one lecture a month. Then from June, she's not going to do any for at least six months."

"Excuse me?!" I exhorted in surprise.

"Maternity leave, B." He glared my way.

Oh, maternity leave...now why didn't I think of that? I had just been planning my schedule for months in advance and it had never crossed my mind! It made it worse when Declan was the one who was anti-pregnancy.

"Yeah, you'd better take note of that, Aneet." I glared back.

"Would you like me to book you into seeing an obstetrician at the Hodge Endeavor Hospital in Anchorage?" She offered.

Aneet didn't know I was a Circulator or what that meant. However from her confidentiality training, she knew that her boss was 'different' and my medical requirements had to be kept from the public eye. But since I was also a Werewolf, I was hardly ever ill and if I were injured; the blood of my Werewolf kin could revive me. I also had the tribe's Medicine Man whom was another Werewolf to treat me, or even the Medical Lab at Circulate HQ, which was run by the Circulate Mainframe. The computer also oversaw Hodge Endeavor's Hospitals and the Legal Department, providing my mate and I with falsified birth or death certificates, to hide our real ages.

Abruptly, Declan darted forwards to cover the speaker with his hand, so she couldn't hear.

"No, we do this with Ki." He frowned. "A human doctor isn't going to know jack about how Werewolves do blood transfusions, which is going to be a guarantee when you have this."

I snatched my phone out from underneath his hand to say, "Thanks Aneet, but it won't be necessary. We have our own medical staff."

Declan wasn't put off by my rudeness or glares. Instead, he sat on the side of the bed to look on my schedule. To stop him, I slammed shut my laptop.

"However, I will notify the Board of this news." She organized. "Would you like me to contact your English relatives, the Worthall's?"

"Um," I thought on this, "I don't think it's necessary. When Jarrod Worthall - the Engineer in ISF I told you about - calls next, I'll let him know myself."

"Very well." She acquiesced. "Is there anything else I can help you with, Dr. Baker?"

"No thanks Aneet, I think that's it." I signed off.

My mate looked on unimpressed, "Mr. Baker?"

"It's my latest name in the academic circuit." I shrugged it off.

He asked grumpily, "And how old are you for this latest trip around fantasyland?"

"In my early forties." I answered. "So getting 'knocked up' won't look too unusual."

He reopened my laptop to look on my schedule again, when I snapped it shut once more.

"Quit it!" He said in annoyance. "I need to see how busy you're gonna be in the next couple of months."

"Why?"

"This isn't a normal pregnancy B, this baby is going to drain you! Can you imagine what it's going to be like when you venture off tribal lands?"

"What's that supposed to mean?!" I fired up.

"A baby Werewolf will probably move around a lot more than a human baby. You could be standing there on a podium, doing one of your lectures when all of a sudden your stomach goes all wibbly-wobbly. Your audience is gonna think you're giving birth to an alien!"

I growled in frustration at his continued negativity, before I rolled onto my back to stare up at the ceiling.

Declan continued studying my schedule, as if he were making mental notes. His newly youthful face was a mask of consternation, as his bright blue eyes were wide. I could almost see the cogs turning in his brain, as he was planning for the future.

"I don't think you should speak at the University in Cairo." He spoke again.

"Oh yeah and why is that?"

"Because it's in January and it's gonna be 40°C in Egypt that time of year. I'm a European Werewolf, which means I'm hot blooded and you've seen how excessive heat makes me go nuts. With the half breed inside you, it's gonna create problems."

"Ever heard of air conditioning, Declan? They've had this nifty invention since the 20th Century." I said sarcastically. "Besides, I've never had problems with heat and I doubt I'm gonna start now."

"Oh yeah?" He raised his eyebrows. "Remember Wendy Wisetail's first pregnancy, five years ago? She kept fainting all over the place! Pregnancy screws up your blood pressure, blood sugar and everything else."

"Wendy's only human!" I scoffed.

"Yeah, but all she was carrying was a future Lokoti Werewolf who's born human! You may be a Lokoti Werewolf, but you're carrying a mini European Werewolf in there, who's already a supernatural creature."

"Would you please stop being so pessimistic about all of this!" I cried out, exasperated.

His eyes narrowed and he looked like he was going to say a biting remark, but he changed his mind. Instead, his voice lowered, with a tortured expression overtaking his face.

"B, you want to have this baby so we're having this baby, all I'm trying to do is prepare. You may be the pregnant one here, but out of the two of us, I'M the European Werewolf. So if I say it's going to be too hot for our half breed daughter, give me the benefit of the doubt, would you?"

This made me pause as I realized he might be right, which made my defences lower.

My husband used this momentary 'white flag' to lie beside his wife. He helped himself to lifting up my jumper to look on my flat abdomen. Then he lightly ran his hand over the bare skin, which made me feel tingly and my eyes fluttered closed.

"Do you feel that?" He asked softly. "It's my aura touching your aura. Every time I touch you and our auras meet, I get all tingly."

"Same here." I admitted.

I lay still, as I watched him stroke the skin around my belly button. He was even looking on in partial awe, which made me curious.

"You're not gonna believe this," he began, "but the aura around your abdomen is a different colour to the rest of your body."

"Huh?" I raised my head. "What do you mean?"

"Your aura is an opal white, sparkling with different colours. But around your belly isn't, it's peach coloured." He looked on hypnotically.

Intrigued, I glanced from him to my body. All I could see was skin and clothes! I wished I could see auras like he could.

"Hang on," I partially sat up, "I thought you said my aura turns peach coloured, when we have sex?"

"It does." He gave a cheeky grin. "So knowing that your belly is permanently peach coloured, because of what I put inside you? It's a hell of an ego trip."

I returned this by picking up my pillow to whack him over the head!

"You little...!" I growled out.

He laughingly tossed the pillow aside to move closer to my stomach.

At first I watched a little wary as his mouth moved over my belly. Then my cheeks heated up, when he bent his head to lick around my belly button before sticking his tongue inside! He tenderly mauled my stomach with his mouth, as the hot wetness made me giddy.

Next, he talked to my abdomen. "OK baby, this is your father speaking. You'll soon get to know me as the one who yells a lot, but who can still make your mother blush."

"As well as growl and curse." I added on.

He flashed a mischievous look my way before he continued. "We have a lot riding on this. Hell, you're even supposed to have siblings one day. Your responsibility as the oldest, is the safety of others. In a few years time I may ask you to look after your little sisters occasionally? But right now, if you could just look after your mother, I'll be open to negotiation with pocket money."

Declan's first pep talk made me laugh as my heart warmed at his words.

"I thought you said that right now our baby is 'just cells'." I taunted.

"Nup, not this kid." He shook his head. "Not if she can already make her mother glow a happy colour."

My hand ran through this spiky, blonde hair. "You know, sometimes her father can do the same thing."

"Yeah?" His smile widened before slowly fading. "When he's not scaring the future mother, right?"

"Lets just try to enjoy this pregnancy, Declan." I said firmly. "Lets just go with the flow and see what happens. But since I don't have a bad feeling about this, it isn't going to turn into a catastrophe."

"I hope so B, I hope so." He sighed unhappily.

Then his hands made a move at unbuttoning my jeans...

"Declan!" I stopped him. "What are you doing?"

He chuckled, "I wanna make the rest of you turn peach coloured."

"But -" I objected.

He sat up to take off his jumper as he joked, "What's wrong B, scared you're gonna get even more pregnant?"

"I'm still pissed about this morning!" I cried indignantly.

My mate casually kicked off his jeans, "Of course you are, I'd be surprised if you weren't."

Within seconds, he had removed all his clothes and now he made a move to take off mine too.

"Stop it!" I grabbed the other pillow to whack him over the head. "What if something supernatural happens, like I end up carrying twins which you also try to stop?!"

"Are you referring to the case where that human woman delivered a Caucasian baby and an African American baby, at the same time?"

This made me pause and the horny male used this chance to remove my jeans in one tug.

"Do you think that could really happen?" I wondered aloud. "Getting pregnant twice, at the same time?"

"Well B, if you give birth to twins and one of them isn't a European Werewolf? Then I'd be worried." He guffawed. "But as long as both of them are half breeds, then I won't go out and kill something."

By now, I was undressed and my mate snuggled into my side. I used this as my chance to cup his face, so I could look him in the eye. Our gazes met and held as he ran his hot hands over my body.

"You really scared me this morning, Declan."

His expression mirrored mine, "You scared me too, B."

"Me?" I scoffed. "How did I scare YOU?"

"Because you're so obsessed with this baby business, you'd risk your own life and leave me in this existence alone; all for the sake of being pregnant."

In surprise, I let go but he quickly caught my hands. He held them against his hot chest as his eyes watered. He tried to hold my gaze for as long as possible.

"Tell me I'm being an idiot." He said soberly. "Tell me I'm imagining things. Tell me that my own wife who couldn't bare to lose me, so she turned me into a Circulator like her? Didn't act like a lemming by diving over a cliff, all for the sake of having a baby."

"Declan, I - I - I -"

"If you couldn't bear to lose me to old age, what makes you think I could lose you to pregnancy? You changed me into a Circulator and if your life was at risk, I'd change you to being non-pregnant. That's all there is to it."

The European Werewolf's jaw was set in determination, as his body hardened.

"But Declan -"

He interrupted, "You said this pregnancy wouldn't be a dangerous, so I believe you. You said you were carrying a daughter and I believe that too. You said that you and I will remain as the only Circulators, and that makes me ecstatic. So we're having this baby and we'll see what happens."

With that, he pushed himself on top as he closed his eyes and moved slowly, as if he could have even been a little fearful.

What we were doing now, we'd done millions of times in our centuries of marriage however, it had never felt like this before. His perpetually hot skin heated up mine, as my body adjusted to his greater strength. He dug his sharpening nails into the mattress, as his human blue eyes flashed their glowing green colour.

However, our movements felt a little mechanical, like we weren't really connecting because of this white elephant between us; the baby issue. But at the same time, I tingled all over, which must have been from the friction of our auras rubbing together.

Declan kept his eyes closed for most of the time. The couple of times they did open, I noticed they were glowing green as he gripped onto the mattress above my head. I felt a little helpless and I wondered if so did he? We were both slaves to our passion, or the bloodlust which came from being Werewolves. We both hungered for what the other could give, as we hungered for fresh kill.

Then I heard it, the dead giveaway to his inner turmoil. He cried out when he came and instead of sounding like a sign of pleasure, it sounded like a cry of pain. Normally, his taught body would loosen with release, but he remained tense, almost like he was angry with himself. Then as he started to move again, he moved stiffly, as if he was even cursing himself for the urges which drove him onwards.

"Declan," I stopped him, by cupping his reddening face, "I was only joking about the getting pregnant twice."

He laughed bitterly, "But it feels different, doesn't it? Knowing our sex can produce something now."

"It's always produced something."

"But we haven't created life from it." He sighed before he continued. "I promised your father as well as your grandfather, that I'd always look after you. Now this pregnancy has thrown a spanner in the works. You'd think I would have learned from my mistake? But like some kind of addict, I can't give up having you."

I rolled my eyes. "Declan, cut the 'poor me' crap!"

Then I pushed him off so I could sit up and crankily glare down.

"Oomph!" He landed face first into the mattress.

"Stop being so negative about this!" I snapped. "I've told you this will be a safe pregnancy! I've told you that you've got your hearts desire, a female Werewolf who ISN'T a Circulator! Hell, you once told me that you wanted only daughters, so you could be the King of the Castle, in a house full of women. You've got that so stop whinging!"

Grumpily, I rolled off the bed and proceeded to put on my robe, to leave the bedroom.

"Where are you going?" He whined.

"To have my evening shower!" I shouted back, before I slammed the bathroom door behind.

*****

No matter how angry we were with each other, it didn't interrupt our centuries old pattern of sleep. Last night in bed, we lay on our sides, facing in opposite directions. However, in our unconscious state, we inevitably came together with me curling up in his strong embrace.

Thanks to his supernaturally hot body temperature, we never used an electric blanket, nor was the central heating left on overnight. Winter evenings in Alaska could drop to -52°C and last night the fall temperature plunged past zero. It made my nose ache from the cold, so subconsciously I dove my face into his hot chest, to warm up.

I was in such a comfortable sleep, tucked into my mate that when he suddenly sat upright, it startled me.

"Hmm?" I stirred. He sat still with his eyes wide, whilst staring at the end of the bed. "Declan, what is it?"

"We're about to have company." He said stiffly.

“Huh?” I sat upright. “Was that a call from the pack? Are we about to fight something?”

Dazedly, I looked at the clock in the dim light of the morning, to see it was 7.23 AM.

“No, Caesar’s coming over with Forrest, Tyson and Ki.” He reported, having received the message telepathically from our First.

“Oh... hang on, what?” I had trouble processing, since I was still half asleep. “But why?”

“Why do you think?” He sneered. “You think they’re bringing us breakfast in bed? It’s about this baby business.”

“Oh.” I watched him climb out of bed and start to dress, by pulling on a pair of jeans and a long-sleeved t-shirt. “But why is Caesar coming over so early, to talk about the baby?”

“Because he wanted to make sure he was the first to give us a Baby Shower present.” He said sarcastically. “Wake up, B! You’re carrying another European Werewolf inside of you. Why do you think Caesar is coming here as First of the pack, bringing your Riverclaw relations with him?”

“I don’t know!”

“He, Forrest and Tyson, have the same concerns as I did yesterday.” He said sourly, as he sat down to pull on a pair of socks then shoes.

“But what’s it to them?” I asked in annoyance. “What, is the whole pack going to get involved with this pregnancy?!”

“I wouldn’t be surprised, I think everyone knows.”

“What?!” I squawked. “But isn’t that a breach of privacy?!”

Declan turned to give me an incredulous look, “What, are you going to sue our Medicine Man for misconduct?”

“How about I maul him instead?” I growled out.

“You maul someone? Now that IS funny.” He stood up and left the bedroom.

“Hey, what’s that supposed to mean?” I threw off the bedcovers, before storming around the bedroom to dress.

Once I’d finished, I stomped down the stairs. I found Declan in the kitchen making himself, his mate and three other cups of coffees for our expected guests. Crankily, I sat up on the kitchen bench, which made him move two of the cups aside, so I wouldn’t knock them over. I watched him pour the boiling water into the mugs which had instant espresso in them, before he applied the milk and sugar, as he recalled who drank theirs which way.

“What was THAT supposed to mean?” I glared however, his youthful face remained impassive as he carried out his task. “Declan?”

“I’ve never seen you maul someone, B.” He said coolly. “The only time I’ve seen you attack something with teeth and claws, was an animal during a hunt. Whenever you fight a foe, you reach for your silver sword.”

"You mean my Katana." I corrected. "It's a Japanese sword, remember?"

"Whatever." He stirred all five cups, before tossing the teaspoon into the sink. He handed me my cup before picking up his. I held my mug in between my hands, savouring the warmth before I took my first sip. Declan continued, "This fact also worries me."

"Why, because you've never seen me maul an enemy?"

"Sometimes you're more Circulator than you are Lokoti Werewolf. You don't hunt as much as the male Lokoti Werewolves and you don't use your predatory instincts as much as they do either. You'd rather use your Circulator abilities instead. This worries me about your pregnancy and I know it's also worrying your Werewolf relations as well."

I looked back in surprise, to find his eyes were waiting to hold my gaze.

I asked stiffly, "What's this got to do with my pregnancy?"

He spoke plainly, "Because we're worried that you may not be Lokoti Werewolf enough, to carry a half European Werewolf inside you."

But before I could rebuke him for saying something so stupid, we were interrupted by a loud KNOCK KNOCK KNOCK!

"Come in, Caesar." He called out knowingly.

We heard the front door open and the footsteps of four large males, enter then shut the door behind them.

A second later, the elderly face of the 156 year old Forrest came to the fore, as he stood in our kitchen entryway.

He was followed by the middle-aged appearance of our First, Caesar, who was 131 years old. His son Tyson who stood behind him, looked like he was in forties and he was turning 100 this year. Ki, who looked like he was in still his thirties when really he was 68 years old, stood beside our leader. Such was the slower aging process of the Lokoti Werewolves, who could live for two hundred years.

All four sets of dark brown eyes were trained my way and their expressions were grave.

"Aunt B," our First greeted.

"Caesar," I said perfunctory.

"I understand that yesterday you and Declan received some news which will affect your family." He began.

"Yes." I shot off a glare to Ki.

However, he didn't look remotely guilty for sharing my condition with the rest of the pack.

"I would ask that you consent to another scan by Ki this morning, and perhaps an examination." Caesar said seriously.

"Excuse me?"

"We need to take some readings of the cells that are growing inside you." Ki stated.

"Say what?" My mouth fell open in surprise. "Why?"

"We need to ascertain how much the baby may resemble either you or Uncle Declan." Our Medicine Man elaborated.

"But why?" I asked, taken aback.

"You know why, B." My mate said softly.

My overprotective Lokoti Werewolf instincts roared inside me first then outside second.

"Is that some kind of slur on Declan?" I raised my voice. "Are you worried about more European Werewolves being created? I don't care if I create an army of his breed, male or female! I love my husband and I'm sick of the hypocrisy - "

Then I was interrupted by a loud growl emitted by our First.

"Right now Aunt B THAT is the least of our worries! We have to make sure that your body is even able to carry just one European Werewolf child."

"Oh please!" I rolled my eyes. "Declan's already been through all of this! He tried to scare me yesterday, with a series of worst case scenarios and you know what I told him? That he's barking up the wrong tree! This baby is also HALF Lokoti Werewolf!"

"But Lokoti Werewolves are born human, Aunt B." Tyson said gravely. "This child will be born a Werewolf. You're carrying a half European Werewolf inside you, a creature with teeth and claws."

"Er, newsflash for you Tyson; DECLAN'S ALREADY BEEN THROUGH THIS!" I growled out between gritted teeth.

"Aunt B please," Forrest said awkwardly, "we're concerned for your safety."

"Of course you are!" I sung sarcastically. "Just like you'd be concerned for Tyson here, if he were knocked up by a European Werewolf too!"

"Yeah, but I'm stronger than you, being a male Lokoti Werewolf." He tried not to laugh.

Caesar spoke in a low voice, "Bianca Grace Wisetail Elm Sabre, when your grandfather Emanuel Riverclaw chose my great, great grandfather Chiron Riverclaw, to be First upon his leave? He made Chiron swear to keep a close eye on you. When your Circulator mother took your Lokoti Werewolf father Hunter Wisetail, to the space time continuum with her? He made Chiron swear again, to look after his only child; the tribe's first female Lokoti Werewolf who's also the world's last Circulator. Before Chiron left this life for the next, he passed the oath onto me."

"Right that's it!" I hopped off the bench, to stand on my own two feet.

"Oh oh," Declan muttered, as he watched warily.

I squared off my shoulders to say, "You're First and I'm in your pack. If you say, 'tonight we hunt caribou' then I hunt caribou. If you say, 'tonight we fight Vampires' then I'm right there with you. But I am your great, great, great,

great, great grandaunt. Right now, having a little boy who's almost two centuries my junior, stand in my kitchen and tell his elder how she can procreate? It's pissing me off!"

"B!" My husband came forwards to pull me away. "Caesar is not just First of your pack, but he and Forrest are the heads of your Riverclaw family!"

"Oh right, even though I'm the longest living member of the Riverclaw family; I'm not the head am I, because I'm just a female! Declan, you're the longest living member of the Sabre's, and your little brother's progeny all look to you as the head of that family. But with me, nope! Now my daughter who will be half Lokoti and half European Werewolf, has to deal with this male chauvinism in the 24th Century?" I ranted.

"You are shown the respect of an Elder in your Riverclaw family," Forrest said evenly. "But we are descended from Julian Riverclaw, who was born before his twin sister Jessica; who was your mother. Our family follows the old ways, of deferring to the first born as you well know, Aunt B."

But his words hit a wall because I wasn't listening, I was too angry.

"You can all drop dead!" I said vehemently. "Unless of course I do from this pregnancy, which is the reason you're all using, to try to tell me what I can do with my own body! If I reach the space time continuum as a spirit instead of a Circulator, I can tell your forefathers how the pack..." then I tearfully glared at Declan, "...and my mate screwed up, for making me do this alone!"

Then I barged through the line up of males, to storm through the living area and upstairs to my bedroom.

BAM! – was the sound the door made from slamming it behind.

I dropped to my knees on the floor beside the bed, to reach under and pull out my suitcase. I tossed it open on top of the bed, when I attacked the tall boy next. I opened the drawers to pull out my clothes and had just thrown in my underwear, when the bedroom door opened.

However, it wasn't just Declan who walked in, but so did Caesar and Ki.

"Oh look, it's 'The Three Amigos'." I said in a surly manner, as I continued.

"Oh look, as usual B is packing her bags." My mate responded in a similar tone, before he spoke to our First and Medicine Man. "You see, at least once every fifty years, B says she's gonna leave. Now for human couples, this wouldn't be seen as a major thing. But when you've been married for 273 years, it adds up."

"She's done this that many times?" Ki asked in consternation.

"Hmm," Caesar frowned, "this is worse than I thought. Aunt B truly is more 'Light Person' than she is Lokoti Werewolf."

"Don't give me that crap about loyalty!" I turned on them, before seething Declan's way. "I stood in the kitchen and told the leader of the pack to go to hell, for putting down my husband! And he STILL sides with the pack over his wife!"

"Loyalty...? LOYALTY?!" Declan roared as his face reddened in anger. "WHEN HAVE I EVER PACKED MY BAGS AND THREATENED TO LEAVE YOU, B?!"

Next, the European Werewolf picked up my suitcase and hurled it against the far wall, scattering my things all over the place!

"Er, maybe we should leave and let them sort this out...?" Ki looked on uncomfortably.

"We stay." Caesar ordered.

"Fine!" I retorted. "I can buy new clothes!"

I started to walk over to my handbag, but Declan reached it first. He picked it up and threw it out of the bedroom doorway, with Caesar coolly moving his head to the side. He was acting like he was accustomed to my husband's ferocious temper, whereas Ki looked nervous.

"Fine!" I repeated. "I can easily get replacement credit cards, from my PA at Hodge Endeavor!"

"SIT DOWN B!" My mate snarled.

He grabbed onto both of my arms, forcing me sit on the side of the bed. I glowered back as my dark blue eyes burned turquoise. He seethed in return, with his bright blue eyes momentarily glowing green.

"OK, now we're going to talk about this calmly." Caesar began. "Aunt B, although you outwardly have the appearance of a woman in her twenties thanks to being a Circulator; I acknowledge you as the oldest living member of the Riverclaw family. I do not wish to offend you, nor do I want to downgrade your role over the many years. Our families have always turned to you for counsel."

I crossed my arms and stubbornly looked away, as the three males stood over me like they were trying to impose their will.

"My father and I may share the titles of heads of the Riverclaw family, but you might recall the many times we've come to you for advice. Even the Council of Tribal Elders, have called on you for your unique insight. However, when you act more as a Circulator, it concerns us that you act less like a female Lokoti Werewolf. It's for this reason, we are worried about what kind of strain this pregnancy will put your body under." Caesar continued.

Forrest agreed as he walked in, "I remember well, how much you and Uncle Declan were there for Maia and I, in the beginning of our marriage." He smiled sadly as he remembered his late wife with fondness. "I remember how you helped her after her miscarriage. I'm still grateful to you for saying exactly the right things she needed to hear, such as 'it's not your fault, problems with fertility happens to everyone'."

Tyson walked in after, "When Samuel was born and Tania went through postnatal depression, I remember how you took her out for coffee all those times. She would come back with renewed strength after talking to you. She'd tell me, 'Aunt B is nearly 300 years old and she still gets depressed from PMT every month. If she can carry on then so can I'."

"B's PMT must be my worst enemy." My mate grumbled, as he sunk onto the bed beside. "It's thanks to those mood swings that I've nearly burnt our luggage set, to stop this nonsense of her trying to run away all of the time."

This made the other males in the room chuckle in sympathy, thinking of their own war stories with the female curse.

"Aunt B, we know of the little things you and Uncle Declan do, behind the scenes for your families." Caesar continued. "So now it's your family's turn to help you through this pregnancy."

I arched my eyebrows, "Help me with it, or try to end it?"

This question made all of them look on puzzled, but it was Ki who cottoned on.

"Hang on," the Medicine Man spoke up, "I think I can see why Aunt B is getting so worked up."

"Then enlighten us, please!" Declan cried out, exasperated.

"Yesterday you frightened her, by trying to talk her out of having the baby." Ki frowned at Declan before looking to Caesar. "With our appearance this morning, she must have thought we were trying to do the same thing. It's the Lokoti Werewolf in her which is acting defensive. She thinks she has to protect her baby."

"Well, do I?" I hugged my stomach, as if I were hugging my daughter.

"What?" Caesar blanched, as did all of the male Lokoti Werewolves.

Suddenly the room was full of guilty expressions, except for my husband.

"Aunt B, no! We certainly haven't come here this morning, to try to force an abortion on you! We came here to scan you and the baby and come up with a strategy on how to see you safely through this pregnancy." Our First promised.

"Oh really?" I looked on skeptically.

YOU AND YOUR CHILD ARE NOT IN ANY DANGER FROM US – Caesar thought my way – *WE ARE ACTING TODAY TO ENSURE YOU REMAIN OUT OF DANGER.*

"Seriously?" I asked, still suspicious.

"Aunt B, you're going to need our help when it comes to the delivery." Ki spoke frankly. "I'm willing to bet this won't be as straight forward as a human delivery. Caesar will be putting the entire pack on standby for the day you give birth, incase you need the blood of your kin to heal."

"Are you for real?" I blinked in disbelief.

"I'm going to scan you once a week and track your baby's development." Ki organized. "Your daughter will no doubt be bigger than a human child, but we're unsure yet of her growth rate. That, and I have to make sure your body is able to carry the child to term, or if you'll make it to the last trimester."

Then my husband surprised everyone, when he stood up to say firmly, "If B needs blood, it's going to be me that gives it to her."

"But Uncle Declan, we don't know how much blood Aunt B will need -" Ki began but he was interrupted.

"B is MY mate and she's carrying MY child. If she needs blood, then it's gonna come from me." He said determinedly.

Our Medicine Man opened his mouth to argue but our First spoke instead.

"Uncle Declan is a European Werewolf and Aunt B is carrying a half European Werewolf. It might be best for both Aunt B and the baby, if Uncle Declan does this. Especially since European Werewolves are the fastest healers of all of the breeds."

Forrest pointed out to Ki, "Think of when Jenny delivered your three kids and how you opened your wrist for her. Didn't you want to provide for your mate in that manner, let alone have another Werewolf do it?"

"Fine," he looked away, disliking that his medical opinion was being disputed.

It was then their Second decided to put a stop to the conversation.

"Look Caesar, I appreciate your help and I understand your position. But can we skip the examination of B and the baby this morning? Emotions are running high and besides, right now they're just cells dividing. If Ki comes back next week to scan her, I'm sure he'll get more accurate readings of what part of me or B, this kid is gonna have."

To top it off, my husband's hand started to stroke my hair in a protective manner. Caesar openly looked on Declan's face, as I sensed a couple of sentences pass between them however, they blocked their words from me. But our First made his thoughts known, when he looked from our Medicine Man to his father and son.

"We'll leave and Ki will come back to scan Aunt B, next week and the week after that and then every week from now on." He declared.

All of the males in the room nodded in uniformity.

Then Caesar gave a parting smile before he turned and left. Tyson and Ki were right on his heels with Forrest lingering for a moment. A kindly smile sat on our elderly great x4 grandnephew's, worn face.

"Congratulations, Aunt B." He briskly placed a kiss on my cheek. "Call on me or any of your Riverclaw family, should you need anything."

Then he turned and left both the bedroom and the house, with the rest of my relatives.

Silence... our surprise visitors were gone and we were alone again.

My husband's hand was still stroking my hair, which I thought was a little hypocritical. I moved my head from his touch before I stood up and walked away.

"OK, let's finish the rest of our fight then." He said tiredly, sitting back down on the bed.

"No, I'm tired of fighting." I said emotionally, as I kept my back turned.

"You, tired of fighting? Now that's a first." He muttered.

I looked around to show my hurt, "I am seriously fed up with your negativity about this pregnancy. If I hear one more bad thing out of your mouth, I'll instantaneously phase out of here so fast, you'll have no hope in stopping me!"

"And we're back to running away again." He groaned. "You know what, B?"

"What, Declan?"

"I AM going to get rid of our luggage set!"

He stood up from the bed, knelt down on the floor and pulled out the second suitcase from underneath. Then he walked past, picked up the first case he had hurled across the room and carried both out.

"What's THAT going to prove?!" I exhorted. "I can just buy new clothes!"

"Then I'm hiding your handbag and your purse!" He called back, as he descended the stairs.

"And again, I can simply get replacement credit cards from my PA with Hodge Endeavor!"

"Then I'll eat her so you can't!" He shouted back from somewhere, in the lower part of the house.

"Then I can get replacements from someone else inside Hodge Endeavor!"

"And I'll eat them too!"

"Or the Circulate Mainframe can generate replacements for me."

"If it does, I'll smash the frickin' thing!"

"That'll be interesting, since you can't instantaneously phase yet." I sung back. "How are you going to reach Taurus Six? It's on the other side of the galaxy!"

Abruptly, a bright blur whizzed through the bedroom doorway and came to a stop before me.

I blinked in astonishment as Declan glared my way. He'd just run up here in the speed of light! He was showing off how well he was adjusting to his new status as a Circulator.

"If I can already do that, I can damn well guarantee that I'll soon start to instantaneously phase here, there and everywhere. So tough luck, B! You really are stuck with me, because now I can follow you to any location you run to." He growled out.

"I hate you."

"Sure you do! But guess what, my little Light Person? You turned me into a Light Person too, so we're together for eternity! We swore 'always and forever' and baby, forever is now here!"

"Not if I don't take you to the space time continuum with me!"

"Like I said B, I have the ability to follow you ANYWHERE!"

"Great! So you're a supernatural stalker? I want a divorce!"

"I don't care if we evolve to the space time continuum as ex-husband and ex-wife, but guess what princess? You're frickin' stuck with me!"

"Like hell!"

"Are you furious with me yet, so we can have hot, angry sex?"

"We passed that point ages ago!"

"Then what the frickin' hell are you waiting for, woman?!"

I leapt into his waiting arms, as my sharp teeth went straight for his throat!

Declan snarled back, as he began to rip the clothes from my body. I used my claws to shred his garments, whilst my teeth broke through his skin. I'm not sure who undressed who first, but soon two piles of ruined fabric lay on the floor.

He started to stumble backwards to fall onto the bed. I left bite mark after bloodied bite mark along his collar bone. He gave a hard thrust which could probably paralyze a human woman, as we rolled around on top of the mattress. We were wrestling over who would be on top...

...until a clawing, growling couple, fell off the bed and landed loudly onto the wooden floor.

~~~~~~
~~~~~~

~ 3 ~

20th December 2363

The pregnancy was life altering because everything around me, let alone inside me, changed.

It changed the tribe's previous views of me, as it changed my husband's. Not only was Declan watching closely but so too were the pack. Everyone seemed fascinated as they observed my shape shift, with some closer than others.

I had left behind a vision, a beautiful but barren creature whom people had put on a kind of pedestal; somewhat like a painting on the wall. Like the two-dimensional art, I had always looked the same. But now, everyone instantly noticed my changes, because they made me more life-like.

For 273 years my appearance never altered, unless I did it deliberately to look older with my changing academic identities. And of course, this was excluding the change I went through when I expanded to hunt on a full moon. Otherwise, my breasts, abdomen, hips or bottom, always looked the same. I kept this form for nearly three centuries, which was a broad-shouldered, athletic figure thanks to my Lokoti Werewolf physique.

On this note, my appetite never differed, except for larger meals during the bitterly cold Alaskan winter. However, after the first week of pregnancy, my husband instantly noticed the change in my eating. I started to steal an extra piece of garlic bread, or a second bread roll with dinner, or even an extra piece of toast with breakfast. My meals were increasing and after the first three weeks, I started to snack more.

Declan would come into kitchen with an attack of the munchies and to his surprise, he would find me there. I didn't use to snack, instead I was quite happy with three meals a day. But my cravings were starting up, like dipping celery sticks into a jar of peanut butter.

"You want a sandwich? I can make you a sandwich." He offered, as he looked on pleasantly surprised.

I shook my head, "I don't want a sandwich, I want celery sticks with peanut butter."

The next afternoon, he found me doing something similar but with carrot sticks and cream cheese.

After a couple of days of this, Declan walked out of the kitchen carrying two plates. On one were his sandwiches and on the other, were neatly cut up celery and carrot sticks. He even put on the side two small dipping bowls of peanut butter and cream cheese.

"Oh, Declan!" My face lit up.

"Food is my department, remember?" He kissed the top of my head. "I can't have your cravings putting me out of business."

As was typical for pregnant women to crave odd things, I started to dip my celery sticks into Nutella as well as peanut butter. Declan openly stared as I munched away.

"You're not gonna start eating sardines and ice cream, are you?" He shook his head in disbelief.

"Shut up." I giggled.

Also, I noticed that he began to slowly build up the size of my meals. If one night I craved more mashed potato, the following night I saw my serving had doubled or even tripled. Then he watched closely as I polished off everything on my plate.

I think it gave the European Werewolf satisfaction that my appetite was growing. His bloodlust made him constantly hungry for food or sex. When I started to behave in a similar fashion, his eyes lit up like it was Christmas morning.

Into the fourth week of pregnancy, I finished my afternoon snack and gazed upon my mate as he finished his. He saw the hungry look in my eyes.

"You want more?" He stood up from the couch, to fetch it.

"No." I frowned, a little confused. "I'm hungry, but I don't think it's for celery sticks."

"You want a sandwich?" He offered.

By standing over me to take our plates, I noticed the ample bulge in the front of his jeans. I don't know what came over me, as I brazenly placed my hand over it. I felt the reaction in him immediately.

"I think I've died and gone to heaven." He uttered out.

Quick as lightning, he almost dropped our plates onto the coffee table to pick me up instead.

I was mauling his neck, as he carried me up the stairs so fast, he may have been running.

For over an hour, I claimed the dominant position and rode him hard. His eyes were closed with a blissful expression on his face. His torso had long scratch marks, which were already healing thanks to his speedy regeneration. He barely flinched as I left bite mark after bloodied bite mark, on his shoulders, his arms or even his chest. Instead, he groaned in ecstasy and pushed harder.

It was like I went wild. What am I saying, I DID go wild! Normally, it would be my body which wore the most bite marks, as Declan's bloodlust demanded that he completely have his mate. But this time it was my turn.

I just had to taste his blood as I craved his other fluids. I felt so hungry with desire, like I could have been on fire! I felt my blood almost boil within my very veins! My skin was burning hot, as my teeth and nails sharpened. They raked across his skin and he would heal over in minutes. I was so surprised at myself, I trembled in astonishment.

“Are – are – are you alright?” I stammered, whilst looking on his injuries.

“Huh?” He slowly opened his eyes, as if he were coming out of a pleasure-induced daze. “Don’t stop now, B!”

He flipped me over onto my back and rode me instead. We snapped our dangerously sharp mouths at the other, as my turquoise eyes burned hungrily and his green eyes glowered back. We playfully fought over who’d be on top, which ended in the both of our mouths locked onto the other’s shoulders.

From the force we were grinding away, it pumped the blood straight into the other’s eager mouth. Then we slowed the bleeding with our tongues. The saliva aided our regeneration, so when our mouths moved away, they left behind new, pink skin in its place.

He sighed in a satiated manner, “You know, I think I’m gonna enjoy this pregnancy.”

“NOW you sing positive things about the baby?” I arched my eyebrows.

“If you keep this up, I’m gonna be singing show tunes soon.” He chuckled, before he bellowed out, “Tomorrow! Tomorrow! I love ya! Tomorrow! You’re only a day away...”

However, the other symptom the pregnancy produced, was difficulty with getting out bed in the mornings. I guess I shouldn’t complain, since I wasn’t experiencing morning sickness like other women in my condition. But I felt exceptionally sleepy and sluggish.

BANG! BANG! BANG!

Huh?

BAM! BAM! BAM!

What was this, déjà vu? Sleepily, I raised my head and looked about, to find Declan was missing from his side of the bed. His digital alarm clock read as 9.13 AM, so that’s why. I had slept in again.

BANG! RRRIIIIIIPP! BAM!

What the hell was going on here? I stumbled out of bed in my negligee and meandered over to the doorway of the second bedroom. I found Declan pulling apart our two single beds. He was sitting on the wooden floor, with his tool kit open as he was unscrewing the wooden bed frames. The mattresses had been taken off and were now leaning against the wall.

“G’morning sunshine!” He sung. “Man, after 273 years, your bed hair still cracks me up! But at least I’ve gotten you out of those cartoon cow pajamas.”

“You’re full of shit.” I said back. “I still wear them when it’s in the dead of winter and it’s minus thirty degrees.”

“That’s my B.” He chuckled at my early morning language. “Your coffee awaits, my lady.”

I slid down the doorframe to land on my ass before I reached over to pick up the cup, which sat beside his.

"Mmm." I closed my eyes as I savoured my first sip.

"You know with this pregnancy, you're going to have to start drinking de-caff soon." He warned.

"Blasphemy!" I almost choked on my drink.

"That's what I hear pregnant women drink."

"Yeah, but they're just humans and I'm a Werewolf, so it's allowed."

"Let's ask Ki the next time he's over, shall we?" He taunted.

"Do you want to wear this coffee?" I threatened.

"Man, I love my wife's biting mood in a morning." He laughed to himself. "Maybe if Marcus had come across you first thing, he wouldn't have been so quick to try to steal you."

He was referring to nearly two centuries ago, when I was abducted by the few remaining European Werewolves left. It was the occasion when Declan murdered his treacherous, man-eating breed and made himself the last of his kind. That was until of course, he knocked me up.

I turned silent as I watched him pull apart the bed frame. He unscrewed the end board, before moving up to undo the bed head. He was wearing a pair of old jeans and his favourite blue-chequered, flannel shirt, but his supernatural muscles bulged underneath. Once the bed frame was completely undone, he moved to our second single bed to disassemble it.

Then I sung teasingly, "You're not going to be the last of the European Werewolves anymore. So how do you feel about that, Mr. Sabre?"

"I am still gonna be the last though, Mrs. Sabre." He corrected as he worked. "Our daughters are gonna be half-breeds, which is fine with me."

"Half-breeds?" I screwed up my face. "I don't like that term."

"And why not?"

"I don't know, it just doesn't sound right."

"Then what are you gonna call our daughters?"

"Special."

Declan snickered, before sneaking a look over to where I was sitting. He cast a lazy gaze over my legs, which were unintentionally on display, thanks to the short cut of the negligee.

"With a mother like that, I think all the boys in the tribe are going to agree with you." He said smoothly.

"You're gonna love it aren't you, when they all come to you for your permission to date your offspring?"

"Ha!" He snorted. "Yes I am! You know how Odysseus had to fulfill all those tasks, and it took him years to finally return to his wife? I'm gonna be just as bad! Any applicant that wants to come within ten meters of my girls, are gonna have to be the best of the best! I'm gonna set such an obstacle course, most of them are gonna give up and slink away with their tails between their legs."

"This should be interesting." I tittered, as I nursed my coffee in both hands. "Only, I don't think this planet has any Cyclops or Sirens left, I think they're all extinct."

"That's what people thought about European Werewolves." He pointed out. "Trust me B, if the boys have to get past me instead? They'll be begging for a Cyclops!"

I giggled back, "If the suitors saw you in European Werewolf form, they'd think they're battling Cerberus."

"Except for the fact that I don't have three heads," he said, before he paused. "Then again, what about the tales of the 'Hounds From Hell'? It makes you wonder doesn't it, about how much fiction is fact?"

"Hmm, it does a bit." I frowned pensively. "I mean, your species of Werewolf is the oldest in the world. So anytime a human saw one of you and lived to tell the tale; I wonder how often the truth was distorted and came out as a fable instead?"

"You got that right." Declan declared. "I was used to the fact that I was the last of my kind. Now with our first rug rat you're carrying, I'm gonna have a whole litter to train. I'll have to teach 'em not to become one of the monsters that people fear in the dark."

"Maybe the legends are still being written?" I posed. "Maybe we're creating all new mythology of how the Last European Werewolf and the First Female Lokoti Werewolf, started an all new breed? Their strength and control, the world has never seen?"

"Oh joy," he grumbled, picking up his wrench again. "But if my daughters mirror their mother with their monthly blues; it'll be an all new PMT the world has never seen before."

"Declan!" I griped. "We were having a nice conversation then, why did you go and spoil it?"

"I'm just trying to prepare for the future." He said simply. "I'm gonna get our PA at Hodge Endeavor to start buying up shares in 'Nutella', so we can get unending free samples sent to us. I'll fill this house with choc hazelnut spread, so my moody wife and ferocious female young, will never go without."

I growled under my breath and stood up to leave, when I paused to look back.

"Why are you pulling apart the beds, by the way?"

"We have a two bedroom house, B." He said coolly. "Where did you think the nursery was gonna go, in the dining area?"

"Oh."

Declan's already organizing the nursery? His gesture warmed my heart, at how the reluctant father was planning ahead for the baby. I left him to his task and returned to the main bedroom, to get dressed.

*****

I put on a pair of jeans, a long-sleeved, black t-shirt and a purple, zip-up sweater, before I wandered downstairs to fix myself some brunch. However, just as I opened the fridge, I was startled by a knock at the door.

I smelled whoever it was, was one of the pack. So when I swung open the front door, I wasn't surprised to find Walt Wisetail standing on my icy veranda. Behind him, was his U.S. Forest Service hover-vehicle, parked on the snowy driveway.

"Walt," I smiled on my distant relation. "How are you? How's Wendy and the rug rats?"

"We're well, thanks Aunt B." He smiled proudly.

He was a typical Lokoti Werewolf, being completely devoted to his mate and young. Never in a million years would he gripe about his wife's mood swings. In fact, his grin grew even wider with his next update.

"Actually, Wendy and I are expecting again."

"A third kid on the way?" My eyebrows arose. "Wow, you really are following Lokoti Werewolf tradition there, Walt."

He chuckled as he came in from the cold air, "How about yourself Aunt B, better late than never?"

Declan's voice interrupted, as he jogged down the stairs. "We were stopping to smell the roses, before weighing down the marriage with kids."

"Kids don't take away from the marriage, Uncle Dec." He said affably. "They add to it, just you wait and see."

My mate said sarcastically, "Oh yeah, the messy diapers, the late night feedings and losing your free time for the next 18 years; I can see how you'd say that. Kids take away the need for romantic dinners, annual overseas holidays or even intimate evenings with the wife."

"With that attitude, you're being extremely optimistic that you're still going to have a wife to be intimate with." I passed a glare.

"Oh you two!" Walt laughed loudly at our banter. "Trust me, kids can add to the sex life. Especially when the parents have to think up new ways how to sneak it in quietly, it leaves a lot to experimentation."

Declan and I exchanged raised eyebrows at his candor.

"Now about those beds..." my husband laughed it off, "...this way."

He turned to lead him upstairs when I spoke, "What about the beds?"

"Oh," Walt paused and looked to Declan to explain.

"I'm giving our spare beds to the Wisetail's." He stated.

"You are?" My hands moved to my hips. "When did you discuss THIS with me?"

"Now," he said simply, before he started to make his way up the stairs again.

"Hold on - hold on - hold on!" I interrupted, making the two turn around once more.

"Er, is there a problem?" Our guest looked uncomfortable. "If you still need the beds Aunt B -"

"No, you can have the beds, Walt." I said in annoyance, whilst glaring Declan's way. "But I'm pissed off that my husband didn't mention this before."

"We don't need the beds right now, B!" He snapped. "Let Walt and Wendy have them, since their 'tribe' is growing faster than ours is."

"THAT'S not the problem, Declan! The problem is you didn't ASK me first!" I growled.

"Why the hell, do I have to ask you?" He asked indignantly. "What, every time I talk kids with the guys, I have to fill you in?"

"When were you talking to the guys about kids?" I asked in disbelief.

"When Walt, Forrest and Caesar, were telling me about the kind of things we're gonna need, for the nursery!" His voice rose. "Now quit with the third degree, woman!"

He and Walt disappeared upstairs, as I stomped back into the kitchen whilst snarling obscenities under my breath.

I don't get Declan...even after two centuries of marriage. He runs hot and cold more than the kitchen faucet! One minute he's happy then he's snappy. Who's the pregnant woman here, me or him?

Then I paused...my husband has been talking to the men in the pack, about impending fatherhood? Why, to get advice? This almost made me laugh out loud as I made myself another coffee.

It was funny to think of the former elderly European Werewolf asking the younger Lokoti Werewolves for their words of wisdom. It also seemed like he was embarrassed about it. He's never liked asking for help, maybe this is the reason why he's acting so tetchy about it?

Typical for his breed, he was a control freak and with his ego, he liked being in charge. To ask his subordinates for baby tips must have been a lesson in humility for him. So to repay Walt for his help, he was giving him the beds? Ah, now it made sense.

After the coffee was made, I sat up on the kitchen bench to drink my beverage. I overheard the men make several trips up and down the stairs as they carried the mattresses and furniture out to Walt's hover-car. With their supernatural strength they easily carried the loads individually. Soon my spare beds were strapped to the top of Walt's vehicle.

To say goodbye, my distant cousin appeared in the kitchen entranceway with my husband standing beside. He was carrying an old cardboard box in his arms, which was full of books and old knick-knacks. He must have had them in his hover-car.

"Oh and by the way Aunt B, I've brought a couple of things that you might find interesting. I found them when I was going through my attic last month." He placed the box on top of the bench beside where I was sitting.

"What's this?" I picked up one of the books which looked so old, the pages were yellow.

"It's an old diary from one of my great aunts." He explained. "But I think she'd be closer to you than she is to me. I think it's Ling Wisetail's diary."

Declan's and my eyes widened at the name, as I quickly put down my mug to open it.

"Hey, it's Nana's diary!" I cried out excitedly. "Ling Wisetail was my Dad's mother!"

"She's something like eight or nine times removed from me, but I thought you'd appreciate it." Walt said kindly. "There's also a couple of old photos in there that I think are of your father when he was a boy, as well as of your Grandpa."

The fact that Walt's family had them didn't surprise me, since Wisetail used to be my maiden name. Walt and Wendy even lived in the same house that I grew up in. Gleefully, I rifled through the box looking at what else was in there. I came across a baby album and when I opened it up, I saw it was Dad's.

"Oh my gosh!" I jumped off the bench. "This is my father's baby album! I didn't know your family had this!"

"Family keepsakes such as photo albums and family records, are passed along the males in the family." He reminded. "I guess after your father evolved to the space time continuum, it was among his keepsakes which remained in house when Jake Wisetail took over, who was my forefather."

"That tradition sucks." I sighed. "Declan and I will certainly break it, with our daughters and their daughters."

"We certainly will." He agreed. "Hey B, don't you have a lot of Riverclaw stuff?"

"I have my foremothers Elisha's, Alexandrina's, Arabella's as well as Jessica's, old diaries. I also have their photo albums and baby books. But I don't have Grandfather's things." I realized.

"Emanuel would have passed it to his son Julian, who passed it on to Phoenix then to Chiron, Stone, Forrest and now to Caesar." Walt respectfully recited the Riverclaw lineage, especially since three of them had been First in the pack. "If you asked Forrest or Caesar, they could check for you."

"It's unfair." I shot a hurt look towards my mate. "We were actually alive during their time, so we should have got their things."

Just then I noticed in the box a framed photo which I picked up and showed to my husband. It was a family photo of a ten year old Dad with a younger looking Nana and Grandpa. My heart hurt, as I remembered my family of old.

Declan looked on Walt unhappily, "What else have you got of B's?"

"Um, that's all I could see of Aunt B's father and grandparents." He said awkwardly. "I mean, there are childhood photos of Fern Wisetail, with his brother and sister when they were growing up. But since Aunt B's grandfather was the older brother of Sky Wisetail, who's my forefather? I think my family will want to keep those."

My mate crossed over to my side as I turned tearful at the photo. These people whom I hadn't seen for over two centuries, could still bring a tear to my eye. I had to sniff as my nose began to run with my longing to see my immediate family again.

"Don't worry, B." He put his arm about my waist. "This afternoon, I'll go to Forrest and Caesar myself and ask for the Riverclaw stuff."

"Oh Declan!" I threw my arms about his neck. "I miss them! I miss them so much! I just wish that my parents and my grandparents were here."

"I miss my Mom and my little brother, too." He held me tightly. "She'd be spoiling us rotten, by cooking for us and coming over nearly every day, to check on the pregnancy."

My mate gently lifted me up into his hug, as my legs wrapped about his waist. His right arm held me up, as his left rubbed my back. Our faces came together, as he used his to wipe away my tears, before planting several soft kisses over my trembling lips.

Walt said uncomfortably, "If you like, I'll do another search of our attic to make sure you have all of Hunter Wisetail's things."

"That would be nice, especially since you're living in the house that my father owned." I reminded.

"Yes but Aunt B, when your father left it to my great, great grandfather; we renovated it and made it our own." He joked back.

"Details details." The European Werewolf growled. "If my wife says it's her house then damn it, it's still her house!"

"I take it you procure anything for her that Aunt B says is hers, right Uncle?" My cousin smirked.

"You got that right."

"Yep, this is going to be an interesting pregnancy to be sure." Walt pretended to look nervous.

"It sure is," my mate held me closely, "and together, we're gonna get through it."

His bright blue eyes held onto my dark blue ones, as if silently endorsing his words.

"Then if you two will excuse me, I have my own pregnant mate to return to." Walt cleared his throat. "Oh and by the way, Wendy wanted to invite you over for afternoon tea, for baby-talk."

"Er, our afternoons can get pretty busy." Declan tried to put our recent bedroom behaviour, diplomatically. "How about morning tea instead?"

"That should be fine." He shrugged. "I'll see myself out and thanks again for the furniture, it'll come in handy for my eldest kids."

Once Walt shut the front door on his way out, Declan placed me back on top of the kitchen bench again.

"So this is the last of your Dad's stuff, huh?" He picked up the baby album, to peruse through. "It's hard to think of your father as a baby. Whenever I think of Hunter Wisetail, I remember this disapproving, old Lokoti

Werewolf, constantly looking over my shoulder. It was like he was just waiting for me to screw up."

"He wasn't that bad!" I rolled my eyes. "Besides, you and Dad ended up getting along."

"Yeah, it only took a century of marriage for your father to get it through his head that I truly was your mate." He complained. "In the end we didn't get along, we simply stopped fighting aloud. Trust me, our glares said it all."

This made me recall something about my parent's passing, in particular what was communicated between my father and husband.

"Declan," I began, "just before Mum and Dad left for the space time continuum, what did he say telepathically to you?"

"Huh?"

"You said, 'do you really have to ask?' or something as such." I remembered.

"Oh yeah, he tried to make me swear that I'd always put your safety first." He said bitterly. "And my response to such a stupid question was, did he really have to ask? He was about to leave behind his mortal existence and evolve as a sparkling cloud of energy and light, to the space time continuum. But he still didn't trust me with his beloved, only daughter."

I pulled him in for a kiss. "Yes, but I'm your beloved B now."

"Damn straight," he murmured, just before our lips pressed together. "You always have been and always will be, no matter how hard your father tried to split us up."

"He didn't try to split us up!"

"He married you to another man."

"Oh yeah, there was that." I conceded. "But that was before Dad knew of my feelings for you."

"He suspected MY feelings and he still pushed you onto Grant." He let go to busy himself by picking up the box. "I'm gonna go put this stuff up into the attic."

"No, I will." I hopped off the bench to take it from him. "While I'm up there, I wanna check on something."

"OK then," he watched me walk away. "Hey, have you actually eaten breakfast yet?"

"No." I called over my shoulder.

"I'm gonna fix you some toasted tomato and cheese sandwiches then."

"OK!" I sung back.

I carried the box up the staircase to put it on the floor, in the small upstairs hallway. Next, I reached up and pulled the chord hanging from the ceiling, which opened the hatch to the attic. The fold-up ladder which was attached, unfolded before me.

Using one hand to climb as the other carried the box, I ascended the small ladder up into the dark, dusty attic.

Immediately, I sneezed from the cold and dust! Then I had to engage my glowing eyes for the night-vision, so I could find the light switch. My hand found the long chord which hung from the ceiling and I gave it a gentle tug.

As soon as the light came on, my glowing turquoise eyes dulled back to their dark blue colour. I looked about the disorganized, dusty, dim attic. Many a cobweb hung from the rafters, or even connected a couple of the boxes which were piled high. I was looking on three hundred years of memorabilia.

We haven't been up here in years! Oh hang on, maybe Declan has... my eyes settled on the least dustiest of the items, the two suitcases. So that's what he did with them! I suppose I should be relieved he didn't burn them, like he threatened to.

I started to examine the different labels on the cardboard boxes. Once upon a time, this attic was clean and organized. When we started to accumulate keepsakes from family members who'd passed on, we wrote on the boxes what was in them.

My hand removed some the dust, so I could see the descriptions properly. I read his writing on boxes which read as 'Mom's Stuff', or 'Derik's Stuff' or 'Blanche and Michael's Stuff'. They had been Declan's human mother, brother, nephew and niece. His family's things were stacked neatly against one of the attic walls.

My family's things however, weren't as tidy as Declan's. Boxes such as 'Vincent's Things,' or 'Mum and Dad's Things', or 'Gran and Grandfather's Things'; were all sitting willy-nilly about the confined space. Over the many years, I'd open them upon occasion when I needed to find something, like a photo album. But his boxes were untouched, as I couldn't recall him ever looking, perhaps because the memories were still too painful?

I picked up the box which Walt had given me and carried it over to the box full of 'Gran and Grandfather's Things'. I wanted my paternal grandparents memorabilia to sit beside my maternal grandparents. I'd have to come back with tape and seal it, before labelling it.

Unconsciously, I began to stroke the box as I reminisced on my parents and my grandparents. With my 'bundle of joy', I'd have loved to share this with my family. I never did make my Mum and Dad grandparents however, Aunt Susan enjoyed this delight through Derik.

Just as I turned to leave, I noticed something. It was a red trunk which looked worn with time. It was half hidden, underneath another cardboard box and for the life of me, I don't remember seeing it before. But I felt this undeniable urge to investigate, or maybe it was one of my all-knowing feelings?

"B!" I heard the distant call of my husband. "Your brunch is ready!"

"Coming!"

Quickly, I walked over and lifted the other box off the red trunk then I sunk to my knees beside. When I opened the lid, the hinges squealed in protest as a huge cloud of dust came up. It sent me into a sneezing frenzy!

"Achoo! Achoo! Achoo!"

My sensitive nose objected, as I spluttered and waved my hand through the air to clear it. But when I looked inside, I accidentally let out a squeal! I felt like I just hit the jackpot.

"B?" He hollered. "What are you doing up there?"

"Nothing!"

"Then come downstairs and do nothing, while you eat your brunch!"

"Alright already!" I snapped back.

I looked inside the trunk again at the old baby clothing, a couple of framed photos as well as some old books. But these weren't just ordinary books, they were more diaries! When I opened up the covers, I saw the names 'Clara Winter' as well as 'Jessica Tandy'. They were my great grandmother as well as my great, great grandmother, from my Riverclaw family.

Bingo! They were just what I was hoping for, after my previous conversation. It looks like Declan doesn't have to approach Caesar after all.

I picked up the framed photos for a closer look. There was a picture circa late 20th Century, of a pretty, blonde woman standing with a handsome, Lokoti man. The woman had a baby bulge, protruding through her thick jacket. I was looking on my great, great grandfather Flint Riverclaw and his mate Jessica. She had been namesake of my mother, since she died before Mum was born. According to Grandfather, Mum also inherited the original Jessica's temper too.

"B, your toasted sandwiches are turning cold!" He complained.

"I'm coming!"

Hastily, I put the photo frame back and shut the lid. I stood up again as I dusted myself off, when my eyes landed on the new box I had just brought up. I made myself a silent promise that I'd return to visit my foremothers soon; the women who'd been the mates of my Lokoti Werewolf forefathers. I pushed the box of Wisetail family memorabilia closer to the trunk, so my foremothers would be waiting together.

Lastly, I climbed down the attic ladder, closed the hatch and happily skipped downstairs.

"There you are!" He walked out of the kitchen with his hands on his hips. "I was about to come up there after you."

"You're a bossy boots, you know that?" I poked him in the side. Next, I fetched my plate of toasted sandwiches, sitting on the kitchen bench. I saw Declan had made himself one too, which I handed to him on my way out.

"What was that squeal, I heard?" He followed me into the lounge room. He sat beside on the couch and watched closely, as I began to eat.

"I found Great Grandma's and Great, Great Grandma's diaries and photos." I said happily.

"Oh," he sounded surprised, "that's handy."

"So I put the box with Nana and Grandpa's things, beside the trunk with those. Now my foremothers are all sitting together." I joked.

“And talking about how their progeny Bianca Sabre, is finally expecting?” He smiled softly.

“That would be nice.” I sighed again.

“Don’t worry, B.” He patted me on the leg. “Having our daughters will be just like it’s always been. I’ll take care of you and you’ll take care of me and together, we’ll take care of them.”

I leaned in to rub my nose against his cheek affectionately, which he appreciated. But as he turned his head to give me a kiss, my hand swiped one of his triangles. However, he caught me.

“Hey!” He objected. “Man, you really are hungry, aren’t you?”

“In more ways than one, dear husband.” I giggled, before kissing him back.

*****

My appetite kept growing and growing. Over the weeks, a routine was established that sex was part of afternoon tea. As soon as the food was finished, we feasted on each other.

It was week six of the pregnancy and we were in the midst of an icy Alaskan winter. My Lokoti Werewolf eyes were glowing brightly, which made our dim bedroom in the winter’s twilight, look brighter. Our empty plates sat on the bedside table, as the crumbs were bouncing between the sheets from how hard the bed was rocking. I was riding Declan again, digging my claws into his skin and making the kind grunting noises he usually makes.

My panting escaped between my elongated, sharp teeth. Declan’s face was buried in my breasts, which were looking larger. His large hands hung onto my widening hips, as I was beginning to take on a more rounded figure. I honestly felt like I couldn’t let go, as I held onto him tighter. Half of my brain was saying ‘don’t break the poor guy’, as the other half was roaring, ‘more damn it! More!’

I cried out helplessly, “Don’t stop, Declan! Don’t!”

Vaguely, he mumbled something back, which sounded unintelligible since his face was full of breasts. My face was angled upwards, as my body was taught and moving hard. Then I dove my head into his shoulder and bit hard, before licking his wound shut.

It seemed to serve as the icing on the cake, as he came for his fourth time and finally, so did I. My intense yearning and the slow build up, eventually resulted in the so-called ‘explosion’. It felt like a massive pleasurable release, which satiated my bloodlust. My body started to loosen, as I slowed to a stop. Contentedly, I nestled my sweaty face into his sweaty neck.

Declan was gasping, like he hadn’t been able to breathe properly, but he wasn’t complaining either. His face did look redder than usual, though. I sensed his overwhelming satisfaction radiate outwards, along with his body heat.

"I'm changing," I speculated.

Abruptly, he roared with laughter! When he finished he said, "Yeah, I kinda noticed."

"Before I was pregnant, our sex was different."

"Uh huh," he agreed with his eyes closed.

"When we had sex before I was pregnant, I came more."

"Huh?" His eyes snapped open. "Are you saying you don't come now?"

"I do, but it's different."

"How?"

"It takes longer and until I do, it's like I lose control. It's like a ravenous hunger, where I have to ravage you. When I do finally come, it's stronger than it used to be. The feelings are more intense."

He contemplated on my words, "Is there anything I can do to bring it on faster?"

"I don't think so," I sighed in resignation. "This isn't a foreplay thing, it's deeper than that."

"Hmm," he frowned, "that's strange."

"Why?"

"Because you sound like what I go through."

I gave him a funny look. "I do?"

"Foreplay doesn't get me off, it's intercourse that does. Before you were pregnant, you needed foreplay. Now, it's like you're just as hungry for the main course as I am. It's like you can't get enough of me. I like how you seem to want all of me at once, because it's how I feel about having you."

"I bite more than usual," I went on.

"And you drink more than usual," he added. "When you used to occasionally bite, it was like you were tasting. But with the pregnancy, it's like you're thirsty for me."

"Yeah," I rolled onto my side, so I could gaze down on his face. "That's exactly what it's like."

"B," he looked back in concern. "That's what it's like being a European Werewolf. In all our years of sex, you've never been like this before."

"I've never been pregnant before."

"You've never been impregnated by a European Werewolf before." He specified. "It's like the baby growing inside you, already has my characteristics because they're coming out in you."

"You think that's it?" I listened.

Declan rolled onto his side, so he was facing me too. His hand rested on my waist, as he looked on his mate with longing. What he said next, confirmed it.

"I have to admit, ever since this pregnancy began? I've been feeling a hell of a lot more turned on."

"You have?" I started to smile.

"You're eating almost as much as me. You're lusting as much as me. And..." he ran his hand over my figure, which was becoming curvier every day, "...your physical strength is increasing."

"What?!" I burst out laughing. "Yeah right!"

"B, just then as you were riding me, you almost had me pinned. I could have broken your grip if I wanted to, but I've noticed that you're getting stronger. It could be from drinking so much of my blood lately? But it's like your body is deliberately making itself stronger, to carry the child inside."

I looked down and watched his large hand, circle my tummy with reverence.

"I'm sorry, I'll try not to drink so much -" I began.

"Don't be stupid, I'm relieved that this is happening to you!"

"You are?"

"If your body is building up its' strength now, maybe when you deliver, it won't be so dangerous. Hell, I'd cut open my wrist and feed it to you every day, if it gave me a guarantee this pregnancy would be smooth sailing."

"Declan, I wish you would stop worrying." I groaned. "I'm not some weak human woman, I've always been able to cope with your greater strength."

"I know this, B." He sighed, before he gave a mischievous grin. "And with your physical strength increasing, I'm pushing as hard as I like. I'm enjoying our sex more."

"Really?" I tittered, as I slid up against his muscled body.

He let out a contented growl while his hand continued to follow my new curves.

"To see your body changing, because of what I put inside you? It turns me on even more and I didn't think it was possible, that I could lust after you more than I do now. B, you've never tasted better."

"I do?" A giggle escaped.

"So anytime you want to eat more food, or eat me? You frickin' pounce or else!" He growled louder.

Declan rolled onto his back whilst pulling me over him. Then he used his arms to partially prop me up. He did this so he could enjoy the sight of what was hanging near his face.

"And feel free to try to suffocate me with your bigger breasts too," he lifted me higher, to reach them.

Then I grunted from discomfort, when I felt him bite into the right. But the pain quickly turned into pleasure, with the sensation of his sucking. I started to feel the ravenous hunger build up inside me again. I moved my hips into position over his and he took the hint.

"Oh yes!" I let out a helpless cry, as I felt him push inside. "There is something you can do for me, Declan."

"Mmm?"

"Push as hard as you like and we'll see if I can go back to my multiple orgasms."

"Mmm..." he moaned, as he put my words into immediate effect.

My eyes drifted shut, as the bed began to rock again. "Oh yes - oh yes - oh yes - oh yes...!"

*****

"Hmm."

Ki rubbed his jaw, as he looked on my results somewhat perplexed. Declan and I looked on worriedly, as he read the results on the hand-held medical scanner.

"What is it?" My husband asked in concern. "What's wrong?"

I was lying on the couch in the lounge room, as was the custom for my once a week check-ups. Declan was sitting to the side holding my hand. Our Medicine Man was running a deep, cellular scan, of both mother and baby.

"I can see what Uncle Declan means, by your bloodthirsty behaviour." He reported. "Aunt B, your muscle density has increased by ten percent. Right now, you're as strong as a male Lokoti Werewolf."

"Really?" I sat up right in surprise. "Is that a good sign?"

"I think so," he frowned, appearing the opposite. "Your body is making adjustments for carrying a mini European Werewolf inside of you. It's compensating, by taking on some of Uncle Declan's strength. It's why you're craving his blood right now, for its regenerative properties as well as his physical prowess."

"Yeah, but besides B taking on my faster healing and strength; she's also taking on some of my character traits." He told Ki.

"Declan!" I whacked him on the arm, to shut up.

"Such as?" Our Medicine Man looked on enquiringly.

"The hunger and some of the other urges attributed to my bloodlust," he continued.

"Declan!" I whacked him again, as I sat upright on the couch.

"Can you elaborate?" Ki listened.

"Like some of my needs and wants in the bedroom." He put it politely.

"Declan, Ki doesn't need to hear this!" I objected, in embarrassment.

"Oh dear," our physician frowned. "You're not getting rough between the sheets, are you? Because Aunt B is still in the first trimester, there's the risk of miscarriage and -"

"B and the baby are safe, Ki." He interrupted, taking offence. "I'm letting her get rough with me, but I keep my claws to myself."

"Good." Our medical practitioner instantly looked relieved. "That's good to hear, Uncle Dec."

"I mean, I like it so much that I'm using every bit of willpower I have, not to get rough with her..." he muttered, looking away.

"It's good to hear that you're exercising restraint." Ki cleared his throat.

"...and sometimes I have to do the times tables in my head, so I don't flat-out maul her in the throws of passion..." he said under his breath.

We gave him a peculiar look, but he didn't see. He was too wrapped up in his own thoughts, as he stared at the floor. Declan seemed to be talking to himself, let alone to the two other people in the room.

"...it's just nice to see someone else go through what I have for years; the lust, the hunger, the downright desperation, to devour the person..."

We exchanged glances when Declan finally snapped out of it.

"Huh, what?" He sat up straighter. "You were saying, Ki?"

"So, you've been enjoying the European Werewolf characteristics which have arisen in Aunt B?" He remarked.

"Hell yeah!" My mate proclaimed, as if it were a given. "Not that B was ever a cold fish, it's just nice that she needs me as much as I need her."

"Declan!" I cried out louder, as I gave him a shove.

The Medicine Man regarded him closely then he even waved his medical scanner in his direction. "Can you tell me more about this, Uncle Dec?"

"Like what?"

"How Aunt B's behaviour is suiting you."

"I dunno." He shrugged back. "She's gaining on me with how much she eats now. It's nice to snack with her, when she used to give me and my perpetual hunger, a funny look."

"I did not!" I shoved him again.

A silly smile appeared on the European Werewolf's face. "She bites more. She drinks more. She eats more. She growls more and quite frankly, she's turning me on. It's almost like we're closer than ever."

"Because she's emulating your bloodlust, you don't feel so different anymore?" Ki caught on.

"Yeah, basically." He shrugged.

"Stop sounding so whiny like you're the world's loneliest male!" I rolled my eyes. "Where have I been the past two centuries, living in the woods?"

"See what I mean?" He chuckled, as he affectionately patted my leg.

"Hmm," Ki was now frowning over the readouts of the new scan.

"What is it?" I asked concerned. "What's wrong?"

"This is interesting," he began.

"What's interesting?" Declan demanded.

"Your body Uncle, it looks like you're going through a couple of changes yourself." He lowered his scanner, to look him in the eye.

"Oh yeah?" His eyebrows rose.

"I don't know if this is a direct result of the pregnancy, but your muscle tone has also increased in density by ten percent." Ki announced.

"But how?" I wondered. "He's already a hundred percent stronger than humans. Now he's a hundred and ten percent stronger?"

"It looks like it." Ki shrugged then he reached out to feel Declan's arms himself. "They do feel harder than usual."

"Could it be because I'm young again?" My mate tried to shrug it off. "Maybe my body is adjusting to becoming a Circulator?"

"I don't think that's it." He shook his head. "After Aunt B changed you, I ran a scan on you that morning, if you recall. It picked up your muscle density had returned to the way it was, when you were in your twenties. Now it's increased again."

We exchanged a look of wonder at this news and I even touched his arms to feel them for myself.

Ki went on, "I do have a theory though."

"Yeah and?" He prompted.

"In the animal kingdom, there are males who become stronger when the female is expecting. The male is preparing to become the provider as well as the protector. Maybe that's what's happening now?" Our Medicine Man speculated.

"Are you for real?" I gave a peculiar look. "I mean, European Werewolves aside from Declan, aren't exactly known for being the kind to commit. In the past, if a male European Werewolf knocked up a female, he didn't usually stick around to co-found the next 'Brady Bunch'."

"Thanks a lot!" My mate retorted.

"I did say aside from you."

"True," he conceded. "Remember Leo and Michelle? I never did find out, how long they were together for. We don't know if they ever procreated, or what not."

"If they had, you wouldn't be the last European Werewolf." I tried to joke.

"What if Leo did get Michelle pregnant?" He continued. "He most certainly would have, but what happened to the baby? Did they stop conception from continuing, with the method I used on you in the past? Or, did they kill it after it was born?"

A cold shiver ran down my spine, making me shudder. "I don't think I wanna know."

"What about Marcus and Roberta? What happened to them in the area of procreation?" He went on.

"Again, I don't think I wanna know." I felt sick at the thought of it.

"Hey, you can see the past and the future, in the Viewing Room at Circulate HQ, can't you?" Declan turned my way.

"Er, yeah?"

"Maybe we should look into the past and at other European Werewolves, in relation to pregnancy?" He thought up.

"Do we have to?" I whined, as a horrible feeling sank in. "I don't think I wanna know."

"What do you think, Ki?" My husband looked to our Medicine Man for his opinion.

"It would be wise to find out as much information as possible." He agreed. "Aside from your baby, there has never been an observed European Werewolf pregnancy."

Declan eagerly stood up, "C'mon then, let's do it!"

"What, right now?" I looked up in surprise.

"Why not?" Ki said congenially, as he stood up too. "I'll come along and it'll be included in my 'house call'."

"Are you sure?" I asked warily. "Maybe this isn't such a good idea."

"C'mon B," my mate pulled me up from the sofa. "Now you've got me curious."

"I have?"

"You did bring up other European Werewolf behaviour in regards to kids." He reminded.

However, my horrible feeling turned into dread and I recognized it as a warning of bad news to come.

"Can't we do this another day?" I tried to back out.

"Why?" He gave a peculiar look.

"It's best that we find out the facts, Aunt B." Our Medicine Man, reasoned. "It could even help with your treatment."

I glanced away uncertain, as a tiny voice cried inside my mind, 'no, don't do it!'

Declan noticed my apprehension, "B, what's wrong?"

"Nothing," I lied.

I didn't know what to say, without worrying them.

"Are you feeling unwell, Aunt B?" Our Medicine Man looked on closely. "Perhaps it's morning sickness?"

"Oh no, I'm fine. It's just that..."

"Yeah?" My husband prompted.

"It's nothing." I let out a weary sigh. "Let's just get it over with."

The men exchanged funny looks as I reluctantly rose to my feet.

I placed my hands on their arms and within the blink of an eye, I instantaneously phased the three of us to Circulate Headquarters.

*****

~ 4 ~

In a bright flash of light, we disappeared from our living room to reappear in another, in a corridor of the futuristic stronghold of the once powerful Circulate.

The headquarters was inside a massive glass dome, which housed late 25th Century technology. It had black floors, open ceilings to allow natural light in, frosted-over, sliding glass doors, and computer interfaces adorning many surfaces. The computers were touch screen, with see-through casings filled with crystallized circuitry. Indeed, the computer core of the Circulate Mainframe which was a 'smart computer'; looked like a giant, rotating crystal pyramid, with a myriad of lasers hitting it to access the ingrained information.

Once upon a time, the Circulate was made up of 696 humans, those who could either calculate time or move through it, in the form of its' Circulators. The Calculators chose to place the second headquarters on the terran-class planet inside of a green nebula, on the other side of the galaxy. It was to protect the secret of the society's existence, since the nebula was too unstable to navigate space ships through. The only way the headquarters was accessible, was for Circulators to phase via the Gate or instantaneously phase, directly to the planet's surface.

The secret society left their mortal existences behind in the Final Phase, to evolve as energy to the space time continuum. After their departure, it left behind only my Circulator mother, who met a long-lost cousin who was a Calculator. It was Mum, Vincent and my Gran - who was the only Circulator let alone human, to have been to eternity and back - who trained my abilities as a Circulator. With my family's departure, now it was just Declan and I, as the last of the Circulate to use the empty headquarters.

"This way," I headed for the nearest entryway.

As Declan and Ki followed me through the automatic, sliding glass doors, they noted on the lit up panel beside which read; VIEWING ROOM.

Immediately, the female voice of the Circulate Mainframe, greeted us. "Welcome to the Viewing Room, Circulators Bianca and Declan Sabre."

"Huh?" My mate looked taken aback. "How does it know that you changed me?"

"The Circulate Mainframe knew of your oncoming transformation, for years." I smirked. "It is monitoring our timelines, don't forget."

Our Medicine Man looked suitably impressed, as well as by the futuristic technology.

The room had a glass top, circular desk which went around in a ring. On top sat three crystallized computer consoles, which were spread around. In the centre of the room, was a large, upside down, crystal pyramid, hanging from the open ceiling. Three Calculators used to sit here, monitoring Earth and the entire Universe, when the Circulate still had all of its members. In the three sides of the pyramid, different scenes from humankind's history were on display. One depicted the Roman Forum during Imperial times, the other was of the Forbidden City in the 16th Century and last of all, were the Lokoti Tribal Lands of the era we had just departed.

"Hey that's my house," Ki pointed at the picture.

"The Circulate Mainframe always has its eye on tribal lands, as it keeps tabs on my whereabouts." I said breezily.

"B, would you like me to report on Circulate systems and Hodge Endeavor?" The computer offered.

"No thanks, not today. I'll get a full report the next time I come, unless there's anything urgent?" I said as I sat at the closest computer console.

"Circulate systems and Hodge Endeavor are operating within normal parameters." She promised, before she picked up what I was typing in. "You are requesting to do a search using the Viewing Room?"

"That's correct," I replied, "the boys need to find out something."

"Will Declan be running the search?" The computer guessed.

"Yes."

"Declan, as a new member of the Circulate, I am aware you are unfamiliar with Circulate systems. Should you require any information or have any requests, I also respond to voice commands." She offered.

He looked on in surprise, "Er, thanks."

"You are welcome." The computer acknowledged. "Would you like B to program the search parameters for you, or would you like to give the verbal commands?"

I gave him an encouraging smile to go ahead.

"Yeah alright," he straightened with the responsibility. "Um, I need to find European Werewolves in relation to pregnancy."

"Please specify the time period you would like me to search," the computer requested.

"Um, do I have to?" He looked confused.

I took over again, "Computer, we need to research pregnancy in relation to European Werewolves. We need to find out what happened to the mothers as well as the offspring. The search parameters are wide with no set time frame. From prior records when the different breeds of Werewolves were established, begin there and track through to the 24th Century. Show us any and all European Werewolves in the area of procreation."

"Working," the computer began to process. "Would you like to begin your research from the time European Werewolves were able to morph to and from human form?"

"Huh?" My mate gawked.

I explained, “Up until 1000 BC, European Werewolves always remained in their supernatural form. It wasn’t until then they were able to change between human and other.”

Declan and Ki exchanged puzzled looks, not only by this piece of trivia, but at how I knew this?

Then I spoke to the computer, “Yes please.”

“The search is complete.” The computer advised. “Would you like to view as well as record, the following results?”

“Yes please,” I ordered. "Download a copy of the report onto my laptop.”

“Your laptop?” Ki looked around. “But you didn’t bring your computer with you.”

“It doesn’t matter.” I told him. “The Circulate Mainframe can send information to it via text message or email.”

“You can download through time and space?” He looked impressed.

“Yup,” I stood up from the console and started to leave.

“Hey, where are you going?” Declan wondered.

“I don’t think I want to see this.” I said, to their further astonishment. “I’ll be in the Observation Lounge waiting for you when this is finished.”

They watched me go as the computer chimed, “Declan, would you like me to begin the presentation now?”

“Um, yeah OK.” He said uneasily once I had left.

*****

Over the next fifteen minutes, I sat curled up in a corner of a couch, in one of the three Observation Lounges. I even sipped on a hot chocolate I had one of the food synthesizers create, in the Mess Hall. The lounges were positioned by the outer dome wall, which gave an excellent view of the alien surroundings.

Taurus Six had perpetual storms and the dense clouds created the constant lightning, which shot across the sky. Occasionally, the hot sunlight from the binary star system did get through, but on any given day there could be up to five hurricane-force downpours. The nitrogen generated from the lightning, as well as the regular rainfall, coupled with the hot light from the binary stars; gave the planet thick, tropical vegetation as well as a rich, oxygen atmosphere. However, it was impossible for humans to colonize the planet, because of the ionized atmosphere the storms created, which wouldn’t allow spacecraft to safely traverse. Then there was also the problem of the ships flying through the unstable nebula, the planet was inside.

As I sipped on my beverage, I enjoyed the stillness of the base. I didn’t mind the solitude, as I liked the hum of the environmental systems which maintained the comfortable temperature and light. Right now, I preferred it to what Declan and Ki were seeing in the Viewing Room. My ominous feelings as a Circulator were still singing songs like, 'don't ask, don't tell'.

I knew it wouldn't be a pretty picture, European Werewolves and sexual reproduction. It would attribute to how Declan was created, as most European Werewolves were; by bite or the transference of blood. When he was three years old, he was mauled by the European Werewolf which killed his father and attacked his pregnant mother. Declan almost died, but my Lokoti Werewolf grandfather, saved his life by sharing his blood. Then he was trained by the pack not to turn into the man-eater which nearly destroyed his family.

All his long life, Declan was careful not to turn any human by bite or contaminate with his blood. He was adamant he should be the last of his kind. The humans he had bitten, he tore apart, so there wasn't anything left to change. In these instances, the Police allocated the murders to an 'animal attack'.

So instead of seeing the depressing statistics, I amused myself by staring out at the tropical landscape.

When my fifteen minutes of peace were up, I was joined by two shell-shocked males.

Declan looked distraught at his species history with sexual reproduction whilst Ki looked disgusted. Since Lokoti Werewolves are exceptionally protective over their mates and young, anything untoward in this area was frowned upon. From the look on our Medicine Man's face, his frown was so ingrained, I thought it would give him new wrinkles.

"Hot chocolate?" I offered to cheer them up.

The two looked like I had just offered to put a simple band-aid on a broken artery, gushing out.

"B, did you know this already?" Declan asked accusatorily. "Is that why you didn't stick around?"

"No," I spoke calmly, "I just had a bad feeling that's all."

"A bad feeling...? A BAD FEELING?!" His voice rose. "When you swore to me that first morning that you'd live through this pregnancy, you LIED!!"

"No I didn't!" I said indignantly, as I sat up straighter. "I did NOT lie about MY pregnancy! I didn't want to come here to do the search, nor watch the results with you, because I knew they wouldn't be pretty. I SENSED it would have been dire at best for other females, but I KNOW it's not dangerous in my case."

"How can you know?" His face screwed up in pain. "How can you know this isn't going to happen to you?"

"Because our daughter will be the eldest, remember?" I pointed out. "If I don't live through this, I can hardly give her sisters now, can I?"

Ki slowly sunk onto the couch next to mine, as he stared vacantly at the lush vegetation outside the glass wall. He truly appeared to be suffering post traumatic stress, whereas Declan was furious. The Medicine Man who would occasionally counsel his patients, looked like he needed to recover.

Altogether, we watched the bright sunlight disappear, as the light green sky was darkened with oncoming storm clouds. I thought the flashes of lightning were poetically timed with the men's moods at the moment. The thunder was so loud, the rumble could be heard as well as felt, through the protective dome.

Declan stood with his back turned, as he watched the lightning rip across the blackening sky. His human blue eyes switched to his glowing green colour in anger, which made him look like he could be a native of Taurus Six. His dissatisfied growl rumbled out just like the thunder outside.

"OK, lets talk about this." I sighed, as I put down my empty mug. "Let's get everything out into the open and deal with it now, so we can just move on."

"Maybe we should," Ki said flatly, "preparations are certainly going to need to be made."

"Instead of panicking and crying out, 'oh my god we're all going to die', let's review the first fact that I obviously live through this pregnancy. The second fact is, I will be having girls." I looked up at Declan, thinking this would make him feel better. "The third fact, what you just saw in there happened to OTHER females. It's not going to happen to me."

"How can you be so sure, B?!" My mate whirled around in anger. "I just saw female European Werewolves die in childbirth, women with twice your strength!"

"Was the male European Werewolf who knocked them up, with them?" I asked knowingly.

"No -" he began, but I cut him off.

"Were any werewolves male or female, around to share their blood with the injured mother?" I asked again.

"No, usually the mothers were alone and gave birth in hiding." He answered.

"So there you go." I said simply. "I'm not going to have this baby alone, so if I need blood, I'm sure my mate or pack will back me up."

Ki spoke distantly, "The female European Werewolves weren't just impregnated by the males of their species, but also by humans. However, their babies still developed as full-blooded European Werewolves. We saw a couple of images of the baby, morphing into its larger European Werewolf shape whilst inside the mother. It ruptured the amniotic sack, as well as split the mother's stomach wide open, which in most instances killed both."

"But that's not going to happen to me," I said firmly.

Suddenly, Declan roared in anger, with his face bright red and tears streaming from his eyes. "HOW CAN YOU BE SO SURE, BIANCA?!"

The volume not only made me jump, but it also made Ki snap to.

"Uncle, please." He said quietly. "Yelling at Aunt B isn't going to solve the problem. We have to remain calm."

I glared back, "Because this baby is half Lokoti Werewolf, so she's got my genes too."

Our Medicine Man rubbed his face, "I asked the computer to show us your future, so we could confirm your pregnancy will have no complications? However, it said it has difficulty calculating your future at times. It said a white light from an unknown energy source, blocks your timeline, so it can't predict your path. All it could say is that you have three children, which are all girls. It said it saw you in the distant future, when the girls were grown, but it couldn't project what the deliveries will be like."

"What good is this frickin' smart computer, if it can't tell us THAT?!" Declan growled out.

Then he kicked an unused couch so hard, it squealed across the floor several meters away!

"Vincent used to say the same about trying to predict my future." I sighed.

"When you're six months along, I'll put the pack on alert." Ki took a deep breath. "As soon as we sense your labour, you'll have fourteen male Lokoti Werewolves on standby as blood donors... as well as Declan, of course."

The father of my child turned back around to glare tearfully out at the storm. It had begun to rage outside, drenching the land in a thick downpour as its strong downdrafts blew fiercely. We saw the vegetation bend and flex in the gale, as its' roots struggled to hold on.

"I just can't believe it..." Ki looked like he was still in shock, "...I've never come across a species that would seem so – so – so programmed, to destroy itself by means of sexual reproduction. I mean, the mortality rate for both mother and young, it's astronomical! I thought the European Werewolf lust was so strong, because it was to ensure its species survival? But it appears to be another method to kill."

"OK, give me some statistics here." I prepared myself for what was ahead. "What happened in the cases of Roberta and Marcus, as well as Michelle and Leo? Were they ever pregnant? Did they go through labour? Did children occur?"

"Roberta and Michelle were impregnated dozens of times. But Marcus and Leo, used the method I wanted to use on you to end the pregnancy each time." Declan spoke in a low voice, with his back turned.

"Since 1000 BC, there have been billions of instances of female European Werewolves being impregnated. But actually going through with the pregnancy, drops to a third. Or, surviving the pregnancy, it drops to a third again. Then the infant Werewolf reaching maturity, drops to another third. So we went to something like less than a hundred times, of both the mother and child surviving procreation." Ki prattled off with wide eyes.

"Less than a hundred...?" I gaped. "From 1000 BC to 2363 AD, there's less than a hundred cases, of both European Werewolf mother and European Werewolf child surviving?"

“Correct,” our Medicine Man rubbed his face again, from stress. “I won’t even tell you what happened to the human mothers, which were impregnated by a male European Werewolf.”

“Dead every time?” I guessed.

“Correct,” he repeated, whist staring at the floor.

“I thought human women wouldn’t survive the experience of being with a male European Werewolf, anyway.” I looked on, blankly.

“From what we saw, eighty percent of the time they didn’t.” His face paled, before he shook his head. “Amazing...it’s like even European Werewolf sexual organs have the bloodlust. Instead of reproducing, they kill.”

“So as I always thought, most European Werewolves are created by bite or blood transference, rather than sex.” I summed up.

“Yes.” He said stiffly.

“Well, it kinda makes sense.” I tried to put it objectively. “The different breeds were primarily created from the prey that survived an attack by the First Werewolf.”

“All except Lokoti Werewolves,” he added on. "We’re the only breed NOT descended from the First Werewolf. We were created from the biological and spiritual convergence of Lokoti Wolf and human.”

“You never know,” I tried to joke, “the changed prey ended up reproducing with members of the canidae family, which includes wolves.”

Our Medicine Man’s face fell, “That’s not even funny, Aunt B. Allow me to remind you that a Lokoti Werewolf has NEVER lost a mate in childbirth.”

Declan snarled in displeasure at our conversation, as he turned around and stormed off down the corridor. I remained in my seat and watched him go, as I sensed he had to walk this off. Right now, he was feeling angry and embarrassed of his breed’s family history.

I turned back to Ki, “What about the male European Werewolves who impregnated the female; did any remain through the pregnancy? You said Declan was stronger because of it, what about them?”

“Um, we didn’t really see what happened to the males.” He mused. “The presentation was centred on females through the pregnancy or the birth. Often, they were alone without the father with them.”

“C’mon,” I stood up, “let’s do some more research.”

“Just give me a minute,” he faltered. “I’m still getting over the last history lesson on the fate of the females.”

“I’ll start on the search parameters and I’ll meet you in the Viewing Room.” I organized, before I headed that way.

*****

Five minutes later, not only did Ki join me in the Viewing Room but so did Declan.

He must have stormed back, asked where I was and was told what we were going to do. However, his whole demeanour had changed. Before I was wary of what happened to the females, now he looked worried about hearing what happened to the males.

"The results have been collected and collated for your perusal," the computer chirped.

"Display," I gave the order, as I sat back in the chair.

I was sitting behind one of the computer consoles, as Declan and Ki came to stand behind.

"Before we begin, can I say now that I know the males of my kind are the very definition of the term, 'bastard'?" My mate nervously wet his lips.

I reached behind to take hold of his hand, to give it a sympathetic squeeze. He latched onto my gesture and wouldn't let go. Then he rested his other hand on my shoulder, as we looked on.

The computer narrated, "Since 1000 BC when a male European Werewolf mated with a female human or female European Werewolf, the encounters were brief with 91% of couples severing their association."

As she spoke, a series of images were shown on the large crystal pyramid, which slowly turned.

We saw a collage of European Werewolves through the ages, in their supernatural forms. Just as the male's sexual organs would disappear behind muscle bulk, so did the female's breasts. But we could differentiate them in their monstrous shapes, by the males being slightly larger.

"Over the 3,363 year period, there have been 97 successful births, where both European Werewolf mother and infant survived. The presence of the father at the delivery occurred ten times." The computer continued.

"Only ten?" Ki's eyebrows rose, in astonishment.

We looked on several different images of female European Werewolves throwing back their heads and howling in pain, as they delivered. The male European Werewolf would use its clawed hand, to pull the enlarged baby out. It was also born in its European Werewolf shape, albeit smaller than the parents.

"Shit," I blanched at the baby's form. "Computer, are European Werewolf children always born in their supernatural body?"

"Negative," she answered, which made me emit a sigh of relief. "European Werewolf young are also born in human form."

Then the computer illustrated by changing the images in the pyramid.

We saw footage of some kind of Viking-like culture in a northern European country, back in time. There was some kind of feast, where there was plenty of drinking and eating. A large, bearded man bounced a large, lusty wench on his lap. The man and the woman's eyes briefly glowed green, showing their true natures.

The man and woman left the revelry, to stumble drunkenly outside whilst carrying their mugs of mead. We caught a glimpse of the man have the woman up against the wooden wall of the long house, with lots of biting and snarling involved. Once they were satiated, they stumbled back inside again. Whereas the woman was content, the man was still hungry.

The male European Werewolf reached out for another woman, when the one he had just had, flew into a jealous rage.

The female swung out her hand at the woman who must have been only human. She fell to the ground dead, with her jugular severed by several claw marks across her throat. Next, the female European Werewolf took a swing at the male and he swung back at her... then it was on! The surrounding humans all leapt out of harms way. Several pieces of broken furniture later, the male and female stormed off – or limped away angrily – seemingly never to talk again.

Then the images cut to several months later, of the large lusty wench looking much larger now. Her baby bulge was huge! She stumbled out of a wooden hut, with a strange man walking out after her, doing up his pants. She fell face first into the snow, crying out in pain and we saw a trail of blood behind her.

Just then the male European Werewolf from the feast reappeared, picked her up and carried her back inside the hut.

Thankfully, the computer fast-forwarded through the messy and painful delivery and slowed again, to show the male European Werewolf using his sharp teeth, to cut the umbilical chord. Next, the male bit his wrist and shared his blood with the female, to regenerate. When the new mother passed out, to sleep through the rest of her healing; the male picked up the crying newborn, whose eyes were also glowing green.

The male European Werewolf carried the baby out of the hut, by carelessly dangling it by its tiny feet, as he headed over to a tree.

BAM! BAM! BAM! BAM!

"Omygod!!" I squealed in horror, jumping out of my seat in alarm.

The male just dashed the baby's brains out! Then he flung it away, into the snow. He must have thought his job was done, instead of returning to the hut to see to the mother; he walked into the larger wooden house, to drink more mead.

As he swaggered away, I noticed that his muscles did look bigger, especially on his arms which stuck out of his fur vest.

"B..." my mate started to reach for me, but I moved away.

I looked from his hands, back to the Viewing Screen almost terrified. I could see what was happening now! It all started to make frightening sense.

Quickly, I ordered, "Computer, show more relationships between male European Werewolves and their young."

The next series of images showed a baby European Werewolf, learning to hunt with its' parents who had stayed together. When the infant couldn't contain its' bloodlust and tried to go on a feeding frenzy, the male tore the tot apart! We saw it was always the father which performed the extermination.

With the trouble-maker out of the way, the parents didn't hesitate to copulate again.

Lastly, the computer zoomed in on a castle somewhere in Eastern Europe. It was the medieval era, with some of the men carrying swords on their belts. In the large dining hall, another feast was occurring but upstairs in one of the bedrooms, a woman cried out from labour. The woman's eyes were glowing green and so were the man's who was looking on. A midwife was seeing to the delivery and moments later, she raised her bloodied hands in the air and in them was a baby boy, also with glowing green eyes. The man took the baby and held him warily, as the midwife saw to the woman's afterbirth.

Then the computer fast-forwarded through the years, as I paid particular attention to the father/son relationship. I watched the man's muscles get bigger, the older his son grew. The man used brute force to lead both his rowdy men as well as his rebellious young. We saw many of the people in the castle were also European Werewolves, as several medieval battles took place against other men, carrying silver swords. They had snake-like fangs and glowing white eyes, indicating they were European Vampires.

This must have been the only time recorded in history, when European Werewolves fought together, against the powerful covens of European Vampires. I remember reading this in the SSIT Report on the Different Breeds of Werewolves. Otherwise, the breed were volatile nomads who didn't like to share their kill, so they lived apart.

However, we saw the teenaged son make some kind of deal with a European Vampire overlord. From which, we saw many European Werewolf soldiers fall, with hundreds of 'fang heads' feeding on them. The father looked on his son knowingly, guessing his betrayal. The computer activated the sound, so we could hear the conversation later back at the castle.

"I raised you, I trained you and I let you live." His furious father spoke, with glowing green eyes. "Every instinct I had, whispered warnings that you were dangerous, but for your mother I stayed the urge to kill. Everyone said that by creating a European Werewolf by birth and not bite, the child would become stronger than the parents. I smell your strength, you are twice as strong as I was, when I was turned at your age. It's a pity your weak character doesn't match your physical strength."

Suddenly, the father pounced on his son and tried to rip his throat out! The son fought back, attempting to slash his father's jugular with his claws. Both males morphed into their bigger and stronger European Werewolf bodies, to battle it out. It was a fight to death, with the boy already a match for the grown male.

When the mother came in, the son tried to attack her too. But the father leapt onto his huge, hulking back, to protect his mate. The mother also expanded into her European Werewolf shape, to help her husband since the son was starting to win. Together, they snapped the son's neck, before completely ripping it off to ensure he couldn't regenerate. Hell, they even tore off his arms and legs, as if to finish the job...

I had to stare at a corner of the room, as I felt my stomach lurch and my mouth turn sickeningly salty.

“This conclude the results of your search, B.” The computer finished. “Do you have any further queries?”

“Um…,” I stared blankly at the glass console, feeling shocked and disgusted, “…no thank you, computer. I think I’m just going to stand here.”

Ki put his hand on my arm, “How about we return to those comfortable couches in the Observation Lounge?”

His voice sounded far away and I sensed he was trying to attract my attention however, I didn’t feel up to answering.

“B,” my husband spoke softly, “let’s get out of this room and talk things through.”

In the corner of my eye, I saw his hand reach for me but I leapt back before he could touch me!

I turned my betrayed eyes towards my mate, who was looking my way and dare I say, even a little guilty?

Declan’s previous words echoed in my mind; *“I WILL NOT abide another threat to come along and destroy everything! C’mon B, just give me ten minutes and it will all be over.”*

It all made sense now, he’s always been adamant he didn’t want sons, let alone any children at all. As soon as he found out that I was pregnant, he tried to kill his child. Declan was behaving just like all the other male European Werewolves, who eliminated their young.

I took another step back then another and another, as I slowly backed away. My watering eyes never left his direction. My head even started to shake by itself, as my heart cried out, ‘say it isn’t so!’

“Aunt B, just breathe.” Ki said concerned, as they watched the blood drain from my face.

I rasped out of my aching chest, “…it’s why you said you never wanted a son, isn’t it Declan? Why, so a girl would be easier to kill? A girl who can’t fight back, because she’s not as strong as a boy…?”

“B,” his voice lowered, “don’t do this.”

However, I started to hyperventilate. “…it’s why you wanted to kill the baby as soon as you found out I was pregnant, isn’t it? Your European Werewolf instincts, were telling you to kill your young…!”

“B, you don’t want to do this,” his head lowered, as he fixed a steely glare in my direction.

“…it’s why you tried to force an abortion on me…!” I wheezed tearfully, as I continued to stumble backwards.

“Aunt B, just breathe!” Ki instructed. “C’mon Aunt B, let’s just concentrate on your breathing right now.”

“…what are you going to do when our daughter is born, dash her tiny head against a tree…?” I uttered out.

Not only did my chest feel like it was constricting, but my throat did as well.

Clumsily, I backed out of the Viewing Room via the automatic, sliding door, but I banged my shoulder into the reinforced glass. Then I fell on my arse, onto the cold, hard floor. When I saw my mate start towards me, I scurried further away until I had inadvertently backed myself into a wall.

"...every instinct inside you, is telling you to kill her, isn't it...?" I croaked out. "...as soon as she does one little thing wrong, it'll be the excuse you've been waiting for...!"

"Aunt B!" Ki rushed forwards, to kneel by my side. "Your heart is racing at 180 beats per minute, you're hyperventilating. I need you to calm down, I need you to take deep breaths for me and calm yourself."

"...it's why you're getting stronger, because your body is preparing to eliminate her...!" My hot tears spilt over.

"Aunt B? Look at me Aunt B, please look at me." Our Medicine Man tried to angle my face towards him.

However, I couldn't take my eyes off the threat in front. I watched the tall, strong figure of my so-called mate loom before me, as he walked into the corridor to stand over. His normally bright blue eyes had turned ice-cold, as his face hardened. He looked on my cowering on the floor, not just unimpressed but dispassionate.

"C'mon Aunt B," the medical practitioner started to pat my cheeks. "Take some nice, big, deep breaths for me. You're not in danger, so let's all remain calm and breathe deeply, shall we?"

Just then Declan crouched on the floor to fix his steely gaze in my direction.

"You're right, B," he spoke coldly. "Not only does my bloodlust hunger for human, but it's telling me to use my claws to rip that child out of you."

My breath caught in my throat, as my eyes bulged at hearing him say it in such a detached voice!

"Uncle Declan, please!" Ki snapped. "We're trying to CALM her, not induce a heart attack!"

But he continued speaking in a voice so low, it was beyond threatening – it was terrifying!

"My instincts are telling me what we saw was right; that European Werewolves created by birth and not by bite, are stronger. Even if you're carrying a daughter, my bloodlust is infuriated that the baby is taking over my territory. My green-eyed monster wants to destroy the child which is coming between us. It doesn't want to share you, it wants you to be my B and nothing but my B."

The Medicine Man looked on in alarm, as he kept a protective hand on my shoulder. Poor Ki, he was probably wishing we were home right now, so he had the back up of the other Lokoti Werewolves. In fact, so was I.

Declan stood up angrily as he growled out, "But as usual, I hold myself back. For you B, I continue to hunt animal and not human. For you B, I'm letting you keep this child. For you B, I'll allow this child to live. So don't go all 'dingo ate my baby' on me!"

With that, he spun on his heel and stalked off down the corridor. We watched him depart, before Ki collapsed exhausted, beside on the floor. He too leaned against the wall as he let out a weary sigh.

He admitted, "I swear by the Lokoti Wolf, this has to be the most difficult pregnancy yet, I've had to oversee."

My heart pounded and I said vacantly, "You're telling me...?"

"The most difficult pregnancy for the tribe's most argumentative couple," he shook his head.

"Thanks a lot!"

"Aunt B, have you or Uncle Dec, ever considered relationship counselling?" He passed a tired look.

"Oh sure!" I scoffed. "I can imagine our sessions now with the non-Lokoti counsellor. Yes, Werewolves exist and yes, we've been married for nearly three centuries. However, getting knocked up has affected our relationship."

"It doesn't have to be with a non-Lokoti counsellor off tribal lands." Ki shrugged. "You could go to one of those marriage groups the Tribal Elders hold now and again in the Meeting Hall."

"Oh yeah, I can see Declan now; sitting there, growling under his breath and scaring away the other couples." I snickered.

"Sometimes I don't know what the hell he's thinking. His mood swings thanks to his bloodlust-fuelled temper, are volatile enough. Then you walk into the room and it's like throwing petrol onto a fire. Tell me Aunt B, with all of your fighting, how do you usually work things out?" He wondered.

"Well..." I wondered how to put it politely, "...make-up sex."

"I see," his eyebrows rose. "I suppose that would be typical in a marriage with two Werewolves, let alone one with a European Werewolf."

"He's usually not this bad," I tried to apologise. "But this pregnancy has really thrown him. We were supposed to evolve to the space time continuum, but that's been put on hold. Declan's not only the father of my child, he's the man I pictured spending eternity with. So if he's not up to fatherhood, I'm screwed."

"Now you do sound like a Lokoti Werewolf," he smirked, "the biological bonding between Werewolf and mate."

"Man it sucks!" I huffed, as I crossed my arms.

"I wouldn't say that," he passed a cheeky grin. "Jenny and I are still enjoying the physical side effects."

"Shut up!" I gave him a shove.

"Hey, that hurt! Watch it with your new strength." He chuckled, as he rubbed his arm. "I think I preferred it when you were hyperventilating."

Then we both took a deep breath, held it and let it out as a loud sigh, as we stared back into the Viewing Room.

*****

It wasn't long afterwards I instantaneously phased the three of us back to tribal lands. Ki picked up his medicine bundle he had left in our lounge area, as Declan crossed his arms and glared at him. I wasn't sure why at first, but I soon found out.

"I suppose you're going to give Caesar the news of what you saw in the Viewing Room today?" My husband asked knowingly.

Ki paused on his way out the front door, to look his way. "Yes, I'll be stopping by Caesar's house on my way home."

"Isn't that just peachy," he grumbled.

"What's wrong?" I queried, looking from my husband to our Medicine Man. "Why do you have to tell Caesar what you saw?"

Ki looked from me, to my husband then back my way. "He's not only our First, but he's your family, Aunt B. After our check-ups, I give him updates of both the mother and baby's progress."

"What?" I looked taken aback. "Doesn't privacy or confidentiality mean anything around here?!"

"YOU'RE pissed off?" Declan arched his eyebrows. "I'm the one who's about to be branded a baby killer!"

This made me feel bad as I sensed my mate was starting to feel like he was being punished for a crime he hadn't committed. It seemed like we were taking one step forwards then two steps back, with this pregnancy. Having so many people involved let alone the parents-to-be, only made things worse.

"Ki," I walked up to him, so I could look him right in the eye as I said this. "I DON'T have any bad feelings about this pregnancy. Also, I don't have any warning feelings that I'm in danger from Declan, either. So can you please stop running to Caesar and blabbing about us?!"

I could see my words affected him as he momentarily looked on, guiltily.

"I'm sorry Aunt B, but I've been given a direct order from my First to tell him everything that occurs with this pregnancy." He said softly, before he passed my mate a knowing look. "Uncle Declan appreciates this, especially since he's Second. When our First gives an order, we follow it."

The two exchanged a long look, before my mate said, "Let Ki go."

Then our Medicine Man along with his medicine bundle departed via the front door. I watched him go before I looked defeated, towards my mate.

"How come every time I speak up in your defence, you side with the pack over your wife?" I asked, hurt.

"Then how come you side with the baby over your husband?" He returned. "You saw what other male European Werewolves were like and you immediately cowered from me. B, you looked at me today like I was a monster, when all I've done was try to keep you safe."

I marched over to where he was standing so our eyes could clash, as well as our words.

"Declan, I got scared because I saw you do exactly what those other male European Werewolves did; you tried to eliminate your young!"

"No B, I tried to protect my mate." He said firmly. "If I was acting like the males of my species, I would have knocked you up and disappeared. Then I'd come back after the baby was born and I wouldn't care if you lived or died, when I came to eliminate my young!"

We stood there in a tense manner, with the both of us so angry, neither of us could back down. Or so I thought, until after a moment he abruptly turned around. He walked towards the backdoor whilst undressing.

"What are you doing?" I watched warily.

"I'm going hunting," he spoke as he stripped. "I'm so angry right now, I have to tear into something!"

"Hunting?" I echoed.

"While I'm gone, I'm sure you're going to pack your bags and run away as usual. Right now, I'm so sick of this pregnancy that I wouldn't care if I returned to an empty house!"

"Declan -" I started after him, but he flung open the door and stepped naked, out into the snow.

I watched him expand into his huge, hulking, hairless European Werewolf body. His hands and feet grew into claws, which left heavy imprints in the snow, as his skin hardened into hide over ripples of supernatural muscle. His bones creaked and cracked, as his bipedal human body adjusted to a four-legged form, with his skull growing a short, stubby snout over razor-sharp jaws. His eyes were glowing green with his circular pupils turning into narrow slits.

He fell forwards from standing in an upright position on his hind legs, to all-fours. But before he could run away, I instantaneously phased to stand directly in his path. I appeared in a bright flash right in front of him.

"Declan!" I cupped his beastly head in the both of my hands. My dark blue eyes desperately tried to hold his glowing green ones. "Declan please, let's just talk about this."

He snapped his dangerous jaws to try to make me move aside, but I refused to budge.

NOT NOW! - he thought my way.

"I'm not going to pack my bags and leave. You just scare me sometimes, especially when I see your behaviour is the same as your kind. But ultimately I trust you, I do."

LIKEWISE, B - He emitted a dissatisfied growl, as he replied *–YOUR ONE-TRACK MIND DOESN'T JUST SCARE ME, IT PISSES ME OFF!*

"Then let's talk about this -" I tried again.

But he rose up onto his hind legs so he could tower over his wife. Like this, he was almost twice my height and three times as wide. However, I stood my ground, as I looked upon his monstrous appearance.

ADMIT IT, IF YOU EVER HAD TO CHOOSE BETWEEN ME AND THE BABY – he thought bitterly – *I WOULDN'T GET A SECOND GLANCE!*

"No..." my eyes watered from my emotional pain as well as the icy air, "...Declan, you're my mate always and forever."

THAT'S SUPPOSEDLY WHY YOU CHANGED ME INTO A CIRCULATOR, BUT I HAVEN'T SEEN ANY SIGN OF THIS! – he let out a vicious snarl.

"Then lets go inside and talk about this properly." I pleaded, as I started to shiver. "C'mon Declan, please?"

This gave him pause when he saw me rub my arms to stave off hypothermia.

He picked me up in his two front claws, to lift me into a tight embrace. I appreciated being squeezed against his hot, hard body, whilst I struggled to wrap my arms about his huge, hulking shoulders. His hot, wet tongue even licked my stinging cheeks. But just as I was starting to warm up, he lowered me to my feet again.

GO INSIDE AND SIT BY THE FIRE – he left as his parting thought.

Suddenly, in the speed of light, he bolted off on all-fours out of the snowy yard. I barely managed to catch a bush quake, from where he brushed past. The snow sprinkled off the leaves to join the rest on the ground beside.

I watched his departure and felt guilty that after 273 years of marriage, the pregnancy made him question whether or not, I still loved him.

We seemed to be at an impasse... Declan wanted things to remain the same whereas I welcomed the changes.

I believed him when he spoke of his bloodlust-fuelled jealousy at the baby encroaching on what he saw as 'his territory'.

For over two centuries, my body, heart and mind had been his and nothing but his. Whenever he felt this was drifting, he would act like the anchor to pull me back in, by yelling or acting out for more attention. If something else threatened our marriage, like the attacks by European Vampires, Voodoo Witch Doctors, or even other European Werewolves, trying to take what was his? He would indulge his bloodlust, by removing the threat in a bloody rampage.

However, with this baby issue, I sensed his bloodlust wanted to attack the threat to his territory, but he couldn't because it would injure me. Then with his role of Second, he was caught in the middle of my family. He was honour-bound to follow our First, which forced him to obey not only the pack, but also the tribe.

Disheartened, I left the cold air outside for the warmer atmosphere of inside.

In the fire place, the last couple of logs were slowly burning away with the tiny flames licking at the charred wood.

Wearily, I sat against the metal safety gauze which felt nice and warm. My mate always kept a fire going in winter even if we had central heating. He knew I liked to sit close to it, if I wasn't sitting close to him instead.

I'm 297 years old and right now, I truly felt my age. Less than two months ago I nearly lost my husband to old age. Now he claims pregnancy instead of death, is tearing us apart. As a Lokoti Werewolf, my biological bond to my European Werewolf mate, wanted to let out a mournful howl at the distance growing between us.

Oh Mum, oh Dad, oh Gran and oh Grandfather... how I miss you all. I could really use your words of wisdom, right now. If it wasn't for this pregnancy, we could be with you, inside the space time continuum. Instead, I sat alone in my quiet house, as I glanced around the living room, with its bits and pieces of family memorabilia.

Next, my eyes wandered over to my small wooden staircase. Those stairs led to the upper part of the house. In the upstairs hallway, is the attic hatch. In the attic, sat boxes and the trunk full of family history, including the diaries.

Hmm... I may not have my mother or grandmother here, but I had the words of my great, great grandmother.

I stood up and left the warm spot by the fireplace and headed upstairs. In the small hallway, I pulled the chord to open the attic hatch, with the ladder unfolding before me. I climbed up into the cold, dusty, small space and pulled the other chord, for the attic light.

Then I headed over to the red trunk, opened it, pulled out one of the diaries and sat back down, on top.

To encourage the central heating to follow me up, I left the hatch open. But it was so cold up here, I had to pull the sleeves of my jumper down over my hands to keep warm. Then like a native of Alaska, I pulled up the top of my jumper over the bottom half of my face, to keep my nose warm.

Like this, I opened the diary and looked upon the pages which had turned yellow with time. The handwriting which was written in blue biro now looked a little green. There were spots of mould on the edges, as well as one or two water marks, but it was still readable.

The first thing I saw, was the name at the beginning of the diary; Jessica Tandy. She had been the mate of Flint Riverclaw, the Lokoti Werewolf in the family where my glowing turquoise eyes came from. They were the couple in that framed photo I saw.

When I turned to the next page, I saw an old and faded photo was stuck down with sticky tape. It was a picture of a slim, blonde woman, posing next to an overweight one with short, dark hair. They looked like they were standing in a city somewhere, which could have been Seattle by the skyline. Written below was, JESS & CHRIS 1999 AND FRIENDS TO THE END.

I noticed by flicking through the pages, there were several more photos throughout the book.

The last photo on the last page had the friends posing with a ten year old boy, standing between them. The three were standing on a large, wooden veranda outside of a familiar looking, log cabin. Then I realized why it rang a bell, it was my grandparents old house! It looked so different, being one story instead of two. Now, it was the house that the widowed Forrest and Caesar Riverclaw, lived in.

Upon closer inspection, the ten year old boy in the photo looked half Lokoti by his long, straight, black hair, but he had his mother's blue eyes. I read the scribble at the bottom of this picture; CHRIS, JESS & DAVID, 2010. It would have been Flint Riverclaw who took this photo of his son, wife and her friend.

I went back to the beginning of the diary, to read the first entry which was dated the year 1999... the end of the 20th Century. But looking at their fashion, it wasn't really that different to the 24th Century. Many Lokoti including my mate and I, still liked to wear flannel, denim or suede, because they were hardy and warm. I had to smile to myself at how the Lokoti lived, like we existed in our own little world, whilst following the old ways.

I gave a quick stretch, before snuggling deeper into my white, woollen jumper and then I began to read...

*****

~ 5 ~

20th August 1999

We pulled up outside of a bar, in some kind of 'one man and his dog' town a couple of miles off the main highway. As soon as the motor switched off, Brian, Abi and Steve were jumping out of the rented Jeep. I looked about this tiny town in the middle of the Alaska Range, and therefore in the middle of nowhere; and I wasn't as eager.

"C'mon, Jess." Steve threw me a tired look. "It's just a rest stop, it's still a four hour drive to Anchorage."

"You said we'd be staying in a hotel tonight, in Anchorage." I whined, as I reluctantly climbed out.

"Gees Steve, you weren't kidding when you said Jess was a city-dweller." Brian laughed, as he took Abi's hand to lead her into the Bar.

Steve was embarrassed about having me as a girlfriend, I could tell. He didn't take hold of my hand, nor did he hold the door open for me. Inwardly, I fumed as I went inside. I toyed with the idea of an immediate break-up once I was safely back in Seattle.

He was the outdoorsy type, who typically played more than one sport but I never pretended to be. I met him at a party and when we were introduced, I told him straight up how I'm a manager at a PR company and I have a pretty impressive resume of events. I own my own apartment and a cat and a fridge, stocked full of frozen TV dinners.

So what if I can't cook over an open fire? So what if I don't know how to pitch a tent? So call me civilized, for having difficulty using the behind of a tree, as a bathroom!

We walked into the bar to find a typical scene for an establishment in the middle of nowhere. Wooden floors which looked like they had never seen a can of polish, and a couple of chairs and tables as well as booths on one side of the room, with a long counter on the other. In the middle, sat burly types who could have been truckers or lumberjacks, for all I knew.

However, there was a pool table at the far end of the bar which was being used by four Native Alaskan guys. They caught my eye as I tried not to obviously stare at their long, black hair, broad shoulders, or their bodies which nicely filled out their jeans and flannel shirts. All four of them had a pool stick in their hands, which implied that they were all playing. Three of them had long hair whereas the fourth had cut his dark hair short.

One of them was taller than the others as well as stronger looking. His hair was also the longest, all the way down to his lower back. Maybe I'd never grown out of my rock band phase, but I thought he was the handsomest although he did look older than me. I was 29 years old and this guy looked like he was 39 years old. I bet he was probably married at his age, oh well.

Just then, the handsome one looked right my way, as if he noticed my gaze. I tried to keep from blushing, as I joined my group in a booth along the wall. When we sat down, Steve immediately picked up a menu so he wouldn't have to look at me.

"Hey, you wanna chip-in for a jug of beer?" Brian asked Steve.

"Sure," he said congenially, to my horror.

"A JUG?!" I exclaimed. "You can't just have one glass of beer each? Why does it have to be a jug? We're driving!"

The men looked on in annoyance and even Brian's girlfriend Abi, looked unimpressed. So I tried to put my complaints in another light.

"I'm sorry, but the last time you two shared a jug of beer, it turned into two jugs then three and even four. We ended up staying in a seedy, local motel for the night. Now you guys said we'd be sleeping in a nice hotel in Anchorage this evening. Our flights back to Seattle are 10 AM tomorrow morning! If I miss that flight, my work will kill me. I have an important meeting with some clients the day after next!"

"I don't think this town has a motel." Brian mused, whilst looking around the mediocre bar.

"We'll just put up the tent," Steve shrugged.

"Good idea. Why pay, when we have our own accommodation?" He laughed back then the two gave each other a 'high five'.

"You're kidding, right?" I laughed nervously.

They must be... you know, this is just a stunt to scare the 'city gal'.

Just then a middle-aged woman who must have been the waitress, came over with a notepad and pen, to take our orders.

"Yeah, can we have a jug of Bud?" Steve ordered, before he looked at Abi.

"Yeah, I'll go for the jug idea." She shrugged.

"Any meals with those drinks?" Our waitress asked.

Just as I opened my mouth to order a cola and burger, Steve jumped in.

"Not yet, we'll have the beer first then see what we feel like later."

The waitress shrugged and walked away to procure our order.

"Don't I get to order, just like I don't get a say on the trip?" I muttered quietly, but I knew Steve heard.

He proceeded to ignore me as he perused the menu again.

My legs jiggled nervously as I tried to come up with a contingency plan.

The three of them, the two guys as Tweedle Dee and Tweedle Dumb, with Abi as the 'Little Miss I'll-go-along-with-whatever-my-boyfriend-decides'; all started laughing over funny stories of the camping trip. My eyes scanned the bar, especially the burly men I hoped were truckers and not lumberjacks. Maybe I could get a ride back to Anchorage with one of them?

I'd pay him cash of course, so he wouldn't expect payment of some other kind. Then I'd make Abi write down the number plate of the truck I climbed into, for safety. If I didn't make it to Anchorage and my body went missing somewhere in the Alaska Range, at least the police would have a starting point to find my murderer aka driver.

The waitress returned with a tray carrying four huge glasses and the jug of beer. She put down the glasses first then the jug second and quickly walked off before I could stop her. Damn it! I don't want to drink beer, I want a cola! And I need to eat something...

My legs jiggled harder and I noticed even my hands were trembling! I don't think it was just from nerves, either. Drat it! I really need to eat something, plus I have to go into the bathroom to check my sugar level. I started counting backwards in my head, from the last time I ate, in conjunction with my insulin shot this morning.

"C'mon Jess," my boyfriend poured some beer into my glass. "Have a drink! You're a lot more fun when you've got a couple under your belt."

"Under her belt, or under something else?" Brian guffawed, with Steve laughing loudly.

To stop myself going into a diabetes-induced rant at the losers, quickly I stood up and crossed the bar. My eyes scanned for the Ladies, as I struggled to keep my composure. I tried not to make eye-contact with the flannel-clad truckers or lumberjacks who watched me leave my friends behind.

"Over there."

What? I looked around for the person who just spoke. It was the tall, long-haired, strong-looking, Native Alaskan man. He was leaning on his pool stick whilst watching me.

"Excuse me?" I blinked.

"Over there," he pointed.

I turned to see where he was indicating, which was a door in the corner with a 'Ladies' symbol on it.

"Thanks," I said in surprise at his perceptiveness.

Then I veered off in that direction as my shaking got a hell of a lot worse.

The bathrooms weren't as dirty as I had imagined, nor were they that clean. I placed my handbag on top of the sink and took out the small pack I always had on me, as per doctor's orders. I pricked my finger, before eying the readouts of my sugar level with dissatisfaction.

I really needed a hot meal. I really needed to shower and climb into a comfortable bed. I really couldn't miss that flight tomorrow, at 10 AM. I really couldn't miss my Monday morning meeting.

The more worried I felt, the worse my shaking grew... I felt like bursting into tears at the lousy time I was having! Back in Seattle, Steve had been a nice guy but with this camping trip, we both had seen a new side in each other. He had turned into a cold, obnoxious male and I had turned into a nagging, nervous wreck!

I'm NEVER going camping again! I hate Alaska! I want to go home to Washington State!

I packed away the diabetics kit before I walked back out. Instead of returning to the booth, I went and sat on a stool at the bar. I tried to sit patiently as I waited to be served, but my trembling went from bad to worse.

When I raised my hand to attract the attention of the bartender who was chatting to another patron, my hand shook uncontrollably.

"Charlie!" A loud voice suddenly boomed. I jumped in surprise just as the bartender did. We both saw it was the handsome, older, Native Alaskan man, now standing beside me. "The lady needs a drink."

The middle-age bartender immediately came over, "What can I get for you today, Miss?"

"Um, can I please have an orange juice?" I managed out.

I had to hug my hands between my legs, to try to stop the shaking.

"And she needs to eat," the handsome man added, whilst looking on my hands.

"What would you like?" The bartender pulled out a pen and pad.

"Um..." I tried to think, but I couldn't clearly.

"Make it a burger with the lot," the man spoke for me again, before he looked my way. "Is that OK? It practically has all of the five food groups, in one meal."

"Hey, Harry? We need a burger with the lot!" The bartender called over his shoulder, to an open doorway where the kitchen must be.

To my further surprise, next the handsome stranger handed over a twenty dollar bill, to pay!

"No!" I cried out, a little loudly by accident. I scrambled for my purse, but the bartender took the man's money and moved away. I tried to hold my purse steady as I pulled out another twenty dollar note. "Here, take it."

"You come from the city, don't you?" The stranger smiled in amusement.

"What has that to do with it?"

"Here, when a person is shouted a meal and a drink, they simply say 'thanks'." He said evenly.

"But I don't come from around here, so I won't be able to pay you back." I pointed out.

He openly looked over my hiking boots, cargo shorts and water-proof jacket, all of which I had bought recently for this camping trip from hell.

"Yeah, I guessed you weren't from around here," the man joked.

Self-consciously, I glanced down at my appearance before I looked back.

"Yeah, I do look like I'm trying too hard to belong in the Alaskan wilderness, don't I?" I laughed nervously.

"Why try?" The man leaned on the bar. "Most people here all come from somewhere else. Except my people of course, we've always been here."

"Yeah, I guess from your appearance, I see that too." I laughed, as did he.

"I'm Lokoti," he said.

"Oh, hi Lokoti." I offered him my hand to shake. "I'm Jessica Tandy."

"No, my name's not Lokoti, it's the name of my people." He chuckled as we shook on it. "MY name is Flint Riverclaw."

"Oh!" I blushed at my stupidity. "Sorry."

The bartender put a tall glass of OJ before me before he moved away to continue his conversation with the other patron.

I tried to keep my hands steady, as I took hold of the glass and raised it to my mouth. But my hands shook so badly, the man kindly put out his hand to help hold it. I felt my face burn in embarrassment as I drank half the glass, before he lowered it.

"I'm sorry, I'm – I'm diabetic..." I continued to blush, "...my sugar levels are a little low at the moment."

"Hmm, I smelled that." Flint Riverclaw frowned in concern.

"You smelled that?" I echoed, thinking that it was an odd thing to say.

Then I watched him flash an angry look towards the booth where Steve was sitting. However, my boyfriend's back was to us, as he was laughing away with Brian and Abi. The three didn't appear to be feeling my absence.

"Your mate should be looking after you." He said in disapproval, whilst glaring at Steve's back.

"My who? My boyfriend? Well, I don't think he's going to be my boyfriend for much longer." I glared into the glass.

"You are unmarried?" He looked on in partial surprise. "I thought you were with the male over there, who's with his friends."

"You mean my soon-to-be 'ex'? No, we were never married. We only started dating two months ago. When he invited me up here, to go camping with he and his friends? I thought to myself, 'well he knows I'm not the outdoors type, but he must be serious about this relationship if he wants me to go away with him'. But this has been the week from hell! He and his friends have done nothing but laugh at me because I couldn't put up a tent, I couldn't start a fire, I couldn't cook over the flames and I hate using trees as bathrooms!"

All of a sudden, all of my grievances came out in one rant!

"He didn't help or provide for you?" Flint further frowned.

“Only when I burned the baked beans,” I said darkly then I started to rub my face from stress. “Now he’s drinking and when he starts, it’s hard to get him to stop. We’re supposed to overnight in Anchorage for our flight back to Seattle tomorrow morning, but I’m scared we won’t make it.”

I wasn’t sure if I imagined it, but I thought I heard a growl? When I looked up sharply, I found Flint looking dangerously on Steve, for some reason.

“Er, so Flint, are you married?” I tried to move the conversation along.

“I have no mate,” he answered, as he pushed my orange juice closer, to hint that I should have more. I smiled at his concern as I picked it up and downed the last. Then he even ordered another for me. “Charlie, can I get two more orange juices?”

“Two OJ’s Flint?” The bartender acknowledged. “Coming right up!”

“Two more?” I echoed. “I’ll probably only drink one!”

“One of them is for me,” he chuckled again.

“You’re not going to have a beer?”

“I don’t drink alcohol,” he said simply, as he pulled another note from his wallet.

“No, let me!” I scrambled for my purse. But he ignored the note in my hand and so did the bartender, as he took Flint’s money instead. “What, is this a conspiracy? Don’t women pay for drinks in Alaska?”

Flint smiled, “So Jessica Tandy, what do you do in Seattle?”

He picked up one of the new drinks which were set down while he waited to hear what I had to say.

“I’m a manager at a large PR firm, called ‘Wildenstein Dreams’.” I said proudly. “I was promoted at the beginning of the year. I’ve won a couple of awards for my event designs and now I earn 50k a year. What do you do, Flint?”

“I work in construction,” he advised.

“Really and how’s that going for you? Do you own your own construction company? How much do you pull in per annum?” I asked congenially.

“In my culture, it’s rude to ask how much a person earns.” He said casually.

“Oh.” I sat up straighter in surprise. Don’t tell me I just offended this nice man? “Sorry.”

“The only time you ask a Lokoti that question, is if you are the father of the woman you want to mate with.” He grinned in good humour.

“No shit,” my face fell. “Er, sorry Flint.”

“The father may not ask that question specifically, instead he’ll ask how the man can provide for the woman, especially when she gives him children. In that respect Jessica, I can tell you that I can provide for a mate should I take one.”

"Oh er, good for you." I patted him on the arm as I wondered what to say to that? But it made Flint laugh again.

"I like your blue eyes." He openly stared at my face. "They stand out the most against your white skin and blonde hair."

"Do they?"

"Tell me about your life in Seattle, Jessica." He sat down on the stool beside mine.

I laughed at the intense look on the handsome man's face, as he came across as very mature. Flint may look like he's 39 years old, but he reminded me of someone in their fifties or older, from his wizened look. He gave the impression of someone who's 'been there and done that'.

"Um, there's not much to tell." I tried not to blush again at the interest he showed. "I wake up at 6 AM, buy a cappuccino on my way into the office, where I work from 8 – 6, Monday to Friday. Then I go home to my apartment which I'm paying off the mortgage and to my cat named Fritz. He's a Persian Blue and usually he's the man of my life. I don't like sport, I HATE camping..." here the two of us laughed, "...and I like to spend weekends with friends, by going to restaurants and seeing movies or shows."

"Alma has a small cinema," he offered.

"Alma?" I gave a funny look. "Where's Alma?"

"This is Alma," he chuckled at my vagueness.

"This town we're in right now, this is Alma?"

"Uh huh," he said patiently. "Alma has a cinema, this bar as well as a diner. It also has a school, which Lokoti kids attend and a supermarket. On our tribal lands, we have a Meeting Hall where we put on dances, bingo, or family celebrations."

"It sounds like you enjoy the quiet life, Flint." I remarked.

"It sounds like you enjoy the fast life, Jessica." He smiled back.

Just then we were interrupted when Steve carried over the empty beer jug to order another.

"Can I get another jug of Bud?" He asked the bartender. Simultaneously, I blanched at the idea they were drinking more as he looked over and noticed me. He fired up, "There you are! We were wondering where you got to."

"I had to get an orange juice." I spoke crisply. "My blood sugar was low."

Flint's eyes narrowed, "Jessica has been sitting here for the past ten minutes, she wouldn't have been hard to spot from where you're sitting."

Steve glared back as he came over to put a possessive hand in my lap.

"So you're drinking orange juice with her?" He asked snidely. "Or is there vodka in yours and hers drinks?"

"I don't drink alcohol." Flint said warily. "And with Jessica being a diabetic, it wouldn't be wise for her to drink either, until her blood sugar level has returned to normal."

"Well thank you for baby-sitting her," Steve said sarcastically. "But she'll be coming back to sit with her friends again."

"No," I shrugged off his hand, "not unless."

"Huh?" He uttered, as his breath reeked of beer.

"Not unless you stop drinking right now and we all hop into the rental and drive to Anchorage!" I snapped.

"Jess, we have the tents! We can camp on the side of the road and get up at dawn, to finish the drive. Brian and I talked about it. You're not gonna miss your flight." Steve rolled his eyes, like I was the one being difficult.

My heart pounded as my eyes widened in fear that I could be stranded...

"I'll drive you to Anchorage." Flint said simply.

"What?" Both our heads snapped around in surprise.

"I'll drive you to Anchorage when you've eaten your burger." He said calmly, as he held my gaze.

"What burger?" Steve tipsily looked around.

Perfectly timed, a hamburger with the lot and a side of fries, was carried out by a younger Native Alaskan wearing an apron. He placed it on the counter before Flint, who slid the plate in front of me.

"Thanks Harry," he patted the younger man, on the arm.

"No problem Flint," the youth smiled back, before he returned to the kitchen.

"Mmm yum!" Steve picked up a couple of fries to jam into his mouth. "Good idea, Jess. I'm hungry!"

Flint didn't like this and he stood up to tower over his opposition. With his height and width, he easily dwarfed Steve. He looked dangerously upon the male who was interfering.

"I bought the burger for Jessica, I didn't buy it for you." He growled out.

"Fine," Steve drunkenly laughed. "If that's the way it is, Jess is getting strange men to buy her burgers in bars? Then it's fine with me! You can make your own way to Anchorage."

"Wait!" I stood up frightened, as this situation went from bad to worse. "Steve, please just take me to Anchorage? Tonight? I'll even get a separate hotel room. You can break up with me in Anchorage and we'll never have to see each other again. Just take me to Anchorage?"

"Oh, now you want to be with me, huh? Burger boy doesn't cut it?" He raised his voice. "Sure this guy is as big as a lumberjack, but I bet he's not a Partner in one of Seattle's top law firms! What's his salary per year? One dollar per tree he cuts down?"

I thought I heard another growl come from Flint as I tried to diffuse the situation.

"C'mon Steve, it's not like that! Flint was just being nice." I said desperately. "He saw me shaking because of my low sugar level and he bought me something to eat and drink. Please just take me to Anchorage tonight? Please?"

"Jess, I told you what our plans are tonight! Stop your nagging! Man, we've only dated for two months and you're already trying to tell me what to do?" He turned away to pay for his jug of beer.

"The lady is frightened, especially when she's unwell and she's far from home. A real man would see to the woman's safety first, particularly the woman he supposedly has feelings for." Flint spoke coldly.

"Oh is THAT what a real man would do?" He taunted. "I bet that you know a lot of 'real' men all the way up north, cold and alone, huh burger boy?"

"Steve!" My face burned bright red. "Don't be such an asshole!"

Now the bartender got involved when he put down the new jug. However, he moved it away again after he heard the arguing. Indeed, the whole bar was watching.

"I think you've drunk enough, friend." The bartender looked on warily.

"Excuse me?" Steve turned on him. "What kind of customer service do you call this?"

The older man looked from Flint to back to him, before he said calmly, "Maybe you and your friends should leave."

"I could sue you for this!" Steve said sulkily. "But you wouldn't be worth the paper work."

As he returned to the table to talk to Brian and Abi, I grabbed my handbag and prepared to go with him.

Flint calmly looked down into my face with his great height, "I'll drive you to Anchorage Jessica, after you've eaten."

That gave me pause, as I looked into his face which seemed open and kind.

"Why?" I wondered. "Are you going to Anchorage yourself?"

"I'll drive you there and make sure you don't miss your plane," he said seriously.

"You're just going to hop in your vehicle and drive me, a complete stranger, all the way to Anchorage?" I asked in disbelief.

"I think it'd be safer than if you remained with your friends, who've been drinking." He said then he leaned in closer and when he did, I got a whiff of whatever aftershave he was wearing. Man, did this guy smell good! He spoke softly, "You have nothing to fear from me, Jessica Tandy. I will make sure you don't come to harm."

I don't know if it was from how deep and gravely his voice sounded then, or his addictive aftershave, or even if it was just his handsome face? Maybe it was all of the above, but my strong attraction made me believe him.

In the corner of my eye, I noticed Abi and Brian get up from the booth and she looked uncertain. Whereas Brian and Steven went over to the door, she walked over to where I was standing at the bar, to speak to me directly.

"Um, Jess? We're leaving for Anchorage now. Are you coming?"

"Jessica has a ride to Anchorage," Flint answered.

She looked over the tall stranger warily, before she leaned in to speak quietly. "Look, I know Steve can be a bit loud when he's drinking. But we are driving back to Anchorage tonight, for our flight tomorrow. I don't think it's a bright idea to get a ride with a stranger you only just met in a bar, Jess."

"You're only driving to Anchorage now because you've been kicked out of the bar, Abi." I replied curtly, offended at how she just made me sound!

"Jessica can call her parents in Seattle and give them my name, address and my number plate. If anything happens to her in Anchorage then they'll know how to contact me." Flint organized.

Abi looked on in distrust, "We're out of range for our mobile phones."

Instantly, he called on the bartender, "Charlie, can we use your phone?"

"Here we go Flint," the bartender who I now knew as Charlie, immediately lifted it up from behind the bar.

Flint told him, "Jessica needs to call her parents in Seattle, to tell them I'll be driving her to Anchorage."

"It's the safe thing to do, Miss." Charlie gave a nod. "I mean, I can speak for Flint, since he's a good man? But if anything happens to you in Anchorage, at least your parents will know where you are."

"Er, my parents are actually in Michigan, I live in Washington State." My face flushed at their attention. "But I have a best friend I can call in Seattle."

"Go right ahead," Charlie pushed the phone closer.

"Jess!" Abi looked guilty. "Just come with us, we're leaving now."

"I'll get Jessica's things from your RV while she makes the calls." Flint told her. "Then she's going to eat her burger and afterwards, I'll drive her to Anchorage."

"I'll speak to the guys and see if they can wait, while you eat." She said annoyed.

Now SHE was getting annoyed at ME? That's it, I've had it up to here!

"Oh, I'm so sorry for having low blood sugar that I need to eat instead of just drink beer. I'm sorry I couldn't cook over an open fire, so I've practically been starving all week! Especially since everybody who's been camping before, didn't offer to help! I'm sorry my college education didn't include putting up tents! I'm sorry I made such a fuss about using a tree for a fucking bathroom, or I can't bathe in a freezing cold river! I'm sorry I've been looking forward to a hotel room in Anchorage all week, where I can shower, sleep in a proper bed and order room service!" I vented.

"Fine!" She said indignantly. "But I've never met anyone that has complained as much as you do, Jess!"

"Of course I've complained!" I shouted back. "Diabetics get shitty when we're cold, hungry and tired!"

Suddenly, the whole Bar erupted into laughter which included Flint and Charlie.

Abi's face turned bright red, whereas Steve and Brian turned and left angry.

"I'd get shitty if I was cold, hungry and tired all week too," one of the men at the counter, chuckled.

"And the showers! Don't forget the showers." One of the men Flint had been playing pool with, laughed along.

"When our pulsating, massage, shower head broke, my wife was shitty for two weeks!" The Native Alaskan man with the short hair, guffawed.

Flint put his hand over mine, which felt warm and strong and even soothed somehow.

"You sit and eat whilst I get your things," he ordered gently.

Unconsciously, I found myself doing exactly what he said as I returned to the stool. I watched him leave the bar with her then I saw one of his friends walk out after him. It was as if they were worried that MY friends were the dangerous ones!

Charlie nodded to the phone, "Don't forget to call your parents and your friend."

I fished out my purse again, "That's two long-distance calls, what do I owe you?"

"Don't you worry about that now, Jessica." He said seriously. "You just call your family and friends, so they know you're alright."

My heart warmed as my face did, at the old-fashioned manners of the people here. I was the one who was sceptical of THEM when I first walked into this bar? So far, the city folk left a lot to be desired when compared to the country.

I dialled my friend's number first however, she was out so I left a brief message on her answering machine.

"Hey Chris, it's me. Um, something's happened in Alaska and I won't be coming back with Steve and his friends. I guess you could say that we broke up. I'm still out of range on my mobile, but I've got a lift with a local to Anchorage. I'll call you tonight from the hotel. Bye."

I put down the receiver and was about to pick up my burger, when Charlie passed me a piece of paper with a name and some particulars.

"What's this?" I queried.

"Flint's name, address and his number plate," he said. "You can give those to your parents."

I think he'd overheard my first call, which I guess was pretty vague. I gave him an appreciative smile as I made the second call. This time my Mom was home, which I wished she hadn't been from the fuss she kicked up!

"Mom, calm down!" I rolled my eyes. "You've got the name and you've got the address. Hell, you've even got the number plate! What? No! No, you don't have to call Uncle Ben in Vancouver. No, I'm NOT stranded in Alaska. Look, I have a ride to Anchorage. Tomorrow morning I'm flying back to Seattle. Uh huh. Well, I'm glad you never liked Steve because now, neither do I!"

When I put the phone down, I also put my head down on the bar, as I felt physically and emotionally exhausted.

"You want me to warm that up for you?" Charlie offered, as he returned it behind the counter.

"Huh?" I looked up and saw he meant the burger. "Um, no thanks. It'll be fine."

"Your mother's a real pistol, eh?" He chuckled.

"Let me put it this way; when I found out that my Dad has high blood pressure, I wasn't surprised." I sighed.

"Eat up, Jessica." He nodded towards the food. "It'll make you feel better."

"Thanks Charlie... for everything."

He gave a wink as he moved away to serve someone else. I felt like I was being watched and when I looked behind, I saw that I was right. Flint's two friends were just standing there instead of playing pool. I got the impression they were looking after me, while he had gone to get my stuff.

I picked up the burger and finally began to eat, bemused by this whole situation. I felt like I was in a time warp with all of this, 'aw-shucks-lets-look-after-the-lady' attitude. But I must admit, it was a nice change.

Flint returned with his friend carrying my large backpack, sleeping bag and the rolled up, inflatable mattress.

"Jessica, this is my best friend John Wisetail." He implied the Native Alaskan man who had the short, dark hair.

"Hi." I offered my hand.

"Pleased to meet you, ma'am." He shook on it. "Is this all the stuff you brought on your camping trip?"

"Yeah, the tent and the other stuff were Steve's, Brian's and Abi's." I answered. "I'd never been camping before and I never will again."

"Camping isn't so bad ma'am, it just depends on who you go camping with." John Wisetail chuckled, before he turned away to rejoin their friends.

Flint sat back down on the stool next to mine and proceeded to watch me eat.

"Oh um, did you want to eat something before the drive?" I asked.

"No, I'm still full from hunting last night." He shook his head

Before I could ask what he meant by that, I had to pay attention to my burger which was falling apart. As I ate, I noticed I still had an audience.

"What?" I wondered if I was making a pig of myself?

"I like the way you eat," he said. "I've never seen anybody eat like that before."

"Like what?"

"You not only look dainty, you eat dainty." He smirked. "Do you want some ketchup with your fries?"

"Yeah, OK." I started to reach for the bottle, when he picked it up and handed it to me instead. "Thanks."

"Take your time," he stood up again. "I'm going to put some gas in the truck then I'll come back and get you."

"Oh," I wiped my hands on the serviette to grab my purse again. "How much would you like for gas? Is fifty bucks OK?"

Flint smiled patiently, "You like to pay your own way, don't you Jessica Tandy?"

"Well, it is the nineties."

"If you lived in Alaska, I would take you home because it's the right thing to do." He stated. "But since you don't, I'll take you to the airport instead."

Then Flint Riverclaw departed the bar a second time, ignoring my money once again.

As I watched him walk off, I wondered if I had offended him? I felt tongue-tied, as I didn't know what to say since in his culture, I kept doing the wrong thing. Maybe I should just shut up and not say anything...

*****

Twenty minutes later, I found myself sitting on the front seat of a blue pick-up truck and riding shot gun down the highway.

The vehicle was old, so the suspension wasn't the best but hey, beggars can't be choosers. Every time there was a bump in the road, I practically went 'boing boing boing' on the seat. The leather seat was so springy, it almost served as the truck's suspension in itself.

Our seatbelts were fastened and the tiny township of Alma was a couple of miles behind. A comfortable silence filled the cab, as I didn't feel obliged to talk and neither did he. Besides, I was enjoying the scenery of the dark green pines, contrasted against the majestic, snowy peaks.

"Oh," he spoke after a while, "I got some snacks and drinks, in case you get hungry."

His hand moved over my lap to the glove compartment, to show the goods. I saw two cans of cola and a packet of plain potato chips.

"Er, thanks."

My heart pounded, as his hand closed the compartment again and moved back over my lap, to return to the wheel.

"How about some music?" He turned on the radio. Country music filled the cabin and I held my tongue. However, Flint Riverclaw was a remarkably perceptive person, as I was starting to see. "You don't like country?"

"Um, if you want to listen, I don't mind." I tried to be polite.

Instead, he moved the dial around to find something else but we didn't have a huge range of stations to choose from. There was more country music, old rock songs from the 1950's, or classical.

"Well?" He asked. "Which station?"

"Er, you don't have any tapes or CD's to listen to?" I thought I'd try.

"Not in the truck, sorry."

"No problem." I tried to be amiable. But I felt bad when he turned the radio off. "Hey, didn't you want to listen to music?"

"I like silence just as much," he said simply.

"It's a four hour drive to Anchorage," I said guiltily. "If you want to listen to country music then go ahead."

"You don't like silence?" He flashed a grin my way.

"OK..." I managed back nervously, "...I can be quiet."

"I don't mind conversation, either." He chuckled. "I like silence, I like talking and I like country music."

Just then I laughed at how he put that, as he made me realize that I was the one who was making me nervous, not him.

So I'm attracted to the guy, so what? I may as well as enjoy his company for the four hours I have it. After tonight, I may never see him again.

"Flint, I feel like I'm always saying the wrong thing around you!" I cried out with a pink face.

"That's a pity, because I like your voice." He smilingly looked out at the road ahead.

"I like your voice too, it's very deep." I decided to give honesty a shot. "Why are you unmarried, Flint?"

"Why are you?" He returned. "I've never met the woman I wanted to marry."

"And I've never met the right man."

"Tell me Jessica Tandy, who is this 'right man'?" He smirked.

"You mean what do I look for?" I guessed and when he gave a nod, I continued. "Well somebody tall, somebody polite, somebody whose company is easy going. I'd like someone intelligent, so I can talk about world news, instead of just sport. What kind of woman are you looking for?"

"I'm not," he said simply.

"Huh?"

"If I fall in love with a woman, I simply will. I can't tell myself who I must fall in love with as it doesn't work like that. The person I end up with will simply be the person I fell in love with."

I frowned, "Then why are you unmarried? If you haven't found the woman yet, whose qualities you weren't looking for anyway, you could have fallen for any old person."

"I haven't fallen in love." He shrugged. "I haven't met the woman whom I wanted to be with, for the rest of my life."

"Oh, so you're looking for the thunderbolt?"

Now he passed me the peculiar look. "Huh?"

"You're waiting for love at first sight?"

"No, I don't believe in love at first sight." He shook his head. "I believe in attraction at first sight, but I don't believe in love at first sight."

"OK Flint, you've confused me." I sounded cross but I was smiling which he saw. "Tell me how you see it then."

"This 'woman' we keep talking about, I assumed I'd be attracted to her in the beginning. After I spend some time with her then I might fall in love. I've been attracted to a couple of women over the years. I've spent time with them. But I didn't fall in love so I did not marry."

"Just like that," I tittered at his easy-going view. "Hey, why did you call Steve my mate, before? In your culture do you -"

"In my tribe, if a man and woman live together, they're mates." He shrugged. "Since you went camping with him, I thought you may have lived together."

"So the woman you live with, will become your mate?" I asked in amusement.

"Yes, she will bear my young and we will be mates."

"Sounds like the animal kingdom," I said to myself, as I looked away.

"Which animal though?" He overheard. "Some animals mate to reproduce then they separate. Other animals, like the wolf or the fox, take a mate and they stay with that mate for life."

"Really, do foxes do that? I didn't know..." my eyebrows rose, "...I didn't know wolves were old romantics either."

"In a pack, the male wolves fight each other to become first, as do the females. Then the first male and the first female mate and the other wolves help them raise the young." Flint explained.

"Sounds like a lot of work just to get laid," I joked.

“Has a man proposed to you, Jessica Tandy?” He asked out of the blue.

“Um...once.”

“Why didn’t you marry this person?”

“Because something just wasn’t right about him,” I sighed. “I mean, he was a nice guy, but there was something missing.”

“Were you in love with him?”

“I thought I was, but now I don’t know.”

“Was it Steve?”

“Hell no!” I cracked up laughing, as did he. “It was two guys before him. I actually did live with this guy I nearly married, for two years.”

“Do you have children?”

“No,” I shook my head, “good ole pregnancy prevention methods, protected me from that catastrophe. But funnily enough, it was the idea that I didn’t want to have children with this guy, which made me not accept his proposal.”

“He did not make you feel safe?” Flint guessed.

“Actually, I think it was something like that.” I looked his way impressed again at his perceptiveness.

“Then Jessica, instead of looking for a man to talk about world news with, why don’t you look for one whom you feel safe with.” He said gently.

I stared out at the long road ahead, tiredly resting my head on my hand which was propped up against the door.

“Maybe you’re right,” I said wearily. “Or maybe I’ll just give up and grow into an old spinster, surrounded by cats?”

Flint laughed aloud, “With your pretty blue eyes, it would be a shame.”

“It’s not a bad life.” I shrugged it off. “I won’t be lonely, my best friend would never let that happen.”

“My friends don’t let me get lonely, either.” He smiled softly. “They have mates and young, but if they think I’ve been alone for too long, they come to visit.”

“So do you have an apartment somewhere?”

“I built a log cabin which is as big as a house. It has three bedrooms, a bathroom, kitchen, living area and front veranda.”

“You built a log cabin by yourself?” I stared and he nodded. “It sounds like you don’t like to get bored.”

“Occasionally I had help, such as with the plumbing or electricity.” He explained. “But I built it myself over two years. The land it’s on has always been in my family. It’s away from the community centre of our tribal lands, so it’s quiet and secluded amongst the trees.”

“It sounds peaceful,” I smiled sleepily, as my eyes started to close by themselves. “Tell me more about your house and your tribal lands, Flint.”

He paused and I sensed he looked over and saw how tired I was. So he started to talk softly as if he was telling a child a story. It suited his deep voice, which lulled me into a relaxed state.

"The Lokoti have always lived in the same place, in the Alaska Range. The majority of it is a large National Park, where my people hunt. We have always lived off the land and will continue to do so. We get our meat, pelts, timber and vegetables from the land. Our tribal lands are older than the township of Alma and older than the state of Alaska. We follow our own ways, which were born from loyalty and love long ago. We live by the old traditions, because it protects our families and it protects the land. What your people call 'land conservation' or 'environmentally friendly', is what we've been doing for thousands of years. By respecting nature and her gifts, we also learn respect for each other. The man who takes a woman as his mate, protects and provides for her, just as the male Lokoti Wolf fights for his mate, in the wild..."

Flint kept talking in a soft manner it soon put me to sleep.

A couple of times I opened my eyes to make sure we were still on the highway and I wasn't being kidnapped. However, the long stretch of asphalt ahead, always greeted me. I wasn't sure what it was about this giant called Flint Riverclaw; but in his company I felt warm, comfortable and most of all safe. The last time I opened my eyes, I found a man's jacket resting over my bare legs which must have been his.

*****

I woke up properly at 6.33 PM or so my watch said, as I straightened and looked out the window. I still saw mountains, forest and highway in the bright 'twilight' of the Alaskan summer. The sun didn't set until late here and when we were camping, it threw my sleeping pattern out of whack.

"We'll be in Anchorage in under an hour," Flint greeted.

"I slept for that long?" I sounded surprised.

"You're very tired and your blood sugar is still a little low." He sounded understanding.

But I wondered how he would know about blood sugar levels, or even mine?

"Do you have a relative who's a diabetic?" I asked.

"No."

"Then how do you know so much about it?"

Flint smilingly shrugged, "I smell it."

"You smell it?" I gave a peculiar look.

Then he changed the subject, "Do you have somewhere to stay tonight?"

"Um yeah, I have a reservation at the Sheraton." I told him, but then I paused. "Oh oh."

“Hmm?”

“I did have a reservation at the Sheraton, but it was for a room booked under Steve’s name.” I frowned. “I wonder...?”

“Hmm?” He watched me take my mobile phone out of my bag.

“Yes, finally! I have reception again!” I cheered then I talked on the phone. “Yeah hi, can you please put me through to the Sheraton Hotel in Anchorage? Thanks.” Pause. “Hi, is this the Sheraton Hotel in Anchorage? Great! Um, I had a reservation tonight under the name of Steve Gingall, but I won’t be checking in with him. Is it possible to have a room of my own, charged to my credit card? You’re completely booked up?”

Flint watched my face fall as he listened in.

“Right. Right. Right.” My expression turned grim, before brightening. “Oh really? Could you please double check? Uh huh. Uh huh. Oh you do? That’s great! I don’t care, just book it in the name of Jessica Tandy. Yep. Uh huh. Well, check-in will probably be in an hour. Yep, OK bye.”

Then I found my driver was half watching the road and the other half was on me.

“You have a room?” He guessed.

“Phew! They were all booked up but then they had a last minute cancellation. Yay! Oh Flint, this is good news! Tonight I’ll be sleeping in a comfortable bed, after a long hot shower and ordering up a banquet from room service!”

“That's good news, it’s just what you were hoping for.” He smiled.

“So what are you doing tonight?” I queried. “Are you staying with friends in Anchorage?”

“No, I’ll be driving home tonight.” He answered.

His reply hit me hard in the face, like a plank of wood. Immediately, I felt like an idiot! That’s me taken care of, but what about him?

“Oh no Flint!” I cried out. “You can’t do that! Look, I’ll call the hotel back and see if they’ve had another cancellation -”

“You don’t have to do that.”

“Let me pay for your accommodation!” I raised the phone to my ear. “It’s the least I can do.”

“Jessica, please.” He kept one hand on the wheel as he used his other to gently take the phone away. “I want to drive back home tonight.”

“But why?”

“I don’t like to be away from tribal lands for too long,” he shrugged.

“Why?”

“Because they’re my home.”

“But you’ve already driven four and a half hours, out of your way for me.” I said guiltily.

“It wasn’t out of my way.”

"Yes it was! I'm just some strange girl that stumbled into your bar, who nearly went into shock because of low blood sugar and a shitty camping trip..." I felt ridiculous as my eyes watered, "...and I must have looked like some social reject, with the crappy boyfriend. You took pity on me and drove me all the way to Anchorage!"

"I was concerned about your health," he admitted. "But you smell better after the food and the nap."

"I smell better?" My eyebrows rose. "Look Flint, let me repay you by shouting you a room in a nice hotel -"

"Jessica," he growled out as he gently cupped my face with one hand. It was so large and hot, it warmed me all over. He looked away from the road just long enough to pierce my light blue eyes with his dark brown ones. "I liked driving you to Anchorage. I'm happy that I got to spend four hours with the beautiful girl who stumbled into the bar where I play pool. I watched your face while you slept and I put my jacket over you to keep you warm. If you lived all the way in Barrow, I still would have seen you home."

Then I don't know what made me act this way, but I held his huge hand in my smaller two and I kissed his palm.

I know it was forward of me to do that but Flint didn't seem to mind. He even caressed my cheek before stroking my hair. When he rested his hand in my lap, the warmth made my legs heat up, as it made my heart pound. I almost wished he would do something else whilst his hand was there, but he didn't and I knew why. He didn't want me to think that I had to pay him back in another way.

We drove through the outskirts of Anchorage which was sooner than I liked. A couple of times, he had to remove his hand to either change gears or use both hands on the wheel. But as soon as he'd finished, he returned it to my lap.

In the city, Flint parked his truck across the road from my hotel. Reluctantly, I climbed out of the warm cab and shivered, pulling my jacket tighter. He pulled out my backpack, sleeping bag and rolled up mattress from the back to carry them into the hotel for me. He accompanied me to the front desk where I checked-in. Instead of giving my things to the Bell Boy, he insisted on carrying them to my room, for me.

In the elevator up, my eyes couldn't leave his darker ones. I literally felt like he had a magnetic pull which attracted me to him. I've never felt desire like this before. I started to argue with myself, how I could invite him to stay with me tonight? Or, would he be turned off by that kind of behaviour? I was still trying to make him out.

I used the electronic card to open my door then I turned around to face him. Reluctantly, he handed over my backpack as well as the sleeping bag and rolled-up mattress. He truly seemed sad to see me go.

"Thanks for walking me to my door." I began. "Um, would you like to come in for a drink or something?"

I watched his eyes widen, was it with hope? But he remained quiet for a moment, as he seemed to be contemplating if he should. Does he need more encouragement?

Just as I opened my mouth to invite him in again, suddenly I found myself pushed up against the doorway, with his lips smothering mine!

His body heat seemed to radiate outwards and into me, as his larger lips moved almost forcefully. We kissed closed-mouth until I offered another invitation by opening mine. Immediately, his bigger tongue entered and felt like it took over my whole mouth.

By this stage, my heart was pounding so hard inside my chest that I felt like I was shaking. My skin turned hot as I tingled all over. This guy smelled so good, kissed so good and – and – and everything good so far!

Flint lifted me up whilst he was still kissing me, as I heard him push my things into the room with his legs.

I vaguely became aware he had carried me in, with the hotel room door shutting behind. It just felt so good kissing him, I took the liberty of running my hand through his long, dark hair. I felt him take my hair out of its pony tail so he could do the same.

"Mmm..." he growled again, "...you smell good, Jessica Tandy."

"I haven't showered in five days."

"I know, your pheromones are concentrated in your sweat." He leaned in to sniff my neck. "I like it."

Next, I felt his teeth scrape along the sensitive skin and it turned me on even more...!

"I mean, I did try to wash myself down a bit. Er, I couldn't jump into the whole river though, because it was too cold. Um, did you want me to have a shower first?" I offered.

Abruptly, I felt my feet leave the floor as my back hit the soft mattress. Flint had just picked me up and lay me on the bed. Our eyes met and held once more, as if he was still waiting for further encouragement.

"Yes, hell yes, what are you waiting for, take me gosh dammit!" I flung my arms about his neck.

His mouth reclaimed mine while his hands ran over my body. I felt them cup my breasts, run over my abdomen, over my hips, down my thighs and then up the insides of my legs. Where his hands roamed, I started to feel my clothes loosen and I realized that he was undressing me.

I started to follow suit only I wasn't as good as he was. Whereas my clothes seemed to be melt off with his touch, I on the other hand tugged clumsily with his. I almost strangled the poor guy when I tried to pull off his t-shirt which had been under his flannel shirt. I suck at the sexily undressing your partner!

"Shit! Sorry!" I cried out in alarm. "Are you alright?"

"I'm fine, are you alright? Are you hungry? Do you want something to eat first?" Flint paused, to look down with care.

"I want to eat you!" I pulled his head back down so I could kiss him again.

I felt him chuckle as he seemed to relax more, by moving his half-naked body up against mine. I started to wonder if he was holding himself back? Why, was he worried he might hurt me? I opened myself up to him as much as I could with my open-mouthed kisses, my sighs, or how I held onto him tightly.

At last we were completely undressed as Flint lowered himself again after removing his jeans. Then he hesitated as he looked me over. From the expression on his face, he looked like he was about to change his mind?

"What is it?" I sat up, worriedly.

"Wait, let me look on you." He gently pushed me back down. Then with one hand resting on my shoulder, his other moved over my body as he touched, teased and taunted the senses! Oh shit, his warm hand doing this to my body, felt good!

He soon found out how good it felt when he placed it over my crotch. His fingers pushed apart my moist folds and how wet I was, seemed to please him. He began to massage whilst further exploring at the same time, as he watched my face.

"Man, you're a tease!" I moaned, before playfully biting his lower lip.

"I like your body, Jessica."

Flint kept massaging, enjoying my response to his constant touching.

A couple of times, he pushed his fingers deep inside which made me moan. He used his other hand to push my legs further apart before he moved to sit in between. He watched closely, the closer I came to climaxing, as if the process of watching me come, fascinated him. His large hand kept moving over my crotch as my pleasure grew. His fingers felt delightful...!

Then it hit! The orgasm ballooned upwards through my torso. My body froze as I tried to hold on to it for as long as possible. His hand held my hip as his other went in and out of my groin, moving with the wetness.

He ducked his head to take my right nipple into his mouth. He gently chewed on it with his sharp teeth which made me a little uneasy. It seemed unusual that they were so sharp. His eyes were closed as I heard his breathing turn faster and faster, like panting. He seemed to gratify himself, by running his nose over my skin, before kissing it and touching over and over again. I think I heard a growl escape, too?

When is this guy going to just have me? What's his game? I've never had foreplay go for so long, isn't he excited enough yet?

"Flint -" I started to speak, as I was going to offer to go down on him, but the words stuck in my throat.

When he looked back, his eyes were glowing! His brown eyes were glowing some kind of bluish colour, or maybe it was turquoise? No, no, I must be imagining it... No, wait! He just looked up at me again and his brown eyes are definitely glowing turquoise.

C'mon Jess, don't be ridiculous! People's eyes don't change colours, nor do they glow! His dark eyes must be reflecting some kind of light in the room. Yeah...that's it.

Flint continued to make growling noises, as his mouth 'mauled' my torso, whilst his large hand kept touching and then touching some more. I felt his sharp teeth scrape over my left nipple, before his warm, wet tongue soothed the sting. I gasped as my head went back into the pillow. I think I'm going to come again!

This guy seemed to be getting off on making me come! His growls confirmed this, as the wetter I became or the louder I moaned, he would follow it with a growl. I had to admit, this was the most 'different' kind of sex I'd ever had, although it certainly wasn't the worst.

As the orgasm grew, I felt my abdominal muscles expand and contract, as I felt one of his fingers push into me, as his other massaged my clit. Shit, this guy was good at this! No wonder he's unmarried, why settle down when he can be doing this with whomever and whenever?

My pleasure climbed higher as I felt my body open itself up inside and out, when Flint gave a huge push. He thrust himself all the way inside in a single heave. I cried out, as I clung onto his back at his oh so perfectly timed manoeuvre. He moved so fast and hard, he was well and truly riding me, as I was riding the wave of ecstasy which hadn't come crashing down yet.

The bed was shaking hard from how forcefully he was moving. He pushed and pulled at my body, which in turn heightened my already escalating pleasure. Flint seemed to be enjoying this as much as I was, when he lost control and I felt a sharp pain in my left breast where he had bitten too hard!

My mouth opened in a cry of pain but it sounded like a cry of pleasure... then I realized it was because I was feeling so much of both. How was he doing this? How was he pushing at the right speed, the right angle and doing the right moves to make my orgasm go on and on...?

Finally, the orgasm completely pushed me over the brink of ecstasy, like it was a cliff with a watery ending to fall into... as Flint came right after me.

It truly felt like landing in a pool of water from how excited he became and came. But I didn't care, I was on the pill. He could come all he wants and I would be safe.

Eventually, his face left my breasts which he'd been worshipping; as he kissed his way up my neck, over my jaw line and back to my mouth. All I could do was just lie there in happy exhaustion, but this guy still seemed to have so much energy! Maybe it's why his muscles are so huge? I recalled he worked in the construction business, so that could be why. His dark eyes peered into mine as he kissed me softly, over and over.

"You're hungry, it's why you feel weak," he spoke with his deep voice. "You wanted to order room service, didn't you?"

What is this guy, a telepath? I snuggled against his huge, warm body which he seemed to appreciate. He held me closely against his larger form.

"Dinner in bed?" I offered.

"Sounds good," he smiled back.

I rolled away to grab the hotel booklet off the bedside table which had the menu inside, but then I didn't have to roll back. Flint moved up behind, so his warm skin was pressing against mine. My body drank up his greater body heat, which he was more than happy to provide. He nuzzled my neck as I proceeded to flick through the room service guide.

"Lets order a bottle of wine," I sighed romantically.

"I don't drink wine," he chuckled.

"Never?" I turned to look into his eyes.

"Nope," he replied then he reminded, "I drink anything but alcohol."

"Then what else do you feel like...?"

"A glass of milk."

"What?" I cracked up laughing.

"I like to drink milk with my meal," he smilingly shrugged.

"Actually, that does sound good," I mused, "with a red meat dish?"

"A rare steak with a gravy or sauce?" He caught onto my thinking.

"Mmm...sounds good." I went along. "Like Steak Diane with mash potato?"

"It does sound good," he chewed on my ear.

"Man, your teeth are sharp." I remarked, uneasily.

Immediately he stopped, "Did I hurt you?"

"No, I'm just not used to it." I admitted.

As if to see I really was alright, he angled my face towards him to examine it.

"I'm OK," I reassured. "It's just that..."

"Yes?"

"...it's just that you're the most different kind of man I've ever been with." I confessed, as I shyly looked down.

I felt silly, like I was a girl losing her virginity for the first time instead of a mature 29 year old woman.

"But you like it, don't you?"

"Yes," I admitted but I couldn't meet his gaze.

He moved his face closer so our eyes could meet. Then as he held them, he slowly kissed me with his sharp teeth lightly grazing my lips. I liked it, as I found myself returning to my back and pulling him over me.

Shit, he can kiss and he smells so good, as well as feels so good! Is this guy real, or am I dreaming the whole thing? I placed my hand on his wide chest to feel his strong heart beat, to fight off the surreal ness of this scenario.

Flint put his hand over my heart too when he frowned. "Your heart is racing and your blood sugar is low again, we should eat."

"Do you know First Aid or something?"

"No."

"Then how do you know all of this?" I wondered.

“By sight, smell, touch...” he ran his nose down my cheek, to my neck where he nuzzled into it, “...and taste.”

My arms tightened about him as I dropped the menu and forgot all about food.

But he stopped himself when he decided, “First we eat, then we continue with the evening’s entertainment.”

I couldn’t stop tittering, which probably made me sound like a chipmunk to the poor hotel employee I spoke to when I ordered our food.

*****

The time on the clock radio which sat on the bedside table, read as 8.33 AM.

My flight was in an hour and a half. One side of my brain was singing, ‘miss it and stay with Flint’, as the other retorted in a responsible tone, ‘you have a meeting with the company’s top clients tomorrow morning, they’re depending on you.’ As usual, the boring side won.

I’d just come out of the shower and silently dressed, careful not to disturb my overnight guest.

I smiled to myself as I looked down on his sleeping form. He was so tall, his feet were hanging over the end of the bed. I gazed over his bronzed, muscled body with the sheet lying carelessly over his waist. His long, dark hair was perfectly contrasted against the white cotton.

He must be exhausted, we’d been up until 4 AM doing things to each other, which could now make me blush. I guess that was the beauty of a one-night-stand; you could experiment and do things you’d always wanted to try without worrying about seeing the person again. It was a pity in this instance, as I could imagine seeing Flint again and again.

Flashbacks ran through my mind of the previous night’s events. The way he seemed to take control and move me into whatever position he liked; normally I’d say no to however, last night I felt ‘safe’ enough to try. I just went with the flow and man, was I rewarded for it! I can’t recall ever coming so much in my life! It was like my body completely opened itself inside out, for this guy.

Now I was showered, changed and packed. I’d done this so silently, he didn’t even stir. I started to write my name and contact details on the hotel stationery by the phone when I changed my mind. Instead, I put the piece of paper in my pocket.

No Jess, just leave things as they are. Why spoil a naughty night of fun with the obligatory ‘I’ll call you’? Maybe he won’t call, I mean why should he try to keep in contact? You’re not from Alaska, you’re all the way in Seattle!

I sighed in defeat as I stood there, looking over his large, masculine form. I couldn’t help but to smile at the nice memory of him. Nup, lets just leave last night as that, without complicating it with reality.

Quiet as a mouse, I picked up my belongings and departed the room.

On my way out of the hotel, I settled the bill for the accommodation and room service. When Flint wakes up, there'll be nothing for him to pay. It was the least I could do for the guy, after driving four hours for me.

With one last look of longing towards the elevator, I climbed into the awaiting cab for the ride to the airport. As it pulled out onto the busy road, I felt this weird, physical pull, to return to him. But I shrugged it off as I took my ticket out of my personal organizer and looked straight ahead.

~~~~~~
~~~~~~

~ 6 ~

24th August 1999

"Jess, you're a mess!" Chris cried in frustration, down the phone.

"I know," I whined, "I don't know what's wrong with me."

Simultaneously, I was talking to my best friend while preparing my nightly glass of wine with dinner.

Using my head to balance the handset on my shoulder, I moved around my small kitchen. I poured the glass of wine first, before pulling a TV dinner out of the freezer. I struggled to even take the meal out of the box because my hands were shaking so much!

"What is with my body lately?" I complained. "Since I got back from Alaska, my hands have been shaking non-stop! Sometimes at night, my whole body trembles."

"It's been that bad, for the past three days?" My best friend asked in concern.

"Yeah."

"How are your sugar levels?" Chris wondered if it was my diabetes.

"Weird, they're either a little high or a little low. They won't plateau in the healthy range, they're all over the place."

"Have you gone to see the doctor?"

"No, I haven't had the time." I sighed. "I've had so many important meetings and presentations the last couple of days."

"Jess, this is your diabetes! You can't just ignore it and hope it goes away." She sounded disapproving.

"I know," I moaned. "But that method worked on Steve, didn't it?"

She laughed loudly before she asked, "You still haven't heard from the guy?"

"Nope."

"Well if you ever do, I hope you give him an earful! Just stranding you in Alaska like that."

"He didn't STRAND me, in fact I ditched him," I said smugly.

"Yeah, for the tall, dark, handsome stranger named 'Flint Riverclaw'. Man, you can't come up with a more rugged, frontier name than that." Chris sounded like a radio announcer, making me laugh.

"No you can't."

Then she said vehemently, "But Steve still STRANDED you, because he made you feel it was safer trusting a complete stranger for a ride, than him."

"Yeah I guess." I paused before I smiled to myself. "But it all worked out in the end, didn't it?"

"Are you wearing that 'cat that stole the cream' grin again, whilst you're thinking about Mr. Tall-Dark-and-Handsome', in your hotel room?" She asked knowingly.

"Yep."

"Maybe you should contact him."

"I wish!"

"I'm serious, Jess." She needled. "Give him a call."

"And say what, 'let's have a long distance relationship'?" I sung sarcastically. "Come off it, Chris! The man lives in the middle of nowhere, in a state far, far away."

"Don't be such a pessimist, maybe he has fond memories of you too?"

"Even if he did, what's it going to prove?" I asked grouchily. "What are we going to do, fly around to see the other a couple of times a year?"

"It sounds like the sex would be worth it."

"Yeah, it would." I sighed wistfully, whilst staring at the cardboard box, my dinner came in. "Besides, I don't know how to contact him again."

"How small was the small town, he came from? Call the bar where you met and ask the bartender who seemed nice, if you could get this guy's contact details? Or even leave the bartender with yours, to pass on to Flint." She planned.

"Hmm," I frowned as I leant back on my kitchen bench, to think about it. "But I don't remember the name of the bar."

"You said there was just one bar, right?"

"Yeah?"

"Then use directory assistance to look up bars or the said bar, in Alma." She said chirpily. "It shouldn't be too hard to find."

"I don't know, Chris." I sighed again. "Maybe it would come across as stalker behaviour and turn the guy off? Maybe I should just move on."

Then I hesitated as I looked down at my trembling hands.

My voice dropped, "But you wanna know something funny? I partly think that my shakiness is because of him."

"Huh?" She sounded stumped. "Like how?"

"The shakiness is worse at night, when I'm lying in bed and thinking of him..." my voice trailed off then I laughed nervously. "Sounds stupid, huh?"

"It sounds like your body is missing the great sex, which you haven't had in so long." She said cheekily. "Out of ten, what would you rate Flint?"

"Ten out of ten."

"And Steve?"

"Five out of ten."

"And Josh, whom you dated before Steve?"

"Four out of ten."

"Then what the hell are you waiting for, woman? Call Flint right now and set up another date! Fly to Alaska and meet him for dirty weekends!" She practically shouted over the phone.

"Chris, times like this remind me why you're my best friend." I giggled.

"Yeah well, out of the two of us; one of us needs to get lucky, so we can talk about it in full detail for the other person's benefit." She muttered.

"You'd get lucky more often if you deliberately didn't scare away the guys. As soon as you start talking about your self-defence classes as well as your evening lectures on feminism, you attend at College? The guy wonders if you're about to break him."

"Ha!" She scoffed. "They're all weaklings, anyways. I can't find a man strong enough to handle me! I really need to find myself a Klingon."

She referred back to her other hobby which was aside from talking about sex, was watching Star Trek.

"Tell me about Klingon sex again?" I tittered.

"If you break your collar bone on the wedding night, it's good luck for the marriage." She recited. "Man, I really need to find myself a Klingon and you need to call this Flint Riverclaw."

"Yeah but Chris, what do I say?" I asked nervously.

Just then my Persian Blue jumped up onto the kitchen bench to sniff at the frozen food. I reached out to tickle under Fritz's chin, as he purred loudly. He even raised his head higher to encourage me to rub for longer.

"Why can't men be like Fritz here?" I bemoaned. "He's straight forward with what he wants."

"If men were like cats, they'd be harder to get along with. Nah, you need to find a man who's like a dog. They're more loyal." She disagreed.

This made me pause as it reminded me of the person I was missing.

"You know, Flint talked about dogs, or more like wolves and foxes." I told her. "Did you know that they mate for life?"

"No, I didn't know that." She said thoughtfully. "Maybe that's why I like dogs so much. If you could marry a dog, you wouldn't have to worry about him being unfaithful."

"I don't think Flint went to College, but he had life experience." I reminisced, as I tickled Fritz's ears and he rubbed against my hand.

"Would you please just bite the bullet and call this guy?" She pretended to sound cross.

"But what if he doesn't want to drive four hours to Anchorage, to see me when I fly up, to see him?" I moaned. "What if he never wants to see me again?"

Out of the blue, Fritz pulled back from my hand and hissed at the front door! Then he jumped off the kitchen bench and bolted into the bedroom. He scrambled across my small apartment within two seconds flat.

I wondered aloud, "What the hell is wrong with that cat?"

"Was that Fritz just then?" She queried.

Next, I heard from my front door, KNOCK KNOCK KNOCK!

"Hang on, there's someone at the door." I told her. "I'll call you back."

"Actually don't." She yawned. "I'm pretty tired, I ran a training group today. I'll call you tomorrow instead."

"OK, bye." I hung up.

KNOCK KNOCK KNOCK!

Whoever it was, was pretty demanding by how hard they hit the door. I walked up and instead of looking through the peep hole, I simply opened it. However, as soon as I did, my eyes bulged and my jaw dropped to the floor.

Flint Riverclaw stood in the hallway of my apartment building.

With his height and broad shoulders, he practically filled the entire doorway. I stared at the Native Alaskan in bewilderment. What the hell was he doing here?

"Er, hi..." I uttered out in shock.

He looked me up and down in my business suit, complete with stockings and high heels. Whereas, he was wearing the same clothes I remember him in, the flannel shirt and jeans. It was like he hadn't gone home yet, since the hotel.

But how did he track me here? I took the piece of paper with my name and address, home with me. Did he somehow find out my information from my credit card details left with the hotel?

His dark eyes pierced mine as he asked in his deep voice. "Jessica, how are you?"

"Er, um... I'm fine."

He gave a knowing look as he said, "The shaking is worse, isn't it."

It was more of a statement than a question. But how would he know that? And why the hell, is he wearing that knowing look? I was about to demand that he explain himself when he spoke again.

"Can I come in?" He asked politely. "We have things to discuss."

"Um, OK...?"

Helplessly, as if I couldn't say no to him, I stepped aside.

As he came in, I caught another whiff of his delicious deodorant or whatever it was, he was wearing. My eyes drifted closed for a second as I held my breath, before I closed the door. But my hand remained on the doorknob, in case I had to make a quick getaway, from my own apartment.

Flint stood in the living area as he gazed around my home. He looked like a giant in the confines of my personal space. I even caught him sniff, as he glanced about.

"You have a cat?" He remembered.

"Yes."

"He's hiding in the bedroom." He looked towards the doorway. "The animal is going to have difficulty with my presence, while I'm here."

What the...? How does he know where Fritz is hiding? Besides, it sounded creepy, the way he was sure the animal would be frightened of him.

Then Flint saw how I was standing by the door and he nodded towards the four seated dining table, "Perhaps we should sit down."

I must admit, by showing up out of the blue like this, seriously had me spooked.

"Please," he said softly, making his deep voice sound even deeper.

Nervously, I came to stand on the other side of the table. I watched him walk up and sit down at the chair across. He was so big, he even dwarfed my furniture.

"We should talk," he nodded towards the chair I was standing behind.

"Talk about what?" I asked warily.

"Please," he repeated.

Again I felt like I couldn't say no to him and I pulled the chair back and sat down.

Just then, he reached across the table to rest his large, warm hands, on my smaller, trembling ones.

To my amazement, immediately my shaking stopped! His body heat travelled up my arms, across my shoulders and warmed me all over. I looked on with wide eyes as he smiled kindly.

"I've missed you," he began.

"I've um, missed you too." I admitted.

"I know, shaking is one of the symptoms." He said mysteriously. "How is your diabetes?"

"Um, it's OK." I lied.

"Your sugar level has been up and down, hasn't it?" He guessed again.

What the hell...? Who IS this guy? Is he stalking me?! Sharply, I pulled back my hands.

I asked accusatorily, "Flint, how did you find me?"

"I arrived in Seattle this morning, after driving here."

My eyes bulged, "You drove here from Anchorage?"

"When I woke up in the hotel room and saw you were gone, I rushed to the airport. However, your plane was taking off and I just missed you. So I got back into my truck and drove here."

"If you were at the airport, why didn't you just fly here?"

"I don't like to fly," he said simply.

"So you've spent the last three days, driving here?"

"Yes."

I folded my arms as I sat back, openly examining him. "Why Flint?"

"Jessica," he took a deep breath, as if he were about to announce something important. "We are mates."

"We're what?"

"We are mates."

"Oh sure!" I cracked up laughing. "So, do you do this to all the girls?"

"No," he answered. "In the past if I've been with a woman, it's been different. We can hold ourselves back."

"You can hold yourself back? But not this time, not with me?" I asked, sceptically.

"With you it was different." He explained. "I tried to hold myself back, but the way we connected and how you opened yourself up to me? I couldn't hold myself back from completely being with you."

His words made my face flush, as it unnerved me how he sensed I had opened myself, more than I had with any other guy.

"Jessica," he took hold of my hands again, "you are carrying my child."

"I'm what?"

"You're pregnant."

"Sure I am!" I burst out laughing, while pulling back my hands a second time.

"You are."

"Um Flint, not to downgrade your manhood or anything, but I'm on the pill."

"It doesn't work on my kind," he said.

"Your kind?" My eyebrows rose. "So you hopped into your truck and drove from Anchorage to Seattle, to tell me that I'm your mate, because I'm carrying your child?"

"When one of us takes a mate, it usually results in pregnancy immediately. But even if you weren't carrying my child, we would still be mates." He continued.

"Oh that's right, because you didn't hold back?"

He looked me in the eye to say, "I couldn't hold back, because I fell in love with you."

"So explain to me why I'm pregnant and the pill doesn't work on 'your kind'?" I crossed my arms again.

He closed his eyes as he sighed deeply, "I have to show you something."

"Oh yeah?" I asked uneasily. "You can't just explain it to me?"

"Very well," he spoke with his eyes closed, "I will tell you first."

"OK," I waited for it.

He opened his dark eyes, to meet mine. "I am a Lokoti Werewolf."

"You're a Lokoti what?"

"I am a Lokoti Werewolf."

"Oh, is that a name for an ice hockey team, or something?" I frowned in confusion. "You play sport, is that it?"

"You do know what a Werewolf is, don't you?"

"Something dog-like with claws?" I shrugged. "Like in the movies, 'The Howling', or 'An American Werewolf In London', or some such?"

"They're more like North American Werewolves or European Werewolves, I am a different kind of Werewolf."

"Right! Of course you are! You're a Werewolf!" I spoke with false bravado. "I have a one night stand with a guy, who drives down from Anchorage to Seattle, to tell me that I'm his mate and that I'm carrying his child because he's a Werewolf? Thank God for this Flint, otherwise I would have been worried you were a crazed stalker!"

He looked on in amusement at my sarcasm as he sat calmly.

I carried on, "Does this mean that I'm carrying a baby Werewolf?"

"Our son will be born human." He declared. "However, after his tenth birthday, if I or one of the pack should die? Then he would turn on the following full moon, to take his place among the ranks."

"A pack...? Oh great, there's a PACK of you? Wonderful, so you're not alone in thinking you're a Werewolf? That's fantastic! Do you have club meetings?"

"We hunt together on a full moon." He chuckled at my way of putting it. "When the tribe is threatened, we fight together to remove the threat."

"Great! Just like a gang of bikies or something..." my bravado dropped as did my head, when I almost banged it maddeningly on the table, "...please say that you're not in the mob?"

"We don't participate in organized crime." Flint frowned upon the idea. "Our existence is kept a secret, protected by the humans in the tribe."

"If this is such a secret Flint, then why the hell did you just drive all the way from Alaska to Washington, to tell me this?" I raised my head to look his way.

"Because we are mates and you are carrying my child."

"And that means?"

"I came to bring you back to Lokoti Tribal Lands, to live with me." He said seriously.

I burst into laughter, "Oh right! So I just pack up my place and quit my job and put my apartment on the market? Then I hop into your old, blue, pick up truck, and let you drive me all the way back to Alma?"

"I'm sorry I didn't wake up, so we could have talked about this in Anchorage." Flint tried to take my hand again, but I moved away. Hurt passed over his face but he continued as if he were being patient with me. "If we hadn't of separated, you wouldn't be feeling so unwell. I could have driven you back to tribal lands with me then."

"Oh you could have?" I looked on like he was a loon. "So this is the way you induct people into your pack; you have a one night stand with someone, you follow them interstate then you try to drag them back?"

"Jessica, please -"

"You said in the bar that you were concerned about my safety and that you would see me to the airport, so I could go home!"

"I did, as I did not foresee myself mating with you."

"Would you please stop calling it that! It was just sex! And I'm NOT pregnant! I'm on the pill and have been for ten years! I'm NOT pregnant, I've never been pregnant and I never will get pregnant! I'm NOT your mate!"

"Jessica, listen to me -"

"Man, I thought you were a nice guy, Flint. My previous memories of that night were also nice. But your behaviour right now, by following me home and saying I have to come back with you? It makes you sound like a FREAK!"

"Jessica, I understand your surprise, I do. It's because our customs would be seen as unusual by outsiders, couplings between a Lokoti Werewolf and human, are usually with Lokoti women. I did not plan for this to happen -" he spoke and he would have said more, but suddenly I stood up and left the table.

"Right, that's it." I defiantly walked into the kitchen to pick up the phone again. I held out the handset so he could see it. "Flint, I have to ask you to leave and never come back, or I'll call the police."

Slowly, he stood up as he tried to hold my gaze, "You are afraid of me."

"Damn straight!" I shouted. "What did you expect?!"

"If I showed you my other form, you'd believe me. But it would also frighten you further. I don't want to do that because your heart is racing too fast as it is. Please tell me what else I can do?" He pleaded.

"Walk out that door and don't come back again!" I pointed the way.

He sighed heavily as he shook his head. Then to make matters worse, he started to take off his shirt then his t-shirt and he kicked off his boots. He's undressing in my living area... why, is he going to force himself on me?

"What the hell are you doing?!" I screeched. "Right that's it! I AM calling the police!"

I turned away so I could dial 911, but it didn't work. I tried again, but I saw my hands were shaking so badly, I kept hitting the 2 instead. I took a deep breath to calm myself, as a little more slowly I pressed the keypad. But I could barely hold the handset properly because I was shaking so much!

"9-1-1, what's the emergency?" A female voice greeted.

Suddenly, the line went dead when a clawed hand, hit the 'end call' function on my electronic phone!

I screamed as I dropped the handset and leapt backwards in fright!

It was a large man's hand with unnaturally long, sharp nails, connected to an impossibly large, muscled arm; which was attached to an impossibly large, muscled torso. His muscle bulk was huge! Then my eyes moved past the bulky neck, to the human head whose mouth had sharp, elongated teeth, jutting past his lips. They stopped at his waiting, glowing turquoise eyes, before swinging down again to see the monster, standing in my kitchen in just his jeans. Oh yeah, the nails on his bare feet, also looked long and sharp.

Glowing turquoise eyes...? Then that means that night in the hotel room, I wasn't imagining things! I recalled how sharp his teeth had felt as I remembered all the growling noises he had made. Right now, he or it, was panting as it stood in the entranceway of my kitchen.

Holy shit, I screwed a Werewolf! Or one screwed me, depending on how you looked at it. I had sex with a Werewolf, albeit it was good sex but nonetheless it was sex. Now this Werewolf is claiming that I'm his pregnant mate?

As cool as a cucumber, the monster used its clawed hand to pick up the handset from the floor and put it back on the phone. But it wasn't the only thing to fall in the shock of the proceedings, as my trembling legs gave out.

My racing heart, shallow breathing and shaking limbs, couldn't take much more of this. I felt my legs collapse from underneath, the same time a curtain of darkness dropped over my eyes. Then so did I, onto my linoleum kitchen floor...

...

...I don't know how long I was out for, but I felt that I was lying somewhere soft and warm. With my eyes still shut, I realized I was lying on top of my bed with a coat over me. I think it was a man's coat, as it was big and smelled like Flint.

It smelled like Flint? The tall, Native Alaskan, who was a Lokoti Werewolf...? The monster that was in my kitchen entranceway...?

My eyes snapped open and the first thing I saw was Flint's human face gazing down in concern. He was dabbing something cool and wet on my forehead, like a damp face cloth. He smiled warmly as if to reassure, but his smile didn't last long.

"Jessica, you are very weak." He said gravely. "Before you, there has never been a case of a Lokoti Werewolf apart from his mate for so long. Your heart rate and your blood pressure are too high."

I believed him since I felt light headed and dizzy. It was like the time I accidentally took too much insulin. The walls of my bedroom looked like they were moving, as if everything was swaying. Were we having an earth quake or was it just me?

"C-c-call an ambulance..." I couldn't speak properly, "...m-m-m-my doctor's n-n-number is on my diabetics c-c-c-card, which is in my p-p-purse."

"I can give you something which will heal you immediately." He said calmly. "You have to trust me, Jessica."

But all I could do was stare up at him, dazed. I was too weak to panic which could have been for the best, especially with what happened next.

Flint was already sitting topless on the side of my bed. Then before my eyes, his muscles expanded to look a hell of a lot bigger. The nails on his hands turned longer and pointer as did his teeth, which protruded from his mouth. His dark brown eyes glowed a turquoise colour, with his black pupils disappearing.

Then I watched him raise his right arm and use the claws on his left hand, to put a gash in his wrist.

When he moved his wound to my mouth, fear took hold. Oh shit, he's trying to feed me his blood! He's trying to turn me into another Werewolf!

"Nooo...," I rolled my head away, "...please don't, Flint!"

"My blood won't turn you into a Lokoti Werewolf, Jessica." He spoke in a thunderous voice. "Only Lokoti are born with the gene to become one of us. But my blood will make you strong."

Using his claw-like left hand, he raised my head to press his bleeding right wrist against my mouth.

At first I refused to let it past my lips, so instead the warm, thick blood, started to trickle down my chin.

"No harm will come to you as my mate." He growled softly as his way to cajole. "Now drink and heal."

Then I don't know why, but I believed him. Against my better judgment or even my control, my lips parted. He gently pushed his wound into my mouth, as I lay there, staring up into his glowing turquoise eyes. I felt his blood pool inside, until I had no choice but to swallow or choke.

Flint sat patiently, as I swallowed reluctant mouthful after reluctant mouthful. As I did, he ducked his head to tenderly run his nose over my forehead. Was he sniffing my state of health? He did say that he could do that.

However, after my fourth time I realized what he was talking about. I DID feel stronger. My racing heart started to slow as the dizziness subsided. I felt my arms and legs, stop trembling. When I tried to sit up, Flint wouldn't remove his arm.

"Just a couple more mouthfuls," he insisted, as he watched my return to health.

Reluctantly, I kept drinking, expecting myself to gag at any minute, but I didn't. This bloodletting didn't taste as bad as I had imagined it would. However, I certainly didn't want people to ever find out that I drank blood!

I noticed as we were doing this, the Lokoti Werewolf started to get turned on.

He kept sniffing around my face or neck as he ran his clawed hand, over my suit. I lay still, almost afraid to move. His glowing turquoise eyes tried to hold my human blue ones, as I felt him hoist up my skirt. Then the heat of his hand felt good against my skin as he stroked my inner thighs.

My heart started to pound in excitement rather than fear. His claws managed to tear the tops of my stockings along with my underwear, but leave the skin unharmed. The ruined garments lay in disuse on top of the bed. Then my eyes almost popped out of their sockets, when I felt his clawed hand separate my moist cheeks, to rub my clit.

Somehow his long, sharp claws didn't hurt, instead they tantalized... how was he doing this? He used the pads on his fingers to do the massaging, but I felt the edges of his unnaturally long nails, touch my sensitive area. It even felt ticklish, adding to the pleasure.

Although the trembling had subsided, it was like I had lost control of my body. I felt my yearning cry out, 'more! more!' the wetter I became. I grabbed hold of his huge, muscled torso, to try to pull him over me. I heard him undo his jeans as he moved on top then I felt him push himself inside.

Immediately, Flint fell into a hard and fast rhythm, which made my bed frame squeal in protest. I repositioned my hips to allow him further access. I liked his hard, strong movements, while I still had the taste of his blood inside my mouth. From the crotch upwards, I felt my body open itself up to him. As if he felt this too, the next couple of heaves were pushing himself deeper before recommencing his fast pace.

My body seemed to be waiting for something, it seemed to be waiting for him to come. I wanted him to fill me, I wanted to feel myself become so wet, just like in that hotel room. I already had his blood inside me, but now I wanted something else of his. It really was like I was turning into a raging, hungry beast, myself!

I think he sensed this, as he grabbed hold of my hips with the both of his clawed hands to push harder. When he did, I noticed there was now a small, pink line in his skin where the gash used to be. Wow, he'd healed that fast? This turned me on even more, as I looked up at this supernatural creature who for some unknown reason, had chosen me as his mate.

Flint raised himself to his knees, lifting my hips up along with him. He held me taught as he pounded hard. From the amount of the squeaking with the force of the bed rocking, I was partially worried the neighbours might hear. In the past, I used to worry about this but now I challenged someone to interrupt us. I almost giggled at the idea, of someone seeing Flint in his huge form between my legs and how they'd be calling 911 instead.

As he came, the hypnotizing, warm wetness engulfed my crotch. When he stopped, I almost lifted my head to beg for more, but I found I didn't have to. He was changing positions to roll me over. I didn't care if my face was being pushed into the pillow, I didn't complain as my business suit was being sullied. All my stockings and underwear were good for now, were the trash. All I cared about was making this hot, hungry desire, be quenched. I noticed that my breathing was coming out like a panting, just like his was.

Here I am, actually having hot, animalistic sex... I am the mate of a Werewolf... Boy, is Chris going to be jealous if she finds out! I wondered if this was what she was picturing, when she spoke about Klingon sex?

For nearly an hour of the male moving me into different positions, of me coming, him coming then changing over; we were well and truly spent.

I lay on my stomach, enjoying the last of my feelings of ecstasy dissolve into physical satisfaction. It felt like my heart was pounding in my crotch instead of my chest. I could feel the blood rush through my veins, as my skin felt like it was glowing, just like Flint's eyes. He was lying on top of me, like a living electric blanket especially with his body heat.

Lastly, I felt him nestle his face into my sweaty hair and growl in a satiated manner. He didn't feel so heavy now, which meant he must have changed back. The nails on his hands which held me close to him also looked normal again.

"Flint?"

"Yes?"

"Do you have any other mates that I should know about?"

"No."

"So I'm the only one?"

"Yes."

"You said before that in the hotel room you couldn't hold back..."

"Yes."

"What does that mean?"

"My kind can hold back from coming, so the female isn't impregnated."

"And you said that usually you could do this?"

"Yes."

"So in the past you've had sex, but you were able to hold yourself back?"

"Yes."

"Then was it still pleasurable for you?"

"In its own way."

"And when you don't hold back?"

"It's EXTREMELY pleasurable." He growled softly in my ear, before kissing it.

"How many women have you been with in the past?"

"A few."

"How many is a few?"

"There have been a few over the many years."

"How few is a few and how many is the many years?" I pressed.

"Jessica, I'm 75 years old."

Pause...my eyes widened as my mouth fell open. "Are you kidding me?"

"No," he chuckled as he kissed the side of my face.

"And you're only taking a mate NOW?"

"Yes."

"Because you never fell in love until now?"

"Yes."

"Why now? Why me?" I turned my head so I could see his face. "I'm a career woman. I have my own apartment and a cat and I'm on the fast track in the company I work for."

"Because you stumbled into Charlie's Bar and you were pretty and you smelled good." He smiled softly.

"So what happens now, I just pack up and move to Alaska with you?"

"Yes."

"And then what?"

"In nine months our son will be born."

"What if it's a girl?"

"It won't be a girl."

"How do you know that?"

"The first born is always a male, so he may turn into a Lokoti Werewolf. He will protect his younger siblings as he will the tribe. He will be the head of his family."

I frowned at the sound of this, "Oh yeah and what about the woman?"

"She becomes the mate of either the Lokoti Werewolf or the Warrior."

"Warrior?"

"A Warrior is a human male. Only fifteen males in the tribe become a Lokoti Werewolf. When a member of the pack dies, a human male is activated to take his place. Usually it's a son or a grandson or sometimes a brother, of the late Werewolf."

"But what if a girl becomes a Lokoti Werewolf?"

"Women are carriers of the Lokoti Werewolf gene to pass onto her sons, but they've never changed."

"Why not?"

"Because males are physically stronger and they're the protectors of their women and children."

"Flint, it sounds a bit archaic and sexist to me."

"Perhaps, but it has been this way for a thousand years and more." He sighed, as he snuggled deeper into my curves.

"You should meet my best friend, Chris." I muttered. "She does self-defence as well as classes on feminism. She would have a lot to say about your tribe."

He chuckled whilst holding on contentedly, "If it sounds like I'm overlooking the importance of a woman's role, I'm not. Women are on our Council of Tribal Elders and help our Medicine Men with herbal remedies. Women are not only our homemakers but they help organize the tribe, as they organize their own families. But the woman is not expected to assist the Warrior or Werewolf, in protecting or providing for the family."

"Flint?"

"Yes, Jessica?"

"If I do quit my job and move to Alaska with you, no offence but from what I remember of that tiny town called Alma? I don't see much work for a PR person." I frowned, pensively.

"Perhaps not."

"So what will I do?"

"Settle down and have our baby."

"And then what?"

"Have another baby, I guess." I felt him shrug.

"But what will I do about a job?"

"Don't worry Jessica, I can provide for you. If you would like to work, it won't be from financial necessity."

"Flint, I know you're saying that to try to make me feel safe? But it's actually frightening me even more. I feel like I'm expected to live with a caveman, while he's still learning how to make fire."

I thought that taunt would annoy him but his voice sounded calm, like he was being patient.

"You will have a comfortable house, with comfortable furnishings. You will have an indoor bathroom with hot showers and will you not have to use a tree for a bathroom." He recited my previous rant, in good humour. "You will have a kitchen with a stocked pantry and a refrigerator. If I see you have difficulty with anything, I will certainly step in to help."

"I'm a bad cook," I warned.

"I'm a good cook," he replied.

"I'm anal retentive about cleanliness." I went on. "I used to fight over how the towels on the towel rack should be left, with the last guy I lived with."

"I'm sure you did, you don't seem to have a problem with speaking up." He chuckled once more.

"What if you get tired of my temper tantrums? If we get divorced, I could be stuck in Alaska."

He moved off my back to roll me onto my side so I was facing him. With his human hand, he caressed my sweaty face. His tender mannerisms surprised me, they showed he was a gentle giant.

"Jessica, taking a mate is held in great reverence by my people. When we are joined, we do not take the wants and needs of our partner lightly. Once a Werewolf claims a mate, the mating is for life. When you invited me into your hotel room in Anchorage three days ago, I accepted because I was already in love with you. I wouldn't have mated with you if I thought you would be harmed by the process."

Flint's words, coupled with his deep voice and his serious expression, made me believe him. What the hell was it about this guy which made him so trustworthy? Maybe it was his supernatural difference which lured me in? A whole new future opened up to me, in ways I couldn't have possibly imagined.

A giggle even escaped, "So, when do we do this?"

"It depends on you, when can you pack up and drive back with me?"

"Well, my work will need four weeks notice -" I began.

"Four weeks?" He sat up startled. "FOUR weeks?"

I sat up too, "Yeah, why?"

"Jessica, the next full moon is in eighteen days."

"So?" I started but I stopped. "Oh yeah, you're a Werewolf. Do full moons really affect you...?" I stopped again when I saw his worried expression.

"The full moon pulls on our psyche, just as it does to Earth's oceans. It makes our bloodlust boil and if we don't hunt animal, we could turn on a human..."

This time he paused when he saw the frightened look on my face.

"... no Jessica, I would never turn on you. Lokoti Werewolves don't crave the flesh of their mate, family or members of the tribe. But being here in Seattle, away from my hunting grounds, would be too risky. Any human that is not Lokoti, is a temptation."

"But what would happen?" I asked, worriedly.

"A century ago, we were able to curb our bloodlust from human to animal. In the National Park, we hunt bear, caribou, moose or other large animals. But I cannot hunt here, in a city. I may turn on a human and become a murderer. It's the reason why my kind prohibits alcohol, as we must maintain constant control of our dangerous hunger."

"Then maybe you should drive back to Alaska tomorrow and as soon as I've got my affairs in order, I'll fly to Anchorage?"

He looked on warily, "We were apart for three days when it affected your pulse, your blood pressure and even your diabetes. We would not be able to be apart for four weeks."

"Wait, all of what I'd been feeling the last three days, was because we were APART?"

"Of course," he said evenly. "When a Lokoti Werewolf claims a mate, the process is for life and it's only severed by death. If they are parted whilst alive, the physical symptoms can be debilitating."

I looked on in annoyance, "But you didn't look like you were shaking, or anything."

"Being away from you makes my bloodlust boil." He confessed. "Not even hunting can purge the hunger for my mate."

Then he nodded towards my messed up bed spread, referring to our prior activities.

"So let me get this straight..." I processed this information, "...your bloodlust will boil if you're stuck in Seattle during a full moon, where you might eat a human? But if you go back to your hunting grounds without me, your bloodlust will still have a hissy-fit because we're parted."

"Yes."

I stood up in a huff. "Man, this mating business BITES!"

He remained seated with his undone jeans, as he watched me take off my rumpled clothes.

I completely undressed and my soiled suit was dropped into the laundry basket, while the ruined underwear was chucked into the bin. Lastly, I pulled on my bathrobe which hung on a hook on the bedroom door. Then I turned around to look on him.

"Wait, what if I didn't want to be your mate?"

He said unsure, "What do you mean?"

"I mean, what if I still tried to kick you out of my apartment? What if I refused to come back to Alaska with you? What then?" I asked demandingly.

Just then Flint Riverclaw stood up so he could tower over me with his greater height. I could even see the muscles across his shoulders and down his arms flex, as if he were restraining himself. It was as if to add emphasis to his next words.

He spoke gravely, "You wouldn't have thrown me out of your apartment, just as you wouldn't throw me out of your life. If it came to the worst, I could use my will on you, to make you submit. But I would rather not, as I love the woman not the puppet, she may turn into."

"A puppet? Your 'will'? What is this crap?" I took a step backwards.

"Do not fear me, Jessica Riverclaw," he growled out as his dark eyes flashed their bright, turquoise colour. "I swore you would not come to harm when we met, and I will keep that promise."

"Answer the question, Flint! What would have happened, if I refused to move to Alaska as your mate? What would happen with the symptoms then? Would they get worse, for the rest of my life?"

He said simply, "I do not know if they'd be a life long illness, because there has never been an instance where the Lokoti Werewolf lost a living mate."

"Why, because your kind can use their 'will' on them, to bring them to heel?" My eyes narrowed suspiciously.

"Jessica," he rested the both of his hands on my shoulders, as he looked me in the eye. "I will tell you this now, however, you will later come to realize this yourself. When a Lokoti Werewolf takes a mate, it is a biological and an empathic joining. I have your scent, which means I will always run to you if I sensed you were in danger. It was how I found you today. Once I was in your city, I tracked you down by smell. I could feel your shakiness so I drove all day to reach you. I felt your shock when you found me standing on your doorstep, as I felt your terror when you saw me, in my other form. I feel it when you're cold, or when you're hungry, or ill. With this in mind, the Lokoti Werewolf becomes overprotective of his mate. Once our lives are settled in Alaska, you will come to know a peace you have never felt before."

I blinked then I blinked again, as I stared at Mr. Tall-Dark-And-Handsome standing before me, in my bedroom. Perhaps, I should call myself, Mrs. Tall-Dark-And-Handsome since biologically speaking, we were 'married'. I felt like all the fight in me had packed up and moved somewhere else. Funnily enough, that would be me too in the next couple of days.

*****

That evening, I showered before we went to bed. When I curled up between the sheets, at first it felt unusual that someone spooned me. With the extra persons' body heat, I ended up kicking off the quilt lest overheat. However, it didn't take me long to slip into sleep, with the feel of Flint's strong heart beat, reverberating through his skin and into mine.

BEEP BEEP! BEEP BEEP! BEEP BEEP!

It can't be 6 AM, already? Sleepily, my head rose to look on the source of the noise when a muscled arm reached over to turn it off. Then I rolled over, to come face to face with the second person in the bed. His long, black hair looked good against my yellow rose, patterned sheets.

"Good morning," he gave a sleepy smile.

"Morning."

"Did you sleep well?"

"How could I not?" I teased. "Maybe you 'willed' me to sleep?"

Flint chuckled as he tried to snuggle with me, however, I squirmed out of his hold.

"I have to get ready for work." I informed.

"That's a shame," he said unhappily. "I could lie in bed with you, all day."

Strangely, I felt the same way when usually, I was a person who didn't like to be idle. I was one of those 'get up and go', kind of people. I used to be one of those 'yuppies' who prided herself with a well-paid job and a future paved in success. I was meant for fast-paced city living instead of a slow country lifestyle.

To my surprise, when I climbed out of bed to get ready for work, Flint acted in similar fashion. Whereas I put on a red business suit with stockings and high heels, he pulled on his pair of jeans and flannel shirt. When I went into the bathroom to fix my hair and make-up, he went into the kitchen to switch on the electric kettle.

"Would you like some scrambled eggs on toast?" He called out.

I paused in putting on my mascara to call back, "I don't have time to eat."

At 6.45 AM I departed the apartment on the dot however, a second person followed me out the door. Instead of catching the tram, Flint insisted on driving me. He obediently followed my directions to drop me off in front of the building where my office was.

"I'll pick you up after work." He offered.

"No, don't do that." My face flushed. "I'll just get the tram."

I climbed out of his truck when he passed me my briefcase which had been sitting on the seat, between us.

"I'll pick you up after work." He repeated, before he drove off through the traffic.

Before I walked through the automatic, sliding doors; my head rose to look up at the glass face of the high rise, like I was never going to see it again.

"Here goes nothing," I muttered to myself, as I carried my briefcase into the building.

The elevator let me out onto the ninth floor then I passed through another set of sliding doors and into the office of 'Wildenstein Dreams'. The familiar faces gave their familiar smiles, as I nodded back. I passed through the administration area to come to my corner office.

Abruptly, I stopped short in my doorway as I surveyed the scene. My laptop sat on the glass top desk, waiting to be switched on. My telephone had several lights flickering on its' panel, indicating numerous messages left for me. My black, high-backed, office chair was behind the desk, with the glass wall behind it displaying views of Seattle's harbour side.

I'd worked hard for five solid years for this office and its view... now I was going to say goodbye to it.

"Damn it," I breathed.

Instead of going inside, I headed towards somebody else's office.

"Hi Jess," my boss's secretary seated at her desk, looked up in surprise. "You don't have a meeting, this morning."

"I know, but I need to speak to Kristy, please." I sighed heavily.

"Oh well, she might be able to squeeze you in before her 8.15." Mona looked at her watch before she picked up the phone. "Kristy? It's Jessica, requesting to speak to you." Then she put down the handset and nodded towards the closed door. "Go on in."

*****

The meeting began well, with Kristy advising the clients I met with on Monday morning were impressed with my presentation. But when I gave her my resignation, things quickly went downhill. At first she thought I was threatening to leave for a pay rise, until I told her I had to give four days notice instead of four weeks. Then she accused me of going to work for one of our competition.

Lastly, she had a security guard escort me back to my office, to watch me pack up my things. My face burned in humiliation as the administration staff stared as if I had just been fired. I was given a cardboard box to put my personal items in, as the security guard confiscated my rolodex in case I'd try to poach clients.

Then the guard escorted me to the elevator, past everyone's desks. I heard a couple of, "bye Jess" as I went, but otherwise they must have thought I'd been caught stealing or something as such. The elevator went 'bing' and the doors opened and at 8.23 am, I left the floor where my office was, unemployed.

My heart was pounding as my legs wavered and on unsteady feet, I wandered out of the building and into the bright light. Uncharacteristically, it was a sunny day in Seattle that morning, the day my resignation turned into instant dismissal. Oh the irony to have beauty and warmth, when inside I felt cold and scared.

Suddenly, I heard a screech of tires when an old, blue, pick up truck, pulled up in the 'no parking' area, in front of the building.

Flint leapt out of the driver's side as he rushed up to take the box in one arm, as his other escorted me to his vehicle.

"Did you sense that I just got fired?" I gaped.

His concerned eyes peered into my own, "Is that what happened? I just felt that you were angry then embarrassed and now, very frightened."

It all poured out, "She just completely overreacted! At first she was singing praises for my work then she accused me of corporate espionage! She even had a security guard escort me out of the office!"

He carefully placed my box of things in the back before he opened the door to the passenger's side for me.

When he climbed behind the wheel, I clutched his arm to say, "She even threatened not to pay out my accumulated annual leave, because I'm not giving a month's notice!"

This made him pause, "How much leave do you have?"

"After all my hard work for the last five years and the first year of not taking any time off; twelve weeks!"

Now he made a move to get out again, "I'll go talk to her."

Imagining an angry Lokoti Werewolf with glowing eyes, long nails and sharp teeth, growling at the bitch; did make me feel better. But I didn't want him to get into trouble.

"No Flint!" I pulled him back. "The security guards have guns, I don't want you to get hurt."

He turned pensive, "As long as they don't have silver bullets, I should be alright."

We sat quietly in his truck for a moment or two, before I heard him chuckle and I couldn't help but to join in by giggling.

"Think of it this way," his arm rested over my shoulders, "you're free now and you'll never have to see her again."

"Actually, I was laughing over the idea of you scaring the pants off her."

He guffawed loudly, before turning the key in the ignition and driving us the hell out of there.

~~~~~~
~~~~~~

~ 7 ~

30th August 1999

"Jessica...? Jessica, wake up. We're nearly there."

Flint's voice was gentle as was his shaking, to stir me from my sleep. I opened my eyes to look out the windscreen. But all I saw was more highway, more forest and more snow-capped, mountain ranges.

"Huh, this is it?" I uttered out. "These are your tribal lands?"

"No, we're coming up to Alma." He put his large, warm arm about my shoulders. "Our tribal lands are outside of town, on the north side."

I snuggled into his side and watched as he turned off the main highway which ran from Anchorage to Fairbanks. We turned onto a smaller, concealed road which had a sign that read 'Alma 5 miles' and underneath, 'Tok 184 miles'. This only accentuated the feeling of isolation out here.

As we approached the small town, we drove past another sign which told us Alma had a population of 709 people. I looked on with new eyes at what would be part of my home. What I originally thought of as a 'one man and his one dog' place to live, I tried to see its good side.

The tiny town had one main street where Charlie's Bar was situated, as well as a small supermarket, a diner and a gas station. The cinema was inside an old, small building, which looked like it also functioned as a town hall. It was advertising its one and only movie which would have opened in the rest of America, well over a month ago. My cosmopolitan evenings of 'dinner and a show' with friends in Seattle; had been reduced to going to Charlie's Bar and attending the small cinema with one movie, for my entertaining pleasure.

The main street was predominantly made up of residential homes which we passed. At the end of the road sat a large building, which served as both Alma's Elementary and High School. This is where my kid will go to learn, one day?

Abruptly the township finished and I found ourselves driving through forest again.

"This is the highway that Main Street is on, which goes on to Tok." He informed. "If you ever wanted to drive to Fairbanks which is the closest, you would drive off tribal lands, through Alma and back onto the larger highway."

Flint drove with one hand on the wheel as his other arm remained about his wife. Then he said proudly, "Now we're coming up to tribal lands."

I sat up straighter to look about. I watched as he pulled off the concealed road and onto a dirt one. We passed a Federal Wildlife sign which read, 'Hunter National Park' then after it, was a much smaller sign which said, 'Lokoti Community Centre.'

After another mile, the forest cleared to show a tiny village made of wooden houses with stone chimneys. The dirt roads were only one-lane wide, with the odd pick up truck or RV's passing each other by driving on the fringes. The wooden houses weren't large, but they had mown lawns.

I saw Lokoti children run from one house to the next, as they played together. Occasionally, adults came outside to check up on them and when they saw us drive by, they raised their hands in greeting. Flint nodded back, he seemed to know everyone.

He drove past a large, grassy block, which must have served as a sports field, as I saw some boys were playing soccer. Next to the field, was a small, wooden building with a sign up, advertising it was a general store. Out the front, I saw one gas pump, where a Lokoti was filling up his RV.

At a small intersection, Flint turned his truck away from the village, towards a forest encrusted hill. His old pick up truck, chugged up the steep, dirt road. Along the way he pointed at a log cabin, sitting on the slope.

"That's John Wisetail's place." He said. "I helped him build his house after he helped me build mine. He lives there with his wife Unka and their three kids."

"I met him in the bar, didn't I?" I remembered.

"Yep," he answered, before he continued. "I built my house first and John built his house second. Then the Riley's built theirs a couple years later and now the Windchime's are building theirs, on top of the hill."

"If you built your house first, how long ago was that?" I queried.

"Oh it was back in the sixties," he thought aloud. "I guess it would have been '64 that I started and completed it in '65."

My eyes widened over the fact that my new 'husband' was old enough to be my grandfather, even if he didn't look it. Flint caught my look of surprise, which made him chuckle. Then he pulled me close to deliver a kiss to my forehead.

"What's the population of your tribe, Flint?" I queried.

"We have around 167 people," he shrugged, "which now includes you."

"So I'm number 167?" I smiled.

"You sure are, so our son will be number 168."

He turned off the steep, dirt road and into a dirt driveway. The sight of a long, wooden veranda out the front of a large log cabin greeted us. There was no yard or garden to speak of, just surrounding forest. But in spite of myself, I liked this house immediately. It looked homey and even welcoming.

Flint pulled up in front of the wooden, porch steps and I climbed out immediately. Instead of making a move to get my things from the back, he took hold of my hand to lead me to the front door. He rattled his keys as he made a move to unlock it, when he paused.

"Oh, I forgot to lock up when I left." He smiled in good humour then he simply turned the door knob.

"You forgot to lock up?" I gawked. "You've been away for nearly two weeks! What if you were robbed?"

"We don't have break-ins, here. If somebody needed to borrow something of mine, they would leave a note of what they took and how long they need it for." He shrugged it off.

Then he swung open the door and stood back to let me go in first before turning quiet, to watch my reaction.

I walked into the large living area which was a lounge and dining room combined. A stone fireplace was situated in the lounge area, which had two old, leather couches and a couple of bookshelves, full of books. The walls were rough, showing concealer between the large logs, which gave the house a rustic appearance. The wooden floors were polished and there was a pine dining table set that could seat six.

I wandered into the kitchen which was small and old fashioned, with an old gas stove. I hate gas, I'm going to change it to an electric, as well as buy a microwave. Then I saw a bathroom which had the laundry beside it, to find both had polished wooden floors too, instead of tiles. In the bathroom, was an old, wrought iron tub, with a shower head over it and a shower curtain around that. I decided I'd have this bathroom redone to put in a separate shower.

Flint followed me down a small hallway to look in on the bedrooms. I saw two tidy guest bedrooms, with single beds and hand-woven quilts on top. When I poked my head inside the main bedroom, I found a queen-sized bed with another hand-woven quilt. There were two bedside tables and a large wardrobe. Aside from the leather couches in the lounge room, all the furniture in the house was constructed of pine. I wondered if they were made here, from the trees in the surrounding forest?

"Was the pine furniture built here?" I asked.

"Yes, some of the families in the tribe run furniture construction businesses." He answered then he watched me dawdle back into the living area. "Well Jessica, can you see yourself being happy here?"

His voice sounded casual but I detected he was nervous. When I looked on his face, I saw an anxious expression. The old giant was worried if his house stood up to my standards? I thought that was so sweet!

"I love it!" I beamed, which made his face light up. "I even love the rustic walls, coupled with the polished wooden floors."

"You do?" His eyes widened with hope.

"But there are a couple of things I'd like to change, please?" I asked, feeling hopeful myself.

"Yes?"

"I'd like new couches." I pointed at his old leather ones then I waved towards the kitchen. "And can we please get an electric stove instead of a gas one? I've never liked gas, especially when I nearly burnt my face off, trying to use my grandmother's."

"Sure."

"Plus a microwave, they're easier to use." I went on. "And I want a new bathroom with a separate shower."

"It's the safe thing to do," his hand settled over my stomach. "When you get bigger, you shouldn't climb over the sides of a bathtub, to shower."

My heart warmed at how easy going he was instead of refusing my demands.

"Oh Flint, I have a good feeling about this!" I threw my arms about his neck.

He squeezed me back, "I told you it would all work out, Jessica."

I pulled out of his embrace as I began to plan aloud. "With the proceeds I have from selling the apartment and paying off the mortgage, leaves me with twelve thousand. Then after selling my car, makes it fifteen and a half thousand dollars, we can use to do up the kitchen and the bathroom. We could hire contractors from Fairbanks, as it's a hell of a lot closer than Anchorage."

He pulled back his shoulders to declare, "You will not use your money towards the house. I have some money, saved up over the years."

"But Flint, what if what I want is expensive, or out of your price range?"

"Jessica," he cupped my face, "when we go shopping, you'll point out what you want and I'll pay for it. Then we'll bring these things back in my truck and I'll install the stove and redo the bathroom myself. If I need extra hands, my friends in the tribe will help."

"Yeah, but what if I want a really expensive stove -" I tried again.

"You keep your money for yourself," he said adamantly.

"Flint, please let me help -"

"Invest it," he said simply. "You never know if times will turn hard and we may need it for the children."

"On that note, it's a good thing my best friend is a financial adviser," I snickered.

He chuckled as he recalled meeting Chris, before we left. On their first introduction, she gave him a good going over, asking what he did for a living and about where he lived. My new beau took it all in his stride, never losing his patience and affording her the same respect as if he were meeting my family.

"So, do you think Chris will like the house, when she comes to visit?"

"When we've done up the kitchen and bathroom and living area, she's gonna love it!" I beamed back. "Leave it to me, Flint. I'm a PR person, I design events, from catering to decoration to entertainment to publicity!"

Flint wore this silly smile on his face as he pulled me into another embrace.

"I certainly have faith in you Jessica Riverclaw, there's no doubt about that."

As his lips smothered mine, I almost turned to jell-o with the feel of my softer body pressed against his firmer one. It felt like nothing could go wrong, whenever he held me in his larger, stronger arms...

"Knock, knock!"

Abruptly we pulled apart to see a familiar looking Lokoti man, standing with an older looking Lokoti woman, in the front doorway. Behind them were three Lokoti youths in the shapes of two teenaged boys and a girl. They looked like they were trying not to laugh at the soppy scene they had just stumbled onto.

"John and Unka," he smiled warmly, "come on in."

"Well howdy there Jessica, it's good to see you again!" The father came inside first with his hand reaching out to shake mine.

I shook his large, strong hand back. "I bet you're surprised to see me here, John Wisetail."

"Not really," he laughed back. "I saw my best friend was smitten, the moment you walked into Charlie's Bar."

He did? I flashed Flint a look of surprise as he stood back to let the introductions take place. I thought I'd noticed him first, the day we met.

"Let me introduce you to my lovely wife, Unka." His best friend waved towards the older looking woman who shook my hand next. Then he indicated his two eldest sons and younger daughter, "And these are our handful, Mark, Sean and Alice."

The children appeared to be in their mid to late teens and very curious of me. Alice stared at my clothes, as her brothers checked out my hair and figure. I guess my black jeans and dark pink, velvet top looked a little city, compared to their country wear of blue denim and suede.

"It's a pleasure to meet you, Jessica." Their mother held onto my hand, before she passed Flint a frown. "It's good to see the old bear finally start a family! Did you know he's the only member of the pack, to wait this long to take a mate? The Tribal Elders began to worry, if it was the end of the Riverclaw line or what!"

"It took a special one to finally catch my eye, Unka." He smiled softly.

"Oh, I can see that!" She laughed good naturedly. "With your pretty face, fair hair and bright eyes, I can see why Flint has stars in his!"

It wasn't just his face that flushed, it was mine too, at her cheekiness.

"Now Jessica," she turned my way. "I don't know how much of our customs Flint has explained, but when a couple moves in together, the tribe throws them a Housewarming."

"Really?" I asked in surprise.

"But because the old bear built this house long ago and it's fully equipped, he's beaten us to the punch line." Unka passed him another frown.

"We're getting new living room furniture and we'll be redoing the bathroom and kitchen." He announced.

"Good!" John cried out, relieved. "You see, there's going to be a Housewarming yet."

"Unka, are you stirring up trouble again?" Flint jested.

John turned my way, "My wife has been stewing about this, since she heard of your coupling. She and a couple of the women in the tribe, even had a meeting about it!"

"Tradition is tradition," she said sternly. "Since Flint is First in the Lokoti Werewolf pack, he should know better than to try to skip his own Housewarming."

This gave me a jolt, at having another person know about my husband's supernatural condition.

"Er, you know about that?" My eyes widened at their candour.

"Know about it...?" John chuckled. "I hunt with the old bear, every full moon."

The news made my eyes bulge when I realized that there were two Lokoti Werewolves in the room. Then I remembered something else they said. "Hang on, what do you mean Flint is First in the pack?"

"Exactly that," John shrugged, "he's our leader."

My surprised eyes swung in his direction, "You're the leader of the pack?"

Flint simply smiled as his answer, as if it wasn't a big deal.

"Yes and what kind of example were you setting to your younger members, waiting so long to take a mate?" Unka chastised.

He answered with, "I was waiting for Jessica."

This made my heart warm as I took hold of his hand and he squeezed it back.

Unka moved on with the conversation when she put her arm about my shoulders and together we looked about the house.

"Well my dear, are we going to add 'the woman's touch' to the old bear's bachelor pad, or what?"

"We certainly are!" I laughed along with this friendly and funny woman.

"Now what kind of couches do you want?" She started to plan.

"Um, I don't know." I pondered. "I was thinking of ordering some catalogues, or looking up some furniture stores online."

"Online?" She gave a funny look.

"The internet, Mom." Mark advised.

"The internet?" She quizzed. "I thought that was just a school thing?"

"We got a new computer room at school," Sean explained. "We've been telling Mom how we surf the internet during class."

"And email our friends," Alice put in.

Unka rolled her eyes, "Emails are electronic letters that are sent down phone lines, apparently... however that works!"

"Ah yeah, I use the internet frequently." I tried not to snicker. "I'll be emailing my best friend back in Seattle, on a regular basis."

"Sounds too complicated for me!" She waved it off. "Mark, where's my bag?"

Her eldest handed over her large handbag which he'd been carrying for her. Out of which, Unka pulled out a small pile of decorating magazines. This woman had more savvy than I gave her credit for!

"The kids can keep their internet, while I go about things the old fashioned way." She said stubbornly. "Here you go Jessica, you can have these. Some of them are a couple of months old, I have John pick them up for me when he's in Fairbanks. But it'll give you an idea of what to do with this place."

"Thank you Unka!" I gushed appreciatively, as I gazed upon the magazines as if they were the best thing since sliced bread.

"This one is exclusively on furniture and these ones here, are about interior decorating. Some of the shops and companies they mention are in Fairbanks. We can pick up whatnot and bring them back here. Give us a month and we'll have your house set up good and proper!" She promised.

"A month long Housewarming?" John chuckled to Flint. "Sounds like it's goin' to be some month, now don't it?"

"It does," he agreed.

"But don't you two fret," John went on. "The pack as well as the tribe, want to get involved. Many hands make light work, so you're not going to be doing it all, yourselves. I think everyone wants to take part in celebrating the tribe's oldest bachelor finally taking a mate."

I felt my face heat up in humility, as everyone looked on me like an exciting change had come.

"Let's not stand here all day, let's get her things in from the truck." Unka organized. "Now Jessica, as the men bring in your boxes, you wait inside with me and tell us where you want everything."

Then I watched the males in the shapes of Flint, John, Mark and Sean obey her command by streaming out the front door.

I saw that although the Lokoti had their established roles of men and women; women were by no means trodden on. This filled me with relief, as a couple of times I'd been scared by Flint's sexism. I can't imagine a Lokoti male ever telling Unka what she could or couldn't do.

The rest of the afternoon went by with laughter, fun and organizing and I saw how far Unka's influence extended. She'd not only decided that I was a friend, but she was kind and mothering in a way, I didn't find condescending. Whenever somebody was about to put a box somewhere, she halted them and asked me if I wanted it to be moved somewhere else. Then as soon as I had spoken, the males obeyed.

Unka seemed to know exactly what she was doing. As she helped me organize, she'd pause and ask me how I liked my linen folded, or kitchen utensils arranged. I could tell she was trying not to step on my toes, or overrun my house. Instead, she acted like a second-in-command by issuing orders to the men or children, which were requests she received from me.

Once my household goods from Seattle were put away, she sent her husband and eldest home to pick up the food she'd made. While they were gone, I told her my ideas of tiling the bathroom and laundry. She nodded along, envisioning my plans and especially agreed to the separate shower idea.

When John and Mark returned, they unpacked large Tupperware containers full of cold chicken, slices of ham, potato salad, green salad, bread rolls and butter. We all sat down at the dining table and ate, particularly me since I was so hungry! Also, I felt appreciative towards the older woman for cooking for me on my first night in my new home.

"Thank you so much, Unka." I said repeatedly, as I spooned some extra potato salad on my plate. "This is delicious!"

"I thought you'd be tired from your journey," she said understandingly. "I'd prefer not to cook, after driving three days straight."

"Especially in your condition," her husband added on.

Their children watched as I also helped myself to a second bread roll, which I slathered in butter. Having an audience made me feel a little self conscious. Was I making a pig out of myself?

"Um Flint, would you like half of this bread roll?" I offered weakly, although I would have happily eaten the whole thing myself.

"No, you eat up, Jessica." He put it back on my plate. "Eat as much as you want."

"You are eating for two." His best friend agreed. "And the food is all yours, since we're leaving the leftovers behind."

"Really?" My face lit up, giving away my delight.

"Women who carry the young of a Lokoti Werewolf, always eat more than women who are mated to human males." Unka declared. "Just you wait until the cravings start."

Right as she said that, I'd picked up the potato salad again to put even more on my plate.

"I think they already have." John chuckled and soon he was joined by the rest of the table.

"Whoops," I blushed and put the container down again.

But Flint picked it up, recommenced with my serving then he did the same for himself. Next, he picked up the chicken and lastly, the ham. As he picked up his fork to eat his second large helping, he passed me a wink.

"Don't ever feel bad about eating, Jessica." She giggled. "Because your Lokoti Werewolf husband is always gonna eat more than you."

*****

I became further acquainted with the bathroom when I had a leisurely, long, hot shower. Using the wall to lean on, I climbed out of the tub before proceeding to the sink to brush my teeth. By the time I exited, a cloud of steam billowed out behind.

Wearing my flannel, yellow pajamas, I walked in to find Flint reading in bed. He was perusing the pages by his bedside lamp. But I could tell he was waiting for me, for as soon as I came in, he put his book aside before pulling back the covers, to welcome me.

Instead of lying down beside, I climbed into his lap to straddle him. Then my hands ran up and down his bronzed, bare chest. He smiled softly with his dark eyes looking particularly warm.

"Flint...?"

"Yes, Jessica?"

This made me smile, the way he always said my name in full. It also made me ask something else instead of what I had been wanting to. "Why don't you ever call me 'Jess'?"

"I like your full name." He said simply.

"Everyone else back in Seattle calls me Jess, but you and the Wisetail's, call me Jessica."

"Do you prefer, 'Jess'?"

"I don't mind, I was just wondering."

"Jessica is a very pretty name." He said fondly.

I tittered back, "I like your name, too. It's very natural sounding... like a scene stolen from nature."

Teasingly, I brushed his lips with mine which I could tell he also liked, by the way he gripped tighter to my waist.

I pulled back to ask my next question. "Flint...?"

"Yes?"

"How and when did John and Unka, get together? She looks so much older than him, does he have a 'cougar' fetish?" I joked.

"John's actually twenty years older than Unka."

My mouth fell open in surprise, "You're kidding me!"

"No," he chuckled. "But outsiders think it's the other way around, because of our slower aging process."

"You mean the Lokoti Tribe's slower aging process, or a Lokoti Werewolf's?"

"A Lokoti Werewolf's."

I sighed as I momentarily looked away, "It answers the question why I originally thought you were 39 years old."

He said optimistically, "But it's a good thing that I'm older than you."

I gave a funny look, "Why?"

"A Lokoti Werewolf can live for two hundred years." He explained. "If you should die before me, I won't be left alone for years until I join you, in the next life."

My hands rested on his warm chest as I examined the earnest expression on his face.

I tried to joke again, "Yeah but you can marry another, 'young bit of stuff', when I'm gone."

"No," he said seriously.

"No?"

"Just as the mating process is for life, we mate once and never again." He frowned. "If anything happened to you, I would mourn you all my remaining years."

"Oh." I sat up straighter, in further surprise. "So if I got hit by a truck tomorrow -"

"Then I would be alone for the rest of my life, starting tomorrow." He interrupted. "Now let's talk about something else."

The idea clearly disturbed him, so he comforted himself by holding his new wife closer.

I felt his large hands slip under my pyjama shirt, to stroke the skin underneath. Then my right hand caught a wisp of his long, black hair and playfully, I tickled his face with it. It made him chuckle quietly, as his hands moved up and down, underneath my clothes.

After another moment, I had to ask because the curiosity was killing me, "Why would you remain alone, if something happened to me?"

His dark gaze met and held mine, "The same reason why you shake, when we're apart."

I remembered, "Because mating is a biological and empathic joining?"

"Yes."

"Is this the same for the other Lokoti Werewolves?"

"Yes."

"So if Unka dies before John..."

"He will live out the rest of his life, alone."

My face screwed up, "That does sound depressing, let's not talk about it anymore."

Flint was more than happy to. He switched off his lamp then lay lower in the bed, while ensuring I remained on top. As such, I found myself lying over him, basking in the heat coming off his body. The hypnotizing rocking of his chest, rising and falling with his steady breathing, lulled me into a relaxed state.

Sleepily, I yawned out, "G'night, Flint."

"Sweet dreams, Jessica Riverclaw."

~~~~~~

TO: christine_steel@smartfinancestrategies.com

FROM: jessicariverclaw@warmmail.com

SUBJECT: The Quiet Life

DATE: 30/ 10/ 1999

Dear Chris and Fritz,

I hope you two are getting along better, back in Seattle. Sorry Chris, about Fritz scratching up your furniture. I don't think he hates you as he always used to love your visits. Maybe he's marking his territory, in his new surroundings? Give him time and soon you'll have a warm, little, purring machine, sleeping soundly on the end of your bed.

My house isn't chaotic anymore with all the renovations done. It was completed in two weeks, thanks to the help we received from our friends and neighbours. I think I mentioned in my last email, Flint took another two weeks off work, to do the house? His best friend John Wisetail did the same, so the two could work together. He and his wife Unka, also came shopping with us in Fairbanks when we bought the new couches and electric stove/ oven. What we couldn't fit in the back of Flint's pick up, they kindly put in theirs.

John is a plumber by trade but he and Flint are also handymen. I love John and Unka's sense of humour, especially when they tease Flint. They always call him 'the old bear' and when they were renovating, I'd hear:

"Flint, we can't tile the new shower recess yet, until I put the pipes, taps and shower head in. Now hold your horses and go make us some coffee."

"Then put the pipes and taps in, so I can tile my new shower."

"You can't see straight since you got married, you old bear. It's a good thing you've got me, helping you. You'd tile the entire bathroom before realizing you forgot the plumbing! What's Jessica supposed to do, stand in a cubicle with no water and pretend to wash herself?"

Unka and I were sitting at the table, drinking coffee and munching on some cookies she'd made; and we burst out laughing when we heard that!

I think you'll love the bathroom and laundry when you come up. I chose terracotta-red tiles for the floor, to go with the wooden floors of the house. Then on the walls, there are slate-grey tiles so it's keeping to the rustic, country style. The couches are a navy blue material to go with the dark red curtains. By the fireplace is a bear-skin rug we purchased off somebody in the tribe who makes them, as well as suede jackets made from either caribou or moose hide.

Flint bought me one and it looks authentic, complete with tassels and the odd bead work. It's very warm as it's lined with fur. I'll take you to see them when you visit, if you'd like one to take back to Seattle. They also make fur-in-lined, suede boots, which are also water proof and guaranteed to stave off frost bite.
~~~~~~

It's already snowed a couple of times, usually at night. The snow melts during the day, but with the daylight getting shorter, reminds us that winter is coming. We have a fire burning every night and we've put radiator heaters in the bathroom, main bedroom and the two smaller bedrooms. You'll be warm and cosy, I promise.

You'll also enjoy Flint's cooking as well as Unka's. Funnily enough, you'll have the chance to sample the rest of the tribe's culinary expertise too. I don't blame Unka, John or Flint since the secret that I'm a bad cook, has come out. But the tribe's people keep paying me in food – LoL! Our fridge and freezer almost always has Tupperware containers full of casseroles, pasta bakes, stroganoff or something that someone has brought over.

What happened was, people heard from Unka that I know my way around computers and I was experienced in organizing events. At the end of the first week when she came over for coffee and cake (which she made), she brought somebody with her. The woman wanted to organize a birthday party for her eight year old daughter, with a fairy theme since she was obsessed with them. The mother couldn't buy what she needed in Alma, so I showed her how to look up places online in Fairbanks or Anchorage, which she could order from. I helped organize a fairy costume for the birthday girl, as well as a pink, glittery, themed party.

It took us the whole afternoon ordering online using my laptop, as well as phoning a couple of places. But the mother was so appreciative, the very next day she returned with a massive Tupperware container full of caribou casserole! It was delicious too, with lots of herbs and the meat was so tender, you hardly had to chew on it. I ended up dividing it into several smaller containers and put them in the freezer, to eat during the week.

The party was a success and word got round. Sometimes when I'm picking up milk from the general store on tribal lands, or shopping in the supermarket in Alma, I'm approached. An older Lokoti will say they just got a new computer but they don't know how to set it up. I'd go over and set up the desktop, along with their printer/ scanner and show them how to use the internet, email, photocopy, scan, send attachments, fax, print etc. Then the next day, the person will turn up on my doorstep, with a meal they cooked up.

I met the council of Lokoti Tribal Elders when they asked for my help in organizing a tribal celebration in the Meeting Hall. Then a couple of days later, one of the Elder's called by with smoked salmon... Mmm, authentic, fresh, smoked salmon! A couple of the families in the tribe make it and it tastes so much better than that what we used to buy in the supermarket. Once you try it Chris, you may not want to leave!

I only do these things one or two days a week, otherwise, my life could be called very quiet. Every couple of days, Flint will get a lift with somebody in the tribe he works with, so I can use his truck. However, I like to go grocery shopping in Alma with Unka because we chat so much, it turns into a social event. She'll pick me and drive me into town with her, with us sometimes grabbing lunch in the diner or Charlie's Bar, beforehand.

Often, I'll go walking. The first couple of times, Flint took me to show me more of the community centre. Just outside the residential area, are the Holy Grounds which have the three Sacred Totems. My husband would point out the painted and carved animals and tell me stories, which explained their importance. Now I like to walk by myself whilst listening to my Walkman. There's a dirt path that runs from my house, through the woods to the river. The water is such a dark blue colour, it's meditative to just sit by the side and stare at the current. Then with the breath-taking backdrop of the mountainous peaks of the Alaska Range, I feel like I'm inside a postcard.

At first it felt surreal, not going to work five days a week. Then my body felt like it let out a huge sigh of relief, as the tension in my shoulders slipped away. It's relaxing not having to worry about meetings, presentations, reports, invoices or moody bosses. It's almost like I can do whatever I want, whenever I want. If I want to go shopping for clothes for me or the baby, I do the 1.5 hour drive to Fairbanks. If I want to chat, I drop in on the Wisetail's. Flint's incredibly easy going too, we hardly ever argue. He likes to read and I like to send emails, surf the net or blog, so often our evenings are filled with comfortable silence.

Thanks for sending me those DVD's by the way, I enjoyed the movies. I watched a couple of them with Unka one evening when our husbands were out. You see, Flint and John are members of something of a 'club' per se. There's a group of 15 men, who follow this kind of tribal custom of hunting altogether on a full moon. The males are the tribe's strongest and fastest and with their keen hearing and smell, they hunt large animals in the National Park. The first time it happened, Unka came over to keep me company and we made popcorn and it turned into a movie night. The second time, I went to her house and played board games with her and her kids.

Another member of this 'club' is the tribe's Medicine Man. Although he hasn't gone to medical school, he has this uncanny knack of accurately diagnosing illness. He always knows my sugar level without the blood tests. His name is Philip and he comes by every two weeks to check how the pregnancy is affecting my diabetes. Yes, you read that right Chris, a 'doctor' that goes to see the patient, instead of the other way around.

He recommended that I visit a GP in Fairbanks to get a new prescription, since my dosage of insulin had to be changed. When I did, the doctor who did go to medical school, verified what he had said and wrote out the script. I think he knew him, as he told me how he was amazed that Philip always knew exactly what was wrong with the patients he sent to him.

Well that's about it for now. Before you pay for your airfare, look up flights that go to Fairbanks instead of Anchorage, as it's closer. Flint's also looking forward to your visit next month, he's told all our friends. I think Unka is planning on having all of us over for dinner during your stay.

Give Fritz a tickle under the chin for me,

Love Jess.

~~~~~~
~~~~~~

30th May, 2000

Two weeks ago, David Emanuel Riverclaw entered the world. It was a home birth, since the labour was so short there wasn't time to drive to Fairbanks' hospital. But it was also a difficult birth and I'd have to say the most painful experience of my life.

Everything happened suddenly; Flint and I were at the Wisetail's for lunch when I got my first contraction. After the second, my water broke and drenched the seat of my husband's truck. When we arrived home, the Medicine Man arrived shortly after us, having been called.

Flint carried me into the bedroom then followed the instructions issued by Philip. Every single towel in the house was used to try to soak up the blood. But I didn't care about the linen, with the excruciating contractions.

Outside of the bedroom I heard voices which belonged to John and Unka, who came to offer their help. Unka turned into my midwife, with Philip as my physician and Flint as my birthing partner. John busied himself by carting off the soiled to the laundry, before fetching new towels or sheets. My husband sat behind me on the bloodstained bed, rubbing my back or holding my hands.

"Breathe deeply, Jessica." He tried to soothe. "Your heart is racing and your puffing is too shallow."

"I don't care about the fucking breathing exercises," I growled back. "I just want this kid out of me!"

"If you keep breathing the way you are now, you'll hyperventilate." Unka frowned.

"C'mon Jessica, breathe deeply with me." Flint instructed. "Hee hee, hoo hoo. Hee hee, hoo hoo."

Philip passed a concerned look to his makeshift assistant, "Her blood sugar has dropped which is why she's feeling weak. She needs a glass of juice to bring her energy back up."

Immediately, she left the bedroom and when she brought back the beverage, I swear a glass of apple juice never looked so good! However, my hands trembled terribly when I tried to drink, so Flint had to hold the glass for me. I was even in a worse condition than the first day we met.

After two hours of agony, bearing down, bloodstained towels and sheets; a bloodied baby appeared in Phillip's hands.

"He's here!" Unka beamed down. "Your son is here!"

The Medicine Man cut the umbilical chord then passed the newborn to the older woman, to clean up. Then he looked from me to my husband with a serious expression.

"As we proceed with the afterbirth, we need to slow down her heart rate and stabilize her blood pressure."

I wasn't sure why he looked at Flint when he said that. As if he could do something, my husband held me closely as he gazed upon my sweaty face. His dark brown eyes were full of love, which shone down.

"Jessica Riverclaw, you can relax now." He spoke softly in his deep voice. "You did good. Our son is here and soon you can meet him. But right now, I need you to concentrate on my heart beat. Can you do that for me, Jessica? Can you feel it beating out of my chest and into yours?"

Since my back was resting against his chest, I could indeed. I recognized he was talking in his soothing manner, which put me into a relaxed state all those months ago that day he drove me to Anchorage. I felt his chest rise and fall with his steady breathing, the same rhythmic movement which lulls me to sleep, every night. His eyes never left mine, so I could see them begin to glow turquoise, with the black pupils disappearing.

"No harm will come to you as my mate." His changed voice rumbled out like distant thunder. "Now drink and heal."

Flint had put a gash in his wrist again, which was being pressed against my parted lips. His glowing turquoise eyes held mine, as I supped. I sensed what he was trying to do, impart his will and his life force onto his mate.

"Good...," Philip's voice sounded far away, "...her heart rate and blood pressure are slowly returning to normal."

"But wait," I heard Unka say unhappily, "look at how much blood that's come out with the afterbirth."

"I know." He replied, gravely. "She shouldn't conceive again, it's just too dangerous."

Soon afterwards I fell asleep, or perhaps I passed out? All I remember, was waking up when it was dark and feeling a lot cleaner. The sheets on the bed had also been changed with no sign of blood anywhere.

Flint walked into the bedroom in new clothes, holding our 'bundle of joy'. Our baby which was wrapped in a blanket, looked tiny in his large arms. The gentle giant carefully sat on the bed beside, so he could pass me our child.

"This is David Emanuel Riverclaw?" I looked on, in awe.

"This is our son," my husband put his arms about the both of us.

Momentarily, I looked away from his cute little pink face, into the larger and mature one of Flint's.

"I overheard what Philip said, before I fell asleep..." I began.

"Yes?"

My throat constricted but I forced out; "...is it true, that our first child will be our only child?"

"Yes."

"Oh Flint, I'm so sorry -"

"Sssshhhh!" He held me closer, while resting my head against his chest. "There will be none of that, Jessica Riverclaw."

"But -"

"You and my son are alive and well, how can I find fault with that?"

"But you were hoping for more children." I sniffed disappointedly.

"It was a difficult birth and I would not risk your life to put you through it again. Remember, we are mates and this process happens once in our lifetime. I would not risk losing you, nor would my body. It will change, so I won't impregnate you again."

"What do you mean, your body will change?"

He looked like he was trying not to laugh at my curious mind, which was still so full of questions, even now. Instead, he ducked his head to tenderly run his nose along my forehead before planting a kiss there. I closed my eyes and took a deep breath, inhaling his attractive scent and relishing his body heat. Then together, our attention returned to the baby.

My eyes filled with tears as I stared at this little miracle, which we had created. I found it ironic, with all the time and effort that goes into preparation and presentation of events; here was the crowning achievement and he was created by accident. Oh what a story we would have to tell him, one day...

~~~~~~
~~~~~~

~ 8 ~

Back to the future, 2363

Sitting here in the attic, I could feel the cold seep through the cracks. I sensed it was getting late without looking at the time. I wasn't wearing a watch and I couldn't see any clocks however, I felt the darkness approach by the chilled air dropping further below freezing.

I staved off the cold by keeping the top of my woollen jumper over my nose, as well as the sleeves over my hands. But I couldn't stop reading Jessica Riverclaw's words, I found her story engrossing. The similarities yet differences in our lives, were fascinating.

I must admit, sometimes my head can get lodged up my arse, with my supernatural differences as the Last Circulator and first female Lokoti Werewolf. So it was nice seeing outside the square I live in, by reading about somebody else's problems.

Jessica had been an everyday human, with her own career, friends and a life, before she met Flint Riverclaw. But one fateful night spent with a stranger in a hotel room, changed her life irrevocably. Sure, she kicked up a fuss at first, then the 1990's career woman simply did what had to be done. So did Flint Riverclaw.

I could guess what the pack thought at the time, by bringing in an outsider. But Flint's best friend John Wisetail and his family, simply made the best of the situation. They welcomed Jessica with open arms, which helped smooth over the rough edges of her transition.

When Flint learned that his diabetic wife couldn't have more children, did he curse the heavens above? Nope! Instead, he counted his blessings that his wife and baby were alive. I could tell he would have cherished both for the time they were with him. What made the story of my ancestors a sad one, was that Flint ended up outliving them both.

I remember the stories told by my grandfather Emanuel Riverclaw, whom had been Flint's grandson. Towards the end, Jessica widowed Flint, dying from a diabetes related illness when she was 59 years old. Before she died, she'd been made a grandmother by her son David mating with Clara Winter. Flint would have been 105 years old at the time of his mate's death, although he would have had the appearance of a man in his fifties. True to Lokoti Werewolf behaviour, he didn't take a second mate after the death of his first.

Sadder still, David Riverclaw died at the age of 32, when he saved his son from getting hit by a logging truck. So Clara moved in with Flint, to have his help with raising her son who went through the change after his father's death. At the age of 18, Grandfather married my Gran and Flint stayed on, to help raise my mother and uncle, as she prepared the tribe for the oncoming war. It was thanks to Gran's foresight as a Circulator, which ensured the tribe became self-sufficient whilst the outside world was in chaos. It was shortly after World War Three, Flint Riverclaw was murdered by looters in 2063, which he and the pack fought to keep off tribal lands.

I was holding history in my hands... the actual lives of people who were served with bad luck however, they lived in love. Did they mope and sulk? Well, maybe for a little while, but they climbed back onto the metaphorical bike and pedalled on.

It was hours later when my husband found me, still sitting on the trunk with the diary in my hands. I was so caught up, I didn't hear him come home. But here he was, in human form once more and wearing a change of clothes.

Declan climbed up the attic ladder as he tracked me down by my scent. He frowned as soon as he spotted me, reading under the single light globe hanging from the rafters. I noticed with his height and broad-shoulders, he took up more room than I did.

"What are you doing?" He sounded surprised.

"What does it look like?" I replied curtly. "I'm reading."

"Why are you sitting up in the attic, reading?" He gave a peculiar look. "Why aren't you downstairs, reading by the fire?"

I said coolly, "I'm reading my great, great grandmother's diary."

"Really?" His eyebrows arose.

"I told you I found them the other day, when I carried the box of Grandpa's things up here. I found them in this trunk." I patted my seat.

He came closer to see, "Oh yeah?"

"I found them with some old photo albums. Grandfather must have given them to Mum, when he and Gran evolved." I continued. "It probably came with the stuff we packed up, after Mum and Dad left for the continuum. I forgot how much stuff we have up here."

"Who knows what's hidden away." He remarked, as he looked about the dust and cobwebs. "I keep meaning to do a spring clean, but I keep forgetting."

I pointed out, "I think in those boxes over there, are mine as well as my parents' old baby clothes and toys."

"Yeah, I think my Mom also kept some baby stuff left over from Derik's and my childhood. They're in those boxes in the corner." He nodded in another direction. Then he frowned when he saw me squint, whilst trying to read in the poor light. "Again I ask, why are you sitting up here, reading that? Why don't you bring it downstairs to read?"

"I like it up here."

"It's frickin' freezing up here and you hate the cold."

"It's quiet and it's peaceful and I'm among family," I said flatly.

"In other words you're avoiding me," his hands moved to his hips.

I didn't look up, “You can storm around and growl and hate this baby as much as you like. Up here, the baby and I have peace and quiet, as we spend time with other women who've been in my condition.”

“I don't hate the baby...” he said unhappily, “...I just hate what it's done to us.”

“Can you please stop calling her ‘it’?” I said unhappily.

“I thought Elisha's diary was on her laptop," he changed the subject.

“Elisha's diary IS on her laptop," I retorted, "but I'm reading the diary of Jessica Tandy, the mate of Flint Riverclaw.”

“Flint Riverclaw?” He recognized the name. “Isn't he your great, great grandfather? Wasn't he your Grandfather's grandfather?”

“Yup, Jessica had a one night stand with Flint then three days later, he tracked her down to say she was pregnant and she was his mate.”

“You're kidding?” He chuckled in amusement. “What year did this happen?”

I answered whilst looking down, “In 1999 and Jessica Riverclaw was a diabetic, too. Pregnancy was a risky thing for her back then, but Flint Riverclaw helped her through it. She had to give up her job and move to Alaska, which was then seen as the middle of nowhere. However, Flint helped her to adjust as they established a new life together.”

Declan turned quiet for a moment or two as my words sunk in.

Then he said quietly, "So you're up here, reading in the cold and dust, to get away from the husband who is acting anything but helpful?”

“Uh huh.”

Next, I heard him take a couple of steps away, but still I wouldn't look up. I thought he was about to climb back down the ladder, but he didn't. Instead, his footsteps crossed over to the boxes in the corner, as he proceeded to unstack them. Eventually, I glanced upwards to see him open one and pull out a couple of baby jumpsuits and even an old toy.

“You remember this, B?” He held up the worn and faded, stuffed dog.

I sat up straighter in surprise, “Didn't that used to be Derik's?”

“Yup.”

He tossed the toy over which I put the diary down to catch.

“Hey, this is Frisbee!” My voice rose in excitement, as I examined it. “This ‘Pound Puppy’ was Derik's favourite toy. Whenever he slept over or I had sleepovers at your place; I remember he'd curl up with it.”

“Ready for another old friend?” Declan called.

Then he tossed over an old, stuffed rabbit. I put Frisbee in my lap along with the diary, to catch it next. This time it was a ‘Bugs Bunny’ doll, with long, floppy, grey ears. It still had the pull ring in its side, which I couldn't help but to give it a gentle tug.

“Hee hee, you're a cute bunny!” Bugs Bunny's voice, chuckled.

"It still works!" I laughed aloud.

"Do you remember his name?" He smiled on.

I pulled a face for asking such a stupid question. "Bugs Bunny, but wasn't he your toy?"

"Uh huh," he gave a nod, "my Dad bought him when Mom became pregnant with me. She told him that she was expecting and Dad was so ecstatic, he came home from work the next day with Bugs. It was one of the few toys they brought when we came to Alaska to live, after the War."

Next, I watched Declan round up his and Derik's old baby clothes from the box he'd opened. Then he walked over to the other boxes I was sitting near, to open them. He found more baby clothes to add to our collection.

"I'm going to give these a wash and see how they turn out." He advised. Then he added on, "Wouldn't it be nice if our daughter could wear the same clothes that we or our family, used to?"

Then he loaded his large arms with the tiny clothing and made a move towards the ladder.

He started to disappear down the attic hatch as he carried out his plan. But before he completely vanished, he left his parting words, "If you take that diary down to read by the fire, you might find a mug of hot chocolate with marshmallows waiting for you. Hell, you may even find a plate of celery sticks and cream cheese, too."

I laughed aloud at his mood swing. But I was also touched that this was his way of apologizing. I wondered if my words about Flint Riverclaw kicked him into gear?

*****

When I thought it was safe to return, I tucked Jessica's diary into my jeans so I could use both hands to climb down. Once I had, I folded the ladder and pushed it along with the attic hatch, closed. As soon as I came down the stairs, the warmth hit me like an old friend.

Declan was true to his word, sitting on the coffee table was a mug of hot chocolate, as well as a plate of celery sticks with a side bowl of cream cheese. A roaring fire was crackling away in the fireplace, thanks to the new wood he fed it. Warily, I looked about but I couldn't see him in either the kitchen or the living area.

I skipped down the remaining steps and blithely settled in the lounge area. I sat on the stone step of the hearth, to continue to read. As I did, I dunked a couple of celery sticks into the cream cheese to munch on. Once the savoury snack had been consumed, I went for the mug of hot chocolate.

It was around this time that Declan emerged from the laundry, carrying a basket full of freshly washed and dried baby clothes.

This caught my eye, as he looked like a natural carrying this sort of thing. I watched him place it on top of the dining table and one at a time, take out the clothes to be folded. After a couple of minutes, he noticed my gaze.

"What?" He wondered.

"You look at home with the baby clothes, like you're an old father instead of an expectant one." I smirked.

"B, I'm 300 years old. Aside from helping my little brother when he had kids, I helped with his grandkids, his great, grandkids, the great, great grandkids and so on. Derik may have died years ago, but his progeny didn't."

"Now you'll have progeny too." I said quietly, as I looked back down.

This made him pause and look my way whilst I pretended to read.

"I know B," he said quietly. "OUR progeny, it just takes a bit to get used to, that's all."

"When will you get used to the idea?" I asked coolly.

"I dunno, when somebody tells me that Genies exist and that they really do live inside lamps or bottles, which get washed up onto the beach?"

I joked back, "If Werewolves, Vampires and Circulators exist, who's to say Genies don't?"

Declan didn't respond, he seemed to be concentrating on the folding up. I found myself lowering the diary, to watch the care and attention he treated the baby clothes with. He separated into neat piles the jumpsuits, the cardigans and anything else, such as bibs, bonnets or booties.

"There's a fair amount there," I commented.

"Uh huh," he agreed as he finished up. "I don't think we'll need to buy any cardigans, booties or bonnets for our little rug rat. But we'd probably need a couple more jumpsuits, especially with how many times a day, you have to change the small fry, with all the spitting up and soiling they do."

I found myself lowering the diary, standing up and moving over to his side to look down on our baby bounty. Out of habit, my arm moved to his wide waist to rest there. Contentedly, he put his arm about my shoulders and together, we looked on.

"This was Derik's, I remember him wearing it." He pointed at a jumpsuit, cardigan, bonnet and pair of booties. "So was this and this."

"I think that was mine," I pointed at another garment. "I think I saw in a photo somewhere, of me wearing it."

"I remember you wearing it," he said softly.

"You do?" I turned his way, in surprise.

"I'm three years older than you, don't forget." He shrugged. "I think you wore it on your first birthday."

"You remember my first birthday?"

"Remember it? I frickin' got in trouble for it."

"You did?" I gave a funny look.

He glared at the memory, "I got into a fight with Grant over you. I was four years old and sitting on the couch holding you, when the eleven year old walked up and pulled you from my arms. So I punched him for it and got a telling-off, by your Dad."

"Actually, this story sounds familiar..." I turned thoughtful.

"I told you about it before, the day that the pack asked me to remain as Second after Chiron's death."

"Yeah I remember now," my frown deepened, "which I still think is unfair."

"Don't do this again," he let out a tired moan, as he pulled his arm back.

"You're the oldest living Lokoti in existence!" I started up. "The Second is meant to become First when our leader dies. It's only fair that you should have been asked!"

"You know why I can't be First, B." He crossed his arms as he leaned back against the table. "You're my first priority and you always will be. I can't be objective enough to organize the pack, when I'm always worrying about you."

"There you go again," I folded my arms too, "making it sound like such a hindrance to have a mate. Now you have young on the way too? Oh poor Declan!"

Rather than getting angry, he started to laugh. But as he laughed, he rubbed his face wearily. The gesture truly showed how long we'd been married.

"This is the real reason why they call Circulators eternal, isn't it? Because all of the constant bitching and moaning, it never stops." He sighed.

"And now you're a Circulator too...?" I began.

"...I'm gonna get it 24/7 for all eternity, no matter how many times the universe is crushed, blown up then recycled again." He finished.

"Well..." I thought about it, "...you could try to shoot yourself in the head when you're in biological form. But you'll still end up in the space time continuum, only you'd never be able to leave."

"Thanks a lot, B!" He let out an indignant laugh. "So for all essential purposes, you're telling me I'm handcuffed to you, for eternity?"

"No, I'm saying that you'd remain in the space time continuum similar to a dead star. I could come and go, as a living Circulator, but you couldn't because you'd be a dead Circulator. So I'd promise to avoid you at all cost, by spending as much time outside of the continuum as possible."

My husband turned quiet as he studied my profile for a moment, as I glared in his direction.

He asked wryly, "How did we go from a joke about your nagging, to a conversation about me blowing my brains out?"

"I don't know..." I looked downwards, "...you made it sound like such a negative, being with me. It's just like you're making everything about this pregnancy sound like a negative too."

"What a load of crap." He spoke in his typical, blunt fashion. "I told you to turn me into a Circulator. I told you we would have this baby. I told you my concern about this pregnancy, was it killing you then being without you. I wasn't made First of the Lokoti Werewolf pack, not because I'm a European Werewolf, but because I'm too obsessed with the tribe's first female Lokoti Werewolf. B, you're the one who's getting bitchy."

"Oh...!" I moaned loudly, as I leaned backwards on the table next to him. "Frickin' hell! Maybe you're right? Maybe I'm not acting like myself lately, just like you're not acting like yourself lately. Maybe I'm taking everything out of context, because we're crossing into the realm of surrealism?"

"What the...?!" He laughed. "You know what B, maybe you're just tired at the moment and whacked-out on pregnancy hormones."

I realized he was right, it was me picking this fight and not him. I emitted a frustrated growl while I buried my face in my hands. I rubbed hard at it, as if I could rub out my mistakes.

"B, open your eyes."

"I don't want to."

"Please?"

"Why?"

"Just open your frickin' eyes," he said softly.

Only my husband could make cursing sound tender... When I did, I found Declan standing before me, holding up a small baby jumpsuit against his wide chest. The sight of them together made me giggle girlishly.

"Your middle name is Grace, isn't it?" He remembered. "Just like your mother's and your grandmother's middle names were?"

"Er, yeah...?" I wondered why he was asking.

"Can you see Lucia Grace wearing this?" He held out the jumpsuit.

Slowly, I took it out of his hands and held it in the both of mine, to examine the pink garment.

I asked in amusement, "Lucia Grace?"

"Lucia was my grandmother on my mother's side." He advised. "I only have one memory of her, as she and grandfather died soon after the War."

In 273 years of marriage Declan's never talked about this. I just assumed he had no early memories of his family before he and his mother were taken in by mine. He tried to talk about it casually, but I sensed his sadness.

"What's your memory of her?" I asked.

"Nonna made me banana custard, because it was my favourite food then." He sighed. "I remember her standing by the stove, cutting up the banana and dropping it into the custard. As she did, she sang 'Ava Maria' in Italian to me."

"Declan, I – I – I didn't know," I began, "I mean, I didn't know that you remembered anything of your life, before your move to Alaska."

"It's just the one memory, it's no big deal." He tried to shrug it off. "They were my mother's parents, who died before Mom and Dad decided to get out of town. But I remember Nonna and Nonno were losing their hair from radiation sickness. They were minding me on this particular afternoon when my parents were at the doctor's, because Mom was pregnant with Derik. They were running late and I was scared that something had happened to them, with all the shooting and stealing that was going on. So Nonna cut up their last piece of fruit they had left, to make me feel better. Fruit was scarce at the time and they must have been looking forward to eating that banana, but they used it on me."

My eyes watered as I watched him blink back his tears. When he saw this, he cleared his throat and picked up a set of booties, cardigan and bonnet from the table. He held the old knitting in his large hands, to look on.

"These have kept well." He changed the subject. "I wonder who these belonged to?"

"Lucia Grace is a lovely name for our daughter," I tried to hold his gaze.

"Yeah well, I thought so." He shrugged it off. "I was tempted to name our first born Susan Grace instead. You know, after my Mom? But I thought if we're gonna give Lucia sisters, the name can be used later."

"How about Susanna?" I shrugged too. "Then it will be a nod to your Mum and it will be a nod to my family tradition."

"What family tradition?" He gave a funny look.

"Elisha, Alexandrina, Arabella, Jessica, Bianca..." I listed off.

"Oh yeah, I get it," he snickered, "names that end with an 'a'?"

"Yup, so Lucia will go perfectly." I grinned.

"Elisha, Alexandrina, Arabella, Jessica, Bianca and now Lucia." He repeated, as he wrapped his arms about my waist. "I like the sound of that."

"And Susanna," I added on.

"You said Lucia will be the eldest of three girls, right?" He held me closely, as he thought aloud. "Then do you think we can throw a Sophia in there, too?"

"Sophia?"

"It does end in an 'a'," he smirked.

"Who's Sophia?"

"My other grandmother on my Dad's side." He informed. "If we're naming one kid after one grandmother, it's only fair we name another, hers."

"Do you have any memories of your grandmother Sophia?"

"Ironically just the one, like my Nonna." He let go to lean against the table again.

I stepped up closely to wrap my arms about his waist instead.

He explained, "My parents begged her and grandfather to leave Indianapolis with us, but they said that they were too old and would slow us up.

I remember when they saw us off, they gave my parents money and jewellery, to trade. Years later when the government got organized again, Mom made enquiries about what happened to them, but she never got an exact answer. All she found out was shortly after we had left for Alaska, some strangers moved into their house. Nobody knew what happened to the original owners, although in those days it probably wouldn't have been uncommon to find their remains underneath the floorboards."

I let go of his waist as my objection to such a fate. "Declan!"

"Yeah I know, it's depressing."

I shuddered, like a glass of icy water had been thrown over me. "Can't we just hope that somehow things turned out for the best?"

"And say that unicorns carried them off, over the rainbow?" He arched his eyebrows. "You know what life was like after the War."

"All too well," I scowled.

"At least we had it good up here. I mean sure, patrolling once a week for nearly forty years wore thin. The pack protected our land and loved ones, from what was outside trying to get in. I would have lost control if you or my Mom, went missing and I found a new family was living where you used to. If I found your remains under the floorboards, the residents wouldn't know what hit them! They'd end up on the walls and ceiling let alone the frickin' floorboards." He growled, as he reclaimed his mate.

"Declan, let's look on the bright side shall we?" I adjusted to his hold. "Let's talk about the life we're creating instead of ending. We are going to have three little girls and their names will be Lucia, Sophia and Susanna."

"How about Lucia Grace, Sophia Arabella and Susanna Jessica?" He offered.

"It's do-able." I slowly nodded. "But we don't have to name them after my Gran and Mum, too. Besides, the original Jessica was honoured when they named Mum after her. We'll see Mum and Gran in a couple of years anyway, inside the space time continuum."

"A couple of years?" He arched his eyebrows.

"Alright, in more than a couple of years." I smirked. "But what if we named them Sophia Clara and Susanna Ling, after my Great Grandma and Nana?"

"Lucia Grace, Sophia Clara and Susanna Ling..." his face broke out into a grin, "...it's do-able."

Teasingly, I ran my nose up his neck as I inhaled his maple syrup scent.

When I reached his ear, I sung, "You're going to be the father of three little girls."

"Three little female Werewolves," he closed his eyes, enjoying the sensations.

Next, I started to chew my way along his jaw. "You're going to be the proud papa bear with three little cubs."

"Damn straight..." he breathed, "...and if any looters tried to come near my mate and young; the authorities would find their remains on the walls, ceiling, floor and the front veranda."

I ran my nose across his cheek, "And if any strange men come a courting your daughters, I can see you doing it to them too."

"Trust me B, if an undesirable looked sideways at our little girls? I'd do worse."

Declan started to pant as he gathered up my clothes. Momentarily, I pulled away, so I could tug off his jumper and allow him to do the same. The garments were whipped over our heads and discarded on the floor.

I liked hearing him using the words, 'our little girls'. "Say that again."

"I'd maul, tear and downright torture with my claws, any male who looks their way."

"Not that!" I giggled. "Say the other part again."

"'Our little girls'?" He chuckled, as he made a move on my jeans next. "Our itty bitty female Werewolves; Lucia Grace, Sophia Clara and Susanna Ling Sabre."

"Mmm...!" I moaned as my head fell forwards to rest on his bare chest. "I like the sound of that."

When I started to bite into his muscles, it pulled on his self control. I felt myself lifted up and sat on top of the dining table, beside the baby clothes. With my feet off the ground, he had no problem in removing my jeans and underwear.

"You better believe it baby!" He growled out, as he rubbed his hot, hardening body, against mine. "I'm the father of your children."

"Say that again." I lay back on the surface, whilst pulling him along.

Declan climbed on top of both the table and his mate, whilst unfastening his jeans. "I'm the alpha male, the papa bear and the stud for your now fertile womb."

"Say that again." I breathed, as I moved my hips into position.

"You're my B who's having my babies and nothin' but my babies."

"Say it again...!" My eyes drifted closed, as I felt our two bodies become one.

However, he paused which made me open my eyes to look questioningly into his.

He spoke in a low voice, "I'm your true mate just like you're mine. You were never meant to breed for anybody but me."

I dug my sharpening nails into his back as my teeth grew elongated. My dark blue eyes glowed turquoise, which were met by his glowing green ones. As a rhythm began, my back arched off the table.

I managed out in my rumbling, changed voice, "I'm yours Declan and nothing but yours."

Now his eyes drifted shut, as his strong movements made the table creak. It looked like he was getting lost in the moment. But he still managed to pant out, “Say that again?”

*****

Our ‘marital activities’ ended with eating pizza on the rug, by the fire. We ordered the food to be delivered via the internet on his phone, with his credit card details. When the delivery girl came to drop them off, Declan retrieved two spare blankets from the linen closet, to answer the door.

By the time our door chime sounded, we were ready and waiting in our semi-dressed state. As soon as we heard her hover-car power down on our snow-covered driveway, my husband fetched the covers. The delivery girl stared at the blanket wrapped around his waist, whilst her eyes bulged at how big and half-naked, he looked.

“Howdy.” Declan greeted the teenager.

“Er, delivery for Sabre?” She managed out.

She took the pizzas and garlic bread out of her thermal carry bag and handed them over.

“Thanks," he took them.

As he did so, the girl in her uniform caught sight of me lying on my side, on the rug by the fire, wrapped in my own blanket. However, she tried hard to carry on as normal.

“Er, ‘Alma Pizza Palace’ is having a promotion at the moment. Only 29 credits were charged to your card instead of the usual 33.”

“Sweet," he answered.

“Enjoy your night in," she tried not to blush.

“You drive safely now," he returned, as I gave a wave.

Awkwardly, she turned around to go down the icy front steps, back to her vehicle. Declan watched her for a moment to ensure she didn’t slip, before he closed the front door. It shut out the freezing night air as he rejoined me by the fire with dinner.

“Here’s your ‘Alaskan Special’ with the smoked salmon and avocado.” He handed me one box. “And here’s my pizza with the lot.”

Happily, he opened both boxes and I watched him serve the food. He grabbed half of my pizza to sit with his whole one. Then he placed three slices of garlic bread on my box, before claiming the rest. He was practically salivating at the sight of one of his favourite foods.

“I think I’ll have more garlic bread tonight,” I spoke up.

“Of course, you’re eating for two.” He chuckled, then he put another three in my open pizza box.

I shook my head at his huge serving compared to mine, “After 273 years of marriage, your huge appetite still amazes me.”

"With another European Werewolf on the way, I think we're gonna need a bigger fridge and pantry, for all the food we're gonna buy." He mused with his mouthful. "Speaking of which..."

"Yes?"

"...if we're gonna have three kids, especially three half European Werewolves, we're gonna need a bigger house." He looked around our cosy abode.

I objected, "But I like this house, I don't want to move!"

"We don't have to move, but we're gonna have to renovate," he said matter-of-factly.

"Hmm," I looked around, "we could get an extension to make the downstairs larger and put in two more bedrooms upstairs?"

"Let's make it three more bedrooms," he haggled. "Then downstairs, we'll put in a study, so you'll have your own work area for your essays and lecture preparation."

I smiled at how he was planning ahead, "What will you be doing, while I continue with academic work?"

"It looks like you've nominated me to be the 'house hubby'."

"But if you wanted to work, what would you do?" I continued. "I thought you didn't want to go back to the Garage."

"I don't." Declan declared. "I've worked for nearly three centuries in the same job and I need a change."

"It sounds like you're looking forward to the role of 'house hubby," my smile widened.

"B, in a house with three female European Werewolves, even if they're half-breeds; trust me, you're gonna need a 'ringleader' in this circus."

"So you're going to keep the little trouble-makers in line?"

"I'll become a drill sergeant," he chuckled at the thought. "I'll have a well-run house with four beautiful, strong and intelligent females. As the mother dresses up in her fancy suits and brings home the bacon? Her handsome husband will keep the small fry in line. I'll keep human flesh from passing my daughters lips, by shoving pasta down their throats instead."

"Hmm..." I thought on his words, "...you think it's going to work?"

"Yup, it's what my Mom did with me." He explained. "I mean, sure the bloodlust could make my blood boil; which is why your Grandfather spent night after night, sitting with me or taking me hunting. But my Mom helped, because she realized my bloodlust was its worst on an empty stomach. So she cooked and cooked and cooked some more. When she wasn't teaching or marking homework, she was cooking or teaching me how to. This is what I'm gonna do with my daughters."

"OK." I mulled over what he said. "So if we're going to add extensions to the house, maybe we should renovate the kitchen too?"

"Good idea." He nodded eagerly. "Our kitchen is pretty outdated for what it should be like in the 24th Century."

“Yes, but you won’t let me buy pre-made meals that other people eat, so they don’t have to cook.”

“I’m not talking about pre-made, or buying one of those meal synthesizers which replicates food or drink. There'll be no artificial crap in my kitchen, thank you very much!” He repeated his old argument. “But I’m talking about getting new, whiz-bang gadgets, which make cooking easier.”

“Fine, you can take charge of renovating the kitchen.” I rolled my eyes. Then I looked over at the baby clothes which were still sitting on the dining table. “I suppose we’re going to have to start putting together a nursery, first.”

“Good point.” He gave a nod, before he scoffed down another slice of pizza. “Let’s get a nursery sorted out then after Lucia is born, we’ll organize the other renovations.”

“We’ll have to do the building during the summer months, so there won’t be any snow hindering construction.” I planned aloud.

“Uh huh," he agreed, as he started on his half of my pizza.

“Do you think we’ll have to live away from home while they build?”

“Maybe," he shrugged, "before we contact the contractors, I’ll speak to the Tribal Elders about getting a temporary house on tribal lands.”

Before a house was built which meant more land was cleared, permission had to be sought from our Tribal Elders. They reviewed which part of the land could be settled on or which had to remain untouched, for nature conservation or spiritual reasons. It was preferred that old houses were reused and renovated, rather than more land cleared. As the Lokoti Tribal Lands grew in time with the size of our tribe increasing, our Elders could act as unofficial Real Estate Agents or Land-Grant Government.

“You know what?” I mused, as I munched on my dinner. “In the diary entries, I read about what life was like in 1999. Alma only had a population of 709 and the tribe had 167 people.”

“No kidding," his eyes widened in surprise. “That makes sense, as your Grandfather told me before the War, Alma had a population of just over a thousand. Three hundred years later with the world going through the ‘Third Renaissance', its population is pushing 7,000 and our tribe is around 600.”

“Hmm,” I frowned, "you don’t think Earth is going to have an over-population problem again, do you?”

He shook his head as he picked up a piece of garlic bread. “Not with the off-world colonies being built on the terra formed planets, in the nearby star systems.”

“Declan,” I began, “do you ever wonder what it would be like to visit a terra formed planet?”

“Nope," his answer was quick. “I feel uncomfortable just visiting the Circulate HQ on Taurus Six, for short periods of time. I couldn’t spend more than 24 hours off Earth.”

“Why not?”

"No matter what science can do to an alien planet, by embellishing vegetation or an oxygen-rich atmosphere; it's not Earth. The gravity isn't exactly the same and when I visit Taurus Six, I feel a little nauseas. Werewolves are affected by the Earth's moon, so what's an alien planet with no moon or more moons than one, going to do to us? Werewolves rely on the familiar smells of our territory, I hate the sterile smell of the Circulate HQ. Sometimes, I get a whiff of the alien vegetation on the other side of the glass dome wall, and I hate that nothing smells familiar."

I smiled softly, "You really are a little homebody, aren't you?"

"And damn proud of it," his chest rose.

I lost interest in my meal, so I crawled into his lap instead. I wrapped my arms about his neck, as I murmured, "I love you, Declan Domitian Sabre."

"I love you, Bianca Grace Sabre."

Then I squealed with laughter when he abruptly flipped me onto my back. I continued to giggle, as he placed the last piece of garlic bread in between my breasts. He ducked his head and snapped it up with his teeth to gobble it down. Lastly, he took his sweet time, to lick the garlic butter off my chest.

I closed my eyes as my hands ran through his short, blonde hair. I wished it was longer. A while ago he had grown it past his ears, but he returned to a crew cut when his hair turned white. Since he was young again, I wished he'd grow it once more.

"Declan?"

"Hmm?"

"Could you grow out your crew cut for me?"

"I already am B, can't you tell?" His voice was muffled, with his mouth full of breasts.

I watched my fingers run through his hair and realized it wasn't as short and spiky as before. The length was just long enough to cover my fingers. However, he made me giggle again when I felt his teeth tenderly chew my nipple, before sucking on it.

"Declan?"

"Hmm?"

"I'm glad we haven't evolved yet. I like doing naughty things with you, in our biological forms. Sometimes when I think about evolving to the space time continuum; I'm worried that we're going to have to behave like angels, or something."

"Screw that!" He objected to the idea so much so, it made him look up. "I'm a Werewolf through and through. If we're supposed to behave ourselves when we evolve to a higher form of life? I'd rather stay on Earth."

I cupped his face. "And you know what?"

"What?"

"I'd stay with you." I spoke plainly. "If you'd prefer to live for a thousand years in biological form, I'd be right there with you."

He grinned at my words. “Always and forever?”

“Always and forever,” I repeated our old promise.

“Then let’s really misbehave, shall we?” He bared his teeth which grew longer and sharper, before my very eyes. Then his human blue ones flashed their glowing green colour.

I squealed louder as he dove his sharp teeth, into my neck and ‘mauled’ his wife, complete with snarling and growling.

~~~~~~

20th January 2364

Yesterday morning we were woken by his digital alarm clock at 6 AM. The latest Trance music on the Internet Radio, blared out. Declan hated Trance, Dance and Techno music with a passion, whereas I liked it.

SMASH!

His hand flew out with his new light speed reflexes. Instead of hitting the ‘snooze’ button, his European Werewolf strength killed his twentieth clock. I raised my head to survey the damage.

“And another one bites the dust.”

He growled bad-temperedly, “I’m retired, so why the hell are alarm clocks still waking me up?”

I yawned as I sat upright, “I have a presentation at the University of Paris.”

Next, I stumbled out of bed whilst Declan rolled over to go back to sleep. I made my way over to the wardrobe to pull out the outfit I'd picked last night, to wear. I pulled off my singlet top and flannel pyjama pants, to put on my haute couture suit. But I caught him peek through half-closed eyes, when I sat on the side of the bed, to pull on my black lacy stockings and high-heels.

Once I'd finished dressing, I surveyed the results by looking into the mirror on the inside of the wardrobe door. The black, lacy stockings suited the dark purple, satin skirt and jacket. However, I noticed that my pregnancy looked more pronounced in this outfit.

I was about to go into the bathroom to do my hair and make-up, when I found Declan lying on his back with his hands behind his head, watching.

“Not bad, Mrs. Sabre.” He grinned. “Now make sure that your wedding ring is on display, so the male professors know you’re taken.”

I patted my growing abdomen, "You don’t think the baby bulge is a good indication?”

Then I departed the bedroom. As I stood at the vanity brushing my teeth, I stared critically into the mirror. I was trying to decide if I should wear my hair up or down? I'd decided last night when I picked the outfit, but with typical last-minute jitters, now I wasn’t sure.
~~~~~~

It's funny, even after lecturing for the past 250 years, I'd still get stage fright. I'd worry if I had enough pictures to display, or I'd worry if my notes were interesting enough, or had enough scientific fact? Or, I'd worry if I looked formal enough, without being too dressed up. So what the hell do I do with my hair today, up or down?

While I was inwardly panicking, I was interrupted by my husband. He sleepily shuffled past, in his 'Loony Tunes', silk boxers. He walked up to the toilet, raised the seat and went ahead with relieving himself.

"Declan!" I objected. "Do you mind?"

"Huh?"

"I'M using the bathroom!" I snapped. "Can't you wait until I'm finished?"

"Nope."

"Declan," my face turned hot, "you don't see me using the bathroom when you're shaving or in the shower, do you?"

"It's called peeing B and I wouldn't care." He yawned loudly. "Besides, with your pregnancy, you've been peeing more than usual. So, I wouldn't be surprised if you had to."

Angrily, I turned the taps on full ball to rinse my toothbrush then my mouth. My husband flushed the toilet before he came over, to wash his hands. I noticed he took his time too, as he looked on my reflection through the mirror. I had started to put on the moisturizer before the make-up.

"I like that colour on you," he inferred the suit," it goes with your black hair and dark blue eyes."

"Should I wear my hair up or down?" I tested.

"You know I prefer you with your hair down." He spoke plainly. "But I don't want you looking too pretty for strangers, so wear it up."

"Then I'll wear it down," I smirked.

He shook his head, as he dried his hands on the towel. "I knew you were gonna say that."

Then he paused before he left the bathroom, to look on our reflections together.

I gave him a funny look. "What?"

"Man, I really do look younger than you," he remarked.

"Thanks a lot!"

"I mean, I look like a 20 year old kid, when I'm standing next to you looking all mature, dressed up like that." He frowned.

"Well you're about to look younger still." I said sulkily, "I'll be altering my appearance to look like the forty-something year old, for the academic identity of Dr. Bianca Baker."

His face fell in horror, "What? No!"

"What do you mean, 'no'?" I almost laughed.

"B, isn't manipulating your age going to affect the baby inside you?"

"Oh," that made me pause, "I never thought of it."

He continued, "I mean, if you're altering your age by nearly twenty years, aren't you going to make our kid twenty years older, too?"

"I don't know..."

"You once told me that when you make yourself look elderly, you feel elderly too. So what about the rug rat inside you? Is she going to suddenly shoot up into an adult?"

"Oh shit..." my face fell, "...you may be right."

"Don't make yourself look like you're in your forties. If anybody asks, say you've had plastic surgery." My husband ordered.

"What?" This time I did laugh. "Of my whole body, let alone my face?"

"Yes."

"But Declan -" I began but he cut me off.

"Or don't lecture today, or do any more as Dr. Bianca Baker." He said sternly. "Tell your PA at Hodge Endeavor that you're going to start a new life with a new name. Then you can reset your age back to your twenties again, with this new persona."

"But – but – but -" I faltered, "but it will mean I'd have to start from scratch! I'd need new academic papers and new findings and whatever else!"

"So?" He shrugged. "You've done it before."

"Yes, but not right before a lecture!" I complained. "Declan, they're expecting me -"

"B, you're pregnant and you've always wanted to be pregnant." He stated. "Now act like a mother and make the necessary adjustments."

I saw through the mirror that he was wearing his determined look, with his jaw set. His blue eyes hardened, giving them a cold quality like the Arctic Ocean. I saw there was no budging his stubborn temperament.

"Frickin' hell!" I threw down my bottle of moisturizer, in anger.

The white liquid splashed all over the vanity, with even a few droplets landing on the mirror.

Coolly, Declan walked out of the bathroom and went back into the bedroom. I thought he had gone back to bed or to get dressed, until he came back, carrying my mobile phone. He pushed it into my hands, as he ordered:

"Make the call."

"Fine!" I snatched it up, as I growled fiercely, "But stop telling me what to do!"

He walked off, "I'm gonna get dressed and make us some breakfast, which you're going to sit down and eat, now that you have the time."

"I said, stop telling me what to do!"

Then he called back from the bedroom, "Afterwards, we're going to go shopping for the nursery."

"Stop frickin' telling me what to do!"

"Then tonight, I'm gonna make your favourite dinner, fettuccine carbonara. You're going to eat it all up and later give me 'thank you' sex."

"Declan, shut up!"

BAM!

I slammed the bathroom door shut, before I began to pace up and down in the small space. My high heels made 'clicking' noises on the tiled floor. However, after I took a deep breath, I forced myself to make the call I didn't want to.

"Hi Aneet. Yes, I am calling about my lecture today. Um look, I can't make it. Yeah, I'm going to need you to call and cancel. Yes, I'm aware that they're not going to pay me for cancelling at the last minute. Yeah, I know they may not reschedule for another date. But um, look...I'm going to have to retire from my academic identity as Dr. Bianca Baker. Yep, so you can produce a death certificate or whatever the Legal Department of Hodge Endeavor does. But I'm going to need an all new birth certificate, passport, driver's license and credit cards. Yep. Uh huh. OK. What do I want for my new name? Um, I don't know. Can I think about it and call you back later? OK, bye."

I ended the call as I leaned against the glass shower screen, in resignation.

Oh well, Jessica Riverclaw nee Tandy, had to give up her working life too. Albeit she didn't have to give up her passport, credit cards and identity... but still. I growled under my breath, as I fumed about what a man had to give up, when compared to a woman.

*****

Two hours later, we walked out of the house breakfasted and in a change of clothes. We headed over to his hover-car parked in the garage. Although it was 8 AM, with winter's shorter daylight it was still dark out.

I'd taken off my suit and instead wore jeans, a pale blue, turtle-neck jumper and a brown suede jacket. I'd gone from 'city chic' to 'country gal', complete with wearing my long hair in two, loose piggy tails. It didn't seem to bother Declan, as he wore his customary work boots, jeans, grey jumper and his old, black, leather jacket.

He hit his remote key, to release the central locking and the automatic doors opened. I remained quiet and he knew I was sulking, as I slid into the passenger's seat and he sat behind the wheel, as usual. We put on our seat belts and he powered up the engine with the vehicle lifting gently, into the air.

That was the good thing about owning a hover-car in Alaska; you simply glided over the boggy snow or dangerous ice. Because of this, people didn't need to be so fastidious about shovelling snow off driveways. Also, it meant less accidents on the road, too.

Once we hovered out of the external building, the garage door automatically closed itself. Declan reversed out of the snowy driveway, before he turned the vehicle mid-air, to cruise down the icy, steep road. We were both quiet as we left tribal lands and cruised through Alma, to reach the main highway. After giving away to the other vehicles, soon we were zooming towards Fairbanks.

"Why are we shopping in Fairbanks and not Alma?" I wondered.

“There are more baby stores there," he answered.

I folded my arms in front as I glared out the windscreen. Declan ignored my bad mood by switching on the Internet Radio and selecting a classic rock station, to listen to. Ironically, the first song that came on was ‘Wild Thing’ by The Troggs.

“Wild Thing, I think I love you..." he sung away, "...but I wanna know for sure!”

He switched the plasma-powered engine over to cruise control. I tried not to laugh at his singing and I had to cover my mouth with my hand, to hide my smile. However, he sprung me, as he rested his hand in my lap, whilst he continued to sing out of tune.

“Wild Thing, I think you move me... But I wanna know for sure... So, c’mon hold me tight... You move me.”

So what if I’m temporarily unemployed, being between identities right now? What the hell, I started to flick my head along to the beat as I 'chair danced'. Declan's large hand squeezed my thigh as we sang together.

“Wild Thing! You make my heart sing! You make everything... groovy. Wild Thing!”

In the old days it was a 1.5 hour drive to Fairbanks. But now with hover-cars cruising at speeds of 150 km/h, it only took us 45 minutes. During the drive, we happily bopped along to classics from the 1960’s, 70’s and 80’s.

As soon as we entered Fairbanks, Declan gave the GPS the command to list all the baby boutiques. Then he decided which one we'd hit first, before the GPS began to issue instructions on how to reach it. We had to turn down the music though, so we could hear the computer's directions.

We parked behind some kind of superstore called ‘Baby Universe’, which was advertised ‘to stock everything in the universe a baby would need’. It was supposed to have nursery furniture, clothes, equipment and everything down to biodegradable disposable diapers. As we walked through the car park to go inside, I observed it was still dark out.

We walked hand-in-hand through the sliding glass doors, when we both halted in surprise.

This place was HUGE! There was nursery furniture on display, as well as massive aisles full of clothes, toys, bottles, potties etc. If it was baby-related, it was here.

“Frickin’ hell..." Declan blanched, "...I think we’re gonna need a day, just to get through this one store.”

I grabbed a store scanner to record the barcodes of the large items we wanted. Then he led me by the hand, towards the furniture section.

“OK, what kind of furniture does a baby need?” He pondered. “I guess a cot is a must.”

“Um...yeah?” I shrugged.

Then I saw a country-style, wooden nursery setting I liked and when I started to walk to it, Declan pulled me back.

“Not wooden furniture," he frowned, “OUR baby would break it.”

“Oh,” I realized he had a point, so I looked around at what else was on offer.

“How about this one?” He pulled me in another direction, towards a stark, metallic, ‘modern art’ design.

Now I pulled him back. “It looks too penal code.”

“But it looks strong,” he debated.

As we looked around at the nursery layouts, I must admit I felt a little lost. I think Declan did too, as we stood together, turning our heads in a wide circle. I could tell this wasn't going to be an easy decision.

Next, he guided me over to a new setting. “How about this one? It looks wooden, but it’s really made of metal.”

I shook my head, "Too fake.”

“Well what about this one? It’s metallic but it looks more spacious.”

I shook my head again, “Too space cadet.”

“Then what about this one? It’s metallic but it’s curved in a kind of ‘The Jetsons’ design.”

“Too futuristic.”

“And that one?” He didn’t bother to move this time, he simply pointed.

“Too... cold.”

“Look B,” he took a deep breath to keep his temper down. "We can’t have wooden furniture and that’s that. As soon as our rug rat has a temper tantrum, the wooden furniture would be in pieces.”

I frowned as I pulled my hand back, so I could cross my arms.

It was at that moment, a sales girl wearing a ‘Baby Universe’ uniform, approached us. She looked just out of her teens, but I hoped she had experience. She too was carrying a store scanner, which also had a feature to scan credit cards.

“Hi, can I help you?”

“Please!” He cried out in relief. “We need metallic, nursery furniture, or even if it’s just a metallic crib.”

“Is this a present for someone who’s having a baby?” She asked.

“Nope, we’re the parents.” He answered.

"Oh," the girl looked disappointed by this, as she looked him over. "Er, congratulations."

"Thanks." I said flatly, before flashing him an unhappy look.

"Well you're in the metallic furniture section," the sales girl waved her arm. "Do you know what kind of look you're after, for the nursery?"

I explained, "Our house has a 'country' kind of feel, with a pine dining table and pine coffee table. Our bedroom suite isn't pine, it's a different kind of wood. I was thinking the nursery would follow suit."

"We can't have a wooden crib and that's that." Declan declared. "So let's look at metallic cribs then we'll look at wooden furniture, for the rest of the nursery."

"Good idea," the girl grinned, as her eyes moved over his tall, strong frame appreciatively. "We'll sort out the crib first and go from there."

What the...?! I found her subtle-as-a-sledgehammer attraction, vaguely insulting.

The sales girl had short, brown hair in a pixie cut and she looked barely 20 years old. I think she thought Declan was her age. Then here he is, rocking up with an 'older woman' he had knocked up, like he was trapped into being with me.

Just as I opened my mouth to tell her we'd be fine without her help, she spoke.

"I think we have what you're looking for."

Then she led the way towards a nursery setting on the far side. As she walked, she threw a couple more glances over her shoulder at the blonde stud by my side. I felt the growl build up in my throat, which he heard.

Declan said quietly, "Let's just see what she has to show us then we'll get rid of her."

"Does getting rid of her mean I get to maul her?" I asked through clenched teeth.

"Not in public," he snickered, as he retook hold of my hand.

However, what she showed us almost redeemed her behaviour.

She waved her arm once more towards a beautiful, metallic crib which was in the design of an antique, wrought-iron bed. The metal bars complimented perfectly the curved and decorated, metallic bed head. It came with an antique style, wooden chest of drawers with metallic ringed handles, an antique-style, wooden change table and even a wooden rocking chair.

"Oh Declan, this is it!" I cried out excitedly.

"Yup, we'll take it." He told the sales girl.

"Great!" She beamed. "You'd like both the crib and the nursery furniture?"

Declan looked upon my expression, before he said, "Pretty much."

"Awesome, I'll scan everything for you and charge it to your credit card." She said perkily.

The girl began to scan the pieces for us, as I walked over to examine everything. As she processed the sale, Declan pulled out his credit card for her to scan last. The nursery furniture was now ours.

"Would you like the furniture delivered, or will you be taking away the furniture kits today?" She asked next.

"We'll get the kits delivered," he instructed.

"When it's delivered, it comes constructed for you." She offered.

"Thanks, but I wanna build it myself," he shook his head.

"Sure," she smiled wider, as if she liked his answer, "so is this your first baby?"

"Uh huh," he answered, as he put his card back into his wallet.

"Is it her first baby?" She nodded my way whilst talking softly, so she didn't think I'd hear.

"Huh?" He gave a peculiar look.

"It's just that you look younger than her." She gave a teasing grin. "I'm guessing that this baby wasn't planned?"

His voice turned cold. "Why do you say that?"

"You look like you're still in College," the girl tittered. "What happened? Were you having a fling with an older woman and either yours, or her contraceptive injections lapsed? That happened to my cousin and her boyfriend. They were both late in getting their next injections and bam! She ended up having a termination."

My hands were shaking with fury, so much so, they started to rattle the side of the crib I was holding onto. My eyes stung as my face burned and I had to spin on my heel and stalk off, before I attacked that little bit of a sales girl! Hers and Declan's heads turned at my sudden exit, almost seeing the metaphorical steam, hiss out of my ears.

"You're new at this job, aren't you?" He asked icily. "Because you just talked yourself out of a huge commission, as my wife and I go elsewhere to buy the rest of our baby stuff."

Then she watched him follow me out the front doors, before she shrugged and moved on to serve another couple.

I stormed into the dark car park where Declan caught up.

"B...? B!" He grabbed hold of my arms.

"Let go of me, toy boy!" I growled out. "I'm going home!"

"Shhh..." he pulled me into an embrace, "...shhh."

"Let go of me, Declan!" I struggled to pull free.

However, he refused to break his stronger hold. Whilst he was holding onto me with one hand, his other began to rub my back. He tried to hold my gaze as he spoke.

"C'mon, don't let that silly little girl, who's over two hundred years younger than us, spoil our day." He tried to console. "I saw how happy you looked when we found the right furniture. Let's go to another store and finish our shopping."

"What a morning!" I started to cry. "First, I'm told by my older husband who now looks younger than me, that he looks like a kid beside me! Then my younger looking husband tells me, I can't make myself look older because it could harm the baby. Then my younger looking husband makes me quit my job, as well as my career in my current academic identity. Now I'm getting insulted, because sales girls think my younger looking husband, is trapped into being with me by pregnancy?"

I felt him chuckle as he stroked my hair, "Welcome to my world."

"What the hell would you know?!"

He pulled back to hold me at arms length, so he could meet my tearful glare. "Three months ago, I was an old man beside a young wife. Three months ago, I looked like a seventy year old man beside a twenty-something woman. People used to tell me I could get a Seniors discount, or tell my wife how sweet it was that she was taking her grandfather shopping!"

"But Declan, we're practically the same age -" I began my old assurances.

"Exactly B." He cupped my cold face between his warm hands. "I'm three years older than you and I aged and I nearly died. You changed me, so now we both look like we're in our twenties. I just happen to look like I'm in my early twenties, that's all."

"I don't want to look like the 'older woman'!" I turned away, to march towards our hover-car. "I don't care if I sound vain or if it was hard on you, when the roles used to be reversed! I don't like you looking younger than me!"

He turned me back around, to give a funny look. "Then why the hell did you make me look younger than you?"

"It was by accident!" I confessed. "I wanted to make you look the same age as me, not younger! But when we were in phase, I almost lost control because I'd never done it before. We almost evolved then and there!"

"We did?" His eyes widened by this news. "We nearly evolved then?"

I gave a tearful nod as my bottom lip quivered.

He asked in disbelief, "You mean after I almost died of old age, I could have come to, as a cloud of energy and light, floating in outer space?"

I nodded a second time as I waited for him to explode and yell, for nearly making him leave his biological existence without being asked.

"Oh..." he stared as his mouth fell open. "...no wonder you looked a little shaky that morning, with your aura fluctuating."

I looked down at the icy asphalt, "Go on, yell at me."

"Yeah you're right B, you do sound vain." He smirked. "I can put up with a century of you seen as my 'young bit of stuff', but you can't take three months?"

"No, I mean yell at me about the 'almost evolving' thing." I scowled.

“What’s to shout about?” He shrugged. “It would have been a bit of a shock, dying as biological life form and waking up permanently in phase, on my way to the space time continuum.”

I sighed wearily, “Let's just go home.”

“So you can hide on tribal lands, where everyone knows I’m older than you and not the other way around?”

“Yes.”

“OK, how about this; let’s drive back to Alma and finish the baby shopping there?” He offered as he pulled out his remote key. “We’ll visit the Bakery Café and buy an early lunch then we'll hit the baby boutiques.”

Typical, the male European Werewolf was thinking with his stomach.

It made me laugh back, "Why not...?”

Then Declan pulled me in for another hug, before he bundled me out of the icy air and into the warmer hover-car.

~~~~~~
~~~~~~

~ 9 ~

24th January 2364

I was in the kitchen making two cups of coffee, when I heard the door chime. It was 10.15 AM and outside it was still dark. During winter, from the 18th of November to the 24th of January, we experienced less than four hours of sunlight per day.

"I'll get it!" I yelled out.

Temporarily, I left the beverage preparation to answer the front door. I could smell whoever it was, wasn't Lokoti. When I opened it, I found I was right.

Standing under the porch light was a well-dressed man in his thirties, wearing a dark grey coat over his tailor-made, light grey suit. He had neatly cut, blonde hair and blue-grey eyes. He came complete with a platinum Rolex, which was peeking out underneath his sleeve, as he carried an expensive, black leather briefcase.

The stranger openly looked me over, standing there in my jeans, jumper and Ugg Boots, before he smiled.

"Mrs. Bianca Sabre?"

"Yes?"

"My name is Jonathan Bourne, I work in the legal division at the London office of Hodge Endeavor." He introduced in an English accent.

"Oh," I tried not to smirk, "no wonder you look like a lawyer."

"Quite." He smiled back. "May I come in? I have the documents you were waiting for."

"OK," I opened the door wider, for him to come in.

The human walked into my living room and I shut the door once he was inside. Just as he gave me a good stare, he openly examined my house. He seemed amused for some reason by the country décor.

"Jonathan Bourne," I recalled his attention, "you look like you're the kind of lawyer that charges hundreds of credits, by the hour." This made him chuckle and I continued, "So why did you come all this way, to Alaska in the middle of winter, instead of sending some lackey to do it?"

"I wanted to meet you." He spoke plainly. "I must admit, I'm rather surprised by your appearance and by the way you live. Why would the Head Chairwoman of one of the world's most successful companies, live as such?"

My hands moved to my hips in a defiant posture, "You care to elaborate?"

“I’m not on the Board of Directors, but I own three houses all of which are five times the size of this one.” He spoke brazenly.

“I like the little things in life,” I said coolly.

“You must.” He walked over to the dining table, to place his briefcase on top. He opened it as he went on, “You continue part-time work with your lectures and papers, instead of enjoying the benefits of what your position can afford.”

“Sounds boring,” I said flatly, "besides, I like to live quietly.”

“And stay out of the limelight?” He asked knowingly. I watched him take out several documents. “This is your new birth certificate, your new passport, your new driver's license, your new bank account, as well as your new credit cards.” He placed them all on top of the table. “As well as your new Bachelor of Arts in History, your Masters and your Doctorate from Cambridge University.”

I walked over to peruse through the papers and cards. “What of the identity of Dr. Bianca Baker?”

“We didn’t generate a death certificate." He declared. "A demise at the age of forty-six, would raise questions from the authorities. Instead, I left a paper trail that the former Professor moved to the off-world colony on Eurasia. If anybody asks, your PA will say that she retired from her academic career, to start a family. It will be in line with your recent cancellation at the University of Paris, with 'morning sickness' cited as the reason.”

Next, I watched him take out a small laptop from his briefcase. He switched it on, to show the electronic records. I saw how efficient he was, my previous I.D. for my last academic identity showed the off-world address instead of the Alaskan one. As did my old bank account details and so on.

“Good," I said impressed, "complete with a fake address?”

“Oh no," he shook his head, "fake addresses are too risky. Dr. Bianca Baker is living in a Hodge Endeavor owned house, on a tropical island. It just so happens to be the only house on the small island, so there are no neighbours to witness its unoccupied state. On that note, you could even use it as a holiday home, if you so wish.”

"Not bad,” a small smile escaped.

“Here is my card,” Jonathan handed me the small piece of fancy stationery. “You still have your PA at Hodge Endeavor of course, but should you get any uncomfortable questions about your old life or even the new? Or should you have any legal concerns, contact me directly. If I’m not in the office to take your call, my PA knows to forward you to my private line.”

My eyes narrowed, as I wondered why was he being so helpful?

“So you came to freezing Alaska to make yourself known to me?”

“Yes," he said simply.

“Why?”

He spoke plainly, “I was recruited by Hodge Endeavor straight out of Oxford. I put in many hours as I worked my way up. Now I’ve become the company's best lawyer and I will continue to prove myself. I was hoping that by doing this, I might become privy to the company's secret."

"The company's secret?"

"Why the Head Chairwoman maintains an anonymous position, whilst never making a bad investment yet." He smiled charmingly.

Since I didn't know him from a bar of soap, I kept my mouth shut.

Jonathan boasted, "I earned my first promotion by winning the gag order on the executive who was fired for corporate espionage. As you may recall, after he was fired, he tried to blackmail the company by going to the media with information on you. The court ruled in our favour and I took away his evidence. I earned my second promotion by successfully petitioning for the 'Anonymity Order', which protects the privacy of high-profile people. This in turn, stopped several members of the media from digging into your private life."

All of this did sound familiar, as I recalled the Circulate Mainframe mentioning them when it reported on notable events. The Mainframe also sent me emails to this effect, when it thought I should be made aware of something. However, the smart computer never said the name 'Jonathan Bourne', only that it monitored the legal department's work in each situation.

"So you came here to get another promotion?" I pondered.

"In a sense," he grinned. "I came to introduce myself and to prove my usefulness. I can see privacy is your highest priority, as your PA and the Board of Directors make every effort to this affect, as well. Your hold on the company is phenomenal and the rewards for the people who perform well, are astronomical. Yet here you are, living in a small, wooden cottage, in cold and dark Alaska, whilst your employees live better than you."

This made me laugh, "It's only cold and dark in winter."

Just then we were interrupted by Declan asking indignantly, "Who's this Jackass?"

Both of our heads turned to see him standing at the top of the staircase, glaring at the intruder.

I saw the two men were sizing each other up. The stranger stood there in his expensive clothing, as my husband wore his typical jeans, t-shirt and an undone, flannel shirt. Then he came down the stairs, so he could stand close to my side, to mark his territory. I could sense he wanted use his tall, strong appearance to intimidate the human. However, the lawyer didn't seem put-off, I caught him smirk at my husband's youthful features. I think he took him for a cocky college kid, or something.

I did the introductions, "Jonathan Bourne meet Declan Sabre."

"The husband and proud father-to-be," he rested his hand over my growing baby bulge.

"Ah, of course," Jonathan seemed to recognize his name somehow. "Please accept my congratulations over your happy condition."

"Thanks," Declan said stiffly, as he eyed him warily.

I moved the conversation along, by picking up my passport to show my husband. “Look, do you like my new name?”

He took it hold of it before he smiled, “Bianca Sabre!”

“I thought you'd like me taking your name again.” I planted a kiss on his cheek.

“Speaking of which,” Jonathan took out another large envelope from his briefcase. “I have the new documents for Mr. Sabre as well.”

“You do?” I said in surprise.

That’s strange, I hadn’t requested these...

“Here's your new birth certificate, driver’s license, passport, bank account and credit cards.” He handed them to my husband. “However, the age on these documents state you’re 29 years old, the same as your wife. Perhaps I should alter your date of birth, to reflect your appearance?”

“No," my mate said firmly, "if B is 29 years old, so am I. Besides, I’m really three years older than her, anyways.”

This made the human’s eyes widen but he was quick to reclaim his professionalism.

The lawyer continued, “Your previous balances in your old bank accounts will be transferred to your new accounts today. Then the old accounts with small amounts remaining to show they're still being used; will be transferred to a financial institution on Eurasia.”

“Huh?” Declan gave a funny look.

“Instead of ‘killing off’ my last identity, they’ve made it look like I’ve moved to an off-world colony, instead.” I brought him up to speed.

“But B,” he frowned, “why didn’t you tell me that you were ordering new ID for me too?”

“I didn’t,” I shrugged helplessly.

“That’s strange,” Jonathan frowned, "the order for the new documents came from the Board of Directors, which you preside over.”

“Oh, I get it,” I realized aloud, "the Circulate Mainframe did it.”

“The computer can do that?” Declan wondered at the technology.

“The Mainframe is always issuing commands and instructions, to the Board of Directors.” I told him, before I shot off an uncomfortable look towards Jonathan, who was listening in. “I have a personal computer that I give orders to, who in turn sends those orders to the Board.”

What I told him was half true, but I left out that most of the time it was the computer making those decisions for me.

Declan caught on that I didn’t want to share this with the stranger, so he went back to glaring at him.

“Of course," Jonathan straightened. "However the word ‘Circulate’, has come up before.”

This raised alarm bells inside my head, “It has?”

"The executive who tried to blackmail the company after his dismissal, said he had information pertaining to a secret society, who were the real controllers of Hodge Endeavor. He said they were called the Circulate."

"Did he just?" My mate growled out, making the human give a funny look. "Who is this guy and where does he live?"

"Declan!" I nudged him to keep a hold on his temper.

"The said individual was silenced with a gag order, whilst his assets were seized when we sued him." Jonathan said casually. "He is of no concern to you now."

"But where is he?" Declan demanded. "How do you know if he's keeping his trap shut?"

"We obtained permission from the European Police Force to tap his video-phone and computer, so we can monitor his calls as well as his emails. We also have a private investigator who observes him at regular intervals." He promised.

"I still think I should take care of this guy," my mate looked my way.

"Mrs. Sabre, if I may?" The lawyer tried to recapture my attention. "If this individual suddenly went missing, after all the media attention he initially attracted when we took him to court? It would bring more attention to this matter."

The European Werewolf started to growl threateningly at the human for his interference, when I whacked him on the arm to stop it.

"Of course you're right, Jonathan." I spoke again. "Besides, it's not like we're in the Mafia or anything, taking out people like that."

"Certainly not." He chuckled at the analogy. "However, it might be in your best interest if I become privy to words that you don't want the media to hear, so I can stop any untoward enquiries?"

"How about you pack up your things instead and I let you leave here in one piece?" My husband returned.

"Declan!" I blushed, as I whacked him on the arm a second time. I said embarrassed, "Sorry, my husband is very overprotective at the moment, from the pregnancy."

"It's understandable," the Englishman waved it off. "If I had a beautiful, intelligent wife, who was in charge of one of the world's wealthiest companies; I'd be clinging to her too."

I snickered at how he made Declan sound like my 'toy boy', but a low growl of displeasure, emanated from my mate.

"Thank you for the documents and for your efficiency, in the past." I rounded up the visit. "But you don't need to monitor the media for me, I have my own system. It's best that you don't know all of my affairs, right now."

"Very well." Jonathan gave a nod, before he closed his briefcase and picked it up from the table. "Thank you for seeing me this morning Mrs. Sabre, I won't take up any more of your time."

Declan walked over to the front door and opened it wide, as his non-violent means of kicking the lawyer out of the house.

But as he passed by, I said, "B."

"Pardon?" He paused, to look back.

"Call me B," I explained, "everyone calls me B, or those that know me. If your PA says 'B' called while you were out, you'll know to contact me on my private number."

Jonathan beamed at this, whereas Declan cleared his throat, to move him along.

"You'd better keep my card close in that case," he sounded pleased.

As he passed my larger husband, he gave him a wide birth though. Once the lawyer was through the front door, Declan slammed it shut! Then the incensed European Werewolf turned to give a glare.

"You don't need that leech looking after you." He said unhappily. "You have me as well as the pack, watching your back."

"I know this," I walked up to wrap my arms about his waist. "But as much as you guys are good in a fight; occasionally, we're going to need a lawyer to take care of other matters."

"He's an 'ambulance chaser', B!" He complained. "I heard him simpering to you, trying to ingratiate himself, when I was upstairs."

"I know." I shrugged again. "But I have one of my feelings, Dec."

"You've got a warning feeling about that guy?" His eyes bulged.

He looked like he was about to run after him, to maul the human.

I held him still, "No, I've got one of my tell-tale feelings which are saying we'll need him in the future."

Declan emitted another dissatisfied growl before he headed back upstairs. I walked over to the window and parted the curtains, to look outside. From the light of the veranda, I watched Jonathan Bourne walk over to a luxurious hover-car which was parked at the end of the driveway, complete with a driver. The man opened the back door for him as he approached. Then the lawyer hopped in without a second thought, as if he were used to this servitude.

What a toff! But I couldn't help but to smirk that he was 'my' toff, at my beck and call. I wasn't offended that Jonathan Bourne was 'brown-nosing' the Head Chairwoman of the company. He was bucking for more money and success, which could prove useful. But to be on the safe side, the next time I'm at Circulate HQ, I'll request that the computer keep an eye on him.

Lastly, I left the front window and dawdled back into the kitchen, to finish the coffees. Then I carried the mugs upstairs as I joined my husband in the second bedroom. I placed his mug by him on the floor, before I sat in similar fashion with mine.

"So, how are we going?" I asked.

Declan was sitting on the floor with our disassembled nursery furniture lying about. His tool kit was open beside him, with a pile of screws next to it. The instructions lay on the other side however, he barely glanced at them. His bloodlust detested being told what to do, even by a sheet of paper.

"I can see why these things usually come constructed, because machinery on a production line was meant to do this." He shook his head in frustration.

"What do the instructions say?" I queried.

My husband gave an incredulous look for asking such a thing.

"Look, give me the instructions and I'll see what it's going on about." I held my hand out.

Declan slapped the sheet of paper into it, as if he were happy to be rid of them. Then he asked unhappily, "So B, when were you going to tell me?"

"Tell you what?" I asked vaguely, as I was studying the picture diagrams. I even turned the paper upside down, to get a handle on what it was supposed to convey. "Hey, did you differentiate the screws?"

"Huh?"

"The screws, are they separated into small and large?" I replied.

I glanced at the pile which were mish-mashed together. Yet another growl escaped as he began to separate them. Whilst he organized the bits and bobs, he continued.

"When were you going to tell me about the kind of role you play, or even what the computer does, with Hodge Endeavor?"

"You know about the role I play." I said flatly. "You know I control the company via the computer."

"Then why the hell did that guy come here, to suck up to you?"

"You'd have to ask him that," I tried not to laugh, "but I think he'd call it, 'initiative'."

"Initiative?" He paused in his work, to flash a wary look.

"Sucking up to the boss to get more money and prestige." I spoke plainly. "Hey, do you need a hand with that?"

Declan had finished separating the screws and now he was trying to hold up both the base and the bed head at the same time. I left my place on the floor and held the pieces for him, so he could drill the large screws in. Once the bed head was done, I did the same for the bed end too.

"Now that I'm a Circulator, is the Circulate Mainframe going to start 'calculating' for me too?" He asked, petulantly.

"It's already started." I observed. "It ordered the new ID and bank details for you, didn't it?"

"Well tell it to stop." He said sourly. "Or I'll stop IT."

"Declan," I rolled my eyes, "it's a computer and it's programmed to look after us. It monitors the timeline and any changes we make to human history. It's meant to run Hodge Endeavor, to protect our assets. It's supposed to send requests to the company for help, should we be in trouble. Vincent spent years programming the computer, to act as my Calculator in his stead."

“B, I don’t like having a frickin’ computer doing things for me!” He snapped.

“Obviously!" I snapped back. "You don’t even like reading instructions on a piece of paper!”

"Hey, I don't need instructions telling me how to build a bed for my baby." He retorted. "Besides, I'm gonna have to get more screws from the garage, to reinforce the joints for our rug rat."

I sighed tiredly, “Declan please, don’t get all ‘princess’ on me.”

“Say what?” He looked on in amusement, for using one of his favourite taunts.

“I trust the Circulate Mainframe just as I trust you and the pack. I want you to trust the computer, too. Now that you’re a Circulator, you can give it orders just as I can. Hell, you can even tell Hodge Endeavor what to do via the computer.”

“I can?” He broke out in a grin. “So if I told the Circulate Mainframe to fire everyone at Hodge Endeavor, including that leech who was just here?”

“It would," I confirmed. “But it would warn if you’re making a bad decision, or how it would affect the timeline.”

“I can live with that," he chuckled, "now what’s next?”

Just as I turned to reach for the instructions again, I felt a jab in my left side. I opened my mouth to say ‘oow’, thinking it was a stitch, until I felt it again. It was coming from deep inside, rather than the outside.

“Declan, she kicked! She just kicked!” I cried out.

He dropped the drill and leapt to my side to place his hands on my abdomen.

“Did she hurt you?" He asked fearfully. "Are you alright?”

“I’m fine!” I gushed. “But this is the strongest I’ve ever felt her.”

Then I moved his hand to where I felt her kick last and we waited. After a full minute, we felt another jab. I looked on my mate amazed, as a silly grin overtook his face. He even laughed for some reason.

“Yeah, I’ve felt her before.” He admitted. “She’s pretty active at night, especially when you’re asleep. Last week you bitched at me, thinking I elbowed you when it was really her.”

“Huh?” I gave a funny look.

“I think it was last Tuesday night, when you were curled up in my arms. I felt her kick and so did you, but you thought it was me. You whined out ‘Deeeeclllaaaan!’ then you rolled over and went back to sleep.”

“Really?” I listened eagerly.

He saw that he had his wife's full attention, which made him go on.

“You can tell she’s my daughter, being the most active at night.” He patted my stomach. “When I felt her kick the first time, I thought I was imagining it. Then I kept my hand on your tummy and waited for fifteen minutes, until I felt her again.”

"Really, Declan? Really?" I giggled excitedly.

"Yup." He turned tender, as he looked down at his wife's ecstatic expression. "You're having my baby, Mrs. Sabre."

"We're having a baby, we're having a baby!" I started to chant.

"My B's having my baby!" He chanted along.

"Daddy Declan," I cupped his face, to pull him closer for a kiss.

"Momma B," he chuckled back, before his mouth engulfed mine.

~~~~~~

20th February 2364

I was nearly 16 weeks pregnant however, what concerned Ki was the foetus was already the size of a five month old. Declan and I weren't surprised though, we always knew Lucia would be different. My mate was just happy that her other European Werewolf tendencies weren't coming out, such as clawing at my womb. I was relieved that I didn't experience a common symptom in pregnancy, such as morning sickness.

Instead of experiencing nausea I'd have phenomenal cravings! They felt just as strong as the bloodlust during a full moon. Instead of feasting on fresh kill, I snacked more, or ate larger servings, or even drank more milk. My craving for dairy products ran at record levels, where sometimes I'd drink two litres of milk, a day! My husband would go to make himself a cup of coffee in the morning, but found he had no milk to put in it, since I drank it all.

Another strange thing about the pregnancy was a change in my hunting pattern. The bigger my stomach grew, the less I hunted. I didn't want to feast on flesh, but on cheeses, dips, or creamy foods.

Two nights ago it was a full moon and I told my husband to hunt without his wife.

His mouth fell open in surprise, "Say what?"

"I don't feel like hunting this month," I shrugged.

I was curled up on the couch by the fire, reading a history book.

"But B, it's a full moon! We get to kill things! Sure, it's not human, but beggars can't be choosers." He looked on like I was nuts.

As he protested, I noticed his leg jiggling restlessly. Even after three centuries, the European Werewolf never got bored of hunting. I guess his bloodlust wouldn't let him. He loved expanding into his beastly body and behaving like a monster. He'd run on all-fours in supernatural speed and tackle large animals, using his gigantic muscles. His bloodlust delighted in taking down his prey fighting. He's said they tasted better when they fought back.

"No, you go on without me."
~~~~~~

He began to strip in the lounge room for his change. However, he thought he'd check, "Are you sure you're sure?"

"Yes I'm sure," I promised, "happy hunting."

He removed all of his clothes under a minute then I watched his naked form depart via the front door. Through the front window, I saw him morph into his larger, stronger, dangerous body. When he was standing on all-fours, his glowing green eyes threw me a parting glance before he leapt into the forest.

After a couple of minutes, the rest of the pack wondered where I was. They were probably curious why my mate rocked up without his. I felt their concern and heard them with my mind:

WHERE'S AUNT B? - Forrest pondered.

SHE'S AT HOME, READING ON THE COUCH BY THE FIRE – Declan answered.

ARE YOU FEELING OK, AUNT B? – Ki asked worriedly.

DO YOU NEED US? – Caesar offered.

I'M FINE, GUYS. FEAST WITHOUT ME THIS MONTH. AS I SAID TO DECLAN, 'HAPPY HUNTING' – I thought back.

Our telepathic communication died down as they closed in on a small band of moose. Although they were over fifty kilometres away, I sensed as usual, Declan took on the strongest male. When his competitor collapsed, he ate alone. The rest of the pack shared three of the fallen females, up to four or five Werewolves per prey. Whereas the Lokoti could feed in a pack, the European's bloodlust, refused to share its kill.

I guess I was feeling a little restless, thanks to the full moon's impact on my brain chemistry. The later it grew, I didn't tire instead I got a rush of inspiration for my next paper. I put on my MP3 player and blasted my ears with Trance, as I moved to the dining table to write up some notes.

At 4 AM, my husband in his naked, human form, walked through the front door. He had blood on his hands and feet from when his claws tore his food apart. I could also smell blood around his mouth, from the flesh and bone crushed inside his massive jaws.

"You didn't wait up for me, did you?" He asked in surprise, to see me still up.

"Huh?" I had to remove the earphones, so I could hear him. "What did you say?"

He walked over to the table, picking up his clothes on the way. "What are you doing?"

"I'm writing up my next paper on 'Ancient Gods In Mediterranean History; Light vs Dark In Creation Mythology'." Then I lifted up my notepad to show him the pages and pages I'd written. "I got the idea tonight. It's fascinating, analyzing the different gods and goddesses and the roles they played in the creation myths."

“Uh huh," his eyebrows rose, as he glanced at all the open books, piled on top of the other. “B, I think this pregnancy has done something to your bloodlust.”

“I think you may be right,” I admitted. "I don’t feel tired, which I think is from the bloodlust. But instead of going out and killing something, it’s brought inspiration instead.”

“I’m gonna go have a shower," he implied his dirty and sweaty body. "How about you finish up and come to bed?”

“But I’m not tired," I shook my head. "I want to write a couple more pages.”

“OK, let's say that again...B you’re pregnant, so you tire easily. You may not feel tired, but I can see how puffy your eyes look, which shows me how tired you really are. Now, I’m gonna go shower and I’ll meet you in bed.”

“Declan, I am NOT tired!” I giggled at his behaviour. “You can shower and go to bed, but I’m staying up to write.”

I turned back to the books as he stood there, holding his clothes in one arm and stroking his chin with his other.

Suddenly, I felt my chair pulled back from the table and my body rise into the air, as he hoisted me up into his arms.

“Declan!” I squealed in laughter.

He roared like he was claiming me, just like he claimed his kill that evening. Then he carried me up the stairs and into the bathroom, to shower with him. Besides, I got my revenge later that morning...

We emerged from the bedroom around the middle of the day. Declan went to make his much-needed coffee, the morning after a hunt. Low and behold, there was no milk left. I overheard the snarling under his breath, on his way out the door to go buy some more.

Today it was my turn to leave the house however, it wasn’t to buy milk, but to buy more books.

I stood up from the bed with my boots done up, grabbed my handbag and departed. But as I was passing the second bedroom doorway, the sight made me pause. I smilingly looked on the nursery setting.

It was almost complete with the furniture built, the linen purchased and the chest of drawers had some baby clothes inside. We still had to buy a high chair, baby capsule, pram, as well as more baby clothes. But I patted my protruding tummy, as I thought to myself, ‘there’s still time’.

After a moment or two, I went downstairs. My husband was sitting at the dining table, preserving sun-dried tomatoes, marinating olives and other ingredients for antipasto, in the spare jars he'd accumulated over the years. He glanced up upon my approach and saw I was carrying my handbag.

He enquired, “Where are you off to?”

“I’m going to hit the bookstores in Alma,” I answered.

“Why don’t you just order the books, over the Internet?” He asked.

“I want to see if the bookstores have these particular titles first,” I shrugged.

“Wait a minute," he made me pause. “Can’t you just download them off the internet now, from the publishers’ websites?”

“Do you mean eBooks? With most you can, but not all. Some publishers still sell the information in hard copy, instead of electronic form.”

I pulled on my coat then I opened the front door, to be hit with the frosty air.

“Why don’t you stay home?" He offered. "You'll be warmer and you can talk to me, while I prepare the delicacies you enjoy eating, especially in your pregnant state. We'll work together, I preserve and you download.”

“The bookstore called ‘Dominion Of Knowledge’, has a huge history section.” I disagreed. “I’ll be back soon.”

I walked out onto the veranda when I heard him call out, “Have you got your phone on you?”

“Yes."

“Be home in an hour!” He ordered.

“Dream on!” I shut the door behind.

*****

It was nice getting out of the house even if it was for a little while. I parked the hover-car in the bustling, commercial centre of Alma. But before I hit the bookstores, I popped into a café to purchase a takeaway, hazelnut mocha, to drink while I perused. Mmm, hazelnut mocha's taste like liquid Nutella...yum!

After the first hour of shopping, my mobile phone alerted me to a text message.

IT’S GETTING DARK, WHERE R U? – Declan.

I rolled my eyes and sent back - IT’S WINTER, IT GETS DARK EARLY.

THANX 4 THE SEASONAL LESSON - he retorted - WHEN WILL U B HOME?

I’LL LET U KNOW, OR SO WILL THE SOUND OF THE HOVER-CAR POWERING DOWN ON THE DRIVEWAY – I replied.

After the second hour, I carried the bags of books I'd bought, back to my vehicle. It was only 3.30 PM and already the sun had set. The pale, starry sky of winter’s twilight, put the streets in a silvery glow.

When I climbed into the driver’s seat, my stomach rumbled and my mouth watered. I blanched, as one of my cravings, hit me full-force. The nails on my hands almost extended into claws, as my teeth sharpened.

I wanted to eat, no I just HAD to eat, smoked salmon. Yes, that's what my mouth is watering for; succulent, savoury, smoked salmon. Only, I don't think we have any at home. The batch we bought off someone in the tribe, ran out two days ago. Declan had put it into a creamy pasta dish, so I'd have to buy some more.

The hover-car powered up and instead of driving home, I parked behind the supermarket. I engaged the central locking, before I rushed into the large building. My mouth was watering so badly, I was worried I might change then and there!

That's all I need, my photo appearing on the World Wide News on Internet TV, as a drooling Lokoti Werewolf. I could imagine the caption underneath; PREGNANT WEREWOLF ATTACKS SMOKED SALMON IN REFRIGERATED SECTION.

Instead of using a hover-trolley, I grabbed one of the carry baskets, as I didn't expect to buy that much. But once I started shopping, my bloodlust urged me to buy more and more. Four packets of smoked salmon ended up in my basket, as well as several packets of rice crackers and two tubs of caviar dip. Just as I turned away, my eyes fell upon the cheeses...

Finally, I made it to the self-service check-outs. My carry basket was straining from the amount of food as I lined up. My foot tapped impatiently, all I wanted was to get out of there, go home and eat.

"Aunt B?"

My head turned to see Peta Sabre approach. She was married to Antonio, who was something like seven times removed from Declan. Antonio was one of Derik's progeny, my husband's late human brother. Peta and Antonio were the parents of Holly, who made the cute card for Declan's 300th Birthday Party, last year.

"Hi Peta," I held the bulging shopping basket next to my baby bulge.

"Are you OK?" She noticed the amount of food. "Would you like me to get a trolley for you?"

"No, it's cool." I blushed. "It's not heavy, it's just awkward to carry with a certain other weight."

She smiled in understanding, "When I was pregnant with Holly, my back and feet would ache something fierce! How's yours?"

"Actually, they're pretty good." I said. "Sometimes I get the odd twinge, but everything else is fine."

"That must be handy, being one of your kind," she hinted at my supernatural state. "Wendy told me that you don't experience morning sickness either, is that true?"

"Yeah, but there is a downside as well," I indicated my over-stuffed basket. "My cravings can get pretty bad."

She cracked up laughing, "So I can see! Um, would you like me to carry some things, for you?"

"Thanks Peta, but I'm fine." I reassured. "I'm stronger than you are, remember?"

“Of course," she rolled her eyes, jealously. “Anyways, I better let you go. Say hi to Uncle Declan, for me.”

“Take care," I gave a wave.

I watched her stand behind someone in the line for the self check-out, next to mine. Then the person who was ahead of me, moved off and I proceeded to process all my purchases. Once I was finished, I carried my groceries out to the car park.

It was then my phone rang with the call I'd been expecting for the past forty minutes.

My husband barked out, “B, where the hell are you?!”

“I thought I’d get some groceries on the way home,” I said calmly.

“If I’d known you were going grocery shopping, I'd have met you at the supermarket.”

“What?" I laughed at him. "I can go shopping by myself, Declan."

“Look, just stay there and I’ll come and get you.”

“Too late,” I sung, "I’m loading up the car.”

“B!”

“I’ll see you at home in fifteen minutes.”

“B, I don’t like you being in the supermarket's car park, after dark." He snapped. "I heard some lady was mugged there, late night shopping.”

“Declan, that happened a year ago and it’s only 4.20 PM!” I objected.

“Yeah, but it’s winter so the sun sets earlier.”

“Look, I’m trying to put the groceries in the boot." I huffed. "I’m going to hang up now and I’ll see you in fifteen minutes.”

Before he could object I hit the 'end call' button. I shook my head to myself while I put the phone back into my pocket. Then I put the last of the shopping into the vehicle as I contemplated my mate’s behaviour of late.

Man, this pregnancy hasn’t only brought out the nesting instinct in him, but his territorial tendencies are ten times worse! It’s like he's ready to tear out anyone’s throat who comes near his mate. It didn't just worry me, but I sensed it caused the pack some concern as well. Half of its members' were treading on egg shells around their grouchy Second.

After all the bags were in the boot, I closed the lid. But just as I started towards the drivers' door, I froze. My body tensed up as my eyes widened, by what was blocking the way.

An African American man with a dirty appearance, was leaning against my hover-car. He looked underdressed for an Alaskan winter, wearing only a black leather jacket over a stained white shirt, with muddy, black jeans. He came to stand directly in front with a hungry look in his bloodshot eyes.

In this situation, a woman let alone a pregnant one, might worry about a mugging or something else; being accosted in a dark car park. But what worried me, was that this man smelled dank and decrepit...

...meaning he was a Vampire.

As I sniffed at his half necrotized body, I pondered what kind of Vampire I'd stumbled across? He smelled unlike any 'fang head' I'd met before. He didn't have the stench of the European species, nor the stink of the South American one. I bet with my pheromones though, he knew I was a Werewolf. I just hoped that he didn't see I was a pregnant one, underneath my thick jacket.

He smiled with his sharp, dirty teeth, "Can I help you with your groceries, Miss?"

"It isn't miss, it's missus." I replied curtly.

Next, I looked around, worried about witnesses, in case I had to fight.

"Of course, especially with that 'bun in the oven'," he licked his cracked lips, whilst looking on my abdomen.

Frickin' hell, he can tell I'm pregnant! I sensed that not only did he find the idea of drinking from a Werewolf appealing, but a pregnant one made me seem like gourmet pâté on mini-toasts. I'd have to instantaneously phase home as I couldn't risk a confrontation, especially without my sword.

Just then another male Vampire stepped up from two car spaces away. Then a female Vampire popped her head up, three vehicles over. They thought they had me surrounded, as they stalked forwards in their dirty clothing. The second male had long red hair, whereas the female had a short, blonde bob.

The first 'fang head', chuckled evilly, "We can do this the easy way, or the fun way."

To which the second agreed, "Please kick up a stink and make us drag you from here."

Then the female smiled, "Please beg mercy, for your unborn child."

As she grinned, her snake-like fangs grew in size, before she made a hissing noise.

"A pregnant female Werewolf, do you know how rare you are?" The first 'fang head' looked me up and down. "We ate a pregnant human last week, but we haven't eaten Werewolf, male or female, in years."

"Not since we took down that North American mongrel, in Wyoming," the second chimed in.

At that moment, a hover-car pulled into a space nearby and powered down. I watched a man step out, lock his door behind then walk towards the supermarket. I didn't want to call for help, as I knew the Vampires would make a meal out of him, if I did. But I was waiting for the witnesses to depart, so I could disappear in a bright flash of light.

"But you're a different breed we haven't come across before," the first continued.

The female came closer, as she stared at my stomach. "How far along are you? Five months, maybe six?"

"The baby will be just big enough for us to tear out and eat separately." The second smiled broadly, whilst allowing his two fangs to extend.

I watched their eyes begin to glow a reddish-yellow colour, as their foreheads changed to take on demonic ridges. The first proceeded to hiss at me with his snake-like fangs, whilst the other two moved in to flank him. As the three came closer, I saw their dirty nails also extend in length.

That's it, I've seen enough to report to the pack. I was prepared to instantaneously phase out of there, when an inopportune witness stumbled by. Talk about the wrong place at the wrong time!

"Aunt B, are you alright?" Peta called out.

She was pushing her hover-trolley into the car park when she saw the three strangers close in on my position.

"Er, fine thanks Peta!" I lied to make her go away.

But she took one look at their glowing reddish-yellow eyes and fangs, when she whipped out her mobile phone.

"Hello, 911?" She began, but was too late...

In a lightning fast move, the female Vampire rushed up and picked her up by the throat! As Peta's feet wavered in the air, her attacker crushed her phone in her claw-like hand. The broken technology clattered onto the icy asphalt.

Frickin' hell, not Peta! She's just an innocent bystander! Now what do I do?

"Leave her alone!" I called out. "Look, I'll come with you. Just put her down and leave her out of this!"

"Where would be the fun in that?" The second male grinned menacingly.

I took a deep breath as I readied to run in light speed over to Peta's position. I'd have to knock the female Vampire off her and instantaneously phase her home with me. It would give away the fact of Circulators existing, but what choice did I have? However, things grew worse when we were interrupted by another voice:

"Hey, what's going on here?!"

Another shopper had come out of the supermarket, when he caught sight of our kafuffle. He saw the males corner me, whilst the female choked Peta. Oh no, not another witness!

"Now this is more like it!" The first 'fang head' laughed, with his two long teeth hanging over his bottom lip.

"Turn around and run you idiot!" I cried out in frustration.

Instead, the man stopped and stared at the three Vampires glowing eyes, demonic ridges and fangs.

"What kind of drug addicts are you three?" He gave a peculiar look.

Next, he too started to take his phone out of his pocket...when the second Vampire rushed up and grabbed him about the throat too! His phone fell to the ground as well, as he sputtered helplessly. Then the female choking Peta, saluted the male who was choking the other human, in a 'cheers!' gesture.

As things went from bad to worse, I saw I was going to have to call for back up.

VAMPIRES IN ALMA! – I thought to both my mate and the pack - *VAMPIRES IN ALMA HAVE ACCOSTED TWO HUMANS! ONE OF THEM IS PETA SABRE!*

WE'RE COMING - Caesar immediately replied - *INSTANTANEOUSLY PHASE HOME NOW!*

I CAN'T, THEY HAVE HOSTAGES! – I thought frightenedly.

Then I thought of using the fact that I had backup against my attackers.

"Look, just let the humans go and you'll live. You have no idea of who my mate is! As soon as he sees you encroaching on his territory, he'll rip your heads off!"

"You're not alone?" The first 'fang head' stepped up closely. "Guess what, neither are we! We were sent to bring you in, which would lure the male Werewolves to us when they try to rescue you."

I blanched, as I wondered how they'd heard of the Lokoti Werewolves? We were a well kept secret, except when we're accosted in car parks, with witnesses stumbling onto the scene. However, the scenario became a lot more noticeable, by who next appeared.

Suddenly, we were interrupted by the loud sound of metal crunching and glass breaking. It sounded like several of the vehicles in the car park were being crushed! When our heads turned at the ruckus, what we saw made the humans and vampires stare in terror, but filled me with a sense of pride.

A huge, hulking, hairless European Werewolf, bounded towards us on all-fours. He leapt from hover-car to hover-car, galloping over the vehicles. The tops of the hover-cars crumpled at his great weight, thanks to his muscle bulk and hardened hide. His glowing green eyes, were trained our way as his razor sharp jaws, were open and ready.

"Holy mother of..." the first 'fang head' started to utter, but didn't have a chance to finish.

Quickly, I ducked and my mate sailed over my crouched form, to land on both the male Vampires at the same time. His greater strength coupled with his larger jaws, were more than a match. Soon Vampire blood was splattered over the sides of the hover-car, as well as over the icy asphalt.

I backed away, whilst simultaneously pulling the man free from the second Vampire's hold. The 'fang head' could hardly protest, with his face being eaten through. I dragged the human several meters away, to sit on the ground gasping from his bruised neck. Then I turned on the female Vampire who was still holding Peta.

The female 'fang head' was looking on in horror at her cohorts' demise. My eyes glowed turquoise, my nails and teeth extended, as my body began to bulk up, for battle. She noticed my change and finally dropped her hostage, to take me on. We circled the other whilst Peta rolled away, gasping for breath.

First, she swiped at me with her long, sharp nails, but I easily wove between her blows with my light speed reflexes. She tried to claw me again and again, but missed every time. Lastly, she hissed in frustration and prepared to leap on top of me...

...when she went flying backwards instead from a European Werewolf, leaping on top of her.

"Declan, that's MY kill!" I growled out, in my changed voice.

CHANGE BACK B, THAT'S AN ORDER! – He mentally commanded.

Then I saw why, as a small crowd was assembling just outside the supermarket's entryway.

Hastily, I turned around as I reverted to my human appearance. When I looked back with my dark blue eyes, I saw the crowd hadn't noticed my transformation. They were all pointing at Declan's monstrous form, instead.

The female 'fang head' tried to scream, but her cries were cut short. The wet, crunching sound of him eating through her skull, made the humans wince. In several chomps, he devoured skin, bone and brain. Within a matter of seconds, she was headless, with just a bloody stump of a neck remaining.

"What is THAT? Is it a bear?" One onlooker, cried out in fear.

"It's a mutant, hairless, albino, grizzly bear!" Another witness, agreed.

The European Werewolf rose from his third victim – slash – meal and snarled warningly at the humans. It did exactly what he wanted it to do, it frightened them back inside. Then he stood on all fours, as he surveyed the scene of a saved mate, a rescued relative and three deceased attackers.

I'LL SEE YOU BACK AT HOME – I telepathically told my husband.

I watched him bolt out of the car park in his monstrous form, past the mangled bodies of my assailants. Their remains lay there on the cold, hard ground without their heads. Around the partially devoured bodies was blood spatter, bits of skull and brain, as well as small bloodied tufts of hair.

THE VAMPIRES ARE TAKEN CARE OF – I overheard Declan's thoughts to the pack - *DON'T COME TO B'S POSITION IN WEREWOLF FORM, AS THERE ARE TOO MANY WITNESSES.*

I knew why he told me to change back to human; because I'm the only female Lokoti Werewolf, I could easily be identified. I let out a sigh, seeing the after effects of the fight I wasn't permitted to partake in. Then I turned to check on Peta Sabre, as I helped her to her feet.

"I'm OK," she wheezed, from her sore throat. "I'm still trying to catch my breath."

"Same here," the man agreed, as he sat a short distance away. Together, the humans looked around in shock at the dead bodies. "What was that thing that attacked us?"

"Drug addicts looking to steal credit cards, I suppose," I tried to lie, until I realized they were talking about Declan.

"Was it my imagination, or did a hairless, mutant, grizzly bear, eat our attackers then run off?" The man coughed out.

“It WASN'T your imagination," she rubbed her sore neck.

These two just barely escaped with their lives from three thirsty Vampires. Instead of talking about them, they're pondering the creature who saved them? I don't understand humans, sometimes.

“Are you alright, Aunt B?” She looked me over. “What did those three people want with you, anyway?”

“I'm guessing they were drug addicts, who thought they could mug the pregnant lady in the dark car park.” I tried to shrug it off.

“Man that girl was strong!" She remarked. "I've heard of drugs making people stronger from an adrenaline rush, but did you see her eyes?”

“The same with that guy," the man agreed with her, "it must have been one hell of a 'high', to make their eyes like that.”

Then we were interrupted by the sirens of two police hover-cars arriving. The car park was soon lit up by flashing red lights. Meanwhile, the people who had rushed back inside of the supermarket, all came out again, to gawk at the crime scene.

The police hover-cars were soon joined by two more, before a black coroners vehicle arrived, to take away the bodies. As the officers used their forensics scanners to record the evidence, I tried to stand away, so I wouldn't be. When an ambulance also arrived on the scene, I politely refused to be seen to, as I was wary of their medical scanners too.

Man, it's a bitch being a Werewolf in the 24th Century. Everyone is just so accustomed to scanning everything. This was an inconvenience when one was a supernatural species, trying to keep their existence a secret. Our Shape Shifter DNA would be picked up, if we were scanned at the cellular level.

I was standing off to the side, telling my version of events for a third time to a Detective. Momentarily, I looked away as he made notes in his PDA; when I saw Declan, along with Caesar and Ki, appear. All three were in human form, looking anxious to see me. However, police tape and several officers blocked them when they tried to come to my position.

“You have to stand back behind the perimeter," a female officer, ordered.

“That's my WIFE over there!” He growled in protest.

“Declan!” I waved his way, before telling the Detective, "that's my husband and relatives.”

He gave a nod to the policewoman and she lifted up the tape, to allow the men through. Declan rushed forwards and engulfed me in his arms.

“B!” He held me at arms length, to look me over. “Are you OK?”

“I'm fine.” I told him, before I looked at the other two. I let the three in, on the story I was using. “It was just an attempted mugging, that's all.”

“That's an interesting way to down play it," the Detective smirked. "Your wife is leaving out the wild animal attack, which followed.”

“A wild animal attack?” Caesar asked obligatory.

“Eyewitness reports have the animal as a large, mutant, hairless, albino grizzly.” The Detective checked his notes on his PDA. “This is going to be fun, to take to the Federal Wildlife Services. We're going to run a search of the Lokoti, Denali and Matanuska National Parks, for the creature.”

“We can help you with that, Detective.” Caesar said smoothly. “If there is such an animal, our people who work as Rangers inside the Lokoti National Park, will track it.”

“I'd believe that," the officer said appreciatively. “You guys never have a problem finding a missing hiker or camper, in your neck of the woods.”

“Can we take B home and out of the cold?” Ki asked the Detective.

“We still have a couple more questions and the paramedics would like to check her out.” He replied.

“I don't need to be checked out by the paramedics!” I objected for my fifth time.

“Pregnant women's mood swings, don't you just love it?” Declan tried to laugh it off.

“I'm a Medicine Man and I'm seeing to her, through her pregnancy. I can make sure she's taken care of. I'm the only medical practitioner she trusts in her delicate condition.” Ki advised.

Declan looked on the Detective like he would be doing him a huge favor. “C'mon man, let me take my pregnant wife home and get her out of the cold.”

He let out a reluctant sigh as he relented, “Alright, I'll release Mrs. Sabre into yours and the Medicine Man's care. She's been through a lot tonight, it's best she's taken somewhere warm, especially when in shock. But she's going to need to be available for further questioning.”

“We'll see to it.” Ki nodded, as Declan held me closer.

However, when he tried to escort me to the passenger's side of our car, the Detective interrupted.

"You can't drive your vehicle home."

“Why not?” My husband gave a peculiar look.

“It's part of a crime scene, Mr. Sabre," the Detective said staunchly. “Your car is covered in evidence. The victims' blood are all over the side and back panels.”

“Oh," he acted like the sound of blood turned him off. I guess he had to, since he was responsible for putting it there.

“But the groceries are still in the boot -” I started to complain.

“Can we get the shopping out of the car?” Caesar asked.

“That should be OK, but don't touch the vehicle. We don't want to contaminate it with further traces of DNA," the officer warned.

We watched the Detective snap on a pair of latex gloves before he escorted us to our vehicle. Declan hit the remote key to open the boot then the policeman passed he, Caesar and Ki, the groceries. Before we departed, the

Detective gave me his card and the final instruction should I remember anything else, to call him. Otherwise he said, he'd see me in a couple of days.

Declan carried a bag of food in one hand and held mine, in his other. Caesar and Ki carried the other two shopping bags, for me. Then I left with my mate and kin, as they escorted me from the scene.

As we walked past the ambulance, Declan shot a look towards Peta. She was being checked out by paramedics when she noticed his gaze. She gave him a nod, to show she was OK then mouthed the words, 'thank you'. Tonight was only the second time she'd seen her Great x7 Grand Uncle in his frightening form. I think it still unnerved her, but she knew it was because of him that she was alive.

The police lifted the tape to let us pass then we walked quickly through the crowd to Caesar's hover-car. I felt antsy and just wanted to run away from the police, their scanners and the staring people. But I also wanted to tell the men that the three Vampires had a coven, nearby.

Caesar hit his remote to open his boot in which they put the bags of food. Then he and Ki sat up the front with Declan and I in the back. As soon as our First sat down at the wheel, he powered up the vehicle.

"Damn it!" I cried out, when the vehicle rose into the air. "My books are still in the car!"

"The books won't go off like the food would have, B." My mate said flatly, as he glanced out of the rear window. "You'll get the books back when I get my car back."

The hover-car glided down the main street and towards the outskirts of town. However, I noticed how tense the men were, as they continuously looked about. It was quiet inside the vehicle as we drove out of town and headed towards tribal lands.

"Guys, I have to tell you something." I leaned forwards in my seat. "The Vampires said that they weren't alone. I think their coven is nearby. They said they were sent to bring me back, to the others."

However, that didn't get the reaction I thought it would. Declan remained quiet although alert, as he looked out the windows. It was Caesar who finally acknowledged what I had said.

"We know, Aunt B." He spoke calmly. "When Uncle Declan ran to you tonight, the rest of the pack scouted the outskirts of Alma. We've tracked the North American Vampires to an unused building, on the edge of town."

"North American Vampires, so that's what they are?" I echoed. "I wondered why they looked different to the European or the South American species, we've seen in the past."

Nobody said anything else, as our driver pulled off the highway and onto the smaller road which led onto tribal lands. I thought the atmosphere was quiet in a way that was suffocating, as if something else was going on that I wasn't aware of. Then something clicked inside my mind...

"Hang on, why are we driving home? Why aren't we going to join the rest of the pack who I assume, are staking out the Vampires' nest?" I wondered.

"We're taking you home first," Declan said simply.

"Oh, to get my silver sword? Good idea." I thought aloud. "I hated facing off those fang-heads tonight without my Katana. Then I'll instantaneously phase us back into Alma."

This was met with further silence which I thought was strange.

The hover-car cruised up the steep hill, all the way to the top where our house sat. As soon as the vehicle powered down on the snowy driveway, I hopped out. Next, I rushed up the veranda steps and hurriedly unlocked the door.

Once inside, I raced up the stairs and into the bedroom, to fetch my silver-coated weapon. I picked it up in its sheath before heading back downstairs. I put the belt over my shoulder as I went, to carry the sword on my back.

When I returned, I found the men were calmly putting away the food, into either the fridge or pantry.

"OK, let's go." I tried to move them along.

It was then that Ki cast an awkward look at his First and Second, as if he were waiting for them to say something.

"B, you're not going," my mate said.

"What do you mean, I'm not going?" I almost laughed. "I'm a Circulator who can fight with the speed of light, which is necessary when fighting Vampires."

"You're also fifteen weeks pregnant," Caesar said sternly.

Then the men all walked out of the kitchen and over to the dining table. There, they started to kick off their shoes and remove their upper clothing. Whereas Ki and Caesar could keep their jeans on, Declan had to completely strip. No fabric lasted long on his huge, hulking body.

"Guys, it's OK." I tried to reassure. "When I'm sword fighting, the 'fang heads' won't be able to get close enough to get their teeth into me."

This was met by more silence, as again Ki looked at Declan and Caesar, to say something. The Lokoti Werewolves wore just their jeans but my mate seemed to hesitate in taking off his. His eyes were fixed on the sight of the sword on my back, coupled with my protruding stomach.

"You can take that sword off B, because you're not going." He said curtly.

"Excuse me?" My hands moved to my hips. "Who died and made you Ruler of the Earth?"

"B, we don't have time for this and you're NOT going!" Declan barked.

"Fine, I'll instantaneously phase without you and beat you there!" I challenged.

My bloodlust boiled at being treated like this! Who did they think they were talking to, a weak woman or another Werewolf? There was no way I was going to miss this fight.

I stomped past the table where they were standing. It was then that I felt Declan's arms close around, to hold me back. I opened my mouth to yell at him to let go, whilst preparing to instantaneously phase out of his grasp. Then a sudden, sharp pain erupted in the back of my neck...

...and I don't remember much else after that...

...one minute I was walking towards the door then my neck got a spasm and I blacked out. I didn't feel my legs anymore, nor do I remember hitting the floor. I passed out so quickly, I wasn't even sure if I fainted or not.

Darkness - complete and total blackness - that's all that I recall.

However, in the outside world, Declan was holding me upright in his arms. His mouth moved away from the back of neck, leaving a bite mark in its stead. In one heave, he scooped me up and carried me over to the couch that was closest to the fire.

Gently, he laid me out, even fixing a cushion behind my head to rest upon. Then he straightened and looked on my unconscious form, whilst he dropped his jeans. Lastly, he turned and walked naked out the front door, with Caesar and Ki, walking behind.

"Uncle Dec, you and Aunt B really should consider 'couples counselling'." Our Medicine Man cast a concerned glance my way, before closing the front door. "In a normal marriage, husbands and especially father-to-be's, DON'T knock their pregnant wives unconscious, when they want them to stay home."

"Shut up, Ki." He growled, as he walked out into the freezing night air.

On the veranda, the Lokoti Werewolves shape shifted first. The nails on their hands and feet turned long, hard and claw-like, as their teeth grew longer, sharper and jagged, jutting out of their mouths. Caesar's eyes glowed a blue colour, as Ki's glowed pink. Their upper bodies bulked up with extra muscle, which supplied their supernatural strength.

The European Werewolf stood by himself on the snowy driveway, as his height began to increase as did his width. His bones made soft cracking noises, as his skeleton expanded into a larger, canine shape. His transformation came complete with a short, stubby snout over razor sharp jaws. He fell forwards to stand on all-fours, as his hips and shoulder joints were manipulated into place. His hands and feet turned into claws, as his eyes glowed green, with his circular pupils turning into narrow slits. His human skin was replaced by a tough hide, over his hardened muscle bulk, which rippled as he moved.

In this shape, Declan was not only faster than the Lokoti Werewolves, but he was twice as strong. However in his role as Second, he dutifully waited in the snow for his First to step down from the veranda. Then Caesar leapt into the woods and ran in supernatural speed, back into Alma, to rejoin the rest of his pack. Declan and Ki ran after him on either side, flanking their First.

*****

I felt warm and also like I was lying down on something soft. I expected to wake up and find myself on the floor, where I thought I had fainted, but I didn't. I opened my eyes and waited for them to focus, before I realized I was lying on a couch in the living room. I felt warm because I was lying on the one closest to the fireplace, which was my favourite seat during winter.

Just as I turned my head, a sharp pain shot up my neck. Man, my neck is sore! It felt like a pinched nerve or something. I groaned, as my hand moved towards it, to try to massage the pain away.

"You want an icepack?" I heard Declan ask.

I tried to turn my head, but I couldn't as it hurt too much. Instead, I had to peek from the corners of my eyes, to find him sitting on the other couch, reading a book. He smelled soapy, like he'd showered and I think he was wearing a change of clothes.

Then I saw him put aside his book, before standing up and leaving the lounge area. I heard him walk into the kitchen and open up the freezer. Then he returned to stand over me, whilst wrapping a tea towel around it. He sat down on the side of the couch I was lying on, to carefully lift up my head and place the icepack behind my neck.

"Here we go," he said softly.

"Oow oow oow!" I whimpered, as my pinched nerve objected to any kind of movement. However, as soon as my head was lowered, with the icepack resting against the sore spot - bliss! "Oh thank you... that feels good."

Declan remained by my side as he looked on in concern. One of his hands rested over the baby bump, as his other began to stroke my hair. His blue eyes looked wide with worry, which I thought was sweet.

"W-w-what happened?" I managed out. "Did I faint or something? Did I knock my head when I fell? Or did I twist my neck when I landed?"

"I knocked you out."

"Huh?" I blinked, thinking I had misheard. "What happened?"

"I bit you on the back of your neck and knocked you out."

What the...?! My eyes widened as I focused on his face. Was he kidding around? From his earnest expression, I thought perhaps not.

"Say that again," I said.

"You heard me."

"Hang on..." I pushed his hands away, "...I thought I heard you say that you knocked me out?"

"I did say that I knocked you out."

He didn't look remotely guilty. His expression said it all, he wasn't ashamed of what he'd done. I bet he wouldn't be adverse to doing it again, either.

"You did what?!" I tried to sit up when the sharp pain became blinding! "Oow oow oow!"

"Woah there," he gently pushed me back down, "take it easy, B."

He even repositioned the icepack for me again.

“It’s your fault that I’m in this condition!" I flared.

“Yeah whatever," he said dismissively. “If you weren’t as stubborn or as stupid as a horse’s ass, I wouldn’t have to.”

“What?!” My voice grew shrill, which I knew bothered his sensitive ears. He even flinched from the noise, as I carried on. “You frickin’ knocked me out?! Your own frickin’ wife?! To stop me from – from -”

But then I paused, to try to see the clock on the wall.

Anxiously I asked, “What’s the time? How long have I been out for? What about the Vampires?”

“It’s 3.23 AM and all the 'fang heads' are dead," he said simply.

“What?” I gave a funny look. “What do you mean all the Vampires are dead?”

“We fought them in their hide-out and afterwards, we buried their mutilated corpses in a mass grave inside the National Park.” He said perfunctory.

“How many were there? Is everyone alright? Are you OK?” I asked worriedly.

He smiled on my fears for his safety.

“There were seventeen North American Vampires at the hide-out and everyone is fine.”

“Well you won’t be, as soon as I can move again!” I whacked him on the arm! He jolted from the impact as I flinched from the jarring to my neck, before I ranted. “You bastard! You complete and total bastard! You frickin’ knock your wife unconscious and fight seventeen more Vampires without me? You were outnumbered and you could have used my help!”

“Oh could we just?” He arched his eyebrows. “Ask me how many 'fang heads' I killed tonight, B.”

“No!”

“Ten! Altogether, I killed ten 'fang heads' tonight! After the three that attacked you in the car park, I killed seven more at the hide-out! It was like I was unstoppable. With my European Werewolf strength and my new Circulator speed, I WAS unstoppable!”

“Declan, you’re NOT unstoppable! That’s just your gigantic ego, talking." I rolled my eyes. “If push comes to shove, I’m still faster than you.”

This gave him pause, “What do you mean that you’re faster? As soon as I learn how to instantaneously phase -”

“That’s not it," I closed my eyes and took a deep breath, as my sore neck was bringing on a headache. “Your ability comes from me, so you'll be able to instantaneously phase one day. But my bio-electromagnetic frequency is still higher than yours. We can both move in light speed, as well as turn ourselves into light, but I'll always be faster than you.”

“What? Why?” He looked offended by this.

"I don't know, it has something to do with our frequencies." I sighed, before I gave him a glare. "So you're NOT unstoppable Declan Sabre!"

"Oh yeah? Well, I'm a damn sight stronger than you!" He said indignantly. "Plus, those North American Vampires were stronger than the European ones we encountered in the past. There was no way in hell I'd put you against that, pregnant or not!"

"Declan...!" I moaned, as I rubbed my face. "Why can't you see the light that's shining on your face?"

"Why can't *I* see? Why can't *you* see, B? You're my frickin' mate! You're MY B! If anything looks at you wrong, I'll frickin' end it! No matter how much you jump up and down and squawk about women's liberation, or whatever? I'm frickin' stronger than you and that's that!"

My headache was starting to make my head pound, as I tried to massage my temples and take several deep breaths to calm down.

"Declan, you're not 'Superman'. Besides, we're supposed to be equals. I didn't turn you into a Circulator to make you better than me, just as I've never seen you as less than me."

"Less than you? You'd never see a European Werewolf look less than anything! We dominate over everything!" He scoffed. "Wait here, I'll go get you some Ibruprofen."

He stood up from the couch and left the lounge room again. I heard him open up the fridge as well as a couple of cupboards, in the kitchen. Then he returned with a glass of water and two tablets. He placed the medication inside my mouth, before raising my head, to help me drink it down. Once I was finished with the glass, he put it on the coffee table and then sat beside.

"If you dominate over everything, what do you call this?" I smirked.

"Shut up." He snickered back. "Besides this isn't servitude, this is protecting my territory."

"Oh yeah?"

"I can't have you sick or injured, or it's no fun when I dominate you...or try to." He gave a wink as his hand returned to my enlarged abdomen. "If you ever stopped fighting back, I don't know what I would do. So please don't make me go looking for another argumentative female."

"If you like it when I fight back, why did you knock me unconscious?" I glared again.

Declan let out a loud sigh, before gazing back down into my eyes. "Because when you disobey a command that's issued for your safety, you scare me."

"Even if the command is unfair?" I raised my eyebrows. I was going to say more, but he interrupted.

"I like it when you bite back during sex. I like it when you snap back, when I tell you to do something. I like it when you yell at me. But I don't like it, when we say, 'don't go near the dangerous Vampires' and what do you do? You're either injured, or you're nearly injured, when you go near the dangerous Vampires."

“Declan that happened ONCE!" I objected. "The first time I fought the 'fang heads' on our European vacation, I won that fight! The second time in Scotland, you would have run right onto that silver knife, if I hadn’t of taken that fang head down with me.”

However, my argument was like water off a duck’s back. Declan didn't look affected by my words, his head was turned in another direction. He even stroked his chin, as if he were contemplating something.

“To hell with it!” He growled out. “Look, I have to tell you something. I think I had my first ‘all-knowing feeling’ as a Circulator today and it was a bad one.”

“You did?” I asked in surprise. “What did you feel?”

He stared into my eyes, “I sensed you were in danger as soon as you came downstairs with your handbag. When you were out for so long, a sickening feeling overtook my stomach. When I called you as you were leaving the supermarket, the sickening feeling turned into this horrible, darkness inside. It felt like my blood turned cold and I'd already started to undress, before we got your call for back up.”

“You did?” I stared back in bewilderment.

“I ran to the supermarket in light speed, I didn’t care about being seen. I’m hoping that I just looked like a bright blur to the passers-by. When I arrived at the car park and I smelled the decrepit stench of those half-dead murderers surrounding you; I literally saw red. B, they weren’t just attracted to your aura as a Circulator, or your Lokoti Werewolf pheromones. But they wanted the baby inside you, the baby I put in there.” He stroked my abdomen.

“Oh Declan, I know.” I murmured, placing my hands over his.

“And since it’s a female you’re carrying, Lucia is going to have just as much trouble as you’ve had. Vampires are going to try to feed off her, or male Werewolves will try to claim her, or if she has the same pheromones you do? All the boys in Alma will be knocking on her door.” He gave a rueful grin.

“I don’t care, I’ll teach her how to fight.” I said stubbornly. “She won’t be made helpless by the world we’re bringing her into, Declan. My daughter may not be a Circulator, but she'll have our strength. I'll train her to become a strong and independent woman.”

He entwined his fingers with mine, as he grinned, “And this is where I love it when you fight back.”

We exchanged soft smiles before he turned serious again.

“I’ll be right beside you B, teaching my daughter with you. But please, give me some small benefit of doubt? If I say she can’t do something because she’s part European Werewolf; then believe me. If I say something is too dangerous for Lucia or even for you; then take my word for it.”

I turned quiet as his words sunk in. He sat there, stroking my large tummy as his eyes shone with love. Just this once I'll let him win, since his first gut instinct as a 'Light Person', turned out to be true. I also liked the idea that his 'all-knowing feeling' was for the safety of his mate and young.

“Oh alright," I groaned, which made him chuckle at my reluctance. "You win this round."

"I'll put it on the scoreboard," he joked.

“But because it's YOUR fault that I can't move properly and I’m tired and I wanna go to bed…?”

I didn’t have to say another word, as Declan scooped me up into his arms, stood up and carried me upstairs. Carefully, he laid me on top of the bed, before changing me into my pyjamas. He acted so considerate, I almost forgave him for putting me into this position – almost.

He stripped down to his boxer shorts and came to bed too. When I rolled over, adjusting my pillow, I used it to whack him in the face! Then I settled onto my side, to dream up other ways to torture him.

“Oow.” He chuckled out, before spooning me from behind.

~~~~~~
~~~~~~

~ 10 ~

4th April 2364

I lay in bed, listening to the noises of the night. Considering it was spring here in Alaska, including our small part of the Alaska Range, I thought it was relatively quiet. The majority of bird life hadn't returned yet. Since there's still a lot of snow on the ground, there were no crickets or frogs either. Yep, the beginning of April was relatively a quiet month, naturally speaking.

I couldn't sleep. So typically when you can't sleep, the stupidest and most mundane thoughts creep into your head. Particularly about birds flying north in spring, or when do crickets come back out.

Although I was tired, I couldn't find a comfortable position to lie in. I'm only six months pregnant, but my baby bulge was huge. It was such an effort to roll over and my favoured position used to be sleeping on my stomach. You can guess it's a bit impossible now, as well as for the next three months.

Declan was quietly snoring away, in a deep sleep. The pregnancy could tire him too, I noticed. In the past, with his predatory instincts he'd wake up just by my rolling over in bed. With my huge shape, it took much more effort to roll over yet he didn't stir. Lately, not only has he been doing all of the cooking, but half of the cleaning, too. If I tried to do any heavy duty chores such as the bathrooms or the floors, I'd get growled at.

I looked over at his digital clock and stared disheartened, at the glowing green numbers; 1.33 AM.

I'd been lying awake for two hours. I was bored! I was tempted to get out of bed, go downstairs and fix myself a snack, but I didn't want to get any bigger. Ki was concerned about how much weight I'd put on with the pregnancy.

"Declan," I said softly.

"Hmm, what?" He immediately stirred. "Is it time?"

"Time for what?"

"To have the baby."

"Declan, I'm not in labour."

"Oh..." his head fell back into the pillow, "...have you got a craving?"

"No."

"Are you in pain?"

"No."

"Then what?" He moaned.

"I can't sleep."

“Yes you can, just close your eyes.”

“I can’t, I’ve been lying here awake for two hours! Well, since we went to bed at 11 o’clock, it’s really been two and a half hours.” I argued.

“Alright alright!” He rolled over to spoon me from behind. “Is this better?”

“No.”

“Then what, B?”

“I can’t sleep on my stomach.”

“Huh?” He opened his eyes, to give a peculiar look.

“I always used to sleep on my stomach, but now I can’t!” I huffed. “I think it’s why I can’t settle.”

“Frickin’ hell woman, you're a classic!” He laughed loudly in the dark bedroom. “Now you don’t want the baby after 300 years of trying, because you can’t sleep on your stomach?”

“I never said that!”

“Here," he snuggled closer, to wrap me up in his arms and his legs. “Close your eyes, relax and do what you used to, when you couldn’t sleep. Didn’t you listen to my heart beat, or inhale my scent or whatever?”

“I used to lie on top of you, with either my head resting on your chest, or I buried my face in your neck. When I did this, I was usually lying on my stomach.” I said sulkily.

“You can still put your head against my chest, by lying on your side.” He offered.

We both adjusted in bed, or it was more like Declan waiting for me to move around. I rolled onto my side so we were facing each other, before he wrapped me into his arms and legs again. He held me closely, so my face could bury itself in his wide chest. Even with my stomach protruding, he could still press himself against my form.

He was right, I did feel much better. His greater body heat started to relax my muscles, as I inhaled his maple syrup scent. His strong heart beat pounded away, as its melody carried me off into 'sleepy land'. Even the baby moved less, as if she too could feel the warmth and it comforted her. That was until...

“Oow!” We both cried out at the same time.

The baby gave an almighty kick, which went straight through me and into Declan.

“She’s getting too hot," he moved away and as soon as he did, the kicking subsided.

“But I was falling asleep!” I whined.

“Wait, I have an idea," he thought up, "roll onto your other side.”

“Why?”

“Just do it.”

“Do you know how much of an effort that is?” I complained.

“C'mon B," he gently pushed me onto my back.

Then he helped me roll over so I was facing away from him. I was about to object, when he spooned me from behind. A contented growl came out of my mouth, as he rested his leg over mine and his arms encircled my large waist.

His heart pounded into my back, which coupled with his steady breathing and excessive body heat; it was like sleeping with a huge, hot water bottle that was gently rocking. Next, Declan lowered the bedcovers past my stomach, which could remain cool. This way the baby wouldn't get too hot, and both baby and mother would be happy.

“Is this better?” He murmured in my ear, before kissing it.

“Mmm... I love you, Declan Sabre.”

“In unan, B.” He rubbed my baby bulge. “In unan.”

The last thing I felt before I slipped into unconsciousness, was the feel of his large hands, slowly stroking my belly. Like the proud papa bear, he was claiming his territory. I didn't mind, in fact the melodious stroking aided sleep to finally take over. Within a matter of minutes, I fell into a deep, relaxing slumber.

*****

The next morning after breakfast, I was ushered out of the house and into the hover-car. Typical of getting ready for a social event, I underwent my last minute nerves over my appearance. As usual, Declan growled that we were going to be late, as he stood in the bedroom doorway.

“B, you have ten seconds to get your pregnant ass downstairs!”

“You can't pick me up and sling me over your shoulder anymore.” I taunted, whilst waving my hand over my enlarged abdomen.

“Trust me woman, I can still carry you out of the house.” He said grouchily. “Now c'mon, it's 8. 53 AM! This thing starts in seven minutes!”

“OK OK OK!” I rolled my eyes as I closed the wardrobe doors. I picked up my handbag and began to depart when I paused. “Maybe I should wear my red jumper instead?”

“It's a frickin' birthing class! Do you think the expectant mothers will be worried about fashion?” He rolled his eyes back, before he grabbed my arm. “Now come on.”

“Wait,” I pulled back, “I feel like we're forgetting something.”

“Yeah, your brain since you're so forgetful thanks to this pregnancy!” He snapped. “I've made sure everything is turned off, unlike you leaving the oven on last week.”

Declan pulled me from the room and marched me downstairs and out the front door. Once I was outside, I was pulled over to the garage. He hit the remote key and our doors automatically unlocked and opened. Then he helped me into my seat, slammed the door shut, before going around to the driver's side.

"Man, it still stinks of human, in here." He grumbled, once he was behind the wheel. "Maybe I should deodorize the car this afternoon."

He was referring to when the police temporarily impounded our vehicle, as evidence in a mugging and wild animal attack. We got our hover-car back three days after the incident, although it could have been longer than that. All it took was one call to my lawyer at Hodge Endeavor and within hours, our vehicle was returned. It was delivered by two police officers who drove it over and since then, Declan's always complained our vehicle smelled like human. The officers didn't smell bad, but he was trying to downplay how it tempted his bloodlust.

Hurriedly, he reversed the hover-car out of the garage, not even slowing down. He careened backwards out onto the concealed road then he gunned down the hill, towards the community centre. Our birthing class was being held in the Meeting Hall, by our Medicine Man and one of the Tribal Elders.

"Man, you're eager." I commented.

"You know I hate being late!" He snapped. "Now we have to walk in last when everyone will be sitting down."

Declan didn't slow until we reached the intersection at the bottom of the hill. We cruised around the sports oval, where some Lokoti kids were in the midst of hockey training. He pulled up in an available car space outside the hall, powered down the vehicle then climbed out.

I was pulled out of the car and towards the large, wooden, carved and painted, building. He opened the door first and ushered me through before walking in behind. We found he was right, everyone was already seated. Chairs formed a small half circle with Ki and Feather, standing up the front. It looked like class had already started, as everyone stared at the latecomers.

"Aunt B and Uncle Declan," the elderly Feather smiled on our arrival. "I'm glad that you could make it."

He flashed me an annoyed look, as he led me over to two available chairs. We sat between two other couples, Walt and Wendy Wisetail as well as Jay and Gina Shallow Water. They smiled in greeting, as Declan did a double take over the Wisetail's.

"What are you two doing here?" He asked in surprise. "I thought with this being your third rug rat, you two would be old and experienced with this birthing business."

"Thanks a lot!" Wendy snorted.

"You can leave out the 'old' but you can keep the 'experienced' part." Walt grinned in good humour.

"Wendy and Walt came for a refresher on breathing techniques during delivery." Ki told him.

“Yeah, this is our second ‘rug rat’." Jay put his arm about his pregnant wife. "But Gina liked the classes so much, we came again.”

To which she enthusiastically agreed, “When they teach the man how to massage the woman’s lower back during delivery, it’s a godsend!”

“And don’t forget the massages before the delivery," Wendy added on. "You’re taught methods the Chinese developed. They're amazing because when you do it correctly, it can help your lower back, let alone your aching feet.”

“Oh," I looked on, impressed.

Declan joked, “What about massages for the expectant father?”

He started to laugh, but he stopped when he saw all of the women were staring, unimpressed.

“OK, let’s get started.” Ki looked towards Feather, who nodded in agreement. “Thanks to Wendy and Gina for sharing some of what will be taught in these classes. Over the next four weeks, we’ll be going through both theory as well as practical. You’ll learn what’s happening to a woman’s body in the lead up to delivery then during the birth. We’ll also go through the after birth procedure and how your bodies will continue to change, during your first few months with your baby.”

“Isn’t it obvious what’s happening to your body during and after pregnancy?" Declan leaned in to whisper. "The baby is inside you then it’s out.”

I nudged him to shut up as I straightened in my chair, to show I was paying attention.

“First of all, we’ll go through the theory of how the baby gets into position during the last month. If you could all take out your pamphlets and open them on page two.” Ki ordered the class.

Declan looked around at everyone taking out the information they were given, when I moaned out, “I KNEW we were forgetting something!”

“If you weren’t so insecure about your looks, I would have remembered instead of having to rush you out of the house.” He rolled his eyes, before he turned to Walt. “The bigger B gets, all I hear these days is, ‘I feel fat’ or ‘my clothes don’t fit me anymore’.”

This time Walt nudged him to quiet down, as Wendy gave him a glare.

“Here you go Aunt B,” our Medicine Man handed me a spare. “Now on page two, you will see a picture of a baby that’s moved into position -”

“Hey that kid is upside down!” My husband interrupted, as he looked at the pamphlet.

“Yes Uncle Declan, the baby is meant to be upside down," Ki frowned.

“Then what happens if the kid isn’t upside down?” He asked.

“Then it’s called a breach birth, which can lead to complications for both mother and baby.”

“Say what?” His mouth fell open. “THAT’S a breach birth? When the baby isn’t upside down?”

Ki pointed out, “If the baby isn’t upside down, then it isn’t born head first, is it Uncle?”

My mate turned to look on my protruding stomach with wide eyes and he even put his hands over it.

“How do we know if it’s upside down or not?”

“Since Aunt B is only six months pregnant, you don’t have to panic yet. The baby doesn’t have to be upside down until the eighth month. Now if you don’t mind Uncle Dec, I’ll explain how the baby gets into position and why.” Ki said coldly, showing his patience was running thin.

I felt my face heat up at the attention Declan was attracting, as Wendy passed me a sympathetic glance. My mate glared back at our Medicine Man and his subordinate in the pack, as he sat back in his seat again. However, he kept one of his hands possessively on my large stomach.

Class went for two hours, with the first one on theory and the second was spent on the practical.

We moved onto some padded mats which were waiting on the floor a short distance away. Here, Ki and Feather began to teach the men how to massage their pregnant women’s feet. According to Ki, this particular massage if done correctly was meant to relieve the pressure points, which could also ease the tension in a woman’s lower back.

However, my feet were so ticklish that every time Declan tried, I couldn’t keep still! He already knew how ticklish they were, which could work to his advantage when he wanted to torture me. But I squealed every time he tried, as he turned into the embarrassed party. He looked on the other males in the room as they proficiently massaged their female's feet.

“C’mon B, just let me massage your frickin’ feet!" He said abashed. "What if the baby doesn’t turn upside down because we didn’t do this?”

“Erm Uncle Dec," our teacher overheard his concern, "if Aunt B doesn’t want her feet massaged, it won’t affect the baby moving into position.”

“Are you sure?” He asked sceptically, whilst looking around at all the other women who were enjoying their foot massages.

“Yes I’m sure," our Medicine Man smirked. “If she doesn’t like foot massages then I’ll teach you how to massage her lower back instead.”

“Trust me Ki, I’ve got plenty of experience massaging B’s lower back thanks to 273 years of period pain!” My mate exhorted, to my humiliation. Then to his surprise, he noticed all the dirty looks the other women in the room threw him. He wondered at their disapproval, "What?”

Sharply, I pulled my feet back from his lap and silently fumed, whilst pulling on my socks and shoes.

“Aunt B, if you wouldn’t mind lying on your side for me; I’ll show your loud husband how to massage a pregnant woman’s lower back. This will ease the tension that the baby weight causes to your spine.” Our medical practitioner spoke, as he knelt down behind.

With a pink face, I obeyed, while noting the pairs of eyes which remained our way.

Wendy promised, "You're gonna love this massage, Aunt B."

"Now do you see where her spine meets her pelvic bone?" Ki proceeded to demonstrate, as he ran his hand down my clothed back. Next, he gently touched several parts of my lower back and hips. "The nerves you need to concentrate on run here, here and here. You'll need to rub in a circular motion as you move your hands across here, here and then up here."

Oh my gosh that felt good! My eyes bulged and I even gasped in surprise. Ki's massage felt heavenly! The twinges of sharp pain instantly began to dissolve into blissful relaxation.

Declan worried over my exhale, "Are you OK, B?"

"Man that feels good!" I accidentally cried out a little too loudly. "Ki don't stop!"

The territorial European Werewolf didn't appreciate this. Ki received a hard shove out of the way, as Declan took his place. My mate tried to copy his hand movements, but with his overbearing strength, it wasn't the same.

"Oow!" I objected. "Declan that hurts!"

"Use less force and more circular motion," our teacher instructed. "You don't want to just poke her, remember that this is supposed to be a massage."

"OOW!" I sat upright. "Now you're deliberately hurting me!"

"I am not!" He returned. "You're just frickin' ticklish!"

"THAT was not tickling!" I rebuked. "THAT was torture!"

"Fine then!" He said sulkily. "I won't massage you at all!"

"Ki..." I looked on pleadingly, "...can I please have another massage?"

He let out a sigh, as if to say, 'I can't take you two anywhere'. Then he risked Declan's wrath by moving behind me again. I lay on my side on the mat once more then as soon as his hands touched my back, immediately I relaxed.

The Second in the pack gave his subordinate a dangerous look, which Walt told me later. I couldn't see what was going on behind, but I heard what happened instead. According to Walt, the Medicine Man was flirting with death, by telling the European Werewolf how to look after his mate.

"Just try to be gentle, Uncle Dec." He lectured. "Remember your physical strength has increased, so you may not mean to harm her, but you are. After all, you're dealing with an already sore part of her body, so your wife just needs a little TLC. Lucia may be six months old, but she's the size of a seven month old. Since she's a big baby like her big father, it's putting a lot of strain on Aunt B's body. When you massage the right way, it will ease much of the tension in the spine."

Then I heard a low, threatening growl come from my mate, which was usually the sound he made right before he attacked something.

In alarm, I looked over my shoulder to see his eyes had turned their glowing green colour and he even bared his sharpening teeth...

Quickly, I sat upright again. "Declan!"

Finally, Ki saw the invisible shovel in his hands, as he realized he may have just dug his own grave. He blanched at the sight of the infuriated European Werewolf, who was within mauling distance. Slowly, he began to back away as Walt looked tense, like he was worried he might have to come to his rescue.

Declan's body remained taught, his teeth sharp and his eyes burned bright green in anger. It was literally like the saying 'the green-eyed monster rearing its ugly head'. Once he had scared off the male that was encroaching on his territory, he silently turned my way.

Gently, he pushed me back onto my side then he began to massage. I lay tense and anxious, expecting him to hurt me again...but he didn't. His rubbing was harder than Ki's however, this time it didn't feel like he was just poking. His large hands moved in a circular motion and after a minute, it did start to relax me, which I think was helped by how hot they felt, too.

"Er, Declan?"

"What?" He replied in a flat tone.

"It's um, working." I admitted.

"Of course it is." He growled out. "If anybody says again, that I can't look after you? They'll have my claw marks embedded in their skin, let alone their thick skulls."

"Oh but you can go around calling me ditzy for being forgetful from the pregnancy?" I replied coolly.

"I never called you ditzy." He spoke in a low voice. "I just pointed out how much you're forgetting lately."

"Forgetfulness is a common symptom in pregnant women." Feather said, as she walked past whilst offering advice to different couples. "When I was pregnant, I accidentally left the grill on all day, after making grilled cheese on toast. I almost burned down my kitchen."

Then she moved off to answer the Shallow Water's questions on massaging during birth. This left Declan and I to exchange a long look. I watched his teeth return to normal as did his eyes, showing his calmer state.

"OK, I'm sorry about the comments I made about your forgetfulness." He said quietly. "It just pisses me off that you wanted this baby so bad, but you'll whine about your clothes not fitting you. Or, people bag me out for having a big baby from my European Werewolf genes, when I warned you all along it could happen."

I rolled my eyes, "I'm always making comments about my clothes when I'm nervous about how I look, pregnant or not."

"I know, which I also don't get." He gave a peculiar look. "You're pretty and you know it, so why the hell are you fishing for more compliments?"

I sat upright indignantly, "What, my whining about feeling unattractive, or when I change an outfit two or three times, is because I'm confident of my looks?!"

Declan looked about, realizing we had an audience who were watching while they were massaging.

"Well isn't it?" He wondered.

"No!" I turned my back on him again. "Maybe I ask those questions because I want to know if I fit in? I have to stand in front of people and look like a professional, when I lecture. Maybe I'm scared of looking like a freak?"

"B, you're a frickin' Werewolf and a Circulator, of course you don't fit in!" He rolled his eyes. "Because you're a Lokoti Werewolf, you've got the pheromones working for you. Then as a Circulator, you have the aura that makes you stand out in a crowd. When you put the two together, you have one hot female. I mean, why the hell did I nearly maul our birthing coach, for touching you?"

Pause...my eyes remained downcast but I managed out, "Really?"

"Yes!" He said shortly. "So quit whining and sit pretty for me, so I can massage my pregnant mate."

Giggling, I rolled onto my back and pulled him over me. He chuckled as he willingly came along. We used our sharp teeth to graze the other's lips, as he emitted another growl, this time in arousal.

"C'mon guys, can you please NOT do this in my birthing class?" Ki asked tiredly.

The room erupted into laughter which made us pull apart. I lay on my side again as my mate resumed his post as the massaging, expectant father. However, I did feel his large, hot hand, slip under my jumper to rub my skin directly, which felt nice.

We overheard one woman say to her partner, "I thought being the tribe's longest married couple, let alone the longest living ones; they wouldn't argue anymore."

"I can't believe how Uncle Dec can make cursing sound tender," another joked.

"I wish I was a Werewolf with the kind of sex lives they have," one man complained. "They've been married for nearly three hundred years and he still gets some."

"Oh excuse me for having nausea, dizziness and tension headaches!" His pregnant wife whacked him on the arm.

The three male Werewolves in the shapes of Declan, Walt and Ki, exchanged raised eyebrows at the unhappy couple in the class.

"As well as the birthing classes, perhaps you'd like to come to our couples counselling here at the Meeting Hall, on Thursday nights." Feather said diplomatically, as she continued walking around, observing.

~~~~~~
~~~~~~

14th April 2364

Once again, I lay awake in bed, listening to the noises of the night. I could hear the hoot of an owl or two, from the trees in the surrounding forest. However, the predominant sound which invaded my concentration was my husband's quiet snore. I raised my head to look over his large sleeping form, to see the time; 12.53 AM.

I couldn't sleep again. So I gave up trying to force myself unconscious and simply laid there. Declan slumbered away on his side, with his mouth hanging open. The corner of his mouth even looked a little wet, with drool.

"Oooaaahhggrrrr!" I growled in frustration, as I rolled over onto my other side, so I was facing him.

I reached out my hand and pinched his nose closed, which stopped his snoring and did something else, too.

He instantly woke up. "Huh? What?"

"Oh good, you're awake." I sung, as I perched my head on my hand.

"Aw B, I was sound asleep!" He whined as he rolled onto his back. "I was having a good dream, too!"

"Really?" I asked out of interest. "What were you dreaming?"

"I was dreaming I was sound asleep," he said with his eyes closed.

"No," I poked him in his side, "tell me what you were dreaming about."

"You don't wanna know," he grumbled back.

"Yes I do."

"No, you don't."

"Why, were you dreaming about another woman?" I asked suspiciously.

"I was dreaming about LOTS of women." He smirked, whilst keeping his eyes closed. "I dreamed that I was still working at the Garage where women paid me in sex, to keep their engines running."

"Say what?" My mouth fell open, before my hand lashed out to slap his bare chest. "Declan!"

"Heh heh!" He didn't even wince. "You were in my dream too."

"And what was I doing in this dream, while women were paying you with sex?"

"You were my manager, deciding on what woman would be strong enough in the sack for me." He grinned like he was picturing this. "When I got bored with the humans, I'd recharge my batteries with you."

"Eew!" I cried out in disgust, as I rolled away.

"Yup, it was a good dream." He sighed wistfully. Then I felt him move up behind and begin to massage my lower back. "You can't sleep again?"

"Do you care, or would you rather return to your harem?" I retorted.

"The dream was OK, but I've had better."

"You've had better sex dreams?"

"Yup," he spoke so casually, it was as if we were discussing the weather. "Remember your first trimester, when you craved me like you'd crave food?"

"Er, yeah?"

"Those were the best three months of my life!" He exclaimed. "Sometimes I dream that you're always like that, where your abdomen is just a tiny bump but your hips and breasts are bigger. You're riding me hard all day, every day, whilst crying out, 'don't stop Declan, don't stop!'"

"You LIKED that?" I looked on like he'd gone mad. "I was worried I might kill you from exhaustion!"

"Trust me B, I would have died a happy man." He chuckled, as he massaged.

"You're in luck then," I said dryly. "We're supposed to have two more daughters, remember?"

"So we'll go through those first three months again and again?" He smiled widely. Sulkily, I looked away, still annoyed about the other kind of dream he had. He was quiet for a minute or two, as he rubbed my lower back. Then he said, "You know what, B?"

"What, Declan?"

"I think I know of a way which will help your sleeping problem and fulfil my fantasies too." He gave a mischievous grin. "These lower back rubs are all well and good for pregnant humans. But with our kind, it calls for another kind of massage."

"Huh?" I gave a funny look, until his hand moved to the front and went straight into my underwear. I gasped, as I accidentally dug my nails into his arm. "Oh Declan!"

He chewed on my shoulder, whilst keeping his eyes on my face to watch my reaction to his new 'technique'.

*****

The next morning, I was rushing about the bedroom trying to decide on what to wear again. The only difference this time was instead of growling impatiently, Declan calmly sat on the bed. Beside him, was my handbag and coat he had ready.

I looked on my large appearance in the mirror, on the inside of our wardrobe, with dissatisfaction. My maternity jeans were sitting comfortably over my large bulge, but I couldn't decide on what top to wear. I eyed my reflection, analytically.

"I don't think I'll wear the red jumper."

"OK," he shrugged.

I tugged it off and pulled on the light blue coloured, woollen turtle neck. Then I looked into the mirror again. This time I thought I looked too uniform, wearing dark blue jeans and a light blue top with my dark blue eyes.

"I look too blue," I said unhappily.

"What about your dark purple jumper instead?" He offered helpfully.

The turtle neck was whipped off and I grabbed my v-neck, dark purple, woollen blend. Once it was on, I checked myself in the mirror. I let out a sigh of relief, as I liked this much better.

"Thanks," I said surprised at his assistance. "But now my hair is all messed up, so I have to go do it again."

"OK," he said, whilst looking at his clock on the bedside table.

"I know we're late!" I snapped, as I hurried out of the bedroom.

"Well, it's 11.18 AM and I told you Wendy's lunch starts at eleven." He called back.

I stood in front of the bathroom mirror, brushing my long, black hair. Then I applied a dark purple lipstick, to go with the jumper. Once the hairbrush and lipstick were back in the drawer, I checked my appearance one last time. Lastly, I walked back into the bedroom to find Declan was standing up, holding out my coat and bag.

"Well?" I demanded.

"You look like the prettiest pregnant female Werewolf in the tribe." He said perfunctory. "Now let's go."

My husband led me by the hand down the stairs then out of the house. I marvelled at how he continued to remain calm instead of acting cranky. He lowered me into the passenger's seat, closed the door for me and walked around to the driver's side.

Slowly, he reversed out of the garage, down our gravel driveway and out onto the road. Then he glided down to the next driveway, on the hill. To my astonishment, we found six other hover-cars, either parked on the road or in the Wisetail's driveway.

"Wow, there's a lot of people here for Wendy and Walt's lunch." I commented.

"Hmm," he agreed.

Declan parked behind what looked like to be Tyson's family car. Once the engine had powered down, we climbed out. I took longer with my huge bulge, as he waited patiently. Then hand-in-hand, we walked up the driveway past the three other vehicles parked there.

As soon as we went up the steps of the front veranda, Walt opened his front door.

"Aunt B and Uncle Dec!" He beamed. "It's good to see you."

"Sorry we're late." I kissed his cheek.

"Late?" He looked on, puzzled. "It's only 11.30 so you're early."

"Early?" I echoed in surprise, before my eyes swung in Declan's direction.

"I told her this thing started at eleven," he smirked to Walt. "I figured if I told her the wrong time, instead of rocking up half an hour late, we would be half an hour early."

Walt cracked up laughing, before he clapped him on the back, "Nice one, Uncle!"

He held the door open for us to come inside, whilst I passed my husband a dirty look for his deception.

"They're here already!" Wendy cried out excitedly, as she came out of the kitchen. She kissed both of our cheeks as she went on, "We're just setting up the food and nibblies. I didn't expect you guys to be early."

"Blame him," I elbowed Declan in the ribs.

"Uncle Dec lied about the time to Aunt B, to get her here earlier instead of later." Walt laughed to his wife.

"You two are a classic!" She tittered. "You're just like that arguing married couple from that old TV show, 'The Honeymooners'."

Then she turned around and waddled back into the kitchen, thanks to her own pregnant state.

Tyson and his wife Tanya came forward to greet us next, as did Caesar and Forrest, Derik and Uma Elm, Antonio and Peta Sabre, Ki and Jenny Lightfoot then lastly, Jay and Gina Shallow Water.

As we did the rounds of 'hi, how are you?', we noticed that all of our families were present today, as well as the members of the pack. Those who weren't here already, were soon knocking on the Wisetail's door. I shot a puzzled look towards Declan who shrugged back, as he was thinking the same thing. We were beginning to suspect that this 'lunch' wasn't just a social gathering. Another funny thing was that people were arriving with presents.

Sodas were being served and I held a ginger ale in my hand, as Declan was drinking orange Fanta. The Wisetail's dining table was completely covered in nibblies, which many of the Werewolves happily congregated around, with their constant hunger. Declan was talking 'pack business', such as security concerns to Forrest and Caesar, whilst they gobbled down cabanossi and cheese. However, Walt was in the kitchen helping Wendy make sandwiches.

I grazed on some water crackers and brie, whilst looking about the Wisetail's living room.

Although I've been back to the house several times over the long years, I still felt nostalgic about being in my old childhood home. When Mum and Dad evolved to the space time continuum, my father handed over the house to a cousin. The house had seen several generations of Wisetail's be born, live and die; with the families altering and expanding the abode, with each ownership.

As I was reminiscing, I vaguely overheard the pack's discussion.

"Did you guys see the news report last night, on the escalating murders throughout the Lower 48 and Canada?" Declan asked.

"We did," Forrest frowned.

"I think they're being caused by several covens of North American Vampires." My mate gave his opinion. "The whole 'smash and grab' approach, with the police finding the victim's drained and mutilated bodies, days later?"

"Hmm," Caesar turned grave. "There was a case in Anchorage two months ago, which fitted a North American Vampire's MO. But I'm hoping the coven we eliminated, were the perpetrators of that offence."

"Yeah, but I think there are way more out there, than anyone realizes." Declan continued. "With the decrease in the world's Werewolf population, the natural or the supernatural balance, has been thrown out of whack. Vampires are reproducing like cockroaches, with not enough Werewolves to cull the numbers."

"Then what do you suggest, Uncle?" Caesar asked warily.

"Instead of playing defence and not doing anything until we get attacked; what if we went on the offence and did some attacking of our own?" He said seriously.

"You mean leave our tribal lands to go and pick a fight?" Tyson objected, as he stood across the table. "That would bring on trouble even faster! Lokoti Werewolves are relatively unknown to the separate species of Vampires. If the 'fang heads' knew about us then we would have a lot more trouble than we do now."

"I agree." Ki spoke up, standing beside his friend. "Our existence is still a myth to many outside of Alaska, let alone the inside of it. By taking on the responsibility of ridding the world of the murderous parasites, would be like putting up a neon sign and inviting trouble. We would be endangering the lives of our human families."

"Then just send me," Declan looked directly at Caesar. "A lone European Werewolf. No-one will know of the Lokoti Werewolves this way, they'll think I'll have my own vendetta."

"Huh? What? No!" I snapped to. "No frickin' way!"

"B, stay out of this," he glared back.

"No!" I stood my ground. "No Declan Sabre, no you cannot go on a killing spree and risk your life like that!"

"B, I wouldn't be in any danger." He said coolly.

"You may be the strongest in the pack, Uncle." Our First spoke. "But you're also going to be a father soon. What you're suggesting is just too risky, even for a European Werewolf – slash – Circulator."

"Can you instantaneously phase yet?" Ki asked knowingly. "We've seen you run in the speed of light, you ran so fast down Main Street that day Aunt B was in trouble, not even the traffic cameras picked you up. But can you instantaneously phase from Alaska to somewhere else in the States, to wage your one-man-war on the fang heads?"

"No, not yet -" Declan began but Ki cut him off.

“Then how can you not give away our existence, let alone our location? The Vampires could track you back here, when you run home.”

The Second started to growl threateningly at our Medicine Man again for his intrusion, but our First put his hand on his arm, to silence him.

“Ki’s right, Uncle.” He decided. “Your offer is admirable, but I'm going to say no. Besides, today is a day to celebrate yours and B’s upcoming parenthood.”

“It is?” I asked in surprise.

“Why yes," Caesar smiled warmly. “I’m surprised you haven’t guessed yet, by everyone arriving with presents. Today is yours and Uncle Declan’s Baby Shower.”

“It is?” My mate's eyes widened. “I thought that was just a 'chick thing'?”

“It is the 24th Century now, Uncle.” Forrest shook his head at his younger looking elder.

“Walt!” Caesar called on his fellow Werewolf and the host of this shindig. “Today was Wendy’s idea, so how about we let her propose a toast?”

Walt escorted his pregnant mate out of the kitchen, as she wiped her hands on a tea towel. Tyson was quick to hand the couple another two cups of soda he'd poured, as the room quieted to hear Wendy speak. She looked nervously upon her husband, who returned it with an encouraging grin, which prompted her to begin.

“Thank you Tyson.” She acknowledged. “Well, first of all everybody, thanks for coming and bringing a dish and a bottle of soda, let alone your presents.”

“Thank you for hosting today, Wendy and Walt.” Caesar raised his drink.

“Yeah, thanks Wendy and Walt.” I seconded that, whilst Declan placed his arm about my shoulders, to smile on.

“Uncle Dec and Aunt B, not only are you the tribe’s longest living members, but you’re the longest married couple. We’ve witnessed your many arguments...” Wendy giggled out, which also earned guffaws from the crowd, “...but we’ve also witnessed that there are no other people in the world that the two of you would rather argue with."

"Here here," my mate planted a kiss on my forehead.

She continued, "When Uncle Dec nearly passed away last year, right after his 300th Birthday Party, it gave us all a fright. We were worried that we might lose you either in two ways, death or evolution. But then the news that Aunt B was expecting came out, which meant you'd have to delay your departure. I must admit, I was glad because I can’t imagine the tribe without you both. You’ve helped your family with babysitting, advice and your protection. So giving you this Baby Shower today, is just one of the ways we wanted to thank you.”

Everybody raised their cups, "To Aunt B and Uncle Dec!”

As they sipped on their sodas, I turned to look up at my mate whose bright blue eyes seemed to be waiting to hold my dark blue ones.

"Here's to parenthood," I tapped my plastic cup against his.

"Did I tell you how beautiful you look today, Mrs. Sabre?" He smiled softly.

"You can tell me from here to eternity, my handsome husband." I tittered back.

His head ducked so his mouth could smother mine...

"And they're at it again!" Ki cried out, making the whole room laugh.

"OK, let's at least do the presents before you two retreat into your own little universe, you seem to exist in." Antonio taunted.

Declan passed his great x7 grand nephew, a warning look. "You'll keep Antonio, you'll keep."

There was more laughter before Peta and Wendy led us over to a couch in the lounge room, so the gift giving could begin. Instead of sitting beside my husband, I sat in his lap. Then Wendy sat beside us, with Walt sitting on the arm rest, beside her. Everyone crowded around with their presents, to take turns handing them over.

We were given the smaller presents first, such as more baby clothes, toys and other accessories. Then in the end, we were presented with the larger ones, such as a hover-pram, a highchair and even a baby capsule, the families all chipped in to buy. My husband and I unwrapped everything together, touched by everyone's thoughtfulness and consideration.

For three centuries, we'd given countless Housewarming or Baby Shower presents. We've watched other couples get married, have kids then grandkids. When we thought I was barren, we were forced to watch from the sidelines, but never participate. Now it was our turn and we were overwhelmed at everyone's celebration of our condition.

"Speech! Speech!" Tyson called, when the gift giving was finished.

Declan and I were surrounded by so many new things, I didn't know what to say. I was so emotional, I couldn't open my mouth in fear of sobbing, so I looked on him to say something. However, even my loud-mouthed mate, was gob smacked.

"Er..." his mouth hung open, "...thanks."

Everybody guffawed at the stunned couple in the room.

Declan forced out, "I mean er, thanks so much guys, we didn't see this coming. It really means a lot to us, um it really it does."

"It must, because I've never seen you speechless before." Caesar gave a wry grin.

"This man has an opinion on everything!" Forrest laughingly agreed.

"I still remember his advice on marriage, when I told him that I was going to propose to Peta." Antonio smirked.

“Is this the one where he tells the husband-to-be, to start buying up stocks in ‘Nutella’?” Tyson smilingly shook his head.

“Yep that’s it," he answered. “That and, ‘if you’re gonna provide for your woman then at least learn how to frickin’ cook! My mouth is still recovering from your over-cooked mushroom risotto’.”

Peta affectionately messed up her husband's hair, "Well it has improved over the years."

“You’re lucky, he was nice to you.” Walt smirked. “When Wendy and I became engaged, he said to me, ‘Walt I have two words for you; take-away’.”

The room erupted into loud laughter over their experiences with the European Werewolf's bluntness.

“Remember in High School, when you did that semester of cooking classes? You set off the fire alarms when you incinerated that self-saucing chocolate pudding.” Antonio teased.

“That was so funny!” Wendy laughed along. “It was winter and below freezing when the whole school was evacuated.”

“So, has Walt’s cooking gotten any better?” Peta asked her.

“He can be trusted with making sandwiches or cutting up fruit or vegetables." She tittered. "But I won’t let him near the stove or oven.”

Then she pulled in her cooking-challenged husband for a kiss.

~~~~~~

5th May 2364

I slept fitfully on my side as I couldn’t maintain a deep sleep. Lucia was moving around like hell and it felt like she was doing somersaults, inside me. Declan spooned me from behind, periodically rubbing my enlarged belly or even my lower back, when he heard me whimper.

On the sixth time I woke up, I opened my eyes to see it was 2.33 AM.

“Frickin’ hell!” I moaned in exasperation.

“Huh?” He sleepily raised his head.

“It’s only two-thirty.”

“Yeah and?”

“I can’t sleep properly!”

“Oh,” his head flopped back into the pillow. Then he mumbled out, “You wanna have sex?”

“No...” I moaned a second time, “...we can’t have sex every time I can’t sleep.”

“Why not? The last couple of times you couldn’t sleep and we had sex, you were out like a light, afterwards.”
~~~~~~

“I didn’t think you noticed, you passed out before I did.” I snickered.

“Yeah, but I woke up and saw you fell asleep right after me.” He chuckled, as he began to rub my lower back.

“Talking about sex though,” I cleared my throat.

“Oh oh," his massaging stopped.

“What?”

“Every time you start that way, I know I’m about to be hit with something I won't like.” He spoke with his eyes closed.

“What I was going to say,” I continued, “is what’s going to happen about sex when we have the baby?”

“Huh?” He opened his eyes to give a peculiar look.

“We’re constantly going to have a third person in the house, so we’re going to have to be quiet. We can’t growl as much or break the bedroom furniture.”

“Aw, why not?” He asked indignantly, as he raised himself as his objection.

“The baby will hear us.”

“So?" He scoffed. "The baby is just a baby! It’s not like she’s gonna know what we’re doing behind closed doors.”

“Yeah but maybe we should practice 'quiet sex' from now on?”

“Quiet sex?!" He turned loud. "It sounds like frickin’ boring sex!”

“It doesn’t have to be.” I said petulantly. “But I want to stop the bed from rocking.”

“Say what?”

“It squeaks from all the commotion we’ve put it through. We’ve had to buy ten new beds over three centuries, from wear and tear.” I reminded.

“Then I’ll put some WD40 on the hinges!”

“Yeah but we should just try to... you know.”

“What?” Declan demanded. “Try to what?”

“I don’t know, try to be more quiet or gentle, or whatever.”

“I tried being gentle once B, but you got bored and bit me!”

I burst out laughing, as I recalled what he was talking about. “I did too! I think I also slammed you into the coffee table, didn’t I?”

“Look, we’ve bought a new bed for the baby, so we’ll buy a new bed for the parents, too. We’ll get an even sturdier bed frame as well as a thick, cushioned mattress. Hell, I’ll even soundproof these walls if I have to!” He knocked on the wall above the bed to demonstrate. “But c’mon, I’m a European Werewolf! Quiet and gentle sex, are you NUTS?!”

Declan proceeded to demonstrate, by growling loudly as his mouth dove into my right breast!

I squealed in further laughter as he 'mauled' his wife, complete with sound effects. I felt his hands pull up my maternity nightgown and fling off my underwear. I used my hands to tug off his boxer shorts, which fell beside on the floor.

Then I parted my legs which he readily leapt in between. His arms were extended, as he held himself over my baby bump, to fall into a quick rhythm. The wooden bed frame creaked and even the inner-spring mattress, squeaked. I noticed the noises immediately, as I worried about anybody else hearing it too one day.

“Damn it!” I complained. “We really do need new bedroom furniture.”

“We can afford it!” He grunted out, as he kept up the pace.

“Do you think we should buy an entire bedroom suite, to go with the new bed?” I wrapped my arms about his neck.

“I'll buy you all new linen, if it makes you happy!” He gasped.

We both exhaled loudly, as our heads rolled backwards. My nails dug into his back as his dug into my thighs, while he held me against his almost vibrating body. When I turned my head back round, I found his mouth waiting for mine.

His eyes were glowing green and his teeth looked sharper. As soon as we were face-to-face, he bit down on my lower lip! I growled in both pain and pleasure, as my eyes burned turquoise. Next, he used his tongue to lap at the bloodied teeth marks, which numbed the sting. His rhythm slowed but remained steady.

“Mmm – mmm – mmm!” He moaned in delight. “If we tried ‘quiet sex', our second let alone third daughter, may not be born!”

He claimed the dominant position to move over my bigger body. A couple more times, he sucked on my fast-healing wound. Then I felt his right hand push down the neckline of my nightgown, as it sought out my left breast to squeeze.

“Yeah well, with your strong 'swimmers', I could be wearing underwear and still get knocked up!” I breathed hard as I came hard.

His hot skin, coupled with his angle and speed, was just the right combination. I felt my inner muscles ripple in an upwards motion, sending waves of ecstasy throughout my torso. My nails dug into his upper arms as my body turned taught, to hold onto the exquisite delight. He recognized my orgasm by three ways; my claws detracting, my crotch wetting and my aura changing colour.

Declan tried to maintain the pace, to make my delight last as long as possible, before I felt him come too. His hot fluids mixed with my warm moisture. Then he stopped moving so he could hold my hips still and enjoy his release.

Eventually, he uttered out, “Well, we aim to please.”

I tittered as I sung mockingly, “Thank you, come again!”

“Oh I thought you'd never ask!” He cried out, mockingly.

'Round Two' commenced, as the bed frame creaked louder and the springs in the mattress squeaked to the same rhythm...

~~~~~~
~~~~~~

~ 11 ~

5th June 2364

What amazed everyone about Lucia's birth was how hard and fast it hit, like a tornado. Although we knew she was coming for eight months, her arrival happened in the most sudden way. We didn't even get a storm warning, or a siren to sound the alarm.

It was a Tuesday night and I was in and out of consciousness. Since the baby bulge interrupted my sleeping pattern, I seemed to subsist in a half-awake state. Whenever I rolled over in bed which affected the lean of my stomach, I had to wake up to do it.

In the back of my mind I was aware of the noises of the night. An owl hooted in a nearby tree and I heard the cricket's singing in our garden. I even heard a breeze rustle the leaves with a 'sssshhh' noise, as it blew through our part of the Alaska Range.

Downstairs, the refrigerator hummed away as per normal. The kitchen faucet dripped into the sink, producing a steady tap, tap, tap. An old clock on the wall in the living room gently ticked away, showing the time as 2.58 AM.

It was a typically quiet Tuesday night. Hardly anything happened here on a weeknight, unless of course it was a full moon. Otherwise, social gatherings within the family or tribe, usually happened on a weekend.

The clock continued to tick, now reading as 2.59 AM.

Declan's soft snoring came to my ears as his familiarity filled my senses. His large arm rested over my waist and even in his sleep, he'd give my tummy the occasional stroke. We'd kicked off the covers this summer's evening with only our sleepwear remaining. He was wearing satin boxers and I was in a loose, white, cotton nightie.

I lay still, not awake but not asleep either. However, I was content and comfortable. Our bedroom windows were open to let in the cool breeze, as my husband hated hot weather. Even our baby objected, since she was half European Werewolf. Whenever she got too hot, she'd kick extra hard.

Then the living room clock ticked over to 3.00 AM...

"AAAAAAAAGHH!"

...I sat upright as the most hideous agony, worse than any period pain imaginable, ripped through my abdomen!

In a single leap, my husband jumped to his feet from fright, probably thinking we were under attack.

"Aaaaaaagh!" I screamed as I parted my legs. "Aaaaaaagh!"

No sooner than I did, there was a gush of a watery substance along with some blood, staining my panties, nightie and bed linen.

"Frickin' hell...!" Declan's eyes bulged.

"Aaaaghh!" I parted my legs wider as if I were bearing down. "Aaaaagh!"

KI GET HERE NOW! – His Second commanded.

ALREADY ON MY WAY, THE PACK CAN FEEL AUNT B'S LABOUR PAIN – Our Medicine Man replied.

All his months of worry and preparation kicked Declan into gear. Speedily, he left the bedroom to get some towels. He returned as quickly as he could and started lying them over the bed.

I gasped in distress with my hands clenched into fists, which Declan noted as he put down the towels. Then he lifted me up to place several underneath, to absorb the messy delivery. It was just in time too, as another gush came out which we guessed was the last of the amniotic fluid.

"Frickin' hell...!" Declan repeated under his breath.

When he lowered me back onto the soaking towels, I panted in pain. I even started doing the breathing exercises. I had to, my hips and lower back were putting me through torture! It felt like my body wanted to deliver this baby as fast as possible.

Declan's eyes almost popped out of his head when he saw me start to push.

"B, you're not pushing already are you?" He gaped and I threw him an indignant look as my answer. "The frickin' Medicine Man isn't even here yet!"

Next, he grabbed hold of my saturated underwear, tugged them off and dropped them onto the bedroom floor.

My eyes glowed turquoise as I felt my body begin to bulk up with extra muscle. Subconsciously, I was changing into my Lokoti Werewolf form to help with the delivery. With my clawed hands, I grabbed onto my mate's arms as he sat on the bed in front.

"Breathe, B! Breathe!" He started to mime the breathing exercises. "Hee hee, hoo hoo! Hee hee, hoo hoo!"

"Mmmmmeeeeeeeeoooooooorraaaaaaagh!" I grunted out in agony.

"Just breathe B, breathe! We've both just gotta breathe!" He panicked. "Where the hell is our frickin' Medicine Man?! You're gonna have this thing before he gets here!"

The splitting sensation in my abdomen turned into a torturous tearing. Then blood appeared between my legs and lots of it. In the birthing classes, I never understood what dilation meant, but I could feel my crotch widen as the baby sank lower. I think it was causing the tearing inside, by her large size moving down my birth canal.

"Oow! Oow! Oow" I howled. "This hurts! This really hurts, Declan!"

"Then stop pushing already!" He cried out.

“It’s not me pushing, it's my body!" I growled out. "It wants her out NOW!”

“Hee hee, hoo hoo! C’mon B, breathe with me!” My frightened husband tried to coach. “Hee hee, hoo hoo!”

At that moment, we heard our front door downstairs was flung open so hard, it banged against the wall.

Next, we heard this somebody bolt upstairs before stopping short in surprise, in our bedroom doorway. Ki looked on dumbfounded at how wet the bed was, with Declan in his boxer shorts playing coach to his wife in labour. The pack's female Lokoti Werewolf, complete with glowing eyes and elongated teeth, sat in a drenched nightie, doing her breathing exercises amidst her panting.

“WHERE THE HELL HAVE YOU BEEN?!” The European Werewolf bellowed.

“How far apart are her contractions?” Ki asked, as he sat his medicine bundle on our dresser and took out his medical scanner.

“What contractions? It's just been one long contraction! She’s having this baby NOW!” He barked back.

“Aunt B, are your contractions right on top of each other?” Ki asked, as he waved the medical scanner over my sweaty body.

I emitted a growl between my sharp, clenched teeth as my answer.

With the excruciating pain in my pelvis, hips and spine, it felt like my lower body was being contorted. The tearing sensation became worse and my sweaty face became wetter with tears. Ki's eyes however, seemed to be glued to the monitor on his medical scanner.

“Holy Mother Earth...!" Our Healer exclaimed. "Aunt B’s dilation just went from seven centimetres to fifteen in a matter of seconds. The baby literally moved into the birth canal before our very eyes!”

“Gee, you don’t say?” Declan said sarcastically. “How about turning off your machine and actually helping us?!”

The Medicine Man turned off the device and placed it on top of the dresser as well. Next, he took out a couple of medical tools, one of them a cutting instrument, from his medicine bundle. Then he moved over to the couple on the bed.

“I need you to move away.” Ki said shortly. “I need to make sure the baby comes through the birth canal properly.”

“Move away...?” Declan's eyes flashed their glowing green colour. "Not frickin' likely!"

“Move behind Aunt B, so I can see to her delivery!” He snapped. “Or shall I just leave you to it, Uncle?”

Instantly, the parents-to-be exchanged a look of dread...

“Right, I’m outta here.” Declan jumped to his feet a second time that night. However, he reclaimed my clawed hands once he was sitting behind. “I’m right behind you B, I’m not going anywhere.”

Affectionately, he placed a kiss on my wet cheek and he didn't even flinch when I squeezed his hands with my supernatural strength.

“Mmmmmooooaaaaarrrrww!!” I roared in pain.

Another wave of blood gushed out onto the towels, which couldn't hold anymore and began to drip the redness onto the floorboards.

To Ki’s credit, he didn’t even blink at the mess my bedroom was turning into. He moved me around so my legs were propped apart on the edge of the bed. Declan moved with me, to provide support for my back. Then our Healer knelt on the floor in front of my privates, so he could see better.

“The baby is crowning! I can see her head." He looked up in amazement. "This has to be the fastest delivery I've ever seen to.”

“Well, she is a Circulator.” My mate made my excuse. "It's light speed or nothing, with this gal."

Our Healer spoke as he worked, “It’s like her body knows it will be a difficult birth, so its way of dealing with it, is quickly.”

“The sooner the baby is born, the sooner I can give her my blood, right?” Declan checked.

“I’ve already asked Walt and Tyson to be back up donors, as a just-in-case.” He reported.

“Like hell she’s going to drink their blood!" Declan snapped. "She has one donor and that’s ME!”

“Mmmeeoorraaaww!” I growled fiercely as right then, I wished the two would shut up and stop arguing.

Sweat was pouring out of me similarly as the blood was and all I could do was push.

Ki cried out excitedly, “That’s it Aunt B! Her head is starting to come out! You’re doing a great job!”

I felt like my vagina was being ripped open, as the splitting sensation went from agony to indescribable suffering. The baby was huge which is probably why I’m delivering her in the eighth month instead of the ninth. But even with my pelvis adjusting, I didn't think she'd fit.

“No! No! It hurts! It hurts!” I sobbed in my thunderous voice. “Push her back in! Do a caesarean! She’s too big!”

“No Aunt B, you have to keep pushing! You’re nearly there!” Ki encouraged.

“Look, if she says she can’t push anymore then she can't frickin’ push anymore!” Declan rallied to my side.

“She can’t just return it and ask for a refund!” He retorted. “She’s doing well! So far neither she nor the baby are in any distress -”

“Not in any DISTRESS?!” The European Werewolf shouted. “Look at her you idiot! She’s bleeding everywhere!”

"Then get ready to give her your blood, Uncle. But unless you have something helpful to contribute, shut the hell up!" The Lokoti Werewolf yelled back, with his eyes glowing pink in anger.

"Do you want some blood now, B?" My mate leaned forward to catch my gaze.

I closed my eyes and tried to concentrate on using my own regenerative ability to dull the torture. If I could just stop the pain and rest a moment, I might be able to do this. Right now, my vagina felt like it would never be able to be used again.

"C'mon Aunt B, you can do this!" Ki tried to hold my gaze. "Look at how far you've come, I can see her forehead!"

"You want some of my blood, B? It might make you stronger to push." He offered.

When Declan's shared his blood to heal, it's also eased the pain. What, no more pain? Hell yeah! I turned my head to nod back.

He raised his wrist but instead of him using his sharp teeth to put a gash in it, I simply grabbed hold and bit it.

"Grrmph!" He grunted, now in pain himself. But he didn't pull away, either.

I drank and drank like I was dehydrated. My body hungered for what his could provide. I swear his blood never tasted so good! Sweet and savoury together, quenching my thirst and making me feel stronger.

It took the sharp edge off the tearing sensation however, the agony remained.

My back ached and painful spasms overtook my abdomen. I knew they were the contractions and thanks to Declan's blood, they were stronger. It was as if my internal muscles took on a life of their own and started pushing by themselves. My Lokoti Werewolf muscle combined with his European Werewolf strength and together, they were going to deliver this baby!

Ki looked on unhappily, "Er, Uncle? I think we should get Walt or Tyson in here to take over. You're looking a little pale."

Declan declared stubbornly, "Nobody gives blood to B, but me!"

Feeling reinvigorated, I pushed his bleeding wrist away. I even sat up straighter, as Declan moved closer to support my back. Once I was sitting upright on the edge of the bed, I gritted my elongated teeth and bore down. I pushed and pushed as I literally willed this thing out of me.

"GGGGRRRRAAAAAAAAWWWWLLL!"

My fierce growl sounded just like my husband's when he was in Werewolf form.

"Go B! Go B! Go B!" He cheered. "Let's punch this thing out of you!"

"The head is all the way through!" Ki called out gleefully. "Hang on, the baby's shoulders are getting stuck... no wait! I've freed the one on the left... now I have to free the one on the right... man, this baby has broad shoulders! You can see she's her father's daughter."

"Well? What's happening? Have you got her?" Declan peered over my shoulder.

"Mmmmrrroooooaaaawwwrrrr!" I roared, as I gave a final push using up the last of my strength.

Ki carefully pulled her out, freeing each limb as she went. Once she was all the way out, I felt my entire body let out a sigh of relief! Every single muscle in my being went kaput. I lay limp in Declan's arms as I tried to catch my breath.

"I've got her! Can you see her? She's beautiful, Aunt B! Just look at her! Here's your daughter!" Ki held her up in the air, so we could see.

I saw a flailing, bloodied baby in his hands... this is Lucia? This is Lucia Grace Sabre? This is my baby girl?

The Medicine Man didn't have to induce the newborn to breathe, as Lucia automatically opened her tiny mouth and wailed.

When she did, we saw that she had tiny, sharp teeth. Then I noticed the nails on the ends of her little fingers and toes, were claw-like. But I didn't care, she looked mostly human. She didn't morph into a European Werewolf shape when she was inside, which could have killed the both of us. And I thought she was the most perfect looking, baby Werewolf, I'd ever seen...

"Lucia...? Lucia...!" I reached out for her with my clawed hands.

Gently, the Healer placed her into my arms, which were supported by Declan and he held the both of us together.

"Lucia..." I growled softly, "...hallo Lucia."

We heard the cutest little growl come from her tiny mouth, as she opened her eyes. The sight of them made my heart leap with joy. They were identical to Declan's European Werewolf eyes; glowing green with narrow slits for pupils.

"Awww...!" Declan and I mooned over our daughter.

"She's beautiful...! She's so beautiful!" I cried over her, which sounded weird in my deep, rumbling voice.

To our surprise, even the toughest guy in the room turned emotional.

I gazed on my husband's face which was next to mine. I saw his eyes and nose were red with tears streaming down his cheeks. In three centuries of marriage, the amount of times I've seen Declan cry like this, I could count on one hand.

"We did it, B." He tearfully looked into my eyes. "We have a daughter who's a half and half. She's exactly half Lokoti and half European."

I bumped my forehead against his, "I love you Dec."

"In unan, B." He delivered several soft kisses all over my sweaty face.

As we were holding Lucia, our Healer cut the umbilical chord. He was frowning as he worked though. I noticed how quickly he knotted Lucia's umbilical stub, like he was rushing.

“Aunt B, before we do the afterbirth, I think we should give you some more blood.” He announced.

“Huh?” Declan’s head snapped around. “What is it, Ki? What’s wrong?”

“It’s just what we talked about, Uncle.” He spoke in a serious manner. “Lucia is a large baby and if Aunt B was human, I would have had to perform a caesarean. Although she was able to deliver naturally in her supernatural form, I'm concerned how she's still bleeding heavily -"

However, he didn’t get to finish for as quick as a flash, Declan put his wrist into his mouth before jamming it into mine. As his left arm bled into my mouth, his right remained wrapped around his wife and child.

“Aunt B’s going to need a lot of blood.” Ki warned. “I think we should let Walt and Tyson step in -”

But he was cut off again by the dangerous growl from my mate's parted lips, as he bared his teeth. This changed the Medicine Man's mind and he even took a step back from the territorial male. Emotions were already running high without aggravating the new father.

I thought it was strange how I wasn’t aware of the bleeding that Ki was talking about. I remember feeling it during the birth, but now as I was holding Lucia in my arms, I didn't feel anything else. If a human woman gave birth to something with sharp teeth, claws and glowing eyes; she'd faint from fright. But as I held her in my muscled arms, I thought she was the cutest thing I’d ever seen! Even her little growls were cute. I would have cooed at her, if I didn’t have a man’s wrist blocking my mouth.

I continued to drink in Declan’s hot, delicious, life-giving blood. With each mouthful, I felt a new strength course through my veins. Like this, I went through the afterbirth with a newborn in my arms and my husband's wrist in my mouth. The big, strong male continued to sit behind, holding his arms steady for his wife and child.

Our Medicine Man proficiently oversaw the last of the delivery. He wrapped up the afterbirth in a blood-sodden towel then headed for the bedroom door. To my surprise, in the doorway I saw not just Walt and Tyson, but Caesar as well. All three looked grave instead of happy for some reason. Then I saw what they were looking at, the blood-soaked bed and puddles on the wooden floor.

Ki handed the afterbirth mess to Forrest, who was standing behind his son. The elderly, great grandfather was no stranger to the birthing procedure. He simply took the bloodied bundle downstairs to dispose of it.

Next, Tyson started to roll up his sleeve, to share his blood too, but Ki shook his head.

“You’ll be chased out of the house by a territorial European Werewolf," he warned.

“Oh," our relative looked daunted by the prospect. Automatically, he rolled his sleeve back down, as he observed his Second. “Are you OK, Uncle Dec? You’re looking paler by the minute.”

The European Werewolf's reply was another threatening snarl, which made both Tyson and Walt, step backwards.

"So this is the newest member of our pack," Caesar said, as he came in.

He gave a kindly smile, which prompted me into loosening my hold so he could pick her up. Caesar held her closely as his brown eyes glowed blue. He did a partial change so he could proclaim in his deep, rumbling, Werewolf voice:

"You, Lucia Grace Sabre, are following in the footsteps of your mother, Bianca Grace Wisetail Elm Sabre. She was our first female Werewolf and now you are our second. Yet you are the world's first half breed. Welcome, Little Wolf."

Declan and I looked on proudly from the bed, as did Ki, Tyson and Walt from the doorway. Then Caesar started to clean Lucia by placing her onto an unused towel and wiping away the blood. He may have been our great x5 grandnephew, but today he acted like a proud grandfather.

"OK people," Ki clapped his hands to return our attention. "There's one last medical procedure we have to do, which is sanitizing the room."

Immediately, Tyson and Walt snapped to, helping our Healer to clean up. Firstly, they picked up all the wet, bloodied towels and carried them down to the laundry. Next, I saw Derik Elm appear in the doorway with a bucket full of hot water and disinfectant. With him, was the elderly Phil Cloud, carrying an armful of sponges. Without wasting time, the two men got on their hands and knees and proceeded to scrub the floor.

With all the voices coming from downstairs, I finally realized the whole pack was here. Did my labour pain send them all running? The camaraderie touched me, how they all chipped in to help. Fourteen male Lokoti Werewolves cleaned up the blood, coming in and out of the bedroom, either bringing up cleaning products or carrying down the mess.

I was feeling much better now, so I started to lap at Declan's wrist with my tongue. My saliva closed his wound and when I moved his arm away, I saw it flop onto the bed. Concerned, I turned around and my eyes widened...

Declan was as white as a sheet! Even his lips looked drained of colour. He also appeared dizzy, as he started to sway.

"I'm alright B..." he saw my fear, "...I've just got to rest."

I reached out for him but he collapsed face-first onto the bed, into the amniotic-soaked sheets.

"Declan!" I cried out fearfully.

Instantly, Ki came over to check on him. He helped me roll him onto his back then I watched the Medicine Man examine him. He checked his pulse first and eyes second.

"He'll be alright, he's just fainted." He shook his head disapprovingly. "I told the old fool that you'd need a lot of blood! But what does he do? He'd rather give his last drop than let another donor step in."

Then Ki and Tyson lifted the unconscious Declan off the bed and over to a chair in the corner.

I felt torn in two as I looked from my husband to my child. Who do I tend to first? But the rational Medicine Man made the decision for me. He noticed my fretting as my eyes flitted to and fro.

"Let's just get you and the room cleaned up first, Aunt B." He organized. "Then we'll return the husband and baby."

*****

All three of us were washed down and changed as the bedroom was cleaned. I put on another nightie after reverting into my smaller, human shape. Although I had healed, I was very tired. So was Declan, he remained out to the world as he was changed too. His previous pair of boxers he had on were taken away to be washed with my sleepwear.

"We should soak these before washing them," Phil said, as he carried them out of the room.

"Nah, it's cool." Derik replied, as he followed him out with the bucket of dirty water. "Just put the stain remover in when the machine is full of water, before the cycle begins. It'll come straight out."

"I still think we should soak them."

"Trust me, when I wash my jeans after a hunt, I tip the stain remover in with the laundry detergent. The blood comes right out." He promised.

Within half an hour, there wasn't a trace of blood on me, the baby, my husband or the bedroom.

I sat on the bed dressing Lucia for the first time. Forrest had retrieved a biodegradable disposable diaper and some baby clothes from the nursery, for us. Then he smilingly looked on, as did Caesar, Ki, Tyson and Walt. Once she was dressed, I held her close and let her slumber against my breasts.

"I have to admit, this birth was a lot less complicated than I thought it would be." Caesar thought aloud.

"Tell me about it," Ki agreed. "Aunt B had this baby in far less time and less complications, than I'd feared."

"It happened pretty quickly," Tyson nodded. "When I felt her labour, I came as quickly as I could. I swear the baby arrived minutes after I did."

"How long exactly was Aunt B's labour?" Walt wondered.

"Hmm, good question." Ki began to count in his head. "It was three o'clock when labour started. Then it was just after half past when Lucia came out."

"It was 3 AM exactly when Aunt B went into labour and it was 3.33 AM when Lucia arrived." Caesar declared. "Her labour went for thirty-three minutes."

"Wendy would love that!" Walt let out a laugh. "When Kurt was born, she was in labour for two hours. When Edwina came, she was in labour for an hour and a half."

"Maybe with this latest pregnancy, you could get down to an hour." Tyson joked. "Time seems to be reducing with each rug rat you have, Walt."

"You might be right." He chuckled back.

"Lucia Sabre was born at 3.33 AM, after labour lasting for 33 minutes and today's the 3rd of June." Caesar spoke gravely. "Her father is 300 years old, after being turned into a Circulator in the year 2363."

"Wow, that's a whole lotta threes." Ki caught on. "You think this means something?"

"We should ask the rest of the Tribal Elders, they're always saying things happen for a reason. The tribe's second female Werewolf is born, when there are hardly any female Werewolves left in the world? Not forgetting Lucia is half European Werewolf, when Uncle Dec was meant to be the last of his kind?" Our First speculated.

"Oh," all of them men frowned in consternation.

"Here's another three for you, Lucia is supposed to be the eldest of three sisters." Ki added on. "It all must mean something."

Uneasily, I looked up at the men standing over as I rocked my daughter.

"Guys, can you please not be so grave, today?" I dismissed their concern. "It's Lucia's birthday."

"Sorry Aunt B, of course we can." Forrest said understandingly.

Then my elderly great x4 grandnephew came to sit beside on the bed, to stroke his newborn great x3 grandaunt.

"This is a nice turn of events," he smiled. "I remember when you and Uncle Declan visited Maia and I, when Caesar was born."

"I remember Aunt B and Uncle Dec visiting Marie and I, right after Tyson was born." Caesar went along.

"And they visited me and Tania, after Samuel's arrival." Tyson chimed in. "Now here we all are, visiting Aunt B and Uncle Dec, to welcome Lucia."

"Hey, Aunt B is a Wisetail as well as a Riverclaw, she's my relative too!" Walt said indignantly, which made us laugh.

Just then Declan woke up. "Huh, what?"

Dazed, he looked around the room from his seat, before his eyes settled on his mate and young, on the bed.

We watched his eyes widen when he saw the newborn in my arms. She was wearing pale pink pyjamas and her eyes and mouth were closed. The only sign of her Werewolf nature were the tiny claws on her fingers and toes.

Forrest stood up when Declan did, to let my husband take his seat. As my mate moved to sit beside, he stared at what I was holding. I held our daughter out him and carefully he took her out of my hands. He treated her so tenderly, as if she was the most precious thing he'd ever held.

"Lucia Grace Sabre," he breathed out her name.

My eyes watered as I watched him duck his head and run his nose along her forehead, inhaling her scent. A sob almost escaped, when I heard Lucia take a deep breath, as if she was learning her father's smell too. She opened her glowing green eyes and gave her Daddy a curious look.

"Lucia," he repeated in his deep voice.

Then his human blue eyes glowed green back to her, to show he was her father.

She looked up into the eyes which matched hers. Now call me nuts, or exhausted from labour? But I swear I saw an understanding pass from European Werewolf father to half European Werewolf daughter.

I leaned into Declan's side as I tearfully looked down onto the new life we brought into the world.

"Hallo, Lucia Grace." I said emotionally and I flashed my glowing turquoise colour at her.

She looked from my eyes to her father's then she emitted another little growl!

"Oooohhhh...!" Her parents melted at the sound of it.

The other Lokoti Werewolves all came forward for a better look, as they watched our interaction. Caesar's eyes glowed blue again, as Forrest's turned yellow, Walt's went orange, Tyson's turned purple and Ki's glowed pink. It was their way of showing she was one of them.

"Guys, this is my daughter!" Declan looked up tearfully. "Now I'm a Dad too!"

"Welcome to the club." Caesar clapped him on the back.

Out of the blue, Lucia screwed up her face and began to squeal like a human baby.

"What?" Declan looked back down. "Is she OK? What's wrong with her?"

However, I sensed what was wrong with my empathic ability.

"She's hungry," I took her back and readied to do my first feeding.

"Already?" Tyson sounded surprised. "She was born only half an hour ago. Samuel didn't feed until an hour later."

Ki smirked, "She already has her father's appetite."

All of the men watched as I took out my left breast and put the nipple into her mouth. I wondered if I was doing this right however, Lucia instantly latched on. She started to suck as well as even chew a little, which tickled. I giggled as I held her steady.

"What is it?" Declan watched closely.

"She's chewing as well as sucking, it tickles!" I tittered.

"She's chewing already with the teeth she was born with?" Caesar's eyebrows rose. "She's really showing off her European Werewolf character."

"It's a good thing Aunt B's skin is tougher than a human woman's," Ki frowned, "as Lucia could damage a normal breast."

"It's a good thing my wife is the sexiest female Werewolf in the world, putting human women to shame." Declan said proudly, before kissing my cheek.

"Don't let Wendy hear you say that," Walt chuckled. "Otherwise she'd rally the women in the tribe to go on strike."

As the men guffawed, I pried my breast away to check if I was lactating. When I did, I saw some white liquid spill onto Lucia's lips. It seemed my supernatural body was ready and willing for the role of motherhood.

Ki must have been thinking the same thing, for he leaned in to examine the feeding. "Look at how quickly Aunt B's milk has come in."

"Hmm," all of the males observed.

"Usually it takes a couple of days for it to go from a yellow colour to a white one." Walt agreed. "It took a week with Wendy."

"The yellow colour is colostrum which is filled with antibodies for the new baby." Ki educated. "But since Lucia is a Werewolf with a powerful regenerative ability of her own, it isn't necessary."

I was starting to feel like a spectator sport with everyone watching and commenting.

"C'mon guys," I said uneasily. "I may be a female but I'm still a Lokoti Werewolf. You guys changed when you reproduced. Can you please stop gawking?"

Forrest apologised a second time, as he moved back from the bed. "Sorry Aunt B."

"Right." My mate stood up to address our First and the males under his command. "Thanks guys for your help and being here as our back up. Now Caesar, I say this as respectfully as possible as your Second; please get the hell out of my bedroom."

Our leader didn't look offended at all, as he looked around the room. "How about we give the new parents some time to rest and bond with their child?"

"Of course!"

"Sure!"

"No problem."

Then the First and Second exchanged a long look and I suspected a couple of sentences telepathically passed between them.

As they silently conversed, their subordinates departed via the bedroom door. Their communication ended with Declan giving Caesar a respectful nod before my relative gave a parting smile. Once he was downstairs, we overheard him give the order to disband, since the danger was over.

"G'bye Aunt B! See ya, Uncle Dec! And congratulations!" Derik Elm called out, as he left the house.

My husband stood by the window and watched them walk down our gravel drive as they headed off home.

It was approaching 4 AM and the sky outside was already light with summer's longer daylight hours. Then he turned away from the window and wearily collapsed onto the bed. He snuggled down, wrapping his arm about my waist, while I was sitting upright feeding Lucia.

"Would you mind if I got a couple more Zzz's? I'm whacked out." He asked tiredly.

"I'm not surprised. You turned so white, you made me scared I drank your last drop." I passed a guilty look.

"So what if you did? I can regenerate." He shrugged it off. "Nobody shares their blood with my wife, but me."

Lucia stopped feeding by removing her mouth from my breast. I tucked it back into my nightie then I moved her to my shoulder. I didn't have to rub her back for long before a small burp erupted. We chuckled at the sound of it.

I rested her in the middle of the bed between us, before lying down myself.

"It should be alright if she sleeps here with us, shouldn't it? The cot isn't made yet and I want catch some Zzz's, too." I yawned.

"She'll sleep wherever you want her to sleep." He rested his arm over the both of us. "If you want her to sleep in bed with us, then she'll sleep in bed with us. If you want her to sleep in her cot, then I'll get up and make her cot."

I entwined my fingers with his as we watched our daughter fall asleep.

"I love you, Declan Domitian Sabre." I murmured.

His response was using his free hand to reposition my long, black hair. He fanned it out so it wasn't just spread across my pillow, but his as well. Then he plonked his head down and fell asleep like that, with his face in my hair.

Within a matter of minutes, he slipped into a deep sleep and I sensed his body was working overtime, to replenish his blood loss.

So there you go...I was snug as a bug in a rug, in bed with two of the world's greatest predators. Yet, I had never felt so at peace or so much love. These blissful feelings soon lulled me into unconsciousness. I slept so soundly, it was like my body was making up for the last few months.

*****

The next time I opened my eyes they settled on Declan's digital alarm clock which read as 9.33 AM. Aside from Lucia, I was alone in the bed. I raised my head to glance around when I heard noises coming from the kitchen.

Next, the smell bacon and eggs sizzling filled my nose. Oh yum! I'm starving! Bacon, eggs and hashbrowns right then, sounded like a godsend!

I left Lucia in bed as I slowly climbed out. Although I felt stiff and sore in the pelvis and hips, otherwise I was fine. I left the bedroom to use the bathroom first.

When I used the toilet, I was worried it would sting. However, I encountered no discomfort, which meant the tearing had completely healed. That's a relief, the last thing I needed was an infection.

I returned to the bedroom to find Lucia still sleeping in the middle of the bed. I slipped off my nightie and put on a maternity bra. But when I pulled on my maternity jeans, I wondered why they felt so loose? I walked over to the wardrobe, opened it and peered into the mirror on the inside of the door.

That's weird, most of the baby bulge is gone. I thought it was supposed to take weeks or months to go down? My tummy looked a little flabby and my hips were rounder, but I no longer looked like I'd swallowed an inflated beach ball. However, I noticed my breasts did appear bigger, which made me wonder if the bulge moved upwards, instead?

What am I saying, my breasts were huge! And it wasn't from the padding of the maternity bra, either. I looked like a model from a porn magazine. When I leaned in to examine them, I noticed tiny blue veins stand out beneath the skin.

"Shite...!" I breathed as I looked on, embarrassed.

I grabbed a maternity t-shirt to put on, to try to hide the size. Although my stomach had shrunk, I hoped it would hide my breasts. Next, I darted into the nursery to grab the baby carrier, to take Lucia downstairs with me. However, what was inside the nursery, made me pause.

The cot was made which Declan must have done when he got up this morning. I smiled at the sight of it, clean sheets complete with a teddy bear sitting in the corner. Also, I noticed he'd filled the diaper bag hanging in the corner of the room. A clean towel rested over the change table and the baby-wipes, baby powder and nappy-rash treatment were ready and waiting.

The baby carrier was in the style of a backpack, with two straps you wore over your shoulders. You could wear it on your back or front and I put it on my front. Carefully, I picked up my sleeping baby and put her inside, making sure her legs went through the two small holes in the bottom. Lucia growled at being disturbed, but as soon as her head was resting against my breasts, she went right back to sleep.

When I came downstairs, Declan poked his head out of the kitchen at the sound of my approach.

"B, shouldn't you be resting?"

"Why?"

"Er, because you gave birth six hours ago," he gave a funny look. "I was going to bring you breakfast in bed."

"I'm fine." I waved it off, as I came into the kitchen. "You need a hand with anything?"

"Nope." He replied, as he returned to work. "I'm making bacon, eggs, sausages, hashbrowns and pancakes."

“Yum!” I beamed. “I LOVE your work, Declan Sabre.”

He gave a gentle push out of the kitchen entryway, “OK, go sit at the table and I’ll serve up.”

“I’ll set the table then.” I made a move for the cutlery drawer.

“Nah ah," he caught my hands. “Go! Sit! Now!”

When he gave another push by putting his hands on my hips, he saw me flinch.

“What is it?” He wondered. "What's wrong?"

“Um, I’m OK to walk around but I’m still a bit sore.”

“Did I just hurt you?" He instantly backed off. “Look B, I think you should be in bed.”

“I’m fine, just don’t get rough with me.” I joked.

Concerned, Declan watched me walk over and sit down at the dining table. Once I was seated, I adjusted Lucia’s little legs which were hanging out of the baby carrier. His frown turned upside down when he watched his wife deliver several kisses to the top of his daughter's head. I caught the smile on his face as he turned off the stove.

Within minutes a huge plate of bacon, sausage, two eggs and a hashbrown, was sitting before me, with two side plates for the toast and pancakes. I picked up the bottle of maple syrup and drizzled it over the pancakes, to allow the sweetness to soak in whilst I devoured the savoury food. Declan followed suit, except his three plates were piled high. I saw four eggs on his overflowing plate, along with three sausages, bacon and three hashbrowns.

We ate in a comfortable silence, following the mantra of Homer Simpson, "Can’t talk, eating!" We ate with gusto, as our bodies craved sustenance to finish healing. Although there was a greater amount of food on his plates, we finished at the same time. I ate slower because I made sure I didn't drop food onto Lucia's head. The idea of taking off the carrier to eat never occurred to me. I relished the feel of her small, hot body against my front, like I was still carrying her on the inside.

Just as we were chewing on the last of our mouthfuls, we were interrupted by the sound of, knock! Knock! Knock!

Declan swallowed before he called out, “Come in!”

Walt and Wendy came in with their two children in tow. When they saw us sitting at the table, it gave them pause. Wendy was carrying a large Tupperware container full of something that smelled like a casserole. But seeing me sitting at the table with Lucia in the baby carrier, made her stare.

"Hi guys," I put down my cutlery. "How are you?"

“Aunt B, are you alright?” Wendy gave a funny look.

I exchanged glances with my mate, before I answered, “Fine thanks.”

Then she roused on her husband, “You said Aunt B gave birth last night, which is why you took off so suddenly!”

“Aunt B did give birth last night,” Walt smirked.

"But look at her, she's right as rain! Her stomach is flatter and Lucia's the size of a two month old!" She gawked.

"Last night, it felt like I delivered a two month old, I promise." I snickered.

"If you'd given birth to a big baby just six hours ago, there's no way you could be sitting at the table, eating your breakfast, like it's just another morning!" She shook her head in disbelief.

Declan chuckled, "If it makes you feel any better Wendy, I was probably in worse shape than B, this morning."

"Why?" She looked on, confused.

"Uncle Dec shared a considerable amount of blood with Aunt B last night." Her husband brought her up to speed.

"Because of it, I feel right as rain." I shrugged.

"Maybe you should be at my next birth, if your blood is that potent?" She said enviously. "Every pregnant woman on tribal lands will be calling on your services."

This made Walt look on askance but it was Declan who explained.

"Er, perhaps not. I'd be creating an army of European Werewolves. I don't think Walt or the rest of the pack, would be happy about their wives craving human flesh."

"Oh," her face fell. "Perhaps I'll stick to Lokoti Werewolf blood then."

Next, she helped herself to our kitchen by putting the Tupperware container in the fridge.

"I brought you caribou casserole, I thought with the recent addition to your family that you'd be too tired to cook."

Declan grinned, "You're a good cook Wendy as well as a good woman, we certainly aren't complaining."

He stood up from the table, picked up our plates and carried them into the kitchen. He helped her shift some food around in the fridge, to make room for the large container. Walt sat down in the chair he'd just vacated, whilst pulling his small son and daughter onto his lap.

"You're looking much better, Aunt B." He began. "Your aura is back to normal."

"Did it fade when I was giving birth?" I asked in surprise.

"Uh huh." He gave a firm nod. "Well, you did lose a lot of blood last night."

I opened my mouth to repeat I was fine when I was interrupted a second time.

"Knock, knock!" A familiar voice called out and our Medicine Man came in, carrying his medicine bundle.

I smiled at the sight of him, feeling a huge wave of gratitude at how he helped last night.

“Ki, how are you?”

“I’m fine thanks, Aunt B.” He came over to the table. “The question is, how are YOU feeling?”

“Just a little sore but other than that, I’m fine.” I promised a third time.

As if he wanted to see for himself, Ki set his black, leather doctor's bag onto the table, opened it up and pulled out his medical scanner.

Slowly, he waved the medical instrument over me then read out the results.

“Your blood pressure is normal and so is your pulse, but there's some bruising in the expected areas after delivering a baby. Otherwise, you’re exhibiting the symptoms of a woman who gave birth a week ago, instead of last night.”

Wendy griped from the kitchen, “If only we could all be female Lokoti Werewolves.”

Then she and Declan carried out the coffees they made and placed them on the table. Next, my husband brought out a plate of shortbread he'd baked a few days ago. He put it in the middle of the table but Kurt and Edwina were quick to claim a piece each. Walt chuckled as he watched over his young. Wendy came to sit in the chair to his left and Declan sat in the seat beside mine. Ki remained standing although he did acknowledge the cup made for him.

“Now, let’s look at the newest member of the Sabre family.” He declared, as he reached down and pulled Lucia out of the baby carrier.

This earned another dissatisfied snarl from the miniature Werewolf.

“But she’s asleep.” I objected, missing the feel of her hot body against mine.

“How about asking first, before grabbing her like that?” Declan stood up in a protective manner.

“OK...” His eyebrows rose as he took a step back, whilst holding the baby. “Er, Uncle Dec and Aunt B, would you mind if I do a check-up on your daughter?”

My arms were outstretched towards my baby girl with Declan's hands on my shoulders.

“Oh alright, if you must,” I sighed reluctantly.

Lucia emitted another unhappy growl at being woken and squirmed in the stranger's arms.

Carefully, Ki laid her on top of the table, aware that Declan was watching his every move. My mate moved even closer as he hovered over his young. With the territorial European Werewolf in close proximity, the Medicine Man began his examination.

Firstly, the Healer waved his medical scanner over the wriggling newborn.

"Her heart rate, blood pressure and antibodies are way above normal, making her the healthiest newborn I've ever examined." He reported. "Now that her vitals are taken care of, I want to run two other tests."

"What kind of tests?" Declan asked warily.

"I want to analyze her blood and saliva, to test the communicability of her European Werewolf DNA." Ki announced.

"Huh?" He gave a peculiar look.

"You mean you want to test if Lucia can turn people by bite or blood transference?" I stood up too.

"Yes," he confirmed, as he looked on the new parents. "As we all know, Lokoti Werewolves can't change a human by bite or by sharing blood. Only those in the tribe change when their Lokoti Werewolf genes are activated."

"Oh," Wendy realized, as her eyes widened. "Is that why Uncle Dec can't donate his blood? People will instantly turn?"

"That or if he bites them." Walt said seriously.

Declan looked clearly disturbed at the idea of his daughter doing this too. He let Lucia grab onto his finger, which she held tightly in her small, clawed hand. Then an expression of hope lit up his face.

"But if she's half Lokoti Werewolf, maybe she can't change people just like her mother can't?" He wondered.

"Maybe...but we should find out." Ki said firmly.

I took hold of Declan's other hand, which he squeezed tightly and together we looked on.

The Medicine Man took out of his medicine bundle a small, glass slide, like the kind used in forensics or science.

He slid it into Lucia's mouth but before she could bite down on it with her sharp teeth, he removed it. Next, he slid the slide into a slot in his medical scanner. As the technology analyzed the saliva sample, he prepared another glass slide. At first, we wondered what it was for, when we watched him produce a tiny needle. He pricked the skin at the bottom of her right foot, making her growl angrily.

Ki put a drop of her blood onto the second glass slide and slid it inside another slot of his medical scanner. Then he rested the device on top of the table, to allow it to work. But he stood in a tense manner, with his arms folded as his eyes never left the technology.

Lucia, who was still lying on top of the table, started to cry. Immediately, I picked her up and held her close. Declan took hold of her bleeding foot, held it higher then licked it, using his saliva to close the tiny wound. Instantly, it sealed shut and her wailing came to an end.

"Good girl Looch," her father cooed, as he lifted his daughter out of my arms and into his. "Who's a good little girl? Who's a gorgeous little girl? Lucia Grace is my gorgeous girl!"

Then she opened her glowing green eyes to look up into her father's face and Wendy gasped.

"Oh my god, her eyes are glowing!"

"And she has sharp teeth and claws, to boot." Walt smirked, as he sipped on his coffee.

"A baby's eyes can change colour in the first nine months of their life. I suspect that as Lucia grows, she'll learn how to switch from Werewolf to human sight. But for the first few months, it's probably easier for her to see with her Werewolf eyes." Ki advised.

Then his attention was taken away by the medical scanner beeping, showing it was done.

Declan anxiously asked, "Are those the results?"

The Medicine Man picked it up and then beamed, giving away the good news. Next, he shared the information on the small screen of the technology. He read aloud so enthusiastically, it made him sound like an announcer.

"Lucia's saliva and blood has zero communicability." He declared. "She can't transform a human into another Werewolf by blood or bite."

"Are you sure?" Declan leaned in to see the results for himself.

"I'm positive." He said, as he angled the medical scanner our way, to show us. "She has both European and Lokoti Werewolf DNA in her genetic makeup, but the Lokoti part seems to be acting like a seal, preventing the transference of the European Werewolf genes."

"Phew!" Walt let out a sigh of relief. "That's great news! This means you won't have to worry about Lucia accidentally infecting anyone."

But Ki's elated mood seemed to evaporate and his frown returned.

"However..." he continued to interpret the results, "...Lucia may not be able to create any Werewolves by bite or blood, but she will by birth."

"Huh?" Declan looked on peculiarly.

"As we know, when a male in the tribe is activated to replace a member of the pack, it's after the age of ten." He began.

"Yeah, so?" My mate shrugged.

"Lucia was born a Werewolf and when she has young, they too will be born as Werewolves." Ki went on.

"If Lucia can't turn people by bite or blood, what's the big deal?" Walt said dismissively.

"Walt," the Healer looked on like he was an idiot, "what if Lucia has a son one day and he mates with a human female?"

"Oh," his mouth fell open. "They could be giving birth to kids who have already turned, or what if they turn inside the mother...?"

"Exactly!" Ki pointed out. "If Lucia had a son who mated with a human female, what's going to happen to her when she's carrying a baby Werewolf? She'll have inside her, no matter if it's half Lokoti, something with claws and supernatural strength."

Wendy flinched at the very sound of it. "Ouch!"

"But B got through it..." Declan began to debate, but Ki interrupted.

"Aunt B has forty times the strength of a human, which means her amniotic sack was stronger so Lucia's claws didn't break it."

Walt and Wendy exchanged looks of horror. Then the father gave his human children in his lap a hug, showing his relief at their ordinariness. The gravity of the situation was lost on Kurt and Edwina, though. They were more interested in the shortbread sitting in the middle of the table. Wendy passed them another piece each, which they happily gobbled down.

“Another fact that should be taken into consideration is how this is going to affect the pack." Ki's frown deepened. "Before, we've always had fifteen Lokoti Werewolves in the ranks. Now, Lucia is our sixteenth member and her sisters will become numbers seventeen and eighteen. One day, they'll grow up and have young of their own. The pack will continue to expand with their progeny. Our ways have been changed forever."

Warily, I looked on Declan and saw he was feeling the same way. Then together, we looked down on our sleeping young. Our first born was oblivious to the change she's made to thousands of years of tradition. Instead, she slumbered peacefully in his large arms, leaving some drool on his flannel shirt.

As a Circulator, I had to be careful of the changes I made to the timeline. Temporal causalities had been drilled in to my psyche, just as my training in self-defence had. A leads to B which results in C; I changed my mate into a Circulator, it altered our marriage and we had progeny as the consequence. The ramification which resulted from this action, I saw as a blessing. But what Ki was forecasting, the repercussions were still rippling onwards, well into the future.

Next, the Medicine Man began to pack up the medical scanner and the slides into his medicine bundle.

“I have to report my findings to Caesar," he said unhappily. “He needs to hear the results of my check-up today."

“I'd better come with you." Declan said unhappily, as he put Lucia back into the baby carrier.

“I'll come too," Walt stood up. “There could be a pack meeting about this."

As the males prepared to leave, Wendy rounded up her kids to take home.

I was left holding the baby as I stood there by the table. Instead of feeling abandoned, I started to feel something else... My heart began to pound, my eyes widened and my skin tingled, like I'd been electrified.

Just as everyone headed towards the door I cried out, “Wait!"

The sensations grew stronger and I recognized it was one of my all-knowing feelings. Often when I 'saw' something or sensed danger ahead, my stomach would tighten. This time it was a tingling sensation running over my skin, which felt similar to when I went into phase.

From my cry, everyone turned my way and then stared.

“Aunt B, your aura is getting brighter." Ki looked on, puzzled.

"And your skin looks like it's glowing, too." Wendy added on.

I felt my body buzz with energy, so much so, I felt giddy. I had to sit down at the table again as I was scared of my legs giving away. The last thing I wanted to do was drop the baby.

“B...?" My husband came back. “What's wrong with you? Are you having a vision?”

"Does she always glow like that, when she 'sees' something?" Wendy wondered.

But her husband shrugged, showing he didn't know the answer.

Ki walked over to the table, “Aunt B, what do you see?”

“Right now, your aura is so bright, human eyes can see it," Walt remarked.

Declan rolled his eyes, “C'mon B, use your mouth as well as your 'sight' and tell us already!”

Instead, I simply sat there and stared vaguely into his face. Yet, I didn't see him or his look of concern, as he knelt before me. Another image overtook my concentration, like finding myself in a daydream.

Actually, it wasn't one image I saw, but a collage of them, like a preview for a movie or in my case, a preview of what's to come...

... I saw a teenaged girl with broad shoulders, long blonde hair and bright blue eyes, with a teenaged boy who looked as strong as her, but with a Lokoti appearance. There was another teenaged boy, who was thin and pale and his faded blue eyes turned completely white, indicating he was a European Vampire. When he did that, the other boy's eyes glowed red, showing he was a Lokoti Werewolf and the girl's eyes glowed green with narrow slits for pupils, indicating she was part European Werewolf. I guessed I was seeing a grown Lucia, but who her friends were, I didn't know. They were sitting on the steps of the front veranda, laughing together like friends sharing a joke...

... then I saw Declan walk into the house with a shorter Asian man. The stranger's eyes briefly turned white with tiny black pupils remaining, indicating he was an Asian Werewolf. Together, they sat at the table which was set for dinner. Declan sat at one end as I sat on the other and in between, sat our three daughters, one with straight, black hair and the other two with wavy, blonde hair. The Lokoti Werewolf teen and the European Vampire boy were also there, as well as an African girl, with frizzy, black hair. She sat in between Lucia and the Lokoti boy, with the boy showing his attraction to her by serving her first then himself second. But when he reached for the salad bowl, it seemingly moved itself across the table towards him. This display showed the African girl was a telekinetic. However, the teen Vampire didn't eat, but sipped on a glass of something that looked like milk. Declan talked quietly to the Asian Werewolf sitting to his left and both wore serious expressions. Then our guest helped our youngest daughter by passing her the garlic bread...

...all of these different elements of the supernatural combined like a paranormal melting pot. The future had been altered yes, but it was changing for the better. Four separate species, who were meant to be enemies, all sitting at the same table. They converged to become one and this hinted that we were moving into a new era, perhaps one of peace?

As abruptly as this vision came, it also went. I heard first then saw second, fingers clicking in front of my face. As my eyes refocused, I saw they were Declan's.

“B...?” He called. "Earth to B, come in, B.”

"She's not having a seizure or a stroke, is she?" Wendy asked worriedly. "When my grandmother had a stroke, she looked like a zombie too."

“Uncle Dec, is this normal for when she has a vision?” Our Healer queried.

"She has them in her sleep or if she has them when she's awake, her eyes glaze over." He frowned. "But she’s never ‘tuned out’ this bad before.”

“Let’s get that baby carrier off her and I can examine her properly -” Ki made a move but I stopped him.

“No!” I pulled back sharply, giving everyone a shock. I held Lucia even closer, as I said, “I’m – I’m fine, I saw lots of things, that’s all.”

Everyone looked on concerned as they stood over the crazy woman holding the baby.

“You were completely unresponsive for five minutes.” Ki said seriously. “It was like you were in a catatonic state!”

“B, what did you see?” My husband tried to hold my gaze.

“Lots of things,” I repeated then I rattled off excitedly, "it’s meant to happen! The changes to the pack and our future as a whole, all of it’s meant to happen!”

“What’s meant to happen?” Walt wondered.

“Think of the SSIT Report on Reincarnation for a moment," I continued. “The Circulate noted that each time a Circulator is created, it affects space just as it does time. A change is going to happen and it’s going to be big and it’s going to be for the better.”

“What the hell is that supposed to mean?” Declan shook his head in confusion.

"Our daughters and the new era they usher in, is the affect from your change into a Circulator." I prattled on. "A leads to B which then results in C, remember? Instead of a spatial anomaly occurring in this galaxy or another, the change is happening on Earth! The pack and the tribe and even the world will change for the better, because of Lucia, Sophia and Susanna."

Declan straightened before he shot off a surprised glance to Ki and Walt, who looked just as baffled as he was.

Wendy thought she'd try, “You didn't happen to see the winning lotto numbers in all of this, did you?”

This lightened the mood and the room was filled with chuckling.

Then my husband wandered away and indicated for Ki and Walt to join him.

He said quietly, “You two go and talk to Caesar without me, as I stay here with B. I don’t want to leave her alone with the baby, in case she 'zones out' again.”

“Good idea," the Medicine Man concurred. “But contact me if it happens again.”

Next, Declan opened the front door to let our visitors out.

“Enjoy the casserole,” Wendy gave a wave on her way.

“Take care you two.” Walt said, as he ushered along their young.

Ki followed behind, taking his medicine bundle and Lucia's test results with him.

Once everyone had departed, my husband closed the door then turned to look on his wife sitting in her seat, gently rocking his daughter to sleep.

It gave him pause then slowly a soft smile settled over his youthful features.

“You know what, B?”

“What, Declan?”

“I think I’m having a vision myself.”

“Huh?" I looked up in surprise. "What are you 'seeing'?"

He walked over to the table, gently raised me to my feet then he sat down and lowered me into his lap. Like this, he could hold both his wife and daughter at the same time. I looked into his bright blue eyes which held my darker ones.

"Right now, I'm seeing the most beautiful female Werewolf in the world, nurse the prettiest one." He said with his deep voice. "You're gonna make one hell of a mother, Mrs. Sabre."

~~~~~~
~~~~~~

~ 12 ~

7th July 2364

After Lucia was born I noticed a change in Declan's behaviour. He acted differently by growling or cursing less and keeping a tight reign on his temper. He treated his wife and daughter with kid gloves, as he behaved so considerately it was unusual. Perhaps when a male is faced with fatherhood this wasn't abnormal. But in this case, I found his new attitude paranormal.

When I awoke from the baby crying, I found he was already awake. In the beginning, I thought it was his instincts as the greater predator, by waking up first. It soon turned into the standard that he would leap out of bed, retrieve the baby and bring her back to be breastfed.

When he brought in Lucia, he'd lie on his side with his head perched on his hand and watch her feed. He wore this wistful expression on his face and once I burped her, he would take her back to the nursery. Most nights he'd also change her nappy before putting her down. He was a very hands-on father, so I thought he was just enjoying parenthood.

However, into the second week, I rolled over in bed and got a fright!

Declan was lying on his side, watching me sleep with his glowing green eyes. His Werewolf sight enabled him to see better in the dark bedroom. His head was perched on his hand again, as he gazed down on his mate.

"Frickin' hell!" I gave a start. "Declan!"

"What?"

"What are you doing?"

"Nothin'."

"You're watching me sleep!"

"So?"

"It's creepy, stop it!" I snapped.

Next, I rolled over so my back was to him and his glowing eyes wouldn't be so distracting.

"Sorry, that's not gonna work," he said.

"What's not going to work?"

"I can still watch you sleep like that." He said before his voice turned soft. "I can see your smooth skin and how it dips between your shoulder blades. I can see the curve of your waist, your gorgeous thighs -"

"Declan!" I interrupted. "I'm tired!"

"I know you are, B." His voice dropped. "Get some sleep."

As I lay there, it occurred to me that it's been fourteen days since any bedroom activity. The last time we had sex was before Lucia was born. And the last time he went without for this long, it created a frustrated European Werewolf.

I sighed as I rolled onto my back, "You want a quickie?"

"No, I just like watching you sleep."

"Are you sure you don't want a quickie?"

"No, I want you to go back to sleep."

"Declan...!"

"B...!" He mimed my whiny voice. "Look, you're understandably tired and I don't want you biting my head off tomorrow, from exhaustion."

"I don't mind," I rested my hand on his chest.

"Nope, go to sleep." He put it on my own chest.

Then we both noticed how high it was sitting thanks to my larger breasts and we laughed.

"I feel like one of those Playboy Bunnies who get those huge boob jobs," I said uncomfortably.

"You look like a Madonna." He sighed happily. "Your motherly body, with enlarged breasts, rounded stomach and wider hips? Coupled with your milky scent and bright aura, I feel like I'm sharing a bed with a fertility goddess."

I giggled back, "Declan, you don't have to butter me up for sex."

"I'm not trying to get laid, B." He sounded offended. "Besides, I wouldn't use the religious term 'Madonna' in relation to the woman I was trying to hump."

Crankily, he rolled onto his back to stare up at the ceiling and no longer at his wife.

I too lay on my back as I stretched out on my side of the bed. My knee accidentally knocked into his side, but then I kept it there because I liked the feel of his hot skin. However, I felt him shiver because of it.

"Hmm?" I raised my head in surprise. "Are you cold?"

"Are you kidding me? It's 20°C at the moment!" He complained. "When you touched me and our auras connected, I felt a pleasurable electric shock."

"Oh sorry," I moved my knee away.

Then he growled as he returned it, so it was touching his upper leg again.

He said gruffly, "I said a PLEASURABLE electric shock, didn't I?"

I settled back down and stared upwards as I contemplated something.

"Declan, why can you see auras and I can't? In the beginning, I thought it was because I was a Circulator. Now we're both Circulators and not only can you see auras, but you feel them more than I do."

“I dunno," he said flatly. “Maybe it's because I'm still a European Werewolf?”

Then I felt him take hold of my hand again and rest it over his heart.

"Sometimes I wonder about it, myself." He continued. "I haven't had visions yet, like you have all the time. All I've had is a bad feeling, which turned out to be true. I haven't phased yet either, all I've done is run in light speed."

I rolled my head in his direction. In the dark, I could see his supernatural eyes glow brightly. I found them as comforting as his strong heartbeat, pounding away inside his chest.

“Hmm...” I thought out loud. “Although the mechanics of Circulating pretty much stays the same, I think each Circulator is different. We all have differing bio-electromagnetic frequencies. Elisha’s was always the highest, even if she was one of the nine most powerful Circulators within the Circulate. The nine, including myself, are the only Circulators to have visions of anytime and anywhere. Other Circulators could only see through time from the location they were visiting. Like they couldn't 'see' when Stonehenge was built, unless they were standing in Stonehenge. Then of course, the nine were the only ones who could instantaneously phase. All the others had to use a reflective surface, like a window or a mirror or even water, to travel through time.”

He appeared to be listening intently, for he rolled onto his side and perched his head on his hand again, as I spoke.

I continued, “Elisha turned Mike Sabre into a Circulator and her female progeny became Circulators, but our bio-electromagnetic frequencies are different to hers. Although I made you a Circulator by putting your bio-electromagnetic frequency into temporal flux, you register at a different frequency, too. Your ability to phase comes from mine, but our frequencies aren't identical. One thing I learned from my training as a Circulator, is no two Circulators' frequencies are the same.”

My husband remained quiet as he appeared to be processing my words. Next, he gave me a good look up and down, maybe seeing my aura in a new light? But what he next said, blew all my assumptions out of the water.

“You look hot in that white, cotton nightie by the way, especially how it accentuates your huge breasts.”

Pause... I looked on Declan as he looked on me then we both burst into laughter!

“Ladies and Gentlemen, I present to you the one-track mind of a European Werewolf!” I guffawed.

He laughed along, “Oh I heard everything you said. Blah blah blah, every Circulator is different. Blah blah blah, differing bio-electromagnetic frequencies. But it was nice watching your breasts rise up and down, as you were saying it.”

Momentarily, my hand left his heart to deliver a playful slap to his chest. He chuckled as he reclaimed it and gave an affectionate squeeze. Then I rolled onto my side so I was facing him too.

My free hand stroked his square jaw, “You know what? I think you’re the only Circulator in the entire history of the Circulate, who can see auras.”

"I'm one of a kind then?" He sounded pleasantly surprised.

"I could have told you that, years ago," I sung liltingly, as I pulled him closer for a kiss.

However, I noticed Declan responded differently this time. Usually, he was the first to turn passionate but instead he pulled away a little, like he was holding back. His kisses were soft but they were restrained. So my mouth engulfed his and when I slipped in my tongue, he sharply withdrew.

"What? What is it? What's wrong?" I asked concerned.

"Nothing, I'm tired that's all." He said awkwardly. "Let's just get some sleep."

Then he pulled me into his strong arms and held his mate in a tight embrace.

Appreciatively, I buried my face in his neck and inhaled his maple syrup scent. In return, his hands ran up and down my back in a soothing manner. Our fronts were squashed together like nothing could tear us apart. That was what I thought, until he spoke again.

"Er, B?"

"Yeah?"

"I think we're gonna have to wash your nightie in the morning."

"Why?"

"It feels a little wet, I think your nipples are leaking again."

*****

Since Lucia's birth, on two different occasions has she shared our bed again. If she was hard to settle after a feeding, I'd lay her down between us. Declan didn't mind, in fact he was happy to lie there with his head perched in his hand and watch us fall asleep together.

I got the impression he idolized his wife and daughter. He practically waited on us hand and foot, doing all the cooking and half of the cleaning. Or, as soon as Lucia cried, he'd instantly stop what he was doing to pick her up. Firstly, he'd check her nappy, change it if necessary then carry her over to be fed. As she suckled, he either sat beside or leaned on a wall to watch.

The next afternoon when I gave her a bath, again we had a spectator, this time from the bathroom doorway.

I washed her in the bathtub using a special baby float that prevented drowning. The warm water was at a low level and my hand was behind her head. Even with all the safety precautions, my overprotective Lokoti Werewolf instincts weren't about to take any chances.

I cooed at her as I washed her down with a yellow, duck-shaped sponge, we'd received at our baby shower. Occasionally, Lucia growled back as she stared up into my face. I noticed she did this a lot and sometimes she could look completely transfixed.

Just then her glowing green eyes dulled to a human blue colour, before they turned glowing green again.

"Hey, did you see that?" I called over my shoulder. "Looch's eyes just went a human blue colour, your bright blue colour."

"Really?" He asked interested, as he came to sit on the side of the tub. "Are your human eyes coming out, Looch? Can you show Daddy your human eyes?"

Lucia looked up at her father next, with a frown on her little face, like she was concentrating. Momentarily, her eyes dulled to a human blue colour, before returning to their supernatural state. As soon as they glowed green once more, her frown evaporated.

"Wow!" I marvelled. "It's like an effort for her to switch to human, when for me it's an effort to switch to Werewolf."

"Yeah, I think she gets it from me." He sighed, as he reached down and let her hold his finger in her tiny, clawed hand. "For me, changing from human to Werewolf and back again is hard. When I'm in my human form, I have the bloodlust urging me to change and go hunting. It hurts like hell when my muscles and bones contort like that. It would be easier to remain in my Werewolf body, especially when there's nothing urging me to return to human. If my bloodlust had its way, I'd permanently stay in European Werewolf form."

I tried to keep my face from falling at the thought of being married to something which was always a monster.

"Oh really?" I kept my tone neutral. "It makes sense actually, because European Werewolves couldn't revert to human until 1000 BC."

"It'd be weird though, huh?" He mused. "If you and I were a couple before then, I'd be coming home to my wife and daughter, perpetually in Werewolf form."

"How would we be able to have sex?" I asked, as I kept my eyes averted.

"Good point," he sighed. "Maybe we wouldn't have had Lucia? One, I couldn't knock up my wife, if intercourse in my gigantic body was so dangerous. Two, if you happened to live through the experience then Lucia would be in European Werewolf form, inside you. Either way, leads to one dead wife."

"Let's change the subject." I cleared my throat. "We're here in the 24th Century with our beautiful, little girl."

"You got that right," he agreed.

Next, he watched me raise her out of the bathwater then move her onto some towels I had waiting on the vanity. As she lay on one, I used the other to gently pat her down. She growled appreciatively, as she reached up with her clawed little hands. I lowered my face so she could touch it, as I cooed at her again.

In the corner of my eye, I saw he was watching with an enamoured expression. He remained sitting on the side of the tub as he saw me pick her up and rest her against my breasts. She always stopped squirming when I did that.

“Would you mind letting out the bathwater?" I recalled his attention. "I’ll dress Looch.”

“Huh?” He snapped out of it. “Oh sure.”

Quickly, he pulled the plug then followed us out of the bathroom.

However, when I lay her on the change table, he came in to help. Declan handed me the baby powder then took it away, before handing over a diaper. I chose a cute yellow jumpsuit to dress her in which he helped button up. It was one of the few left in our collection whose feet weren't worn through from her miniature claws.

“There we go!" He picked her up to rest her on his right arm. "Look at the prettiest, little, female Werewolf in all of tribal lands.”

With his left hand, he gave her a tickle which made her gurgle away happily.

Next, we all went downstairs to the kitchen where Declan opened up the fridge. I sat up on the kitchen bench then held out my hands, into which he placed Lucia. Then I snuggled with her as I watched him prepare something.

“You want a snack?” He offered.

“I won't say no.”

“Celery sticks and peanut butter?”

“Yum!” I grinned.

“Stick with me kid,” he gave a wink, “I’ll take care of you.”

Then to my delight, he prepared some carrot sticks and cream cheese to go with it.

*****

At 7 PM we put the baby to bed and at 10 PM the parents retired.

It was another warm evening thanks to the heat wave on top of the extended daylight. We'd heard on the news that day Fairbanks reached 32°C whereas tribal lands which were high up in the Alaska Range, hit 28°C. Right now, the temperature was sitting around 22°C.

We lay on our backs with our arms and legs stretched out. Declan was in a pair of satin boxers and I was in another cotton nightie. Our windows were open to invite the breeze and the bedroom was in a pink hue from the late sunset.

Fairbanks may have four hours or less of daylight in December and January, but in June and July it experienced four hours or less of darkness.

Extended daylight in summer affected people just as the shorter days in winter did. Whereas depression and lethargy were higher in the darker months; hyperactivity and a greater libido, were prevalent in the sunnier period. People bloomed just like their garden beds did, with flowers or vegetables expanding beyond normal size.

Summer's always made me restless which coincidentally, also made me horny. It was the same with Declan, where the only activity he enjoyed sweating over, was sex. In the greenhouse, our vegetables would grow faster and larger without any UV lamps or fertilizer. In the bedroom, the husband and wife would be growling and grunting, with the bottom sheet turning damp.

Ah, the memories... the last two centuries of summers together, always brought out a smile. I lay there, staring up at my white ceiling which looked pink, grinning mischievously. When I looked over at my mate, he appeared to be asleep but I sensed he wasn't.

I rolled onto my side so I was facing him and began to caress his torso. His eyes snapped open to look my way in surprise. He even moved away from my touch.

"Er, can I get you something?" He asked uneasily.

"Well, as a matter of fact..." I moved up against him.

Suddenly, he sat upright, looking nervous for some reason. "B!"

"What?" I raised myself. "What's wrong, Declan?"

"Do you want a glass of water?" He offered.

"No."

"Then let's just get some sleep." He lay back down whilst turning his back on his wife. "Who knows when Lucia will wake up for her nightly feed."

That was the cold shoulder if ever there was one!

Dejectedly, I too rolled over so I was looking the other way. Then I glanced downwards, as I wondered if I looked repulsive? Were my breasts leaking again? I didn't want to wear a padded Maternity Bra to bed, so I could let my nipples air. My stomach was still flabby, maybe he doesn't like the baby weight?

"No, it's not because I think you're unattractive." He sung knowingly. "Lets just catch some Zzz's, OK?"

"But I'm not tired."

"B, you need the rest."

"Why do you keep saying that?" I sat upright, in annoyance. "Declan, I'd completely regenerated within 24 hours of giving birth!"

"Good for you." He said flatly. "But with all the adjustments your body is undergoing, you need your rest."

"What adjustments?"

"Well...milk production for one. It's like your breasts are on tap, with your body as the factory." He rolled onto his back to look up at my chest.

"Producing milk is NOT exhausting!" I laughed out. "Why, is the fact that I'm lactating, turning you off?"

"What?" His eyes widened. "Don't be stupid, of course not!"

"Then why are you acting so strangely?" I demanded.

"We just had a baby!" He cried out indignantly. "Gimme a break!"

He turned his back once more before pounding his pillow with his fist then settling down.

I frowned as I lay down too and returned to staring at the ceiling. It now looked purple in the oncoming twilight. Instead of concentrating on the bedroom slowly changing colours, I pondered something else.

Is he still recovering after sharing his blood? If he was, he'd be physically tired and not jumping up and down all the time, to fetch the baby. Then why is he acting this way? I've heard of human women losing interest in sex, after they've given birth. But that's a biological thing that happens to their bodies. So how could his body change after Lucia's birth, for him to lose interest?

Just then it occurred to me a male Lokoti Werewolf's body changes, when they stop reproducing. But they still maintain physical relationships with their mates. All that changes is the sex no longer results in impregnating their wives. Has his European Werewolf body changed? Instead of like a male Lokoti Werewolf, it's made him lose interest in sex altogether?

The thought of Declan no longer wanting to have sex, was just so - so - so wrong.

The very idea of it wasn't just supernatural, but unnatural. I'd become accustomed to his hot-blooded behaviour, that the thought of never having sex again seriously daunted me. I couldn't even envision such a future...

Hang on, Lucia is supposed to be the eldest of three girls. After seeing them in my vision, I knew he was the father. So what's his problem?

At last my eyes began to close, as I came to a resolution that brought some small comfort. If it continues, I'll ask Ki for advice. He's arranged to come by and do monthly check-ups on our daughter. If her father's peculiar behaviour continues, I'll ask for a check-up on him, too...

...

...I wasn't sure how long I was asleep for, but when I opened my eyes, the sun was rising.

Half-consciously, I raised my head to check the time, when I found him watching me sleep again.

"Declan!" I gave a start. "Would you stop doing that?!"

He chuckled back, "You make this cute little snore, sometimes."

"What's the time?" I asked, as I wearily rubbed my face.

"Oh er, it's 2.55 AM." He looked over his shoulder at his digital clock, before turning back my way. "But as I was saying, sometimes you make this cute little snore. You sound like a squirrel or some other furry, little animal."

"Declan, have you gone to sleep yet?" I asked tiredly.

"Um, I got about an hour's rest."

"Then please, follow your own advice and get some sleep!"

Exhausted, I flopped onto my stomach with my face half buried in the pillow. I settled as such, hoping that sleep would return. Instead, I was distracted by what happened next.

After a moment, I felt Declan move closer. His hot skin pressed against mine as he wrapped his arm about my waist. I felt his large hand stroke my hips as his other, rearranged my hair to expose my neck. I felt him lean in and nuzzle there first, before gently pulling down my nightie. Then he placed a tender kiss between my shoulder blades.

He whispered in my ear, "I love you B, more than life itself."

Sleepily, I picked up his hand and pulled it upwards, so it was resting in between my breasts. He hesitated at first then he started to relax, by resting his body against mine. Together, our eyes started to close and our breathing came into sync and then...

...Lucia's cry pierced the air just as it pierced our slumber.

*****

The next morning, I noticed he had an exceptionally long shower. Usually he was a ten minute guy, which included when he shampooed. So after twenty minutes, I knocked on the bathroom door.

"Declan...?" I called out.

"What?"

"Are you OK in there?"

"I'm fine!"

I tried the doorknob but it wouldn't move, showing it was locked. Now that's weird, the only time he locked the bathroom door was if it was an extended trip to the toilet. He's never locked the bathroom door before when showering. In fact, he had an 'open door' policy, in case the other person wanted to join in.

"Why is the bathroom door locked?" I wondered aloud.

"B, do you mind?!" He barked back. "Can I shower in peace here?!"

OK...! I turned around and walked off with raised eyebrows. Something fishy was going on, but I thought it best to let it go.

*****

After lunch, we went outside to work on the greenhouse and garden.

The greenhouse was a big job, the new bags of fertilizer had to be stacked, as well as the potting mix, planters and packets of seed. Each summer we bought greenhouse supplies so we'd be prepared for winter. Our crops of vegetables, herbs and his orchids needed TLC, especially in the frozen months. I offered to help, but Declan banished me with a tender-loving-care shove, out the greenhouse door.

It was a sunny afternoon but not too hot, with the temperature sitting at 24°C. So I retrieved Lucia from the nursery and put her in the baby carrier. With a slumbering baby against my front, I caught up on some watering.

The yellow Daffodils and pink Tulips had finished, but a colourful variety of Daylillies were in bloom. We had the dark Autumn Red mixed in with yellow Stella D'Oro in one plot then in another, a mixture of white Gentle Shephard with pink Strawberry Candy. The third garden plot, which ran in a strip in front of our veranda, had wildflowers native to Alaska. There were red and dark pink colours of Fireweed, blue Forget-Me-Nots, yellow Wild Geraniums and a mix of purple and blue Lupine. Along the gravel drive we had a couple of Hydrangea bushes, some pink, some purple and some blue. Then along the side of the house which faced the front garden, we had red, pink and white Camellia bushes. Yet my favourite, was the huge Jacaranda tree standing in our front lawn, which flowered for an extended time, leaving a purple 'snow' on the lawn.

I pulled the hose along with me as I watered the flower beds first. I was wearing denim shorts, an old v-neck t-shirt and my hair up, to keep cool. It was nice being outside, with the sweet scent of the garden and the contact with my baby girl.

Next, a noise attracted my attention and I turned my head. I saw it was Declan, who was working in dark blue, cargo shorts. On each bare shoulder he carried a large bag of fertilizer, which he stacked by an outside wall of the greenhouse. The load could make a human stumble over however, he carried the bags with ease. But he slowed to a stop when he saw me watering the garden with Lucia.

He stood still with his mouth opening a little. His eyes moved upwards from my bare feet, to the denim shorts then the old t-shirt. I think it gave away more cleavage than I thought, as it was enough to capture his attention. Yet I was guilty of staring too, as I ogled his sweaty, muscled body.

It was like time came to a stand still by the sight of each other. That or it moved in extremely slow motion. The water spraying out of the hose, now lingered like a frozen waterfall. The leaves swayed so slowly, it was like the wind was waltzing with them. Even my own heart felt like it had slowed, with the rhythm changing from a fast beat to a lengthy boom.

Declan was the first to break the spell however, as he turned around to get more bags. I watched disappointedly, as he retrieved two large sacks of potting mix and stacked them next to the fertilizer. My eyes were glued to his muscles and how they rippled as he moved. By this stage, my heart was literally pounding in my chest.

“Please don’t be changed...!” I murmured under my breath, as I returned to watering. “Please don’t be, please don’t!”

“Huh?” He gave a peculiar look from overhearing.

“Oh nothing,” I lied. “I was just talking to Lucia.”

He looked on in disbelief, "What don't you want to change about her?"

"Long story," I waved it off.

Then I tugged the hose along to water another section of the garden.

*****

Once the flower beds were watered, I noticed something else felt wet too, Lucia's nappy.

I carried her inside and changed her upstairs. But before I could put her down for a nap, she cried for her afternoon feed. So I sat down in the rocking chair, tugged up my t-shirt then unfastened my Maternity Bra. Once she supped on the left breast, I moved her to my right. She drank so much, I swear I went down a bra size.

The feeding made her restless and I knew she wouldn't go down without a fight. So I rocked her in the chair whilst singing softly to her. I must admit, I didn't know many lullabies, so I resorted to using my favourite Kiss song, 'God Gave Rock 'n Roll to You.'

I think I got a couple of the verses wrong, but my two-week-old didn't seem to mind. She fell asleep against my clothed breasts, panting softly. I thought I could make my getaway, until I looked up. Declan was standing in the doorway, watching as usual, even if he was covered in dirt and sweat.

"I think our little girl is gonna grow up to be a head-banger," he grinned.

"Why do you say that?"

"Well, you just sang Kiss to her and last night I sang Alice Cooper's 'Poison'."

"When did you do that?"

"When you were in the shower and she needed a nappy change." He shrugged, before he looked down at the dirt sticking to his skin. "Speaking of which, I'll just jump in the shower then I'll start on dinner."

"You did such a good job with the greenhouse, I thought I'd cook and give you a night off." I smiled.

"Nah ah," he shook his head. "Food is my department."

Slowly, I stood up from the rocking chair then gently put her in the cot. Next, I tip-toed out of the nursery and partially closed the door behind. When I thought was in the clear, I put my hands on my hips to confront him.

"Declan, stop it." I spoke quietly but firmly. "Since Lucia's birth, you've been waiting on us hand and foot. Now, I'm not an invalid, I can help in the greenhouse and I can make dinner."

This made him pause and I thought my argument was working. That was until he looked from my eyes, down to my cleavage, then back to my eyes. A silly smile spread out across his face.

"Not on my watch," he said coolly. "Now go and read your grannies' diaries or something. If I even catch you in the kitchen -"

"You'll what?" My eyebrows rose as I challenged him. "You'll do what, Declan?"

He paused a second time, like he was trying to think of something. Then he snapped his fingers as the idea hit him. He said smugly, "I'll tell Wendy that you didn't like her caribou casserole."

"You wouldn't..." my face fell.

"Try me," he folded his arms across his bare chest.

"You wouldn't dare!" I rebuked. "You've seen how hormonal Wendy is, in her last few months of pregnancy. You wouldn't risk the Wisetail's never talking to us again."

Out of the blue, Declan picked me in his arms and hoisted me up into the air. I was held so high, it was close enough for him to playfully bite into my side. He pretended to maul me as I squealed with laughter.

He growled out, "Say you'll behave!"

"Never!"

Next, he pretended to toss me into the air and catch me again. I laughed and laughed, loving every minute of this! He appeared to be the same, as he was in no hurry to put me down.

At last he returned me to my feet but his arms remained about my waist. My dark blue eyes looked up into his bright blue ones. I saw how they widened and his lips parted. I thought this may have been the end of our dry spell. My mouth opened and I started to stand on my tippy-toes to kiss him...

"Waaaaaahh! Grrrr! Waaaaaahhh!"

...when we were interrupted by Lucia's cry. I sensed our mayhem roused her and now she was overtired and grumpy. Great, it's going to take a while to get her back to sleep again.

"I'm gonna have that shower then I'll cook dinner." He took a step back. "Tend to our waif, wench, and behave yourself!"

Cheekily, he delivered a smack to my bottom then ducked into the bathroom, locking the door behind. I knew it was to prevent retaliation from his spouse. Smilingly, I shook my head as I went into the nursery and picked up our daughter. I sat back down in the rocking chair and held her against my chest.

I sang Alanis Morissette next, "An old man turned ninety-eight, he won the lottery and died the next day."

*****

After dinner, Declan insisted on stacking the dirty dishes into the dishwasher. So not only did he cook, he cleaned up afterwards as well. I know this is the dream of every new mother, feeling frazzled being at the beck and call of a baby. But the way he waited on us hand and foot, started to piss me off. What am I, weak and useless?

"Hey, it's still sunny out." He observed through the kitchen window. "There's a cool breeze now, so it's not so hot. How about a walk down to the General Store and I'll shout you an ice cream?"

I gave a funny look, "It's past 7 PM and you want to go for a forty minute walk there and a forty minute walk back, just to buy an ice cream?"

"The sun isn't gonna set until eleven o'clock." He replied. "C'mon, let's take Lucia for a walk."

"Alright," I sighed out. "I'll put her in the baby carrier."

"Nah, lets use the hover-pram instead." He decided. "We haven't tried it yet."

Declan readied the technology in the living room by turning it on and taking it for a 'test drive' around the dining table. When he deemed it was safe, he called out. I carried Lucia downstairs after changing her into cotton shorts and a singlet. Once she was in the pram, I rested just a sheet over her. I didn't want her overheating, she felt especially hot after being in the garden.

My mate insisted on pushing the hover-pram like a proud papa bear. I locked the front door behind and the technology sailed smoothly down the wooden veranda stairs. We walked down our gravel driveway then we descended the steep, concealed road. We were both wearing sneakers, jeans, t-shirts and sunglasses.

As he pushed the pram, I walked quietly beside, deep in thought.

Tomorrow morning, Ki was coming to do his check-up on Lucia and I was tempted to ask him to scan Declan too. I wanted to make sure my husband hadn't changed biologically as he had mentally, towards sex. I was also tempted to bring up the rest of his behaviour to our Medicine Man. Maybe his medical scanner could pick up if the European Werewolf had been replaced by a 'Stepford Wife'?

Where's the man who'd pounce on his wife and wrestle for the dominant position? Where's the man whose snarls could make a human jump in fright? Where's the man who'd get cranky if sometimes he didn't have sex twice a day?

When we had walked halfway down the hill, Declan broke the silence.

"You're quiet."

"You've gone quiet," I returned.

"I'm not quiet, I'm the one who's talking first."

"But you've turned quiet." I frowned.

He turned to look my way through his black shades, "Maybe I'm content with the way things are."

"What, with slave labour and no sex?"

"Nope," he chuckled back. "I'm happy having a healthy, beautiful wife and a healthy, beautiful daughter. I plan on keeping it this way too."

This made me stop in surprise, "What's that supposed to mean?"

"C'mon, B." He took my hand and rested it on the handle. Then he put his hand over it and like this, he pushed along his wife and child.

"You've turned creepy," I looked away, sulkily.

"Thanks B, I love you too." He snickered.

“I mean it, Declan." I said seriously. "It’s like an alien has taken your place.”

"Sure.”

“An alien who doesn’t know how European Werewolves behave." I went on. "Instead of growling or pouncing on your wife, you constantly cook and clean. The next thing I know, you’ll start knitting, or crocheting, or something just plain wrong.”

“It’s a full moon in a couple of days.” He noted. “So if I stay home and knit, then you’ll know something's wrong with me.”

“Can you please stop being so nice and bite my head off?” I said crankily.

He leaned forwards and snapped his teeth together in front of my face, before he walked onwards.

“Is that better?” He asked.

I passed him a sideways glance, “Can you please stop being so polite and have me up against that tree or something?”

He laughed it off as he removed his hand from mine and tucked it into the back pocket of my jeans. Like this, he easily pushed the pram one-handed. He even gave my backside an affectionate squeeze.

“Is this better?” He asked congenially. “Don’t ever change, B. You have the perfect attitude for the mate of a European Werewolf.”

“What, bad-tempered and bitchy?”

“Exactly.”

Contentedly, he walked the rest of the way, only removing his hand when we entered suburbia.

We walked past the sports field where a twilight game of soccer was playing. The game was paused when Samuel Riverclaw and some of the other players ran over to greet us. In fact, any tribesperson who happened to be outdoors and saw us, came over to offer their congratulations.

Everyone wanted to look on little Lucia. We received well-wishes after well-wishes, as a proud Declan kept one hand on the handle and the other on my waist. He beamed as people fawned over his progeny and asked all sorts of questions about her weight, or delivery.

We received the same reaction inside the General Store. The automatic glass door opened and everyone noted our arrival. All eyes were upon the new parents and the hover-pram they had with them.

“Look at what we have here, the Sabre family!” Uma Elm gushed, as she came forwards with her teenaged daughter. “Can we see her?”

Declan bent down and carefully picked her up, making sure she was wrapped in the sheet, before handing her over.

“Oh, isn’t she gorgeous!” She looked down into Lucia’s face. Her eyes were closed and her clawed hands were tucked in, so she looked like any other baby. But then she opened her glowing green eyes to look up at the person holding her. Instead of acting aghast, Uma cooed, "Look at this beautiful little girl! You can see both her father and mother in her."

"She has her mother's beauty and her father's strength," he joked along. "You can't complain about that, can you?"

"You can't indeed!" Uma beamed. "A Sabre and a Wisetail-Riverclaw, all rolled into one!"

He put his arm about my shoulders and grinned at all the attention. Once upon a time, people had anticipated an Elm and a Wisetail-Riverclaw baby, by my arranged marriage to Grant Elm. The union wounded Declan, so much so, he couldn't bear to be in the same room as us. Now it was to his delight, people were congratulating our procreation instead.

"Anytime you need a babysitter, just give a holler," Helena Elm volunteered.

"OK, I will." I accepted the offer.

"Can I hold her now?" She asked eagerly.

Reluctantly, her mother passed her over and ensured the sixteen year old held her correctly by supporting the head.

Several other Lokoti crowded around to look on the newest addition to the tribe. Even Becca Barley who was working behind the register, came over for a closer look. All throughout, I sensed a deep satisfaction radiate from my mate. I guessed this was the true motivation behind his ice cream request, to show off his newborn. He truly acted like a proud papa bear, while holding mama bear against his side.

"Excuse me? Excuse me!" A stranger sung out, demandingly. "Can I get some assistance?"

Our heads snapped around at the foreign voice, to see a male of Indian appearance, wearing a shirt, shorts and hiking boots. He was standing in an aisle and trying to attract Becca's attention. I guessed he was a hiker or a camper, stopping at the General Store on his way in or out of the National Park.

Instantly, I froze in fear whereas Declan immediately went on guard.

Uma turned hers and Helena's backs to the strangers, to block their view of Lucia. At the same time, Declan came to stand in front, to use his larger size to cover them. An uncomfortable silence filled the General Store, as everyone quieted because of the outsiders in our midst.

The stranger looked around before he asked in a haughty fashion, "Does someone actually WORK here?"

I heard a growl crawl up Declan's throat, but it was Becca Barley who stepped forwards.

"I work here," she said calmly. "Can I help you?"

"Yeah, all I can see are these 'Wet Ones' anti-bacterial wipes." He complained. "But have you got any other brands?"

"I'm afraid we don't, sorry." She answered politely. "There's a large supermarket in Alma that would sell more of a variety."

“In this day and age, who only sells one brand?” The man pretended to mutter to himself, but loud enough so all could hear. “Come along, Roshana! We have to go to the BIGGER supermarket in town.”

“But Nagendra, we’ve just come from there!" An Indian woman whined, as she walked down another aisle. "We’re supposed to be setting up camp now. At this rate, we won't have our tent up by dark.”

"I need anti-bacterial wipes and you know I don't like using 'Wet Ones'." He stomped towards the door. “Now we have to go all the way back to civilization, which offers more than just ONE product!”

Disgruntled, she started to follow him out until she saw the teenager holding the baby.

“Oh what a cute... WHAT IN THE NAME OF SHIVA?!”

Helena tried to turn Lucia away from the strangers, but in curiosity, she moved her head around to see what was making all the noise.

That was when catastrophe struck...

“Look at the baby's eyes!” The man stopped and stared, along with the woman.

"They're glowing green!" She pointed at my little girl.

"And look at her - her - her pupils!" The man spluttered out his surprise. "They're not round, they're weird! I don't think it's human!"

I didn’t have a chance to react because Declan did, but it wasn’t the reaction I was hoping for.

In a lightning fast move, he grabbed the man about the throat and lifted him into the air. Simultaneously as he was choking him, he moved in front of the automatic door, to block the woman’s escape. His eyes glowed green in anger, making this already bad situation worse.

“Declan!” I yelled. “Put him down!”

“Nagendra!” The woman cried at her husband being dangled in the air. “I’m calling 911!”

No sooner had she pulled out her mobile phone, the European Werewolf whipped it out of her hand and crushed it in his larger one.

The woman emitted a terrified whimper as the man made choking noises.

An idea formed in my mind which made me lift Lucia out of Helena's arms. I carried her over and held her in front of my enraged mate, who was going nuts in the overprotective department. It was like the expression, 'all he saw was red', with his bloodlust ignited.

“Declan, put the man down NOW!”

He looked away from his targets just long enough to notice his wife and child. Then his eyes lingered on the baby in my arms and like a flick of a switch, he released the stranger. The gasping man fell to the floor, spluttering, as his wife knelt down to help him.

"H-h-here, use my phone..." the man wheezed as he retrieved it from his pocket, "...c-c-call the police."

His wife took it from him and started to dial as she looked up, frightened.

The European Werewolf loomed over them in a threatening manner and I knew the strangers' lives were in danger.

I had to think fast and take action before a bloodbath occurred.

Next, I handed Lucia over to Declan, as he wouldn't attack with a baby in his arms. Then I too took out my mobile phone. It didn't ring long before my lawyer answered.

"Hi, Jonathan? It's B. I need you to use Hodge Endeavor's contacts in the U.S. Government to run a background check on some people."

By naming the huge, international company and its powerful friends, gave the woman pause but she continued.

"Hallo 911? This is an emergency, my husband and I are being held up inside of a convenience store!"

"Can you do a trace on the number plate..." I peered out the front window at the hover-car in the car park I didn't recognize, "...UZNS 5611."

"It's on a reservation beside a town called Alma." She started to cry then she snapped. "No, we're not in Alma, the reservation is beside Alma!"

"Nagendra and Roshana Kumar?" I repeated the information and their eyes widened. "That sounds like them. Their address is Apartment 311, 2118 Sunshine Terrace, Palm Beach, Los Angeles? Yep, I want you to do a full background check on them. Find out where they work, their bank account balances, the whole shebang."

The outsiders' mouths fell open when I said aloud their address.

"Nagendra is self-employed, huh? He owns his own accountancy firm. What, it's marked by the IRS? Gee, you don't say... he's been receiving large deposits that aren't declared as income. Do I want you to pressure the IRS to act? Now that's a good question."

Their faces paled and the woman looked like she'd forgotten she was supposed to be on the phone.

"Hello? Ma'am, I can't hear you anymore," the operator spoke. "But I've tracked your position by your mobile phone signal. A Sheriff's vehicle from Alma is being dispatched to your location."

My determined eyes met her terrified ones in a silent challenge, as both women wanted to protect their loved ones.

"I'm sorry, it's all a misunderstanding." Roshana said hastily. "I don't need a Sheriff. Thank you, good bye."

She hit the 'end call' button and handed the phone back to her husband.

"Yes Jonathan, I'm still here." I said after a moment. "Stand down with the IRS, but keep this information in a safe place. You never know if we might need it again. Thanks for your help."

I too ended my call and put the small technology back into my pocket.

The human couple looked up at the Werewolf one, in horror.

“Who ARE you people?” Nagendra gaped.

“People who stand tall and stand together," Uma walked up to rest her hand on Lucia’s back.

“And for your information, you’re not on a *reservation*." Helena said coldly. "You're guests on Lokoti Tribal Lands.”

"Which is inside the Lokoti National Park," Uma finished. "World Heritage Listed Land that belongs to its' original owners."

Becca smirked, “I think you’ll find the anti-bacterial wipes your looking for, in Alma.”

Browbeaten and worse for wear, Roshana stood up first then helped her husband up, second.

Glaringly, Declan moved aside whilst holding his infant and let them depart via the automatic door.

The outsiders rushed to their vehicle, aware that the eyes of every person in and outside of the store, were on them.

On their way, they passed two tall, strong-looking, Lokoti men. One stood outside the Garage which was beside the store, the other in the car park. They stood as still as statues, but their large muscles which were evident under their clothes, looked tense. Their dark brown eyes narrowed as they watched the strangers leave.

To top it off, a US Forest Service hover-car powered down, with a Park Ranger jumping out. To the strangers, he looked just as tall and strong as the other two, and just as foreboding. He stood in his uniform, beside his off-road vehicle and watched the outsiders get into theirs.

As soon as the strangers' seatbelts were buckled, their hover-car rose into the air and zoomed out of the car park.

With the danger now passed, Tyson left the Garage to come into the Store, as did Derik and Walt.

"Hey hon, are you OK?" Derik approached his wife first. "I felt you were scared about something."

"It's alright now," Uma hugged him. "There were two outsiders who got a look at Lucia."

"But I don't think they'll be bothering us again," Helena said, before hugging her father next.

Then Tyson and Walt approached their Second who was holding his young closely.

Walt grinned in good humour, “Trouble in paradise?”

“A near miss,” Declan said curtly. “B scared them off by having Hodge Endeavor's government contacts, look into their tax records.”

“Nice!” Tyson looked on, impressed. “Nothing scares a human like death or taxes.”

Next, Walt tickled Lucia under the chin to make her smile. He chuckled down to her, "You're stopping traffic already, are you Looch?"

Everyone started to relax as a couple more jokes flew around the room. But there were two people weren't able to laugh it off, me and Declan. The European Werewolf's eyes were still glowing green in anger. Also, his muscles were so taught, they made his veins stand out.

He would have strangled that man! And it wouldn't have stopped there, the woman's life would've ended right after his. Seeing my mate overreact scared everyone in the store. It also taught me that his bad-temper hadn't disappeared. Now I knew his bloodlust was hiding deep inside, just waiting for a threat to his mate and young.

*****

At 11.13 PM the sun set and the parents took advantage of the darkness by going to bed.

Both of us lay on our sides, facing in opposite directions. Neither of us could sleep though, I sensed that this evening's excitement was foremost in our thoughts. Eventually, I rolled over onto my back to talk about it.

"What would you have done if Hodge Endeavor weren't able to help tonight?"

There was a moment of silence, before he turned his head to say gruffly:

"What the hell do you think, I'd take them out for tea and crumpets?"

"Declan..."

"B, shut up." He said tiredly. "You know what I'm capable of, if I think you're in danger. Now we have a daughter, times it by two."

Indignantly, I sat upright so I could glare down on the obstinate male.

"Declan, you gave yourself away tonight!"

"Gee, you think?"

I ranted, "I like living here with our friends and family! If the Police were pulled in, we'd have to go on the run! We'd have move to a new timeframe! You almost killed two people tonight! You even jeopardized the anonymity of the pack!"

Angrily, he sat up to face me with his eyes glowing green once more.

"B, nobody is going to threaten my mate and young! Do you hear me? NOBODY! If that means I have to kill any strangers who get a look at the two of you, then so be it!"

"Oh goodie," I sung sarcastically. "I can see my grandfather's years of training your bloodlust to hunt animal instead of human, has paid off."

"Don't give me that!" He snapped. "If your Gran or Mom or even you, were in danger, your Grandfather would've acted the same way!"

"WRONG!" I yelled in his face. "Grandfather once fought off a bunch of drunks outside of a bar in Alma, for sexually harassing Gran. He fought them in human form, not giving himself away! He'd only show his Werewolf nature if it was a last resort, like when he patrolled after the War. Declan, tonight WASN'T a last resort. You turned in one second flat!"

"Of course I did, I'm a European Werewolf! I still crave human flesh every frickin' day and I'm 300 years old! If a human acts untoward my mate and young, it's a safe bet that I'm gonna act untoward them!"

"Declan, you're a father now," my voice dropped. "Fathers act with restraint. Fathers lead by example. It's great that you don't feed on human, but let's work on the urge to kill humans, just for looking at your young."

Silence... his eyes widened as his mouth wavered at my words.

After another moment, he spoke with a helpless expression on his face. "Man, I really am a murderous sociopath, aren't I?"

A loud sigh escaped as I briefly looked away. Then I took a deep breath before looking into his eyes again. The glowing green started to fade back to their blue colour. I felt his regret and it made me put a sympathetic hand on his shoulder.

"You're not that bad," I said with a sad smile. "Compared to the other European Werewolves we saw in the Viewing Room, you should be awarded a medal."

Guiltily, he glanced away as his shoulders slumped at whatever was weighing on his mind.

He confessed, "I liked strangling that guy tonight. I liked killing those North American Vampires. I like the fact that I'm the biggest and the strongest in the pack and if only one is sent out to fight, it's me. My bloodlust is revelling over my change into a Circulator and the fact that I can run in light speed. The cold voice inside that tells me to eat human, is now saying that being so strong and fast, I don't have to follow a moral code anymore."

"Declan..." I began, "...I know that voice, I used to hear it too."

"You did?"

"It said the same thing to me when I first changed. I think it scared the pack when they empathically felt its influence over me. The voice said I was faster than them, so I shouldn't have to obey. It's why I was drugged and locked in the bathroom, so I couldn't escape."

He moved closer as he rested his hand on my thigh, "I remember the first night you changed and ran towards Alma, to hunt human. You outran the pack and I knew the only way I could stop you was head-on, at the border."

I rested my hand on his wide chest, "I remember when you stepped out in front. I thought you were so big that there was no way I'd get past you."

Then he grinned, "But you still tried."

And I giggled, "You pinned me to the ground and it resulted in our first kiss."

"It was my first kiss, period." He said. "I'd never kissed a girl before."

"Really?" I looked on in surprise. "I knew we were each other's first time, but I didn't know I was the first girl you kissed."

"You're the first everything." He spoke plainly. "You're the pack's first female Lokoti Werewolf and the first woman I could safely be with. You were my first kiss, first sex, first mate and now, you've delivered my first child."

My hand moved up his chest, over his jaw line and briefly touched lips.

He continued, "When we're in the same room, I don't hunger for human, I hunger for you. When I feel your aura, the cold voice knows it can't compete. Now I see you with Lucia and how happy you are with the child that I gave you? I'm frickin' ecstatic, so much so that my aura has turned yellow, the same colour yours turns when you're happy. When you were pregnant, your aura was a peach colour. After the delivery, it looks part peach and part yellow. Basically, your aura is an orange colour and it's never been that before. I'm on top of the world, knowing that I was the one who made you turn a new colour."

Just then I climbed into his lap so I was straddling him. He looked surprised by my advances but he didn't put a stop to it. I wrapped my arms about his neck as I peered into his eyes.

Next, my lips brushed his as they moved to murmur into his ear, "In unan Declan...always and forever."

He responded fervently, kissing my shoulder then my neck and lastly, on the mouth.

Our tongues entwined as my fingers did, through his scruffy, blonde hair. His mouth smothered mine, over and over again, with his lips latching on. He breathed hard through his nose which sounded like loud sniffing.

I felt his fingers dig into my hips as his hardening member met my crotch. But our intimate areas were separated by his satin boxers and my cotton panties. My nails dug into his back to show I hungered for him just as much as he hungered for me.

I felt his heart rate quicken as he responded eagerly. His hands held tightly onto my waist, pulling my crotch downwards as his member moved upwards. The fabric of our underwear strained against our arousal. I found myself being lowered backwards onto the bed, but instead of feeling the weight of his body on mine, it and he had vanished.

A bright blur jumped up from the bed and whizzed out of the bedroom in light speed!

Simultaneously, I heard a loud BANG which was the bathroom door slamming shut. After a second, I heard the shower turn on. It was louder than usual too, like the water pressure was on full strength.

What the...? Has Declan gone crazy?! He was about to - to - to - why did he race away? This will be the third shower he's had today!

I lay on my back, panting hard from my ignited lust, which was answered with rejection and frustration.

*****

~ 13 ~

“Everything seems A-OK," our Medicine Man said chirpily.

Ki was leaning over Lucia, who was lying on a blanket which we'd put on the coffee table.

He read off his medical scanner, "Her heart rate is strong, her blood pressure is better than normal and her immune system is the strongest I've ever seen in an infant. With her regenerative ability, you can forego the usual inoculations and vaccines children have these days."

Next, he clicked his fingers near the right side of her head then the left. Her head moved side to side at the noises, with her glowing green eyes following his movement. This impressed him for some reason.

"What is it?" I wondered.

"Lucia's not only the size of a two month old, but she's surpassed the development of one." He reported. "At three months, babies react to sound by turning their heads. Your newborn is developing quickly, as I suspected would happen."

"Is that a good thing?" I queried.

"Well, its part of her predatory instincts as a Werewolf." Ki shrugged. "I'm willing to bet that her academic learning will be on par with a human child. But her physical developments will occur at an accelerated rate. Think of it as nature's way of preparing her for hunting as soon as possible."

This made Declan frown down on his squirming young, in concern.

Ki turned off his medical scanner then put it inside his medicine bundle. I picked up my writhing baby, sensing that she wanted contact. As soon as I did, her little legs and arms stopped flailing.

“How much longer are her eyes gonna glow like that?” Her father asked.

“I'm guessing Lucia’s human colour will become permanent anywhere between nine months to two years.” He shrugged. “I've noticed her claws are starting to weaken into human nails. Only time will tell but until then, I wouldn’t suggest any trips into Alma.”

He started to snicker at his joke until he saw my mate's expression and he stopped.

Our Healer picked up the old, black leather, doctor's case and prepared to leave.

“Actually...” I stopped him, “...that’s the baby checked out, but can you scan my husband too?”

This gave him pause. “I'm sorry...?”

"B, don't!" My mate objected. "Ki, it's fine."

"No it's NOT fine!" I snapped. "There's something wrong with you!"

"There is not!"

"There is too!" I retorted, before I looked to our Medicine Man. "Can you please scan him?"

He pulled out his medical scanner again and switched it back on, as he enquired, "And what am I looking for?"

"I said I'm fine!" The European Werewolf barked.

"Yeah right!" I rebuked. "Ki, can you see if he's turned into an alien, or a robot, or make sure he hasn't got a virus or something?"

"I haven't been sick since I was three, when I was turned!" He huffed.

Ki ran the scanner over him then checked the read outs.

"Your pulse is faster than usual and your blood pressure is a little higher than normal." He told my mate before turning my way. "But they're nothing to be concerned about. Officially, Uncle Dec has a clean bill of health. Why, what seems to be the trouble?"

"B, don't!" My mate growled.

"We haven't had sex since Lucia's birth," I proclaimed.

"I can't believe you just did that." He rubbed his face, as he walked away.

Ki struggled to hide his surprise, "Er, can you tell me more about this?"

"He – he – he - " I fumbled, unsure how to put it.

"The equipment isn't in working order?" Ki tried to put it tactfully. Declan emitted a dissatisfied snarl at the suggestion, which made him quickly continue. "Or is there lack of stimulus or motivation?"

"Hey!" I cried out, offended. "He tells me everyday he loves my motherly body, but he won't seal the deal!"

The Healer sat down on the couch to hear this out.

"Uncle Dec, how about we hear your side of events?" He called him over. "After all, it is your body. Can you tell us if what Aunt B is saying is correct?"

Restlessly, the European Werewolf began to pace up and down. He growled out between gritted teeth, "I can't believe we're having this conversation."

"What was I supposed to do?" I complained. "I've asked you again and again, but you won't talk about it."

"I've told you why!"

"No you haven't!" I objected. "Except some half-ass excuse that you want to let me recover from Lucia's birth."

"That IS the reason why!"

"Ki, can you please tell my husband that I'm fully regenerated after the birth." I said coolly.

"Ki, can you please tell my wife that I'm not willing to put her life at risk again." Declan retaliated.

"Ki, can you please tell my hard-headed husband that my life isn't at risk."

"Ki, can you please tell my stubborn wife that I plan on keeping it that way."

"OK - OK - OK!" Our Healer put up his hands for silence. "How about we all sit down and talk this through rationally."

"You're asking my wife to be rational?" My husband feigned surprise. "How about walking up to a Hindu and demand that they eat cow?"

"You're telling my European Werewolf husband to be rational? This is after he nearly killed a pair of Hindus, just for looking at his daughter!"

"Now that's enough, you two," the Medicine Man took charge. "Can both husband and wife sit down and we'll calmly talk about this?"

Declan walked back over and sat on the couch first then I sat down with Lucia, second. He sat on the left as I sat on the right, leaving a gap between us. But the territorial male didn't like that, so he moved closer to put his arm about his mate and young.

"You see?" I waved his way. "He's always hovering nearby. He even stays up all night watching me sleep. But if I make a move on him, he goes running for the hills. That or into the bathroom for a shower. Yesterday he showered THREE times!"

When Ki looked in his direction, Declan cleared his throat.

"If I'm having cold showers, it proves my 'equipment' is in working order, doesn't it?"

"You're having cold showers?" The Medicine Man's eyebrows rose.

"Yeah and believe me, they're COLD!" He emphasized. "The water is frickin' freezing!"

"Well, I think we can rule out physical malfunctions." Ki tried to maintain a professional air. "It sounds like Uncle Dec is suppressing his sexual urges. So what we have to ask is, why is he denying his physical needs?"

Declan removed his arm as he reached the end of his already thin patience.

"Am I the only person in this room who doesn't have the memory span of a goldfish? What is so frickin' hard to understand, people?! Ki, you saw how much blood there was! You saw what Lucia's birth did to B! Why am I the only one here, who's not rushing head-first over a cliff?"

"I'm fine!" I rebuked. "What's so frickin' hard about that YOU can't understand, Declan?"

The Medicine Man cast a concerned look over the baby, worried that our fighting may upset her. But she rested against my breasts, looking the very epitome of the word 'peaceful'. She was already accustomed to her parent's growls and snarls.

"Uncle Dec, correct me if I'm wrong, as you're so fond of doing..." Ki said wryly, "...but Aunt B did say that Lucia would be the eldest of the three sisters, did she not?"

"It's not like we're never gonna have sex again!" He scoffed. "But I am going to give my wife breathing space, as well as breeding space, between rug rats."

"Sounds reasonable," Ki conceded, before looking my way.

"But it's not in Declan's case!" I refuted. "He's changed since Lucia's birth. He's politer than usual. He waits on us hand and foot. Hell, he even growls and swears less! Well, he did before today."

Our 'marriage counsellor' opened his mouth again then he hesitated. He caught sight of what my husband was doing and stared. There was a tender expression on the European Werewolf's face, as his large hand caressed his daughter's small forehead. Then a grin broke out at the tiny growl she made.

Ki Lightfoot was accustomed to seeing Declan Sabre as Second in the pack, who answered only to the First. He's seen my mate tear apart his prey with his claws, or devour flesh and bone in his large jaws, in battle or on a hunt. His reputation as not only the pack's but the world's most dangerous Werewolf, was well-earned. Now here he was, over the moon with his new family.

"Aunt B, I heard what happened at the store. The pack has always been aware of how Uncle Dec reacts when he feels that his mate is threatened. Seeing him like this, explains a lot about his change in attitude." He began.

My husband had placed his little finger inside Lucia's mouth for her to chew on, when he looked up. "Huh?"

"Your husband is caring for his wife and child in the manner he thinks best." Ki continued. "I doubt there's anything he wouldn't do for the pair of you, which includes protecting you from himself."

"You got that right," Declan declared.

He went on, "Looking at the pair of you, sitting together on that couch; Aunt B your aura right now is orange, which I've never seen you glow before. Uncle Dec's aura is yellow, which I understand is a happy colour. Seeing the two of you together, with your positive auras alongside of your baby, is one of the perks of my job. I see a couple who were supposedly barren, be granted the miracle which is sleeping in her mother's arms."

"But Ki..." I faltered, "...tell Declan that if I get pregnant again, I won't be in danger. I mean, how else are we supposed to have our other daughters?"

"Breathing space B," my mate repeated, "as well as breeding space."

Now our Medicine Man stood up with a sigh as if to say, 'well my job here is done'. Then he picked up his medical scanner and returned it to his medicine bundle. While carrying his doctor's case, he headed for the front door.

"This is a conversation for husband and wife... not husband, wife and Medicine Man." He chuckled once more at his own joke. "As long as all three Sabre's are healthy, my work here is done. I'll just see myself out, shall I?"

"See you round, Ki." My husband gave a dismissive wave before turning back to his wife. "You see B, the only one with a problem with this, is you."

I glared back before I stood up and carried Lucia upstairs to change her.

*****

After lunch, I put my baby in the carrier and took her into the greenhouse with me.

Coolly, I walked past Declan, who was sitting at the dining table preserving antipasto mix. He looked up from the second-hand jars he'd sterilized, but I averted my gaze. I walked out the back door and down the pathway to the glass door.

Lucia slumbered against my front as I potted some new radishes, lettuce and celery, at the workbench.

I planted the seeds in several long trays. Once they were sown, I prepared to pick up the crop of radishes and move them over to a shelf. I reached out my arms to ensure it wouldn't knock against the baby carrier when two larger arms extended past mine. They proceeded to pick up the planter, raise it over my head then place it on the shelf.

My husband had slipped into the greenhouse unseen and proceeded to do the heavy lifting for me.

"I can carry it," I said coldly.

"You're already carrying something; the baby."

Next, he did the same with the planters for the lettuce and celery.

Since he'd taken over, I went outside to fetch the hose. I tugged it inside the greenhouse and turned on the setting for a gentle spray. Like a fine mist, the tiny water droplets moistened the soil then the rest of the vegetation. He smiled appreciatively as he watched me water his orchids as well.

When I moved away, he walked over and plucked an orange flower from his most precious of plants. I looked on his offering in surprise and my eyes widened further still, as he tenderly tucked the flower between my breasts. I was wearing a v-neck t-shirt, which gave him access to my cleavage.

"An orange orchid for the girl with the orange aura," he smiled softly.

With that, he turned and left the greenhouse to return to the main house. I watched the back of his strong build disappear, before looking upwards in a dreamy state. As I gazed up at the clear blue sky, I noticed something white and round.

It was a full moon...

My heart began to pound as my hand holding the hose, started to shake. My breathing turned into panting as my muscles tensed up. It's been months since I hunted and now that I was no longer pregnant, I felt the bloodlust in full force.

Just then the sleepy, little growl my daughter emitted, made me look down.

Oh, how was I going to hunt with a baby? Lucia's too young to carry while running in supernatural speed. I didn't want to ask anyone to babysit, as I wasn't sure how she'd behave. What if the full moon affects her too?

I turned off the hose, rolled it back up then went inside to pose these questions.

Declan was sitting at the dining table again, only he'd finished preserving. Now, he was about to make a fresh batch of pasta. He had the bowl of dough and his tools ready, but upon my approach he looked up.

"Tonight's a full moon and I don't think I can take Lucia in the baby carrier when I'm running in supernatural speed."

He didn't look surprised by this, in fact, he looked resigned.

"Yeah, I figured as much," he sighed. He slapped down a glob of dough on the board then pounded it with his fist. "We can't carry her when we take down our prey, either. She could be kicked in the head by a caribou or moose, or whatever else we hunt."

"What are we going to do?" I asked unhappily.

"I guess we stay home."

Then he took a deep breath, as if he were mentally preparing himself for the hardship ahead.

I stood there watching him flatten the dough with his palm, before he squashed it with a rolling pin. His brow was furrowed, like he was trying not to think about it. His shoulders looked tense and I sensed the stress build up inside him.

"Maybe you should go hunting without me." I sighed, defeated. "I mean, I didn't feel like hunting when I was pregnant. My maternal instincts dulled the bloodlust then, so maybe they'll do it again."

"But you feel like hunting tonight?" He asked knowingly.

"Well... yes."

"Then I'll stay home with Lucia and you go out." He said as he worked. "It's only fair, especially since you've missed the last five months."

His offer was admirable, but I noticed he didn't look up as he said it. Instead, he pretended to concentrate on the task at hand, which was making pasta. I sensed he was trying to be strong for his family, but I felt his bloodlust boiling.

"No..." I moaned, "...you go hunting and I'll stay home with Lucia."

"Then it looks like neither of us will be hunting this full moon."

"But Declan -"

"If you can't hunt because of our daughter then neither can I." He interrupted. "Now pass me the spaghetti maker."

*****

By the time we went to bed, his digital clock read 11.33 PM.

The light of the full moon overtook summer's pale twilight, making the evening seem more magical.

I could tell the light of la luna was turning my husband into a lunatic. His foot was jiggling so hard, it made our bed vibrate. I knew he had to go hunting, otherwise neither of us would get any sleep.

"Declan, would you please just go?" I said tiredly. "There's no point in fighting it."

"But it's unfair if you can't, coz you have to stay home with the baby."

"Yes, but my bloodlust isn't driving me as mental as yours is." I said simply.

I watched him sit upright to look on the moonlight spilling onto the bedroom floor and his eyes began glow. I heard the growl under his breath, as I heard his heart pound. He looked longingly out the window then down on his mate.

"I'm sorry B, but I have to get out... I have to kill and feed."

"I know you do."

"Do you wanna come too? Maybe Lucia will be alright in the baby carrier, just stand back and let me do the killing then you feed." He offered.

"No Dec, you'll be hunting alone this month." I said reluctantly. "Lucia's too young to come and running in supernatural speed might be too jarring for her."

He emitted a low whine in frustration and guilt, as his leg jiggled as restlessly as his foot.

"Please go." I said softly. "Purge your bloodlust."

Next, a large, bright blur leapt up from the bed, out of the bedroom and simultaneously downstairs, I heard our front door open and slam shut.

All that remained of him were his boxer shorts lying discarded on the floor.

I imagined him changing into his huge, hulking, hairless body as he rushed out. With my keen hearing, I heard him bolt out of our yard then gallop into the surrounding woods, on all-fours. I sensed he was racing after the pack to hunt with our First.

Perfectly timed, I was reminded why I wasn't with them, by the sound of crying from the next room. Wearily, I heaved myself to my feet and went into the nursery. As I looked down into the cot, I noticed her eyes were glowing brighter than usual. Even her tiny teeth were bared, as she flailed her small, clawed hands. It looks like the full moon was also impacting my newborn Werewolf.

Carefully, I picked her up and carried her over to the rocking chair by the window.

Sitting in the moonlight, I breastfed my half-breed daughter. As she suckled, she stared up at the haunting, white circle in the sky. I noticed she did drink more than normal, which must have been her own bloodlust peaking.

*****

After feeding, burping, changing and placing my tiny tot back into her cot, I meandered back into the main bedroom.

I fell face first onto the bed and sighed audibly into my pillow. As I lay there, I noticed my right foot was jiggling, although not as hard as Declan's whole leg had. With another sigh, I rolled onto my back and stared out at the moonlit woods.

Maybe because I was wishing I was outside too, I swear the trees never looked so inviting. The breeze which teased the leaves looked so tempting. I closed my eyes and pictured running through the woods so fast, my hair billowed behind.

Disgruntled, I kept tossing and turning as I couldn't settle into the one position. I even grabbed my MP3 player out of the top drawer of my bedside table. Once the earphones were sitting over my ears, I blasted them with Trance music, to try to use the rhythm to channel my excess energy.

My jiggling foot now tapped along to the tunes. My heart still pounded though, as it pushed the blood faster through my veins. I noticed my hands tremble from the effect, which made me fidgety. I toyed with the chord for the earphones, as I tried to concentrate on the bass. The music played so loudly, I almost didn't hear the call.

AAAAAARRRRROOOOOOOOOOOOOOOOOOWWWWLLLLL!

Instantly, my glowing turquoise eyes snapped open. I even felt my nails tingle, as my claws appeared from the supernatural sound. It was so loud, like it came from right outside the house.

AAAAAARRRRROOOOOOOOOOOOOOOOOOWWWWLLLLL!

It was Declan, I'd recognize his howl anywhere. I leapt up from the bed, leaving my MP3 player behind, as I bolted out of the bedroom. Then in a single jump, I leapt over the entire staircase! Unharmed, I landed on all-fours on the wooden floor, before jumping up to throw open the front door.

On the gravel driveway sat my mate in his European Werewolf form.

Fresh blood dripped from his razor sharp, canine jaws, as well as from his four claws. He was so huge that even sitting on his hind legs like a canine sits, he was the height of a human male. His glowing green eyes with his narrow slits for pupils, were trained my way.

Next, his beastly head nodded towards something on the ground in front of him. I walked forwards onto the veranda to see what it was. There on the gravel was a bear claw...

Now in human terms, it's not unusual for a husband to bring home his wife a 'bear claw', but this was no sweet pastry. It was an actual claw from a bear, attached to what remained of an arm, which was still bleeding freely. From the looks of things, the furry arm had been torn off and kept for later.

COME AND GET IT! – He telepathically declared, as if he'd just served dinner.

What the...? In shock, I stared at the bloodied offering then back to my husband. My hesitation was obvious as I stayed on the veranda.

Declan NEVER shares his kill, his European Werewolf bloodlust wouldn't allow it. Whereas Lokoti Werewolves killed and feasted altogether, Declan attacked and fed alone. He's NEVER shared his kill, in all of the centuries I've known him. Hell, he doesn't even like it if I sneak food off his plate at the dinner table.

My husband growled impatiently, as he bent his huge head and nudged his offering closer.

C'MON B, HURRY BEFORE THE BLOOD BEGINS TO CONGEAL – he thought.

"But you don't share your kill." I said warily, as if this was some kind of trick.

SCARED I'M GONNA POUNCE ON YOU? – his canine mouth upturned in grin, as I heard him pant out a chuckle.

My disbelief was his answer as I refused to come any closer. I wasn't afraid of him attacking his mate rather, he'd knock her out of the way. He's done it before on a hunt or in battle.

With an amazing amount of patience shown in his dangerous body, he picked it up with his mouth, stepped up to the balcony then deliberately dropped it on my feet! Blood splashed onto my bare feet and white, cotton nightie. Then he returned to his sitting position on the gravel drive.

Whilst keeping a watchful eye in his direction, I knelt down and picked up the still-warm, bloodied arm. My gums tingled as my teeth grew longer and sharper inside my watering mouth. My human body expanded into my Lokoti Werewolf one, with my muscles inflating while simultaneously hardening.

Using my keen senses, I sniffed my meal to ensure it was fresh. Next, I used my claws to rip away the bloodied fur then my mouth dove into the warm, tender flesh. Mmm, it tasted divine! My sharp teeth tore the meat off the bone, like I could have been eating a juicy, chicken drumstick. Instead of honey-soy as the marinade, warm blood trickled down my chin and all over my white nightie.

Declan growled in approval at seeing his wife in her monstrous form, become covered in blood.

Contentedly, he sat and watched as I ripped all the meat off the bone, leaving blood and fur all over myself and the front veranda. A small voice inside my head remarked, 'that's going to be fun to clean up in the morning'. But it was soon silenced by my bloodlust roaring satisfactorily.

When all that was left were bones, Declan came forward. He knew I couldn't eat bone whereas he could. So along the lines of, 'waste not, want not', he devoured them. The bone crunching sound could send chills down a human's spine, but not mine. I looked on admiringly, as his large, strong jaws chomped away. The bones were crushed to smithereens and within a matter of minutes, he'd gobbled it all down.

Once it was all gone, his head moved closer then his hot, wet tongue came out and lapped at my mouth. He licked the blood off my lips then my face, before moving down my neck. I tried to kiss him back when I was nearly knocked backwards from his overpowering strength. Determinedly, I wrapped my arms about his thick neck and his large jaws settled over the bottom half of my face.

As I was holding him in my arms I felt him decrease in size. His hardened hide turned into softer skin, his muscle bulk shrunk and his canine shape, shifted into a human body. His jaws digging into my cheeks withdrew, along with his short, stubby snout and soon a flatter, human mouth moved against mine.

My naked husband then picked up his Lokoti Werewolf wife in her blood-spattered nightie and carried her inside the house. Vaguely, I made out that I was being transported upstairs to the bathroom. I barely noticed the journey, because my mouth was still attached to his.

Declan kissed hungrily, as he pulled off my bloodied nightie then he looked longingly at my reddish breasts from the blood soaking through.

I was lifted onto the vanity and there I sat, so his mouth could engulf each of my nipples. He half kissed and half licked the blood stains off my skin. My eyes closed as I pulled his hips closer so our crotches were touching. But as soon as they did, he pulled away and moved us into the shower.

With the warm water streaming down, the husband sponged down his wife before passing her the loofah so she could do the same to him.

He took his time as he drizzled my mango-vanilla shower gel onto the accessory then he slowly moved it over my body. Considerately, he lifted up my long, wet hair to massage my broad shoulders. Once I turned around again, his mouth reclaimed mine, with his tongue moving just as slowly.

Oh frickin' hell's delight! My legs almost gave away, but Declan caught me by pushing me up against the shower wall. I started to part my legs, expecting him to claim the rest of me when instead he knelt down to lather my legs. But before he stood up, his mouth smothered my crotch in a long, sensuous kiss. His lips parted the folds as the tip of his tongue tickled my clit.

Again, my legs nearly gave out and I almost fell on top of him, but he caught me.

Declan pressed his mate against the wall before pressing himself against her front. He looked down to see how my breasts were squashed against his wide chest and he moaned. I tried to wrap my legs about his waist, but he pushed them back down.

“No," he growled.

I snarled as I bared my teeth at his dominating behaviour. My eyes glowed turquoise as his green eyes glowered back. My bloodlust demanded that I have him, but he pinned me to the wall.

“No.” He growled again.

I snarled a second time as my teeth sharpened.

He smirked in satisfaction at my viciousness. As he pressed himself against my form, I felt his arousal between my legs. Slowly, he rubbed his crotch against mine before his head rolled backwards and his mouth fell open, in a silent roar. Then the rubbing stopped and he simply held his mate instead. My heart was racing so fast, it made me tremble.

We stood like that for a while; the man pressed against the woman, who was pressed against the wall. The warm water poured over our muscled bodies as the last of the soap suds disappeared down the drain. His heart pounded out of his chest and into mine, as he held on tightly. I sensed he was regaining control of his primal urges. The physical confirmation was that I no longer felt his arousal between my legs.

Eventually, he let go of my arms to take a step back. Next, he turned off the shower and two water-logged Werewolves stepped out. I stood on the bathmat as he pulled his large towel off the rack and used it on his wife, first.

Considerately, he patted me down before drying my hair. When he dried himself after, I picked up my toothbrush and toothpaste. There was something that felt like gristle between my teeth, which I wanted to remove. Once he returned his towel to the rack, he brushed his teeth, too.

I must admit, the mint flavour of the toothpaste was like tasting reality. The removal of the taste of blood made me feel human again. Together, we left the bathroom, leaving my bloodied nightie in the dirty washing basket.

We returned to our bedroom where he picked up his boxers from the floor and I pulled on a new pair of panties and another cotton nightie.

He climbed into bed first and as soon as I joined him, he spooned me from behind. His arms held fast and his skin felt hotter than usual. So did his breath, which I could feel on the back of my neck. Next, his hot, wet mouth enveloped my ear before gently chewing on it. It pulled on my self-control, which didn't help the remaining bloodlust.

“Declan, how long is this going to go on for?” I asked unhappily.

“I like the shampoo, conditioner and the shower gels, you pick." He said softly. "They go well with your natural scent.”

"Declan."

“I dunno.” He sighed. “I just want you fully recovered for the next half-breed we have.”

“How many times do I have to tell you -”

“Yeah yeah - you'd completely regenerated after 24 hours of giving birth - blah blah.” He interrupted. "But as soon as I pounce on you, kid number two will be on the way."

"Why do you think I'll immediately become pregnant?"

"C'mon B!" He said crankily. "I knocked you up as soon as you turned me into a Circulator!"

"So it's up to you when we have sex now, is it?"

"If we have sex then I try to use my breed's method of birth control afterwards; you'll turn defensive and refuse to let me do my job."

"Oh so your job is instigating as well as ending pregnancy?" I asked in a surly manner.

"If I do it right afterwards like I did on our first time," he said coolly, "then it's stopping pregnancy instead of ending it."

I noticed that although we were arguing, he hadn't let go. I was still lying on my side with the obstinate male still curled up behind. If anything had changed, his arms had actually tightened. I lay there quietly for a minute or two, as I pondered his words.

Then I asked, "What exactly is it you're doing, when you do *that*?"

He hesitated for a moment, before he spoke. "I don't know the specifics, but it's something to do with my saliva."

"Huh?" I turned around in his arms so I could meet his gaze. "But why would your saliva stop pregnancy?"

"Well, you know how I can change a person into a European Werewolf by bite or by blood...?"

"Yeah?"

"Then my saliva's different from a human's isn't it? I don't know exactly how it works, but the saliva kills the fertilized egg."

Next, I rolled onto my back to stare up at the ceiling and think. Declan's explained before, a long, long time ago. But until fertility became a reality, I'd never given it a second thought.

"How does it kill the egg?" I pondered.

"I dunno... how does my saliva turn a person into a ravenous, man-eating, monster?"

"Because there's European Werewolf DNA in your saliva," I remembered.

"And my saliva and whatever's in it, kills the newly fertilized egg."

"But how?" I rolled in his direction again. "Why doesn't it transform the egg instead of just killing it?"

"Well there's no point in transforming it, if it's been fertilized by European Werewolf semen." He shrugged. "It's already gonna be born as one of my breed."

"So how does your DNA, or whatever else is in your saliva, kill the egg?"

"Like I said, I don't know." He shrugged. "I think my saliva is more acidic than a human's."

"What?" I screwed up my face in disbelief. "You don't have acid saliva like those creatures in 'Alien' have acid blood!"

"It's not THAT acidic." He said. "But humans can't digest bone like I can. Nor can they process food as fast, which is why I'm always hungry."

"Oh," I saw his point.

"Remember, I only have a matter of days for this method to work." He continued. "And don't forget how small your eggs are, no bigger than the head of a pin. So my saliva would be acidic enough to destroy it and maybe even my own sperm."

"And then what, the rate of reproduction would be too far advanced?"

"Yep and with my strength, it'd be far more resilient."

We both lay on our backs to stare upwards and contemplate our conversation.

"When you kiss me, your saliva doesn't burn." I observed. "And you've even healed me with your saliva, in the past."

"That's because the DNA which changes a human, gets inside your wound and heals you." He rebuked.

I raised my eyebrows impressed, "You know a lot about biology."

"No I don't."

"You know more than me."

"Yeah and why is that, Little Miss University Professor?" He teased as he poked me in the ribs.

"Shut up," I giggled. "Besides, I have a doctorate in history, not biology."

"Whatever," he yawned, "any kind of study, bores me."

"Actually, I was impressed that you remembered how small the egg was."

"One of the few times I paid attention in class, was during Sex Ed."

"Why am I not surprised...?" I smilingly shook my head.

He continued, "And I read my Mom's high school textbooks on biology again, when I got a crush on you."

"Huh?" I gave a funny look. "Why?"

"I was a seventeen year old European Werewolf with a crush on a fourteen year old Circulator. Sure, you were a Light Person but biologically speaking, you had the body of a human female. There was no way the pack, let alone your father, would allow a European Werewolf kiss you, let alone mate with you."

"Why did you study biology again after you'd left school?"

"I was trying to figure out a way we could be together, without injuring or turning you."

"Really?"

"Yup."

"And what did you come up with?"

"Zilch."

"What about condoms?"

"Condoms can break and I know with my strength and stamina, they wouldn't last long." He said matter-of-factly. "Which was the second problem, my strength could harm you. Then of course there was the third problem, if the condom broke and you were knocked-up, what carrying European Werewolf would do to your human body. Which leads us to the fourth problem, I couldn't use my saliva to stop the pregnancy, coz it could turn you."

"So either way, we were screwed."

"Like I always say, the day you turned, I thought you turned just for me."

Then he rolled onto his side so he was facing in my direction, to possessively wrap his large arms about his mate again.

I smiled softly as our human eyes met and held in the dimly lit bedroom. "You're being open and honest tonight."

"Yeah well, if I can't be physically intimate with you, I'll have to settle for being emotionally intimate instead."

"I like it."

"Thanks."

"Declan?"

"B?"

"I believe you love me, truly I do. I mean, you're the walking example of 'Patrick Bateman' and his violent fantasies but -"

"Who's Patrick Bateman?"

"The main character in 'American Psycho' by Brett Easton Ellis."

"OK."

"But I know you love me and it's our love that keeps your darker urges at bay."

"And your question is?"

"The question is, why don't you just make love to your wife and make her and yourself, happy?"

"B."

"You're an animal and a beast, I get that." I spoke plainly. "Hell, it even turns me on!"

"Why thank you," he chuckled, as his gaze lowered towards my breasts.

I grabbed hold of his scruffy hair and lifted up his head, making him meet my eyes again.

“I’m an animal too and I want you just as much as you want me.” I rambled on. "I thought that was the appeal of our relationship, our sexual attraction and that we could be ourselves with each other."

“Not just as much.”

“Huh?”

“You don’t want me just as much as I want you." He said. "I want you more.”

“Then prove it!"

“I mean, if I earned a credit for every dirty daydream I've had about you? I’d be richer than frickin' Hodge Endeavor.”

“So have me already!”

“Hell, I’d even give Hugh Heffner a run for his money back in the day, with his lust nest of ‘Playboy Bunnies’." He chuckled. "But I don't think I could ever eat a 'Playboy Bunny'. Their fake blonde hair would stink of bleach and their fake tits would be full of plastic.”

“Declan!”

“What?”

“I just said I wanted you to have me!”

“Seriously, can you imagine what silicone would taste like? Eugh! I may as well visit our grandniece and chew on one of her dolls.”

“Grrrr!”

I gave up as I flounced onto my back and seethed up at the ceiling instead.

He chuckled as he nuzzled my neck, “I love making you angry.”

“Shut up.”

"Your aura's turned blue and you've got these little sparks flying off it."

"I said, shut up."

“I love your growls and snarls." He continued. "I love it when you bite and claw me, too.”

“Roll over and die.”

He murmured into my ear, before licking it, “I love you B, always and forever.”

I turned away from him by lying on my other side, so I was facing in the opposite direction. However, he wasn't put off by my body language and he spooned me from behind. His arms weren't about to let me escape, which showed as they wrapped about my waist.

His strong heart beat pounded out of his chest and into my back, as his breathing turned slower and deeper. It was a sign he was settling down to sleep. The other indicator was, he buried his face in my damp hair, so he could inhale my scent as he drifted off.

Within ten minutes Declan was in a deep slumber. Just like how a cat sleeps by flexing their claws in their unconscious state; I felt his nails periodically dig into my 'love handles'. I knew he wasn't trying to hurt however, it was just a sign of his obsessive nature.

*****

The following evening after Lucia's bath I carried her downstairs. I'd dressed her in a light blue jumpsuit which had 'Donald Duck' embroidered on the front. She smelled of baby powder as she jutted out her strong little legs. Playfully, she kicked my flabby abdomen which tickled, however if I was human I would have been bruised.

I found her father sitting on the couch whilst watching the world wide news. He frowned at the Internet TV whilst nursing a notepad and pen in his lap. I wondered what was so fascinating that he had to take notes of current events.

"What are you up to?" I asked, as I sat beside.

"Oh nothing," he quickly shut the notepad so I couldn't see what he was writing.

Next, he picked up the remote and changed channels. The news disappeared and 'The Vicar Of Dibley' took its place, an antiquated BBC comedy. Then he stood up, taking his pen and notepad with him.

"I'm gonna get started on dinner, I was thinking of making spaghetti bolognaise." He said. "We have some fresh parmesan in the fridge that I got from the supermarket. I know you prefer it instead of that fake, powdery crap."

"Sounds like you prefer it, too."

"You got that right."

I watched him walk into the kitchen and I heard him open up one of the cupboards to pull out a saucepan and a frying pan.

Then my stomach tightened as my shoulders tensed up. I recognized the physical sensations were the onset of one of my all-knowing feelings. He was hiding something and by the warning signs, it wasn't good.

I reached for the remote and hit the 'back' button to return to the last channel. A female newsreader was reporting on a crime which occurred somewhere in Europe. As she spoke, a small box in the corner of the screen showed footage. I saw what looked like a body-bag on a hover-stretcher, being pushed towards a coroner's vehicle. All around it were police hover-cars with uniformed officers interviewing civilians.

"European Union Law Enforcement has set up a special task force to investigate the escalating murders throughout the continent and the UK. British Police have advised they are cooperating with the investigators by sharing evidence which matches the MO of the killers. Both the British Police and the European Union Police Force suspect that the crimes are being carried out by several individuals working in collusion. What links these murders is the fact that the victims' bodies are all drained of blood before they are burned..."

I stood up and carried Lucia out of the lounge area before coming to a stop in the kitchen entryway. I stood there, bouncing a baby on my hip, as I glared at my husband. In return, he paused in the middle of his dinner preparation to innocently look back.

With purpose, I walked into the kitchen and placed Lucia in his arms, so he couldn't stop me. Then thanks to another one of my all-knowing feelings, I opened up the bottom drawer where the tea towels were kept. I lifted up the pile of folded linen before pulling out his notepad which he'd tried to hide.

“B don’t -” he started, but it was too late.

I flipped it open and in light speed, I read his messy writing. The pages were flicked over so fast, it was like they were cards being shuffled. He'd made a lot of notes, the pad was almost full. Declan had written down dates, locations and how the human victims were found.

2ND JANUARY 2359 SAN JUAN, PUERTO RICO... PARTLY EATEN AND DRAINED MALE BODY FOUND ON BEACH. MULTIPLE TEETH MARKS INDICATE SOUTH AMERICAN VAMPIRE

6TH SEPTEMBER 2361 NEW YORK, USA... DRAINED AND MUTILATED FEMALE BODY FOUND IN DUMPSTER INDICATES NORTH AMERICAN VAMPIRE

19TH OCTOBER 2362 JOHANNESBURG, SOUTH AFRICA... PARTLY MUMMIFIED MALE BODY FOUND IN ABANDONED HOUSE INDICATING WEST AFRICAN VAMPIRE

6TH JUNE 2363 PARIS, FRANCE... DRAINED AND BURNED FEMALE BODY FOUND IN UNDERGROUND TRAIN STATION INDICATING EUROPEAN VAMPIRE

1ST JULY 2364 THE HAGUE, NETHERLANDS... DRAINED AND BURNED MALE BODY FOUND IN CAR INDICATING EUROPEAN VAMPIRE

Although I was so angry that my skin burned, a cold shiver shot down my spine. What gave me the chills was the fact that he'd been taking notes for some time, years before I'd turned him into Circulator. I tossed the notepad onto the kitchen bench and it landed beside the chopping board covered with sliced onion and garlic. My hands moved to my hips as I took a defiant stance, while my eyes burned his way in a demanding fashion.

“What excuse do you wanna try on me first?” I asked in low voice.

“I was getting bored eating the animals here in the National Park, so I was thinking of hunting some 'fang heads' instead,” he gave a glib reply.

“You’re not allowed to, Caesar said so.”

“That's only because he thinks that I can't instantaneously phase yet.”

Pause...my eyes widened at what he had just said in not so many words.

“Yet...?” My mouth fell open. “Do you mean you can?”

Declan gently rocked his daughter in his arms, purposefully making her sleepy, before handing her over to her mother again.

"Something funny happened to me last night, B." He said casually. "I raced after the pack as fast as I could, so I wouldn't be left behind. I realized I was running in light speed when I started to feel all tingly. The next thing I knew, I was glowing. Suddenly I found myself in the Brooks Range instead of the Alaska Range, with no idea how I got there. So, I started to run back as fast as I could, when the same thing happened again. I tingled all over, I briefly glowed then I found myself back inside the Lokoti National Park."

I'd turned into a statue, as I stood there frozen to the spot, staring at my husband in shock and even in a little bit of horror...

His European Werewolf body was adjusting to his Circulator status in leaps and bounds. His bloodlust not only spurred him to kill and feed, but it made him phase through time and space to do it. I'd always imagined I'd train his Circulator abilities in the manner I was, with patience, logic and reasoning. But his dangerous European Werewolf body was training itself. It made me fearful of what else his bloodlust would do with his new powers? I guess I saw my answer in that notebook of his.

My mouth hung open as my heart began to pound. I felt afraid that his new powers were going to his head. His ego was big enough as it is, it didn't need fuel added to the fire.

"Watch this," he said.

Next, Declan straightened as he took a deep breath. He fixed his gaze ahead at the dining table in the living area then he started to walk towards it. However, as he walked past, I caught his eyes close as he frowned in concentration.

Suddenly, in a bright flash of light he disappeared before my very eyes! It looked just like how I instantaneously phased, with the same side effects. The temperature in the kitchen momentarily dropped, as I felt the hair on my body stand up from the electrostatic charge.

"B."

I whirled around at the sound of his voice to find him standing on the other side of the dining table. Declan beamed at his mate and young who were still in the kitchen. He looked so proud of what he'd accomplished.

"It's a lot easier than I thought it would be." He grinned. "I thought it would take months of training, like you had. Mind you, I haven't tried phasing through time yet, so maybe that's the hard part."

My chest constricted as my breathing turned shallow. I almost hyperventilated, but the weight of the baby in my arms acted as my anchor. I inhaled slowly and steadily as I tried to stop terror from setting in.

"Why...didn't you tell me this...last night?" I managed out.

"I wanted to surprise you." He smiled, which slowly faded. "What's the matter, B? You look like you're trying not to cry or something. I thought you'd be happy about this."

"Oh Declan..." my eyes stung as I looked on, "...this is so wrong!"

"What's wrong?" He walked around the table and returned to the kitchen. "Seriously B, what's the big deal?"

I didn't want to argue about this with a baby in my arms. So I left the kitchen and headed upstairs. Carefully, I put her down in the cot when we were both startled.

In another bright flash of light, Declan appeared beside us. His manner of arrival made me jump and Lucia also gave a start. Then she screwed up her face to cry.

"Do you mind not doing THAT in the nursery?" I snapped before returning my attention to my daughter. Reassuringly, I rubbed her tummy which I knew she liked. "Sssshhhh."

"Sorry," he walked around to stand on the other side of the cot. He reached down to caress the top of her head. "She'll get used to the bright flashes, especially when she travels with us."

With the attention of both parents on her, her fears soon faded away. We watched her eyes flit from her father and mother before they began to close. I kept massaging her stomach in a soothing manner, which expedited her nap.

“So, what’s the big deal about me instantaneously phasing?" Declan asked softly, as he watched his young fall asleep. He looked up to joke, "Or are you just jealous that you're not the only one who can do it now?"

“Emotions, Declan." I whispered back.

“Say what?” He gave a peculiar look.

“It’s what’s driving you to instantaneously phase, which worries me.”

“What’s that supposed to mean?”

“Most Circulators phase or instantaneously phase for their first time, because of an emotional reaction. A powerful feeling like fear or love, charges up our bio-electromagnetic fields, causing the Circulator to go into phase. Last night when the full moon turned you into a lunatic, that acted as your trigger. Your bloodlust demanded you run out and kill something as quickly as possible, and it engaged your abilities as a Circulator to do it. Your murderous behaviour is dictating your learning.”

All the while I was speaking softly, my hand kept rubbing Looch's tummy. Our quiet voices and the rhythmic movement of my hand eventually put her to sleep. When I sensed this, I pulled back then gestured for him to follow me out. We exited the nursery with Declan closing the door behind us.

“So, you’re a Werewolf and a Circulator." He retorted. "When you instantaneously phased for your first time, wasn't it when you were hunting?"

I walked into the bedroom to take our argument out of the hallway and we stopped beside the bed.

“No, it was fear of my bloodlust that made me instantaneously phase for my first time." I told him. "As you know, Grant, Dad, Grandfather and Ian took me hunting, to teach me to crave animal and not human. I fought a grizzly with my bare hands, or should I say my claws, and I shredded my prey. They wanted me to finish it off and feed... but I couldn’t. I looked down on that animal groaning in pain and I bolted in the opposite direction! I was so sickened at what I'd done, I ran so fast I slipped into light speed before I turned into light. Fear was my trigger because I was afraid of myself.”

My words gave him pause as he examined my upset state.

I sank onto the bed and sat in a slumped position on the side. He emitted a heavy sigh as he sat beside. Then I felt his hot hand begin to rub the back of my neck.

"Yeah, I remember that night." He said. "I found you sitting in that field, shivering, so I carried you home."

I continued, "The morning we discovered I was pregnant, you ran in light speed to block the door, because you wanted to end the pregnancy. You ran into Alma in light speed, to attack the North American Vampires. Last night, your bloodlust made you instantaneously phase for the first time. Now you want to instantaneously phase all over the world to hunt Vampires? It keeps escalating Declan, your murderous inclinations are your trigger."

He stopped his mini massage and the both of his hands flopped onto his lap, while he looked downcast. I didn't want to hurt him, but the message had to get through. Eventually, he asked, "Do you regret creating the kind of monster I've turned into?"

"I don't regret stopping you from dying of old age." I said emotionally. "If you had died that morning, so would've I."

His watery, bright blue eyes met my watery, dark blue ones.

Then he asked in a tight voice, "But you regret turning me into a Circulator, to keep me alive?"

"I don't regret turning you into a Light Person, to remain together for all time." I said honestly. "But I want you to start exercising self-control double time -"

However, I was interrupted when he stood up with a frustrated growl.

"Exercise self control...?" He snapped. "What the hell do you think I've been doing with this 'no sex' routine?!"

"Maybe it's not worth it, if one of the repercussions is you lose your control over the bloodlust!" I stated. "You told me when you feel my aura, the cold voice can't compete."

"Great, so either I knock up my wife and endanger her life; or I'm a danger to others? Thanks a lot!"

With that, he spun on his heel and stormed out of the bedroom. I heard him stomp downstairs to continue making dinner. However, probably all of tribal lands heard him too, as he banged around the kitchen.

The noise was enough to wake Lucia but I sensed she was also hungry. Her cries summoned me to the nursery, which Declan heard too. I think he berated himself for waking her, as he stopped cooking so loudly.

I picked her up and as soon as I held her against my clothed breasts, her mouth tried to latch onto a nipple. I carried her downstairs and sat down in one of the chairs at the dining table. Then I raised my t-shirt, undid my maternity bra and fed my daughter while I talked to her father.

"Declan, you're a monster and so am I." I said plainly. "But usually, you're a loveable monster, whom everyone affectionately calls 'Uncle Dec'."

"Usually?"

"Yes, usually." I gave a wry smile. "When you're not plotting warfare with the separate species of Vampires, that is."

"Ha ha," he said deadpan, "very funny."

Then my smile faded, "I love you so much that sometimes it hurts."

This made him pause a second time. He'd just picked up the chopping board with the onion and garlic, to tip them into the frying pan, when he stopped. He put the board down again and walked over to where I was sitting.

His hand caressed the back of my neck as he bent down to plant a kiss on my forehead.

"Welcome to my world." He said. "These past few weeks have been an endurance test for me."

While breastfeeding my newborn, I turned my head to press my face against his torso. I felt his hot skin through his t-shirt and I inhaled his maple syrup scent. In return, he put one arm about my shoulders as his other hand stroked my hair.

"You're my beloved B and my little Looch." He said. "If you don't want me to hunt 'fang heads' then fine, I won't. But I am going to keep an eye on their activities. And if one of them shows their ugly face to my mate and young? Then trust me, no order from a First or Tribal Elder will stop me from wiping out it and its' coven."

I was enjoying our contact and I inhaled him one more time before I pulled away. What he said triggered something in my memory. I recalled what the newsreader said and what he'd put in his notepad.

"So those burned bodies that are popping up all over the UK and Europe...?"

"Are victims of European Vampires." he answered. "What better way to eliminate any DNA left in the teeth marks?"

"So they burn the evidence."

"Yup."

Then he left my side to return to cooking. I watched him tip the sliced onion and garlic into the hot frying pan and they instantly started to sizzle. As he let that cook, he retrieved the minced beef from the fridge.

He talked as he worked, "They don't kill all of the humans they feed on, the trail of bodies would be too great. But occasionally, the entire coven will feast on a single human as a special treat, milking every last drop out of the poor bastard. Then they burn the remains with a laser rifle and since the bodies have been emptied of blood, they burn easier."

I sensed he knew all of this by instinct, particularly since European Vampires and European Werewolves were natural enemies. It was like the hate as well as the information, was coded in his DNA. But he's always had an uncanny knack in dealing with members of the supernatural world. What I know comes from the SSIT Reports, but what he knows comes from intuition.

Next, he tipped the mince out of the packet and into the frying pan too. The smell of the meat cooking with the herbs was divine. However, hearing it sizzle especially after our conversation, unnerved me. I wondered if human flesh made that noise when it was burned? Another cold chill shot down my spine, making me hold onto Lucia tighter.

Periodically, Declan would look away from the stove and watch us together.

His face was a curious mixture of adoration and determination. His expression was softened by love but his eyes were hard with resolve. I don't know if it was my empathic joining to him, or centuries of marriage speaking? But it was as if I heard his promise to himself, "no way will I let a 'fang head' come near my wife and child."

~~~~~~
~~~~~~

~ 14 ~

8th August, 2364

When we heard that Wendy had delivered hers and Walt's third child, we went to congratulate the couple.

My husband had prepared a large lasagne, a huge green salad and four loaves of garlic bread for the Wisetail family. We rested the Tupperware containers full of food in the bottom basket of Lucia's hover-pram then walked half way down the hill. I offered to push the pram, but the domineering male who always insisted on driving, took over the technology too.

"Aunt B and Uncle Dec!" Our host greeted with characteristic exuberance upon opening his front door. "Come in, please."

"Walt," my mate shook his hand as he came inside. "Congratulations."

"How wonderful!" I kissed his cheek. "What have you called him?"

The proud father waved his arm, "Allow me to introduce you both to Kevin Lewis Wisetail."

He indicated where Wendy was sitting on the couch in the living room, breastfeeding their newborn.

Immediately, I walked over for a closer look as I came to sit beside.

"Oh Wendy, he's gorgeous!"

"He is, isn't he?" She mooned over the latest addition to her family.

"We come bearing gifts." Declan brought out the Tupperware containers. "Here's a lasagne, salad and some garlic bread. There should be enough to feed your family for a couple of nights."

"Thanks Uncle!" He eagerly took the offering. "I'll just put them in the fridge. Then would the two of you like a cup of coffee?"

"Sure," my husband followed him into the kitchen.

Next, Kurt and Edwina went over to Lucia's hover-pram to look on her. The two were fascinated with her glowing green eyes. However, they soon discovered that they weren't tall enough to see over the side. So the four year old tried to climb up...

"Woah woah woah!" I jumped up when I saw the hover-pram begin to tilt.

"Kurt, get down!" His mother scolded.

Dejectedly, the boy returned to the floor as his little sister turned sulky at being denied.

I picked up Lucia and carried her over to rest her in my lap. Once I was seated beside Wendy again, her eldest children came over. Eagerly, they crowded around to compare the newborns.

"I want to see her eyes," Kurt pouted. "Open your eyes, Looch!"

However, the miniature Werewolf slumbered on, which Edwina didn't like.

"Tickle time!" The two year old declared and poked her in the side.

"Edwina!" Her mother warned. "Stop it."

Lucia emitted an unhappy snarl at being woken then bared her tiny, sharp teeth.

"Mommy, look at Looch's teeth!" He stared. "How come Kevin doesn't have teeth, too?"

Wendy and I exchanged smiles of amusement, before I explained, "Looch was born with teeth because she's half European Werewolf."

"And Kevin?" He wondered.

"No, Kevin is not half European Werewolf," his mother laughed.

"Daddy?" Edwina queried.

"Your Daddy is a Lokoti Werewolf." Wendy educated.

"Then are we half Lokoti Werewolf?" The four year old tried to figure.

"You may turn into a Lokoti Werewolf after your tenth birthday, if one of the pack dies." She shrugged back.

Edwina piped up, "Me?"

"No, Ed." Her brother answered. "Girls besides Aunt B can't be Lokoti Werewolves."

Evidently, Edwina didn't like this, for she stomped off to go play with her dolls.

Carefully, Kurt began to stroke Lucia's forehead like he could have been petting a puppy. When she emitted a contented growl, he grinned. He beamed upwards, so proud of what he'd accomplished.

For his benefit, my dark blue eyes momentarily glowed turquoise. Softly, I growled down to Lucia, who opened her glowing green eyes to growl back. Wendy and I saw how this made his day, by seeing her supernatural eyes.

"Awww, she's so cute!" He leaned in with an enamoured expression.

"I think Lucia has her first admirer," his mother gave a nudge.

"You might be right." I snickered, as I watched Kurt stroke her head again.

Once tiny Kevin had fed enough, his mother redid her maternity bra and buttoned her shirt back up.

Gently, she raised him to her shoulder and rubbed his back, to rid him of any wind.

“But that could be a good thing,” she went on, “if Kurt did turn and Looch ended up with a Lokoti Werewolf.”

I laughed at her, “Wendy, are you setting up my two month old daughter with your four year old son?”

“I'm just saying...” she blushed, “...that Looch ending up with another Werewolf would probably be better than if she ended up with a human.”

“What's this?” Declan overheard, as he helped Walt carry out the coffees for everyone.

“Wendy's matchmaking our two month old daughter,” I informed.

“That's my wife, always thinking two steps ahead.” Walt chuckled, as he put down her cup close by to her.

“Oh well,” my husband handed me my beverage, before he and Walt sat on the opposite couch with theirs. “I heard that Hunter Wisetail fell in love with Jessica Riverclaw when he was two years old. Maybe it's a Wisetail trait for early courtship?”

“Yes but Mum and Dad didn't get together until she was eighteen and he was twenty.” I reminded.

Declan guffawed, “I heard that every time he asked her out, she turned him down. It only took a World War to get her to change her mind.”

Walt laughed, “Yeah I heard that too.”

“The tribe's most argumentative woman bred with the pack's quietest werewolf and low and behold, we got our first female Lokoti Werewolf.” My husband gave a wink.

Wendy pondered, “Yes, but don't you think it's odd that no other women in the tribe turned, after Aunt B? Why is she the one and only female Lokoti Werewolf?”

“Fate just designed it that way.” Her husband shrugged. “The Tribal Elders are always telling us that things happen for a reason.”

“But it's also genetics, since women are meant to be carriers of the gene and not activated themselves." Declan added on. "I tell B that I think she changed just for me. I fell in love with her when I was seventeen, but because she was human, I knew that there was no way that her parents, or the pack, would let me touch her. Whadyaknow, she turns just before her eighteenth birthday."

“Too bad I was married off to someone else.” I said wryly.

“Yeah but you didn't breed for him, did you?” He replied. “Besides, after Grant's death, you simply returned to your first and one true mate.”

“How do you figure?” Walt listened with interest. "I was told that Aunt B was mated to Grant Elm first."

“We were secretly involved before B married.” He spoke casually on what used to be a taboo subject.

“You were?” Wendy's eyebrows arose. “That must have been hard on you Uncle, seeing her with another man.”

"Let's just say that fighting my urges not to hunt human those five years; paled in comparison to what I wanted to do to Grant Elm." He said sourly.

Walt and Wendy exchanged raised eyebrows at the European Werewolf's glare, which prompted her to change the subject.

She looked on her husband, "I remember the time I met Walt in High School when my family just moved to Alma. He stared so much, he forgot to pay attention to a self-saucing pudding our class was baking. The fire alarm went off and the whole school was evacuated in the middle of an icy winter."

"Ah, so this is the infamous fire alarm event we heard previously." I tittered. "And why Declan said the famous two words at the announcement of your engagement, 'take away'."

"He's getting better." She smiled. "He made pancakes this morning and only burned two."

"What can I say?" Walt grinned in good humour. "When my wife is in the room, concentrating on cooking is the last thing on my mind. How can I pay attention to the stove when Wendy is all I see?"

The human glowed at his words as I'm sure they made her feel like the most beautiful woman in the world. In return, she passed her husband a shy smile. This made him look on in adoration with their love for all to see.

Next, all of our attention was taken away by Kurt, who climbed up onto the sofa. He pushed himself in between Wendy and I then leaned into my side, so he could stare down at my daughter. Coincidentally, it was the same look on his face we'd just seen on his father's.

Declan frowned, "Hey buddy, I have three words for you; grow up first."

*****

It was lunch time when we left the Wisetail's and walked back up the hill towards home.

Again Declan pushed the hover-pram, although thanks to the anti-grav units, it was just as easy to push the pram up hills as it was down them. You could even push it up and down stairs, the technology simply glided over everything. The smooth sailing of the carriage made Lucia fall fast asleep.

It was a beautiful summer's day and I looked on admiringly at the sunlight bringing everything to life. The gentle breeze teased our hair as it did the leaves in the trees. I took a deep breath of air which was scented musk from the abundance of pine.

"It's a nice day," he remarked.

"It is," I agreed.

"I can tell you think so, your aura is brighter."

"Is it?"

"Uh huh," he verified then he waited a moment before asking, "So when are we going to start my training?"

"Huh?" I looked back in surprise.

"When are we going to start my training as a Circulator?" He asked again. "I mean, you had your Mom and Gran to teach you how to phase through time. Don't I get any lessons?"

"Oh, I don't know... you almost seem to be teaching yourself."

"Yeah, but I can't phase through time yet, like you can." He pointed out. "All I do is instantaneously phase to different locations."

"Can you see through time yet?"

"No." He frowned, before he said grumpily, "Hence the word, 'train'."

"Have you had a vision of something in the past or the future?"

"Are you even listening to me?" He retorted. "I can't 'see' anything."

"I don't know, Dec." I stared off into the forest. "Circulators start by having visions. It's when they see through time to the era they want, they put their bodies into phase and circulate there. It's part of that 'trippy time travel' stuff you don't like hearing about; A leads to B which then results in C. You have a vision, you learn how to go into phase, then you pass through time like light passing through glass."

"So how do I see through time?" He gave a peculiar look.

"I dunno...you just do." I sighed, as I thought out loud. "Circulators start with visions long before they learn how to phase. But you're doing things backwards, you phased before you've had any visions."

"Hey, I may not have seen things yet, but I had a warning feeling which turned out to be true." He sounded offended.

"Yes, but it was about an event in this time frame."

"Well, can you train me to have visions of another time then turn myself into light?"

I was still staring off into the distance, which was the surrounding woods, as we walked and talked. It helped me to think aloud. Besides, the beauty of nature was a nice distraction.

"I suppose we could start off with some basic exercises." I contemplated. "I remember reading in Elisha's diary about the kind of classes she did at Hamilton's College. We could try that way."

"Great!" He said enthusiastically. "So when do we start?"

*****

After eating the delicious lunch that Declan prepared, I tidied up the kitchen then went upstairs.

On my way into the bedroom, I looked in on the nursery. I saw my husband was rocking his daughter to sleep, which made me smile. He'd just changed her and now he was trying to put his restless young down for a nap. Whereas I would've used the rocking chair, he used his large arms.

The sight of the 'papa bear' making "shhh" noises whilst gently swaying his young side-to-side, made me sigh. It proved to be an effective technique too, for her glowing green eyes started to close. As she drifted off, her father edged closer to the cot to put her down.

Next, I walked into the master bedroom and over to our wardrobe. I opened the doors wide, particularly the one which had the full-length mirror on the inside. Then I stood in front of it and stared into my reflection.

Declan's voice startled, "Yes you're still beautiful."

"I wasn't checking." I blushed. "I was trying something else."

"Like what?"

"Come over here." I held out my arm which he walked over to. Then I moved him to stand in front of me, so he was directly in front of the mirror. "Now I want you to stare."

"Stare at what?"

"Stare into the mirror." I instructed. "Let your eyes glaze over and think of a time you've always wanted to visit."

"But I don't have a time that I've always wanted to visit." He turned to give a funny look. "I'm not into history like you are."

"Hence the reason why you haven't had any visions yet." I smirked. "Oh I know, you mentioned how you wished you could show off your first born to your mother. Think of a time when she was with us."

"OK." He closed his eyes as he thought back.

"Now I want you to think hard on a particular year when your mother was here." I ordered. "Concentrate on a particular month and then a week and then a day, when you were with her. Do you remember when we had lots of dinners with her and your brother?"

"Yeah, I remember." His eyes squeezed shut as he faced the mirror again. "I remember one of our Sunday night Sabre dinners. You and I were there and so was Derik, Rachel and their two kids. Mom had cooked up beef cannelloni with green salad then afterwards, a tiramisu for dessert. You and I washed up after dinner, as Mom helped Michael and Blanche with their homework. Derik and Rachel sat on the couch, watching."

"What was the date of this particular dinner?" I probed.

"It was a couple of years after you and I finally got together." Declan thought aloud. "I remember it was winter... oh, I know! It was just after Christmas so the date must've been Sunday the 19th January 2098."

"Now open your eyes and stare into the mirror, picture this moment like it's a photograph." I advised. "As you do, let your eyes glaze over. It will help you focus on the image in your mind instead of the image of yourself. Once your eyes have glazed over, focus hard on the memory."

I watched his eyes open and he stared into the reflective glass. I saw a distant expression on his face, as he continued to replay the scene inside his head. After a minute, I overheard his sharp intake of breath, like he just had a surprise.

"Frickin' hell B... how are you doing this?"

"Doing what?"

"How are you making them appear in the mirror like that...?" He looked my way in amazement, before looking back. "Aw, what? No way! They're gone!"

"That's because you lost your concentration." I explained. "You looked away from your vision, which you can't do unless you deliberately want it to end. Just imagine if you were in the middle of phasing there and your destination suddenly disappeared. You could end up anywhere."

He turned away from the mirror to look on his wife.

"So that's why when you're phasing us somewhere, I hear you mutter the date over and over?" He guessed.

"Yup."

"Did you see my Mom and Derik and Rachel?" He wondered.

"No, how could I? It's YOUR vision Declan, it's the moment in time you've chosen. I can't see it, unless you grab my arm and phase us through the mirror and take me there."

"What, that's it?" He straightened in surprise. "I see where I want to go then I put myself into phase and go there?"

"Essentially, that's it." I nodded before adding on, "But you have to 'see' your destination clearly. You can't just put yourself into phase and circulate anywhere, or there's no telling where you'll end up. Remember those times I couldn't instantaneously phase somewhere, because I couldn't picture the location?"

"Oh yeah, like in Peru when you couldn't instantaneously phase to Machu's house, because you didn't know where it was."

"It's the same thing," I nodded. "That's when Circulators use the Gate at Circulate Headquarters to target where they want to go."

"So if I picture that moment in time with Mom again and I concentrate hard enough so I see it in the mirror; I could put myself into phase and pass through the mirror to that scene?" He checked.

"Uh huh," I nodded again. "Or, if you know the date you want to go but you're unsure of the geography, you use the Gate. All you need to do is concentrate on the time frame as the Gate moves your phased particles to the location. Circulators who can't instantaneously phase, only move backwards and forwards through time in the location they're already in. So if they want to phase to somewhere else, such as Circulate Headquarters, the Gate moves their light particles there as they circulate through time."

"But how does the Gate know if they want to phase from Earth to Mars, or to Taurus Six?" He wondered.

"Each Circulator has an assigned Calculator, yours and mine is now the Circulate Mainframe. She's always monitoring us via the Viewing Room.

But in the old days, Calculators also operated the Gate. It used to be manned 24/7 by a Calculator who could 'see' when a Circulator needed to come to Headquarters. These days, since you and I can instantaneously phase, we can move through time and space without using the Gate all the time."

"So not all Circulators can instantaneously phase?" He remembered.

"In the beginning, it was just four Circulators in the Circulate who could; Elisha Worthall, Sophie Wilcox, Lucas Hodge and Rufus Kell." I explained. "Then the four became nine; Elisha, Lucas, Rufus, Mike, Alexandrina, Arabella, Jessica and me, Bianca."

"Wait," Declan frowned, "did you just say the name Lucas Hodge?"

"Yes, he was the Lead Councillor on the Circulate Council for many years. He's the one who started 'Hodge Endeavor' in the 1940's, to act as the Circulate's political stronghold and 'cash cow'."

"Wow." He looked on, impressed. "The guy who started the massive international corporation that you're now head of; used to be one of four Circulators who could instantaneously phase?"

"Bingo." I smiled.

"Small world," he commented.

"Not really." I reasoned. "It's temporal causalities -"

"- A leads to B which then results in C." He smilingly interrupted. "Gees, one day if I didn't hear you say that, I'd think you were a 'Body Snatcher'."

I gave him a playful slap on the arm before I turned serious again.

"As a Circulator, you're going to have to learn it, too." I pointed out. "You can't change history whenever you feel like it, without realizing the repercussions. Think of the timeline like a chain."

"And if you change something, it can break the chain?" He guessed.

"Or creates a chain reaction that runs in another direction," I warned.

"I prefer to think of the 'Butterfly Effect'," he said. "You know, a butterfly flaps its wings then on the other side of the world there's a hurricane, or whatever."

"They're basically the same thing."

"Cool." He grinned as he said proudly, "I'm a Circulator within the Circulate. I'm the tenth Circulator who can instantaneously phase. I see through time and I'm part of a secret society that owns one of the world's richest companies."

I took hold of his hand and came to stand beside then together, we looked at our reflection in the mirror.

"Officially, we're the last two Circulators in human history." I said solemnly. "When you and I evolve to the space time continuum, the Circulate will cease to be. The Mainframe on Taurus Six would initiate the self destruct sequence and our existence will slip into obscurity."

"Unless you and I change more people into Circulators," he shrugged.

I shook my head, “We can’t.”

“Huh?” He gave a funny look. “Why not?”

“When an energy signature is taken out of the timeline by being put into temporal flux; the ramifications reverberate through time and space.”

“In English, B.” He rolled his eyes again.

“You need to read the SSIT Report on Reincarnation,” I frowned. “But basically, each time a Circulator is created, it impacts the surrounding space and time. When Gran turned Grandfather into another Circulator, it affected the birth of a new star which didn’t end up igniting.”

“Wait, I remember you saying something about this, the morning we first found out you were pregnant.” He realized. “You said something like, ‘because their mother changed their father, our daughters will be born but not as Circulators’.”

“Precisely.”

“Frickin’ hell...” he moaned, “...as Werewolves we have to be constantly on the look out for the bloodlust. Now as Circulators, we have to be doubly careful, watching out for changes we make to the timeline?”

“We do have to be wary of any changes we make.” I confirmed. “But the other good thing about having a Calculator is, that’s their job. The Circulate Mainframe sends me messages when she thinks I should know something, or when an action will impact the future.”

Declan paused for a moment before he passed a wary look my way.

“Is this why you freaked out when you heard I could instantaneously phase?” He asked. “You ranted about my European Werewolf bloodlust taking control of my abilities as a Circulator. Is it because you’re afraid of what else it might do? Are you worried about what the ramifications would do to the timeline and to the human race?”

I turned side on so I could look him right in the eye, “Yes.”

“B...” he pulled me into an embrace, “...don’t you know that would never happen?”

I searched his bright blue eyes and I saw his earnestness, as he continued.

“Don’t you know it, even now? I don’t just have my own conscience, but I have your Grandfather’s voice inside my head, or even my Mom’s. But if the cold voice of the bloodlust talks over the top of them, I’ve also got you. All I have to do is look on your aura, or even hold you so it radiates through me. The darkness can’t compete with that.”

Relieved, I buried my face into his wide chest while breathing in his maple syrup scent.

I mumbled into his shirt, “I love you, Declan Sabre.”

“I love you more, my own, little Light Person.” He gave a squeeze.

I looked up into his waiting gaze, “You’re a Light Person too now.”

"Maybe, but your aura is still brighter than mine." He smirked. "If she could talk, Lucia would agree."

"Really?" I gave a peculiar look. "Why do say that?"

"When I'm holding her, she stares up at my aura. But if you come along, her eyes widen double time." He chuckled. "My aura is like a soft light, but yours is an almost blinding, search light. A couple of times I've even seen her stare hypnotically at you, like a deer in headlights. She probably thinks an angel is her mother."

He made me giggle like schoolgirl, "The sweetest things you say."

"I'm just being honest," he said casually. "You're the light in my life and I wouldn't be surprised if our half-breed daughters saw you this way, too."

"Well, maybe until they're teenagers," I said abashed. "Then they'll temporarily hate me over fights about make-up and clothes, dating and curfews."

"Ha!" Declan scoffed. "Trust me B, they're gonna hate me more when they learn they're not even allowed to date."

I laughed at the overprotective 'papa bear' as he pulled me closer for another cuddle.

~~~~~~

31st August, 2364

It was another warm afternoon with the temperature sitting at 25°C. Sunlight poured through our open windows facing the west, casting the living room in a warm hue. The heat didn't bother me, although it did with my hot-blooded husband. He was crashed on a couch by an open window facing east, to catch the breeze.

I was carrying Lucia around in the baby carrier as I did the laundry. She was resting against my front, emitting the occasional snarl in her sleep. I took out the clothes from our combined washer/dryer then carried them out of the laundry and over to the dining table, to fold up.

Declan laid there in a singlet top and a pair of cargo shorts, with his bare feet hanging over the arm rest. He looked the very epitome of relaxation on this lazy Sunday afternoon. That, as well as bothered by the heat, as periodically he'd fan himself with the book he was reading.

"Mmm," he commented, briefly looking in my direction. "I love the smell of freshly washed and dried clothes, straight from the machine."

"Same here," I smiled as I worked. "I love how soft they feel when they come out."

Declan laid there, watching me work for a moment or two, before he returned to his book.
~~~~~~

“This is the life, B.” He sighed loudly. “A beautiful day, a beautiful wife, a beautiful baby, clean clothes and a good book.”

“I agree.” I smiled back, as I organized the clothing into neat piles on top of the table. “What are you reading?”

“‘American Psycho’ by Brett Easton Ellis.” He held up the cover so I could see. “My wife mentioned it to me.”

“Oh did she?” I giggled. “You don’t often follow your wife’s suggestions on reading material, or other matters.”

“No, not often.” He said coolly. “Occasionally she makes sense, but it happens about as frequently as buying a winning lottery ticket.”

Then he laughed when I threw a pair of rolled-up socks at his head.

“So, what do you think of the book?” I queried.

“It’s alright...” he mused, “...I like the pop culture references used to show the era it’s based in. But I don’t know why you thought I was like this Patrick Bateman character. He’s pretty tame by my standards.”

“By *your* standards?” I raised my eyebrows.

“Yup.” He said simply. “Humans make such a big deal about being cut up with axes or chainsaws. But that’s nothing to being eaten alive. I don’t think they’d like to meet my kind with our teeth, claws and bloodlust. We certainly wouldn’t keep any body parts around as trophies, either.”

“No?”

“It’d be a waste of food.” Declan declared.

His casual demeanour about the subject of murder unnerved me, so much so, I changed the conversation.

“Patrick Bateman was also a superficial yuppy, consumed with fashion. I don’t know why some people become obsessed with accumulating so much wealth, or amassing expensive things. I’m happy with the roof over my head, the food in my fridge, working in the greenhouse, folding my own clothes and taking care of my kid.”

“Ha!” He scoffed. “This is coming from the Chairman on the Board of Directors, of one of the world’s most powerful companies.”

“But do I live like those other people on the Board of Directors?” I replied.

“No, you’re not like Jonathan Bourne with his drivers, fancy hover-cars and three houses, all five times the size of this one.” Declan recited what he overheard one winter’s morning. “What’s the bet that this guy even has armies of servants in each of these houses?”

“And don’t forget his haute couture suits and the Rolex peeking out from under his sleeve.” I tittered.

Declan put his book down to roll over onto his side so he could look directly my way.

“Why, B?”

“Why what?”

"Why do you choose this way of life instead of the residing in the lap of luxury?"

"I dunno," I shrugged. "I like our lifestyle."

"Do you?" He checked. "Because you seem to like the academic one too, where you dress up and go to seminars at these fancy Universities."

"True," I admitted. "I don't know, Dec. I mean, it's fun to dress up in formal attire and do the occasional lecture or attend academic functions. But whenever I'm away, I think of home. I don't mind the idea of going away, because I know that I have you to come home to."

"Really?" He watched closely.

"Truly."

Then he rolled onto his back once more and picked up his book again.

"I know what you mean, I'm a European Werewolf and we're supposed to be nomads. My breed constantly moved around to hunt human and not get caught by the authorities. But I can't imagine living anywhere else but here, because when I think of the mountains of the Alaska Range and its dark blue rivers? Those mountain ranges remind me of your curves and the rivers remind me of your dark blue eyes, and I know I'm home."

That actually made me stop and stare, pleasantly surprised.

"Wow, you're a poet and I didn't know it." I joked. "As I said before, sometimes I think an alien has replaced my husband."

"I went hunting on the last full moon, didn't I?"

"Yes, but you've never shared your kill before."

"Well, I never had a wife and kid waiting for me at home, before." He shrugged. "I liked the idea of providing for my family."

"Why, so you could feel like the big, strong male?" I taunted.

"Yup." He ignored the sarcasm. "Don't forget my breed is in direct descent of the First Werewolf. Neanderthals aspire to be us one day."

"Wow, good point!" I laughed. "From that perspective, I'm married to a caveman or a dinosaur!"

"You'd better believe it, baby." He chuckled along. "Now go and fetch your husband and therefore your lord and master, a soda from the fridge."

However, what he received instead was another pair of rolled up socks thrown at his head.

Once the laundry was folded, I carried the piles of clothing upstairs to put away.

I opened the drawers in the tallboy and carefully placed the clothes where they belonged. I was obsessed with orderliness and so was my husband. I think it came from our territorial behaviour as Werewolves. If our underwear wasn't where it should be, we'd go on guard and sniff around for signs of intruders.

I lingered on a pair of his 'Tassie Devil' boxer shorts. The red satin felt extra soft, as well as a little warm from the washer/dryer. The garment felt nice to hold, just like Declan did. I held them against my face whilst inhaling the smell of the laundry detergent and my husband's scent, in the fibres.

Man, I miss misbehaving with him... Then I snapped out of it, when I remembered I was still carrying our daughter. What would she think of her mother sniffing her father's shorts?

Next, I carried both baby and the baby clothes into the nursery. There I did the same to the drawer full of her jumpsuits, grouping separately the whites, the pastels and the darks. Again, I lingered on her green 'Kermit the Frog' jumpsuit. With Lucia's glowing green eyes, the clothing perfectly suited her. Everyone melted like butter when they saw her in it and begged to hold her.

Once the clothes were done the last thing to put away was the baby.

I carried her over to the cot then carefully lifted her out of the baby carrier. She emitted a dissatisfied snarl at being disturbed, but calmed once I laid her down. I tucked her under a sheet only, since her body temperature mirrored her father's and she could overheat in summer. As I began to caress her head, she gave a contented growl before falling asleep with her mouth open. Her sharp teeth were on display with a tiny bit of drool appearing on her cheek.

Awwww, she's so cute!

I ended up standing over her cot and watching her sleep. Although she was growing fast, I still thought she was the cutest thing I'd ever seen. A couple of times she emitted more growls and even panted a little, as if she were having dreams of future hunts to come. I watched the way she clenched and unclenched her clawed little hands, before settling once more.

After a minute, I began to feel like I was being watched myself. I looked up to find Declan standing in the doorway. With his height and broad shoulders, he completely filled the doorway. He looked on with longing at the scene of his mate hovering over his young.

"It's time, B." He said softly.

Huh? Time for what? I even checked my watch, wondering if he meant we were about to have company.

Declan snickered when he saw this, so he thought he'd illustrate his meaning.

He walked in, took hold of my hand then he led me out of the nursery and into our bedroom.

I found myself standing beside our bed with the two of us facing each other. The first thing he took off was the baby backpack on my front. Next, his hands began to gather up my t-shirt, which he lifted over my head. As soon as it was tossed aside, his hands made a move on my jeans.

Oh, it's time for THIS...!

I giggled girlishly which made Declan chuckle. Then my hands reached out and similarly undressed him. As soon as I unzipped his cargo shorts, I saw just how ready he was. I had to give him a wide birth when I pulled down the rim of his boxers, to accommodate his arousal. I must admit, the sight of it turned me on, too.

Finally, the wait is over... My heart began to pound as my face turned hot. I felt a warmth spread throughout my whole body, originating in my abdomen.

"I've pictured this moment for nearly three months and it has to be perfect." He said.

To demonstrate, he picked up our mobile phones and put them on silent, before replacing them on the bedside table.

Then he sat down on the side of the bed and using the both of his hands, he moved me closer.

He slowly laid back on the bed as he pulled me along until I was sitting in his lap. He moved my crotch over his as I used my thighs to raise myself. Then I moved into position as his hands gripped tightly onto my hips.

Gradually, I lowered myself and felt us become one, with gasps escaping from both our mouths. We moved slowly at first, so he could retain control and my body could readjust to his size. Then his hands which were holding onto my hips, began to lift and lower them at a steady pace.

"B...?" He looked up, pleadingly. "You know how for the past three months you've teased, taunted, rubbed your body up against mine or even flat out bit me?"

"Yes?"

"Feel free to do all of the above."

My mouth opened as I leaned over his torso and he saw my teeth sharpen. Then I used them to scrape over his left nipple then his right, making him groan. His hands squeezed my hips and he kept moving as I bit into his tough skin. Blood momentarily appeared on his epidermis until I licked it off, tantalizing him with my tongue. His eyes fluttered closed from the pleasure I caused while his mouth fell open.

"Frickin' hell, you're nice and warm and wet...!" He groaned.

He continued to move steadily, but with each push I felt him go deeper inside. It was like my body completely opened itself up to him which he must have felt too, for he pushed himself all the way in. Declan's hands remained on my hips, holding them securely, not picking up speed but increasing in strength. I liked this, my eyes closed by themselves as I let my ecstasy take over.

Suddenly, he sat upright so his mouth could reach mine. At first his hot, wet tongue touched mine then his lips moved away so his teeth could graze my jaw line. Lastly, his mouth went south, nibbling his way down my neck then across my right shoulder.

By now, his fingers were digging into the soft flesh of my buttocks as another part of him delved into a softer, moister part of my body. Since he was sitting up, he couldn't gyrate as much, so his hands took over. I felt them lift me up and down at a greater velocity, as his head fell backwards and his mouth opened.

"B - B - B!" He cried out. "I need to hear you say it, B! Say the words to me!"

His face contorted in what looked like both rapture and pain, as he strained to keep a hold on his control.

"I need you Declan, I need you now!"

No sooner did these words leave my mouth, I felt his release. Declan's eyes were squeezed shut with his mouth agape. He didn't even stop moving, as his large hands pumped me up and down on his throbbing member.

After another minute or so, I felt his hands loosen and our movements slow down.

What, we're not going to stop after only one round, are we?

No sooner did these words drift through my mind, out of the blue I found myself flipped onto my back with the domineering male climbing on top.

He gave a smug grin, "Now let's really christen this new bed."

A growl escaped from between my sharp teeth as my body was borderline from changing. Declan half raised himself using one arm as his other held onto my waist. In this position, he started to move once more, only this time picking up speed as well as intensity.

The faster we went, the less I tried to hold onto him. Instead, I raised my arms over my head to hold onto the edge of the mattress. The bed shuddered with our fierce rocking, but I didn't care. I closed my eyes as he rode me and I rode the hypnotic waves of pleasure that were rising upwards like it was high tide.

We grunted, groaned, moaned, made helpless noises, but we kept on moving. Sweat beaded on our skin before trickling off, further dampening the sheets. He came a second time as I came for my first then we pushed some more. We became completely wet, inside and out, as our mattress took the brunt of our desire.

"Change, change, change...!" I uttered, as I moved out from underneath.

As soon as I rolled onto my stomach, I felt his weight on my back as he climbed on top again.

My hands clung to the side of the mattress with his hands over mine. The sweat was virtually pouring off us by this stage, but like slaves to our passion, we carried on. We found a rhythm that suited us both and I gyrated my hips, as his lower body slammed into mine. Both the rhythm and the vibrations sent my ecstasy sky high and my whimpering let him know it.

My internal muscles spasmed over and over again, as the multiple orgasms ballooned outwards. The ripples started from my crotch then they moved upwards through my torso, out to my arms and even down my legs. The rapture made my claws detract as my body went taught, to hold onto this bliss.

I felt him let go of my hands as his larger ones ran up my arms, over my shoulders then followed my curves. As they did so, his mouth planted several kisses on the back of my neck. His tenderness showed his satiated state.

That was until the both of our gazes were redirected to the bedside table. Declan's mobile phone alerted him to a call as it gently vibrated on the wooden surface.

“Aw, what?” I complained.

“This isn’t what I’d imagined!” Declan snarled, with his blue eyes flaring green. “Somebody had better be dying!”

Bad-temperedly, he pulled me across the bed with him as he reached over to snatch up the technology.

“Don’t say that.” I berated, as I partially sat upright.

Through our long years of marriage we actually had been interrupted by news of this kind.

“It’s frickin’ Antonio!” He swore when he saw the name on caller ID. “Why the hell is calling us NOW? That’s it, he’s grounded!”

I tittered, “You can’t ground your forty-something, great x6 grandnephew who has his own house, wife and kids.”

“Well I’m not taking his call either.” Declan declared.

Then he swung out his arm and sent his mobile flying through the air!

The ringing phone went out the window and we heard the technology break apart on the gravel drive.

I cracked up laughing as he rolled me onto my back and buried his face into my larger breasts, quickly forgetting the interruption.

*****

The next morning we woke up at 7.16 AM. Instead of lying in, the parents prepared to rise before the baby did. I heard my mate yawn before sitting upright to stretch.

He sat on the side of the bed for a moment, as if getting his bearings. Next, I overheard the sound of sniffing, lots of sniffing in fact. Sleepily, I looked over my shoulder when I jumped in fright!

“Declan!”

He was leaning over his wife, sniffing her, with a puzzled expression on his youthful face.

“Not again!” I complained, as I rolled onto my back. “Can’t we find out these things like normal people? That’s why pregnancy test kits were invented!”

“B, you’re not pregnant.”

“Huh?”

“You’re NOT pregnant.” He looked stumped by this. “I thought for sure you would be.”

I sung teasingly, “Are you worried your swimmers are on strike, or something?”

However, my husband didn’t look amused by the joke, not at all...

He glared my way, “With our catch up session yesterday, I could have knocked up twenty females! So why didn’t I knock up just the one?”

“What, were you deliberately trying to impregnate me?” I sat up, defensively.

“No, but it should be a given.” He frowned, before he leaned in to start sniffing again.

I pushed him away, “Would you stop it!”

“Why aren’t you pregnant, B?” He asked accusatorily.

“I don’t know!”

“Maybe we should get Ki to scan you.” He said, concerned.

“Why?”

“Why? What do you mean, why?” He looked on like I was an idiot. “How are we supposed to have two more daughters if I DON’T load your metaphorical oven with my bun?”

“Maybe we don’t have them right away...?” I shrugged.

However, my speculation didn’t placate my husband, but it perplexed him instead.

He threw off the covers, took one last sniff of his wife then he stood up from the bed.

“I’m getting Ki here first thing after breakfast to check you out.” He said as he started to get dressed. “We have to make sure.”

“Make sure of what?” I gave a funny look.

“That Lucia’s birth didn’t damage you permanently.”

I groaned loudly as I fell back onto the mattress...and we’re back to that again.

“And you tell me that I’M the broken record player?” I groaned, as I rubbed my face.

*****

After getting dressed, feeding and changing Lucia then eating the huge, hot breakfast Declan crammed down my throat; I found myself sitting on the opposite couch to our Medicine Man.

Next, he asked me to lie down like I did when I was pregnant, so he could scan me that way.

Declan stood off to the side while rocking Lucia in his arms. His attention was half on his daughter and half on his wife. Distractedly, he tickled a gurgling baby while watching Ki work. When the scanning was finished, I sat upright as my mate came to sit beside.

“OK,” our Healer read out the results. “There’s no residual scarring around the ovaries, fallopian tubes or the uterus. This means that Lucia’s birth did not leave any permanent damage which would stop pregnancy from reoccurring."

Instantly, my mate looked relieved. "Phew!"

"Told you so." I shot off a glare.

"But..." the Medicine Man took a deep breath, as his eyes remained on the technology.

"What?" Declan anxiously leaned forwards. "What is it, Ki?"

"The lining of her uterus has changed, but I believe it's only temporary." He announced.

"Say what?" My husband's mouth hung open.

"It's fascinating, really." He continued. "You've heard male Lokoti Werewolves stop breeding if they suspect pregnancy may endanger their mate? A male Lokoti Werewolf's body can also suspend their fertility. Let's look at Wendy and Walt for a moment, with their children who were born two years apart. Walt's body temporarily suspends its fertility without changing irreparably, to ensure Wendy isn't constantly breeding."

"So you're saying that something similar is happening to B's body?" My mate queried.

"Exactly," he turned off his scanner before putting it away. "Right now, the lining of Aunt B's uterus is coated in antibodies which are repelling the fertilized egg. With the fertilized egg unable to embed itself, pregnancy can't proceed."

"Oh," Declan looked surprised. "So my swimmers are working, but they're being repelled?"

"Oh they're working alright." Ki snickered. "Your swimmers are very active, Uncle Dec. If this was an Olympic swimming event, your 'swimmers' would win gold, silver and bronze. Hell, they'd probably even destroy the other competitors in the pool to take the trophy, or the egg."

"Woo hoo!" Declan let out a cheer. "You hear that, B? I'm Superman in the sack!"

Wearily, I rubbed my face. "Thanks Ki, now I'm never gonna hear the end of it."

"On that note, I'll take it as my cue to leave." He stood up, picking up his medicine bundle to take with him.

"Thanks for your help." I stood up too, to walk him to the door.

Declan followed after, holding his baby girl securely in his right arm. But just as I opened the front door to let Ki out, my mate stepped in the way. He blocked the exit to interrogate the Medicine Man further.

"So B's resistance to my swimmers is just temporary?" He wanted to double check.

"I believe so." Ki spoke honestly. "I think if her body wanted to stop reproducing permanently then her ovaries would shut down."

"So this is her body's way of taking a hiatus between rug rats?" Declan drilled.

"Yes," he answered. "If you're concerned about this, or if you and Aunt B wanted to start on expanding your family right away? Then we could set up a series of appointments where -"

"No thanks, Ki." I interrupted. "I don't mind taking a hiatus between rug rats. Besides, I'm still getting to know my firstborn before giving her sisters."

Declan looked on my objection in astonishment.

"That's understandable." Ki smiled sympathetically. "Well if there's nothing else, I'll see you next week when I come back for Lucia's check up."

Reluctantly, my huge husband moved aside to let the slightly smaller male, out.

Together, we watched our Medicine Man go down the veranda stairs and cross over to his hover-car which was parked on the driveway. Funnily enough, the driver's side was also next to a small pile of broken technology on the gravel. Ki passed it a peculiar look, before looking our way in a knowing fashion. Then he opened his door, hopped inside his vehicle and reversed out.

Out of the blue, Declan turned on me, "What the hell is wrong with you?!"

"Huh?"

"You're the one who was gung ho about getting pregnant! For three hundred years all I ever heard was, 'I can't get pregnant when all I want is to have your babies'. Now we know we can have kids, but your body and your attitude are against my 'Superman Swimmers'. Why B, don't you want to have any more of my children?"

"What the...?" I stood back from his blast. "Declan I never said -"

"Yes you did! Just then you said it in front of our frickin' Medicine Man! He said he could set up a series of treatments and you cut him dead!"

"No I didn't."

"Yes you did!" His face reddened as his eyes blazed.

I was about to protest my innocence when I paused.

Clearly, I could see how fired up he was. But he was still holding Lucia safely and securely, tucked into his big, strong arm. No matter how angry he'd get, he still put the safety of his loved ones first. I think I can see what's happening here.

To his further surprise, I smiled at him. In fact, I beamed at the sight of him standing there with our young. It was like our roles have been reversed, where in the beginning he was the reluctant father. Now he was leading the parade for parenthood, as the commander in chief.

"You're clucky." I announced.

"Say what?" He blinked.

"You're clucky."

"What the hell...?" He blanched. "B, I'm a European Werewolf and trust me, we DON'T cluck!"

"You're the proud papa bear who wants more cubs to care for." I carried on. "You're the proud duck, waddling along and wanting more ducklings to follow after. You want another baby Werewolf in the house."

"Hey, I'm just 'sowing my seed'." He turned defensive. "It's not my fault if the field I'm trying to plant in, is not letting me produce a harvest."

"You want another baby, you want another baby..." I sung, "...papa bear Declan wants a new cub to care for."

"Whatever."

His face turned pink as abashed he turned away and headed for the stairs.

"Declan is clucky, Declan is clucky..." I sang louder as I followed him up, "...Declan wants another baby, Declan wants another baby."

"Shut up." He snapped, as he ducked into the nursery to change Lucia.

"Declan Domitian Sabre wants more children." I taunted, as I leaned on the doorway to watch. "It's a good thing you're the last of your kind. If another European Werewolf found out, you could be thrown out of the club."

"Shut up, B."

Gently, he lay Lucia down on the change table to quickly and proficiently change her. As he did, Looch gurgled up at her father. Declan softly growled back, to which she responded by baring her sharp, little teeth.

"That's my girl." He chuckled over his young.

~~~~~~
~~~~~~

~ 15 ~

5th May 2365

Lucia's first eleven months passed in busy happiness. The same time as our baby developed into a walking, talking, toddler; her father learned along with her, developing his abilities as a Circulator. There were first steps for the both of them, whereas one learned how to use her legs, the other learned how to instantaneously phase through time. Sometimes, all I could do was stand back and watch as their natural and supernatural skills progressed.

Last September, I found Looch sitting upright in her cot. She sat there grinning with her glowing green eyes looking extra bright. I halted in surprise in the nursery doorway.

"Oh my...!" I stared at my three month old in wonder. "Declan! Declan, come quick!"

"What? Why?" He called back. However, he came running up the stairs to stop short beside. Immediately, he smiled on his little girl, "You're sitting up, Looch! Is this your first time sitting up?"

Lucia squealed in delight at the sound of pride in her father's voice. Then she held out her clawed little hands, showing she wanted to be picked up. Her father responded by lifting her up then holding her close.

"Aren't we a clever little girl?" He gently rocked her. "Aren't we a cute and clever, baby Werewolf?"

I leaned in to rub my nose against hers which earned further squeals of happiness.

Later, we told Ki what happened at Lucia's check-up. Our Medicine Man's eyes widened in astonishment and remained that way when Declan sat Looch on the floor. She sat upright and alert, as she examined her surroundings.

"Remarkable...!" The Healer said impressed. "Normally, babies sit up around six months and even then with support. Her bone and muscle density must be forty times stronger than a human's."

"Nah, it'd be stronger than that," her father dismissed. "B's forty times stronger than a human and don't forget that this kid is half of me, too. I'd say Looch is sixty times stronger than a human. As she grows, I bet she'll get stronger too."

Ki's eyebrows rose warily, "I believe you."

During the third month, Declan and I witnessed another development in our little Werewolf... her growing bloodlust.

On the full moon, the father went hunting with the rest of the pack as the mother stayed home with the baby.

Eagerly, I waited for a body part from whatever animal Declan tore apart. My bloodlust burned over the fact that this was another full moon I missed a hunt. But I would soon satiate it with whatever tasty morsel he brought back, still bleeding of course.

However, this time when the European Werewolf sat on the gravel driveway and howled upon his return, I didn't come running.

He paused before he howled again, but still his mate didn't come. He looked from the caribou leg which was beginning to congeal, to the front door. He cocked his ears, listening for approaching footsteps, when he heard Lucia crying instead.

Next, he shrunk back into his human body to come inside and see what was going on. On his way, he grabbed his old, stained bathrobe, which was hanging on the veranda railing. He put it on to cover his nakedness then followed the commotion upstairs.

He found me pacing up and down in the nursery, rocking a screaming baby in my arms.

Lucia's face was bright red as she screamed the house down, emitting many an unhappy snarl amongst her sobs.

"She's hungry but she won't feed." I shouted frightened, over the noise. "I don't know what to do!"

He looked from his wife to the screaming baby then he took charge.

Declan walked up and carefully took Lucia out of my arms. He nursed her on his right arm, whilst raising his left wrist to his mouth. I watched as he used his sharp teeth to put a deep gash in the skin, before lowering his bleeding wrist to the baby's mouth.

Like the flick of a switch, she stopped crying and I stood there in shock.

"It's the full moon, it's making her bloodlust peak." He said perfunctory, as he held his wrist still.

"You mean every full moon we have to feed her blood instead of milk?" I blanched.

"During the day she'll still drink breast milk or formula. She did today, didn't she?" He speculated. "But at night when the moon is at its most powerful, we're gonna have to make other arrangements."

As he spoke, he looked tenderly on his young.

"Oh." My face fell. "She drinks a LOT of milk, what if she needs a lot of blood, too?"

"Since it's you that does the breastfeeding, I don't mind being the blood donor." He said simply. "Besides, I regenerate faster than you, so it should be me."

"How long will this go on for?" I asked unhappily.

"I dunno... until she's able to hunt, I guess." He shrugged. "Speaking of which, your meal is growing cold on the driveway."

"I'm not hungry." I said disheartened, but then my stomach objected.

He caught me flinch from the physical pain caused by the bloodlust.

"Go and eat, before the blood congeals any further." He ordered.

Hurriedly, I raced out of the nursery, down the stairs then out of the house.

I found the bloodied leg of a caribou waiting with a great deal of flesh still attached to the hind quarter. It smelled fresh, indicating decomposition hadn't begun yet however, some of the blood on the outside had congealed. The sight and smell of the offering was enough to make me turn and I picked it up in my clawed hands.

I ate a second dinner that night in my Lokoti Werewolf body. My elongated, sharp teeth tore away the hide, to reach the succulent, warm flesh underneath. As soon as my taste buds touched the fresh-kill, my bloodlust revelled in the life that was taken away.

I sat there in my nightie, on the cold, gravel driveway in my bulked up body. My clawed hands held up the huge caribou leg to my dangerous mouth. I felt the caribou's blood spill down my chin then on the front of my clothing. Blood trickled down my arms too and splattered over the gravel.

With my acute hearing, I heard a noise behind and when I turned around, I saw it was Declan. He came to sit on the veranda steps in his bathrobe, with Lucia sucking on his bleeding wrist. He sat there so casually, like he could have been bottle feeding her instead. His eyes were glowing green just as his daughter's were, to see clearly in the dark. I sensed his bloodlust delighted in watching his wife gorge herself on what he killed for her.

Now all of this made sense - we were a family - a family of Werewolves.

We had Papa Werewolf to do the hunting and bring back the fresh kill, Mama Werewolf to do the breastfeeding and eating of the fresh kill and Baby Werewolf to suckle from her mother and now occasionally, her father. All three had the infamous bloodlust which demanded the taking of life, which gave us our strength and longevity. It was Declan's regenerative blood which was in direct descent from the First Werewolf that healed his wife and daughter. We were interconnected in so many ways and as much as we were supernatural, we were still part of the natural.

*****

In December, our six month old gave her parents another surprise. It happened in the self-defence training room at Circulate HQ. Lucia now enjoyed instantaneously phasing with her mother, as her father hung on. I didn't want Declan instantaneously phasing to another planet on his own yet, as I was scared of what could go wrong. I didn't fancy the idea of him floating off into outer space.

The bright light which momentarily blinded, no longer frightened her. She barely batted an eyelid at this mode of transport anymore. Contented, she sat upright on a blanket on the floor, putting toys into her mouth. Periodically, she looked up at her parents who were circling the other warily. She didn't understand that her Mummy was teaching her Daddy how to fight in the speed of light, but it didn't seem to concern her, either.

Declan and I wore work-out clothes; me in a purple, elasticized singlet top and three-quarter pants and him in grey tracksuit bottoms with a white singlet. We were sparring in the white, padded room, which had the massive weapons display on the wall. The swords, crossbows, muskets and automatic guns, showed off humanity's own bloodlust through the ages.

We weren't throwing actual punches at the other, but mainly blocking or swerving the jabs the other threw out. I wanted him to develop his speed and I must admit, I was impressed at how easily he engaged his light speed reflexes to duck or block. Speed as well as strength, appeared to be at his command.

"Good..." I commended, "...very good, Declan."

I was in an attack posture as he stood in a defensive stance. I threw out a couple more jabs, which he swerved from the first then blocked the second. His reflexes were so fast, they didn't just look like a bright blur, but a couple of times I couldn't even see his movements.

"This is great!" I dropped my fighting posture to stand normally. "How do you feel? When you engage your light speed reflexes, does it feel like time is slowing down?"

"Yeah, why is that?" He asked, puzzled.

"You're moving in another time differential." I declared. "Think of space ships that travel in light speed -"

"Yeah yeah." He cut me off. "Since I'm moving faster, to me time seems to be slowing down. But to somebody else, I'm speeding up."

"Basically." I shrugged it off.

Then I looked away to check on Lucia, when time seemed to stop completely... She wasn't sitting on her blanket anymore and in fact, she was nowhere to be seen.

"Hey, where did Looch go?" Declan voiced my thoughts, as he looked in the same direction.

Hastily, I looked around as fear grabbed hold of my heart. Then I spotted her crawling – yes crawling – towards the weapons display on the distant wall. I think the shiny, sharp things attracted her attention.

Just as I was about to run over, Declan beat me to it. He disappeared from my side and I wasn't sure if he instantaneously phased, or if he ran in light speed? But he scooped up his six month up from the floor and held her up, so her face was the same level as his.

"No Lucia Grace," he shook his head. "Not only are those things sharp, but some of them are made of silver."

"Declan..." I uttered in shock, "...Looch just CRAWLED!"

"Er, yeah B, I kinda noticed." He smirked at my stunned expression.

"No, it was her FIRST crawl!" I elaborated. "That was Lucia's first crawl!"

His bright blue eyes widened as he looked from his wife to his daughter.

Next, a silly grin overtook his youthful face. "Did you just crawl, Looch? Did you just have your first crawl?"

In reply, she smilingly gurgled back at her surprised Daddy.

"Put her on the floor and let's see if she does it again." I prompted.

I moved back by about ten metres then we both crouched down. Gently, he put her on the ground and watched as I held out my arms and called to her. Looch cast a last look at her father, before crawling towards her mother on her strong little hands and knees.

"Good girl, Looch!" I cheered her on. "Good girl!"

I picked her up to deliver showers of kisses over her cherub face.

"Woo hoo!" He stood up to cheer. "Ladies and gentlemen, this kid can crawl!"

Thoughts of light speed and self-defence were soon forgotten as we played with our daughter instead.

A couple of days later when we told Ki this news, the look on his face was of befuddlement.

"But Looch is just six months old..." he uttered, "...babies aren't meant to start crawling until around nine months."

Smugly, her father lowered her from his lap and onto the living room floor.

Our six month old giggled at this grant of freedom, before crawling towards the dining table. She scuttled along the polished, wooden floorboards on her hands and knees. Her wavy, dark blonde hair bounced around, as she easily skedaddled across the room.

Gloatingly, her father looked back at the Healer, "You were saying?"

"This is amazing..." Ki shook his head in disbelief. "And how's her eating pattern?"

"She's still on formula, but we've started giving her solids once a day." He reported. "I feed her pureed raw meat and vegetables."

"Raw meat?" The Medicine Man's eyes widened in alarm. "Not cooked meat?"

"The first meal I made for her was cereal and banana and she spat it back up. Then I tried pureed cooked vegetables but she refused to eat it. The third time I tried pureed cooked meat and vegetables and she had a few mouthfuls. So I made pureed raw meat with vegetables and she gobbled it all down."

"You mentioned formula..." Ki looked my way, "...isn't she still on breast milk?"

"Er, no." My face heated up, as I shifted uncomfortably. "She's on formula instead."

"Why?" He noted my unease.

"Last week B's body stopped lactating." My mate spoke for me, as he rested a supportive hand on my leg. "Well look at her, her body's changed back to the way it was before the pregnancy. Her motherly curves have disappeared and we're back to her athletic build, since her breasts have shrunk."

Our Healer openly looked me over. "Oh, I see."

"It happened pretty quickly, too." Declan frowned. "One day my wife's breasts are on tap then the next they're not. It was like overnight B's body reverted. When she got out of bed last week, I noticed the changes immediately."

"That is unusual." Ki stared at my smaller breasts, flatter stomach and thinner thighs.

"I think I know why." I began. "When Gran and Mum had children, their bodies reverted to their pre-pregnant states within the first three months. As a Circulator, my body isn't meant to change unless I deliberately alter my age. But I think it was the Lokoti Werewolf part of me that kept my motherly body for longer, to care for my young. But it's weird, because as soon as we put Looch onto solids, my milk dried up overnight."

Ki took out his medical scanner and waved the instrument in my direction. Then he lowered it to check the results, as it hummed away. My husband leaned forwards as he waited to hear the verdict.

"Fascinating..." Ki breathed out, "...you're right Aunt B, your breasts have completely reverted to their pre-pregnant state. Normally it can take months for the transition, I've never heard of it happening overnight."

"Well, now you have." My husband took hold of my hand. "We certainly wouldn't be self-defence training if you still had your motherly body."

"Why?" I gave a funny look.

"I'm not taking a swing at you when you have soft, motherly curves and huge breasts." He said indignantly. "Now that you're back to your athletic build, your muscles are harder and you're far less fragile."

"I wasn't fragile!" I objected.

"Alright, softer then... you were softer in your motherly body." He said then we caught him mutter, "It was a damn turn on, man I miss it."

I let go of his hand to deliver an elbow to his ribs, to remind him of his manners.

He snapped to and looked at our medical practitioner. "So, what are we gonna do about B's 'antibody uterus'? Bring on the rug rats!"

In annoyance, I moved away from him on the couch.

Ki tried to retain his professional decorum, "Are you currently trying for more children?"

Simultaneously, as Declan answered "yes", I answered with a "no," then we gave each other a peculiar look.

"We're not?" Declan arched his eyebrows.

"We are?" I replied in similar fashion.

"Er, hello? What do you think we've been doing every night?" He gave a peculiar look.

"The same thing we did every night when we thought I was barren!" I snapped back.

"We ARE trying for another." Declan said sharply. "So if her body is still battling my swimmers, what's the next plan of attack?"

"Well, there are several kinds of medicinal herbs we can try..." Ki began but he stopped when he caught me wince, "...or you can wait."

"Wait? It's been six months! C'mon people, let's make another baby here." He clapped his hands together as if he were rallying the troops.

"Maybe it's just nature and her body deciding to space out your children," our Healer said patiently.

"Or we can give them both a nudge with the medicinal herbs." My mate refuted.

Ki opened his mouth to say something else when I exploded.

"I AM NOT TAKING ANYMORE DRUGS FOR INFERTILITY!"

Pause...Ki looked on sympathetic as Declan appeared confused.

BANG!

All of our heads turned at the loud noise, to see Lucia sitting under the dining table. She had deliberately knocked over one of the chairs with her supernatural strength. Then she giggled at her accomplishment and made a move to knock over another.

"Lucia Grace!" Her father growled as he quickly stood up to retrieve her. We heard him grumble as he carried her back, "If all female Werewolves in the house would remain calm, we could talk about this in a logical manner."

As soon as he sat down again, I pulled her out of his arms and into mine instead.

"If all male European Werewolves in the house could go out and buy a clue...?" I muttered back.

Declan opened his mouth to retort when Ki jumped in.

"Erm hmm, getting back to Lucia's developments," he cleared his throat. "Have her eyes turned blue any other times?"

My mate passed an annoyed look my way before returning his attention to the Medicine Man.

"Yeah, usually in the morning her eyes turn a blue colour." He spoke. "When she first wakes up, her eyes are glowing green but by mid morning, they fade to blue. Then in the afternoon when it starts to turn dark outside, her eyes glow green again."

"How about her claws?" Ki wondered.

"They're occasionally soft enough for us to cut, but they grow back after a couple of days." I told him.

"Does she accidentally scratch herself?" He guessed.

"Yup." Her father answered, as he smoothed back her hair. "When her nails grow back, they're strong like claws. But after a day or two, they weaken enough for us to cut again."

"I think it's around once a week that we cut the nails on her fingers and toes," I looked to Declan which he confirmed with a nod. Then I continued, "But I think she's beginning to sense how different she and her parents are."

"How so?" Ki listened.

"When Looch accidentally scratches herself, either Declan or I lick her wound which seals it shut. Over Thanksgiving, we had the Wisetail's over and Kevin was lying on his blanket on the floor with Lucia. When she reached out, she accidentally scratched him. Then it looked like she tried to put her mouth over his wound to try to heal him, like she's seen her parents do."

"And then what happened?" His eyes widened.

"Wendy picked up Kevin when he began to cry. She watched Walt lick Kevin's scratch which healed him, but she noticed how Wendy didn't. I think she's realizing that not everyone is a Werewolf." I explained.

"Wendy looked pretty freaked out." Declan added on. "We had to remind her if Looch had licked him, he wouldn't have turned into a European Werewolf."

"Hmm," Ki frowned. "I wouldn't be offended by Wendy's behaviour, it's just the protective motherly instinct."

"We know." I said flatly. "But it also made me wonder what other mothers may be like if we tried to take Looch to a playgroup or something."

Supportively, Declan moved closer on the couch to put his arm around his wife.

"I'd give her some social training first, before that happens." Ki started to laugh at his own joke.

"No, we're just going to let her loose on the other toddlers." Her father said sarcastically as he glared back. "Of course we're going to teach her! Do you think we're gonna encourage antisocial behaviour? At Thanksgiving Dinner, Edwina picked up her roast vegetables and started throwing 'em at Kurt. It looks like the Wisetail's have some social training to do too, don't they?"

*****

Ironically, the full moon cycle for December fell over the Christmas period. As we celebrated the holidays in the Christian fashion, we also celebrated it Werewolf style.

This was Lucia's first Christmas and we wanted to make it extra special. Two weeks before, Declan went out into the woods with Walt in his U.S. Forest Service vehicle. They took the larger hover-car with the rear carriage, to bring back their respective trees.

Although Walt was Lokoti and traditionally, our people didn't celebrate this holiday; many members of the tribe including Wendy, came from family backgrounds which did. Wendy's father was Athabascan and her mother was French Canadian. She grew up celebrating Christmas and Walt didn't mind carrying on the tradition.

Around 4 PM, Declan kicked open the front door and dragged in the thickest, bushiest, most perfect looking pine tree. It was so tall, it almost touched the ceiling. With his physical prowess, he easily carried it inside and soon he had it sitting upright in a pot, in the corner of the lounge room.

I put on 'John Denver and The Muppets: A Christmas Together' for us to listen to, as we decorated the tree. The album used to be on a tape, which was then converted to CD and now it was saved onto the hard drive of our Sound System. It was an old family tradition to listen to it while putting up Christmas decorations.

"Nothing says Christmas like listening to Kermit, Miss Piggy and Fozzy Bear, singing carols." Declan smilingly shook his head.

Lucia sat on the rug by the fireplace looking at all of the tinsel in fascination.

She watched her father hoist her mother onto his shoulders, so I could put the Sabre family Angel on top of the tree. It was an antique which had been in Declan's family for years. It started when the Sabre's left Italy after World War Two and his parents kept it when they left Indianapolis after World War Three.

Then a week before Christmas, Declan and I took turns in staying home with Lucia as the other person went out to do their shopping.

When Declan babysat, he invited Walt over, who arrived with his small fry in tow.

Coincidentally, the same day that I went shopping, so did Wendy. Since we were both out on the town, we met up for lunch at the old Bakery Cafe. We showed each other what we'd bought for our kids as well as for our husbands. However, I kept hidden in the hover-car a couple of gift baskets to dole out to the Wisetail's, the Sabre's, the Riverclaw's and to our Medicine Man.

The following day, the men went out to do their shopping as Wendy brought over her kids again.

We sat at the dining table, sipping non-alcoholic eggnog whilst looking over our children who were playing on the rug by the fire.

"Are your parents coming to stay this Christmas?" I asked.

"Mom and Dad miss a Christmas with the grandkids? Never!" She giggled.

"You should bring them over for plum pudding again." I offered.

"We just might take you up on that." She smiled at the invitation. "My parents respect you and Uncle Dec. They often ask how you are and they can't wait to meet Lucia."

"So um, I guess they know we're Werewolves then?" I thought I'd check.

"Yes, we told them before we came over last year." She verified. "Dad grew up hearing stories of Lokoti Werewolves. So when I told my parents I'd married one, they didn't faint at the news. Dad knew the legends well enough to know they're the protectors of the tribe. Then Walt explained that Uncle Dec was a different kind of Werewolf, but he wasn't a man-eater either, and my parents were as right as rain."

"Cool." I smiled in relief.

If only the rest of the world could be as well informed...

Suddenly, Wendy cried out, "Edwina, no! Kurt, stop Edwina from throwing the toys into the fire!"

The four year old quickly caught the two year old's doll before she could launch it over the fireplace's safety grill.

"Your daughter just loves to throw things." I frowned.

"Your daughter just loves to chew things." Wendy replied, while looking on the new teeth marks in Looch's glow-worm doll.

Kurt in his role as the eldest thought he should help the mothers by taking charge.

Dutifully, he kept an eye on Kevin and Lucia, who were sitting upright and salivating on their respective toys. Or, he kept guard over Edwina, keeping her from hurtling them over the safety grill. Periodically though, he would place a kiss on the top of Looch's head as well as give her an affectionate pat.

"So, shall we make it a spring wedding?" Wendy giggled.

Christmas Eve was the night of the full moon. It was also the night that children dreamed of what Santa might bring. Whereas, I fantasized about what blood-dripping, body part, my mate might bring.

Instead of wearing a red suit, the European Werewolf left the house without any clothes on. He walked past the decorated Tree with its presents below. Then he stood in the snow outside to morph into his frightening shape. I watched his change from our bedroom window, as I rocked Lucia in my right arm. I'd put a gash in my left wrist and she was suckling on the blood flow.

Before he departed, he said, "Don't give her too much. Stop as soon as you start to feel dizzy. Don't worry if she's still hungry, because I have an idea."

"Oh yeah?" I arched my eyebrows. "And what bright idea is this?"

"Trust me," he gave a wink with his glowing green eye.

However, my energy and patience had considerably thinned by 2 AM. I paced up and down in the nursery with a sobbing baby in my arms. I was feeling dizzy and Lucia was still hungry.

Just then I heard the backdoor downstairs open loudly. Along with it, came Declan's heavy footsteps. However, instead of coming upstairs, I heard him go into the kitchen.

He called out, "Come downstairs and bring Lucia with you."

The unhappy little Werewolf writhed in my arms. I managed to keep a grip on her, as I struggled down the staircase. I found Declan in his bloodstained robe preparing something in the kitchen. His hands, feet and mouth were bloodied and they became bloodier by what he'd brought with him.

A hind quarter from a moose was sitting on top of the kitchen bench, still bleeding. Its' blood trickled over the side and down the cupboard doors, pooling onto the floor. Although it smelled delicious, I wasn't looking forward to cleaning that up.

"What the hell...?!" My face fell at the sight of the mess. "Couldn't you have done this outside?"

"I couldn't do THIS outside," he replied, as he worked.

Lucia's cries escalated into screams and I sensed her bloodlust was putting her through agony.

Declan worked quickly, partially changing so his nails turned into claws and his teeth were jagged and sharp. Next, he used them to strip the hide and rip off a handful of flesh too. Then he dropped it into the food processor and turned it on. Once the meat had been minced into mush, he turned it off, lifted up the lid and sniffed it.

"It's still warm and fresh," he noted.

Then he dipped his claw-like hand into the red mixture and took out a tiny bit. Using his fingers, he carefully placed it inside Lucia's open mouth. As soon as she tasted the fresh kill, she stopped crying. She chewed on the offering, whilst looking on gratefully with her tearful, glowing green eyes. Declan's eyes were also glowing green, as he looked on his young in understanding.

Over the next half hour, the Werewolves had an early Christmas feast.

Declan and I sat together on the bloodied bench top, getting even bloodier. He sat with Looch in his lap, as he fed her the minced moose from the processor. Meanwhile, her mother sat beside in her Lokoti Werewolf form, eating the remaining meat off the bone.

I used the back of my hand to wipe my mouth, feeling full. Then I burped loudly, which Lucia copied, making Declan chuckle. She too was satiated and now was falling asleep against her father's flannel robe.

Next, I caught sight of the time on the microwave which read as 3.03 AM. Children on the east coast would be waking up about now, to see what presents Santa left them. Here in Alaska, I'd just indulged in my first Christmas treat.

"Merry Christmas, Dec." I said in my deep, rumbling voice as I grinned with my elongated, sharp teeth.

"Merry Christmas, B." He smiled back with his own messy, dangerous mouth.

Affectionately, I leaned in to lick the blood off his face before I felt him do the same back.

*****

In March when Lucia was nine months old, she gave us another surprise.

I was getting dressed for the day when I heard Declan call out from the nursery:

"Hey B, come here a sec."

"Hang on," I called back.

I walked into the nursery then I froze... Lucia was standing up in her cot whilst holding onto the railing.

"Check it out," her father grinned proudly, as he stroked the top of her head. "Looch's first stand."

"Oh, Lucia Grace!" I squealed like she did. "Look at you, little girl! Look at you, all grown up! You're standing up like a big girl does!"

Lucia squealed back as she clapped her hands. But because she let go of the railing, she landed with a bump onto her backside. She giggled at herself then again when her father picked her up. He carried her over to the change table to put her into a new nappy.

Expertly, he held her still while changing her, as she wriggled and writhed and giggled some more.

"I was thinking of making scrambled eggs for all three of us, this morning." Declan said as he worked.

"What, instead of giving her mashed banana?" I checked. "But she's just started getting used to fruit."

"We'll see how she goes with the scrambled egg and if she doesn't like it, then I'll give her mashed banana."

Then he handed me a changed baby to hold as he went to go wash his hands.

Half an hour later, all three Sabres were sitting at the table, eating scrambled eggs for breakfast.

Looch sat at the head of the table in her high chair, with Declan and I sitting to her left and right. Her father was feeding himself and his daughter with her little plastic spoon. I knew he did it to encourage her and make it look more natural.

Mmm, yum!" He said loudly for her benefit, eating some scrambled egg off his plate.

Then he scooped some up from her plastic bowl and put it into her mouth.

"Mmm – mmm – mmm!" She copied, obediently swallowing.

She liked it so much, she dipped her fingers into the bowl and tried to pick it up. A little reached her mouth however, most of it toppled down her bib, leaving debris over the highchair's tabletop.

Next, Declan picked up his glass of freshly-squeezed OJ. Slowly, he began to drink it in front of her. She watched with interest with her wide, human blue eyes. So I picked up her straw cup with the juice inside and held it for her. She began to drink from it while making sure her father was watching.

"Way to go, Looch." He tenderly ruffled her hair.

"How did you..." I began, but my voice trailed off.

"How did I what?" He enquired.

"How did you know that Looch was ready for other foods?" I pondered.

"Woman's instinct." He joked. "No seriously, she's a Werewolf. Human babies are fragile lil critters, but this kid's got pluck. She was born with teeth and she already craves raw meat. I mean if I were her, I'd get bored of eating the same thing all of the time."

Out of the blue, I left my chair to sit in his lap instead. I straddled him whilst wrapping my arms about his neck. Teasingly, I leaned in to chew on his lower lip before his upper one then smothering both in a passionate kiss.

I growled out, "I must have the hottest property on the father market."

"Mmm..." Declan kissed back, "...you'd better believe it, baby."

"Mmm – mmm – mmm!" Lucia mimed again, making us laugh. However, what came out of her mouth next, really made our day; "Mumumum... Dadadada... Mumumum."

"Say what?" Declan sat back and stared at his nine month old in her highchair.

"Did you hear that?!" I stood up, excitedly. "She just said her first 'Mummy' and 'Daddy'!"

Declan jumped to his feet then picked up Looch and held her high in the air.

"Say it again, Looch!" He cheered her on.

"Mumumum... Dadada... Mumumum... Dadadada." She repeated.

"Woo hoo!" I jumped up and down like we'd won the lottery. "Our daughter just called us Mum and Dada!"

"Say it again, Looch!" Her father spun her around. "Go on, say it again!"

"Mumum... Dadada... Mumum... Dadada." She chanted over and over.

He lowered her to hold against his wide chest and I leaned in to caress her cheek with my nose.

It's funny, looking back we can't remember what else we did that day... All I remember was Looch's first stand then being called 'Mum' for the first time and everything else blurred into pale comparison. I think it was the same for Declan. The outside world could have blown up again but inside the Sabre household, we existed in our own little universe. There was Papa Bear, Mama Bear and Baby Bear and if Goldilocks deigned to sleep in our beds, we hardly would have noticed. Except maybe Dec would have turned to me after putting Looch down for the night, "Hey, who was that strange, blonde chick we kicked out of Baby Bear's bed?"

*****

It was April and although Looch was ten months old, I'd still put her in the baby carrier.

Today was one of those days and I carried her around with me whilst I did some light housework. I did the laundry as Declan emptied the clean dishes out of the dishwasher. Then I wiped down the benches as he stacked the dirty dishes into the machine.

Afterwards, I sat down at the dining table and turned on my laptop. It blinked to life as my baby slumbered against my front. She may have been ten months but she was the size of a fifteen month old. Right now, my big baby was drooling on my t-shirt, in her sleep.

However, what concerned me was the paper I was working on, was older than my child. Normally, it took me six months or less to ready a paper and its corresponding presentation. However, motherhood and a possessive husband consumed much of my time. I hadn't even been able to go back in time to collect further evidence, because I'd been so busy. But today, I wanted to collate my research so far and type up my introduction.

Expertly, my fingers touched typed a hundred words a minute, thanks to centuries of practice. Music played softly in the background from Sigur Ros' album, 'Med Sud I Eyrum Vid Spilum Endalaust'. Declan was in the kitchen, checking on his jars of antipasto mix, as well as his olives and feta preserve.

Around four o'clock, I had to stop typing and rub my weary eyes from staring so long at the computer screen.

"Take a break." He said simply.

"I can't." I moaned, rubbing my eyes harder. "I'm behind with my academic work. So far I haven't published or lectured yet as Dr. Bianca Sabre."

"Give up your day job." He said flatly. "Retire completely, like I have. You're a mother now, so take up full-time parenting."

"I can't, OK? I just can't!" I whined. "I'd be lost with out my papers and research."

He didn't reply as he stood in the kitchen with his jars and preserves. It sounded like he was opening them, but I couldn't see. He'd even pulled out a plate from the cupboard and I wondered if he was sampling them? Whatever he was doing, he was doing it in a moody silence.

"Besides, my academic work is only part-time." I continued. "I still have plenty of time for you and Lucia."

"When we give Lucia sisters, will you have time for them too?"

"Declan, lay off!" I passed a glare. "We already agreed that I'd keep working and you would be the 'house hubby'."

Finally, he looked my way, "And when are we going to give Lucia some sisters to play with?"

"What is this, 'pick on B day'?" I gave a peculiar look.

He returned to whatever it was he was doing with the jars, before putting them back in the pantry. I watched him open the fridge and return the jar of feta preserve as well as a packet of something I couldn't see properly. Next, he picked up a plate he'd been fiddling with and carried it over to where I was sitting. When he put it down on the table, my eyes practically popped out of my head.

There sat a gourmet feast of mini-toasts topped with prosciutto, feta preserve and various antipasto, such as olives, eggplant or sun-dried tomato.

"Wow." I looked on, impressed.

"Yeah, I'm the bad husband for pampering my wife and preparing her such delicacies."

Gloatingly, he sat up on the dining table and popped some food into his mouth.

"Then what are you doing?" I looked on warily.

"I dunno..." he sighed loudly, "...it's just that I've been so happy lately, I thought you've been feeling the same way."

"I am happy."

"So why don't you wanna have anymore kids...?" He whined like a five year old.

"Who says I don't?"

"When you sit there typing madly away instead letting your husband knock you up, it makes me wonder."

"Declan, I do this maybe once a week and I'm 'with' you every night." I used the innuendo around my daughter. "Six days a week I'm the devoted wife and mother and hell, right now I'm working while still holding the baby. So don't make me out to be a bad parent!"

To press my point, I pinched him on the leg.

"C'mon B!" He brushed my hand away. "Let's have another rug rat."

"No."

"Why not?"

"I dunno, ask my body." I said coolly. "But it, or fate, or maybe even the timeline is saying, 'not yet'."

"Screw fate." Declan muttered. "I'd say screw your body too, but it's obviously not working."

He made me laugh loudly which momentarily disturbed Lucia. Sleepily, she opened her eyes which were glowing green again. Then she turned her head and settled down once more. Reassuringly, I rubbed her back which made her give a contented growl.

When I was sure she was back to sleep, I pinched him on the leg again.

"You're a father now, you can't talk like that around your kids."

"Trust me B, if they grow up talking like me? I ain't gonna punish them for it." He smirked. "Anyway, there was something else I wanted to talk to you about."

"Hmm?"

"I instantaneously phased to Taurus Six yesterday while you were in the shower -"

"Say what?" My mouth fell open in surprise. "You instantaneously phased to a planet on the other side of the galaxy?"

"B, don't start."

"But you're not ready for that yet!" I sat up straighter in alarm. "You need to practice phasing through time first! Do you know how dangerous that was or -"

"Would you calm down and let me finish?" He rolled his eyes.

As if in agreement, my ten month old emitted a dissatisfied snarl at all the commotion.

"What were you doing on Taurus Six?" I demanded.

"Hiking, what the hell do you think?" He replied sarcastically. "I was using the Viewing Room dumbass, coz I wanted to check something out."

"Did you just call me a dumbass?"

"Can you just listen to what I have to say?"

"Not if you're going to call me a dumbass."

Offended, I returned my attention to my laptop, but the obstinate male lifted it away.

"As I was saying..." he cleared his throat, "...I was checking out the Viewing Room because I've finally thought of where I'd like to go for my first time travel trip. I want to go back in time to when Mom was still alive to show her Lucia."

"Well, since you can instantaneously phase to other planets now and I'm a dumbass, you don't need my help."

"Yes I do." He gave a funny look. "I need your help to plan this perfectly."

"Are you sure you want the help of a dumbass?"

"Man, what is up with you today?!" He exhorted. "Are you getting your period or something?"

To answer his own question, he left the table and went into the kitchen to check the calendar. He looked on where I put my appointments, social engagements, academic functions, as well as an asterisk on certain days of the month. Then I saw his jaw drop to the floor.

"Oh shit, you are."

Instantly, he sprang into action as if he were carrying out a rehearsed emergency procedure.

I watched him open the pantry and rifle around for something on the top shelf and I saw him pull down a jar of Nutella. Next, he opened up the cutlery drawer and take out a teaspoon. Then he marched back to the table and held out his peace offering.

He said soberly, "I'm sorry for calling you a dumbass."

"What, if it wasn't my period you wouldn't apologise for calling me a dumbass?" I asked coldly. "You really think that if you shove a jar of Nutella in my face, you can make everything alright?"

"OK then, I'm the dumbass," he said.

"No, you're a clucky, domineering, control freak, who jumps up and down whenever he doesn't get his own way." I snapped, as I snatched up the jar and spoon. "You make dumbasses look good!"

Declan tried not to smile at my retort whilst I tore off the lid and dove the spoon into the soft, dark brown, chocolate-hazelnut spread. I loaded up the cutlery with a huge amount, before lifting it up to my mouth and slowly licking it, like it was a lollipop, relishing the taste. Lastly, I closed my eyes as I delivered the whole spoonful to my mouth, before eventually removing it then opening my eyes again.

"Was it good for you?" He joked.

"Mmm..." I sat back in a relaxed state, "...now you were saying you want to go back in time to see your dead mother?"

"Uh huh, and I think I've even pinpointed the exact date." He explained. "Remember the weekend in 2130, when we went to Blythe?"

"I think it was in um, November?" I ate as I listened.

"It was the 10th November 2130, Veteran's Day weekend." He confirmed. "Now, I'm no time travel expert, but I thought it would be a good idea that we visit when the other B and Declan are away."

"Good thinking, so we won't bump into our past selves and tamper with the timeline."

"If the past B and Declan saw you with a baby in your arms, isn't that gonna affect the timeline?" He pondered. "What if you try to change me into a Circulator sooner, so I can knock you up?"

"You are getting the hang of temporal causalities." I grinned. "If I did change you into a Circulator sooner so we could start a family, then we wouldn't have done so much travelling. We may have never met Nairn in Scotland or Paulo in Peru and who knows if they would've died because of it? Nairn by the European Vampires or Paulo by the South American Vampires."

"That's a scary thought, whether we meet someone or not, can mean life or death." His eyebrows arose.

"OK, so we have to visit your mother when the other Declan and B are away." I concurred. "But if we ask your mother never to tell them, do you think she can keep our secret?"

His face hardened, "Are you saying my Mom can't be trusted?"

"It's a big responsibility, knowing an important event in the future and not being allowed to talk about it." I said seriously. "What if her daughter-in-law is crying about being barren and your Mum decides to share what she knows, to cheer her up?"

He glanced away with a thoughtful frown on his youthful features. His pensive look lasted a full minute until his expression changed as he suddenly sat upright on top of the table. He looked like he'd just had a revelation and he clicked his fingers, to boot.

"Remember just before my Mom died and all the time I spent with her?" He spoke quickly. "On the last night she was alive, she said something peculiar. I was putting her to bed when she started talking about you. She asked again why you were unable to have kids and observed that you could obsess about it. I told her I'd stop you from talking about it, hoping it would stop you from thinking about it, too. Then she grabbed my arm and looked me right in the eye and said, 'you do take care of her, Declan. I know you'll take care of her until the very end, like you've taken care of me. And remember, often miracles happen when you least it expect it. You would make a wonderful father one day, just as you've been a wonderful husband and son'."

"Oh." I looked on, in surprise. "Do you think she said that from seeing you as a father?"

"I bet she did, or she will." He gave a confident grin. "So you see? My Mom can be trusted. We did go back in time to see her and she did keep our secret. She may have hinted about it on her death bed, but she never said a thing."

"Hmm," I turned pensive, "maybe if we time this right, we could kill two birds with the one stone."

"Huh?"

"What if we see Derik and Rachel too?" I asked, brightly. "Or, what if we include my Mum and Dad, or even my Gran and Grandfather?"

"You mean like a family reunion?" He smiled at the idea.

"Exactly!" I stood up to pace which helped me think. "The Circulate Mainframe can communicate through time like sending text messages or emails. What if we sent Aunt Susan, Derik, Rachel, Mum, Dad, Gran and Grandfather a text message to meet them somewhere?"

"Yeah!" He cried out exuberantly. "We could text message them to meet us at somebody's house at a certain time. They would think it's from the Declan and B in their era."

"Right on!" I pointed at him. "Now, Aunt Susan was always going to my grandparents' house for coffee. What if we sent Aunt Susan, Derik, Rachel, Mum and Dad a message to meet us at Gran and Grandfathers? But we would have to time this right. We have to send the messages after their B and Declan have left, in case they're asked about them."

"OK," he nodded along.

"I think we left on Friday afternoon for Blythe and came back on Sunday night?" I checked which he confirmed with a nod. "So what if we send messages to their phones at 10 AM on Saturday morning and tell them to meet us at my grandparents' at 4 PM that afternoon?"

"B, you're the sexiest and smartest female Werewolf in all of existence and after this, you can work on your papers all you like." He promised.

"I think the Circulate Mainframe would have their phone numbers saved, or it would know how to find them." I continued to think. "I'll organize with the Mainframe to send the messages to their phones."

Impressed, my husband looked down on the open jar of Nutella sitting on top of the table.

"Man, I love the effect this stuff has on my wife." He picked it up and sampled some using his finger. "Mmm, this stuff is good."

"Declan," I froze as soon as I saw what he was doing. "Put down the jar of Nutella."

"Sorry." He obeyed. "I don't know what came over me."

"Never touch a woman's jar of Nutella," I said in a low voice.

"Yeah I know." He held up his hands in surrender. "Like I said, I don't know what came over me."

Just then Lucia woke up, she didn't cry but she did squirm to be let out of the baby carrier. Carefully, I lifted her up then lowered her to the floor.

Looch crawled over to one of the dining table chairs and used it to stand up. Then while she was standing on her own two feet, she looked up at her Daddy with her glowing green eyes. Next, she proceeded to stumble over to where he was.

"Oh my gosh, did you see that?" I uttered in shock. "It's our ten month old daughter's first walk!"

Declan beamed as he knelt down on the floor to her level. "Hello there."

"Dadada." She giggled out, before turning around to stumble over to where I was.

I knelt down to meet her, but as she was half way over, she tripped over and fell! Instead of crying, she emitted another giggle as if she were laughing at herself. Then she returned to her own two feet and continued on, straight into my waiting arms.

"Lucia Grace!" I hugged her as I felt overwhelmed with pride.

"Mumumum." She rubbed her little face against mine, before she squirmed to be freed.

Our tiny, ten month old daughter next toddled around the living room.

Her steps wavered but stubbornly she continued onwards. We watched as she made herself used to this new mode of travel. Whilst walking around, she became acquainted with the downstairs of her home. She walked in and out of the kitchen then the downstairs bathroom-combined-laundry.

"She's exploring." Declan observed, as we remained crouched on the ground. Then we heard her sniff as she reached out her clawed little hand to touch the dining table. He marvelled, "B look at her, she's claiming her territory. She's learning the feel and smell of things, to memorize them."

In wonder, we watched our baby Werewolf get to know her home better. When she toddled into the kitchen a second time, we moved over to the kitchen entryway. We saw Looch sniff closely the bottom cupboard doors. She remained like that for a good two minutes, as she sniffed up and down the wood. She even got down on her hands and knees, to sniff the floor.

"She's tracking the smell of blood." Declan's eyes widened. "She can smell where the blood spilt from that piece of black bear I brought home."

"No way...!" My mouth fell agape. Of course there was no longer any blood there, as we kept a clean kitchen as well as a clean house. But she could track where it used to be?

Declan spoke to his half European Werewolf daughter, "The blood and bear are all gone, Looch."

She looked up sharply with her glowing green eyes.

"It's gone, Looch." I sung. "It's all gone."

I think she understood us which upset her. We watched her little face screw up and she began to cry. I sensed that the smell of blood made her hungry. Her father must have sensed it too, for he announced:

"It's dinner time for all the little Werewolves in the house."

I picked up my crying baby then moved to sit up on the kitchen bench and hold her in my lap.

Lucia watched with interest as Declan took out the raw meat as well as the vegetables from the fridge. Her eyes were wide as she watched her father's every move. Deftly, he chopped the broccoli, carrots, pumpkin and potato first before tipping them into a special container then putting it in the microwave. Once the vegetables were steamed, he took them out and tipped them into the food processor along with the raw beef. When her meal had been mushed together, he put the pureed food into her blue Donald Duck bowl.

"Here we go." He said softly.

He held the bowl in one hand and the matching blue, plastic spoon in his other.

Looch accepted the food, eagerly gobbling it down. As she ate, she didn't spit up and looked like she relished every bite. Since there weren't any spills, a bib wasn't called for. She even reached out her hands to grab hold of the bowl and eat straight from that.

"No Looch," I gently restrained her.

"Nah ah." He moved the bowl away. When she looked like she was about to cry again, he said sternly, "We eat with cutlery, not just straight from the bowl like an animal would."

Our little Werewolf growled angrily and reached for the bowl again, so Declan took a step backwards. She started to cry as if to use tears as her method, but he took another step back. So she stopped her sobbing and behaved, turning completely calm. Then her father came forwards once more and proceeded to feed her with the spoon again.

Declan frowned as he fed his young. "I think I can see what's happening here."

"See what?"

"Ki's right, Looch's development is different to other babies, because it's her predatory instincts kicking-in." He explained. "She's learning to talk at the same rate as a normal baby, so her mental development is on par with a human. But her physical abilities are developing faster, because it's her bloodlust preparing her to hunt as soon as possible."

"Hmm," I thought on this, "remember in the Viewing Room when we looked on other European Werewolves with their young? I think the offspring were very young indeed, when they started hunting. I think they were toddlers when they began, with or without their parent."

"Yup." Declan sighed unhappily. "As soon they were able to walk or run, they were able to hunt. You saw the second thing she did once she learned to walk, was track the trail of blood."

My eyes widened, "Do you think Lucia is going to try to hunt human?"

"As we've fed her animal from the beginning, I'm hoping that it's curbed her bloodlust to crave that particular flesh instead." He said gravely. "But we also have to train her that it's unacceptable to hunt without us. When she hunts, it's when we hunt. If her bloodlust plays up in between full moons, then I'll take her. We have to be tough on instilling human codes of conduct, which will also help her battle her bloodlust. If we let her eat without cutlery or behave too much like an animal, then her bloodlust will turn her into an animal."

"What do you suggest?" I listened intently.

"We keep doing what we're doing." Declan shrugged. "We teach her to use cutlery, to dress, to bathe, to talk and good manners. If she can't go to school in Alma because she craves the other school children, then we home school her. But we'll continually have the Wisetail's over, or go to social events within the tribe, so she can be trained how to behave around people."

"Do you think it's safe for her to socialize within the tribe?" I asked concerned.

"Yup." He confirmed. "I've been watching her closely the last couple of months, especially when she's with the Wisetail's. She doesn't crave them. She isn't interested in eating them at all. I think it's the Lokoti Werewolf part of her, she doesn't crave the blood of her kin. Otherwise, she would have tried to bite them already."

"Phew!" I let out a sigh of relief. "It's too bad we can't predict when her eyes will be blue, otherwise we could take her into Alma and see how she reacts to the town folk."

That got an immediate reaction and it wasn't the one I was after.

"B, don't ever take Lucia into Alma without me. Don't you ever, ever, take her off tribal lands if I'm not with you. Don't even think about it for the first ten years of her life. Don't you dare until I tell you it's safe."

"What?" I asked indignantly. "Who died and made you Lord and Master?"

"You saw what she was like when I momentarily took the bowl away. At first she growled threateningly then she tried to use cunning by crying. She may be ten months old, but the predator is still there. Her bloodlust would manipulate her into manipulating us. Lucia could fake it, pretending that she doesn't want to eat the people in Alma. Then as soon as our backs are turned, she would make a run at a human."

"How will you know if she's faking it or not?" I wondered.

"Trust me B, I'd know." He looked me right in the eye. "If she ever says she isn't tempted to eat a human, then I'll immediately know she's lying. It's how well she's able to control her bloodlust, which will make me trust her."

I frowned at his words as I looked on my daughter sitting in my lap. She continued to eat her meal, blissfully unaware of our grave conversation. Patiently, Declan fed her with her small plastic spoon however, he was quick to move the bowl away when she tried to grab it again.

~~~~~~
~~~~~~

~ 16 ~

10th November, 2130

Emanuel and Arabella Riverclaw sat on the couch opposite to the stone fireplace.

The flames cast the living room in a warm hue and heated the couple who were each engrossed in a book. Although they were reading separate novels, they still read together. Gran's legs rested comfortably over Grandfather's, with his hand giving them an affectionate rub in between turning pages. It was rewarded by her sneaking a smile over the rim of her book, before they giggled like love-sick teenagers and returned to reading.

As a Circulator, Gran maintained a physical appearance of a twenty-something, when in actuality she was 102 years old. Grandfather was the same age as she, although he had the appearance of a well-built fifty year old. Such was the slower aging process of the Lokoti Werewolves. The two were told about each other's differences the very first day they met. Rather than being put-off, it ended up working out as opposites attract.

Outside, it snowed softly in below freezing temperatures but inside, the two were toasty warm.

Their relaxation was partly due to the fact that their children and their grandchildren were grown and had homes of their own. This made their solitude seem like a prize for successful parenting. However, they were in no way neglected by their progeny, since they lived on the same hill as them.

Just then, Gran put down her book to look directly at her husband.

"I feel like a cup of Earl Grey Tea," she declared in her English accent.

"Cool," he replied in his American accent. "I won't say no."

Next, she let out a groan as if she were physically in her hundreds, as she heaved herself to her feet. She meandered into the kitchen and switched on the electric kettle. But just as she reached for the mugs, she was interrupted by a sudden knock at the door.

"It's Jess and Hunter." Her husband announced, recognizing their scent.

She watched him stand up from the couch and cross over to their front door.

"I wonder what brings them here this Saturday afternoon?" She mused.

Grandfather shrugged before he swung open the door for the arrivals.

"Hey Dad!" Their daughter greeted cheerily.

Mum gave him a kiss on the cheek on passing. Following her was her faithful mate and my father. He gave Grandfather a handshake on his way in.

My mother also looked like a woman in her twenties, although she was 83 years old. My father looked like he was in his forties, when really he was two years older than his mate. He, like his father-in-law, was a Lokoti Werewolf and besides aging slower, he too had a muscled build.

"What's up?" Gran asked, as Mum went to give her a kiss on the cheek too.

"I dunno." She said vaguely, whilst looking around the living room.

She began to take off her coat, gloves and beanie which Dad instantly stepped forwards to take for her.

"What do you mean, you don't know?" Gran gave a peculiar look.

"We got a text message from B, to meet her here." Dad announced.

Then he hung Mum's coat and winter things on the coat rack, before hanging up his own.

"But aren't B and Declan at Blythe for the long weekend?" Gran looked on, puzzled.

"They left last night." Grandfather nodded. "I saw Declan yesterday afternoon, at the Garage. He said he was heading home early to pack an overnight bag. Then B would instantaneously phase them to England. The Worthall's were expecting them for dinner."

"They must be home early for some reason?" Mum shrugged.

"Maybe Declan lost his temper again and morphed into his European Werewolf form?" Dad muttered. "That or he ate someone."

Then he realized he said this a little louder than expected, as Mum, Gran and Grandfather looked on, unimpressed.

"Declan's control over his bloodlust is admirable." Grandfather stuck up for his grandson-in-law, as usual.

"I like Declan." His wife agreed. "I thought you did too, Hunter. You formally acknowledged him entering the family, all those years ago at their Housewarming."

"I had to, or risk alienating B." He said unhappily.

"If you keep this up, you'll be alienating your wife soon." Mum glowered before turning to Gran. "I like Declan, because I think he's good for B. I like the way he brings her back to reality. If she moans about this barren business, he's quick to snap her out of it."

"I don't like the way he talks to her." Dad disagreed. "B's infertility is a touchy subject."

"Come along, Hunter." Gran shot him a pointed look. "B obsesses over this issue, you must admit."

"The pack can feel her pain." Grandfather frowned. "We've all seen her aura fade when she feels inferior over her infertility. Declan sees this too, so he'll deliberately argue with her to get her fired up again."

Just then the four were interrupted by the sound of a plasma-powered vehicle pulling into the snowy driveway.

"Aren't we popular today?" Gran shot Grandfather a look of amusement.

He crossed over to the front window and peered through the curtain, "It's the Sabre's."

Through the glass, everyone watched a sixty-something Rachel and Derik climb out of their four-wheel-drive. Then he turned around to open the back door, to help his elderly mother out. With Aunt Susan on his arm and Rachel in tow, the three humans carefully trod up the icy veranda steps. By the time they reached the front door, Grandfather opened it for them.

"Em!" The white-haired, old woman beamed. "Perfect timing! My, it's cold out there. The weather report says it's something like - 20°C."

Grandfather shut the door behind them as Mum, Dad and Gran all came forwards to greet them with more handshakes or kisses on the cheek.

Dad helped Derik take his mother's as well as Rachel's coats and hang them on the coat rack.

"I was just about to make a cup of tea, would anybody like one?" Gran offered.

"Or perhaps a coffee?" Grandfather counter offered, as he walked over to assist.

"That would be lovely!" Aunt Susan said exuberantly, as she rubbed her hands together. "Then I can warm these by holding onto the hot cup."

"Sure Aunt Arabella, that'd be great." Derik answered, before he looked around. "Where's B and Declan?"

"Huh?" Mum gave a funny look. "Did you get a text message to meet them here too?"

"Yeah, we did." Rachel pondered. "But I thought they went to Blythe this weekend, to visit your English relatives?"

"That's what we thought too." Gran speculated. "But suddenly Jess and Hunter turned up, announcing they got a text message to meet them here. Then you three arrived, saying the same thing. We didn't know they were back early, or why they'd want to meet here and not at their house."

Next, Mum, Derik and Aunt Susan pulled out their mobile phones to show each other the messages they realized they got at the same time.

"Anyway, how about that tea or coffee?" Grandfather recalled their attention.

"Coffee for me please, Em." Dad chimed in, "And for Jess too."

As Grandfather went into the kitchen to procure these, Gran went with him. Whilst he focused on the coffees, Gran served the tea. She also carried out plate of shortbread biscuits to the dining table, where everyone had sat down.

Everybody talked animatedly about the text messages and why Declan and I could be back so soon. However, with Aunt Susan in the room, Dad held off on making anymore disparaging remarks. Gran and Grandfather rejoined everyone with the beverages before they too sat at the table.

"I'm gonna text message B and see where she is," Mum frowned, "after all she did arrange this."

"Oh don't rush them, Jess." My mate's mother waved her hand dismissively. "Maybe they're unpacking from the trip."

"They were meant to be away for two nights, so how much unpacking do you think there'll be, Mom?" Her other son chuckled.

"Shhh!" She playfully whacked him on the arm, making Rachel giggle. "Stop giving me cheek and instead give me news on how my grandchildren are going?"

"They're good." Rachel answered. "Both Blanche and Michael are well and so are their kids."

"Anthony is doing well in pre-school." Derik reported. "He won an award for one of the pictures he painted."

That was met with the whole table issuing their congratulations and not just from Aunt Susan.

"I remember how much you used to like art." Gran looked Mum's way. "You were always painting or sculpting something."

"I remember how much you used to like moulding the 'Playdoh', as well as throwing it at the other kids." Grandfather shook his head.

"Remember that perfect sculpture of a cat she made?" Gran agreed. "Before she ruined it by throwing it at her brother."

"Yep, Jess still likes throwing things." Dad smirked. "The only thing that's worrying is, after all these years her aim is improving."

Mum whacked him on the arm to hush up, which earned further guffaws from the table.

"Remember the flour and water fight you, Rachel, Mandy and B had when you were ten years old?" Aunt Susan looked to Derek. "You four got the bright idea in your heads to throw it at each other! I came home and found all four of you covered in wet flour, with Declan supervising you on clean up."

The human husband and wife cracked up laughing as they recalled the day she was talking about.

"I remember how he woke up, saw the mess we made and roared in anger." Derik smilingly shook his head. "I remember being so scared of him when we were growing up."

"Hmm, we all do." His wife nodded along as she sipped her tea.

"I hated making him angry because of his eyes would glow green and boy, could he yell." He continued. "Personally, I'm not surprised that he and B ended up together. She was scared of him too, but she never backed down."

Rachel added on, "She's the one who smeared the wet flour on his shirt when he came outside and yelled at us to stop."

“Why am I not surprised?” His mother rolled his eyes. Then she cast a sideways glance at Dad as she said next, “I’m not surprised that the two ended up together and it’s not just because of this Werewolf business. They’re both hard-headed as two rocks clashing together, which is the result of all their fighting. But I know for a fact that there’s no-one else they’d rather argue with.”

Dad knew she said this for his benefit although he silently disagreed.

“Speaking of which, where are the couple under discussion?” Gran looked up at the clock on the wall. “B did say 4 PM, didn’t she?”

Derik pulled out his phone once more to check. “Yeah, they did.”

“It’s now 4.15 PM so I’m going to call her,” my mother picked up her mobile again.

However, before she could hit the speed dial function, she and everyone else received a surprise.

Suddenly, in a bright flash of light, Declan instantaneously phased into the living room.

He grinned at the table of shocked onlookers, who stared open-mouthed at the manner of his arrival.

The fact that he’d instantaneously phased there, attracted their attention first. Secondly, he somehow looked younger, like he was in his early twenties instead of late. Thirdly, his crew cut had mysteriously grown out overnight and his hair was now just past his ears.

Declan’s eyes moved over his older looking younger brother and his sister-in-law, before settling on his elderly mother. His bright blue eyes watered, as the force of emotion of seeing his human family again after all these years, hit him harder than expected.

“Hi Mom,” he grinned tearfully, “you look well.”

“Declan, did you just...?” She tried to find the words.

“Instantaneously phase here like a Circulator? Yeah Mom, I did.” He answered in a tight voice. “B turned me into one the day after my 300th Birthday, when I nearly died of old age.”

“Old age?” Derik stared at his younger looking older brother.

“Yeah, don’t worry Derik, I aged and I nearly died when I hit my expiration date.” Declan chuckled in good humour. “I was an old man but when B changed me, she also reversed my biological clock.”

My father jumped out of his seat in alarm, as he looked on fearfully. My grandfather also stood up slowly, not in fear but in consternation. The only two people in the room who didn’t look taken aback, were my mother and grandmother. In fact, they appeared delighted by the news.

Dad demanded, “You’re a Circulator?!”

“Yeah, I am.” Declan glared back, guessing what was on his mind. “And don’t worry Uncle Hunter, my new power hasn’t tipped my control over the edge. Besides, I may be the strongest in the pack but I’m not the fastest. B’s still that little bit faster than me.”

"Of course it hasn't." Grandfather shot a warning look Dad's way. "But Declan, if you're from the future, why are you here?"

"Sorry for all the secrecy, but we had to time this when your B and Declan, wouldn't be here." Declan explained, as he looked from Grandfather to Aunt Susan. "So while they're away in England for the weekend, there's someone that I'd like you to meet."

"So you're the ones who sent the text messages!" Mum realized.

"You sent them back in time via the Circulate Mainframe," Gran pieced the puzzle together.

"Yup," he grinned.

Then in another bright flash of light, I appeared beside him holding our daughter in my arms.

The gasps from everybody recognizing Lucia as our biological child, were clearly audible.

Dad's eyes almost popped out of his skull, as Grandfather's gaze softened. Both Mum and Gran melted upon the sight of the three of us together. The Sabre's appeared stunned, as Derik and Rachel stared whereas Aunt Susan's eyes watered.

"Oh she's so cute!" Rachel accidentally cried out.

"Are you the B from the future, too?" Derik wondered, looking on my face and hairstyle closely.

"Declan, is this...?" Grandfather nodded towards my baby girl.

"This is our daughter Lucia Grace Sabre." Declan announced proudly, as put his arm about my shoulders. "And today is her first birthday."

"She was born on the 10th of November?" Rachel wondered.

"Actually, she was born on the 3rd of June, 2364." Declan declared. "But we're visiting today the 10th November 2130."

"But B..." My mother slowly stood to her feet, as did Gran. "How did you...? I mean, I thought that you couldn't...?"

"How did I get knocked up?" I laughed out what they couldn't say. "Lucia was conceived the same day I turned Declan into a Circulator."

"But how?" Gran frowned in confusion. "You're supposed to be the Last Circulator and that's what stopped you from carrying on the line."

"Well, you see Aunt Arabella, when a man loves a woman -" He cheekily began.

"Declan!" His mother reprimanded, to the older Derik and Rachel's laughter.

"Sorry Mom."

"You're still a smartass." Derik stood up too, as did Rachel then Aunt Susan.

"You're still as ugly as all hell..." he walked forwards and to his brother's surprise, he hugged him, "...but I missed you, bro."

"This is coming from the 'Incredible Hulk'?" Derik snickered. "Careful, I'd better not make you angry!"

Declan laughed as he purposefully hugged Derik so hard, it made him splutter!

"Really, you two!" Rachel rolled her eyes. "You're apart for two centuries and this is the way you carry on?"

I looked on my best friend fondly as I missed her frank mode of speech.

"Rachel," I smiled tearfully, "how are you?"

She caught my eyes mist over as I turned away to look on all the familiar faces of old.

My eyes met my mother's and grandmother's, who looked on my wrought expression with understanding. Then I looked on my father and grandfather and whereas Dad looked shocked, Grandfather smiled softly.

"Declan, can I...?" Aunt Susan looked eagerly at her newest grandchild.

It was just what he'd been waiting to hear, for he carefully lifted Looch out of my arms and into his. Then he walked her over to his mother to introduce the two. He stood in front whilst holding his daughter out to her.

"Mom, meet your youngest granddaughter from your eldest son."

"Oh my son, oh Declan Domitian Sabre!" She tearfully exclaimed. "This is Lucia Grace Sabre?"

The whole room turned quiet as everyone watched him gently place his baby girl into her arms. Aunt Susan adjusted to Lucia's weight as she cooed down. This made the other women crowd around, as they all fawned over her.

"B?" My father anxiously looked over to where I was standing. "Are you OK?"

"Dad!" I rushed into his arms to hug him tightly. "It's so good to see you again! I'm fine, I really am fine. In fact, I'm so happy it's unbelievable!"

Next, Grandfather came over for a hug too before he went to shake Declan's hand.

"You look good for a three hundred year old." He joked to the older Werewolf in the room.

"I don't feel a day over twenty-one." Declan chuckled.

"But B, how did you do it?" Gran looked our way. "How did you get pregnant?"

"Well you see Gran, sometimes when a Circulator loves another Circulator -" I tried again.

"Oh please!" Derik cracked up laughing. "You can tell that the two of you have been married for three centuries."

"Our bio-electromagnetic fields match now, even if my bio-electromagnetic field is slightly higher." I put it simply.

"It gave us a shock, I can tell you." Declan explained. "The very next morning after my change, I woke up to find my wife was pregnant."

"Lucia was a surprise, even if she was a special one." I cooed over at my daughter. "Weren't you Looch?"

Our baby girl giggled back, as drool dripped from the corner of her mouth. Her human blue eyes flashed their glowing green colour, which made everyone in the room gasp a second time. Mum was holding one of her little hands and she examined how long the nails were. Dad frowned as he noted all of this from where he was standing.

"Dude...she's got your glowing green eyes!" Derik marvelled.

"Of course she has." He said proudly. "She's also got my bright blue colour too, as well as my lighter hair."

"What else has she got of yours?" Dad wondered aloud, before looking my way. "How was the pregnancy? How was the delivery? Were there any complications?"

"Dad, the pregnancy was fine." I laughed off his concern. "Looch was a large baby so I delivered her early, but it was all good."

"She was premature?" Dad's eyes widened. "Was it a difficult delivery?"

"No, not really." I tittered. "Oh it was funny when Declan fainted though."

"Declan fainted?" Grandfather echoed in amusement. "At the birth?"

"It didn't happen like B is making it out to be." He rolled his eyes. "I passed out after sharing my blood with her."

"Why would you need to share your blood with her unless she was in danger?" Dad's eyes narrowed.

"She WASN'T in any danger, Uncle Hunter." He said gruffly. "She had the whole pack on standby in case anything went wrong."

"The pack wouldn't have been on standby, if it was a routine pregnancy." Dad said icily.

"Of course it's not going to be a routine pregnancy if B is carrying the world's first half Lokoti and half European Werewolf baby." He said coolly.

"But it didn't stop you from impregnating her as soon as you were turned into a Circulator," my father said in a dangerously low voice.

"Dad!" I snapped, as I supportively took hold of Declan's hand.

"Hey, I tried to talk her out of it in the beginning!" Declan fired up. "We damn well had a fight about it and she hated me for days afterwards! But B had one of her all-knowing feelings that it would be safe, so I let her go ahead with it."

Dad opened his mouth again as he looked murderous upon my mate, but Grandfather interrupted.

"That's enough, Hunter." He said softly. "B and the baby are safe and that's all that matters."

Abruptly, my father spun on his heel and walked over to the front door, opened it, then slammed it shut behind.

Grandfather looked on his departure sadly, whereas Declan was livid. I could feel his bloodlust-fuelled temper boil inside. I squeezed his hand supportively and after a moment, I felt him squeeze it back.

I said, "I got plenty of THAT when my pregnancy was first announced."

"You did?" Grandfather asked in mild surprise. "What happened?"

"Our First, Caesar Riverclaw, ordered our Medicine Man to run weekly check-ups during the pregnancy." I huffed unhappily. "And every time the baby kicked, Declan panicked that I could be injured."

"But you weren't, were you?" Our elder checked.

"No."

Next, I looked over to the women who were still cooing over the baby. Aunt Susan had reluctantly relinquished Lucia to Mum, who was now holding her. It was her turn to be the proud grandmother, as Gran and Rachel tickled her feet. Lucia happily giggled away, relishing all of the attention.

"Where's Hunter?" Mum looked around. "He should hold his only grandchild."

"Your first grandchild, Mum." I smilingly corrected.

"You mean you're...?" Derik looked on my flat stomach.

"No, she's not." Declan said. "But according to B's visions, Lucia will be the eldest of three girls."

Aunt Susan looked around for another baby to hold. "Oh, did you bring them too?"

"Not yet Mom, not yet." Declan chuckled at his clucky mother. "Give us time to make 'em first."

This was met with more laughter, as Declan let go of my hand so he could return his arm about my shoulders.

Together, we stood with Grandfather, looking on our one year old daughter be kissed and cuddled by her relations who in our time period, could be called her ancestors. With Dad's absence, I could feel Declan's temper fade away, as the sight of his mother with his daughter, gave him a deep sense of satisfaction.

Derik walked over to stand beside his youthful older brother. "So you're a family man now?"

"Damn straight." He grinned.

"I remember what you were like looking after my kids when they were growing up." Derik reminded. "I don't think Lucia or her future sisters will be game to skip school, let alone misbehave."

"Oh Looch can misbehave, trust me." He told them. "Last week she ran for her first time, which eventuated by trying to run away from me. She started to knock B's books off the shelf and when I told her to stop, she kept at it. When I got up from the couch to physically stop her, she tried to skedaddle at top speed, but she tripped over her own feet."

"She can run already?" Derik stared in amazement, which Grandfather shared.

"Yup." He verified. "She still likes to crawl when she's tracking something, but otherwise she can walk and run. Now she loves to run barefoot in the garden."

"You have a lawn?" Grandfather listened with interest.

"Yeah, we were the first house on the hill to put in a proper garden." He informed. "Now all of the houses have lawns and garden beds, including this one."

"Who lives here in your era?" Grandfather looked around his large, two-story, log cabin as if he were trying to imagine it.

"More Riverclaw's." He promised. "Just like more Wisetail's live in Uncle Hunter and Aunt Jess' place. Derik, your progeny still lives in Mom's old place too, as well as your house."

"Cool," he seemed pleased by the idea.

"What's this?" Aunt Susan looked our way, after catching some of that.

"The continuity of family in our era," Declan brought her up to speed.

"So how are my great, great grandchildren?" She enquired.

"They've passed away now, Mom." He smiled sadly. "We're up to your great, great, great, great, great, great grandchildren."

"Wow, so the Sabre family are alive and strong?" Derik sounded impressed.

"I'm still the head of the family, don't forget." My mate said matter-of-factly. "They've got me to watch their backs."

"And he does," I winked at Derik.

He looked on his older brother with renewed respect, "Yeah, thanks for that."

"Don't thank me for doing my job." Declan frowned. "I was the eldest growing up and I still am the eldest."

"So are my great x6 grandkids afraid of you too?" Derik ribbed.

"Yeah, but their parents appreciate picking up well-behaved children." He joked.

"Holly Sabre is our fourteen year old great x7 grand niece and she's not afraid of her Uncle." I told Derik. "She even asks him to make his eyes glow green."

"Really?" He listened.

"Holly saw Dec in his European Werewolf form when he pulled her to safety after her family's car crashed. So on his 300th Birthday, she made him a birthday card and put a picture of a European Werewolf on the cover." I said.

“Except that she made me look like an albino grizzly bear,” Declan chuckled.

“Holly and her family were in a car crash?” His eyes widened.

“Relax Derik, she and her parents are fine.” He promised. “They haven’t got a weak, little human looking after them, they’ve got me.”

“What, the ‘Incredible Hulk’ instead?” Derik jovially elbowed him.

“Whatever you say, pencil neck.” Declan nudged him back, which made him lurch from his greater strength.

However, Grandfather turned serious once more as he looked our way.

“Declan, tell me about Lucia’s eating habits.”

We all understood what he meant and why he frowned when he said it.

Declan advised, “She has the bloodlust too, which peaks every full moon. When she was four months old, we had to share our blood with her. At six months, I fed her fresh kill from the food processor. At twelve months, we don’t have to puree her food anymore, just tear it up into small pieces. She’s needing more and more, so we’ll probably take her on her first hunt soon.”

“Your little girl craves fresh kill?” Derik’s face fell.

So did Grandfather’s, as the two looked askance on the giggling one year old.

Gran pulled Looch from Mum’s arms to hold her next, with Aunt Susan and Rachel still crowded around her.

“My, she’s a big girl...!” Gran commented on her weight.

“She’s as heavy as a two year old, isn’t she?” Mum agreed.

“Our Medicine Man says she’s the size of an eighteen month old.” I told her.

“We officially took Looch off formula two weeks ago.” Declan continued. “She’s started eating whatever we eat, either mashed or chopped up. She can stomach anything and she eats four times the amount that a human child her age, would.”

“I remember what your constant hunger used to be like.” Derik frowned. “Now there’s two European Werewolves in the house, I’d hate to see your grocery bills.”

“We still grow a lot of our own vegetables and herbs in our greenhouse, which helps.” I told them.

“Can she play with other children?” Grandfather queried.

Again, we knew what he was really asking, so I let Declan answer once more.

“Yeah Uncle Em, Looch is safe around other Lokoti. The Wisetail’s with their kidlets come over on a regular basis, which she plays with. We’ve also taken her out and about on tribal lands and she hasn’t tried eating anybody.”

“What about off tribal lands?” Grandfather asked knowingly.

"We haven't tried that yet." He said gravely. "We never know when her eyes are gonna glow green, so we can't. But as I told B, when we try taking her into town, I'll be present."

"Yeah, because I'm weak and helpless, so I need a male around." I said sarcastically.

"No, because Lucia will grow up to be stronger than you and you'll need the strength of a male European Werewolf who'll be stronger than her." Grandfather spoke in a low voice.

Next, he and Declan exchanged a long look of understanding, almost like a silent agreement between the two.

"Don't worry B, you're still stronger than me. Can you imagine how easily Lucia would knock my old, human body to the side?" Derik pointed out.

"A gust of wind could knock your old, human body to the side." Declan ribbed.

Then he laughed when Derik elbowed him in the ribs a second time.

As the brothers 'male bonded' I noticed a shadow in the front window.

It was Dad standing outside on the veranda, looking in. I sensed that as much as he was infuriated with Declan, he still had to look in on his young. It must be freezing out there but he wouldn't come in. So I made the decision to go outside to talk to him.

Temporarily, I retreated from hearth, heart and home via the front door. Derik, Declan and Grandfather noticed, but after catching sight of my father's outline at the window, they didn't ask why. I closed the front door to keep the heat in, before rubbing my arms in the bitter air.

Although it was only 4.30 PM it was already dark. The ice outside looked a pale blue in the winter's twilight, contrasted against the warm yellow light of inside. The two met on the front veranda, which acted as the border between inside and outside of the house.

"Dad?"

"You should go inside B, where it's warm." He said gruffly.

"Don't give me that." I said coolly.

I crossed over to where he was standing in a square of yellow light spilling down from the window.

"Go inside." He ordered. "I'm OK, I just need to be left alone. I'm cooling off."

"Literally," I smirked.

He paused as he looked long and hard on my face and hair, which I think was a different style to the B in this time period.

"Since when did you become so disobedient?" He asked wryly.

"Dad, I'm turning 299 this year." I retorted. "Right now, I'm older than you."

My father openly examined my appearance of a woman in her twenties before he shook his head at himself.

After a long moment, he asked quietly, "Why didn't you immediately leave for the space time continuum with Declan, after you changed him?"

"I don't know..." I looked away, "...that was the plan, but Lucia happened."

"The two of you should have left the moment you turned him." Dad said unhappily. "The longer you remain here, the more you risk your light fading."

I swallowed, "Is that what you're worried about?"

"It's part of it." He cleared his throat. "Also, what will having Declan's children do to you?"

"Dad, I'm not in any danger." I moaned wearily.

I was getting sick of saying the same thing over and over again.

Ignoring the tone of my voice, my father looked me right in the eye to say his piece.

"You were the Last Circulator which was why you couldn't breed. Then you used your power to turn him into another Circulator. Now that you're breeding for him, what's gonna happen to your bio-electromagnetic field?"

"Having children has nothing to do with my bio-electromagnetic field - " I began, but he cut me off.

"B, it has EVERYTHING to do with it!" His dark brown eyes momentarily glowed red. "Your body is a battery which is just gonna wear down -"

"Dad!" I interrupted. "If Declan even suspected that kids were weakening my bio-electromagnetic field, he would NOT have gone ahead with it. You have NO idea of how protective my husband is over his wife!"

"No B, you have no idea of the type of monster Declan is -" he began but I cut him off this time.

"His bloodlust? His constant hunger? His fierce nature?" I rattled off. "I have seen Declan do some horrific things when he thought my safety was threatened. Believe me, I KNOW what my husband is capable of. But what you don't know about, are the good things he's done. You've seen some of them, but not all. He's generous and he's caring and most of all, he's loving."

As if he were breaking bad news, he clasped my cold hands in his warmer ones as his eyes tried to hold mine.

His voice dropped, "I've seen his kind do some despicable things. I've seen a European Werewolf hunt a pregnant woman," he alluded to the night Declan's family arrived on tribal lands. "And I've seen a young European Werewolf harm its own mother, when she tried to stop him from hunting human," he referred to my mate's early years. "So what's your half-breed European Werewolf children going to do to you?"

I let out a long sigh as I looked away, wondering how I could change his mind?

"Do you know what Declan's reaction was when he found out I was pregnant?"

"No, what?" He asked obligatory.

"He was ninety percent concerned about my safety with the remaining ten percent determined to destroy his seed." I spoke bluntly.

This made my father straighten in surprise and I carried on.

"He swore he'd be the last of his kind, because you and the other members of the pack trained him to think his seed is rotten. It took me months to alter his low opinion of himself, so he would be ready to be a father. It took me decades to work on his self loathing for being the breed he is. Declan has saved lives, he's acted with compassion and he's fought for what he loves. So I would appreciate it if you could cut him some slack, stop sulking and come inside and be with your granddaughter."

I wasn't completely sure if my speech worked, but as soon as he heard the word 'granddaughter' from his only child, his eyes widened.

No matter how prejudiced he could be, my father was still a Lokoti Werewolf. Their whole existence revolved around mate, young and tribe. Now that his family had expanded, it tugged on his heart and on his sense of responsibility.

Then we looked in to see Mum pull Lucia out of Gran's arms to nurse her once more. Seeing his granddaughter in his wife's hold, seemed to have an effect on Dad. He looked on with longing then without another word he headed inside.

We came in from the cold with Dad staring at his granddaughter in his mate's arms. He saw how Mum glowed whilst holding her. He left my side to go to hers, with Rachel and Aunt Susan stepping back to give them some space.

"Careful Jess, your tough exterior is slipping." Dad smiled fondly.

Mum picked up one of Looch's little hands to make her wave at him.

"Hallo Grandpa," she mimed, as if it were Lucia speaking.

"So this is my granddaughter, Lucia Grace Sabre?" He reached for her.

Mum loosened her hold so he could gently lift her out of her arms and into his. Dad held her closely as Lucia looked on her grandfather with curiosity. I even caught her sniff, as if to confirm that this strange man was family.

I came to stand beside Declan again and instantly his hand sought out mine to hold. Then we stood there, smiling on. Derik stood on my left with Grandfather on Declan's right.

He turned our way, "You'll stay for dinner, of course?"

"Yes!" Gran agreed. "You must."

"Consider yourselves kidnapped." Rachel snickered. "Besides, I haven't held Lucia yet, so there's no way you can go."

"I haven't held her either." Derik sided with his wife. "So don't even think about leaving."

"Declan has always been a good son," Aunt Susan joined in, "of course he wouldn't break his old mother's heart by leaving so soon."

We tittered at everyone's determined invitation before Declan turned my way.

"It wouldn't hurt the timeline if we stayed a bit longer?" He checked.

Then Gran caught my eye, "There's roast pork in the freezer and your Grandfather will make your Great Grandma's special gravy."

"We're in!" I cried out, sending more guffaws through the room.

*****

While I helped my grandparents cook, Declan sat at the table and answered Aunt Susan's questions about my pregnancy and the birth.

As he did, Derik and Rachel had a play-fight with Mum and Dad that it was their turn to hold the baby. I melted at the sight of Derik playing 'This lil' Piggy' with Looch's toes as Rachel held her in her lap. Now it was their turn to be an Uncle and Aunt and it looked like they relished their new roles.

During dinner, Declan sat with Looch in his lap as he fed her from his plate. I sat beside, also popping a small piece of meat or vegetable into her mouth. When Looch tried to take our plates by force, Declan gently restrained her. Then he moved his chair backwards from the table, so she couldn't reach them.

Grandfather put the rarest pieces onto our plates, from remembering our daughter preferred raw meat. Although the meat was partially cooked, Lucia still gobbled it down. In fact, she liked the roast pork so much, she began to cry when Declan held her back.

"I have some rare meat on my plate she can have," Rachel offered.

"No thanks." Declan frowned on his little girl. "Looch has to learn to eat slowly with cutlery and in moderated amounts. Otherwise, she'd eat straight from the plate then attack the remaining roast in the middle of the table."

"She's always hungry and she even tried to eat one of my books the other day." I told everyone. "It was an antique too and now it's got a bite mark in the hardcover."

"Dada!" She cried as she pointed at his plate. "Dada! Mumum! Dada!"

"Eat slowly, using the cutlery and you'll get some more." He said firmly.

However, with a whole table of relatives looking on, Looch's bloodlust refused to be told what to do.

Her tearful blue eyes glowed green as she angrily began to growl. So Declan picked her up and carried her over to the couch. He sat her in his lap as she continued to snarl threateningly, while squirming to be freed. Calmly, he held her still whilst rubbing her back and talking softly to her.

The frightening noises her bloodlust produced made the humans look on askance, bar one.

Aunt Susan shrugged it off, "I had the same problem with Declan when he was a new Werewolf."

"I remember." Grandfather smiled fondly. "One night he completely emptied your fridge and pantry, didn't he?"

"He even ate the spice out of the spice jars." Aunt Susan laughed. "But with Em's help and a hell of a lot of patience, I taught him the way he's teaching her. Instilling self-control in a human is hard enough, but a young Werewolf?"

Just then Looch's temper dissolved into loud sobs. He continued to rub her back as he spoke softly to calm her. It looked like it was working too...until Looch jumped off his lap and tried to run back to the table. We all watched as Declan easily caught her and swooped her up into his arms. Then to everyone's surprise, he took her outside onto the front veranda, shutting the door behind them.

"He's taking her outside?" Dad sat up straighter. "It's below freezing out there!"

"She won't get frost bite." I smiled on his concern. "Her body temperature is as high as her father's, consistently sitting at 42°C. She also overheats as easily as him, too."

"Declan's removing Lucia from temptation." Aunt Susan explained. "With all of us eating in front of her, it's working against him. Outside she'll listen to what he's trying to say."

"That or freeze." He frowned at the front door.

"Relax Dad, Declan knows what he's doing." I promised as I continued to eat. "Although she's just a one year old, her bloodlust is pretty cunning. Declan's had to chastise her overeating and instead of listening, she'll look at my plate. Sometimes she'll cry pathetically to distract you and when you're not looking, she'll snatch up some more food."

"Michael used to do that." Derik sighed.

"Michael was the worst at that." His wife agreed. "When he misbehaved and he wasn't allowed any dessert, he used to steal his sister's."

"Then he looked so surprised when we'd take it away from him," he said.

"You and Julian would get into some spectacular screaming matches over your Grandma's special gravy." Gran looked at Mum.

"Well, he did try to hog it." She retorted.

"So did you." Grandfather snickered.

"How is Uncle Julian?" I asked out of interest.

"He and your Aunt Danika are well." Gran nodded. "They're travelling around the UK at the moment. They're supposed to meet up with the other B and Declan at Blythe tonight."

"Oh that's right." I remembered. "Uncle Jules came back with that blurry photo he took in Scotland, which he tried to make us believe was a picture of the Loch ness Monster."

Then I snickered at the memory as everyone looked on peculiarly.

"Oh yeah, it hasn't happened yet... sorry." I inwardly kicked myself. "Forget I said anything."

Mum rolled her eyes at her twin brother. "That sounds like Jules."

"I can't believe that we're sitting here, having dinner with the B from the future." Derik smilingly shook his head. "And that she and my 'Incredible Hulk' for a brother, have a mini-Hulk for a baby."

"Even Looch's eyes turn green just like her father's does." Rachel giggled along.

"Maybe we should call Fern and invite him over to meet Lucia?" Mum suggested.

"No!" I accidentally cried out in alarm, which made everyone look on strangely. "I'm sorry and I mean nothing against Grandpa, but no."

"Why not, B?" My father wondered.

"The timeline." Gran guessed. "I think B's about to ask us not to tell anybody about tonight."

"Oh?" Grandfather sat back to look on quizzically. "Why not?"

"Because the B in this time frame can't know that one day she does get impregnated." I spoke frankly. "She and Declan must remain childless right up until Declan nearly dies of old age. If your B changed your Declan into a Circulator tomorrow, then it would alter the future."

"Oh, you mean like the cause and effect scenario?" Derik caught on.

"So tonight was a one time thing?" Aunt Susan asked, hurt. "But I would love to see Lucia grow up. You also mentioned you were going to have more daughters, when will I meet them too?"

"I'll see what we can do, but otherwise...?" I said guiltily. "Please push tonight to the back of your minds like a distant memory, or even a weird dream."

"If you're so concerned about the timeline B, why did you come at all?" Mum asked in annoyance.

"It was Declan's idea."

"Figures," my father sneered.

"Dad, that's enough." I glared his way, before looking to Aunt Susan. "He really wanted his mother to meet his first born and tonight was his first trip through time as a Circulator."

Her eyes watered from the sentimentality shown by her usually thick-skinned first born, which Derik saw. He reached out and put his hand over hers. Mum's eyes watered too, so she looked down to hide them. Even Dad looked affected by this news, as he guiltily looked at his mate.

It was then that Grandfather decided to take charge of the situation.

"We'll do our very best not to speak of tonight to the Declan and B in our time, or to any other person."

"Thank you." I said gratefully.

At that moment Declan returned, carrying a calmer daughter on his right arm.

As soon as he did, he instantly noticed that every eye in the room was on him. He passed me a puzzled look as he came to sit back down at the table. I reached out to caress Looch's tear-streaked face.

"So, what did I miss?" He asked, breezily.

"I was just asking everybody not to talk about tonight." I said dismissively.

"And that tonight was your first trip through time as a Circulator, which you used to introduce your daughter to your dearly departed mother." Aunt Susan said emotionally.

Then her tears overflowed and she had to use her napkin as a handkerchief.

"Oh." My tough-as-nails mate looked uncomfortable that his soft side was showing. "Well er, yeah. Sure we've got the next generations of Sabre's, Wisetail's and Riverclaw's where we are, but I thought it'd be nice to introduce Lucia to you."

"It was nice, thank you son." Aunt Susan reached out her other hand across the table and Declan took it.

"You can also thank B for this enterprise," he said modestly. "I told her where I wanted to go and when, and she masterminded the whole thing."

This made my parents smile softly on their only child sitting next their grandchild.

Aunt Susan smiled from Declan to Derik. "I had a very nice evening with my boys tonight," then she looked at Rachel and I, "and their lovely wives," then she beamed at Lucia, "and my beautiful little granddaughter."

Mum asked out of interest, "Do you know what you're going to name your other daughters?"

I recited, "Our three daughters will be named Lucia Grace, Sophia Clara and Susanna Ling."

Our choice in names resulted in a cause and effect scenario by itself. Nearly everyone at the table turned misty-eyed and I could tell Dad and Grandfather were touched by the nods to their mothers. There were several glances shot across the table between the parents and grandparents.

"Where do the names Lucia and Sophia come from?" Mum queried.

"They were the names of mine and my husband's mothers." Aunt Susan told her. "They both died after the war, one from radiation sickness and the other from looting. But they did their damndest to make sure Anthony and I were safe, by sending us to Alaska with food, money and even jewellery to trade."

"I've still got the Sabre family angel." Declan squeezed her hand. "We get it out every Christmas, don't we, B?"

"That and 'John Denver and the Muppets: A Christmas Together'." I passed a smile from Aunt Susan to Gran.

"Really?" My grandmother cracked up laughing. "Goodness that tape has been in our family awhile!"

"It sounds like you and B are moving into the future while honouring your past." Grandfather smiled in approval then his eyes fell upon our daughter. "That's an important lesson to instil in our young."

Next, he stood up, walked around the table to where Declan and I were sitting and he lifted Lucia into his arms. Finally it was his turn to hold her and hold her he did. We looked up proudly at the head of the Riverclaw family smiling kindly on his great granddaughter.

"You are the world's first half Lokoti and half European Werewolf." Grandfather stroked Looch's hair. "You are legacy little wolf."

Then he planted a tender kiss on her forehead and we saw her close her eyes as she accepted his blessing.

"Yep, she sure is." Derik grinned on his niece. "Just don't make her angry."

~~~~~~
~~~~~~

~ 17 ~

12th December 2365

I kissed him again and again...in fact, our lips never left the other's. With our mouths smothered, it effectively stifled our growls, grunts and panting. I could feel his sharp teeth dig into the soft tissue of my bottom lip, as my own claimed his top. Occasionally our teeth banged together which made a bone-tingling 'crunch' by the clash of the calcium.

Our breathing moved hard through our noses which sounded like constant sniffing. His fingers dug into my thighs as he held my crotch taught against his. My nails grew longer in excitement and broke the skin on his back. He didn't complain either, the only noise he made was a slight whimper, but in pleasure instead of pain.

Declan moved hard, making our bed shudder and shake, albeit quietly. I was impressed at the stress our new bedroom furniture could take. Our nightly acrobatics could scare off a crash-test dummy, but so far they proved lasting.

Our bedroom door was locked as the idea of children accidentally stumbling in was a pet paranoia of mine. As much as we rolled around or fought over the dominant position, it was all done silently. Barely a sound escaped through the door which would give away our marital misbehaviour.

I could feel the climax build up inside with each of Declan's movements. I slammed my crotch into his, telling him by body language how I was approaching the precipice. But just as he began to push even harder with the same strength that could push a hover-car up a hill; our bed betrayed us with a loud squeal!

Our eyes widened in worry, which we could clearly see on the other person's face.

Whilst he was holding onto my waist, he moved us in a single heave to another part of the bed. Then we quietly continued our activity. However, the change of position also restarted my climax. It took another couple of minutes to reach my prior point of pleasure.

Helplessly, my sharp nails clawed at his back as Declan pushed some more. I sensed he was holding on for as long as possible until he felt me come. After centuries of marriage, he recognized the physical signs like he could have been looking on a sign post; Fairbanks to the right, Anchorage to the left and of course the classic, 'you are here' with the pointed arrow.

And then I felt it...the orgasm ballooned upwards and outwards, making my body turn tense as I tried to hold onto the ecstasy. After one last push, I felt his pleasurable release mix in with mine. Our glued together mouths stopped us from moaning aloud however, we felt the other's satisfaction instead.

We both turned limp and relaxed and Declan finally removed his mouth. He ducked his head to graze his lips down to my collar bone, while I overheard him inhale my scent coming off my sweaty skin. I felt his tongue extend to lap at the crevice between my breasts, before licking his way back up.

My husband's eyes met mine and I saw his hungry look as clear as a cloudless blue sky.

I tried not to giggle at Declan's constant appetite, which certainly made a woman feel wanted. Humans have wondered how our sex-life hasn't faded over the years, whereas I'd wonder how theirs had? It was impossible to imagine a day I'd stop hungering for what Declan's powerful body could provide.

His mouth reclaimed mine and I felt his tongue push inside while another part of his body part did the same. A new rhythm was established as I ran my hands up and down his rippling back. Our eyes fluttered closed as the renewed pleasure swept us up.

Just as our physical gratification picked up in strength, abruptly he stopped. Declan moved his mouth away as he turned his head towards the door. I was about to ask why, when I heard it.

Through the locked, wooden door we could hear Lucia cry.

Oh oh...we both froze as we listened. Her cries were irregular and even mixed in with a couple of growls. Then they stopped completely and next, the only noise that came to our ears was silence. This was of course excluding the sound of our hearts pounding.

My protective instincts sensed my daughter was growling in her sleep again. Her short cries must have been her 'sleep talking'. It was a habit of hers but being parents on 'alert status', it still made us pause.

"It's fine, she's still asleep." I whispered.

"Are you sure?" He whispered back, while watching the door warily.

To show we were in the clear, I began to chew on his neck. He groaned as his eyes closed, showing his enjoyment. Then my sharp teeth bit into his muscled torso and he groaned again. After another minute of chewing, his mouth captured mine in a passionate kiss.

Our nightly activity soon recommenced as he returned his attention with gusto.

*****

The next morning, I held Lucia's hand as I helped her walk down to breakfast.

Declan was setting the table when he looked up at his eighteen month old coming down the stairs.

"Did she use the potty again?" He checked.

"She sure did." I smiled proudly.

Next, I walked her over to her highchair which was at the head of the table. Then I lifted her into her seat which she eagerly climbed into. She'd already equated that sitting here meant it was meal time.

Our little girl was as tall as a two year old and her shoulder-length, dark blonde hair flicked around, as she turned her head towards the kitchen. I could tell she was trying to see what was for breakfast. Her bright blue eyes were wide with her nostrils flaring at the delicious smell.

I took my seat at the table as Declan carried out our plates of bacon and eggs, with Lucia's already cut up for her. He put Lucia's plastic plate with her plastic fork down first then he put down mine. He returned to the kitchen to retrieve his and I saw his serving was three times the size of ours.

When I saw my daughter pick up her cutlery to start, I stopped her.

"No Looch, wait for Daddy to sit down."

Obediently, Lucia put down her fork and waited until her father was seated.

Teaching her manners was proving fruitful, as Looch's bloodlust knew it couldn't get around Declan's. It acknowledged him as the dominant and respected him for it. However, it also meant that if I gave an order which she tried to ignore, Declan would pull her up for it quick smart.

Although my husband and I saw each other as equals in our marriage, we ended up falling into a line of command in the eyes of our toddler. Being the biggest, her father was seen as First in the family, with her mother as Second. If she misbehaved, Declan's deafening roars could send vibrations through the floorboards and make our windows shake. Or, if he emitted a dangerously low growl, she paid attention quick smart.

As soon as he picked up his fork and began eating, Lucia copied. Dutifully, she ate her breakfast at the same time as her parents, only pausing to pick up her juice cup periodically. I noted it was usually the same time as her father picked up his coffee.

"B, I've been thinking." He began. "Next summer, we should begin those renovations to the house we talked about."

"OK." I swallowed. "But it sounds like it could be a big job, having downstairs as well as upstairs extended. We can't live here while they're renovating."

"Yeah, I've talked to Caesar about that." He said as he buttered his toast. "There's plenty of room at his house since it's just he and Forrest there, so they've invited us to stay with them over the summer."

"Cool." I smiled.

I liked the idea of temporarily living in Gran and Grandfather's old home with their Riverclaw progeny.

He continued, "I was thinking we could use one of construction companies in Alma. Caesar told me that the company 'Grand Schemes' has half of their employees comprised of Lokoti. This way, we'd be giving work to our own people."

"Doesn't Jay Shallow Water work for that company?" I remembered.

"Yup." He put his buttered toast onto his plate. "He's one of the company's architects."

"Sounds good." I talked in between eating. "Maybe he could do our designs for the place."

"That's what I was thinking." He smiled at how we were on the same wavelength. "I've made an appointment to see him in town, this morning."

"But I want to come!" I objected. "I want to go over the plans too."

He frowned upon the idea, "But who's going to stay home with Looch?"

"We'll take her with us." I shrugged.

"B," his frown deepened, "I don't think she's ready for that."

"Declan," I returned. "Lucia has to start learning that although there are humans that may tempt her, it's the 'look but don't touch' policy."

His eyes swung from his wife to his daughter, sitting peacefully in her highchair and gobbling down her bacon and egg.

"Yeah, I suppose you're right." He sighed heavily. "We can't keep her hidden away on tribal lands forever."

Then I watched him put his second piece of buttered toast on Looch's highchair table-top. Her blue eyes widened at the offering and she eagerly dropped her fork to munch on the crunchy bread instead. She emitted a happy giggle, as she shone a messy smile to her father.

"That's my girl." Declan chuckled, reaching out to ruffle her hair.

*****

Once breakfast was finished and everybody's teeth were brushed, we trod through the snow to the garage. Declan used his remote key to unlock the hover-car and the vehicle automatically opened three doors; two in the front and one in the back. I walked Looch to the back door first and lifted her into her car-seat then did her seatbelt.

He climbed into the driver's seat, entered the security code to start the engine and turned on the heater. As soon as Lucia was buckled in, I shut her door and leapt through mine, to get out of the freezing temperature. Dutifully, my husband aimed most of the air vents my way, as the cold didn't particularly bother him or his half breed daughter.

The hover-car gently lifted up off the cement floor then lingered in mid-air. I wondered why we weren't reversing out of the Garage doorway? Then I looked his way and saw he seemed hesitant to get us on the road.

"Declan, it'll be fine." I put my hand over his. "I'm not having one of my warning feelings about taking Looch into Alma today."

He sighed heavily, "Yeah but she's been so good of late, what if introducing her to town folk is tempting fate?"

"She has to start eventually. If we keep putting this off, what's it going to be like when she's older? If we start her training early, she'll get used to it." I pointed out.

"Yeah, you're right."

Declan flashed a wary look over his shoulder at his young in the backseat then he reversed out of the Garage and down the driveway.

Eagerly, Lucia looked out the windows at the changing scenery. During the drive I kept an eye on her reaction, as did Declan through the rear vision mirror. When Looch realized we were driving off tribal lands, her eyes widened in excitement.

"Mumum...Kurt?" Looch asked in her eighteen month old speech.

"No, we're not going to the Wisetail's." I answered. "We're going into town."

"Dada...Ceesee?" She next queried.

"Nope, we're not visiting Caesar either." He told her. "We're going into Alma."

"Holeee?" She tried to guess.

"No, we're not visiting Holly or your Sabre relations." I smiled. "We're going to see Jay Shallow Water instead."

The hover-car cruised down the highway which turned into the main street of the busy and bustling Alma. Looch's eyes almost popped out of her head at all the unfamiliar people. She gawked at the new sights and smells of town.

I noticed Declan parked as close as possible to the building Jay worked in.

Once the hover-car powered down, Looch squirmed out of her seatbelt to explore her new surroundings. Quickly, I hopped out of my seat as did Declan. When I opened Looch's door she was already free and raring to go.

We walked down the footpath with Lucia in the middle, as we each held onto her hands. Declan and I watched our daughter closely as she stared at all of the new people. She gaped at the mixture Native Alaskan, Caucasian, Asian-descent or African American people on the street. A couple of times we even caught her sniff as they passed by.

We entered the building and crossed the foyer to the elevator. When the doors opened, we stood to the side to let the people disembark first. As the business people exited, Looch sniffed them with a curious expression. Once we were inside, Declan hit the button for the fifth floor and the doors closed.

However, Looch was frightened of the elevator when it began to move and she emitted an unhappy sob.

"Hey, it's OK." I gave her hand a reassuring squeeze. "We're just going for a ride, that's all."

"She probably doesn't like the confined space." Her father appeared uncomfortable himself.

Seconds later, the elevator doors opened and Declan was the first one out with Lucia a close second.

While holding onto her hands, we walked her down a carpeted hallway to an automatic glass door. We went through into a modern office which had an indoor garden in the reception area. Next, we approached the receptionist who was sitting behind a glass desk, with a computer interface.

Declan greeted, "Hi, we're here to see Jay Shallow Water."

"Do you have an appointment?" The man in his pressed suit, looked up at our casual dress of denim and suede.

"Yep, for 9 AM." He confirmed.

The receptionist pressed on his touch screen computer. "Your name?"

"Sabre," he said simply.

Next, the male receptionist spoke into his metallic earpiece which was sitting on his left ear.

"Mr. Shallow Water, your 9 AM is here." Then he looked up at my tall, strong husband, standing over him. "Please take a seat, Mr. Shallow Water will see you shortly."

I led the way over to one of the flat couches and sat down. However, the European Werewolf felt like standing and it became evident so did his daughter. He hung onto her hand as she looked around at the pictures on the walls. Then he picked her up so she could see them better.

"You like the pictures of the houses, Looch?" Declan asked her.

She nodded to her Daddy as she looked on the architectural designs. Then she looked back over at receptionist in his suit. The stranger was of Asian-descent and she stared at him, just as fascinated.

"No," his voice dropped warningly, as he turned her away.

Looch looked puzzled on her father and he gave her a deliberately slow shake of his head.

My senses recognized the way Lucia was looking on the non-Lokoti human, was like a child looking on a strange, new food. Her bloodlust was telling her that the human was edible, but like a typical child she was hesitant about trying something she hadn't eaten before. Silently, I hoped that she would be happy to stick to animal instead.

"Aunt B and Uncle Dec!" A familiar voice called out. "How are you?"

We saw Jay had come down another hallway into the reception area. I stood up upon his approach and came to stand with my family. He shook Declan's free hand first and mine second.

"Not bad," my mate answered. "This is Looch's first outing, off tribal lands."

"Look at you!" He turned his attention to our eighteen month old. "Look at how fast you're growing! You look as big as a two year old!"

Declan and I caught Lucia sniff Jay, instantly recognizing him as Lokoti. Then she looked confused back to the receptionist. I sensed she was wondering why some humans smelled edible, but others didn't?

"Have you got an office somewhere that we can go to?" My husband asked, looking on his daughter warily.

"Right this way."

Jay turned and headed back down the hallway he'd just come from, with us right on his heels.

Looch's eyes remained transfixed on the receptionist. She stared over her father's shoulder until she lost sight of him. Declan and I exchanged an unhappy look, before we sat down in the seats which were in front of Jay's desk. Once we were seated, Jay hit the control to close the automatic door, so Looch couldn't smell the humans anymore.

"Thanks." My husband acknowledged.

"At least she didn't growl or her eyes didn't glow green." Jay chuckled.

"I think so far she's doing pretty well." I reached over to stroke her hair, as she sat in Declan's lap.

My mate looked at the family photo sitting on his desk, "And how's your small fry?"

"Not bad, not bad at all." Jay grinned as he sat behind his desk. "Gina is well and so is Genevieve. But Gerard is teething at the moment so he's been keeping us up." Then he looked on Lucia in curiosity, "I heard Looch was born with a full set of chompers. Are those her baby teeth?"

"Yup," he answered. "Ki thinks she's not going to get a new set until a couple years yet."

"It makes sense." Jay conceded. "Genevieve's five years old and she's just lost her front teeth. Maybe Looch will be the same age when her adult teeth come in?"

"That's what Ki said too."

Then I picked up Looch from his lap and placed her in mine. My mate watched fondly as I hugged her, which made her growl affectionately. Her body heat radiated outwards, which I relished as I held her close. Next, Declan rested his hot hand on my leg, to lend some additional warmth.

"So it's time for the Sabre's to finally expand their small, two bedroom cottage?" Our architect called our meeting to hand.

"Yup." He sat back in his seat. "We're thinking of putting in upstairs another three bedrooms and a bathroom. Then with the downstairs, I want the kitchen expanded, as well as a study put in for B."

"I'm surprised you waited for so long to have your kitchen redone." Jay smirked, since Declan's appetite was renown in the tribe. "With kitchen designs these days, the primary focus is storing pre-prepared foods or even installing a meal synthesizer -"

"No way!" He interrupted. "Our house will NEVER have a meal synthesizer installed. Pre-prepared crap? I make my own meals from scratch, instead of that mass produced rubbish."

Our friend laughed it off, "I know what you mean, we had to program and reprogram our meal synthesizer until it produced a decent dish. And if the bag of bio-matter goes off before its expiry date? Eugh! It's a pain but the technology is handy when you're too tired to cook -"

"Jay, you trying to sell a meal synthesizer to a European you-know-what, is like trying to sell a hover-car to an Amish family." Declan rolled his eyes. "It ain't gonna happen."

He guffawed, "OK, no meal synthesizers in the Sabre house, I get it."

Next, he hit a couple of controls on his touch screen computer. Simultaneously, it dimmed the lights in his office as well darkened the tint of his large, office window. Then a 3-D holographic representation of our small, wooden house appeared over his desk.

"What I was thinking is that with the extensions to your house, we could extend it from the back and side wall here and here." Jay demonstrated on the holographic projection. "I take it you'd like the outside appearance to remain in its current state?"

"Yes." I answered. "Is it possible for the front of our house along with the front garden, to remain the same?" I queried.

"It sure is!" He proclaimed. "By altering the back of the house and this side wall here, the front of your house with its veranda and the stone chimney will stay exactly the same."

Over the next hour, we discussed the plans in full detail with Jay including all of our ideas to the hologram.

The 3-D projection of our small, two-story, two bedroom house morphed into a large, two story, five bedroom house, complete with a study downstairs. It was also decided that the second bathroom would become our ensuite, so the kids would share the current bathroom.

Looch behaved herself as she sat in my lap, looking captivated on the hologram. She giggled and clapped her hands each time the holographic projection morphed to include our changes. But when she started to turn restless, Declan pulled her out of my arms to hold her steady in his own.

We even chose the interior design for the kitchen, the study, the new upstairs hallway and the three extra bedrooms. Jay programmed all of our requests into his computer. Not only were they shown in the hologram, but they were saved as a work order for the construction crew.

When our hour was up, our holographic house disappeared. His office lights came back on as his window allowed in sunlight once more. It was a like waking up from a dream.

"OK with everything we've discussed, I can give you a quote on how much renovations will cost." Jay calculated on his computer, before looking our way. "The damage would be 250,000 credits, but this includes labour and materials. It's so high because you'll have two teams of workmen instead of one, to get the job done faster."

"250,000 credits?" Declan's eyebrows arose. "That's the same price to build a brand new house."

"If you had just one team of workmen, it will come to 199,000 credits. But then construction could go up to three months instead of one." Jay warned.

"No, I want to pay extra to have it done faster." I looked from the architect to my husband. "I want to be back in my own house as soon as possible."

"Will both teams have Lokoti workers?" He checked.

"Yeah they will." Jay smiled, recognizing where our request was coming from. "In each of these crews you have builders, carpenters, electricians, plumbers, central heating specialists, fitters, painters and so forth. The two teams who'll be working on your house will have all of our Lokoti employees, including me as your architect."

"Well B?" My husband looked my way. "Can we afford 250,000 credits?"

To Jay's surprise, I pulled out my credit card then and there.

"Would you like us to pay now?" I enquired.

"Er, you don't want to go home and discuss it?" He marvelled at how quick we were to sign on the dotted line.

"No," we both answered, before my husband added on, "we've already discussed it."

Our friend looked abashed at his computer, as if he really appreciated our vote of confidence.

"Um, maybe I could knock a couple of thousand off the price for you, if we use cheaper materials..."

"Jay, don't worry about it." He frowned. "We can afford two hundred and fifty grand. We don't want cheaper materials, we want our house to last."

"Here you go." I placed my credit card on top of his desk.

"Is that the one which your Hodge Endeavor share dividends go into?" Declan guessed.

"Uh huh."

Jay's eyes bulged in recognition of the name.

"You have shares in Hodge Endeavor?" He asked in surprise.

"Shares?" Declan exhorted. "Dude, you're sitting across from the Head of the Board of Directors."

This really made the architect's eyes widen double time.

"Well, you're also the Head of the Board of Directors, being a Circ – er – I mean being a Light Person too." I almost slipped up.

Jay certainly knew we were Circulators as well as Werewolves however, it was an unspoken rule that it wasn't discussed off tribal lands.

"You're both in charge of one of the world's most powerful companies?" He blinked. "No wonder you can easily afford a quarter of a million credits."

"Yeah, but don't let it go to your head and charge us incidentals." Declan smirked.

~~~~~~

5th July 2366

Construction on our house ran from the 31st May to the 30th June. During which time Lucia, Declan and I stayed in the old Riverclaw house. There was certainly enough space with its five bedrooms. The parents slept in one guest room with Lucia in another.

The elderly Forrest loved having a baby in the house again as his time and attention to Lucia ran at record levels. Whereas, Caesar loved having a chef in the house again since his wife passed. My husband cooked up hot breakfasts each morning, as well as lovely lunches and scrumptious dinners. The looks on the older Werewolves faces when Declan made lasagne or fettuccine carbonara, or cannelloni, complete with salad and garlic bread... it was as if Christmas had come early.

"Do you always eat like this?" Caesar asked, impressed.

"Pretty much." Declan shrugged it off.

"No wonder you need a bigger kitchen." Forrest chuckled, as he played with Lucia on his lap.

The widowed Werewolves in the forms of father and son had become accustomed to living as two old bachelors. However, having a woman in the house again triggered something. Not only was Lucia spoilt rotten, but so was I. Freshly picked flowers would appear in my bedroom or on the dining table. That, or they'd come home with cakes or ice cream for dessert every second day. Forrest had retired but Caesar ran the Garage that Declan used to own.

The second evening into our stay had a waning moon with the moonlight spilling onto the bedroom floor. We've always slept this way, with the blinds up or the curtains open. We liked to be able to see the night sky, or we enjoyed waking up to sunshine. In the pale light, I looked on the small vase of flowers on the bedside table before looking back to my mate.

Declan and I were lying on our sides facing each other. My right leg was slung over his waist with our clothed crotches touching. My husband was amorously kissing my neck and shoulders, as I glanced at the flowers once more.

"I think Caesar and Forrest like having us here." I whispered.

"Uh huh." He replied, as his teeth grazed my skin.
~~~~~~

"I must admit, I like staying here." I spoke quietly. "It's nice being in the old family home. I wonder which room used to be Mum's when she was growing up?"

"I dunno."

"When our house is finished, we should invite Caesar and Forrest over more often." I planned.

"If you say so." He said distractedly, as he ducked his head to reach my breasts.

I grabbed a handful of his hair to make him look upwards. "Are you listening to me?"

"You said, 'I think Caesar and Forrest like having us here,' to which I agreed. You next said -" he crankily recited, as he brushed my hand off.

"Well, what do you think?"

"About what?" He whispered. "B, just say whatever it is you wanna say so I can agree and get laid!"

"Shhh!" I slapped him on the arm. "We're sharing a house with three other Werewolves who have sensitive ears."

"We're WHISPERING!" Declan hissed. "And their bedrooms are upstairs."

"Do you think Caesar and Forrest would mind if we had a couple of people over for Looch's second birthday?" I asked quietly.

"Of course not, in fact they've already offered to give her a little party."

"Really?"

"Yeah, Caesar came into the kitchen to give me a hand with dinner and he said that Forrest thought it up." He confirmed.

"Truly?" I almost squealed in delight. "Aw, that's so nice of them!"

"Yeah it's great!" Declan said with fake enthusiasm. "Now can we please have sex?"

I reached over and grabbed another handful of his hair and yanked on it!

"Oow!" Declan yelped as he swiped away my hand a second time. "What the hell was THAT for?"

"It wasn't very romantic of me, was it?" I snapped. "Well neither are your remarks!"

The husband chuckled as he rolled onto his back and pulled his wife along. "Man, your aura right now is bright blue with these tiny sparks flying off it."

I growled dangerously as my hand reached down to grab another lot of hair, but Declan caught it in time. I tried to use my other hand, when he caught that one too. Since I was unable to use my arms, I used my mouth to bite hard into his chest. Instead of flinching, he closed his eyes and moaned softly.

"Yes, yes!" He breathed out. "Now to the right...down a bit...yes, yes!"

I delivered bite after bite into his tough skin, while his grip on my hands was ironclad. It was almost like he was holding me in place, as he gave several hard thrusts before falling into a steady rhythm. Unfortunately for us though, this bed was much older than the one we had left at home. It started to squeak with every movement we made.

"Oh no!" I pulled away in alarm.

"Screw this for a joke!" He muttered under his breath.

He grabbed his wife and made us topple to the floor. However, we didn't make a sound when we landed, for Declan put out his large arm to catch us. I landed underneath with the male quick to claim the advantageous position. When I tried to squirm out of his hold, he pinned me to the floor.

Soon a round of 'play fight' sex began with us snapping our sharpening teeth at the other. There was the odd clawing as our eyes glowed brightly before rolling over to start again. I struggled to climb on top but each time he rolled over. At one stage I managed to get underneath his defences when my elongated teeth went right for his throat.

Rather than back off, it turned him on even more. He pushed hard as my sharp teeth broke through the skin on his neck and it also broke his self control. I felt him come before I did.

Amidst all of this wriggling and writhing on the floorboards...not a sound escaped through our locked, wooden door.

*****

On the 3rd June, the Riverclaw men held a small gathering for family and friends to celebrate Looch's second birthday.

Tyson, Tania and their Riverclaw kidlets; Derik, Uma and their Elm small fry; Antonio, Peta and their Sabre progeny, as well as Walt, Wendy and their Wisetail horde; reported in with presents and well wishes.

Lucia sat in my lap as I sat in Declan's and all three of us were seated at the end of the table.

Before us was a white chocolate mud cake, decorated with pink icing flowers and two small candles burning on top. Everybody stood around, singing away with their kids at the front of the group. Meanwhile, Forrest, Antonio and Walt captured pictures on their digital cameras.

"Happy birthday dear Lucia...! Happy birthday to you!" Caesar sang the loudest.

"Hip hip?" Declan chanted.

"Hooray!" I chanted along with everyone else.

"Hip hip?"

"Hooray!"

"Why was she born so beautiful...!" Samuel Riverclaw started to sing.

However, Kurt Wisetail didn't appreciate this, so he turned around and punched him in the stomach!

Walt pulled away his struggling son. "Kurt!"

The little boy cried out, "Looch is my girlfriend, not yours!"

"Woah, it's the revenge of the midgets!" Samuel laughed it off.

Just as everybody's attention was taken away by the six year old trying to beat up a twenty year old, Looch tried to dive head-first into her cake!

"Oh shit!" I managed to catch her before her face landed in the icing.

"What the...?" Declan had to help me pull her back.

"Hungry! Dada! Mumum! Hungry!" Looch sobbed as she tried to wrestle her way to the cake.

"Calm down, Looch." Her father frowned.

Then he indicated for me to stand up so he could, then he took our hysterical child from my arms.

However, as soon as he carried her away from the table laden with party food, she began to growl threateningly. Her blue eyes turned glowing green and her nails extended before our very eyes. With her mouth hanging open from crying, we caught sight of her teeth grow longer and sharper.

Everybody paused as they looked on the two year old's tantrum taken aback. The humans gasped at her changes, as the Werewolves frowned upon her loss of control. Before our very eyes, a little girl morphed into a wilder beast all because she was denied diving into cake?

"Declan, her teeth." I pointed.

With everybody staring it added fuel to her tempestuous fire. Abruptly Declan left the house via the backdoor, carrying his daughter with him. Outside, we could hear Lucia's cries turn into angry screams, which also sounded like roaring.

"Er, cut the cake Caesar, we'll be in shortly." I said awkwardly.

I passed the knife to my relative before I too hurried out of the backdoor.

I found Declan pacing up and down out the back, as Lucia kicked and screamed in his arms. Her tearful, glowing green eyes widened when they saw me approach. With her mouth agape, drool escaped from her dangerous jaws. I saw she was digging her claws into her father's arms, deliberately trying to hurt him, so she could run back inside.

"What's wrong with her?" I asked in alarm. "She can't be THAT hungry, she's already had lots of sandwiches and chips during the party."

When I tried to smooth back her hair, she snapped at my hands! Instantly, I recoiled and her father growled angrily when he saw what happened.

"Lucia Grace!"

His warning stayed her temper as her screams turned into sobs once more.

"Declan her teeth..." I said concerned. "I've never seen them extend before."

"I think this will be the month, B." He said unhappily. "Look up."

I glanced up into the sky, scanning the blue backdrop until I saw the crescent moon.

"But it's not yet full." I said puzzled.

"Nope, but I think this coming full moon will be it." He said matter-of-factly. "I think Looch will undergo her first change."

Frightened, I looked on my screaming two year old struggling in her father's arms.

After a moment, I asked, "Do you think she'll change as much as you do?"

"She's a half breed so who knows how she'll end up." He said warily. "But since she was born with teeth, claws and glowing green eyes, I was hoping that would be the extent of it. We'll take her on her first hunt and see what happens."

But it wasn't until towards the end of the month when we realized how close Declan's predictions were...

On the night of the full moon I cleaned up the kitchen after dinner.

It was 7 PM and it was still bright outside thanks to the longer daylight during summer. Caesar and Declan were outside, talking about something which by their expressions looked serious. Forrest was sitting on the lounge, playing with Lucia in his lap.

However, all of this changed the moment Lucia's screams pierced the air.

Then she screamed again, as a baffled Forrest tried to hold her steady. She continued to scream as she writhed in his arms, as if she were in pain. Then she slid off his lap and scurried under the dining table.

"Lucia!"

I made a move towards her as simultaneously Declan and Caesar also came running.

I fell onto my knees so I could reach under, when she screamed again and bolted through the nearest doorway which was the downstairs bathroom. Forrest and I followed her inside, to find her bawling as she cowered in a corner. Her eyes were wide with fear and were glowing green.

We all watched the nails on her hands and feet grow into claws once more. She started to pant, as her body began to expand with muscle, tearing half of her clothes. My poor little girl howled in pain and fear, as her clawed hands began to touch her wet face.

"Looch?" I crouched before my terrified two year old. "It's OK, Mummy goes through these changes too."

"So do I." Forrest said.

Then he began to take off his shirt and shoes to go through a change of his own, to show her.

Next, Caesar walked into the bathroom whilst partly undressing. "We all do."

Lucia's eyes bulged as her older, topless Riverclaw relations morphed into their Lokoti Werewolf forms.

Caesar's and Forrest's upper bodies bulked up, as their teeth grew long and sharp, as did the nails on their hands and feet. Caesar's eyes glowed blue as Forrest's glowed yellow. From between their elongated teeth came the sounds of soft, reassuring growls.

"You've seen Mummy in her other body before." My dark blue eyes glowed turquoise. "Don't worry Looch, you're not alone."

"Wait..." Declan came in to look on his daughter, "...look at how she's holding her face like that, something's wrong."

My instincts sensed that Declan was right and that Looch was only partly through her change.

With four grown Werewolves looking on, Looch's face reddened. She panted harder in pain, as she held her clawed hands over her mouth like she had a tooth ache or something. Then we watched her mouth and nose join together in a canine appearance. Her top lip attached itself to the bottom of her nose, right underneath her nostrils. It forcefully parted her lips and showed off her sharp, elongated teeth.

So here she was, my half breed little girl with canine facial features. Her glowing green eyes with the narrow slits for pupils, looked teary and shameful. I sensed she was embarrassed of her changes, which she felt with her claw-like hands.

Now Declan appeared as the odd one out, looking like the only human in the room.

"Bring Lucia outside." He ordered, before he spun on his heel and walked out of the house.

Looch howled in both physical and emotional pain, thinking her father was shunning her because of how she looked.

"Come on, Looch." I scooped her up into my arms.

With her muscled arms about my neck, Caesar and Forrest stood aside to let us pass before following us out.

I went outside via the backdoor to find him stripping on the back lawn. He was getting ready to go through the change for his daughter's benefit. In the past, she's only had brief glimpses of her father in his other form, but tonight she would see him in his full glory.

I knelt on the ground so Looch could stand on her own two feet, as Caesar and Forrest stood on either side.

As soon as he began to change, she stopped crying and watched fascinated.

Declan's bones made soft cracking noises as they contorted. His human skin turned into hardened hide as his muscles expanded. His height almost doubled as his width tripled before our very eyes. His nails turned into claws, with his human skull creaking into its canine shape of a short, stubby snout over razor sharp jaws.

Once his change was complete, we were looking on a huge, hulking, hairless, canine-shaped monster. His glowing green eyes with the narrow slits for pupils were trained our way. No matter how many times we saw him turn, it always impressed.

"Dada...?" Looch managed out in her deep, rumbling Werewolf voice.

The dangerous giant gave a single nod of its canine head.

"Dada!" Lucia left my arms to stumble towards her father.

He fell forwards so he was standing on all-fours. In this position, he still towered over his young, but his head was around the height of an adult. However, Lucia fell backwards in fright, afraid he was moving into this position to attack her. She started to cry, which came out as a howling noise.

Just as I moved to pick her up, Declan beat me to it by swooping up his young in his front right claw. He held her against his hardened, hot chest as he growled tenderly to her. We heard her crying/howling stop then she growled back to him.

ARE YOU COMING OR WHAT? – Declan thought my way.

His glowing green eyes swept over my appearance. Now everybody had changed except me. My eyes were glowing turquoise, but the rest of me was still in human form.

Normally, I'd put on stretchy gym clothes which could take my expansion. But the t-shirt and jeans I was wearing were fairly stretchy, so I thought what the hell? I simply kicked off my shoes, tugged off my socks and morphed into my Lokoti Werewolf body then and there.

My t-shirt strained over my torso as it inflated with supernatural muscle. I flexed my longer, sharper nails and blinked my glowing, turquoise eyes. My breathing sped up into panting, between my elongated, sharp teeth.

"I'm ready when you are," I growled out in my changed voice.

Declan swung his daughter up onto his hardened back. Lucia must have sensed what was about to happen, for she leaned over to hold onto his bulky neck. He turned his beastly head to make sure she was holding on properly then he gave a nod.

Suddenly, Caesar took off out of his yard and into the surrounding woods, with Forrest right behind. I waited until Declan made a move after them, to run alongside. As the three adult Lokoti Werewolves ran upright, the European one ran on all-fours.

Lucia hung onto his back as she growled in anticipation. She emitted the odd howl of excitement when Declan leapt over log or bush alike, with me a close second. Although being Circulators made us faster, out of respect we remained behind our First.

A couple of times Caesar stopped running and crouched low on the ground. He'd sniff the earth before he'd raise his head and sniff the air. It was then I realized I was watching how a First decides what his pack will hunt.

TONIGHT WE HUNT MOUNTAIN LION WHO'VE STRAYED ONTO OUR TERRITORY – He commanded his men and women.

Gleefully, I growled at the idea of tasting an exotic meat, before I took off running once more after my mate and young.

Mountain lions aren't native to Alaska however, upon occasion a couple may stray across the Canadian border. When a mountain lion hunts on our land, it takes away food from the other predators, such as the wolves or bears. Although we were supernatural, the Lokoti Werewolves were still part of the natural food chain. Having a new predator on our hunting grounds also upset our food supply.

I SMELL MORE THAN ONE MOUNTAIN LION – Forrest thought to his son.

IT'S A FAMILY THAT I'M TRACKING. - Caesar concurred - *THEIR SCENT IS STRONGEST IN THE NORTH EAST MOUNTAINS* .

Caesar and Forrest ran ahead with Declan and I right behind. As we ran along, Ki fell into step beside me and Walt ran alongside of Declan. Next, the rest of the members of the pack caught up to join in the hunt. In speeds reaching 200 km/h we ran hot on the trail of our kill.

But by the time we reached the particular mountainside, there wasn't a single mountain lion to be seen.

THEY CAUGHT OUR SCENT BUT THEY'RE NEARBY – our Second said.

Declan sniffed the breeze, as he craned his beastly head to look around. His glowing green eyes carefully scanned the surrounding night, just as all our glowing eyes did. With our supernatural sight, we could see through the dark as clear as day. I've heard that the other Werewolves could see infrared. It's how they spotted a Circulator or a psychic by the 'aura' produced by their higher bio-electromagnetic fields.

OVER THERE! – Derik mentally declared.

The entire pack leapt from the mountain ridge and into the woods. We darted through the trees, with Caesar running in the front with Derik. Declan and I were a close third and fourth, with the rest of the pack right behind us.

We saw four mountain lions crouched in different positions, watching us come for them. They didn't look surprised we'd tracked them, but poised and ready to fight. Caesar leapt through the air to attack one, as Declan with Lucia still on his back, leapt onto another. The mountain lion landed flat on its back with a massive European Werewolf on top of it.

As the men pounced, I wondered who I should eat with, Caesar or Walt?

NO B, YOU FEED WITH LOOCH AND I – Declan willed my way.

Say what? Declan's offering to share his kill on a hunt? Shocked, I actually stood there stumped. Then I came forwards to pull Looch off his back, so she wouldn't fall off during the fight.

He had his two front claws on the mountain lion, pinning it to the ground. The creature snarled and clawed back as it desperately tried to free itself. As usual, he'd picked the strongest male to fight in this unusually large mountain lion family.

As soon as his young was out of harms way, Declan allowed the mountain lion to climb back to his feet. Next, my mate and his opponent circled the other, sending out their swings and leaving bloodied gashes in the other's skin. However, Declan's greater strength also sent his opponent flying through the air.

Finally, the mountain lion realized it had no hope of fighting his way out, so it tried to bolt to safety. But it didn't get five metres when Declan pounced on top of it. Using his razor sharp jaws, he ripped out the creatures' throat, instantly bringing about its death. Then he used his monstrous head to nod for us to join him.

Looch watched her father fight with wide eyes. Upon the sight and smell of the blood she licked her lips in a hungry manner. After seeing her father's signal, she wriggled out of my arms and eagerly ran over.

Declan and Lucia had already begun eating as I warily approached.

This wasn't the same as waiting at home for whatever fresh kill Declan deigned to bring back. In that situation, it was he who decided what part of the animal his family would feed on. Right now, I didn't trust his unusual generosity.

B, STOP BEING SO OVERDRAMATIC AND EAT! – Declan rolled his eyes – *WE EAT TOGETHER AS A FAMILY SO LOOCH WILL LEARN TO HUNT WITH HER PARENTS.*

Well that made sense, I could understand his behaviour upon that reasoning.

He used his two front claws to split apart the Mountain Lion's rib cage so Looch could reach the organs. However, since it was his kill, Declan's jaws snapped up the heart and swallowed it down in one gulp. Then he looked on in pride as Lucia didn't waste any time getting her face covered with blood. Using her clawed little hands, she began to eat one of the lungs.

I've always been fussy about which organs to eat, so instead I broke off a leg to chew on. Using my sharp claws, I stripped off the fur to reach the flesh underneath. Declan considerately left the other legs for me as he and Looch concentrated on the insides.

As our family ate together, I noticed the surprised glances from the rest of the pack.

This was the first time they'd seen the European Werewolf share his kill. As the pack divided what was left of the remaining mountain lion family, they gawked at Declan eating with his mate and young. Derik almost choked on his mouthful when at the end of the meal, he licked Looch's bloodied face clean.

DO MY EYES DECEIVE ME OR IS UNCLE DECLAN'S BLOODLUST BECOMING DOMESTICATED? – Derik joked.

MAN, I WISH I HAD MY CAMERA WITH ME – Ki joined in.

I THINK I'LL BUY A LOTTERY TICKET TOMORROW – Forrest guffawed.

DO YOU WANNA SHUT UP OR SHALL I SERVE YOU UP NEXT TO MY TWO YEAR OLD DAUGHTER? – Declan threatened.

*****

After Looch's first hunt, she returned to behaving herself around food. We sensed that her bloodlust had been purged and she was able to carry on as normal again. My instincts told me that Lucia had made peace with her 'dark side', especially now she understood it better. By the time we moved back into our house she was a giggling little girl again.

On the 1st July our family and friends stood on the driveway with us, to look on our new and improved home. Jay Shallow Water and his family were there, as well as the Wisetail's, the Sabre's and the Riverclaw's. They all came to see our completed house.

Altogether, we looked over the enlarged, two story, five bedroom, dark brown, wooden house with its original stone chimney.

Caesar commended, "Not bad, Jay."

"Yeah, we just may look you up when we have a spare hundred grand." Antonio joked which made Peta giggle.

"You certainly don't come cheap." Walt chuckled.

"Well I've never been the kind to 'put out' on a first date." Jay hit back. "Just ask Gina."

There was further laughter when his wife with a pink face, elbowed him in the ribs.

The four year old Edwina looked puzzled to her older brother, "Put out?"

"Baseball." Kurt told her. "Boys and girls play baseball coz they're always talking about first and second base."

"But I don't like baseball." Edwina screwed up her face.

Declan gave her a wink, "In years to come, your father's gonna truly appreciate that fact."

"Instead of just standing here on the driveway, let's actually go inside and see the new house." I insisted.

"Yes ma'am." He gave a mock salute.

Then with Lucia in tow, we wandered up our gravel drive to inspect our new abode.

However, once we reached our front door, I found that the lock no longer accepted our electronic key. There was a keypad there instead, hinting that we needed a security code. This made the European Werewolf growl in dissatisfaction.

"What the...?" He grumbled. "Hey Jay, do you mind letting us into our own home?"

"Oh yeah, sorry!" Our architect laughed as he jogged up the veranda stairs. Then like an absentminded professor, he started to rifle around in his pockets, checking each scrap of paper he pulled out. "I wrote down the security code somewhere."

But I was so excited, I was too impatient to wait. Then to Jay's and our onlookers' surprise, I went into phase and passed through the wood instead. One minute I was a biological person then the next, a see-through being made of light.

"Did you see that, Looch? Your Mommy cheated." Declan chuckled.

Looch squealed in delight as she clapped her hands at her Mummy's feat. Declan saw his daughter's enthusiasm for having Circulators for parents, so he must have thought, 'oh well, when in Rome...?' Next, he put his bigger body into phase, as well as his daughter's since he was holding onto her, then they too passed through the wood.

Jay's mouth fell open in shock, as the piece of paper with the security code slipped from his hands. He may have heard of Circulators, but to see one up close and personal? The hairs on the back of his neck stood up as he tingled all over from the electrostatic charge.

My mate reformed by my side with an ecstatic toddler in his arms.

"Again Dada," she applauded.

"Look Looch, this is your new home." He gazed around.

We stood in the centre of our living room and noted how big it was now. Both the lounge and dining areas had been broadened. Our previous furniture which used to fit snugly together, now sat spaciously apart.

Next, we walked over to the entryway of the kitchen and Declan's eyes bulged. He looked awestruck on his new and improved cooking area. His favourite area of the house was three times its previous size. Now it had the latest technology in cooking appliances which looked shiny and new and just waiting to be used. Our new refrigerator was massive and looked like it could have been industrial sized.

Looch began to squirm, indicating she wanted to be put down. Then she proceeded to run around to touch and sniff everything, as she reclaimed her territory. Following her, Declan and I explored the rest of our house.

I slid my hand into his larger one and he gave it an affectionate squeeze. Hand-in-hand, we slowly walked around as our two year old ran. We heard her talk gibberish and we weren't sure if she was talking to us, or even to the furniture.

Our downstairs bathroom - combined - laundry was the same, as well as the wooden staircase was still the original. However, now there was a doorway off to the side that didn't use to be there. We walked through and into our new study and my breath caught with emotion.

The walls were lined with shelves and all of my books were neatly put away. Although I'd have to rearrange them into categorical and alphabetical order again, the sight of them made my eyes sting. In the middle of the room was a large mahogany desk and behind it was an antiquated, high-backed, brown leather chair. Then behind that was a large window which let in as much natural light as possible. It was in the perfect position to catch both the morning and afternoon sunshine, making the room bright and inviting.

"Oh Declan!" I turned tearful. "Oh Declan!"

"Does my wife with the PhD find this working arrangement suitable for her needs?" He asked softly.

"Oh Declan!" I repeated as I didn't know what to say.

Instead, I leapt into his waiting arms and he squeezed me back tightly.

"Tell me B, how much do you love me?" He grinned.

I showered his face with kisses, "This much!"

"So the next time we meet your father on a time travel trip and he intimates that I can't look after my family...?"

"You can yell, 'in your face!'" I mimed loudly, which made him guffaw.

Just then we were interrupted by the noise of our family and friends, making their way into the house.

Antonio teased, "I changed my mind Jay, I don't want you to rebuild my house, otherwise I may never step foot in it again."

"We made it inside eventually, didn't we?" He retorted.

"Yeah, but if you look outside, you'll see winter is right on our heels." Walt said humorously.

"Where have Aunt B, Uncle Dec and Looch got to?" Wendy wondered aloud.

"Maybe they phased somewhere else?" Peta speculated. "Isn't that what Circulators do?"

"Great!" Antonio exclaimed. "We bags the house!"

"Dream on, oh great, great, great, great, great, great grand nephew of mine." Declan sung in amusement, as we emerged from the study.

We rejoined the small crowd in our larger living area which was spacious enough to accommodate everyone.

"Besides, since Aunt B is my great, great, great, great grand aunt? I'm a closer relation than you, so I get first dibs." Forrest joked along.

"Whadyaknow, since I'm your eldest that means I'm the next in line." Caesar joined in.

"And I'm your eldest so I'm after you." Tyson put up his hand.

"Hey, that's unfair!" Antonio objected. "Tyson is the same amount of greats that I am."

"You wish!" Tyson nudged him. "Ant, I am far greater than you."

As the jokes flew around the room to much laughter, Declan pretended to look worried.

"I think we'd better get Jonathan Bourne back here to redo our will."

I tittered along, "I think you might be right."

"Mumum! Dada!"

Instantly, Declan and I looked up, to find Looch standing up the top of the stairs looking worried about something.

"Lucia, remain where you are!" Wendy panicked then she said frantically to her parents, "You REALLY need to install those safety gates on the stairs."

"Wendy, relax." He smilingly shook his head. "Looch has already fallen down the stairs and do you know what happened? She sat up and giggled. Then she climbed back up and deliberately made herself topple down again."

Not only did Wendy's mouth fall open in shock, but so did Peta's, Gina's and Tania's.

"She won't break any bones from falling, but she does enjoy the dizzy spells." I laughed at their stunned expressions. "Remember when we were children and we used to play 'rolley polley' down steep, grassy hills? That's Looch with stairs."

"Aw, cool!" Kurt beamed up at her like she was the best thing since sliced bread. "Fall down the stairs now, Looch!"

"Kurt!" His mother roused, as she pulled her son to her side.

"Mumum! Dada!" Looch recalled our attention. "Nursewee!"

Then she stomped her foot as she looked on demandingly.

"I think I know what's wrong." I said to Declan, as we traipsed up the wooden stairs.

Looch took hold of our hands then pulled us down our new, longer hallway to what she thought was her bedroom, the nursery. Next, she pointed at the bare cot then she walked over to the tallboy. She opened one of the drawers to point out her clothes were missing.

"Oh I get it, she's wondering where her things are." He smiled.

"This isn't your room anymore, Looch." I told her.

"No it's not." He shook his head. "You kept climbing out of your cot as you're getting too big for it."

Looch's face fell and I guessed she was thinking that because the nursery wasn't her room anymore, she had nowhere to sleep!

"C'mon little wolf." Declan held out his hand to her. "C'mon."

Her eyes teared up, as she started to cry and she even stomped her foot as if to say, 'no dammit, this is my room!'

"It's time for all Werewolves in the house to get new rooms, better ones." Her father promised.

"C'mon Lucia Grace, come with us." I held out my hand too.

Tearfully yet furiously, she shook her head as she stood resolute.

So her father growled out, "Lucia Grace, obey!"

That did the job, she reluctantly took hold of our hands and we walked her out of the nursery and into the next bedroom.

This room had pink carpet with yellow walls and a bright green 'Kermit the Frog' quilt cover over a single bed. Over the head of the bed hung an antique style mosquito net and the fine fabric gave her bedroom a 'princess' feel. Her furniture was a lime green colour which went with the quilt cover and coincidentally, her supernatural eyes.

When Looch let go of our hands, she walked over to the tallboy, opened it and smiled in relief when she saw her clothes were inside.

Next, she began to walk around her new bedroom, recognizing her old toys and teddies which were waiting for her.

We were soon forgotten, as Looch plonked herself down on the pink carpet and started to play with her old things.

"Yup, I'd say this has won us the seal of approval." Declan chuckled, as his arm settled over my shoulders.

"When all is right in the world, the parents are no longer needed." I smiled in agreement.

At that moment, Wendy poked her head in with Kevin, Edwina and Kurt, hanging onto her legs.

"Does Looch like her new room?" She thought she'd check.

Declan waved his arm in her direction, "See for yourself."

She came inside as did her children. As soon as Kurt saw Looch, he went over to play with her. As soon as Edwina saw a doll she liked, she went over to play with it. Then a two year old, tumbling toddler in the shape of Kevin, also headed for Looch's position. But on his way, he tripped over his own feet and fell face-first onto the new carpet.

"Now that's the kind of kid that needs safety gates, period." Declan joked, which earned a whack from Wendy.

~~~~~~
~~~~~~

~ 18 ~

11th November 2368

It was a frosty morning outside with a thin layer of snow on the ground. It completely covered the grass and the garden plots. The ice painted our bare Jacaranda Tree white, with its stark branches reaching into the cloudy sky.

I saw this from my bedroom window before I headed downstairs for the warmer kitchen, where my husband and daughter were making pancakes.

Upon my arrival, I found a glass of freshly squeezed orange juice waiting. It was sitting next to two empty glasses which had been Declan and Lucia's. She was sitting up on the kitchen bench, stirring a bowl of raw pancake mix, as her father readied a frying pan on the stove. My arrival earned an immediate grin from my four year old.

"Mummy!" She cried ecstatically.

"G'morning sweetheart." I leaned in to place a kiss on the end of her nose.

"Thanks Looch." Her father reclaimed the bowl. "Now how about you set the table?"

Our strong little Werewolf who was the size of a six year old human, easily hopped off the bench.

She proceeded to open the drawers for the cutlery and placemats, as I stepped back to watch her work. I couldn't help but smile at her enthusiastic efforts. At a young age, she'd learned that helping with food preparation resulted in being fed faster.

Looch loaded up her arms with the tableware and she was about to leave the kitchen. She paused in the kitchen entryway, wearing a puzzled expression. She passed this look my way, before she returned to the task at hand.

What was that all about? I turned to Declan and saw he'd seen it too. My husband was trying not to smile, which looked like he was smirking instead. Casually, he continued cooking by pouring some of the pancake mix into the hot frying pan.

"What?" I wondered.

"Ah nothin'."

I looked down at my clothes to check if they were inside out. They weren't, so what's so funny? Next, I used the glass on the oven door to check my reflection. A woman with long, dark hair pulled back in a pony-tail, wearing jeans and a white, woollen, turtle neck jumper, peered back.

I overheard my husband snicker when he caught sight of what I was doing. I passed the blonde, scruffy-haired male a glare. Silently, I challenged him to make a remark but, wisely, he kept his mouth shut.

"The placemats and cutlery's done, Daddy." Our daughter declared, returning to the kitchen.

"Thanks sweetie, now grab the butter and maple syrup and put those on the table." He instructed.

Instantly, she obeyed by opening up the fridge and taking out the dairy and condiment. But just as she was about to leave the kitchen, I caught her sniff then pass me another peculiar look. Before I could ask why, she went on her way.

"What?!" I cried out in frustration as I turned on Declan. "What is it? What's wrong?"

"Nothing." He innocently shook his head.

I tried to see his eyes but he angled his face away, using his broad shoulders to hide it.

"Daddy..." she came back into the kitchen, "...you're forgetting the strawberries and bananas! We always have strawberries and bananas with pancakes."

"Here you go." He handed over a pre-prepared plate for her to take.

Lucia's face lit up at the sight of two of her favourite fruits neatly sliced and she stole a piece as she carried it away. I watched her carefully slide it into the middle of the table as she stood on tippy-toes. But before her hands moved away from the plate, she helped herself to another slice.

I went over to the kettle and switched it on to make a cup of coffee.

Declan glanced over his shoulder and saw what I was doing. "Yeah, I'll have one."

I retrieved two mugs from one of the top cupboards then the coffee and sugar from the pantry, when I was interrupted.

Looch came to stand in the kitchen entryway to declare, "Mummy, you smell funny."

Say what? I paused in surprise and Declan laughed! He laughed loudly too, which made my hand swing out and whack him on the arm.

My face burned, "Lucia that's not very nice!"

Next, I ducked my head to sniff under my arms...no, I hadn't forgotten to put on deodorant, so what was she talking about?

"It's called pregnancy, Looch." Her father smiled down on his daughter. "In nine months, you're gonna have a little sister to play with."

Her face lit up like it was Christmas morning. She even began to jump up and down whilst clapping her hands. It was like she'd been given the news she was about to get a new toy she'd always wanted.

"Just like Kurt and Kevin have Edwina and Katrina?" She asked excitedly.

"Yup, you'll have your very own little sister to play with." He promised.

Next, my four year old daughter skipped around and around the dining table, chanting:

"I'm gonna have a little sister! I'm gonna have a little sister!"

Smilingly, Declan carried on cooking as he flipped over the pancake.

I passed the smug male a glare, "How long have you known?"

"Two days now." He shrugged.

"Why didn't you say something before?" I asked accusingly.

"Hey, you said you didn't like it when I sniffed you and announced it that way." He reminded. "You said you wished you could find out from a home pregnancy kit. Well B, we didn't have to go out to the store and buy one, instead we have one in the shape of our half European Werewolf daughter."

I leant against the kitchen bench for support, as I stared wide-eyed at the pancake cooking on the stove. I watched him remove it from frying pan before pouring in some more mix to make another. It didn't take long for the tiny bubbles to appear on the surface and he had to flip it over.

"What's wrong, B?" His smile faded. "You don't look as happy as you should."

"It's nothing, really." I said despondently, as I stared off into the distance.

He said crankily, "Look, if a home pregnancy kit really means that much to you, so you can find out the human way, then I'll go out and buy you one."

"Huh?" I gave a funny look. "You think I look like this, because I didn't find out from a home pregnancy kit?"

"I've seen you sulk over some weird things in the past." He shook his head. "I remember when you didn't talk to Peta for a month, because she forgot to mention us in her 'thank you' speech at Holly's Christening."

"Well we DID organize all of the drinks!" I fired up. "Especially when the Elm family dropped out because of Uma's cancer scare."

"Here we go," he smirked once more. "Here's the feisty wife that I know and love."

I could tell he was trying to make me smile but I returned to staring off into the distance instead.

"Alright B, what is it? What's wrong?"

"I dunno..." I sighed.

"You don't have one of your warning feelings, do you?" He asked anxiously.

"No," I shook my head.

"Then what is it?" He rolled his eyes. "C'mon, just spit it out."

"I was hoping for a little more time before baby number two came along."

"Whadya mean more time?"

Then he removed the frying pan from the hot plate, so I could have his full attention.

"We've started teaching Looch to read, but we're gonna have to buy proper text books to home-school her." I thought aloud. "I've also been booked for the next twelve months to lecture on my latest paper."

"Her bloodlust is under control and so is her learning development." My husband reasoned. "We can order the text books we need, over the internet. Her education will be a piece of cake."

"Yeah, but you said it's too soon for her to attend school in Alma. What if she won't be ready to mainstream until a couple of years? Then we'll be raising one child while educating another."

"Hmm," he frowned as he looked out the kitchen entryway, which Looch skipped past. "When I took her to the hardware store with me last Sunday, I caught her sniffing the sales assistant."

"When Jonathan Bourne came over with the paperwork for Hodge Endeavor, I caught Looch sniffing him too." I said unhappily.

Next, Declan came over to where I was leaning on the bench, to rest his hands on either side of where I was standing. With me effectively trapped, he leaned in to rub his nose against mine, which made me smile. Appreciatively, I ran my hands up and down his clothed chest.

"My baby B and I are having another baby Werewolf." He began to chant, which made me giggle. "It'll be alright, you wait and see. Since we're doing such a bang up job with Lucia, fate decided it was time to give us Sophia."

His words warmed my heart, especially since the last time a pregnancy was announced in this house; it was me consoling Declan. Now it was the proud Papa Bear cheering his mate, Mama Bear, that Baby Bear was about to have another cub to play with. I couldn't help but grin like an idiot.

"There we go," he smiled softly, "your aura has turned yellow, which is your happy colour."

"Is my aura ever an unhappy colour when you're around?" I tittered.

"Nope!" He sung gloatingly. "Admit it B, you'd be lost without me."

"Mmm," I stood on my tippy-toes so I could rub my nose against his again. "It's why I changed your temporal signature, to keep you by my side for all time."

"Always and forever B," he muttered before his mouth claimed mine.

"In unan, Dec." I murmured back, before moving my lips with his.

That was until we were interrupted by the shrill voice coming from the kitchen entryway:

"Mummy! Daddy! What about pancakes?!"

We pulled apart to find our daughter standing in a demanding fashion with her hands on hips.

"Sorry Looch." He snickered as he returned his attention to the stove. "Your Mom has a strange effect on your Dad."

"Look who's talking," I giggled, "you leave a lasting impression, yourself."

*****

After breakfast, Declan put some Anzac biscuits he'd made into a Tupperware container. The biscuits were a gift for the Wisetail family with the birth of their fifth child. Then with his wife and daughter in tow, he carried them out of the house and down the hill.

The steep road was icy but the grip on our new boots handled the slippery conditions. Declan and I walked hand in hand as Looch ran circles around us. She ran up and down the dirty piles of snow on either side or she jumped over the muddy slush.

"Five kids..." I thought out loud, "...you think Walt's body is going to stop reproducing soon?"

"I think it already has." He remarked then waited until Looch was out of earshot. "Walt told me two months back that he's noticed his body's changed."

"How can he tell?" I asked out of curiosity.

"Because the sex is different, I guess." He shrugged.

"Hang on," I pondered. "Grant once told me about this and he said they still come, but what comes out is different."

"That's what I just said, didn't I?" Declan said coldly, as he let go of my hand.

He still hated to hear Grant's name spoken, especially by the woman who was once mated to him.

"No, you didn't say that." I spoke crisply. "I'm just wondering if it feels different, as well as IS different."

"Well that makes sense." He said sarcastically. "And people pay you to come and teach them?"

"Shut up." I retorted. "Then how did Walt tell you his body's changed?"

"How the hell am I supposed to know?" Declan's face reddened. "Guys don't share secrets about their bodies like girls do. We don't sit around and discuss when we get our period or whatever."

"You mean you get your period?" I laughed at his choice of words.

"Yeah, I'm surprised you haven't noticed your pads going missing around my time of the month." He rolled his eyes.

"Well, it explains the PMS." I playfully poked him in the side. "Then what exactly did Walt say?"

"Why do you want to know?" He gave a funny look.

"Because I'm curious!" I cried out, defensively. "I wanna know what happens and how."

"Why, in the hope that my body might change too?" He asked in a low voice. "Sorry B, it doesn't work that way for European Werewolves."

"Would you just tell me exactly what Walt said to you?" I stopped walking.

He looked away in annoyance, "I made some comment about having five kids and he said, 'yeah, this one will be the last.' Then he said, 'I noticed that my body's changed.' That's all he said, now do you mind not being so nosy?"

Angrily, I walked off ahead of him, catching Looch's hand on my way past.

"C'mon Looch, let's go and find someone less moody to talk to." I said coolly, knowing he would overhear.

He remained behind for a moment to watch us storm ahead before he sulkily trailed behind.

When I stomped up the steps of the Wisetail house, Walt immediately opened his front door from hearing our approach.

"Aunt B and Lucia! How are you both? Ah, Uncle Dec there you are!" He greeted with cheerful exuberance as we came inside.

We proceeded to take off our boots as Walt closed the front door then he took our coats.

Excited to see her, Kurt ran up to my daughter. "Looch!"

Once her boots and coat were removed, he took hold of her hand and they ran off to play.

I watched the eight year old run off with my four year old, with a four year old Kevin chasing after. The six year old Edwina was sitting on the rug by the fire, dressing her dolls. A two year old Katrina sat beside her playing with some blocks. All of this was lovingly overseen by the mother hen in the shape of Wendy, as she breastfed her newborn.

"So, what's this one called?" Declan enquired, as he handed over the Tupperware container.

"Allow me to introduce Hugh William Wisetail." He beamed proudly.

I went over to sit by Wendy to look closer on her newest bundle of joy. As soon as I sat down, Wendy angled the suckling babe my way, so I could get a better view. My stomach melted upon seeing his dark hair, pink skin and red lips, as he fed with his eyes closed.

"Oh Wendy, he's beautiful!"

"He is, isn't he?" She smiled. "He's our youngest and our last."

"So you know about Walt's body changing?" I asked in surprise.

“Er, yes...?” She gave a peculiar look.

Just then Walt cracked up laughing from overhearing us.

“Since Wendy is my mate, don’t you think that she’d be the first to know?” He asked in amusement.

“That’s my mate for you.” Declan glared my way. “Inquiring minds, want to know.”

Next, the men went into the kitchen to serve up the biscuits with coffee.

“So Aunt B, when is your body going to change back again? It’s been four years since Looch was born. Or, don’t tell me you’re going to have one child per decade, or even per century?” She teased.

“Heh heh!” I laughed nervously. “Funny you should say that Wendy -”

However, the loud sound of Kevin tripping over was enough to distract his mother and I was saved by the bell.

“Kevin!” She called out. “No running in the house! Kurt, that means you too!”

We watched him walk over to help his little brother up, when Lucia thought she should do something. With her supernatural strength, she more than picked up the boy who was the same age as her. Poor Kevin found himself being dangled in the air!

“Looch, put Kevin down please.” I instructed.

A little too obediently, Looch released her hold on the back of his jumper and he landed face-first on the floor again!

“Ouch!” I grimaced. “Gently Looch, gently!”

However, Kevin Wisetail was proving to be a tough nut as instead of crying, he laughed! Then the good-natured little boy picked himself up, much to the respect of his older brother, who gave him a pat on the back. Then the three of them raced upstairs to play.

“Here we go.” Walt reappeared, carrying the plate of biscuits. “They’re still warm and smell delicious.”

“I baked them this morning,” my husband advised. “I should’ve got the kitchen done, a century ago. Everything’s so much easier to cook these days.”

The men carried out the drinks and doled them out, with Walt resting Wendy’s de-caff coffee on a nearby table for her.

Immediately, Edwina’s eyes fell upon the Anzac biscuits which she helped herself to. Katrina looked on the food curiously, but returned to stacking her blocks. However, once Walt was sitting down on the other sofa beside Declan, she left her toys to climb up into her father’s lap for a cuddle.

“I remember when Looch was that age and all she wanted was cuddles. These days, I have to bribe her with food to get her to stand or sit still long enough, for me to get a hug in.” Declan sighed.

"Oh well, with this next one you'll soon have another little cub to hold, Uncle." Walt chuckled in good humour.

"This next one?" Wendy's ears picked up.

"Don't tell me you can smell it too?" I asked in mild annoyance.

"I certainly can." He grinned back.

"Everybody can smell it except me!" I bemoaned in frustration.

"Smell what?" Edwina looked up, wondering what we were talking about.

"But you smelled I was pregnant the last five times," Wendy looked on, puzzled.

"B can smell the change in hormones in other women, just not herself." Declan told her. "So this morning when Lucia told her that she smelled funny, she got a surprise I can tell you."

This gave the Wisetail's a good guffaw over me finding out my happy condition that way.

"Thanks Declan." I passed him a dirty look.

"Any time, B." He toasted me with his coffee mug.

"Goodness..." Wendy looked on her husband, "...there's going to be another half European and half Lokoti Werewolf in the tribe."

"There sure is," Walt smiled back.

"I wonder if this one will she be as strong as Lucia?" She pondered.

However, right as she said that, I felt a strange, fluttery feeling inside, like butterflies in my stomach. I knew it wasn't out of nerves, it was one of my all-knowing feelings I could get as a Circulator. I sensed my next daughter would be unique, just as Looch was. But I also sensed Soph would be different to her older sister, as she carved out her own path. I almost envisioned her, when I was interrupted.

"B?" My husband recalled my attention. "Are you having a vision?"

"Not exactly, no." I said dismissively. "Just a knowing feeling, that's all."

"You've got that glazed look in your eyes." Declan observed.

I rested my hand over my abdomen as I spoke to Wendy, "I don't think Sophia will be as strong as Lucia."

"I knew it!" My mate leaned forwards. "You did just 'see' something then, didn't you?"

"I'm still not talking to you." I seethed back, before I returned to her. "I think each of my daughters will be unique in their own way."

"That's a given for having supernatural parents." She giggled.

"I think Looch was born one way and Sophia will be born in another." I continued.

"Er, hello? It's the father of your children over here." Declan waved his hand. "You mind sharing this with the guy whose job it is to knock you up?"

"I think Sophia's physical abilities will be different to Lucia's." I giggled excitedly.

"B? Earth to B, come in B!" He snapped his fingers.

"What if Looch is born with one set of abilities then Sophia is born with another and then Susanna is born as something completely different?" I prattled on. "I know the timeline has something in store for them, it's so strong I can almost taste it!"

"Right, that's it." Declan plonked his mug on the coffee table. He turned to Walt, "Can you please tell her what it's like for a male Lokoti Werewolf whose body changes?"

Walt almost choked on his coffee. "Er, excuse me?"

"Tell her how your body has changed," he pointed in my direction, "so my wife will talk to me again."

"Declan!" I exclaimed with my face heating up.

Walt and Wendy exchanged baffled looks as their two daughters looked up enquiringly.

"Um, I noticed what comes out is different...?" Walt fumbled out vaguely in front of his children.

Wendy said simply, "Ki explained it as his sperm count lowering, or some such?"

"There you go B, is that what you were waiting for?" Declan demanded.

"No, you hanging by your ankles over a black hole, is what I'm waiting for!" I rebuked.

"Well before THAT happens, how about sharing info on the kids front with the guy who's responsible for giving them to you?" He asked indignantly.

Katrina and Edwina's heads turned side to side, like they were watching a tennis match, as Declan and I bickered back and forth.

"Keep talking like that and our third baby will be born via IVF!" I fired off.

"Like hell a test tube would be able to contain my strong swimmers!"

Walt and Wendy cracked up laughing, with him laughing so hard that he spilled his coffee. Wendy detached Hugh from her breast so she could burp him. She smilingly shook her head as she rubbed her son's small back.

"Can you imagine living for three centuries with that kind of bickering?" She looked at her husband.

"And they're still at it," he snickered.

"At least once a day my wife tells me to drop dead." Declan declared. "It's when she wishes me well that I get worried."

~~~~~~

11th July 2369

My second pregnancy was different to my first as not only were the symptoms dissimilar, but so were my family's reactions. Instead of dreading what could happen, my husband eagerly waited for any changes. Whereas with my daughter, she watched with interest like it was a spectator sport.

Each time Declan noticed something new, he practically gave a cheer. During my first trimester, my body changed from its slim, athletic build to a softer, more rounded figure. He let out a sigh of delight before helping himself to my new curves.

"Any time you wanna ride me, like you did with your last pregnancy? Please go right ahead. Any time of the day, any minute of the hour, I'm at your beck and call." He propositioned.

He was leaning against the ensuite doorway, watching me dry myself after an evening shower. I returned the towel to our heated towel rack, but before I put on my negligee, I examined my reflection in the mirror. My fuller breasts stood out, my stomach looked flabbier and even my thighs looked bulgy.

"It's like my Lokoti Werewolf muscles have changed, too." I observed. "Some parts of my body have remained hard, but others have completely flopped."

"Your stomach muscles have loosened so they won't restrict the baby's growth." He pointed out.

"Hmm, I suppose." I frowned, as I turned sideways to view my small 'pot belly' with a critical eye.

"Hey, I know what we can do." He dropped to his knees with a mischievous grin. "Maybe if we rub the belly it will bring good luck. Isn't that what's supposed to happen when you rub Budai's belly?"

Next, he ran his large, hot hand over my tummy. Then he closed his eyes and kissed it instead. Tenderly, he 'mauled' the flabby flesh, using his lips instead of his teeth. The wetness of his mouth on the sensitive tissue made me giddy.

"Declan?"

"Hmm?"

"I don't crave hardcore sex like I did when I was carrying Lucia." I confessed. "I crave gentle sex instead. I think my body's softer than it was with the last pregnancy. I think this is another sign that our second daughter will be different to our first daughter."

"Yeah, I smell it too." He sighed wistfully, as he looked on my tummy. "Daughter number two will be softer because she's making her mother softer."

"Isn't it amazing the way genetics works?" I thought aloud. "The first time I became pregnant, you were scared of having a baby that was exactly like
~~~~~~

you. Instead, we have Lucia who's half and half. Now our second daughter is softer than Looch, which means she's less like you and more like me."

"The more kids we have who are less like me, is a good thing." Declan said resolutely, before he caressed my tummy once more.

"I wouldn't say that." I stroked his hair. "I wouldn't be opposed to the idea of having a strong, female European Werewolf in the house."

"You're kidding, right?" His whole demeanour changed, like I'd just said the most thoughtless thing in the world.

"No, why?"

Declan stood up to give a cold, steely-glare, "In one word; Michelle."

It looks like time doesn't heal all wounds. Declan's disgust at his own breed had in no way abated over the years. Empathically, I felt his hate or shame or sometimes even both. His misgivings of his own kind were turning into my worst enemy.

"Declan, if one day we had a daughter who was exactly like you? We would train her just as we've trained Looch to control her bloodlust." I said. "She wouldn't be a threat to our family."

"No B, if one day we did have a daughter that was exactly like me? You wouldn't survive the pregnancy, let alone live long enough to train her to do anything." He said coolly.

Then he turned around and walked out of the bathroom. I came to stand in the doorway to watch Declan strip in our dark bedroom. He dropped his clothes into the laundry basket as he readied for bed.

"Stop sulking." I spoke bluntly. "I'm getting tired of your self-loathing, Declan. How you view yourself will one day affect our daughters. They're part European Werewolf and I don't want them to grow up hating themselves for it."

My words gave him pause and he hesitated in the midst of his undressing.

"I don't hate my daughters because of it." He admitted. "In fact, I love seeing part of myself in them. But as much as I'm proud of Looch's strength, I feel prouder still when I see her act with restraint."

I came to stand before my husband to reach up and press my palm against the side of his face.

"You're one of the best fathers I've seen, Declan." I said honestly. "And together, you and I can handle anything."

His bright blue eyes were wide as he drank in my words. Then his gaze lowered as he gave me a good look up and down. I still hadn't put on the negligee yet, which was back inside the bathroom.

"B, any time you wanna do one of your inspirational speeches in the nude, I'm not gonna object. Well, except maybe if it's out in public. Your speech is really inspiring me right now, in fact."

"Is it just?" I giggled flirtatiously.

"You've rallied this soldier."

His eyes indicated to look down and so I did, to admire his alert status.

"Then make tender love to your wife, Mr. Sabre." I sung liltingly.

"Yes ma'am!" He chortled happily.

In one swoop, he picked me up in his arms then lowered the both of us onto the bed.

*****

Our daughter watched as her father turned more attentive towards her mother.

She observed him open doors for her, help her in and out of hover-cars or prepare whatever foods she craved. If I dropped something then made a move to pick it up, he would call out, "I've got it!" and pick it up for me. It was the same with carrying anything; he would pull the washing basket out of my arms and tote this into the laundry for me too.

One morning, I was stacking the dishwasher after breakfast when Looch stopped me.

"No Mummy, you're not supposed to bend over!" She roused.

Next, she came into the kitchen, took the frying pan out of my hands and put it in the lower rack. Then she did all of the cutlery as well as the plates, too. All I had to do was hand her something and she put it in the bottom section.

"I can bend over, Looch." I smiled at her behaviour. "I just have to be careful when I lift up heavy things."

"No Mummy, I'll bend for you!" She said crossly.

Declan was walking past the kitchen entryway when he saw what was happening.

"You've just been told." He chuckled to his wife.

*****

Often when I sat in the study working on my academic papers, Looch would sit at the desk and play on her laptop. I would be touch typing a hundred words a minute, only stopping to check a footnote or other point of reference. Looch would copy, by looking away from her screen to check how a word was spelled in one of her text books.

I took Lucia's education seriously and decided to turn the disadvantage of her not attending school, into an advantage. I bought workbooks on reading, writing, math, science, history, geography and art for Grades 1 – 3. I also bought her a special laptop which was marketed for children as easy to use and with several educational games installed.

The desk was large enough to seat two people, but we also held some of her lessons at the dining table. I would teach her to read and write, as Declan tutored her on math and science. I'd also teach history and art while he tackled geography. Occasionally, we'd take her for long walks in the woods as part of her lessons to explain by example. Looch loved these excursions the most, as she liked the outdoors and she was very inquisitive by nature.

She liked to feel included too. Looch loved to help her Daddy in the kitchen, or she'd do her homework when I did my academic work. She'd sit opposite to me with the both of our laptops turned on and our books open. But if there was a word she couldn't understand, she would climb up into my lap to ask.

"Mummy..." she helped herself to pushing my chair away from the desk to make room, "...what does 'chomp' mean?"

"Hmm?" I looked away from my work long enough to glance at her textbook. "Oh, it means to bite or to chew. When you hunt, you chomp on flesh."

Then I illustrated by picking up her arm and pretending to chomp on it, which made her erupt into giggles.

"OK." Her father walked into the study, carrying a plate of carrot and celery sticks with two small bowls of cream cheese and peanut butter on the side. "It's afternoon tea time for the two of the smartest and prettiest female Werewolves in the world."

"Yaaay!" Looch clapped her hands then we dove into the food on offer.

Happily, we dunked our celery or carrot sticks into the side bowls, as we ate one-handed whilst we worked. I highlighted passages in my readings as Looch started on her writing exercises. The study was full of crunching sounds as we munched away on the raw vegetables.

Now Declan wanted to feel included, so he perched on the side of the desk to look down on Looch's messy writing.

"Hey, not bad." He ducked his head to place a kiss on top of hers. "But you need to make the top of your 's' smaller, but bigger on the bottom."

"OK." She followed his instruction. "You see Daddy, I'm doing acca-dame work like Mummy is."

The parents shared a smirk.

"Yes, you are doing academic work like your Mommy is." Declan stroked her hair. "One day, people could pay you to come and teach them, too."

Lucia grinned proudly at her father's praise which made her try even harder.

*****

Another change which occurred during the pregnancy was the dulling of my bloodlust. What disconcerted my family was that in the second month, I stopped craving fresh kill. My maternal instincts even dominated over my murderous inclinations.

On the night of the full moon, I dressed my little one in her stretchy exercise clothes, but not myself.

"But Mummy, you HAVE to come hunting!" Looch cried out, worriedly. "Otherwise you'll go bonkers!"

"Go without me." I told her.

Then I planted a kiss on her forehead, turned her around and gave her a gentle push towards the front door.

Declan stood there in his bathrobe, holding the door open for his youngest, as she unhappily marched past.

"Are you sure?" Declan thought he'd double check. "When you were carrying Lucia, you hunted up until your fourth month."

"I know." I sighed. "But I just don't feel like it."

"You want me to bring you back something?" He offered, meaning an arm or a leg from one of his hapless victims.

"Hmm," I frowned, "you wanna know something strange? I don't think it's just concern about the baby getting kicked. I don't even feel like eating raw meat."

"You're right B that is strange...in fact, it's flat out weird." Declan shuddered at the thought.

Then he shut the front door behind himself. Next, I watched via the front window as my husband and daughter shifted into their supernatural shapes on the snowy driveway. Declan's bathrobe hung over the veranda railing, waiting for him to revert to human again.

His width tripled as his height almost doubled, while his muscles expanded and his bones contorted. His skin turned into hardened hide over muscle bulk, which made him look like a huge, hulking, hairless, canine-shaped monster, with a short, stubby snout over razor sharp jaws. Then he turned his beastly head to see if his daughter had finished changing.

Her body expanded with muscle bulk, as the nails on her hands and feet grew longer. She retained her humanoid shape, although her face contorted into a canine appearance. Her mouth and nose became conjoined, with her top lip attached to her nostrils. Like this, she sniffed the air then she bolted into the woods with her father galloping right behind her.

A wistful sigh escaped as I felt left out. I sensed it would be the same for the remaining months of my pregnancy, too. Then I shrugged in an 'oh well' fashion before I returned to the study.

By the light of the full moon spilling through the window, I wrote a chapter about ancient rituals to the gods and goddesses. I typed about the worshipping of Athena and Dionysus, of the reputed hunts and orgies which took place. I even lit a sandalwood incense stick to go with the mood. This, coupled with the silvery light of la luna as well as the glow of my computer screen, while I waited for my family to come home with their own bloodlust purged...? How avant garde, I tittered to myself.

As I was madly typing away, my mouth began to water. I felt thirsty as a full-blown craving hit me. I wanted – no I needed – I just had to have milk. Yes, milk and lots of it!

Hurriedly, I stood up from the desk and practically rushed out of the study and into the kitchen. I opened the fridge and picked up the unopened two litres of milk from the refrigerator door. Then I opened it and sculled straight from the bottle like there was no tomorrow.

Gulp, gulp, gulp, gulp, gulp...you get the idea.

Within two minutes, I had downed two litres. I felt replenished and my craving was satisfied, but I realized I had depleted our house of milk. Oh oh, now what will my husband put in his coffee? Or what will my daughter use on her cereal tomorrow morning?

"Frickin' hell!" I cursed my craving.

Then I marched upstairs to get my coat, remote key and purse.

It was 2 AM when I parked the hover-car outside Alma's 24 hour supermarket. Next, I rushed inside, afraid of Declan discovering I ventured into town in the early hours without him. If he learned of this spontaneous shopping trip, I'd never hear the end of it. Hastily, I walked up to the dairy section, grabbed a two litre bottle of milk and turned to leave. But then all the varieties of cheeses, dips, custards and yoghurts available, caught my eye...

"Holy crap!" My husband exclaimed, when he opened up the fridge the next morning. "Ah, B?"

"Yes?" I called back from upstairs, while I was doing Lucia's hair.

"Did you go into town last night?" He sung knowingly.

"Er, what makes you say that?"

"Oh, I don't know..." he drawled, "...maybe because our fridge looks like the dairy section of a supermarket?"

"Well, we ran out of milk so I had to get some more." I said lamely.

"Oh yeah?" He stifled his laughter. "Then what about the one litre bottle of vanilla custard, the one litre bottle of chocolate custard, the sour cream, the strawberry yoghurt, peach and mango yoghurt, cheddar cheese, Philadelphia cheese, smoked cheese, the French Onion dip, Tzaziki and the Hommus?"

"Um, they're for 'in case of emergency'." I tried to say casually. "You know, in case we have last minute guests over."

"Uh huh." He said dead pan. "Next time you get a craving at one in the morning, how about sending your husband on a mission of 'fetch'?"

"It wasn't one in the morning, it was two in the morning." I half said to myself. "Besides, you and Looch were off settling your own cravings."

However, he picked up my retort with his sensitive ears.

"I don't care if I'm all the way on Taurus Six! You went to the supermarket by yourself at two in the morning. The last time you were pregnant and went to the supermarket alone at night, you were attacked by North American Vampires. Next time, you call me and that's an order!"

Looch giggled at the growling her mother got from the person she saw as 'First' in our family.

I muttered under my breath, "So frickin' bossy!"

"Hey, I heard that!" Declan flared from downstairs. "And I don't appreciate your 'whatever' attitude towards the safety of our baby!"

*****

The larger I grew, the worse Declan's overprotective nature became.

During a trip into Alma, he almost attacked a stranger who cut us off in traffic. He had to slam on the hover-car's breaking thrusters, before parking the vehicle on the side of the road. Once he'd checked that his pregnant wife and kid were OK, he made a move to get out and have words with the human male.

"No Declan!" I pulled him back. "Just leave it."

"B, you saw what he did! It wasn't just illegal, it was frickin' dangerous!" He growled as his blue eyes flashed glowing green.

"No wait...!" I lost my hold on him when he stood up from the hover-car.

"Hey, moron! The lights were red! Are you frickin' colour blind or just plain stupid?!" He bellowed at the stranger.

The human looked to be fresh out of his teens, which would explain the reckless driving. The kid took one look at the strong build of my enraged husband and climbed back into his vehicle to make a run for it. To make matters worse, Declan looked like he was about to run up and hold down the vehicle, to prevent his escape.

I climbed out of the car and roared so loudly, everyone on the street heard.

"Declan Domitian Sabre, you get back into this hover-car RIGHT NOW!"

Looch's blue eyes widened as they looked on her mother impressed at the growling she just gave to her Daddy.

He stood still as the stranger's hover-car rose into the air and then gunned down the road, away from him. I sensed he was fuming at what he saw as a threat to his family, was getting away. But I also sensed he realized he nearly gave himself away. After standing in tense manner for another moment, he turned around and headed back to our vehicle.

Slowly, I lowered myself back into my seat around the same time as Declan returned to his. Both Looch and I could hear the dangerously low growl under his breath, as he sat still and stared out the windscreen. He was probably picturing hunting that particular human down on the next full moon.

Just then he turned my way as he rested his large hand over my baby bulge.

“Are you sure you’re alright?” He asked anxiously. “Is the baby OK?”

“She’s fine.” I promised, putting my hands over his. I flashed a look back at Lucia who was watching our interaction, before I met his gaze. “All Sabre’s in the car are fine.”

Just as I said that, Sophia chose that moment to give a kick, as if she wanted to prove her health.

Declan laughed as he gave my belly an affectionate rub, “Yeah, right back at you kid.”

*****

Sophia was extremely active at Looch’s fifth birthday party.

Our guests were our relations from the Sabre, Elm, Riverclaw and Wisetail families. Forrest and Caesar sang the loudest, with Walt, Tyson and Anthony snapping away pictures on their digital cameras. With all the party sounds of children playing, adults laughing then a chorus of ‘Happy Birthday to you’; Sophia didn’t want to feel left out.

Although I was eight months pregnant, we all piled onto my husband’s lap. Looch sat on my legs as I sat on Declan’s and the birthday cake sat before us, on the dining table. This time it was a caramel mudcake complete with five candles.

Just as Looch leaned over to blow them out, Sophia gave an almighty kick which went straight through my stomach and into her back.

“Hey!” My eldest turned around and looked on my tummy with an indignant expression. “This is MY birthday NOT yours Sophia!”

The whole room erupted into laughter and my favourite photo taken on this day was a picture of Looch talking to her sister via my large stomach.

*****

So far, my second pregnancy seemed more normal than my first. Perhaps I should use the word ‘human’ instead, because Sophia’s progression ran along course of a human foetus. Looch was a large baby that my body delivered early. Sophia wasn’t a large baby and I carried her for the full nine months.

After what happened with Lucia, my husband was on stand-by mode as soon as we entered the eighth month.

If I moaned when I rolled over in bed, Declan woke up, instantly thinking I was in labour. Or, sometimes if I awoke during the night, I’d find him lying on his side watching me sleep. His eyes would be glowing green to see better in the dark. They’d swing down to my balloon-like belly before lingering on my larger breasts then they’d settle on my face.

“Ooooaaaarrrggh,” I groaned, as I changed from lying on my left side to my right.

“Are you OK?” He checked.

“I’m not in labour, Dec.” I replied tiredly.

“How’s your back?” He asked, concerned.

“Not good,” I frowned with my eyes closed. “I have shooting pains down the back of my legs.”

As soon as those words left my mouth, I felt his large, hot hand start to massage my lower back and hips in a circular motion.

“Mmmm...thank you.” I mumbled out.

The immediate relief was enough to put me back to sleep.

“I know what my woman wants.” He chuckled softly, only pausing his massage long enough to plant a kiss on my shoulder.

*****

Since Declan was on guard at night, of course Sophia had to surprise us by arriving during the day.

It was the fourth of July and the whole family was working in the greenhouse. I was watering the plants while Declan was harvesting our herbs and preparing them to be dried. Looch was sitting on the greenhouse floor, stacking some empty pots. However, she cast many an upwards glance at her father’s prized orchids, as the delicate flowers captivated her.

When I moved over to water them, I wondered why my maternity jeans felt wet. Then I glanced down, expecting to find that the hose had leaked. Instead, I found the wet patch was spreading out from my crotch.

“Oh shit.” I dropped the hose. “Declan?”

“Yeah?” He replied, not looking my way.

“Er, Declan -” I began but Looch beat me to the punch.

“Oh oh, Mummy’s wet her pants!” She cried out.

“Huh?” He looked from his daughter to his wife, when I saw his eyes widen in alarm. “Oh shit!”

KI GET HERE NOW! – I heard him call on our Medicine Man.

I’M ON MY WAY – He thought back – *CAESAR IT’S TIME.*

DAD AND I ARE COMING NOW – Our relative replied.

“Looch, turn off the hose for Mommy and follow us inside.” Declan instructed.

He sprang into action by rushing forwards and literally sweeping me off my feet. He raised me up into his arms then hurried out of the greenhouse and towards the backdoor. He managed to open it before barging inside and heading straight for the staircase.

Our five year old obeyed her father's orders, first of all turning off the water then racing into the main house after us.

My mate led the way, carrying me upstairs and into our bedroom, with Lucia stopping in our doorway to watch.

"OK Looch, Caesar and Forrest are coming over to play with you, so can you please wait for them in your bedroom?" Declan ordered.

Then he gently lowered me onto the bed before taking off my shoes.

"Is Mummy OK?" Looch asked concerned.

"I'm fine, sweetheart." I promised.

"Your Mommy's having the baby now." He said as he undressed the woman in labour.

"Can I help?" She offered.

This made him pause for a moment before he said, "Open up the linen cupboard and bring in all the towels."

"All of them?" She checked.

"Yup, every single one." He clarified, as he removed the last of my garments.

Next, she skedaddled back and forth, running in and out of our bedroom carrying as many towels she could muster. As she did, I pulled on an old cotton nightie to cover my nakedness. Then Declan lifted me up and placed as many towels as he could underneath, as well as over the rest of the bed.

They had just finished covering the mattress when I sat forwards and began my breathing exercises. A painful contraction ripped across my abdomen and I tried not to cry out in pain in front of my daughter. However, Declan saw my face contort and he gave Lucia a gentle nudge towards the door.

"Thank you sweetie, now wait in your room for Caesar and Forrest." He instructed.

"But is Mummy OK?" She hesitated in the doorway. "Daddy, look! Mummy's bleeding!"

"Lucia Grace, go to your room NOW!" He yelled.

She ran out of our room and into hers crying. I felt bad to hear she was so upset but I felt worse from the labour. I tried to focus on my breathing exercises as I felt the baby sink lower. I swear I felt her move into position and the contractions had only just begun.

In another minute or two, we heard Ki arrive the same time as Caesar and Forrest. Instead of knocking, the three simply walked into the house and headed upstairs. Ki and Caesar came into my bedroom as Forrest went into Looch's. I overheard him greet her and reassure that everything was going to be OK.

"Hello Lucia, I see you've got Bob the Bear there." He spoke in a kindly voice. "Do you mind if I sit with you and Bob, while Ki and Caesar help your parents? It's going to be alright, your little sister's on her way."

In the main bedroom, Ki and Caesar cleaned their hands with a sterilizing gel. It looked like our First was going to take on the role of the Medicine Man's assistant. No sooner than their hands were sanitized, Caesar opened the medicine bundle and took out the medical scanner for him. Ki waved it over me the once then handed it back.

To all of our surprise, he declared, "she's crowning," then he moved my legs over to the side of the bed.

"Already?!" Declan spluttered. "But it's only been ten minutes since her water broke!"

"Thirteen minutes, Uncle." Caesar corrected him. "It's been thirteen minutes since we got the call."

"Who cares!?" I cried out with a reddening face. "She's coming NOW!"

"Just let it all out, B..." my mate rubbed my lower back, "...literally."

With Declan sitting behind supporting my back and my legs propped apart on the edge of the bed, I began to push. I also began to sweat as well as bleed. But since Sophia is a smaller baby than her sister was, she almost coasted along on the contractions alone. I felt her come out with far less effort than my first child.

"Good work, Aunt B!" Ki cheered. "The head is out...and now her shoulders. Excellent job, Aunt B! While you push, I'll pull out the rest of the body...and now she's all the way out!"

Both Declan and Caesar laughed in relief at how easy that looked, as Ki held up a perfectly healthy, bloodied baby girl in the air. Then Sophia opened her mouth and cried. She, like her older sister, didn't have to be induced to breathe and it made me wonder if it was a Werewolf trait.

Our First came forward with a clean towel into which the Medicine Man placed my baby girl. Then Ki cut the umbilical chord which enabled Caesar to carry her away to be cleaned. He rested her on top of the tallboy as he wiped away the blood.

My husband remained behind to support my back as I went through the afterbirth. However, his eyes were on his offspring who was being cleaned by our relative. So were mine in fact, as I tried to hurry through the procedure so I could hold her sooner.

As soon as it was over, I reached out and Caesar placed Sophia Clara into my arms.

"Oh Declan..." I said emotionally, "...this is our second daughter!"

We both stared in amazement at our human-looking child.

Her fingernails looked normal and when she opened her mouth to cry, all we saw were gums. Her crying sounded like a human baby's too, there wasn't any growling. But she stopped when Declan gave her his little finger to suck on.

"Look at how...normal...she looks." He marvelled at his littlest girl.

“It looks like Sophia’s Werewolf physique is going to grow as she does.” Ki mused.

“Also, Aunt B gave birth to Sophia in her human body and not in her Werewolf one.” Caesar speculated. “It makes sense when you think about it; Aunt B in her human body gives birth to a human-like daughter.”

“It’s because I didn’t have to push as much.” I admitted. “She’s a much smaller baby than Looch was.”

And then Sophia opened her pink eyelids to look up at her parents and we saw her eyes were glowing green with thin, black slits for pupils.

Declan joked, “Hey, this kid does belong to me after all!”

Our First laughed along before our Medicine Man looked at his watch.

“Aunt B’s labour was less than twenty minutes.”

“Woah!” Caesar looked on impressed. “Is that a new record in the tribe?”

“I think so.”

“My B always has to be different.” Declan smiled lovingly. “In the beginning she’s the pack’s first female Lokoti Werewolf then she’s the first Lokoti Werewolf to mate a second time. Next, we’re the first Lokoti Werewolf/ European Werewolf pregnancy and now she has the fastest delivery in the history of the tribe.”

Then he delivered several kisses to my sweaty forehead before wrapping both his wife and baby in his big, strong arms.

“Right.” Caesar clapped his hands to call for order. “Let’s get Aunt B and this room cleaned up, so Looch can meet her little sister.”

“Yes sir.” Ki returned to taking orders instead of giving them.

As Caesar began to collect the messy towels, Ki sterilized his medical equipment before putting them away.

Reluctantly, my husband left my side to help our First tidy up our bedroom.

The males made several trips in and out of the room to put the soiled linen in the wash, or left in the laundry for the next load. I was washed down and changed, as well as our sheets and mattress protector. As the two worked, I watched Ki do the same tests on Sophia as he did on Lucia after her birth.

“There’s zero communicability of transferring Werewolf DNA by saliva or by blood.” Ki reported when he was done. “Sophia can’t change anyone by biting them or sharing her blood with them.”

“Well that’s good news.” Declan sounded relieved.

“However, I can predict that when she procreates, her children will be born as Werewolves.” Ki said seriously, whilst looking on our First. “Just as her grandchildren will and so on.”

“So it will be a lineage of baby Werewolves?” Caesar asked gravely.

“Yes, they will all be born as Werewolves.” He confirmed. “The Lokoti Werewolf genes are stopping Sophia and Lucia from changing any humans by blood or bite. However, because of Uncle Dec's European Werewolf genes, their children and their children's children, will always be born as Werewolves."

"Hmm," Caesar frowned. "So if Looch or Soph have sons who mate with human women, we can't guarantee the mother's safety."

Moodily, Declan went to go stand alone by one of the bedroom windows. I saw his jaw clench and the familiar glare he wore when he was filled with self-loathing. It made me feel bad for him, being blamed for his genes.

"Hang on," I spoke up as I rocked Sophia in my arms. "We're talking grandchildren here, so if Looch and Soph have sons? They won't be as strong as Declan, because they won't be pure blood European Werewolves. If they're not as strong, then nobody should be in any danger."

"True," Ki mused. "But as we know, European Werewolves are a hundred times stronger and Lokoti Werewolves are fifty times stronger than a human. Even if the European Werewolf's strength is diluted down, don't forget the strength of a Lokoti Werewolf. A baby with our muscles, or claws or teeth, would still jeopardize the safety of a human woman who carries that child."

"Thank you Ki," our First ended the solemn discussion. "We'll cross that bridge when we come to it."

He gave a nod then he picked up his old, black leather doctor's case and departed from the bedroom as well as the house.

With our door left open, the elderly Forrest came in with an eager Looch. Her eyes widened upon the sight of her mother sitting upright in bed with a wrapped-up baby in her arms. Our great grandnephew let go of her hand to allow her to run over and climb up onto the bed to get a better look.

"Mummy, is that Soph?" She asked excitedly.

"This is your little sister, Sophia Clara." I angled the baby towards her.

Next, she looked on with concern. "Did it hurt?"

"It did." I admitted, before I reached out to tweak her nose. "But it's worth it."

Then all talk of labour was forgotten as Looch leaned in to stare upon her sister. As she did, Forrest came to sit on the side of the bed to smile on the happy scene. When I carefully handed Soph to him to hold, Looch moved over with her, to perch by his side and continue to stare.

I looked up at Caesar who was talking quietly to Declan by the window. The two men were talking so silently, it was like their entire conversation was under their breath. I strained to hear what they were saying and could only make out every second or third word.

"We'll cross that bridge when we come to it, Uncle." Caesar repeated in his normal voice. "But today is meant for rejoicing, as we welcome your newest member of your family and the tribe."

Then Caesar walked over to Forrest to smile down on his elderly father holding his precious charge.

Next, Looch started to chatter non-stop in an excited manner, telling Soph about all the things she was going to teach her, like reading and writing, or even hunting. This made all of the grown-ups in the room laugh...everyone but Declan that is. My mate was still standing with his arms crossed, by the window.

He was looking on the room as if we were a distant picture. I didn't like this and I wanted to bring him back to reality. I reached out for him and I noticed when he came over to take my hand, his movements were mechanical. His reluctance was clear to see and it hurt.

In a strong tug, I pulled him onto the bed beside me before I whispered in his ear, "I'd breed with you any day of the week and twice on Sundays, Mr. Sabre."

His bright blue eyes met my dark blue ones and our gaze lingered on the other.

"I know the seed is as good as the man," I said softly.

To my relief, a mischievous grin appeared on his youthful face, or was it a smirk?

"Since there's still another baby to come, it looks like you're in luck Mrs. Sabre." He said cheekily.

Forrest announced, "Let's return the newest Baby Bear to the proud Papa Bear."

As if they were handling the Hope Diamond, I watched Forrest with reverence, place the baby Sophia into Declan's waiting hands. The tiny tot looked so small in his large arms, I could tell he was trying extra hard to be gentle with her. He held her against his wide chest as he looked down on his offspring.

Again, Looch followed after her little sister and now she was sitting in between Declan and I, so she could continue to stare.

"You want to hold your little sister, Looch?" Her father offered.

Instantly, she jumped at the chance. My husband placed his youngest into his eldest's smaller arms. Looch held onto her securely as she grinned proudly.

"Maia would have loved to have seen this." Forrest sighed.

"So would've Maria," Caesar reminisced about his late wife, too. "The tribe's most argumentative couple turn peaceful by procreation."

"Hey!" The European Werewolf flared. "Don't tempt fate, fellas. As soon as you know it, my wife will be wishing me dead in no time."

"Hey!" I objected. "I've never wished you dead!"

"You've told me to drop dead a couple of times in the past." Then he leaned in to plant a kiss on my flushed cheek. "But I wouldn't have it any other way."

~~~~~~
~~~~~~

~ 19 ~

5th January 2370

Sophia's pregnancy wasn't only the most 'human' I experienced, but so were the postnatal symptoms. Just like human women who've given birth, my mood swings were all over the place. Medically this is defined as 'postnatal depression', only times it by fifty when they occurred in a female Werewolf. It didn't disconcert Declan, but it worried our family and friends.

At first the symptoms weren't so bad since they presented themselves as crankiness and restlessness. I was so restless, I couldn't concentrate properly let alone focus on any academic work. Also, my cravings were stronger.

On a Monday afternoon, I was sitting in the study with my laptop open. Sophia was slumbering peacefully in the baby carrier against my front. The warm sunshine was spilling through the window, putting the small room in a warm glow. I had the window open which not only let in the musk-scented breeze, but the bird song as well.

A loud sigh escaped as I looked out the window, before glancing down on Sophia sleeping away. Her dark hair complimented her ivory skin, which felt warm and soft to touch. So far my second daughter physically resembled her mother the most. She had the dark Lokoti hair and when her eyes weren't glowing green, they were a dark brown colour. Tenderly, I caressed the top of her head while she snoozed.

Who am I trying to kid here? There's no way I can get any academic work done this afternoon. Growling under my breath, I stood up and left the room.

I found Declan and Lucia working together in the kitchen. My mate was checking his marinated olives and antipasto mix and our eldest was helping. Father was teaching daughter of how to check for bacteria by smell, to make sure everything was preserving correctly. I brushed past the two as I opened up the fridge.

"Are you still hungry?" He turned my way. "You finished off that plate of cheese and crackers pretty fast."

"What's that supposed to mean?" I snapped.

"Nothin'." He shrugged. "If you can wait another hour and a half, I'll make an early dinner."

"Hmm," I looked back into the fridge. "I feel like eating something now."

"There's still some smoked salmon dip left." He suggested.

Then he scribbled down today's date on the jars he had just checked.

"Why are you doing that, Daddy?" Looch watched closely.

"I write down the dates that I checked them, so I'll remember which jars are good for another couple of months." He advised. "As Werewolves, we can't die from food poisoning, but it can make us irritatingly sick."

"Have you been sick?" Her eyes widened.

"Tell her about the time you ate that bad boccaccini." I smirked.

Declan flashed a look of annoyance my way, before he spoke.

"Once I ate bad boccaccini and it made me sick for a little while."

"You were in the bathroom for an hour." I snickered.

"Do you mind NOT laughing about the day I had stomach pains and diarrhoea?" He snapped.

"Well I DID tell you not to eat it since it was past its' expiration date." I replied. "But as usual, you followed your stomach."

My husband turned back to our daughter who looked shocked at the idea that something could have weakened her big, strong father.

"It's OK Looch." He tweaked her nose. "Ki said what I had could've killed a human, but your Daddy takes a lickin' and keeps on tickin'."

"Bad food can kill people?!" She looked horrified at the idea, especially since eating was her favourite past time.

"It's the bad bacteria in food which can kill people." He corrected.

It was on this note that I picked up the half-eaten smoked salmon dip and complained.

"Aw, who ate this last and didn't put the lid on properly?"

"Not me, I haven't had any yet." Declan answered.

I glowered at Looch whose eyes dropped guiltily, before I walked over and threw the container out.

"Hey, what are you doin'?" He objected. "That dip is still good!"

"The lid wasn't on properly!" I snapped, as I stormed out of the kitchen.

"Yeah but it still smelled OK!" He reached into the bin to pick it back up. However, since the lid wasn't on, half of it had fallen out so he released it. "Now that was a waste of good food."

I walked out the front door and stood on the veranda in the warm sunshine. The summer breeze teased my hair and it felt so good to be outside that I decided to go for a walk. I started down the veranda steps when Declan followed me out.

"B?"

I called back over my shoulder. "I'm going for a walk."

"But it's coming up to Looch's bath time and I'm going to start cooking soon!" He objected.

I didn't even stop, I simply threw a parting wave over my shoulder as I stomped off into the woods.

The familiar dirt path led me down the wooded hill towards the river. It was a path I knew well, having followed it for centuries. I could even walk it blindfolded if had to.

Sophia stirred from the jarring to the baby carrier the hike was causing. When her eyes opened, I saw they were her dark brown colour which squinted in the sunlight. She gave a dissatisfied snarl at being woken up before she started to cry.

"Aw, c'mon baby," I crooned. "It's a nice afternoon, don't be that way."

Sophia's response was to cry louder and boy could this kid cry! It was as if she was learning that if she kicked up enough fuss, she could get her own way. Her cries escalated into piercing squeals as her eyes glowed green in anger.

"But I'm enjoying the walk!" I complained. "I need to get out for a while and the fresh air will do you good."

As if she disagreed to that, she started to scream.

"Alright alright!" I flinched at the noise. "Home it is!"

Rather than listening to the ruckus on the walk back, I cheated by instantaneously phasing home.

We disappeared in a bright flash of light from the sun-dappled woods, to reappear in another inside of the dimmer nursery. Immediately, Sophia's screams reduced to normal cries, but she wouldn't stop. I sensed she'd soiled herself and now she needed to be changed.

Frickin' hell, it looks like Declan won and it's time for the kids' bath after all.

"C'mon then," I carried her over to her change table to undress her.

*****

After I washed Soph and put her down for a nap, I bathed Looch. Our eldest loved to play with the bubbles produced from the bath formula. But trying to get her to stay still so I could shampoo her hair was the real challenge.

I was running out of patience as my clothes were getting wetter from her splashing. "Looch, sit still and that's an order!"

"But I don't want to wash my hair, Mummy!"

"Lucia Grace, I gave you an order!" I growled.

She knew if she disobeyed her mother then her father would be cross. Her eyes widened at the idea and eventually she sat still. She allowed me to wet her hair with the hand-held shower extension before I turned off the tap and reached for the shampoo. After putting some into my palm, I gently massaged it through her dark blond locks.

That was until the delicious smell of dinner cooking, wafted into the bathroom and made Looch's head turn.

"Yummy! We're having spaghetti bolognaise for dinner!" She cried excitedly, recognizing the scent.

Using her supernatural speed, she leapt out of the bathtub and ran out of the bathroom!

"Lucia Grace!" I shouted. "Come back here NOW!"

Downstairs, I heard Declan crack up laughing at the sight of his wet and soapy daughter standing in his kitchen.

"Er, Looch, did you forget something?" I overheard him. "Like getting dressed or even washing the shampoo out of your hair?"

Next, I heard the wooden stairs creak as he carried his little girl upstairs and back into the bathroom.

"Are you missing something, B?" He asked humorously.

However, I didn't feel like laughing. Crankily, I stood up as Declan lowered Looch back into the tub. I pushed past as I flounced out of the bathroom.

"You can bath her since YOU'RE the only one she obeys around here!" I snarled sulkily.

Then I stormed into my bedroom and slammed the door shut!

"Can you at least go downstairs and turn the stove off, so our dinner doesn't burn?" He called out.

"Fine!"

I instantaneously phased into the kitchen, turned off the hotplates and then I instantaneously phased back. I was just about to sit on the bed when I heard Sophia cry again. Empathically, I sensed she was hungry too.

Frickin' hell, it never ends! Whose bright idea was it to have kids anyway? Man, I missed the relaxing days of being kid-free.

Declan poked his head out of the bathroom to see our bedroom door open and his weary wife emerge. He frowned at my slumped shoulders as I shuffled into the nursery. It was a good minute or so until he heard his second daughter stop crying.

I sat in the rocking chair and nursed my newborn. However, I was starting to see Sophia's personality was a loud one. Although my breast was bared and her mouth was near; she took her time to start suckling. One might even say she liked the sound of her own voice and what a voice she had...

If Sophia got cold, she squealed. If she was hungry, she squealed. If she was tired, she squealed. If she was soiled, she squealed. If she was bored, she squealed. If she wanted attention, she squealed. From the first week of her birth, our second was proving to be a challenge. Although she may not have the physical strength of her older sister, she could deafen you with her screams.

Declan would flinch and Looch would cover her ears as Soph's ear-piercing noise filled the house. I noticed my mate would prefer to spend more time with his eldest than his youngest. He was a hands-on father with Looch when she was a baby however, by the fourth week of Sophia's arrival, a distance was starting to appear between them.

"It's because her screams hurt his ears," I reassured myself.

After her bath, he took his washed and dressed five year old downstairs with him, to help with dinner. With the bolognaise sauce simmering away, Looch set the table. I observed that the father and daughter team enjoyed working together since they shared similar interests.

I was sitting on the stairs watching them, when Declan spotted me as he carried out our cooked meal. He put down the large bowls of pasta and salad on the dining table, with Looch carrying out the garlic bread. Then he came over to the staircase to look up at his wife.

"Is Soph down for the night?" He checked.

"She's fed and now she's sleeping."

"Let's see to her mother then," he took hold of my hand.

He sat his wife and daughter in their respective chairs as the delicious aroma of spaghetti bolognaise, toss salad and garlic bread filled our nostrils. Declan served his daughter first then his wife second and himself third, as Looch and I helped ourselves to the garlic bread. My spirits rose as I ate the scrumptious meal. He watched me eat a mouthful of pasta then some salad and next a slice of garlic bread.

"All good?" Declan looked on and I noticed so did Lucia.

"Mmmm," I nodded with my mouthful.

"Your aura is turning yellow so I'll take it as a yes," he gave a wink.

"How come you and Mummy glow different colours and I don't?" Looch looked from one parent to the next.

"It's because we're Circulators, Looch." He said casually. "It's how we can instantaneously phase from here to Taurus Six in a bright flash of light."

She turned thoughtful, "Is that why Ceesee and Forrest and Walt call you 'Light People'?"

"Good call," he grinned. "That's exactly why Looch."

"But how come you're Werewolves and Circulators and everyone else are just Werewolves?" She asked next.

"Do you mean the pack?" Declan gently corrected and she gave a nod. "Well once upon a time, your mother was the only Circulator. But your Mom loved your Dad so much, she turned him into a Circulator too."

"Can I be a Circulator?" She looked hopeful.

"We'll see," I said.

But Looch looked to whom she saw as 'First' in the family. "Daddy?"

Her attitude was really grating on my nerves which made me sit there and glare instead.

"Your mother answered your question, Lucia Grace." He said firmly.

However, my first born continued to look beseechingly on her father. "But I want to glow too, Daddy."

Then we were interrupted when Sophia's piercing cry rang from upstairs. The European Werewolf and his half breed daughter shuddered at the noise. I sensed Soph wasn't hungry or soiled, but she couldn't sleep and wanted to be held. Since I had tended to her all day and a breast wasn't required, I looked to Declan to indicate it was his turn.

"Don't look at me, I can't breastfeed." He gave a funny look.

"She doesn't want to be fed, she wants to be held." I said coldly.

"If I risk my ears by going up there to hold her, she's gonna keep crying." My husband said unhappily. "She wants her mother."

"Now why would you say a thing like that?" I asked icily. "Because you're 'First' and I'm 'Second'?"

"No, because every time I hold that kid, she won't shut up until she's in her mother's arms." He said unhappily. "You saw what she was like when I changed her this morning, she wouldn't settle until you took over. She may be only five weeks old, but she already knows what she likes and she likes your softer hands and body, let alone your brighter aura."

"What has my aura got to do with it?!" I snapped. "Would you both shut up about auras!"

Declan's blue eyes flashed their glowing green colour as his face reddened in anger. Looch looked wide eyed upon her parents who sat on either side of the table, fuming at each other. Meanwhile, Sophia's cries went up a notch as they turned into a high pitched squealing.

"Fine then!" He seethed.

He marched upstairs to take on the responsibility of his second born.

One minute turned into two then the two turned into three, but the crying didn't stop.

I watched the clock on the wall tick over to five minutes since he went into the nursery but she continued to cry. I tore up a slice of garlic bread in my almost claw-like hands, as I struggled not to change in anger. Looch sat with her hands over her ears, looking irritated herself. She seethed at her 'Second' for disobeying her 'First', which was the result of all the noise.

Ten minutes later, Declan marched downstairs with a screaming baby in his arms. Sophia was in such a state, her face was bright red and her little arms were flailing. Her father looked not only angry, but hurt at how his youngest wasn't bonding to him.

"I tried rocking her, I tried singing to her, I tried growling softly to her and I tried walking around with her." He said wearily. "Just take her B, my ears can't take anymore."

Carefully, my husband 'dumped' our one month old into my arms and as soon as he did, she stopped crying.

I rocked her as everyone watched her glowing green eyes dull back to their dark brown colour. Next, they closed contentedly as she nestled into my clothed breast. Looking the very epitome of peaceful, she dozed off.

"I'm all for equality with parenting, but it doesn't help when I can't care for one of our children, because the only contact she wants is with her mother." He said sulkily.

I stood up with the baby in my arms as I flashed a look towards my eldest before I met his gaze again.

"Now you know how I feel," I said bitterly.

Then I turned away to carry our youngest back up to the nursery.

*****

I remained in the nursery until 9 PM because every time I tried to put Soph down, her crying started up. I walked around and around in circles as I sang Sarah McLachlan songs to her, before I sunk wearily into the rocking chair. After another feed and a little more singing, finally she fell unconscious.

Feeling strung out, I shuffled into my ensuite to have a long, hot shower. The pulsating shower head and the temperature of the water began to knead the knots out of my neck and shoulders. Once I was washed, I stepped out to dry and dress in a negligee.

As I was brushing my teeth, I found myself staring at my reflection in the mirror. I must admit, I didn't like what I saw. I looked tired, with the weariness worn on my face like a mask from a Greek Tragedy. I saw how saggy my boobs looked, as well as my stomach. I didn't look like a Lokoti Werewolf should with muscle tone and stamina, I looked flabby and awful!

The sobs escaped from me so suddenly, it made me drop my toothbrush. I backed away from the hideous reflection and ended up collapsing onto the side of the bathtub. There I sat, rocking myself, while I cried.

What's wrong with me? Why am I so tired and ugly? Why did I always want to be a mother? I have what I've always wanted, but I'm not enjoying it. Why am I so unhappy? There must be something wrong with me, not to find fulfilment in my children.

"B?"

I glanced up to find my younger-looking husband standing in the doorway. His skin looked smooth and tight over his square jaw. His bright blue eyes were wide with worry, giving him a bright-eyed appearance. This was accentuated by his blonde hair looking particularly wavy tonight. It fanned out about his face, making him look like an Adonis.

"Don't look at me!" I turned away. "I'm fat and flabby and old and miserable!"

"Say what?"

"You heard me!"

"Woah, watch it with the decibels!" He flinched at my tearful screeching. "We already have Soph to deafen us with her high-pitch noise."

Then he came in to kneel on the tiled floor and catch my wet face between his hands, but I wouldn't look at him... I couldn't.

"Please go away," I rasped. "Let me just cry and get it out of my system."

"B, you know I hate it when you cry." He said unhappily. "Your aura fades and it makes me want to go out and kill something."

I couldn't help but to titter at our old joke, which gave Declan his chance to hold my watery gaze.

"I'm OK," I lied. "I just need to be alone."

"You're tired." He moved his hands to my shoulders to massage them. "You've spent the last two and a half hours in that nursery with our newborn 'princess'."

I laughed a second time, "So my title has been taken away?"

"Sweetheart, that one month old in the other room could take out the worst of the prom queens." He said matter-of-factly.

Then we both laughed as he gently bumped his forehead into mine and he dried my face by rubbing it against his.

"So we have one daughter who doesn't listen to her mother, because I don't have the strength her European Werewolf father does. We have another daughter who isn't physically as strong as a European Werewolf, but has the mentality of one. Now we have the mother who's wondering why she wanted kids at all and hates her flabby body!" I sniffled.

"We'll sit Lucia down for a serious talk tomorrow." He decided. "But I've always played the dominant because we had to train her bloodlust."

"I know, Declan." I sighed heavily. "But I don't see why we both couldn't play the dominant."

"B, you're the mother so you're supposed to be softer." He reasoned. "Your body has to be, to carry the baby inside you then nurse it once it's out. Looch enjoys climbing into your lap for hugs more than she does from me. Now so does Soph, who's a newborn so she wants to be nestled. When I'm holding her with my hard body, it must be like being held by a brick wall."

"But Looch liked it when you held her when she was a baby," I frowned.

"Yeah but she's tougher than Sophia." He continued. "I think you're right about our newborn, though. Our youngest hasn't got the strength of a European Werewolf but she's got the personality of one instead. She's already showing territorial behaviour around you."

"I don't want our daughters to view us differently, Declan." I said emotionally. "When I was growing up, I saw my parents the same way. They took turns with cooking and cleaning and looking after me."

"You don't cook, I cook." He smiled softly. "It's the way I provide for my family, especially since I'm the house-hubby."

"Are you saying I should quit academic work and stay home with you, so our children will see us as equals?" I gave a funny look.

"I'm not saying that at all." He spoke calmly. "You're the brains and I'm the brawn, it's the way it's always been in our marriage. I used to work at the Garage as a mechanic and I enjoyed that. You've always been a bookworm, with your studies and presentations. We're like your parents in many respects; your father laboured away doing his handyman jobs and your mother was interested in books and circulating. When she was travelling through time, your father minded you. Now I'm staying home with the kids while you're off lecturing."

"If I helped you cook, would it change the way Lucia sees me?" I wondered.

"I doubt it," he said. "We have a five year old half European Werewolf who occasionally craves human flesh. This means we have to deal with a five year old's bloodlust. If you stood between her and a non-Lokoti human, her bloodlust would ram you over to reach its food source. But if I'm standing there instead, it knows it'd be running right into said brick wall."

I examined his face before I asked next, "Do you mind playing Lawkeeper for your young?"

"It's a fact of life." He shrugged it off. "It's either that or having my children turn into man-eaters. At least I can sleep at night, knowing my children aren't murderers."

My anger began to dissolve which made my hand reach out and run through his hair. Declan closed his eyes like he relished the touch, before he parted my legs to move closer. Then he remained like this, holding my legs apart as I felt his body heat emanate outwards from his torso.

"B," he spoke again, "when we first found out you were pregnant, I knew the role I was gonna play. Just as the pack taught me, I'm gonna teach my young. They acted like a wall to prevent me from knocking over my mother to eat the next human I saw and so shall I act for my young."

Next, his hands ran up and down my thighs as his mouth smothered my neck.

"Besides, I like what having my young does to your body..." he mumbled out, "...I like how your body changes and turns all soft like this."

"You mean it turns flabby," I said flatly.

"Mmm, something I can sink my teeth into." He spoke in a muffled voice, as his mouth moved down to my chest.

Then I noticed something strange, I wasn't enjoying my husband's touch. Instead of turning me on, it was turning me off. When Declan removed one of the straps of my negligee to free my left breast, I pulled away.

"Um, I'm not in the mood tonight." I said awkwardly, as I repositioned the garment.

"Of course," he tried to cover his disappointment. "You're worn out from looking after Soph all day."

Then he stood up and left the bathroom and I watched him undress in the bedroom. The sight of his muscled body would usually arouse me but for some reason, it didn't tonight. I even felt a little guilty because this had been the first time he'd made a move on me since Sophia's birth.

Although I'd completely regenerated after childbirth, I wasn't in the mood. I don't think it was a physical thing but it was a mental one instead. All I felt was tired, unattractive and emotionally worn out. Right then the idea of sex was about as appealing as labour pain.

*****

Not only was I feeling down about my appearance, but I was feeling downtrodden in general. Soph didn't help with her constant, high-pitched crying, which put the whole house on edge. It seemed like every time I put her down, she started up.

Our youngest preferred to nap in the baby carrier rather than her cot. It started to become the custom of carrying her this way, sometimes all day. She was quite happy to snooze in the carrier while I sat in the study, working on my papers. Looch would sit on the other side of the desk with her own laptop open, playing the spelling games that were part of her schoolwork.

One morning I moved my chair away from the desk to allow her room to climb into my lap to ask a question. Looch was careful not to bump Sophia who was slumbering away in the carrier. Sleepily, she opened her eyes and saw her sister in close proximity. Then her dark brown eyes glowed green as she started to scream.

"But I didn't bump her, Mummy!" Looch cried out in alarm.

"I know you didn't, darling." I sighed, as I gently lifted her off.

As soon as Soph saw the 'threat' had been removed, her screams died down to a high-pitch whining instead.

"Why does she cry like that?" She covered her ears. "Katrina and Hugh don't cry like that!"

"I don't know, Looch."

"I wish I had a little sister like Katrina, because she's nice and she likes it when I'm around!" Her eyes watered.

Then she ran out of the study, crying too. She must have run for her father, her beloved 'First' to be comforted. Next, I heard Declan speak to her in the kitchen.

"What's up, Looch?"

"Sophia doesn't like me!" She bawled.

"I'm sure she does sweetie, she's just very territorial of your mother." He sighed.

A moment later, he appeared in the doorway, holding our tearful first born in his arms.

"Maybe we should get Ki to check her out," he nodded towards our second born. "She does cry a hell of a lot."

Two hours later, Sophia was lying on top of the dining table with our tribe's Medicine Man waving a medical scanner over her. Of course she was crying again because she was away from her mother. Declan stood to the side, holding Looch in his arms as the two gazed on in dissatisfaction. Her little hands were over her ears and her father's face looked strained.

"I can't find anything physically wrong with her," Ki lowered his scanner. "Some babies can be very demanding, that's all."

I let out another sigh of defeat as I lifted up my youngest and replaced her inside the carrier. Like a switch had been turned off, Sophia turned silent. Not only did Declan and Looch notice, but so did our Medicine Man.

"Hmm," Ki looked on closely and for some reason he engaged his Werewolf vision and his eyes momentarily glowed pink. When his eyes returned to their dark colour, he gave his verdict. "I can see what's happening here."

"Yeah, she's territorial of her mother which is interfering with the rest of the family." Declan said in annoyance.

"She is but the question is why." Ki said coolly.

He packed his medical scanner back into his medicine bundle and looked like he was ready to leave.

"And the answer is?" Declan prompted.

"Sophia is an aura 'junkie'." He smirked.

"Say what?" My mate blinked.

"Well, you've heard of the saying 'a mother's glow'? Only in the case of Aunt B, it's literally." He explained. "Sophia likes to bask in her mother's aura, because she feels it let alone sees it. Whenever Aunt B holds her, or Soph is in the baby carrier, she's basking in her aura. When she's taken away from Aunt B, she loses the sensation which is why she cries."

"But I don't get it!" I cried impatiently. "Declan once told me he can feel my aura let alone see it, but I can't! What's the big deal about my frickin' aura?!"

Ki saw my exhausted appearance so he didn't take offence.

Patiently, he explained, "I can see your aura Aunt B, but I can't feel it." Then to prove his point, he touched my hand. "Nope, I can't feel a thing."

"Hey!" Declan fired up. "Hands off my wife or the next thing you'll be feeling is my fist!"

Hastily, our Medicine Man took a step away. "You see? Uncle Declan who can feel it, is acting with the same territorial behaviour Sophia is."

"Great...!" I growled out between gritted teeth.

I was beginning to feel a little too 'owned' by certain members of this family.

"However, I've heard that some Lokoti Werewolves like your European Werewolf husband can also feel a Circulator's aura." Ki went on. "Caesar told me that your grandfather and father could feel your grandmother and mother's auras. I imagine it's partly what attracted them."

"Actually, I think my first husband Grant could too." I mused.

Now, Declan growled out between gritted teeth, "Great, you just had to bring up THAT guy again, didn't you?"

"I can feel it," Looch volunteered. "Yours too, Daddy."

"Hang on, Looch is right." I thought aloud. "Declan has an aura too, so why doesn't Soph like being held by him?"

"Your aura is brighter than Uncle Dec's and your body is a lot softer than his." Our Medicine Man pointed out.

"Told you so," my mate sung gloatingly.

Ki nodded towards Soph sleeping against my front. "You could always try weaning tactics to lessen the clinginess."

"What do you mean?" I asked puzzled.

"Well, when human babies won't calm unless they're being held or rocked, the parents provide the babies with substitutes." He thought aloud. "Such as buying those vibrating baby bouncers."

My face fell, "How the hell do we find an artificial aura?"

"I don't know, but perhaps your husband could share what it's like when he's touching your aura and we'll see what we can do?" Ki looked in his direction.

Suddenly, my mate's face lit up for the whole room to see. He lowered Lucia to her feet then he grabbed his coat, wallet and remote key for the hover-car. As he headed for the front door, Looch followed him out.

"Daddy, can I come too?" She trailed behind.

As his answer, Declan held open the front door for her and joyfully she skipped outside.

"I'll be right back." He gave a wink then he closed the door behind.

"This should be interesting to see what he comes up with." Ki chuckled. "Unfortunately, I have to leave for another house call, but feel free to send a text message if his plan works."

Then I watched our Medicine Man pick up his old black leather doctor's case and he saw himself out.

I found myself standing alone in my living room as I was left holding the baby.

*****

An hour later, I heard our hover-car power down on the driveway outside. Soon after, the front door opened again and in skipped a reinvigorated Lucia. Her father walked in after her, carrying a medium sized box.

I was sitting at the dining table reading a book when she ran up with her face alight.

"Daddy bought me a hotdog and an ice cream for afternoon tea!" She beamed.

"Did he?" I looked to my husband, before I nodded towards the box he was carrying. "What's that?"

"Give me five minutes and when I call out, bring Soph upstairs." He smiled mysteriously.

Next, he disappeared up the staircase, taking the box with him.

"We have a surprise for you." Looch leaned in to kiss her sister's cheek.

Sleepily, Soph looked back from her snug position before she closed her eyes again.

True to his word, in five minutes we heard, "OK it's ready now!"

I went upstairs with Soph in the carrier and Looch hot on my heels. I walked down the hallway but before I went into the nursery, I stopped in surprise. I stood in the doorway, looking upon a glow lamp which was sitting on a bedside table beside the cot. Its' soft light changed colours from yellow to orange to pink to purple to blue to green and then back to yellow.

"A glow lamp?" I gave a peculiar look.

"It's a pretty, isn't it Mummy?" Looch looked on admiringly. "It looks like your aura when you're happy or mad."

Then Declan walked forwards and carefully lifted his baby daughter out of the carrier. Instantly, Sophia began to cry but he disregarded the noise. I watched him lay his baby down in the cot then pull the covers over her.

I stood transfixed as I watched the following occur; Declan tenderly rubbed her tummy in a soothing manner and Sophia actually stopped crying, as she looked at the glow lamp beside her bed. I saw her glowing green eyes return to their dark brown colour once more as she closed them. While she snoozed, her face remained turned in the direction of the lamp.

"Ladies and Gentlemen, we have a placated two month old." He grinned.

"But – but – but how?" I uttered out in surprise.

He held out his hand and I walked over to take it, before he pulled me close.

Together we stood over our slumbering babe with our five year old peering through the bars of the cot.

"The lamp changing colours like that is similar to your aura." He whispered in my ear.

I turned to look up into his face to find Declan's gaze waiting to hold my own.

He gave me an affectionate squeeze, "I know what it's like for her, coz I can't sleep if I don't have your body next to mine."

This made me wrap my arms about his waist and hug him in gratitude. At last, we have peace and quiet in the house! Declan ran his hands up and down my back in a soothing manner.

"Stick with me kid, I'll take care of you," he used his old joke.

*****

The difference the lamp made in the nursery was astounding. Soph cried less as she slept more in her cot, which was a relief to the whole household. Looch's mood improved and she paid more attention to what I said. I think she felt like she didn't have to fight for her mother's attention anymore.

However, I was still feeling down and the sight of my flabby body didn't help. I even began to face away from the mirror when I brushed my teeth. My cravings were just as bad as when I was pregnant, which I couldn't understand. I'd tell myself 'no snacking between meals', but I couldn't stop myself from opening up the fridge mid afternoon.

My husband didn't mind my post-pregnant body. What I called flab he called curvaceous or love handles. At night, his hands would run over my body as he enjoyed squeezing the soft flesh. I didn't mind this kind of touching but when he became turned on, I was turned off.

This was the third time Declan tried to initiate sex. I was lying on my side with my husband spooning me from behind. His large hand ran down my side as his wet mouth left a moist trail down my spine. I could feel his hot body turn even hotter which indicated how aroused he was. But when I felt him try to remove my negligee, I stopped him.

"No Declan."

"Huh?"

"I don't want to."

"Aw c'mon B!" He moaned. "It's been nine weeks since you gave birth! Surely you've regenerated by now?"

I frowned as I sat upright in bed and readjusted my clothes. "It's not that."

"Then what is it?"

"I don't know..." I said, "...I'm just not in the mood."

"You're never in the mood since Soph was born!" He growled unhappily.

Frustrated, he rolled onto his back as he rubbed his face.

"I know and I don't know why it is," I said in a small voice.

"Do you need some blood to regenerate?"

"No," I gave a funny look. "I said I wasn't injured from Sophia's birth."

"Then what is it?" He asked disappointedly.

"I don't know." My eyes dropped guiltily. "I just don't feel attracted to you or turned on or anything."

He sat up indignantly, "Did you just say you don't feel attracted to me?!"

"No – well yes – I mean no. I don't know!" I snapped. "I don't know what's wrong with me! I just don't want to."

He growled a second time in annoyance then after a moment he put his arm about my waist.

"Maybe you just need more foreplay or something?" He shrugged.

"I don't think that's it." I looked away.

The husband sat in bed beside his disinterested wife as he pondered what to do.

"OK, I'm not a telepath so you're gonna have to tell me what's going on in your head." He spoke bluntly. "What's wrong?"

"It's just that..." my voice trailed off.

"Yes?"

"I mean, I like it when you're stroking me and kissing me but..."

"But what?"

"But that's where it ends," I said uncomfortably. "I don't want anymore than that."

"Say what?" He blinked in surprise, like he couldn't believe what he just heard.

"I know, it sounds wrong!" I cried out. "But that's what's going on in my head right now."

"OK - OK - OK!" He waved his hand for silence. "You like me touching you, right?"

"Yes."

"Then that's a good starting point, don't you think?"

Now that gave me pause as I passed him a peculiar look.

He continued, "When you were pregnant, you wanted gentle sex, right?"

"Er, yes...?"

"Maybe you still need that while your body is all soft like this." He thought aloud.

"Oh." I pondered his words. "But I thought you were getting bored of gentle sex."

"Bored?!" He cracked up laughing. "What gave you that idea?"

"I thought you were thinking that once Sophia was out, we would go back to our bedroom marathons."

"B, right now you could demand we put on moose costumes and I'd agree to it!" He chuckled.

This made me laugh, especially when I pictured the scenario complete with moose noises.

Declan leaned in to kiss my bare shoulder before caressing my cheek with his nose.

"Come here, Mrs. Sabre."

Gently, he lifted me into his lap so I was straddling him.

I hung my arms about his neck as his lighter blue eyes gazed into my darker blue ones. While maintaining eye-contact, the next contact he made was with his lips. Softly, he kissed his wife over and over as his hands ran up and down her back. The massage was relaxing and I began to respond to his advances.

Our tongues touched as his hands pulled me closer so our crotches were touching too. I felt his arousal through our underwear and this time it didn't put me off. His kissing turned sensuous with his mouth occasionally leaving mine to nuzzle my neck or to chew on my ear.

He put such effort into his tender love making that my body couldn't help but to respond...

Afterwards, I laid over him in bed with my face tucked into his neck.

"That wasn't so bad, was it?" He teased, as he held me closely.

"You can be very gentle when you want to be." I remarked.

"Yeah but if you tell anyone, I'll deny it." He joked.

Playfully, I pinched him on the nipple and he laughed out loud.

"If someone told me a century ago that I was married to a gentle man, I would've laughed in their face." I mused. "We were at a very different stage of our lives, back then."

"Yep, we sure were."

Then I raised my head so I could peer into his eyes as I asked my next question. "Do you miss it?"

"What, life with no kids?"

"Yeah."

He hesitated for a moment but eventually he answered with, "Nope."

I opened my mouth to say, "sometimes I do," but then I stopped myself.

"Hmm...?" He looked on curiously, sensing I was holding back.

Guiltily, my head dropped down and I hid my face in his neck again.

*****

The tension inside our home seemed to ease, with our problems in the bedroom and the nursery somewhat solved. The next two months passed quickly and quietly with no great catastrophe. Looch behaved herself and paid attention to her lessons. Declan happily cooked three meals a day, including a little something extra for afternoon tea. The household seemed content and life carried on... until the end of Sophia's fourth month.

Although she was born in human form, her development was very much a Werewolf one. In fact, her growth rate mirrored Lucia's as did her early achievements such as reacting to noises, moving around and sitting up. On this note, her teething occurred earlier and what made it more difficult was not one or two teeth appeared, but all of them came up.

Sophia's teething was not just hard on her, but it was for the whole family. She returned to her constant crying because of the pain. Ki made many house calls during this period as he doled out medication to try to lessen her discomfort.

We tried Children's Panadol which didn't work long on her. He also gave us a special gel to rub on her sore gums which was supposed to numb them. However, when I was using my index finger to carefully apply the gel inside her mouth, Sophia deliberately bit me!

"Oow!" I pulled away in surprise.

Declan came into the nursery. "What's wrong?"

"She just bit me!" I showed him the blood oozing out of the tiny teeth marks.

He looked down on his five month old in mild surprise, before he looked out the bedroom window.

"It is that time of the month," he remarked.

I walked over to the window to see a perfect white circle of the full moon, high in the blue sky.

"Tonight I'll bring back some extra fresh kill." He organized as he rolled up his sleeve. "Some for Mommy Werewolf and some for Baby Werewolf."

Next, I watched Declan raise his wrist to his mouth and extend his teeth so they became longer and sharper. He used them to put a deep, bloody gash on the inside of his right arm. Then using his left arm, he scooped up his young and rested his injury over her mouth.

Immediately, Sophia began to suckle on the wound. Her dark brown eyes looked up appreciatively at her daddy. I saw a new understanding pass between father and daughter that day. Her other European Werewolf features were coming out, which gave her something in common with him.

Declan sharing his blood solved two problems that morning; it appeased her bloodlust and the regenerative properties in his life-giving liquid worked better than children's medicine. The pain in her gums diminished and rather than dosing her with medicine, she drank her father's healing blood.

However at 3 AM that night, I paced around and around the dining table exhausted by Sophia's constant crying. I was waiting for Declan and Looch to come home from the hunt and I sensed Sophia was sobbing in pain. Instead of her gums hurting, it was her stomach. Her bloodlust was spiking and I tried feeding her blood from my wrist, but she wanted her father's.

Suddenly, the backdoor was thrown open and my husband wearing his bloodied bathrobe appeared. He carried in a hind leg of moose which he'd ripped off his prey. Looch ran in after him, still in her Werewolf form and in her blood-sodden gym clothes.

He kicked shut the door behind then he strode into the kitchen. Next, he dumped the dripping hind leg onto the kitchen bench. Our eldest tried to reach for the tasty offering, but Declan gently pushed her aside.

"No Looch, you've already feasted on fresh kill tonight." My mate said sternly. "Now it's Soph's and Mommy's turn to eat."

Our youngest cried louder from the smell of the blood as I rocked her in my arms.

Expertly, Declan extended his nails to rip the hide off then strip the meat off the bone. Looch hung around in hope of more, so he gave her the bone to gnaw on. Happily, she took the offering then sat in a corner of the kitchen floor, nibbling off any remaining flesh.

My arms were sore from rocking Soph all night and her shrill cries had given me a headache. I think my own bloodlust was adding to my irritability. It seemed like forever for him to come home and now to prepare the food.

"What took you so long?!" I raised my voice over the crying. "You left the house at 7 PM and you said you'd be back around midnight!"

"We hunted on the north side of the National Park." Declan said casually, as he dropped the still-warm meat into the food processor. Then he smiled proudly on his eldest, "Looch fought and feasted on a wolverine tonight."

Then he turned on the machine which added to all the noise and made my headache worse.

"She's too young to kill on her own!" I snapped.

"If she tried to take down a bear or another large animal, I'd agree with you." He spoke calmly. "But she attacked that wolverine so fast, it didn't know what hit him. She ripped out its throat before it could react, you should have seen her."

Now that he's mentioned it, I did notice some new holes in her clothes which looked like they could have come from an animal's claws.

"Declan," I marched up angrily, "you're suppose to kill and then she's supposed to feed!"

"Relax B," he turned off the food processor before he took off the lid. "I had my eye on her the whole time. Besides, her bloodlust is growing just as she is. I can't kill for her all the time, otherwise she isn't satiated. Remember, a Werewolf likes to take their prey down fighting."

Declan scooped up some minced moose meat from the processor then he put some fresh kill into his baby's mouth. I stopped arguing to watch her reaction. This would be the first time Sophia's eaten something that's not breast milk, mashed up food, or her father's blood.

Her glowing green eyes widened at first from the strange sensation of using her new teeth. But her crying stopped and she looked to her father for more. Declan smiled softly on her as he loaded up his hand then moved it to her mouth.

"Here," he took Soph out of my arms. "I'll feed the baby and you feed yourself."

He nodded towards the stripped flesh sitting in a pool of blood, on the kitchen bench. But that bloodied body part didn't appeal to me at all. In fact, his previous words, 'a Werewolf likes to take their prey down fighting,' rebounded inside my head. I was getting tired of eating second-hand kill. I wanted to go out and murder something myself!

"I'm going out," I declared, as I walked out of the kitchen.

"Say what?" Declan did a double take.

"I'm going hunting." I said coolly.

Then I opened the front door and shut it loudly behind.

I stood still on the front veranda with my eyes closed, relishing the quiet of the night. I felt my nightie tighten over my body as it expanded with its Werewolf muscle. At the same time, I felt the nails on my hands and feet extend, as did my teeth. When I opened my eyes again, the night was lit up as clear as day, thanks to my night-vision.

Just then the front door opened and my husband came out.

"B, I don't think you should hunt tonight and definitely not alone." He said warily. "Your body is softer than it usually is, even in Werewolf form."

But I ignored his concerns by jumping down the veranda steps then racing into the surrounding woods.

"B!" He called after.

I ran in supernatural speed down the hill. Then I ran in a northerly direction, as if some small part of me was hoping to find the pack and join them. My bloodlust made me sick of being the stay-at-home mother on a full moon. I zoomed through the woods, leaping over log, rock or bush alike, as I felt my hair stream behind.

However, the further I ran, I sensed that the pack were long gone. They'd hunted and feasted and went home the same time Declan had. I'd have to hunt on my own this time, which was a lonely thought.

I sniffed the night air as I ran, to catch wind of something to kill. The bloodlust hurt my stomach and it made me run faster in desperation. I knew I'd have to feed soon before the agonizing cramps started.

Finally, I caught wind of something large and warm-blooded, which made my mouth water. I veered left towards the tempting scent. I raced through the moonlit forest that had a little snow lying around from an early fall. It made the ground cold and hard, but nothing my clawed feet couldn't handle.

Just then I leapt out of the tree line and into an open area. I found myself on a grassy slope which looked brightly lit. Surrounding it was more dark woods and the snow-tipped peaks of the Alaska Range. The snow looked like it shone under the moonlight.

But it was another kind of light in the distance which attracted my attention. It was ground level and orange in colour and from the smell of things, it was a campfire. However, what made me pause was the fact it was also in the direction of the delicious smell I was tracking.

Oh no, don't tell me I'd just tracked some campers? What the hell is wrong with me?! I should know the difference between human and animal scent. I haven't craved human in centuries! Maybe the fact that I haven't hunted in twelve months has disrupted my feeding pattern...

My stomach growled as my teeth grew longer by the intoxicating aroma. I could smell it was a man and woman by their different hormones. They were sitting close to the fire to stave off the icy night and the heat made them smell delicious.

Before I knew it, I'd lowered myself to the ground and was stalking towards them on my hands and knees. I crept closer without making a sound. Drool escaped my open mouth which my sharp teeth jutted out of.

When I peered over the long grass to take another look at my prey, I saw something else. An Alsatian was sitting beside the humans and it looked in my direction. It smelled just as edible as the campers, if not more so, which made more drool trickle down my chin.

The animal began to bark as it leapt to its feet in alarm! Its sudden reaction startled the couple, who also rose. The woman reached for a torch as the man went for a laser rifle, which was resting against a cooler.

I growled back at the dog as I started to go into an attack posture of my own, when the woman shone the torch my way.

Quickly, I dropped to the ground to duck from the beam of light and the force also knocked some sense back into me.

B, what the hell are you doing?! There is NO WAY you can eat the humans, no ethical or moral way at all! You're losing your mind! Now get out of here before they see you and report what they saw.

Slowly, I started to wriggle backwards on my stomach, to get away. However, the Alsatian sniffed I was in retreat which empowered it to attack. My bloodlust made me stop, as it waited to feast on its' flesh.

The dog leapt out of the human's campsite as it ran towards me with its jaws open and ready...

...when I felt myself lifted up from the ground as a large, bright blur running in light speed surprised me, the dog and the humans....

...in the blink of an eye, it ran into the tree line with me slung over its' back, leaving behind a pair of confused campers and a whimpering dog.

It was Declan in Werewolf form, galloping in light speed, which made him indistinguishable to the humans but the Alsatian had caught a sniff of him.

The animal guessed the other canine-like creature had run to the aid of its mate, which made the Alsatian duck to the ground in a submissive posture. It whimpered pathetically, as if its life had flashed before its eyes. The humans didn't know it was caused by one of the world's most dangerous predators.

I didn't see much more after that, so I had no idea what the campers might have said. I was too busy being knocked around by the jarring of his muscled back as he ran on all-fours. I think we were over 20 km's away from the human's campsite, before he stopped.

Safely ensconced amongst the tall, dark trees of the vast forest, he dropped his nightie-clad wife onto the cold, hard earth. As soon as my arse hit the ground, I had the enraged canine face of my European Werewolf husband in mine. His glowing green eyes burned with fury.

WHAT THE HELL ARE YOU DOING?! – He thought angrily – *HUNTING HUMAN, ARE YOU NUTS?!*

But I couldn't answer him, because I was scared he was right. I don't think I would have actually attacked the humans, but I would have given myself away when I ate their dog. What the hell is wrong with me?!

Next, Declan paced around on all-fours where I was sitting, as if he were guarding me from doing anything else so stupid.

"Hang on, if you're here then who's with the kids?" I spoke in my deep, rumbling Werewolf voice.

CAESAR AND FOREST ARE MINDING THE GIRLS – He rolled his eyes – *OR DO YOU THINK I'VE LOST MY MIND TOO, BY LETTING A FIVE YEAR OLD LOOK AFTER A FIVE MONTH OLD?*

My glowing turquoise eyes turned downcast as I felt the hot tears well up. I felt embarrassed, angry and still hungry. I just couldn't shake this caged-in feeling which was driving my foolishness.

I CAME AFTER YOU BECAUSE I WAS SCARED YOU COULD BE INJURED BY THE LARGE ANIMAL YOU TRIED TO HUNT – Declan fumed – *BUT I DIDN'T THINK I'D EVER HAVE TO STOP YOU FROM HUNTING HUMAN AGAIN.*

"I don't know what came over me," I rumbled out, "I didn't even know I was tracking human until I saw them."

WHEN I TOLD CAESAR WHY I NEEDED HIM TO MIND THE KIDS, HE SUGGESTED WE GET KI TO CHECK YOU OUT – My mate continued – *AT FIRST I SAID NO BUT NOW I THINK WE SHOULD.*

"I don't know what's wrong with me, Declan." I said tearfully. "I'm angry all the time. I feel trapped by the kids and I feel guilty for not enjoying motherhood."

THE ANGER IS INTERFERING WITH YOUR BLOODLUST – He thought grimly – *IT'S MAKING IT WORSE.*

"I think you're right." I sighed defeated, which sounded like a soft growl. "And I don't know what to do."

ON THE NEXT FULL MOON YOU SHOULD HUNT WITH THE PACK AND I'LL STAY HOME - He offered.

"But your bloodlust is worse than mine, you wouldn't be able to cope with second-hand kill."

Then I heard him growl under his breath before he thought back - *YOU'RE RIGHT, WHATEVER YOU BROUGHT BACK FROM THE HUNT WOULDN'T SATISFY ME UNLESS I KILLED IT MYSELF.*

He stopped pacing around his mate to sit beside her instead and contemplate what to do.

"It's the kill that's important," I said in my deep voice. "It's the sensation of taking life before consuming it."

YOU GOT THAT RIGHT - He sighed, which came out as a long pant.

"It's the fight and the victory of dominating your prey..." I rumbled out, "...then the sweet sensation of that first taste."

My canine-like husband turned his beastly head to look down on his wife sitting beside.

NOW YOU'RE PREACHING TO THE CHOIR - He agreed.

Frustrated, I rubbed my face with my clawed hands, "I really wanted to hunt tonight."

IT'S BEEN TOO LONG - He recognized where this was coming from.

Then he stood up on all-fours once more and came to stand directly in front.

C'MON B, DOMINATE ME - he said.

"Say what?" I blinked my glowing turquoise eyes in surprise.

TRY TO DOMINATE ME LIKE YOU WOULD DOMINATE YOUR PREY - he challenged.

"What...?" I looked on askance.

DRAW BLOOD, OR TRY TO - he growled, as his front right claw pawed at the ground.

"I'm not hunting you." I gave a funny look.

C'MON, I KNOW YOU WANT TO - He panted hard.

"I'm not hurting you, Declan." I looked away in objection.

WHAT KIND OF WEREWOLF ARE YOU? - He taunted.

Just then he shoved me with his front right claw and I was knocked backwards onto the ground.

That was it... it was all my already heightened bloodlust needed.

Snarling, I sprang to my feet in a crouched position, ready to strike.

C'MON THEN - he lowered his head and bared his teeth - *ATTACK ME.*

I felt an uncontrollable rage inside which made me tremble at its force. It had been steadily climbing the past five months, since Sophia's birth. My heart didn't just pound inside my chest, it beat the blood through my veins with blunt force. The pressure resounded in my ears and turned my skin hot.

Irrationally, I hated him for impregnating me, for putting me through childbirth. I hated him for his body not changing like mine did. I hated him for not spending more time with Sophia like he had with Lucia. I hated him for making me miss out on hunting with the pack.

As if he sensed this, he took a defensive posture as I went into an attack stance.

"It's your fault!" I seethed. "It's all your fault!"

THEN DO SOMETHING ABOUT IT - he leered.

He leered at me, as if I were a weak woman who couldn't defend herself.

I bared my sharp, elongated teeth as I sunk lower to the ground, with my legs tense and ready to spring.

C'MON, WHAT ARE YOU WAITING FOR?

My bloodlust raged at his taunts, but my protective Lokoti Werewolf instincts stayed my claws. He was my mate whom I had to protect. A male Lokoti Werewolf would be tender towards his other half and shelter her from harm. Then again, I'm not a male Lokoti Werewolf and I wasn't married to a human female, I was mated to the worst breed of Werewolf in the world...

WHAT WILL IT TAKE, B? - he pawed at the ground again.

I started to shake by the bloodlust beating down my body.

COME AND GET IT!

We both sprang into the air like two fierce fighters! He looked a lion with his claws closing around and I looked like an enraged female Lokoti Werewolf, with her long nails and teeth ready. However, with his greater weight, I fell backwards with the large male over me.

He tried to pin my arms and legs to the ground, but I writhed out of his hold.

Next, my right fist swung round and hit him on his canine jaw, but he didn't react. Then my left fist pounded him again, but he didn't flinch. The force of my blows didn't even make his head move.

"Change to human!" I growled out. "Change to human!"

I wanted to see my blows do some damage but it wasn't going to work in his stronger body.

NOT YET - he thought back.

I used both of my legs to knee him off before I swung around my right foot and kicked him in the snout. This time his head did turn and it gave me my chance to jump to my feet. He too raised himself onto all-fours then we circled the other warily.

He raised his left claw in a lazy swing and I saw that he deliberately missed. But it didn't stop me from retaliating, as I swung around my right claw and swiped him with my long nails. Four scratch marks appeared on the left side of his canine head, but with his hardened hide they weren't that deep.

IS THAT THE BEST YOU CAN DO? - he goaded.

I roared out a battle cry as I jumped onto his large back and dug my claws in. He roared in return and tried to shake me off, but I clung on. He started to run around in a circle, as he jumped around to loosen my hold, but I hung on.

CAREFUL NOW - he warned.

Then he rolled over on the ground to force me off. Declan did it quickly so that I'd lose my grip but I wouldn't be crushed in the process. As soon as I was down, he tried to pin me a second time.

"No way Jose!" I growled.

I grabbed hold of his thick neck in a strangle hold but it was so wide, my hands couldn't go all the way around.

"I can't fight you in this body!" I cried out exasperated.

HIT ME B, I CAN TAKE IT - he thought - *HIT ME AS MUCH AS YOU LIKE, IT'S WHY I'M IN THIS FORM.*

I blinked in surprise as I looked up at the beast with the scorching breath and the dangerous jaws.

C'MON, DON'T JUST LIE THERE - Declan demanded - *HIT ME AS HARD AS YOU CAN.*

So that's it, he's using himself to placate my bloodlust. He's remaining in his virtually indestructible form to be my punching bag. His selfless act stunned me and instead I lay on the freezing earth, staring up at him.

He used his left claw to try to nudge me back to life, but I simply laid there. To show him I wasn't going to fight anymore, I reverted back to human. I felt my nails and teeth retreat back into my body as it deflated into my flabby form. The forest floor felt a lot colder without my muscle bulk protecting me.

I heard him emit a confused whine as he looked down on his weaker wife.

However, my reversion had another repercussion as I was cruelly reminded why I'd changed to Werewolf in the first place; the bloodlust.

Suddenly, the hideous cramps ripped through my abdomen, making me curl up in a ball on my side.

"Oh shit!" I gasped.

I hadn't experienced stomach pains caused from the bloodlust in centuries! Usually, I'd feasted on fresh kill before the pain kicked-in. It hurt when we didn't eat and right then as I rocked myself in a foetal position, I wished I hadn't of been so fussy by dismissing that second-hand kill back home.

B? - my mate looked on in alarm.

But I couldn't answer as I writhed in agony. My stomach ached as my rocking turned into convulsing because the pain shot down my arms and legs. The torture was immobilising and I couldn't think clearly.

Declan didn't waste any time, he raised his right wrist to his sharp jaws, bit down on it then shoved the bleeding gash into my mouth.

My lips closed around the wound and I drank in his life force.

I've tasted my husband numerous times before but tonight, I swear his blood never tasted so good. The slightly sweet but salty texture of the hot, red liquid filled my mouth and I gulped it down. I even sucked on the wound to draw it out faster, as every mouthful lessened the trauma.

I swallowed mouthful after mouthful as the pain lifted and a sense of satisfaction took its place. His high temperature also lessened the chill of the earth beneath me. My body stopped shaking and in a relaxed state, I rolled onto my back whilst tugging his arm along with me.

"Mmm...!" I moaned in delight.

Declan settled beside me on the ground and I heard the familiar sound of his bones cracking, which meant he was changing. I watched him shrink back into his human body, as his hardened hide turned into softer skin and his four claws turned into two hands and feet. His glowing green eyes remained though to see in the dark. He used them to examine his mate as his other hand smoothed back her messy hair.

"Are you OK?" He asked in concern.

I nodded as I clung onto his arm and kept drinking, I couldn't stop myself. He tasted too good, he made me feel warm, strong and most of all, fulfilled. The sense of satisfaction soon turned into desire and I wanted more of him.

I pulled his naked body over mine and he guessed what I was trying to do. He positioned himself between my legs as his free hand lifted up my nightie. Once it was raised it past my hips, he removed my underwear which was a bit of a challenge using only one hand. I helped him by lifting my hips off the ground then I felt him tug them down my legs.

Now our groins were bared and they pressed against the other's. He raised my legs on either side of him and I knew what he wanted. I squeezed his hips so he could feel ensconced between my thighs. He groaned as he lifted himself higher and rubbed his member around my clit. I groaned too as he did this a couple of times, making me wet with excitement.

To my dismay, he took his arm away from my mouth to use it to hold himself up. Then he slowly pushed himself inside as he lowered himself again. I felt his hand move behind my head and lift it towards his shoulder. I sensed what he wanted me to do and I did it; I bit down. My teeth dug into his flesh until I tasted his blood again. Next, he started to move slowly as I clung to him while drinking in his essence.

He groaned a second time as he felt my body open itself up to him. My legs wrapped themselves about his waist as I enveloped him in a passionate embrace. He groaned as he pushed deeper with each thrust, as if he were trying to make the two of us into one.

He moved at a slow but steady rhythm that wouldn't disrupt my drinking. His hot blood coursed down my throat as his hot body rubbed against mine and his hot member throbbed inside. All of this melted into bliss and I felt the build up to an orgasm begin. My arms wrapped about his torso and I held on tightly, as both of our eyes drifted shut and we moved by instinct alone.

"Oh - oh - oh!" He uttered out helplessly and I felt him come.

The hot wetness in my groin combined with the hot wetness in my mouth was just what I needed. I felt my inner muscles spasm as the prior pleasure and bliss ballooned throughout my body in a single wave of ecstasy. Although it was slow to arrive and it was quick to leave; it left me feeling warm, wet and divine.

"Woah, that's enough now..." he raised himself away from my mouth, "...I'm starting to feel dizzy."

My eyes popped open in alarm at the harm I'd caused but he gave a reassuring grin.

"It's alright, the dizziness feels good with the sex." He joked. "It's part of the pleasure."

I looked on his face to see he was telling the truth and that he really was alright.

"We should have sex like this more often," he snickered.

In concern, I pulled him back down to lap at the wound with my tongue, to speed up his regeneration.

"Oh that feels good," he moaned. "Just a little more and you're done."

I licked at his broken skin until I couldn't taste his blood anymore and when I removed my mouth, I saw new pink skin in its place.

"C'mon, we'd better head home," he sighed.

Declan stood up first then he reached down and pulled me to my feet. Next, he instantaneously phased us home in a bright flash of light. Gone was the feel of the forest floor beneath my feet, now they felt the tiled floor of our ensuite.

My mate lifted up my dirty nightie over my head and dropped it into the washing basket. Then he guided us into the shower and turned on the water. Under the steady stream we lathered up using our individual shower gels and washed off any blood and dirt which was stuck to our skin.

I got out of the shower first and dried myself when he turned off the water and joined me. Together, we brushed our teeth then we went out into the bedroom. I pulled on another nightie as he tugged on a pair of boxers then he put a bathrobe on.

"I'm gonna go downstairs and let Caesar and Forrest know we're home," he said.

I watched him depart from the bedroom before I climbed into bed.

Soon I heard our front door open and close then the sound of my husband's footfall as he came back upstairs.

He took off his robe before he came to bed too. He rolled onto his side so he could hold me better and I settled in his embrace. He ducked his head and inhaled my wet hair before kissing the top of my head.

"Declan," I broke the silence.

"Hmm...?"

"Please don't tell Caesar or Ki that I almost hunted human tonight."

He was quiet for a moment which made me look up so I could see his eyes.

Our gazes met and held and I saw his bright blue eyes fill with understanding.

"I know it wasn't you B and I'm not gonna say anything to anybody." He said.

I was touched by his loyalty and my eyes filled with tears as I ducked my head again.

"Shhh," he leaned in to place a kiss on my forehead. "Don't be sad, I know you didn't mean to."

"It's not that," I sniffed. "You're a wonderful husband who's been burdened with a crazy Werewolf for a wife."

"You, a crazy Werewolf? Yeah right!" He scoffed. "B, do you know how many times in my life I've almost hunted human?"

"Um, I know of a couple..." I thought aloud, "...and in New Orleans you actually did hunt human."

"How many humans have you killed, B?"

"Um, none...?"

"So there you go, you're the wife who's shacked up with the crazed killer Werewolf."

He made me laugh and I buried my face in his chest to show my appreciation.

"I love you B," he gave an affectionate squeeze. "And besides, tonight wasn't all bad. I thought the sex was pretty good. Although, you do need to brush up on your self-defence, your punches were pretty poor."

"Oh shut up."

"Seriously, you could barely hurt an Asian Werewolf with how flimsy they were and they're the weakest of all the breeds."

"Declan, you're ruining the moment."

He snickered as he held onto his wife tighter then he settled down to sleep like that.

*****

"Hmm," Ki stroked his chin as he looked on the readouts of his medical scanner.

I was sitting on the couch after having been scanned. My husband sat beside me, with our young sitting on the rug by the fire. Lucia was colouring in with crayons that Sophia was trying out her new teeth on.

On the opposite couch sat Caesar and Forrest, who came to hear our Healer's verdict. I guess my 'walkabout' last night worried them. Declan had served coffee along with a plate of choc chip cookies in an effort to make this visit a social one, but nobody was eating or drinking.

Ki was sitting on the edge of our coffee table with his medicine bundle open. The medical scanner in his hand was beeping away, alerting everyone of its results. The only eyes which weren't on Ki or his equipment belonged to our young. Lucia picked up another crayon to colour in with, ignoring the tiny teeth marks and drool it had on it.

"What is it, Ki?" Our First prompted.

"Aunt B, can you tell me more about how you've been feeling these past five months?" He queried.

I shared an anxious look with Declan as he rested one of his larger hands over mine.

"Um, I can't stop eating." I confessed. "Sometimes I eat even when I'm not hungry, but I still crave food."

"Her servings have increased." Declan added. "Sometimes she eats as much as I do."

"I didn't think anybody could match your appetite." Forest joked.

"Do you think your emotional well-being will improve with food, but no matter how much you eat you still feel down?" Ki guessed.

"Yes," I looked on in surprise, "how did you know that?"

"It's called binge eating." He said matter-of-factly, lowering the scanner. "It's a common symptom of depression."

Declan sat up like cold water had just been thrown over him. "Depression?!"

"Aunt B has depression?" Caesar asked concerned.

"No – no – no – no!" My mate quickly shook his head. "MY wife does NOT have depression!"

Ki half turned so he could explain to both his First as well as his patient. "After scanning Aunt B's brain chemistry and then hearing of her behaviour, I can say she's exhibiting signs of postnatal depression."

"But I'm a Werewolf, I thought only humans get that." I looked from the Healer to my husband, "So I'm sick then, is that it?"

"I can prescribe a low dose of antidepressants which will correct the chemical imbalance and I also recommend counselling sessions -" Ki began.

However, he was interrupted by my husband's raised voice:

"Don't tell my wife there's something wrong with her, or I'll physically make something wrong with YOU!"

His quick temper made Ki blanch and Caesar frown, but our children carried on as normal. They didn't even look up, as Looch coloured in with a chewed-on green crayon and Soph put the yellow one into her mouth next. Both of our daughters were accustomed to their parents' growls and snarls.

"If you don't believe me Uncle Declan, I can show you the readings so you can see for yourself." Ki said.

However, Caesar caught my mate's eyes begin to glow green so he tried another tact.

"Perhaps you could tell us Uncle how you see your wife's behaviour?"

"Heaven," he summed up in one word.

This made my face warm while the other three Lokoti Werewolves in the room blinked in disbelief.

"But hasn't Aunt B been behaving erratically?" Ki asked puzzled.

"Yeah and so what?" He shrugged it off. "She's the mate of a European Werewolf who has half breed young, so there's bound to be some changes."

"As a medical professional, I understand that Uncle," our Medicine Man said. "But these days postnatal depression can be easily treated -"

"Come near B with any kind of treatment and I'll shove it so far up your behind you'll need at least two operations to retrieve it." He spoke in a dangerously low voice.

Ki looked to Caesar for help, so he cleared his throat as he sat forwards.

"Aunt B, how do you feel about the idea of medication or counselling?" He asked.

"Um," I looked downwards, feeling a little embarrassed. "If Ki thinks I need it, then maybe I do...?"

"C'mon B, so you're a little hormonal?" My mate tried to hold my gaze. "What's different now compared to the last 300 years of your PMS?"

"Declan!" I elbowed him in the side.

"Besides, it's nice seeing you eat more and yell more." He shrugged.

"Declan...!" I blushed as I ducked my head.

"I loved your scent and your temper when you were on heat for over two centuries." He continued. "I loved seeing your body change shape when you carried my young. So you're hormonal after our babies are born? So what? Sweetie, you're a Werewolf so you're supposed to be temperamental. It's a little thing we have in common called the 'bloodlust'."

"Oh Declan!" I giggled out.

Next, my husband wrapped his arms about my waist as he held me close.

“How about I make your favourite for dinner; fettuccine carbonara and tiramisu for desert?” He offered.

“Mmm...!” I licked my lips at the sound of it.

Then he leaned in to kiss his wife tenderly until he was interrupted by the sounds of three different people clearing their throats.

“Food and sex, is that all you think about?!” Ki flared.

In indignation he proceeded to pack up his medical scanner, as Forest and Caesar smiled in amusement.

Lucia looked up, “Are we having tiramisu for dessert?”

Next, the three visitors exchanged looks of amusement at how this piece of news captured her attention, but not the other.

“We sure are,” her father smiled on his young.

Then the room watched Declan lean over to remove the crayon from Sophia’s mouth and replace it with a biscuit instead. Her little hands grabbed hold of the cookie which she removed to examine. Then as if she thought to herself ‘oh well,’ she returned the biscuit and tried to crunch on it.

My husband handed over another biscuit to his eldest, stroked his daughters’ hair, then he sat back and returned his arm about his wife.

“All seems right in the Sabre household,” Caesar remarked to his father.

“If a day goes past where food can’t cure all ills in this family, then I’d be REALLY worried.” Forest chuckled back.

~~~~~~
~~~~~~

~ 20 ~

6th June 2024

My name is Clara Winter and this is the first time I'm using this diary my Dad gave me for my 18th Birthday. He bought it with the idea I could use it as a cookbook, to jot down my recipes. I guess he didn't think I'd use it for much else, as he thinks like the rest of the tribe does, that I don't have much to say.

I'm a quiet person, the tribe calls me 'as silent as a still wind'. Because I don't talk much, people misunderstand me. They take my silence as judgmental, or they see me as boring because they think I have nothing to contribute.

My best friend May Elm knows better, she relies on my silent support. She can chatter non-stop but it's only because she feels she has to fill the silence with conversation, even if it is one-sided. Some people think of her as a chatterbox and my parents say, "that girl can talk the hind leg off a dog!" But I don't mind her noise like she doesn't mind my quietness.

We've been best friends for so long, sometimes she says what I'm thinking. Why talk when May can speak for me? And she likes it when I bake because I let her lick the beaters.

My parents know when we're together, from the delicious smell wafting from the kitchen and the sound of May's chatter. But when they come in to ask what I'm making, they cringe when she starts talking at them a hundred miles an hour. Politely, they come up with an excuse to leave and she looks hurt in my direction.

"Clara, you're gonna have to start pinching me on the arm when I talk too much," her eyes looking haunted by rejection.

"I like it when you talk," I reassured, "you speak for the both of us."

Sometimes when we go to birthday parties for our cousins, we stand alone because no-one talks to us. I like to wear dresses as they look better on my short, rounded body. May is skinny with a flat chest though, so she looks better in jeans and tight t-shirts to embellish what assets she has.

Nearly everyone in our tribe is related by blood or marriage, so we have to be invited to gatherings otherwise it would slight our families. But usually after everyone's said their hellos, they move away to talk in larger groups. Then there's May and me, standing just the two of us. It's been like this since kindergarten. She used to chatter about her dolls, now she tries to cover her hurt by prattling on about her newest crush on a Hollywood actor.

However, something different happened two months ago at Keith Wisetail's 18th Birthday party - he talked to us.

Or rather he stood and listened to May while she chattered away extra fast because of nerves. She was wearing jeans and a tight red t-shirt, which matched her red lip gloss. I think Keith thought she looked pretty, he gazed on her as she talked so fast, she started to sound breathless.

Keith Wisetail is John Wisetail's grandson and the newest member of the pack. Keith joined the ranks when one of its members died. His father Mark Wisetail was too old for the change so Keith changed instead. Another member who was the closest to his age, David Riverclaw, was also at the party.

David is four years older than May and me. He's studying Civil Engineering by correspondence. He changed when he was Keith's age, which ended his mother's plans of sending him to University. Lokoti Werewolves can't leave tribal lands or else they wane. Everyone in the tribe knew who was one of the pack. They hunted on the full moon in their supernaturally strong bodies and acted as our tribe's protectors.

If there was an outsider illegally using firearms in the surrounding National Park, it was the Werewolves who intervened. The Lokoti Werewolves also policed tribal lands, with our Tribal Elders acting as both Judge and Jury. Last year when Martin Grey Sky beat his wife, the Werewolves brought him before the Elders. He was sent away with just the clothes on his back and his wife and child were taken in by her family.

I noticed the surprised looks from the other girls at the party, at how May had captured Keith's attention.

Unmarried members of the pack were treated a little like celebrities by the women in the tribe. When they went through the change, they became tall and strong. Keith's new muscle bulk was evident under his long-sleeved t-shirt. He smelled nice too, which I think were his Lokoti Werewolf pheromones that are meant to lure a mate. I think they were working on May, she was talking triple fast and the hand holding her soda was shaking.

Momentarily, I looked away and observed how David Riverclaw was trying to talk to a human his age named Will about his degree, but they were interrupted. One or two women at a time would walk up, place their hand on his arm and ask him a question. Sometimes they would flick their hair or stand really close to flirt with him, but he would take a step back.

I'd heard the story of how his father Flint Riverclaw, waited until he was in his seventies until he took a mate. The way the females at this party were throwing themselves at him, it was like they couldn't wait. But like his father, David Riverclaw didn't seem to be in any rush and he politely dissuaded them by his distant body language.

Just then he excused himself from his friend as well as the gaggle of girls and walked in this direction.

His dark Lokoti hair was cut short and thanks to his Caucasian mother, his skin was pale and his eyes were blue. But with his father's Lokoti Werewolf genes, he was tall and strong even in human form. He came to a stop beside me with a polite smile, before he looked on his fellow pack member and friend.

Keith looked away from May, "Hey David."

"Hey Keith," he returned, "listen I'm gonna take off, I have an assignment due which I have to email tomorrow."

"Well thanks for coming tonight." Keith shook his hand. "I'll catch up with you on the next full moon."

"That you will," he smiled before he nodded to May and I.

Then he turned and left but as he walked off, I caught a musky scent. It was masculine as well as natural smelling, reminding me of a fur tree. It gave a hint of something tall and strong.

The next day I went with May into Alma where we bumped into him again.

The small town next to tribal lands had a tiny population, with its one and only Bar, Milk Bar, Supermarket, a small Cinema -cum- Town Hall, and a Grade School-combined-High School. Our tribe used these facilities as we only had a small General Store, Garage and Meeting Hall in our community centre.

May was chattering about Keith's attention on her last night. I also heard how he walked her home after the party and when he could get a word in edgewise, he offered to take her to see a movie. She was so excited about this, she was talking four times as fast.

"But I don't know what to wear, Clara!" She wailed. "He's already seen my red top but it's the one that looks the best on me. What should I wear? Is my black t-shirt OK, or should I wear the dark green?"

I was so busy listening as we walked into the Milk Bar, that I wasn't looking where I was going and I walked into somebody who was coming out!

The side of my face hit something warm but hard and when I turned to see who it was, it was David Riverclaw. All of a sudden a strong musky scent hit me even harder than the impact had. It left me standing there blinking, as I breathed in deeply.

David and his friend Will smiled in amusement at my stunned expression. They must have been David's Lokoti Werewolf pheromones! Actually he smelled nicer than a fur tree, he scent was as refreshing as the river running through tribal lands.

He smiled, "You smell like a freshly baked cake."

My face heated up as I replied, "I baked one this morning for my grandmother's birthday."

He stepped aside while holding the door open for us and we went in.

May and I headed towards our favourite booth in the corner, when I paused to watch through the front windows David and Will depart. My heart was racing and I realized I finally had a crush on someone. I'd never had a crush before, but by my racing heart and how my skin warmed, I knew it was love.

That was the peculiar thing about always being overlooked, it does something to your mind. When people don't see you, or not even realize you're standing there, you start to see people the same way. I saw through them like glass in a window.

Leaving my teens, it didn't matter that all I had was May or my family for company. They were the only ones who really saw me, the short, stout, quiet girl who expressed herself through cooking. They came into the kitchen and spent time with me that way, joining in with not just my hobby but my passion. My family and best friend could even guess how I was feeling by my culinary creations.

I don't think it was just a physical attraction I felt for David Riverclaw, but he SMELLED the real me. It was like somebody finally seeing you, the real you, the you that nobody else could see. This 22 year old Lokoti Werewolf with blue eyes, pale skin and black hair, who ignored the other girls, smelled ME.

Over our lunch of burgers and fries, I sat opposite to my best friend and nodded along. She was thinking aloud of how to look for her date. Although physically I was in that booth with her, mentally I was elsewhere. But after twelve years of being best friends, I was adept at nodding in the right places.

A couple of days later when I accompanied my Mom to the supermarket, I saw David again. He was pushing the shopping trolley for his own mother. Mrs. Riverclaw and my Mom stopped to engage in some quick gossip, as David and I looked on each other.

"Hi Clara," he said.

"Hi David," I said back.

"You smell like freshly baked cookies," he grinned.

"I made them this morning for my mother's quilting group this afternoon." I answered.

A couple of days after that, I bumped into him coming out of the General Store on tribal lands.

He was carrying a bottle of milk and a loaf of bread and he brushed past on my way in.

I inhaled his scent deeply, which I think he caught with his acute hearing.

"Hi Clara."

"Hi David."

"You smell like spinach and cheese puffs."

"I made them for my Dad's fishing trip this afternoon."

He stepped aside while holding the door open for me and I went in.

I picked up a carry basket from the stack beside the door as I turned to watch him depart via the shop window. He walked over to his father's truck, opened the door and climbed in. However, he noticed I was watching him and he threw a polite wave as he drove away.

Then a couple of days later, I bumped into him when he was coming out of the Bar from playing pool with Will. I'd just come out of the cinema with my little brother Clifford. Originally, I was going to see the movie with May, but she'd already seen it on her date with Keith.

"Hi Clara."

"Hi David."

"You smell like popcorn."

"I just saw the remake of the 'Terminator' and we shared a bucket."

"Did you like the movie?" He enquired.

I shrugged back, "It was OK, but it relied too much on special effects instead of the storyline than the original movie did."

This made him smile, "I thought the same thing when I saw it yesterday."

"C'mon Clara!" Clifford interrupted as he impatiently looked at his watch. "Dad said he'd pick us up from the corner at 5.15 and it's 5.17 PM."

Embarrassed, I ducked my head as I hurried after my little brother.

Although I didn't look back, somehow I sensed that this time David watched me leave.

At the end of our fourth week of run-ins with each other, he started to look like he expected to bump into me.

David would always smile and I would inhale his pheromones as I shyly smiled back. Each time he'd see me, he would sniff and announce that I smelled like a particular food I'd recently been around. I liked it, especially when he could accurately guess what I'd cooked up.

On one particular Sunday afternoon, I was walking home from May's house. She'd spent the whole afternoon telling me all about her fourth date with Keith and particularly about their first kiss. As usual, she was talking a hundred miles and hour but I didn't mind, she was gushing with happiness.

I passed by the Garage on my way home to find David was filling up his father's truck at the gas pump.

"Hi Clara," he greeted.

"Hi David," I said, coming to a stop beside him.

Even over the petroleum fumes, he could accurately say, "You smell like cinnamon donuts."

"I made some to take to May's house this afternoon," I told him.

Then I watched him remove the nozzle from his gas tank and replace it on the pump, before he screwed the lid on.

"Say Clara," he began, "I think people are starting to talk about us."

I almost stopped smiling but then I noticed he hadn't, which gave away his jest.

"What are people saying?" I played along.

"They're wondering if you're following me around from the amount of times we bump into each other." He winked.

"It's a small town." I giggled.

"I tell them that you can't resist my pheromones," he chuckled.

"They do help." I said.

"Say Clara," he began, "I do a little cooking myself. What would you say to an evening picnic by the river on Wednesday night? With it being summer and all, it won't get dark until ten and I can pick you up at five."

I realized he was saying this because he knew my parents were strict about curfew.

"Alright," I managed to say calmly, although my heart was pounding.

"If you like, I could take you home right now and ask your parents for permission." He turned serious. "Just in case your father is worried about me being four years older than you."

This made me pause and I stared down at the ground, before I looked back into his blue eyes.

"No, it'll be OK." I said. "Since you're picking me up at five and dropping me back at ten, it'll be fine. Besides, our parents know each other."

"I think every parent in the tribe knows each other." He smiled in amusement. "But can I give you a lift home right now?"

I shook my head. "No, I want to walk."

Then I didn't know what else to say, so after one last parting smile I turned and continued on my way home. This time I knew without needing to look back that David Riverclaw was watching me walk away. I felt his eyes on my back as my confidence rose.

That evening after I helped Mom with dinner, our family sat at the table to eat. My parents passed around the corn bread to eat with our rabbit stew. With my new sense of self-confidence, I broached the subject of my date with David Riverclaw.

"Clifford, pass the butter." Mom requested and my little brother complied.

I watched her carefully spread the butter thinly on top of her bread, whereas Dad ate his with gusto.

"I have a date on Wednesday night." I announced.

Then I dunked the corn bread into the stew before putting the piece into my mouth.

"You have a date?" Mom echoed in surprise.

She shared a stunned look with Dad, who looked so taken aback he'd stopped eating.

"With who?" Clifford demanded.

"David Riverclaw is picking me up at five o'clock to take me on an evening picnic by the river." I continued.

"Flint Riverclaw's son?" Dad said in surprise. "But that man is a good four years older than you, Clara."

"I know." I shrugged. "He offered to come and ask you permission himself, but I said it should be OK because you know his parents."

"One of the pack asked YOU out?" Clifford asked in disbelief.

"Uh huh." I nodded.

"An evening picnic is very grown up for a first date." Dad frowned.

"It's summer so it's longer daylight hours now." I pointed out. "He also said he'd have me home by ten, before it gets dark."

This stumped my father who looked like he couldn't object to that, so he looked to Mom to think of something else. However, my mother shrugged back. Then she looked on her daughter with new eyes, as her hand caressed my hair.

"You have nice skin and beautiful long, shiny, dark hair, Clara." She smiled. "With your patient disposition and wonderful cooking, you have a lot of good qualities to offer as a potential mate."

"Joanne!" Her husband objected. "Can you please not talk about mating and my eighteen year old daughter in the same sentence?!"

"She's turning nineteen in December." Mom said coolly. "My older sister married at that age."

"David Riverclaw, the guy who all the girls are goo-goo for, asked YOU out on a picnic?" Clifford asked sceptically.

I hid my hurt by looking down at my dinner.

"I think you should braid your hair the night before so it's nice and wavy for your date." Mom planned. "And you should wear that black dress with the large sunflowers printed over it."

"Joanne, can you please stop trying to get your eldest married off to the first offer she receives?" Dad said indignantly. "She's only just finished High School!"

"You're just afraid of losing her cooking if Clara does get married," my brother snickered. "Then you won't have any more spinach and cheese triangles to take on your fishing trips."

"That's enough Clifford, you're excused from the table," my father glared.

Loudly, my brother pushed back his chair and stomped off into his bedroom.

"It's just a date." I said with a red face. "It's not a marriage proposal or anything."

"Yes but David Riverclaw is one of the pack." He said warily. "When a Lokoti Werewolf sets his mind on a mate, there's no changing it. The next thing I know, my beautiful bunny will be telling me there'll be a Joining Ceremony."

Dad used his old pet name for me from childhood which made me look up and pass a small smile his way.

"Our little girl is growing up, Harold." Mom sighed sadly. "My oh my Clara, are we going to miss your cooking."

"It's just a date." I repeated, as I looked back down.

*****

I was dressed for the occasion an hour before, with my long hair looking wavy from the braids my mother put in the previous night.

I'd also put some macadamia and choc chip cookies as well as some spinach and cheese triangles, in individual Tupperware containers. I know David said he'd provide the food, but I baked extra when I made them for Dad's fishing excursion and Mom's quilting group. I also had a picnic rug ready, as a just in case.

At five to five, there was a knock on the door. I was sitting in the living room with Mom and Dad who were watching some game show on TV. Even Clifford hung around, as if to bear witness that one of the pack had indeed asked his older sister out.

Dad took his time in standing up from his easy chair to answer the door. My leg jiggled nervously at how long he took and I almost jumped up to answer it myself, but Mum put her hand on my arm and shook her head. I realized it was as if some kind initiation ceremony was taking place.

At last Dad opened the door and I heard David greet him politely.

"Hi Mr. Winter."

"Hello David," he said sternly as he permitted him entrance.

My date walked into the living room and with his height and muscled body, it looked like he just fit through the front doorway.

"Hello David," my Mom smiled. "Won't you take a seat?"

"Thanks Mrs. Winter."

I watched him stride over to sit down on the couch opposite to mine.

Once he did, his blue eyes met and held my dark brown ones. "Hi Clara."

"Hi David," I tried not to blush, as my gaze shyly dropped to the floor.

Dad returned to his easy chair and regarded the Lokoti Werewolf sitting on his couch.

Clifford came to lean on a nearby wall and watched what took place.

"Clara says you're taking her on a picnic by the river," my father said gruffly.

"Yes sir," my suitor sat up straighter out of respect. "There's a nice part of the river bank just past the Holy Grounds, I was thinking of taking her."

"Make sure you have her home by nightfall." Dad frowned. "The rocks by the river can get slippery and I don't want her stumbling over in the dark."

"Yes sir," he hastily agreed. "I was going to have her home before nightfall, but even if it turned dark out? I'd see as clear as day and I'd make sure nothing happened to her."

Clifford piped up, "So is it true that Werewolves can see in the dark like infrared?"

"Um, I can't speak for all the breeds out there, but I can for the Lokoti Werewolves. Yeah, we can see in the dark like infrared. It's how we spot our prey by their heat signatures." David said abashed.

"Cool!" My brother sat on the arm rest of Dad's chair, to look on like he was the coolest person in the tribe.

"That's enough now, Clifford," my father patted him on the back. "It's best that your sister leaves now on her date, so David can have her back by ten."

"Yes sir," he stood up as did I. "Clara won't be home a minute later than that."

"I should hope so," my human father stood eye-to-eye with his daughter's date, even if he was a full head higher than he was.

David held open the front door for me and I walked out of the house with the picnic rug and two Tupperware containers in a cotton carry bag.

Politely, he walked me to the passenger's side of his father's truck and opened the door for me. Then he closed it once I'd climbed inside. As soon as he was sitting in the driver's seat, he flashed a familiar grin.

"You smell like spinach and cheese triangles as well as freshly baked cookies."

I nodded towards the bag on my lap, "I made extra for us to take on the picnic."

"Awesome!" He beamed. "I remember eating the caramel cheesecake you made for your cousin's birthday last year. It was the best dessert I'd ever tasted."

With that, he reversed out the driveway and then we cruised down the small streets of the community centre. Because we were driving so slowly, it gave the neighbours a chance to ogle at who was in the truck. I noticed a couple of kids who were playing games on their front lawns, even paused in surprise. Nobody expected to see Clara Winter going on a date with David Riverclaw.

It didn't take us long to park off to the side of the Holy Grounds. Then David walked me down the rocky riverbank to the spot he'd picked out. He carried a picnic rug, two large cushions as well as a large picnic basket. Considerately, he paused as I walked extra slow, to make sure I didn't slip on any of the rocks.

Soon, we were sitting comfortably on the cushions on top of the water-proof blanket. An array of sandwiches neatly cut into small triangles sat on four plates. There were bottles of ginger ale and root beer leaning against the side of the basket. Also, there was an open packet of corn chips and a jar of store-bought salsa.

"Um, I remembered you drank either ginger ale or root beer." He pointed at the bottles of soda, before he indicated the food. "But I couldn't remember what kinda sandwiches you like. So there's ham and salad, as well as egg salad, and there's chicken and avocado, or even peanut butter and jelly."

"You remembered what kind of soda I drink?" I looked on in surprise.

"Well, at parties or tribal gatherings, I remembered seeing these types of drinks in your hand." His face flushed.

"You noticed me at parties or tribal gatherings?" I asked in astonishment.

"Yeah," he smiled bashfully. "You and May would look like you were in your own little world, standing together. Sometimes I wished I could join you and get away from the crowd."

Now it was my turn to blush, "It's because nobody wanted to talk to us."

He looked surprised, "Really? I thought with your quiet disposition, you'd have people constantly bending your ear. Somebody's always looking for someone to listen to them."

I shook my head as I pulled out the containers of spinach and cheese triangles as well as the cookies.

David helped himself by picking up a triangle then dunking it into the salsa. He devoured it while emitting sounds of pleasure.

"Mmm, good spinach and cheese triangles," he munched. "Try them with the salsa."

So I did, I picked it up then dipped it in and nibbled on it. He watched the smile break out on my face as I swallowed. Why hadn't I thought about eating them this way before?

After that, the majority of our picnic was spent in a comfortable silence.

David had picked a pretty part of the riverbank to sit on. There was the murmur of the river with the occasional bird call. A gentle breeze made the branches of the trees sway and my hair billow out, which David noticed. A couple of times we watched birds like Bald Eagles swoop down to catch the fish in the river.

I was starting to see that David Riverclaw was just as quiet as I was. Perhaps it was because of his status as one of the pack, people looked to him to lead, so he felt like he had to say something. But during our picnic, he seemed relieved not to have to talk much.

My Mom says my expressions say a hundred words, it's just that people didn't see them. This evening I saw something similar on David's face, his eyes would soften when they gazed in my direction and it made my skin warm as my heart pounded.

At 9.40 PM I helped him pack up the picnic basket then we walked back to the truck.

It was 9.55 PM when we pulled into my driveway and he switched off the engine.

He jumped out first and walked around to open my door for me, before we slowly meandered towards my veranda.

"I had a great time tonight, Clara." He grinned.

"So did I."

"Can I take you out again this Saturday? I know a lookout which would make another nice spot for an alfresco lunch." He offered.

"Only if I can provide the food." I haggled with a smile.

"OK but how about I bring the drinks?" He counter offered.

"Alright."

Next, he opened the front door for me and held it open as I went inside.

My parents looked his way from their easy chairs, to which he gave a polite wave. After one last smile my way, he ducked his head as he departed and the front door shut behind him. Like that he was gone and my date had ended.

Mom stood up and followed me into the kitchen. I pulled out the now-empty Tupperware containers and put them into the dishwasher. She watched how I moved before she looked on the expression on my face.

"You had a nice night then?" She queried.

I nodded, "He's taking me on another picnic for lunch on Saturday."

"That's good," she said brightly. "Do you like this boy, Clara?"

I paused, "He suggested eating the spinach and cheese triangles with salsa. It's nice, you and Dad should try it."

Then I left the kitchen and went into my bedroom with Mom staring after.

~~~~~~

9th September 2027

David and I saw each other two or three times a week. He was always respectful of my parent's wishes by minding my curfew, as he behaved just as respectful towards me. He'd open doors for me, or carry things for me, or behave in a protective manner by holding my hand while standing closely. Often he took this stance at tribal gatherings, because in the beginning of our relationship, people would stare at our coupling.

Keith would arrive with May and David would arrive with me. People's eyes would widen when they saw us and some of them would whisper. I think David overheard what they said with his acute hearing, but I pretended not to notice. People only saw me now, because they saw me with David. This didn't speak well of certain people in the tribe.

"What are two of the tribe's hottest men doing with a beach ball and bean pole?!" One girl hissed to another, at a mid-summer bonfire we attended.

"Let alone the fact that one can talk her way through wood and the other is like a piece of wood, with about as much she has to say." Her friend hissed back.

David's head turned sharply as did Keith's, but May didn't hear them. I did but I pretended I didn't, as I sipped on my root beer and held onto his hand. I guess being a quiet person, my hearing was almost as good as a
~~~~~~

Werewolf's. Otherwise, people simply wouldn't notice I was there when they were gossiping.

By dating David, people took much more notice when I was around. Perhaps we looked like a mismatched couple, with me being so much shorter than him. But when we sat together on our dates, it felt like we were the same height. In fact, it felt like we were the same everything.

We had our quiet natures in common, but soon we realized we liked the same music and the same movies and had a similar outlook on life. Sometimes he'd even sense when I was feeling cold and he'd take off his jacket to put around my shoulders. Mind you, his jacket was so large, I almost swam in it.

I heard that Lokoti Werewolves would become empathically attuned to their mates, but it occurred after mating. Sometimes David acted like he was already attuned to me, that or he was an extremely perceptive person. I think it must have been both, although once he paid the compliment by saying the same about me.

We both enjoyed being around food and he loved every single thing that I baked. He could always smell what I'd cooked that day and it became part of his standard greeting.

"Hi Clara."

"Hi David."

"You smell like strawberry cheesecake."

"I made one for May's mother's birthday, but I had some mix left over so I made you another."

Most of our dates centred around food; picnics or having lunches or dinners. It was another reason why we were suited, cooking was my favourite past time and eating was his. A couple of times David took me out to lunch at the Milk Bar and sometimes Keith and May would join us, like a double date.

May was so happy, she would giggle amongst her chatter and Keith was getting used to his girlfriend's constant noise, so he was able to interject more. Meanwhile David and I would exchange small smiles and just sit back and listen. They both seemed suited to each other too, they could talk about anything and everything.

On the other hand, May and I became accustomed to David and Keith's large appetites. Where we were happy with a burger and shared fries and a milkshake, the Lokoti Werewolves would eat triple that amount. They'd order onion rings as well as fries, drink a milkshake each then order pie for desert.

David would tempt me into trying some by asking, "Do you think the banana cream is OK, Clara?"

I would take a bite and either frown or nod. If I nodded that it was good, he would order an extra slice as take away, which he would put into my hands at the end of our date. However, when it came to paying for our meals, the guys always insisted on looking after the bill and never let the girls pay.

Our romance slowly but surely blossomed, with most of our time spent in a comfortable silence. On our second date for lunch at the lookout, David held my hand when he pulled me up the steep slope or afterwards when he helped me down. On our third date, he escorted me to my door and left a parting kiss on my cheek.

That was another thing about him, he always escorted me to my front door rather than simply dropping me off when our date was finished.

But it wasn't until our fourth date when he hesitated on the steps of my front veranda, that we shared our first kiss.

Gently, he pulled on my hand which he'd been holding, to make me stop and turn towards him.

I was standing two steps above him, which roughly made me the same height. We both smiled over this, before he leaned in and tenderly pressed his lips against mine. My stomach fluttered when I felt his mouth open which turned our kiss passionate.

As our relationship progressed, I began to feel like a desirable young woman instead of a girl with a crush.

On our twelfth date as we were stargazing from the back of his truck, we made out on the picnic rug and cushions he'd put down.

We both became hot and bothered and I heard the occasional growl escape. His hands had bunched into fists as I felt his teeth sharpen. Feverishly, he kissed me on the mouth then my ear and then down my neck. His head buried itself between my clothed breasts, when suddenly he sat upright while panting hard.

"Clara, did I tell you that I fish too? Maybe I should spend time with your father by fishing with him one day." He panted out.

I saw he was holding himself back but right now, talking about fishing was the last thing on my mind. I grabbed hold of the back of his sweater and in one tug, I pulled him back over me. Next, his hands squeezed my breasts as we kissed long and hard. That was until he sat upright a second time, while panting even harder.

"I have the perfect fishing flies to attract large salmon." He forced out. "Trout too, my father taught me how to dangle the line in the water -"

But I pulled him back down before he could finish his sentence. We kissed hungrily as I ran my hands up and down his clothed chest. At the same time, I felt his hands start to gather up my skirt before he quickly sat up again.

"Salmon swim upstream so you have to dangle the line in the water at the right angle to avoid it snagging on a rock." His voice sounded strained.

"David," I sung, "I don't wanna talk about fishing."

"Maybe we should go fishing on our next date." He rushed out. "Standing in cold water sounds like a good idea right about now."

I sat up too, so I could rub his back in a soothing way as he closed his eyes and seemed to be concentrating on his breathing.

"Clara," he spoke with his eyes closed.

"Yes David?"

"You smell really good, a little too good." He muttered. "I think I'm gonna have to take you home."

Disappointed, I pulled back to ask, "Why?"

When he glanced my way, I saw embarrassment in his eyes.

"I've been with girls before but I've never had to battle my self control like this." He confessed. "I'm in love with you, Clara."

I looked on puzzled, "And this is a bad thing?"

"My - my - my body keeps trying to er, claim you," he admitted with a red face.

Then he looked away like he was ashamed, which made my hand reach out to gently turn his face back my way.

I repeated, "And this is a bad thing?"

This made him pause as he looked back. He blinked in disbelief before staring upon my face. Then his hand reached out and ran through my long hair.

"That's what I love about you Clara, I feel like I can be myself around you." He said softly. "I can eat as much as I want and you give me more food. We don't have to talk because we both prefer silence. We like the same things and think the same way."

I sat there smiling as he said all of this and I enjoyed his touch. His hand left my hair to cup my chin instead. Then holding my head in one hand, he spoke seriously.

"You're soft and you always smell delicious, which are very alluring traits." He continued. "You're always doing something nice for somebody, like cooking them things. I'd be the luckiest guy on earth if I ended up with a mate like you."

Was that a marriage proposal? I decided to take it as one, I felt empowered by our deep attraction and I took hold of his hand in the both of mine and held onto it tightly.

"I will marry you, David Riverclaw."

His blue eyes widened and a grin spread out over his face. "You will?"

I nodded while holding his gaze.

"Clara..." he managed out in shock, "...you'd make me the happiest man alive."

Then we both laughed at the suddenness of this serious conversation.

"After I graduate next year I can get a job in Fairbanks," he began to plan. "We could get married then."

I nodded a second time as I listened to him orchestrate our future.

"When I drive you home tonight, I'll ask your parents for permission." He said. "Dad's already given me this truck and I have savings in a trust fund, from my Mom. I have a lot to offer a mate, just you wait and see."

But he didn't have to convince me, I was head-over heels in love. I would have followed him to the North Pole if he'd asked me to. I would have done anything and everything for him.

"Come to dinner tomorrow night," he continued. "My parents would love to get to know their future daughter-in-law."

"Alright," I went along.

*****

It was 11 PM when David took me home and by the sound of the TV, I could hear my parents were still up. When I told them we were going stargazing, they agreed to extend my curfew. But now I was nervous about telling them. I'd left the house on a date and was coming back to them engaged.

My fiancé opened the front door for me then followed me inside, making my parents look up from their seats.

"Good evening, David." Dad greeted gruffly. "Thank you for having Clara home before midnight."

He nodded before looking my way like he didn't know where to start.

"Mum and Dad, we have something to tell you." I said. "Could you turn the TV off for a minute?"

"Oh Clara," my mother put her hand over her heart. "Is there something wrong?"

"Oh dear," my father's face fell. "This does sound serious."

David's face flushed as he took hold of my hand. He stood so tall, his head almost touched the ceiling. He easily dwarfed my father, who stood up to face him.

"Mr Winter, I'd like to ask your permission to marry your daughter." He began. "We'd like to hold the Joining Ceremony next year, after my graduation."

"Clara!" My mother beamed. "This is wonderful news!"

However, my father didn't smile as he looked on the giant holding his daughter's hand.

"So this will be after you graduate, when you'll be able to support a family." Dad said sternly.

"Yes sir," he nodded.

"And how are your studies going, David?"

"Next year I'll be graduating with a Bachelor in Civil Engineering," he answered.

"Hmm," Dad looked to his daughter. "It looks like I was right after all. My beautiful bunny is telling me to expect a Joining Ceremony."

I didn't know what to say, so I smiled at him to show him how happy I was.

Slowly, his frown disappeared as he held out his arms and I gave my father a hug.

*****

The following evening, David picked me up and drove me back to his place.

His pick-up truck chugged up the steep hill towards his house then he turned into his driveway. I'd never been to the Riverclaw's before, but I'd seen his parents at tribal events. Now I sat on the front seat, looking through the windscreen at his family's large log cabin.

As if they were waiting for us, his parents walked out onto the wooden veranda and waved.

Mrs Riverclaw held hands with her husband as she smiled our way. She had shoulder-length blonde hair, bright blue eyes and fair skin. Although she was wearing jeans and a red shirt, she looked more glamorous than her clothes. Her husband on the other hand, looked at home in his jeans and flannel shirt. His long, grey hair framed his bronzed, worn face and he had kind eyes.

"Hi there!" She waved. "How are you, Clara?"

I climbed the front stairs with David. "I'm good, how are you?"

"Fit as a fiddle," she laughed back. "Now come inside and make yourself at home."

Mr Riverclaw opened the door for everyone then trailed in afterwards.

I was escorted to a couch to sit on in the living room but on my way past I saw that the dining table had been set.

"Now, what would you like to drink?" Mrs Riverclaw organized. "We have diet coke, diet lemonade, orange juice, or chilled water?"

I remembered that she was a diabetic which explained the low-sugar products in her home.

"I'll have an orange juice, please." I said.

"Yeah, me too." David joined in. "I'll get them."

"No son, I will," his father stopped him.

David was standing beside Mr Riverclaw and the men looked identical with their height and stature. Then his father veered off into the kitchen as David came to sit beside me. His mother sat on the sofa opposite to us.

"So Clara, you finished High School last year, didn't you?" Mrs Riverclaw started.

"Yes."

"And what have you been doing since then?" She enquired.

"I've been baking."

"You've been baking?" She echoed in surprise.

"Clara's a wonderful cook," David rested his hand on my leg. "She made that strawberry cheesecake I brought home."

"That's right," she remembered. "I'm not supposed to eat sugary things often, but that cake was a treat alright."

"I bake things for people in the tribe," I told her.

"Oh, is this a business you're starting up?" She wondered.

"Clara doesn't charge people for what she makes," her son explained. "She makes them as gifts."

"Oh," his mother looked puzzled. "Well, you could always open your own bakery with your talent."

"I don't just bake, but I cook lots of things," I told her. "I made the potato salad at the Elm's barbecue and the Caesar salad at the tribe's bonfire."

"Those huge bowls of salad?" Mrs Riverclaw blanched. "They must have taken you hours and somebody said you always bake from scratch."

"I made the dressings myself." I told her.

Mr Riverclaw came back out and handed everyone's drinks to them.

"I went fishing with your father last Sunday and I tried one of your spinach and cheese puffs." He said. "They were delicious."

"I use more than one type of cheese to bring out the flavour," I told him.

"Amazing," Mrs. Riverclaw shook her head. "I just don't have the patience for cooking."

"Jessica's specialty is using the microwave to reheat leftovers," he chuckled, as he sat beside her.

"Hey, I helped with dinner tonight." She poked him in the ribs.

"Mom and Dad made roast beef with seasoned vegetables," David said.

I smiled their way to show I was looking forward to it.

"Well, it was Flint who did most of the cooking," she admitted. "But I did help cut up the vegetables."

"You were a wonderful assistant," he grinned in good humour.

"I'll show you some 'assistance' alright, if you're not careful!" She poked him a second time.

Mr Riverclaw laughed as he caught his wife's hand in his then he raised it to his mouth to kiss it.

She giggled at her husband's affection before returning her attention my way.

"So, the wedding will be next year?" She checked.

David and I exchanged glances before he said, "We'd like to have a Joining Ceremony next year."

"OK," her eyebrows rose. "So no white dresses or tuxedoes then?"

"No, it'll be traditional dress," her husband told her. "I still have my father's skins which David can wear."

"Oh, you mean the suede pants and jacket you showed me once," she said. "But um, do they have Receptions after Joining Ceremonies?"

"There'll be a Housewarming," I told her.

"So the two of you would like a Joining Ceremony and a Housewarming, instead of a wedding and a reception?" Mrs Riverclaw reiterated.

I nodded as David said, "Yeah, pretty much."

"Um, how does one cater and decorate these sorts of events?" She turned to her husband.

"Remember Mark, Sean and Alice's Housewarmings, we went to?" Mr. Riverclaw explained. "Each member of the tribe brings a dish and a drink to share."

"As well as a gift in the form of a household item," David filled her in.

"Oh of course!" She laughed at herself. "Now I get it."

"Something simple and something small..." her son ended, "...that's what we'd like."

"Missy Shallow Water had her reception in the tribe's Meeting Hall, you don't want that?" His mother checked.

We shook our heads at the same time.

"Alright then," she sat back in surprise, "a no frills and no fuss wedding it'll be."

"Joining Ceremony," her husband gently corrected her.

"Wedding or Joining Ceremony, it's the same thing." She waved it off. "They both result in the two of you permanently living together, don't they?"

David exchanged a wry grin with his father as the two men tried not to laugh.

"So does a Housewarming," I smiled in amusement.

"Good point, Clara." She pointed in my direction. "So how come the Wisetail children had a Housewarming but not a Joining Ceremony?"

"They preferred not to," her husband shrugged.

"Why did Missy Shallow Water want a wedding and a reception?" David pointed out.

"Different people prefer different things," I said.

"And on that note," Mr. Riverclaw stood up from his seat, "I'm going to check on dinner."

David smiled softly my way as he took hold of my hand which his mother noticed.

"I'll come and help," she volunteered.

Then she stood up from the couch and left us alone in the lounge area, to give us some privacy.

~~~~~~

Back to the future... 9th September 2370

I lay on my side in between two sleeping children while reading Great Grandma's diary. Lucia was curled up behind me with Sophia slumbering against my front. Periodically, I'd put down my book to smile on my sleeping children, before returning to the words on the page.

The six year old Lucia and one year old Sophia could kick up a fuss when you tried to put them down for an afternoon nap. So Declan and I developed the tactic that one of us would lie down with them. This way the kids couldn't retort, "Why do WE have to lie down but you don't?" Or our eldest would, with a grumpy one year old glaring in agreement.

This worked so well, our little 'cubs' looked forwards to their afternoon naps. They liked to climb up onto our large bed in the main bedroom and snuggle into either side of the parent. These occasions gave me time to read for enjoyment rather than study.

I heard Declan whisper, "Are they unconscious?"

I looked up to see him standing in bedroom doorway, smiling on the sight of his mate and young curled up together.

When I nodded back, I watched him come into the room and carefully lie down on the bed behind Soph.

As if she sensed the greater heat source emanating from her father, she rolled over and snuggled into his clothed chest instead of mine.

His smile widened as he caressed the top of her head, careful not to wake her.

"I was thinking that when Forest and Caesar come over tonight, I'll cook up a roast dinner using the leg of lamb in the freezer." He said quietly.

"With Great Grandma's special gravy?" I checked.

"Is the Pope Catholic?" He smirked.

"Here, you should take a look at this." I handed him the book. "In between Great Grandma's diary entries, she wrote down her recipes."

"Clara Riverclaw's recipes?" His eyes widened like I'd just handed him something sacred.

"Uh huh," I smiled.

"Caramel cheesecake, strawberry cheesecake, choc chip and macadamia cookies, spinach and cheese triangles..." he flicked through the book as his mouth watered, "...I feel like I'm holding onto the Holy Grail, with this legendary work in my hands."
~~~~~~

"It's fascinating to read, especially how different life was in those days." I whispered. "On most of their dates, David Riverclaw took Clara Winter on picnics since there was only one Milk Bar or Bar in Alma to eat at."

"Now there's something like twenty different restaurants or cafes." He commented. "Hang on, did you just call her Clara Winter?"

"Winter was her maiden name." I said. "I forget we're related to that family when we see them around tribal lands."

"Yeah but it's understandable, this diary is over three hundred years old." He replied. "Hey, I think we've got the ingredients needed to make the caramel cheesecake. I'm gonna try it out, it'd be nice to serve it to Clara Riverclaw's progeny when they come to dinner tonight."

He rolled the sleeping Sophia back towards her mummy before he planted a kiss on my forehead then he stood up.

I watched Declan depart with the book as I settled down with our kids.

~~~~~~
~~~~~~

~ 21 ~

5th September 2372

When Sophia was nine months old my body returned to its athletic build. Declan lamented losing my 'love handles' but on the bright side, returning to a pre-pregnant physique lifted my postnatal depression. I stopped binge eating, my appetite returned to normal and so did my general well-being.

Three years later, I appreciated my former muscle as my arms strained with the heavy bags of books that I was carrying. I was walking down a busy sidewalk in Alma with Lucia and Sophia in tow. Older sister held onto younger sister's hand, since mine were full of shopping bags.

This trip was important for two reasons; to top up on educational books and this was Lucia's first time leaving tribal lands without her father. It was important for Sophia too, she had to practice not losing her temper in public so her eyes wouldn't glow green. So far so good, neither daughter had caused a scene.

Lucia had begun to express her desire to attend Grade School in Alma like Kurt, Edwina, Kevin and Katrina did. She knew the reason why she was home-schooled and they weren't; because she had the bloodlust and they didn't. But as I watched her walk down the street holding onto Sophia's hand, she barely sniffed at the humans anymore. She was trying hard to blend in, in the hope of attending school soon with her cousins.

My eight year old had reached the stage where she was conscious of her differences, which made her feel left out. She was as tall as a ten year old and stronger than an adult human, with her muscled little body. She was the only girl her age who hunted on a full moon with the pack. Thankfully, she didn't feel rejected by her supernatural differences, as the Wisetail children treated her like the best thing since sliced bread. She played with them when they came home from school and her lessons at home had finished.

One afternoon, Declan and I listened in to one of their conversations over afternoon tea. My husband had served a plate of choc chip and macadamia cookies with glasses of milk. Kurt, Kevin and Katrina happily devoured them when they came over to play.

"Dad said you took down a female caribou all by yourself when you hunted last night." Kurt looked on in admiration.

"Uh huh," she nodded back.

"But doesn't it hurt if they kick or try to ram you?" Kevin asked concerned.

"When they charge, my Dad tackles them." She shrugged. "But if they kick, I dodge and go for their throats."

"That is so cool!" Katrina beamed.

“I wish I could hunt with you and the pack,” Kurt frowned, “but Dad won’t let me coz he says it’s too dangerous.”

“Soph comes with us and Dad carries her on his back.” Looch said. “But Mum holds her while he takes down our prey and then we eat with him.”

“I wish our Dad would take us hunting,” Kevin complained.

“You’d have to eat raw meat,” Kurt pointed out, “and you don’t even like sushi.”

“Yuck, I hate raw fish!” He declared. “I hate smoked salmon coz that’s raw too.”

“I don’t mind, I’ll eat anything,” she shrugged again.

I was sitting up on the kitchen bench watching my husband slice up the ingredients for our salad tonight. We didn’t talk because we were eavesdropping on the children. But there were a couple of times we exchanged looks of amusement.

Today, Lucia walked down the street behind her mother, firmly holding onto her sister’s little hand. She walked upright in a proud manner, thanks to the trust her father put in her to come into town without him. Declan sensed his eldest was ready for a little independence, but he was wary about his youngest. However, another one of Sophia’s differences was she didn’t seem to crave human flesh. Her bloodlust was already accustomed to fresh kill from the animal kingdom.

Most of the time, Sophia acted like a little girl and a human trait she adopted was vanity. She was already developing a fondness for fashion and her eyes would light up when I’d dress up for my guest lectures. Soph loved my suits and to watch me do my hair and make-up, so much so that she wanted to partake. Declan would laugh when I emerged from the bathroom with make-up on and Soph followed me out wearing some lipstick too. She showed no interest in cooking with her father but she liked to copy her mother instead.

When she changed, Soph also mirrored me because she looked almost exactly like a Lokoti Werewolf, but for her European Werewolf eyes. Her small body would bulk up with muscle, as claws appeared on the ends of her fingers and toes. Her teeth would grow elongated and sharp and she could bolt in a supernaturally fast speed. She didn’t seem to have her father’s appetite, either. Where Looch would gorge herself on intestines and whatever else, Soph would pick at her prey in a fussy manner.

I noticed today in town she attracted many a second glance from the townspeople. When I put her dark hair into piggy-tails this morning, she pointed at the hair ties with the plastic, white daisies on them. The three year old was already showing fashion sense by choosing what she wanted to wear. Once she was dressed and her hair was done, she preened before the mirror. Today she looked especially cute and she knew it.

We rounded the corner that the supermarket was on and headed towards its rear parking where our hover-car was waiting. The girls followed me over to our vehicle when I hit the remote key and the boot automatically opened. Once I dumped the heavy load into the back, I let out a sigh of relief.

"Right," I turned towards my young. "We've just got to duck into the supermarket to get a few things for your father then we'll head home."

"Dad told me to remind you to get some more cream cheese, so he can make strawberry cheesecake for dessert." Looch piped up.

I pulled out my mobile phone which the shopping list was on and input this extra item.

"Thanks Looch," I smiled. "I should take you shopping more often."

She beamed at the vote of confidence, but it didn't last long when a frown took its place. "But Mummy?"

"Yes Looch?"

"I don't like the strange man that's following us," she pointed.

What was that? Instantly, my eyes scanned the area she indicated and I saw him. A dark-haired and bronzed-skin man was standing by himself on the corner we'd just rounded. He was looking in our direction but when he saw that I saw him, he glanced away.

The hairs on the back of my neck stood up as my stomach filled with dread.

"He's followed us since the bookstore and he smells funny." She scrunched up her face in distaste. "He – he – he smells like he's half dead."

Looch's sense of smell was better than her mother's, thanks to her father. So if she said the man smelled half dead, I believed her. From his appearance which looked a little native, I was going to hazard a guess that he was a South American Vampire.

But what was his kind doing so far north? I remembered the SSIT Report and it said their species didn't like cold weather. Mind you, he was wearing a brightly coloured, woollen poncho.

"OK, change of plan." I hit the remote again to open up all the doors of the hover-car. "We're going home now and we'll save the grocery shopping for another day."

"But Daddy said we needed the cream cheese for dessert tonight." Looch said unhappily.

"Then we won't have strawberry cheesecake for dessert, we'll eat the ice cream that's in the freezer." I said brusquely.

Hastily, I ushered my little girls towards the backseat. Looch climbed in first then I lifted Soph into the baby seat. My hands moved quickly to buckle my youngest in, as my eldest did her own seat belt. However, her head craned so she could look out the window, like she was on guard.

"Mummy, he's coming towards us," Looch warned, pointing again.

In alarm, I stood up so fast that I knocked the back of my head on the door!

"Oow!" I cried out, before I turned around and gave another jolt in surprise.

The South American Vampire was standing right behind and his dark eyes looked bloodshot and hungry.

"Hola," he greeted.

"You just made me hit my head on the door!" I snapped.

"Lo siento," his apology sounded hollow. "I wanted to come over and tell you how pretty your daughters are, Señora."

"Oh really?" I asked coldly. "Why, do you like little girls?"

"They make the perfect snack," he returned smoothly, dropping the act. "However, they don't just smell like you, they smell part something else."

I said icily, "They're half European Werewolf, you idiot."

"They are?" He grinned, which showed off his yellow teeth. "This is an unexpected pleasure, I heard that this breed was now extinct."

With his thick accent, when he said "extinct" it sounded like, "esteenct."

"Then you know that he's the most dangerous breed of Werewolf in the world." I glared.

"I have heard that Señora." He said. "But the more dangerous the prey, the more satisfying the hunt, si?"

Then his bloodshot eyes turned completely red as his smiled widened to show off his rows of sharp, pointy teeth. It was the second time I'd seen a South American Vampire's teeth and they still reminded me of a piranha. The same time as his face changed, his dirty nails grew longer and sharper.

"I shall savour the delight of sampling the blood of such a unique source," he hissed.

"You don't scare me, you walking corpse." I growled back. "You think you're tough by accosting a mother with two small children. But did you ever stop to consider that my mate would be nearby?"

"We were actually counting on this, Señora."

Next, I noticed two more male South American Vampires walk towards us from different directions.

Damn it, he came with his coven. Oh well, three against one? Declan's creamed these odds before, coincidentally in the same location. What is with fang heads and supermarket car parks? I was never going to hear the end of it from my husband.

"So, are there any more of you?" I sounded bored. "Three of you isn't much of a challenge."

"We did have a fourth," the second Vampire said in another thick accent. "But we got hungry so we ate him on the way."

"Mummy," Looch undid her seatbelt to move closer. "Can I hunt them? They're not human and they seem mean."

"Put your seatbelt back on, Lucia Grace!" I ordered.

She may have been strong, but she wasn't strong or fast enough yet to take on an adult sized South American Vampire. She pouted as she obeyed by moving back into her seat. But her eyes burned green as she glowered at the threat to her family and therefore, her territory.

"The half-breed is trying to protect her weaker mother?" The third Vampire chuckled to his cohorts. "She's a strong little one too, her regenerative ability will add to all three of us."

Protectively, I stood in front of the car door as I didn't like the hungry way they were looking on my children.

"Take out your phone and call your husband to come and rescue you," the first Vampire ordered, as he used his long, knife-like nails to lift up my handbag. Their completely red eyes and piranha-like teeth gave them a menacing yet starved appearance. "Then you will drive us to a location where we will wait for the rest of the dogs try to save you."

He meant the Lokoti Werewolves, which made a low, dissatisfied growl come out at his insult.

"I have a better idea," I said coolly. "I'm going to duck and you're going to be mauled."

Before they could reply, I did duck and a European Werewolf leapt over the hover-car and landed on all three at once!

"Daddy!" Looch and Soph squealed excitedly.

Hastily, I turned around and shushed them, worried a witness may hear.

Declan in his huge, hulking, hairless body, complete with his short, stubby snout over razor-sharp jaws, was unrecognizable to outsiders. Any time a stranger saw him, they called him an 'albino, mutant, hairless, grizzly'. As our girls applauded their father for his perfectly timed manoeuvre, I had to stop them to make sure they didn't give away his identity.

As soon as the first South American Vampire spoke, I sensed my mate's approach. Empathically, I felt that his intuition as a Circulator had sounded the alarm. Back home he'd stripped off his clothes then he went outside to expand into his larger body. He ran in light speed from tribal lands into town so nobody least of all the 'fang heads', saw him coming.

The wet crunching sound of his huge jaws eating through the Vampire's heads came to our ears.

Looch and Soph watched with interest, whereas a couple of humans who'd been walking past with their hover-trolleys, took off in fright! They bolted back into the supermarket, leaving their trolleys behind. I was tempted to walk up and simply take what items were on my shopping list.

Declan munched his way through two of the Vampires' heads, eating skin, bone and brain. The third 'fang head' which was pinned by his greater weight, stuck his long, knife-like nails into my mate's hardened hide. My overprotective instincts didn't like this and I grabbed hold of it and snapped it backwards! It screamed in pain and flailed it's now broken hand.

B, STAY OUT OF THIS! - Declan telepathically ordered - *YOU'RE SUPPOSED TO BE THE VICTIM WHEN THE POLICE INVESTIGATE.*

"Why do I always have to play the victim?" I complained. "Why can't I taste Vampire flesh too?"

"What does Vampire flesh taste like, Mummy?" Looch asked as she watched.

"Um," I wondered how to explain. "It's not as nice as fresh kill, because it's already half dead. It's a little like eating meat that's defrosted after you've taken it out of the freezer."

"Eew!" Looch and Soph's faces screwed up in distaste.

Their father's jaws now broke through the third Vampire's head and after a couple of mouthfuls, it too lay dead with most of its skull missing.

I'LL GO HOME AND PUT SOME CLOTHES ON – he thought my way – *THEN I'LL COME BACK FOR YOU.*

"See you soon," I said quietly.

Then he winked at his young sitting on the backseat, before he bolted out of the car park on all fours.

The girls giggled at his sign of affection and Sophia raised her arm to wave good bye, but I pushed it back down again.

"People aren't supposed to know that was Daddy," I whispered to them.

My youngest looked puzzled from her mother to her older sister, so Looch demonstrated by raising her finger to her mouth in a 'shhh' gesture.

Thank goodness little children thought secrets were fun, as Soph giggled in agreement.

"Looch, your eyes." I said lastly then I stood up to talk to the approaching humans.

She noticed in the rear view mirror that her eyes were still glowing green, so she quickly shut them. When she opened them once more, they were back to their human blue colour. She looked out the car windows at the small crowd which was gathering.

"Are you alright?" A man asked, as he walked towards us. "I've dialled 911 and the police are on their way."

"Are you OK, sweetie?" A woman bent over to look on the kids sitting in the back.

Then her eyes widened in surprise when Soph giggled and made the 'shhh' gesture to her.

"Soph!" Her sister pushed her hand back down. "You're the one who's supposed to shhh!"

The woman straightened with a disconcerted look on her face. "I think your kids are in shock, the poor little mites."

"You may be right." I pretended to be in shock, myself. "An attempted mugging and a wild animal attack, some shopping trip this turned out to be."

*****

Within minutes the police arrived and after the first hover-car landed, three more appeared. A coroner's van was the next on the scene, as the South American Vampire bodies were scanned before they were 'tagged and bagged'. Lastly, I watched them be pushed away on hover-stretchers.

A female Detective took my statement as the kids squirmed on the backseat, bored. A couple of officers also questioned the witnesses, who pointed in our direction as they answered. All eyes were on the mother and her children who'd been the focus of the attack.

An ambulance was the last to arrive on the scene and the paramedics had to push through the crowd of onlookers. When a female paramedic tried to scan us for any injuries, I politely declined. I couldn't risk our anomalous cell structure as Shape Shifters being identified.

Since I refused medical attention, the paramedics felt like they should help somehow so they put blankets about us.

"You feel cold when you go into shock," the female attendant advised.

"But I'm not cold, I'm hungry." Looch whined, as she tugged off her blanket.

Soph started to whinge in agreement although she kept her blanket on.

"Would you like a juice and some jelly beans? You've been through a lot so your sugar levels may be low," the paramedic offered.

Then she went to procure them from the ambulance, leaving her partner behind to observe us.

"Could you explain why your DNA was on one of the assailants, Mrs. Sabre?" The Detective quizzed.

I let out a sigh at how Declan was right by telling me to stay out of it.

"I broke one of the men's hands when he reached for my kids." I lied.

"Did you know the men who attacked you?" She quizzed, as she made note of what I said in her PDA.

"No," I shook my head. "The first time I saw them was today. My daughter pointed at the strange man who'd followed us into the car park. When we tried to leave he came over to stop us. Then his two friends showed up and they demanded that I drive them to some location."

Momentarily, her face lost its hardened expression. I guessed she was thinking that we just had a lucky escape from sexual predators who preyed on females young and old. She was right about the predator part, even if she was wrong about the motive.

"It's a good thing you know self-defence," her eyebrows rose.

"My mother taught me," I smirked.

The paramedic returned with two small juice containers and packets of jelly beans.

"Here you go dears," she handed them to my children.

"Yummy!" Looch salivated at the treats on offer.

My eldest ripped into the jelly beans first as my youngest struggled with the juice container. I took it and poked the straw in it for her, before returning it.

"Thank you." I smiled appreciatively to the paramedic.

"OK," the Detective returned to the matter at hand. "Man number one approached you first and stopped you from leaving. Then men numbers two and three joined in and tried to force you to drive them somewhere, with your daughters. Is this when you broke one of the attacker's hands?"

"Yes, the third man reached for my daughter and I snapped it backwards," I nodded.

"And that's when the wild animal attacked?" She looked on closely.

"Yes, ironic isn't it." I arched my eyebrows. "One predator saved me from another."

"Eye witnesses are calling this wild animal a 'huge, mutant, albino, hairless grizzly'." She read off her screen. "Is this correct?"

"Sounds about right," I shrugged.

"One witness said that you told them an attempted mugging took place before the wild animal attacked."

"They tried that too, man number one grabbed my handbag." I lifted it up to show her.

She called over another police officer who was holding a Forensics scanner and he waved it over my handbag.

"One of the assailant's DNA is on the leather," he reported.

Then the Detective dismissed him and he returned to scanning the blood spatter on the asphalt.

"You escaped an attempted mugging as well as an attempted assault? This is your lucky day Mrs. Sabre." She remarked, whilst making another note in her PDA. "But there is something that I'm curious about."

"Yes?"

"This is the second time you've been a victim of such an incident and in the same location." She eyed me suspiciously. "Wasn't there a wild animal involved in that altercation too?"

Frickin' hell, by Declan running to his family's aid in his European Werewolf form made things worse. I should have instantaneously phased myself and the kids home. No, that wouldn't have worked, because Declan had already sensed the Vampire's presence. Whether I'd phased home or not, my territorial husband would have come after the 'fang heads' who tried to feed on his wife and kids.

"Mrs. Sabre?" She prompted my response.

"Yes and it looked like the same animal too." I cut to the chase, knowing she was going to bring that up next. "In fact, I'm almost sure it was."

"You've seen this animal before, on the first occasion you were attacked?"

"Yeah, it looked like a huge, mutant, albino, hairless grizzly." I snapped my fingers like it had just come to me. "It suddenly appeared and then disappeared. It ran faster than any grizzly I'd ever seen."

"It attacked the perpetrators in the exact same manner that it attacked your last assailants," the Detective frowned. "Funny that."

Suddenly, Soph cried out, "Daddy!"

"Sophia, SHHHH!" I turned around and shushed her, inwardly panicking that she was about to give up her father.

"No Mummy, it really is Daddy." Looch pointed.

My head spun around as did the Detective's, to see Declan walking my way with Caesar and Ki. When a male officer tried to stop them from crossing the perimeter, the Detective indicated it was allowed. My husband rushed up and engulfed me in his arms, before letting go to check on the kids.

"Are you two OK?" He looked from Sophia to Lucia.

"We're OK Daddy, we were saved by a wild animal," Looch grinned.

"Was there another wild animal attack?" Ki feigned surprise.

"We found some unusual tracks in the National Park recently, next to a mangled corpse of a caribou." Caesar lied to the Detective. "The tracks looked like it came from the same kind of animal that migrates through every couple or so years. We think it comes from Canada, the neighbouring Lynx Tribe has also seen evidence of it passing through their territory."

"I see," the Detective also put this into her PDA. "Could you or a Park Ranger show us these tracks?"

"Of course," Caesar lied with a straight face. "They're on the north side of the National Park, we could take you there tomorrow."

"Wait a moment," she frowned, "you said the north side of the park?"

"Yes."

"But Alma is south of the Lokoti National Park," she shook her head. "Perhaps they're from another animal."

"Maybe, but whatever is on that security camera," Caesar nodded to the small, indiscreet camera by the supermarket's rear entrance, "its large claws will match the type of tracks we found."

"Then you should temporarily close the park to campers until this animal is caught." She said, concerned. "It appears to hunt large prey, such as caribou or human."

"I'll call one of our Park Rangers now." He pulled his mobile phone out of his pocket and made the call. "Walt this is Caesar, there's been another attack by the mystery mutant grizzly. I told them of the tracks you found and the police think it would be a good idea if we close the National Park to campers until we're sure the animal is gone."

“OK,” we heard Walt reply. “I know where a couple of campers are right now. I’ll drive up and tell them they’ll have to stay in a hotel due to a grizzly attack.”

Caesar turned back to the Detective, “We’ll start evacuating the campers immediately.”

Just then Soph squealed with laughter as she thought all of this was very funny.

“Daddy!” She pointed at the topic of conversation. “Daddy!”

“Yes sweetie, it’s Daddy.” Her father unbuckled her and lifted her into his arms. “Daddy’s here to take you, your sister and your Mom home.”

“Can we take them home now?” Ki asked the Detective. “I’m sure all of this has been very trying for them.”

“Alright then, I have Mrs. Sabre’s address in case we have any further questions.” She frowned. “Tonight we’ll see what the security camera recorded and tomorrow morning you can take us to the animal tracks.”

“I can arrange for a Park Ranger by the name of Walt Wisetail to meet you outside the Meeting Hall on tribal lands at 9 AM.” Caesar agreed.

Oh no, the camera would have recorded me snapping back the Vampire’s hand! I’d be seen to be assisting the animal, which would make me an accessory to murder. I flashed a frightened look towards my husband who returned it with a ‘stay calm’ expression. But I felt like there was a huge neon sign pointing in my direction.

“C’mon kids, let’s get you home.” Declan leaned over to buckle Soph into the baby’s seat again, but the Detective stopped him.

“You’re not leaving in this car.” She said adamantly. “Do you see that blood spray on the side panels there? That’s evidence.”

“Not again,” he rolled his eyes.

“This time I’m remembering to get my books out of the car!” I said emotionally.

I walked around to open the boot with trembling hands when Ki joined me. He grabbed two of the bags as I grabbed the other two. Before I closed the lid, he took hold of one of my shaking hands and gave it a reassuring squeeze.

“Do you feel cold and shaky?” The female paramedic came forward, as she’d been watching us the whole time. “They’re symptoms of shock.”

“I’m a Medicine Man, I can tend to her.” Ki said. “I’ll sit her down with a cup of chamomile tea and she’ll be as right as rain.”

Caesar came forwards and took the other two bags of books to carry, as Lucia emerged from the hover-car.

Declan carried Soph on one arm as his other hand held mine. Caesar carried a load of books in one hand and in his other he held Lucia’s. Ki walked last with more bags of books and the six of us left as a group. We crossed the police perimeter and moved through the gathered onlookers. The spectators all stared at the mother and her children who had a harrowing escape, although I felt like I was deeper in trouble than I was before.

I tried not to panic as Caesar led the way to his vehicle which was parked on the street. Declan and I climbed onto the backseat with the kids in our laps, as Ki and Caesar sat in the front. Our First punched in the ignition code and his hover-car rose into the air. I cast a last look through the rear window at the flashing red lights, before I looked to my husband.

"I'm screwed!" I whimpered.

"No you're not." Declan said firmly.

"But the security camera -" I began.

"It didn't record a thing," he said adamantly.

"But -"

"B, do you know why Caesar mentioned the security camera to the Detective?" He asked. "Because when I fought the North American Vampires, the camera hardly recorded anything from electromagnetic interference. You should know when Circulators move in light speed, it causes static with electrical equipment. Caesar saw the recording of the previous attack, when he pretended to help the police look for the 'mutant grizzly' the last time."

Caesar spoke as he drove, "I saw static, a glimpse of Uncle Declan eating one of the male North American Vampires, then more static."

Declan was right, I did know all of this. Hell, I've been teaching him about it as part of his Circulator training. But right now, I was panicking over what that little glimpse may be amongst the static.

"The security camera will show static with maybe a second or two of footage of me eating the fang heads and then more static." He promised.

"What if that second or two of footage is of me snapping the fang head's hand?" I wailed.

"I doubt it." He said dismissively.

"But you can't guarantee it!" I cried. "When that fang head was stabbing you with its knife-like nails, I couldn't just sit there and watch!"

"B, I regenerated within minutes of being injured." He lifted up his jacket and t-shirt to show smooth skin underneath. "I ran home, had a quick a shower to wash off the Vampire blood, then I dressed and got lift back here."

I felt a rush of relief to see my mate was unharmed and I surprised him by hugging him with one arm.

"Oh well, if I get arrested for aiding and abetting a 'mutant grizzly', at least I can rest easy with the knowledge that my mate is OK." I sighed.

"Is Mummy getting arrested?" Looch's eyes widened.

"Would everybody please calm down?" He raised his voice. "Nobody is getting arrested!"

"Aunt B is understandably upset after the attack this afternoon," Ki said sympathetically.

"I was fine right up until the point I found out about that security camera!" I seethed. "Would people please stop acting like I'm some useless female who can't defend herself!"

"Fine, but you're not going into Alma without me ever again." Declan said adamantly.

My head snapped around in his direction. "What?!"

"But Daddy, I didn't try to eat anybody!" Looch whined.

"I know sweetie, but it's just too dangerous." He said unhappily. "Every time I let my guard down, a fang head pops up. It's like those bloodsuckers can sense it and ruin my day."

"The next time a fang head appears I'LL fight them!" I said angrily. "I don't care if people recognize me! It'd be better than having a husband who thinks he can tell his wife what to do!"

"No females in the Sabre family will step off Lokoti land without the accompaniment of their husband or father." Declan declared.

"Bite me!" My eyes glowed turquoise in anger.

"I wish!" My husband's eyes glowed green.

"Alright that's enough!" Ki turned around in his seat to face the family in the back. "The way you two argue, I'm surprised you can teach your children any self-control at all, let alone with handling the bloodlust!"

Caesar let out a snicker as he cruised onto tribal lands then he turned towards the hill our houses sat on.

"But I didn't eat anybody!" Looch complained again.

"Daddy ate the smelly people." Soph smilingly pointed at her father.

My mate gave a wink to his youngest sitting in my lap. When she waved her finger in front of his face, he playfully pretended to bite it. This made both of our little girls giggle.

"Aunt B," our Healer looked my way. "Uncle Declan is not intimating that you're helpless. But you and his children are his entire world, which is why he acts territorial around you three."

"Damn straight," my husband's jaw set.

"Uncle Declan," he looked his way next. "Aunt B can certainly defend herself. But installing strict rules on your family's movements is not going to stop more Vampires from showing up."

"Thank you Ki." I said.

"Yeah yeah," my husband glared at our Medicine Man – slash – Counsellor. "It's all well and good to observe from the sidelines, Ki. But lets see how you'd react if you had fang heads hunting your wife and kids."

Looch pouted, "Mummy wouldn't let me fight the fang head."

This gave Declan pause then he stroked her hair.

"One day you'll grow up to be stronger than the fang heads, Looch." He said seriously. "Until then, it's best to let your parents handle 'em."

Caesar pulled up into our driveway then powered down the vehicle. Everyone hopped out as soon as the hover-car landed with a soft thud. Declan helped out Looch since she was sitting on his lap, as I lifted out Soph.

Instead of walking towards the house with everyone else, my husband headed for the tree line of the surrounding forest.

I called after him, "Where are you going?"

"I have some tracks to leave behind," he returned. "Walt's gonna have to show the police something tomorrow morning."

Then the European Werewolf disappeared into the woods whilst taking off his clothes.

Caesar opened the boot then he and Ki carried inside our bags of books. I sat my three year old down at the dining table then I headed into the kitchen. Next, I switched on the kettle before opening up the pantry.

I offered my guests, "Coffee, gentlemen?"

"I don't think you should have any caffeine after this afternoon." Ki came into the kitchen as Caesar sat at the table with Soph. He helped himself to the pantry by pulling out a box of chamomile tea. "How about this instead?"

"Do you have any of that peppermint tea?" Caesar wondered aloud.

I pointed at the shelf where it could be found then Ki assisted in making the beverages. I gave Looch the biscuit tin to carry over to the table, to share with everyone. However, she stopped short and looked around, with her blue eyes glowing green again. We caught her sniff the air as she scanned the house.

"Lucia?" Our First sat up straighter in alarm "What is it?"

Instead of answering, her glowing green eyes looked up at the ceiling. This made Caesar react by rising to his feet. Absentmindedly, Looch shoved the biscuit tin into her little sister's hands and crept behind our leader as he skulked over to the staircase. She looked like she was going to follow him upstairs, but he gently pushed her back and indicated for her to remain.

"Bickies!" Soph squealed, looking on the open biscuit tin like she'd just won the lottery.

"Shhh!" Ki shushed her, as he tiptoed past to follow his First.

I walked up and pulled Looch backwards, away from the stairs and over to where Soph was sitting. Standing by the table, I watched my Lokoti Werewolf relations morph into their supernatural bodies. Their shirts tore from expanding muscle bulk as their nails extended at the ends of their hands and feet, poking through their shoes. Caesar's eyes glowed blue as Ki's eyes glowed pink.

"Is this another secrets game, Mummy?" Soph asked confused.

Then we heard it with our acute hearing; a scratching sound moving down the wooden floorboards of the upstairs hallway.

"Who's that?" Soph looked up at her mother.

Looch put her hand over her mouth as she whispered in her ear, "There's another fang head upstairs."

I watched the male Lokoti Werewolves sniff as they soundlessly climbed the stairs. By now it wasn't just Lucia with her keen sense of smell, but its' odour of decay was evident to all. I don't know how we didn't detect it before.

Damn it, those three Vampires lied! They didn't kill off their fourth, although I wouldn't put it past them to do such a thing. They must have been sent to bring back the targets to their leader.

My heart pounded as I stood with my arms around my daughters. I felt my kin's determination to exterminate the predator who would prey on their female and her young. I felt torn in two, as half of me wanted to climb those stairs and fight with my First, while the other half wanted to stay and guard my children.

Suddenly, we heard a loud hissing noise and Caesar who'd just disappeared upstairs, was thrown down them! When he landed on the hard, wooden floor, we saw multiple stab marks in his torso from the Vampire's knife-like nails. Next, Ki tumbled down the stairs, breaking a banister or two on his way. He landed unconscious beside his First on the living room floor. He too, had several stab wounds in his chest and abdomen.

With a groan, Caesar forced himself to his feet and I caught him glance our way. My stomach knotted as I sensed that he was seriously injured, but like any Lokoti Werewolf defending his territory, he was going to fight to his last breath. However, he could barely stand upright, as the Vampire descended the stairs.

The fang head wore dirty jeans and a stained white shirt. It was barefoot, with its toenails long and knife-like, just like the nails on its hands. It had long, black, greasy hair and its eyes were blood red. Its piranha-like, pointy teeth were long, which made the hissing noise as it breathed through them.

We watched our First engage our enemy in combat. Caesar swung out his clawed hand but the Vampire ducked. He swung out again, but as the enemy side-stepped him, it stabbed its nails into our leader's ribcage.

We heard him roar in pain as he sunk to his knees. While he was down, the South American Vampire started to kick him. We watched in horror as the knife-like nails on the ends of his feet inflicted more harm.

"Nooo!" Looch tearfully cried out. "Leave him alone!"

The violence ignited something inside and like a soldier on a battle field, I snapped to attention.

To Looch and Soph's surprise, abruptly they found themselves shoved under the dining table.

"Stay there!" I yelled at my daughters.

I expanded into my Werewolf body, as my blue, woollen jumper tore at the seams from my extra muscle. I kicked off my ruined shoes as I flexed my claw-like hands. My eyes glowed turquoise and I felt my elongated, sharp teeth jut out from my mouth. Then to the fang heads' surprise, I moved into a self-defence stance.

"Aunt B, no...!" Caesar wheezed in pain, as he rolled onto his side. "Get your girls and run!"

But I remained in a defensive position, which invited the South American Vampire to engage. It smelled old, almost as old as I was. The style of its stained white shirt looked circa the 22nd Century, which hinted at its age.

"So you like hunting female Werewolves, huh?" I spoke in my deep, rumbling Werewolf voice.

"More than life itsssssself," the fang-head hissed out.

As a last ditch effort to protect the females in his family and pack, Caesar sent out a telepathic distress call:

THERE'S A SOUTH AMERICAN VAMPIRE IN AUNT B AND UNCLE DEC'S HOUSE!

ON MY WAY – Walt thought back – *BUT I'M COMING FROM DEEP INSIDE THE NATIONAL PARK AFTER MOVING ON THE CAMPERS.*

I'M SHOPPING IN ALMA BUT I'LL GET THERE AS SOON AS POSSIBLE – Forrest responded.

It probably looked strange, an elderly Native Alaskan man abruptly dropping whatever he was carrying and bolting out of the shop.

Just then the South American Vampire lashed out in my direction, but I ducked. It continued to swipe with its long nails but using my light speed reflexes, I was able to swerve. I avoided a double swing as it used both of its hands, when I side-kicked it in the abdomen! It went flying backwards and hit the couch in the lounge area.

"You're ssstronger than I thought," it said as it returned to its feet. "I thought femalesss of your ssspecies were not asss ssstrong asss the malesss."

"That's the good thing about being female, we've got stronger lower bodies." I grinned back with my sharp, elongated teeth.

I sensed that Declan would be here at any moment, so this time I attacked. The fang-head didn't know what hit it, one moment I was standing still and then the next, I was punching, kicking and scratching it up with my own nails. I moved so fast, I looked like a bright blur. He was kicked and punched backwards again and again, until he hit the wall beside the front door.

It doubled over in pain, if it had been human, my blows would have turned its torso into mush. I punched its face, knocking the back of its head against the wall. Then I threw in a swipe which left a bleeding claw mark across its face, for good measure.

As I moved in for the finale, I was almost disrupted by the bright flash of light of Declan instantaneously phasing into the room. But before my mate in his large body could eat the threat to his family, I beat him to the chase.

My fist punched through the Vampire's chest until my knuckles hit the wall behind. Then I ripped my hand back and along with it, came its' still beating heart. Stunned, my enemy stared at the sight of his organ, before it watched me move it to my mouth and bite into the flesh.

Blech! Fang heads don't just smell stale, but they taste stale too. I don't know what Declan sees in eating them, they certainly don't taste very nice.

I dropped the half-eaten organ to the floor as my opponent joined it. However, the South American Vampire didn't die. It even started to pull itself along the floor towards the door, whilst making pained noises. I stood and watched, amused at such a slow getaway.

IT CAN STILL HEAL – my husband thought – *YOU HAVE TO REMOVE THE HEAD FROM THE BODY TO STOP IT FROM REGENERATING.*

"Looch," I turned to my eldest who was watching with wide eyes. "Run upstairs and get my sword from my bedroom."

I'VE GOT IT – Declan mentally declared.

Next, our daughters watched as their father ate through his fourth Vampire's head.

His gigantic jaws crunched through the back of the fang head's skull. The Vampire's eyes bulged at the sensation of having his head eaten through. He opened his mouth to scream but after another chomp, our enemy fell flat on his face. Now it was completely dead with half of its skull missing. As if to finish the job, Declan didn't stop eating until there was no brain matter left.

Looch and Soph crawled out from under the table and ran over to their parents. I was standing beside Declan and as Looch hugged one of her father's large legs, Sophia clung to mine. Caesar slowly sat upright, breathing hard in pain while poor Ki was still out to the world.

"I thought you said the head had to be removed from the body." I spoke in my rumbling voice.

LOOK AT IT B, THERE'S BARELY A HEAD LEFT TO REMOVE – He rolled his glowing green eyes.

Then Declan delivered an affectionate lick to Looch's forehead, before he moved away from her. On all fours, he walked over to where our First was sitting. He sat on his hind legs beside, lifted up his front left claw to his mouth and then shoved the gash he'd just made, into his leader's mouth.

As my mate tended to our First, I went over to our Healer. Our daughters crowded around to look on our unconscious friend. I sniffed his injuries and smelled that the cuts had ruptured his liver, lung and stomach. So I lifted my wrist to my sharp teeth and put a gash in it as well. Then I lowered it to his partially open mouth and waited as the blood pooled inside.

"Wakey wakey, Mr Medicine Man." Soph started to slap his cheek.

"Soph, don't." Her sister pulled her hand away.

Next, my youngest stood up and went over to examine the Vampire's body. At first she knelt down beside the shoulders to look on what little head there was left. But when she reached out to touch the fang head's long, sharp nails, I called out.

"Soph, no."

Our three year old didn't like being told 'no' to all the time and I think all the excitement had gone to her head. She went ahead and touched the nails anyway, which of course she cut herself on.

"Oow!" She flinched then she started to cry. "Mummy...!"

"I told you not to." I rolled my eyes. "Now come over here."

However, when she stood up, something supernatural happened. A drop of blood dripped from her cut and landed on the Vampire's heart, as she walked past. The half-eaten organ actually started to beat again and right before our eyes, it began to heal itself.

"What the...?" I uttered in shock.

Since Soph was used to seeing something killed by her parents stay dead, it gave her a fright. Our three year old screamed and ran behind her massive father to hide. She cried pitifully as she clung to his muscled back.

Just then Ki came around from the healing properties in my blood. He spluttered as he sat upright with some assistance. He looked down at his wounds in a daze, before he caught sight of what we were all gazing at.

A completely healed South American Vampire heart sat on the polished wooden floor, beating beside its annihilated body.

"That's new." Ki said vaguely. "I take it that belongs to the Vampire?"

Caesar removed my husband's wrist from his mouth then he stood up from the floor, completely regenerated. The only traces of his injuries were the bloodstains on his clothes. Then he walked into our kitchen, opened up a cupboard and reappeared carrying a bread and butter plate. He knelt down and using the ends of his claws, he pushed the organ onto the dish.

"Do you guys mind if I borrow the plate?" He asked. "I want to keep this."

"Do you want a Tupperware container to put it in, instead?" I offered.

"Yeah, thanks Aunt B."

I left Ki's side and headed into the kitchen. Looch helped our Healer to his feet and then he and my husband moved to stand beside our First, to look on the unusual trophy. I reappeared with the container and Caesar tipped the beating heart into it. The organ continued to thump no matter its surroundings.

"I wonder how long it'll beat like that, before it dies again?" Ki thought aloud.

Caesar snapped the lid shut, "That's what I want to find out."

At that moment, we were interrupted by the sound of several hover-cars powering down on the driveway. It was accompanied by the footfall of numerous people running up the gravel towards the veranda steps. Our heads turned towards the front door just as it was thrown open by the rest of the pack, reporting in for battle. They were changed and topless with Walt and Forrest leading the way, their faces frantic with worry.

"Where's the fang head?!" Walt boomed out in his thunderous voice, looking around for something to kill.

Looch pointed at the body lying on the floor and their glowing eyes dropped in disappointment.

"Uncle Dec, do you think you could let us get in at least one kill before you annihilate the whole coven?" Forrest asked wryly.

IT WASN'T JUST ME THIS TIME FELLAS – Declan panted out a laugh – *THIS TIME IT WAS B.*

Walt looked my way in surprise, "Aunt B?"

"Thanks a lot!" I bristled at their disbelief.

"But you helped her, right Uncle Dec?" Derik asked, dumbfounded.

A dangerously low growl escaped between my sharp, clenched teeth.

Forrest elbowed Derik in the ribs to watch it, as Declan rolled his glowing eyes at his screw up. However, my mate was next distracted by his youngest crying, as she looked on the Tupperware container frightened. Soph crawled in between his two front claws as she tried to hide behind his muscle bulk.

Walt wondered, "What's wrong with Sophia?"

"She's not used to the dead coming back to life." Caesar held up the container. "She prefers the things her parents kill, not to move afterwards."

The rest of the pack crowded around to look inside. Their First opened it again to show his men what their adversary was capable of. I heard their audible gasps or growls, as they looked on their enemy's longevity with dissatisfaction.

"Where did the heart come from?" Derik queried.

"Aunt B ripped it out of the Vampire's chest." Caesar said proudly.

"Yeah, but Uncle Dec helped her do that, right?" He asked again.

Ki shook his head, "Keep digging that grave with the invisible shovel in your hands, Derik."

I passed a scathing look towards my mate who actually flinched in his bigger body at my temper.

"You see?" I growled unhappily. "This is what happens when you fight all the Vampires without me!"

YEAH BUT YOU SECRETLY LIKE IT, GO ON ADMIT IT – Declan delivered a slobbery lick to my face.

"Daddy! Daddy! Daddy!" Soph cried louder. "Make the yucky fang head go away!"

Caesar turned to his men, "And on that note, how about we give Aunt B and Uncle Dec a hand with the cleaning up by taking away the body?"

"Maybe we should dismember it before burial, to make sure nothing else regenerates." Forrest looked on like it was dangerous garbage.

"Good idea." Ki patted his sore stomach. "Trust me, you don't want one of those things coming after you."

Walt and Derik picked up the Vampire's body and carried it outside. Most of the pack went with them, to lend a hand with burying it in the woods. The members who remained behind were Ki, Forrest and Caesar.

Sophia saw the body was removed but she continued to whinge whilst pointing at the Vampire's blood on the floor, as if she were afraid of it too.

C'MON SOPH – her father inwardly sighed.

Then he picked her up in a similar way you see a dog carry a puppy inside its mouth. Carefully, he used his dangerous jaws to bite down on the scruff of her sweater. Then in his large canine body, he made his way upstairs whilst carrying his young with him.

*****

Forrest went upstairs with the kids to read to them in Soph's room. He spoke softly like a kindly grandfather, in an effort to put my overexcited children to sleep. It was past their nap time and we'd learned the hard way not to overlook Soph's tiredness. She could still scream the house down with her tantrums.

In the meantime, the rest of the adults tidied up the living room.

Caesar used a multipurpose spray to clean the Vampire's blood off the wall however, where my fist had landed left a dent. I was mopping up more of the Vampire's blood from the wooden floor and Ki was sitting at the dining table with his medicine bundle open, running tests on the still-beating Vampire heart. Declan, who had reverted to human and dressed, retrieved his tool kit from the garage and was repairing the staircase.

"Next time Ki, when you fall down the stairs would you mind NOT breaking my banister?" He grumbled, as he reset the wood.

"Oh I'm sorry, Uncle." Ki looked up from his work. "How about next time I just stand back and NOT defend your family?"

"Whinge - whinge - whinge." He muttered.

Caesar and I snickered at their bickering before we returned to our cleaning.

Ki hesitated as he watched the European Werewolf work. "Perhaps you can answer a question for me, Uncle."

"Yeah?" He paused in his repairs to look his way.

"You sensed your family were in danger at the supermarket and you came running. So how come you didn't sense the second danger at home, until after our First sent out the call?" Our Healer queried.

"How would you know that if you were out cold?" He goaded.

"I was in and out of consciousness, thanks to my head injuries." Ki said. "But even in our sleep we hear a command from our First, as you well know."

The question made everyone stop working and look his way.

"I was distracted," he said dismissively as he turned to our First. "I was leaving behind my claw marks for the police to find, when I tracked something. I followed the fang head's footprints to a cave in the northern part of the ranges, when I found where they made camp."

This piece of news almost made Caesar drop multipurpose spray in surprise.

He continued, "The South American Vampires knew enough about us to go around the perimeter of the National Park. They camped under one of the rocky overlooks, careful to stay upwind of tribal lands, so we wouldn't pick up their scent. Those bastards had been casing the joint and they knew enough about us to know how we work."

Our First's face paled but he gathered his wits to ask, "From the evidence left behind, could you tell how long they'd been watching us for?"

"At least a couple of days," his Second answered. "There was a masticated corpse of a townsperson they'd fed on."

Caesar frowned as he looked away in contemplation. "It looks like we may have to start patrolling our borders again."

"But how did they hear about us in the first place, to come so far up north?" Declan walked up in a demanding fashion. "Patrolling our territory isn't going to stop more fang heads from coming and looking."

My stomach knotted as I sensed what he was leading up to, which made me drop the mop.

"No Declan." I shook my head. "No way."

"Not now B," he said dismissively before he turned back to Caesar. "It's time I sent a message to the separate species of vampires."

"No!" I cried out in alarm. "Dream on, Declan!"

Momentarily, Ki put aside his testing and he stood up to listen intently.

"Send me to do some attacking of our own." Declan's bright blue eyes turned ice cold. "It will let them know that we are in no way helpless and we can fight back."

Ki snorted, "It will also act as an advertisement to all the other fang heads who don't know about us yet."

Our First looked away from his Second and over to his Medicine Man and I sensed a silent exchange between them.

However, so did Declan which infuriated him all the more. "I am NOT some overreacting father, lashing out against an attack on my family!"

"I'm sorry Uncle, but that's exactly what you are." Caesar said calmly. "And the answer is still no."

"But I can instantaneously phase now, so I won't lead the fang heads back to tribal lands!" He argued on.

"Of course it will bring on further attacks!" Ki cried in indignation. "Either one of two things will happen. One, is that a lone European Werewolf who nobody knows where it comes from so nobody knows you're protecting your mate, goes on a killing spree. In an act of vengeance, the fang heads will actively try to track you down. Or two, the fang heads will know why you're doing this, which will place a bright neon sign above our heads!"

Declan's eyes glowed green in anger and I sensed he'd lost the last of his patience with our outspoken Medicine Man. Ki sensed this too, however he didn't stand down. He thought he was speaking out for the safety of his family and tribe. Caesar called out my mate's name but he seemed too angry to hear.

The taller European Werewolf marched upon the slightly smaller Lokoti Werewolf. But before he could launch himself on his opponent, in a bright flash of light, I instantaneously phased in front of Ki. My husband halted in his attack with his wife standing in the way.

"Uncle Declan!" Our leader roared in his thunderous Werewolf voice as his brown eyes glowed blue in anger. "You will obey!"

He stopped still with a hateful look directed towards the Healer we were protecting.

"Like I said Ki," my husband spoke in a dangerously low voice, "let's see how you'd like it if the fang heads threatened your family."

Our First addressed his Second, "Ki is not the enemy here Uncle and you know it."

To Ki's credit, he didn't even blink about how close he came to death a second time that day.

He said coolly, "Would you like to learn why the Vampires are so interested in hunting your family, or would you like to storm around for longer?"

The atmosphere in the room was tense as Declan stood there seething, so it was Caesar who spoke.

"What have you got, Ki?"

Our Medicine Man returned to his seat at the dining table where the open Tupperware container sat alongside his medical equipment.

"I've discovered why a single drop of blood from Sophia reanimated the Vampire's heart." Ki began, as he picked up a dropper which was sitting next to several vials of blood. "Watch this."

The three of us stood around and watched him dip the dropper into one of the vials of blood. Then he delivered a droplet onto the Vampire's heart. In return, the beating organ began to slow and beat in a sluggish manner.

"What was that?" Caesar wondered.

"I have several blood samples I've collected the past few years." Ki informed. "I just dropped some blood from a Brown Bear onto the heart. As you can see, animal blood will keep a Vampire alive, but it's not their preferred food of choice. Now watch when I drip some human blood onto the organ."

We moved in closer to watch him drip another drop of red liquid onto the body part. The organ reacted by beating a little faster and stronger from the infusion. Ki looked up at his audience with a grin.

"It prefers human blood certainly, but watch when I add a drop of Lokoti Werewolf blood and then a drop of European Werewolf blood." He instructed.

We watched the dropper place a third drop of blood onto the heart and it sped up again. But after the fourth drop though, the organ beat so hard and fast that it made the Tupperware container vibrate.

"Yeah and?" Declan said unimpressed.

"Lokoti Werewolf blood offers strength to a fang head however, European Werewolf blood is the crème of the crop." He announced. "It's like a supernatural steroid which they can use to heal from almost anything."

As if to compound this, Ki stood up to look Declan directly in the eyes.

He continued, "Your blood which now flows in the veins of your young, is like liquid gold to the fang heads. There's a reason why European Werewolves were hunted to almost extinction before you finished off the job. It's because your kind is like the elixir of life to Vampires."

As if he wanted more proof, Caesar lifted up his shirt to look on his torso. We saw that after drinking the European Werewolf's blood, he was completely healed without any scars. Then he lifted Ki's shirt, to find his wounds had pink scar tissue. He was still healing after drinking my Lokoti Werewolf blood.

For the briefest moment, I saw a glimmer of fear on my husband's face before it hardened once more.

"Yeah well, if the fang heads think I'm gonna go down without a fight then they have another thing coming. If they think they can snack on me or my young, I'll snack on them instead. This proves nothing." Declan declared.

Then before our Medicine Man could stop him, his fist pounded the South American Vampire's heart!

BAM! SQUISH!

The remaining blood squelched out of the pulverized organ as it died all over again.

"Hey, I was going to run more tests!" Ki complained.

"Now if you'll excuse me, I have a staircase to repair then a dinner to cook." Declan's jaw set as he moved away.

Worriedly, I watched him return to work before meeting the concerned gazes of my Lokoti Werewolf kin. Declan's stubbornness was both admirable and frustrating. He was determined he didn't need help but the growing dread in the pit of my stomach said he would. I knew this wouldn't be the end of the matter, as one of my all-knowing feelings whispered words of doom.

~~~~~~
~~~~~~

~ 22 ~

3rd March 2374

Last Saturday was a busy one in the Sabre household. Our daughters were running around excitedly over their first sleepover, as the parents organized their overnight bags. My husband looked after our youngest as I took care of our eldest.

"Soph, where are your favourite pajamas?" Declan called from her bedroom.

"Looch, run and get me your toothbrush." I ordered, as I organized her overnight bag.

They ran past each other in the upstairs hallway and just missed a head-on collision. Soph was carrying her favourite pink 'Miss Piggy' pyjamas and Looch was toting her green 'Kermit the Frog' toothbrush. Looch ran up with the requested item and I put it in her toiletries bag.

"B, where's the girls' toothpaste?" He called to his wife.

"Looch has it in her toiletries bag!" I shouted back.

"No!" I heard Soph squeal. "I want my own toothpaste!"

"You share the toothpaste with your sister at home and you can share the toothpaste when you sleep at the Wisetail's." I overheard him say firmly.

He had to, Soph was coming to an age where she kept claiming everything and teaching her to share was proving a challenge.

"But Daddy..." she whined, "...why does Looch get to mind the toothpaste?"

"Because she's older than you and it's one of the things older sisters do." Declan said simply.

Looch went over to her bedroom doorway to taunt. "Ha ha!"

"I hate you, Lucia!" Soph said angrily.

"So what? I hate you too." She said coolly.

Just then the four year old launched herself across the hallway, onto her nine year old sister. Looch fell backwards with a snarling and scratching Sophia on top of her. With her greater strength, she easily flung her off but undeterred, her sibling attacked again.

"Not again...!" I groaned, as I went to separate them.

Declan walked over to the two writhing on the floor the same time as I did. We both shared a tired look then he grabbed Looch as I pulled back Soph. The two had been at each other's throats since Soph's fourth birthday and she began to fight for dominance.

At first, it was funny to watch the tiny Werewolf go up against her bigger and stronger opponent; like watching David march up to take on Goliath. However, when it started to happen everyday, the novelty wore thin.

"THAT'S ENOUGH!" He roared as his eyes momentarily glowed green. "If you two keep fighting, you won't be allowed to sleep over at the Wisetail's tonight!"

"But Daddy, she started it!" Looch pointed at her little sister. "She always starts it!"

"Not always, Lucia." I passed her a knowing look.

"I don't care who started it but I'm finishing it!" He snapped. "If you two want to go out more then start acting like you're ready for the responsibility!"

Their little heads dropped at the chastisement as his hands moved to his hips.

He lectured, "Both of you are stronger than human children and you have the bloodlust to boot. Two very good reasons why you have to exercise self control double time. Now if I hear a peep out of either of you, the sleepover is cancelled!"

Without another word, our daughters disappeared into their respective bedrooms to continue getting ready.

The parents exchanged a look of relief before they followed after.

Although the sleepover was organized at the last minute, the parents were just as excited as the children were. Where the girls were looking forward to staying the night at their cousins; their mother and father couldn't wait to have the house to themselves. This would be the first evening we'd be alone since Looch was born.

That morning when Declan came out of the ensuite, he started sniffing with a peculiar expression on his face. When I passed him to use the bathroom next, he grabbed hold of my waist, leaned in and inhaled me. Then he grinned like a used hover-car salesman.

"You smell extra nice today, Mrs. Sabre."

"I'm not pregnant," I backed off, "so what do you want?"

"Can't a husband tell his wife of three centuries that she smells nice?"

"No."

"Heh heh!" He pulled me closer. "I just love how blunt and honest you are, B."

"Like I said Declan, what do you want?" I pushed him off.

"You look nice as well as smell nice..." he wrapped his arms about my waist, "...you must be the most attractive female Werewolf on tribal lands."

"Since I'm the only female Werewolf on tribal lands old enough to have a lover, that doesn't say much."

"Don't be like that," he held on tighter. "Let's share a shower this morning and get in a quickie."

"No," I tugged myself out of his hold. "The girls will want their breakfast."

"Looch can pour the cereal."

"You promised them blueberry pancakes this morning."

He emitted a frustrated growl as he left me alone and started getting dressed. I shook my head at his subtle-as-a-sledgehammer hints as I continued into the bathroom. Once inside, I noticed a couple of things which gave away his motive.

First of all, I noticed I was spotting. I did feel a little tender in the abdominal area, so I dismissed it as my period coming. Then I realized that couldn't be it, I had it only a week and a half ago. Also, I noticed when I lifted my arms to spray on my deodorant that my body odour was stronger. Hang on, I am grouchier than normal which would also indicate hormonal upheaval.

Just as a dressed Declan was about to depart the bedroom, I surprised him by throwing open the ensuite door and marching upon him.

I waved my deodorant in front of his face as I demanded, "Am I on heat?"

Instantly, a silly grin broke out on his face, which gave me my answer.

"It's time for baby number three, Mrs. Sabre." He pulled me into his arms a second time that morning. "It's like nature has flicked a switch and your body is pro-pregnancy again."

"What, you can smell that too?"

"Uh huh," he murmured in my ear. "I can smell you're ovulating right now in fact. It's like your body is saying, 'take me, take me now'."

"You wish!" I elbowed him away.

He chuckled as he watched me march back into the bathroom and close the door behind.

It wasn't until I came downstairs dressed and ready for my day, I saw how much he really did wish.

Declan was standing at the kitchen bench stirring the pancake mix with Looch standing next to him, slicing some strawberries. A tray of blueberries sat next to the mixing bowl and I watched him tip them in. Soph seemed so excited this morning, she skipped back and forth from the kitchen to the dining table, as she set it.

"Somebody's happy about having blueberry pancakes." I smiled.

"That's not it, Mummy," Looch said. "Daddy said we can sleep over at the Wisetail's tonight!"

What the...? I looked on my husband in surprise at the suddenness of this arrangement. In return, he passed me a wink before he checked on the strawberries his eldest was cutting up.

"Good job, Looch." He commended. "Now put them on the table and cut up the banana next."

"When did this happen?" I asked, as I leaned on the bench beside.

"While you were getting dressed," he shrugged.

"Do Wendy and Walt know about this?" I gave a funny look.

"Well, Walt does and I imagine he's telling Wendy right about now."

"What did you say, 'my wife is on heat so can you baby-sit the kids tonight'?" I mimed his deep, gruff voice.

"Since I thought it to him, I don't know if it sounded like that." He smirked. "But I said we need some alone time tonight and can the kids crash? He thought back 'yeah sure' in his typical, easy going, Walt way."

"This means we'll owe them a sleepover in return," my eyes widened at the idea of minding seven kids at once.

"Five human kidlets and two lil' female Werewolves, what can possibly go wrong?" He asked in good humour.

SMASH!

Quickly, our heads turned to see Sophia and Lucia struggling against each other with a broken plate of strawberries at their feet.

Looch held her little sister in a headlock, "Now look what you've done, Sophia!"

"Hey hey hey!" Declan darted forwards with his wife on his heels. He pulled back his eldest as I got a hold on our youngest. "What's going on here?"

"Soph tried to claim the strawberries!" She pointed at her snarling little sister.

"They're MY strawberries!" Soph's dark brown eyes glowed green.

"I'M the one who cut them up!" She flared.

"Sophia Clara, you can't keep claiming anything you want!" Declan snapped at his youngest before he turned on his oldest. "Looch, you're five years older than her, so you should know better than to let her pull you into a fight."

"But she keeps trying to claim everything, including MY stuff!" She cried indignantly.

"The strawberries are the family's not an individual's!" He raised his voice. "And when it's the family's territory then everybody has to share!"

"I don't want to share!" Sophia proclaimed.

"Get used to it because you're going to have to learn how to." I said crossly.

"No I don't!" She struggled harder to escape my hold.

"Sophia Clara Sabre, do I have to sit on you again?" He threatened.

In a 'normal' family, you would send the tempestuous child to their room for time out. However, in our family, the child could trash the room so other measures had to be taken. When Soph's bloodlust-fuelled temper was in full flight, there was no calming her.

The Papa Bear of the family had come up with the unusual disciplining tool of sitting on her back. The first time it happened, I almost had a heart attack because I was scared he'd crush her. However, I was reminded that since our children were different, so too had to be our disciplinary actions.

Two months ago, Sophia was sent to her bedroom without any afternoon tea because she tried to claim Looch's glittery hair band. When I gave it back, she started up her high-pitched screaming which she knew hurt our sensitive ears. Declan threatened she couldn't have any of the shortbread he made, but it had no effect on her. Soph continued to stand there and scream, so her father carried her upstairs and put her inside her bedroom.

BAM! BANG! SMASH!

"What the hell…?" He uttered in surprise.

We opened her bedroom door and found she had overturned her bed, pushed over her tallboy and smashed her bedroom window by throwing her lamp through it. As soon as she saw her tantrum had won her an audience, she started to claw her mattress. She screamed louder as foam and other material flew everywhere.

"Right, that's it!" Declan's jaw set in determination.

He marched over and pinned his four year old to the floor. She snarled viciously as she tried to lash out at him, so he rolled her onto her stomach. Next, she started to claw at her bedside table, so he moved her into the middle of the room, out of reach of anything. Then to my shock, he sat down on her back to keep her down.

"Declan, get off!" I panicked. "You'll hurt her!"

"Relax B," he said. "Look at the damage to her bedroom, she's stronger than a human kid."

Soph was pinned to the carpet on her stomach and unable to break anything else. She continued to scream as she helplessly kicked her legs and flailed her clawed hands. Her father remained sitting on her back as he picked up a damaged story book from the mess. Calmly, he opened it up and started to read aloud.

"'Or I'll huff and I'll puff and I'll blow your house down'," he read from the torn pages. "Right now, I know how those Three Little Pigs feel."

Twenty minutes later, she lay limp and her screaming had died down to crying instead. As soon as we saw her calmer state, her father stood up then helped her to her feet. Our youngest was embarrassed she lost the fight and couldn't meet our gazes.

Her lower lip trembled as she looked downcast, "I'm sorry."

"You have half an hour to tidy up your room." He said crossly. "The money we're gonna have to spend on the new glass for the window, is coming out of what we would've spent on your summer wardrobe."

The four year old fashion diva's face fell at the further damage her tantrum had caused.

Now at the very mention of her father's disciplining system, Soph's eyes dulled back to their dark brown colour and hastily she shook her head.

"Go and get the dustpan and brush and clean up the mess you made." He pointed to the laundry where our cleaning equipment was kept.

She turned to obey, bowing her little head in a submissive gesture.

"Looch, there are more strawberries in the bottom of the fridge, go and cut them up please." He ordered his eldest next.

"OK," she sighed in resignation.

Then we had peace and quiet in the house again which made me look on my mate in pleasant surprise.

"You see, B?" He gave a grin. "If we baby-sit seven kids or even eight one day, it'll be a piece of cake."

"You're like a sergeant major in the army, issuing orders and instilling a sense of command." I smirked.

"You'd better believe it, baby." His grin widened. "Besides, what sergeant major do you know who cooks for his soldiers everyday?"

Then I watched Declan return to the kitchen to give the pancake mix one last stir before cooking it up. Lucia was busily slicing up some more strawberries, popping a slice or two in her mouth while she was at it. Sophia stomped out of the laundry with the dustpan and brush and proceeded to clean up the broken plate and spilt food. Then she tipped the debris into the bin as she grumbled.

The European Werewolf was smug enough so I hid my smile at his 'Superdad' routine.

*****

Although it was the beginning of spring, the hardened snow on the ground made it dangerously icy. Instead of walking the girls down to their cousin's we ended up driving them. At four o'clock, Declan parked our hover-car on the Wisetail's driveway. Before they could jump out with their overnight bags, he turned around in the driver's seat to give them a long, hard look.

"I want you two on your best behaviour," he began. "The Wisetail's are kind enough to let you crash the night, so I don't want to hear about any fighting. If I'm told of any tantrums or fuss, then this will not only be your first sleepover but your ONLY sleepover."

"Yes Daddy," they chimed simultaneously and made a move to get out, but their father wasn't done yet.

"Looch," he fixed her with a stare, "you're the oldest and you're in charge. Look after your little sister and mind your strength."

"Yes Dad."

"Soph," he looked her way next. "You obey your older sister and mind your temper. You're at the Wisetail's house so it's THEIR territory. If I hear of you trying to claim something then having a tantrum to get it, you won't have a sleepover again."

Our littlest sat back in her seat and pouted at her father's words.

I saw the Wisetail's front door open and Kurt, Kevin, Katrina and Hugh came out to greet their guests. Edwina was nowhere to be seen, which meant she was probably in her room, dressing her dolls. Poor Kevin slipped over on one of the icy veranda steps but he was quick to jump back to his feet. When Hugh laughed at him, Katrina picked up a handful of snow and threw it in his face.

Looch squirmed on the backseat as she looked on her cousins having fun without her.

"Dad, can we go now?"

"OK." He said gruffly.

The girls opened their doors and were about to jump out when he stopped them one last time.

"Hey, where's our kiss goodbye?"

Our little Werewolves rushed forwards to bestow their signs of affection before they jumped to their freedom, out in the snow.

Kurt took Looch's bag to carry for her as Kevin copied off his older brother by taking Soph's. Hugh and Katrina took turns in throwing snow at each other, before waving at their overnight guests. Their play fight was soon forgotten as they converged around to say their hellos.

We watched Walt come out onto the front veranda to call the children inside. We threw him a wave which he returned, before he ushered in our small fry through the front doorway. Once he closed the door behind them, my husband restarted the engine and drove us back home.

Neither Declan nor I said a thing for the short ride home. I could sense he was feeling a little guilty at pushing our young on another family at the last minute. But then I caught his right leg jiggling, showing his own antsy behaviour at wanting some time alone with the wife.

He powered down our vehicle in the garage then hand-in-hand, we walked towards our front door. However, as we began to climb up our own icy steps, I almost did a Kevin by slipping over! My husband's strong arm stopped me from landing on my arse.

"Oh no you don't!" He caught me. "Don't even think about falling over and hurting yourself."

Then I was raised into the air as he hoisted his wife up into his arms.

"Declan, put me down!" I laughed out.

"Nope, I'm carrying you back to my cave, woman!" He laughed back.

I was carried through the front door where the warm air of central heating greeted us. Declan returned me to my feet then he shut the front door and headed over to the fireplace. I watched him lean over to check how much wood was available before he looked my way.

"How about I start a fire?" He offered. "We haven't made love in front of a roaring fire in a while."

"You old romantic," I smiled softly.

Next, he headed out the backdoor to fetch the chopped wood which was stacked by the greenhouse. While he was gone, I took off my mittens and coat, which I hung on the coat rack. Then I heard the backdoor open and close again, as my strong mate easily carried in a large load of wood. I sat on the couch and watched him organize it in the fireplace along with some kindling.

Lastly, using a 'fire starter' which was a small, hand-held laser, Declan ignited the fire. He took off his gloves as he watched the kindling burn before taking off his coat as well. He rested them over the armrest of the couch, before sitting down to take off his boots. For some reason, he looked up at our old wooden clock on the wall like he was expecting something.

"What is it?" I wondered.

"I'm waiting for a call from Walt saying that he can't mind Sophia because of her tantrums." He said ruefully. "If she manages to last a whole night without incident, I'll be very surprised."

Then he stood up and proceeded to undress, starting with his flannel shirt.

"What are you doing?" I gave a funny look. "What happened to our romantic night, if you're going straight to the wham-bam-thank-you-ma'am?"

"I just wannna get a head start before we have to pick up our youngest." He said.

"If you're so sure she's gonna screw up, why did you drop her off in the first place?"

"If I can get in at least one hour of uninterrupted sex..." he gave an evil grin, "...I'll be a happy man."

Declan pulled me to my feet and into his arms. He was standing in only his jeans when I felt his hands start to remove my clothing. As he undressed his mate, his mouth engulfed hers over and over again. He only loosened his hold to tug off my jumper over my head, before he leaned in again. He made hungry noises as he kissed open-mouthed before he pulled away. I overheard him inhale deeply as he stared down at my body.

"Man, this reproducing business never ceases to amaze me," he sighed. "The way your body advertises it's ready for me to plant my seed. Then to watch my seed grow and how your body changes because of it."

"I'm not grass, Declan." I gave a funny look. "You made me sound like you're growing a lawn."

He let out a laugh and I took a step back. He tried to pull me close but I took another step away. He looked on puzzled as I continued to distance myself from his touch.

"What's this?" He queried.

"Maybe I want you to chase me." I sung, as I kept walking backwards. "After all, we have the house to ourselves and there aren't any kids around to hear."

This made the European Werewolf lower his head and fix his wife with a dangerous yet hungry look, as he bared his sharp teeth in a frightening grin.

When he started towards me, I quickly ran around to stand behind the dining table. Then he tried to walk around to where I was and I ran around to the other side. We probably looked weird, people who were over 300 years old and still playing games, but there wasn't anyone around to see.

"You know what, B?"

"What, Declan?"

"First, I'm gonna have you on this table then we're gonna do it on the staircase and then we're gonna finish on the rug before the fire." He planned.

"No Declan, first you have to catch me."

Suddenly, he leapt over the dining table using his light speed reflexes, catching me off guard. I turned and ran towards the study but not before I felt him grab hold of the back of my bra. My heart was racing in excitement at how I was being hunted. I kept running when I felt my bra snap, leaving the torn lingerie in his hand.

"One down and two to go," I overheard him say to himself.

I slammed the door shut then I locked it before backing away. I expected to hear him bang on the wood or even burst through. But with his supernatural strength, all he had to do was crush the doorknob in his hand and it swung open.

"Oh come on, that was too easy!" I complained.

"You're the one who insisted on brass doorknobs when we redid the house." He shrugged, as he came into the small room.

"I wanted you to knock it down!" I retorted.

"And what if I accidentally knocked you out in the process?" His eyebrows rose. "I don't want an unconscious wife, where would be the fun in that?"

I darted behind the large mahogany desk which had mine, Looch's and Soph's laptops on it, as well as our open books.

"Heh heh, you're trapped in here!" He taunted. "I'm standing between you and the door."

"Oh really?" My eyebrows rose in return.

The next thing he saw was his wife disappearing in a bright flash of light before reappearing in another, in the doorway behind.

"Hey, that's cheating!" He turned around and followed me out. "This is a Werewolf game, not a Circulator one."

I ran around the dining table again as I tried to make sure the piece of furniture remained between us.

"Oh yeah and who says?" I teased.

"Your Lokoti Werewolf pheromones telling me you're on heat." He circled the table.

"So what then, we hunt each other like Werewolves?"

"If you like," he returned. "I can do that and lay my woman like she was a lawn."

"Dream on, Declan!"

Just as I was about to dart upstairs, in a loud SCREEECH the European Werewolf pushed aside the dining table. It knocked over several chairs and momentarily cut off my escape route. When I paused in surprise at the force of his action, he pounced.

He pushed me on top of the table using one hand as his other scurried to undo my jeans. However, I was able to swing around my left leg in a high kick which knocked him sideways. I was about to leap off the table when he used his quick reflexes to catch the leg of my jeans. Since they were undone, as I continued to pull away he ended up pulling them off. I landed on the floor running and bolted up the staircase in just a pair of panties.

"Two down and one to go," I overheard him chuckle to himself.

I ran into the guest bedroom which was beside the nursery. Next, I opened the wardrobe door and hid inside. Quietly I shut the door, careful not to make any noise, before I sat on the wardrobe floor and waited. I wouldn't be surprised if Declan tracked me in here with his keen sense of smell, but I wanted to see how long it would take.

Silently, I sat and listened to my mate come up the stairs, walk down the hallway and enter the guest bedroom.

Damn it, that was too easy, I wanted him to search for me!

When he opened the wardrobe door, I glared up at him, "Did you hear me come in here?"

"I heard your footsteps run down the hallway but I didn't hear you come into this particular bedroom."

"What, did you immediately track me in here?" I asked in disbelief.

He knelt down to my eye level and smirked. "Baby, right now with this on heat business; I could be blindfolded and I'd still track you across the Alaska Range without making a mistake."

Then he pulled me into his large arms and our lips locked as I wrapped my arms about his neck.

Declan made a move to stand up and carry me downstairs, but I stopped him.

"Nah ah," I shook my head. "We haven't done it yet in our guest bedroom, let alone in a wardrobe before."

This made him smile as he cast a look around the space. "You wanna mark this room like we're marking our territory?"

I cupped his face before leaning in to gently chew on his lip. "I wanna make tonight different and special."

Then he said the magic words, "B, anytime with you is different and special."

"Then come and claim me, big boy." I tittered.

"Yes ma'am!"

He lowered his wife back onto the wardrobe floor where he helped remove the remaining garments. This time I didn't struggle and in fact, I accidentally broke the top button on his jeans when I tore them off. He discarded the ruined clothing before eagerly moving in between my thighs.

*****

The next couple of hours became a bit of a blur. We kissed a hell of a lot and there were times when our faces seemed permanently attached, just as our groins were. I recalled I kept hitting my head on the back of the wardrobe from the force of his pushing. So Declan lifted me up from the floor and dropped me onto the spare bed. Then I remember thinking a double bed just isn't big enough for two Werewolves, we kept nearly falling off until we actually did.

Sex on the stairs was a unique experience. It helped with the right angles however, it started to hurt after a while having the wooden edges dig in. The dining table was OK, but we accidentally put some new scratches in the floorboards from the table legs being pushed backwards and forwards.

It was 9 PM when I moved my face away from Declan's long enough to glance up at the clock in the lounge area.

We'd migrated back to the rug before the fire and now the logs were just glowing embers. With the removal of my mouth, he started to chew his way to my ear. I felt his teeth tug on the soft tissue which made me sigh in delight.

"Declan, I'm hungry and it's getting late." I spoke. "Let's order pizza or something."

"Or something?" He mumbled back.

"How about instead of ordering pizza, we get chicken wings or ribs?" I asked.

"Chicken wings or ribs?" He repeated again.

"Yeah, I think you can order them from the pizza place."

He stopped moving for a moment to look down on my face. Then he declared, "Man I love my wife! I was just craving some kind of meat."

"And let's get potato wedges with sour cream and corn cobs!" I said excitedly.

"Oh yeah!" He ducked his head as returned to his previous activity with gusto. "Order extra sour cream."

"But I actually have to order them," I laughingly pushed him off.

I reached for his jacket resting on the couch to pull out his phone.

"Hey, where do you think you're going?" He complained, as he grabbed hold of my waist.

"Stop it!" I playfully slapped him on the chest. "I'm not ordering ribs while having sex at the same time."

"B, you're a woman so you're supposed to be able to do two things at once." Declan said dryly.

He rolled onto his back as he pulled me on top. I slapped him on the chest even harder to make him behave but it only made him laugh. Right now in my naked state, I appreciated the fact that we both had the videophone function switched off. All the calls we made were audio only.

"Yeah hi, could we order delivery for Sabre please? Yes, that is the address. Yes, we'd like two servings of ribs -"

"Four servings," he interjected.

"Oh, you heard that?" I pinched him on his nipple which made him laughingly cry out. "Yeah, four servings of ribs please. Plus two servings of chicken wings, along with two servings of wedges with extra sour cream. Oh, and two corn cobs. Yep, that's it. OK then, bye."

He snatched the phone out of my hand and tossed it back onto the couch where his clothes were.

"It took you long enough just to order the food." He growled playfully.

Then he sat up as his mouth went for my right breast to chew on the tender flesh.

However, I grabbed hold of his scruffy, blonde hair and forced him to look up. "Then don't interrupt me when I'm on the phone."

Abruptly, Declan flipped me over so I was underneath him again. He reclaimed the dominant position as he raised my legs on either side of him. He gloatingly looked down, "I like it when you talk back."

"So I've noticed," I said.

As he recommenced pushing, I squeezed his hips in between my strong legs. If he'd been human, I probably would've heard a 'crack' as his back broke. Declan's face did redden more than usual though, as the veins in his neck stood out. However, he continued to push like nothing could stop him. In fact, he even sped up to finish this round before we were interrupted by dinner being delivered.

*****

It was midnight when we fell into bed satiated but exhausted. We didn't put on sleeping attire as we didn't think we had to worry about being woken in the night by children. I caught Declan cast one last look at his clock, impressed at how his young were behaving so far. It had been eight hours since we dropped them off and as far as we could tell, World War Four hadn't hit yet.

I soon fell fast asleep with my mate's hot body resting over mine. He staved off the chill in the sheets as he warmed the bed for the both of us. Declan fell asleep right after I did with his face buried in my long, dark hair. It was just unfortunate though that this state didn't last long...

KNOCK, KNOCK, KNOCK!

My mate jolted awake, "Huh?"

"Hmm?" I stirred from my sleep.

"Stay in bed, I'll get it." He climbed out and reached for his robe.

KNOCK, KNOCK, KNOCK!

Whoever was pounding on the door, was a demanding person, which should have been the giveaway.

KNOCK, KNOCK, KNOCK!

My mate went downstairs fastening his robe. As he told me later, the loud noise put him on his guard so he sniffed the door before opening it. But he couldn't believe whose scent it was, so he swung open the door in surprise.

Our small, four year old daughter stood in her pyjamas, looking up at her gargantuan father.

"Soph?" He said in befuddlement. "What are you doing here?"

Her eyes were glowing green and he was unsure if they were to see in the dark, or because she was angry. Or perhaps it was because of both? However, what she next said answered his question.

She declared, "I'm NOT sleeping in a sleeping bag on the lounge room floor!"

After this announcement, she came inside and headed for the stairs to go up to her room.

"But where's Walt or your sister? Did they bring you home?" Declan looked around the dark veranda before he shut the door.

"No!" She said sulkily. "Looch is sleeping in a sleeping bag on the lounge room floor with the others."

"Say what? Don't tell me you just stormed out of the Wisetail's house in a temper tantrum?" He guessed as he followed after.

"I'm NOT sleeping in a sleeping bag on the floor!" Soph repeated. "I don't want anymore sleepovers, I want to sleep in my own bed!"

Then she stomped into her bedroom, removed her fluffy, pink slippers and climbed into bed. My husband on the other hand, stood stumped for words in her doorway. She'd beaten him to the punch of the 'no more sleepovers' threat.

It was right at this moment we heard Walt's thoughts – *UM, SORRY TO BOTHER YOU GUYS BUT BY ANY CHANCE HAS SOPHIA COME HOME?*

By now I was sitting up, wide awake from overhearing my little Werewolf's words. I had to put my hands over my mouth to try to smother my giggling. But as soon as I heard Walt's telepathy, I burst out laughing.

Declan wondered back – *WHAT'S THE DEAL WITH SLEEPING BAGS ON THE LOUNGE ROOM FLOOR?*

Walt sent back – *SOUNDS LIKE SHE'S HOME THEN...PHEW! WENDY AND KURT THOUGHT IT WOULD BE FUN TO TURN THE*

SLEEPOVER INTO A PRETEND CAMPING TRIP, IN THE LIVING ROOM. BUT WHEN IT CAME TIME FOR BED, SOPH HAD A PROBLEM WITH SLEEPING ON THE FLOOR. WE OFFERED TO PUT HER IN KATRINA'S BED BUT LOOCH ORDERED SOPH NOT TO BE A 'PRINCESS' AND SLEEP WITH THE REST OF THEM. AS YOU CAN SEE, SOPH REALLY WANTED TO SLEEP IN HER OWN BED.

Her father burst out laughing as he looked on his littlest who'd put herself to bed. Smilingly, he shook his head, turned around and came back into the main bedroom. He shut the door behind before slipping off the robe and sliding under the covers.

I thought to Walt as we lay back down – *IS IT COOL IF LOOCH STAYS AT YOUR PLACE AND WE'LL COME AND PICK HER UP IN THE MORNING?*

Obligingly, Walt willed back – *NO PROBLEM, THE KIDS ARE SETTLED NOW. WE'LL BRING HER HOME TOMORROW AFTER BREAKFAST.*

My husband counter offered – *WHY DON'T YOU ALL COME OVER FOR BREAKFAST? IT'S THE LEAST WE CAN DO.*

The response to his invitation was quick – *PASS UP THE CHANCE TO SAMPLE YOUR LEGENDARY COOKING? NEVER! WE'LL BE THERE AT 8 AM SHARP.*

We were still chuckling at what happened while we settled back down and I curled up in his arms once more.

*****

I woke up the next morning from the feel of Declan's hot body lifting off mine. Momentarily, I opened my eyes and saw him climb out of bed and proceed to dress. Next, my gaze fell on his clock and I saw it was 6.39 AM.

"Why are you getting up so early?" I mumbled out.

"I gotta tidy the house before Sophia wakes up and especially before our guests arrive." He said.

I watched him pull on pair of jeans and a long-sleeved t-shirt. But before he left, he placed a parting kiss on my shoulder. Then he raised the covers higher to ensure I stayed warm and departed.

It didn't take me long to slip back into sleep. I felt particularly tired this morning, no doubt from last nights' exertions. However, it didn't feel like I slept much longer until I was disturbed again.

KNOCK, KNOCK, KNOCK!

"Mummy, it's time to get up! Daddy said to tell you the Wisetail's are here." Sophia declared. "Mummy? Mummy!"

"Alright already! I'm up!" I called back.

I listened to her stomp away from the door and back down the hallway towards the stairs.

My eyes swung back to the clock and I saw the time was 8.13 AM.

Reluctantly, I sat up and the smell bacon and eggs cooking came to my attention. Slowly, I climbed out of bed and stood on my own two feet, when they wavered from how beat I was feeling. Last night must have been one hell of an event, I haven't felt this weak in the knees in years!

By the time I finally traipsed downstairs dressed with my hair brushed, it was 8.30 AM. I was met by the sounds of Wendy fussing over the children, Walt's chuckling and Declan snapping at Soph to play nice with Edwina. The two were sitting on the rug in the lounge area, fighting over outfits for their dolls.

I must admit, seeing the young contestants in the 'Miss Princess' competition playing together, made me laugh. The eleven year old Edwina was bossy and liked to have her own way, which was fun to watch her go up against a four year old female Werewolf who displayed similar behaviour. They shared the same interests in fashion and dolls, but half the time their playing ended in a screaming or hair pulling match.

Wendy smiled upon my approach and I took the seat next to hers at the table.

"Aunt B, how are you? How was last night?" She greeted.

"Er," I wondered how to put it politely, "yeah, it was OK. So thank you for looking after our handful."

"You're very welcome." She smiled warmly. "Your handful and my handful certainly keep the hands busy, but I love spending time with the kids."

I saw Walt was in the kitchen giving Declan a hand with breakfast by making the toast. The five year old Hugh who was sitting in Wendy's lap, appeared to have the sniffles, so he snuggled into his mother for sympathy. Meanwhile, Looch, Kurt, Kevin and Katrina were sitting around the table, engaged in a debate on who was fiercer; Werewolves or Godzilla.

My husband walked out of the kitchen carrying a mug of coffee which he placed on the table before his wife.

He teased, "What do you mean last night was 'OK'? You're supposed to say it was frickin' awesome! My wife is supposed to say, 'the earth moved'."

I giggled as I picked up the caffeinated beverage but Wendy looked on unimpressed.

"Uncle Declan, not in front of the children!" She roused.

The European Werewolf laughed as he returned to the stove.

"Huh?" Kurt looked her way. "What's not in front of the children?"

"Never mind, Kurt." She said. "You continue with your conversation and we'll discuss ours."

"Godzilla can make the earth move." Kevin said, thinking we were talking about the same thing.

"Sometimes so can my dad when he's in his huge Werewolf body and he's fighting something almost as big as him." Looch said proudly.

"Yeah but Godzilla is bigger than your dad." Kevin argued.

"But my dad's stronger." Looch refuted. "Aren't you Daddy?"

"Sure I am." Declan said back and we heard Walt chuckle again.

"Dad, are you as strong as Uncle Declan?" Katrina called to her father.

"Er, no." He said modestly. "Your Uncle Declan is a European Werewolf and I'm a Lokoti Werewolf."

"Looch is half Lokoti and half European Werewolf." Kurt looked on in admiration. "Does that mean she's gonna grow up stronger than the both of you?"

All of the adults cracked up laughing which made the children look on in confusion.

As I nursed my coffee in my right hand, my left reached out to stroke her wavy, dark blonde hair.

"Looch will grow up stronger than the Lokoti Werewolves, but she won't be as strong as her European Werewolf father." I smiled softly.

Lucia's face turned pink in modesty as she glanced down.

"What about me?" Soph inquired from the lounge area. "Am I gonna be stronger than the Lokoti Werewolves?"

"Maybe, Soph." I shrugged. "Just maybe."

"I think so," Declan talked to Walt as they worked. "Soph already has half of B's strength and she's not even five yet."

"Hmm, I agree." He said as he buttered the toast. "Soph looks the most like a Lokoti Werewolf but the pack can smell her underlying European Werewolf strength."

"She's certainly got the European Werewolf temper," her father snickered.

"Now THAT the pack has definitely noticed!" He guffawed.

Soon the men served up the five-star feast to their families. Not only did we have the delight of crispy bacon and creamy scrambled eggs, we were spoilt with hash browns, grilled tomatoes and sautéed mushrooms. We also helped ourselves to the pile of toast Walt made when I saw his curse with cooking continued; two of the slices were burnt.

"I'll take these two," he gallantly put the pieces of charcoal on his plate.

Smilingly, Wendy shook her head at her husband's bad luck in the kitchen when he gave her a cheeky grin, making her giggle.

Everyone was seated at the table except for Katrina, Hugh and Sophia who ate at the coffee table in the lounge room. When Sophia started to whinge that she wanted to eat at the dining table, Declan silenced her with a growl. All of the seats at the table were taken.

"That girl really doesn't like sleeping or eating on lounge room floors." Wendy remarked. "With our mock campsite in the living room last night, she refused to eat her hot dogs with us before the fire and went and sat at the table alone."

"Hmm, our little 'princess' is developing some royal pain in the behind behaviour alright." Declan grumbled.

Sophia spoke up, "I don't like eating and sleeping on the floor because it's dirty."

"But you're not actually eating your food off the floor, are you Soph?" He replied.

"I still don't like it." She said adamantly, whilst sitting around the coffee table with her cousins. "But Daddy?"

"Yeah Soph?" He answered amongst his eating.

"How come the house was a mess last night but when I woke up this morning it was tidy again?"

Declan and I almost choked on our mouthfuls as Wendy and Walt tried to cover their laughter. The rest of the children looked on curiously, wondering what the joke was? Her father coughed and picked up his glass of OJ to drink before answering her.

"We had a game of 'Hide and Seek' last night."

"You too?" Katrina perked up. "My Mommy and Daddy play that after they've put us to bed."

Now it was Walt and Wendy's faces which reddened as Declan and I snickered at them.

"Aren't you too old to play that game?" Edwina looked on peculiarly. "Even I don't play that anymore!"

"I'll tell you what Edwina," he looked her way, "when you meet the man or woman you still want to play games with when you're an adult, you'll know you've met your mate."

Both my heart and face warmed when Declan said that. It made me pause in eating and he noticed my gaze and gave me a wink in return. Next, he picked up the plates of bacon and mushrooms and put some more on my plate.

"No more, Declan!" I objected. "You've already piled the food high enough as it is."

"You need your strength," he insisted.

At first I thought he saw how tired I was feeling after our 'games' last night. But then I caught a knowing look pass between him and Walt. It made me sit up straighter as I gazed suspiciously on the two. Walt tried to act innocently by averting his eyes as he continued eating.

*****

That night my suspicions were justified when I readied for my evening shower.

I had the bedroom to myself with my little girls asleep and my husband downstairs, putting the leftovers from dinner in the freezer.

I turned on the bedside lamp and proceeded to undress. Each piece of clothing I took off ended up in the dirty laundry basket and I noticed yesterday's garments were in there, too. Declan must have put them in when he tidied up this morning.

Once I had removed all of my clothes, I noticed my body odour had changed again. I guess I'm not on heat anymore which was a relief. It's disconcerting having other people knowing what stage of your cycle you're in. I thought everything was back to normal... that was until I went into the ensuite.

In surprise, I stopped in the doorway and stared at what was sitting on the vanity.

There sat a pregnancy test kit beside an orange orchid, freshly cut from the greenhouse.

~~~~~~
~~~~~~

~ 23 ~

4th April 2374

I lay on top of our king-sized bed watching the storm come over our part of the Alaska Range via the window. I could hear the distant rumble of thunder and the dark clouds looked heavy with snow. Meanwhile, I felt snug-as-a-bug-in-a-rug, lying on top of my warm quilt wearing jeans, a long-sleeved t-shirt and my favourite black, woollen cardigan. The central heating kept the chill inside our home to a minimum with only the weather outside reminding us of the cold.

The delicious aroma of dinner simmering away wafted upstairs and from the scent, I guessed we were having Hungarian Goulash. The giggling of my daughters playing a board game downstairs also came to my sensitive ears. I think their father pulled out our old 21st Century games to keep our young's fighting to a minimum and allow their mother some rest.

My husband was doing his best with looking after a pregnant wife who was experiencing morning sickness as well as tension headaches. Normally, these symptoms weren't cause for concern in expecting women. However, in the case of a female Lokoti Werewolf who'd never experienced these sensations before, it was unusual.

During the first week of pregnancy, I was watching a movie on the Internet TV with my husband and daughters when I experienced heartburn. Being Werewolves with our large appetites and regenerative capability, we were hardly ever burdened with digestive problems. I'd almost forgotten what heartburn felt like. I went into the kitchen to drink a glass of milk, which temporarily helped.

Then the next evening during dinner the food began to repeat on me. We were eating beef cannelloni with Caesar salad when I felt my stomach churn. I burped loudly, which made my husband's eyebrows rise and our little girls erupt into giggles. Next, Looch burped too then so did Soph and their Daddy belched out the father of all burps, making our children laugh harder. When we had company, Declan and I made sure the kids minded their table manners. But since it was just ourselves, we ate as a family of Werewolves with our supernatural stomachs.

I laughed along with them when my heartburn turned into nausea. Then I could taste my mouth turn sickeningly salty...oh oh. What the hell is going on here? I couldn't remember the last time I threw up.

To my family's surprise, I jumped up from the table and looked like a bright blur when I ran in light speed into the downstairs bathroom-combined-laundry. I landed on my knees on the cold, hard, tiled floor by the toilet and wretched as my dinner came back up. Partially digested cannelloni and salad, now there's a sight I could live with never seeing again.

"B?" My husband followed me in and snatched up some toilet paper before passing it to me. "Are you OK? I haven't seen you throw up in centuries!"

"I can't remember the last time I was nauseas," I moaned.

I flushed the toilet and tried to stand up but Declan had to help. He held on as I stood by the sink to rinse out my mouth. I splashed some cool water on my face and my husband passed me the towel.

"Your skin looks pale and pasty," he said unhappily.

"I feel pale and pasty," I groaned.

"Go to bed and I'll clean up tonight." He ordered. "Maybe I should call Ki to come and check on you."

"No, don't do that," I shook my head. "I'll just retire early and sleep this off."

Reluctantly, he let go of my waist and watched as I slowly walked over to the doorway. I had to lean on the door frame to get my bearings before I continued on my way. Dazedly, I walked past the table as I headed for the staircase.

"Mum, are you alright?" Looch asked, concerned.

"Mummy, you look terrible!" Soph declared.

"I'm putting myself to bed." I told them.

I gripped onto the banister hard as I used it to pull myself up the stairs. My husband stood by and watched me climb up, which was a good thing. When I almost fell backwards, he zipped up behind in light speed, to stop my fall.

"B!" He cried out. "What the hell's wrong with you tonight?!"

"Woah..." my head rolled backwards, "...I haven't felt this dizzy in years."

My mate swung me up into his arms then carried me the rest of the way. Vaguely, I made out I was hoisted down the hallway and into the master bedroom. Feeling sick, hot and dizzy, I welcomed the sensation of being laid on top of the bed. I rolled onto my side and curled up with a pillow as my eyes closed.

"I'm DEFINITELY asking Ki to come over tonight." He grumbled, as he took off my shoes.

When I opened my eyes again, I saw my young were standing in the bedroom doorway, looking on worriedly.

"Dad, what's wrong with Mum?" Looch enquired.

"Is Mummy dying?" Soph asked next.

"Your mother is NOT dying!" He snapped. "Our Medicine Man is gonna come and check her out."

"Does Mum need some blood to heal? I can give her some." Looch offered.

"That's nice of you sweetie, but we'll wait to hear what Ki says first." He said.

Then he pulled his mobile from his jeans' pocket and phoned the tribe's Healer.

Ki came over within half an hour of being called. He stood beside the king-sized bed, waving his medical scanner over the patient. Anxiously, Declan paced up and down in the bedroom as our girls watched from the doorway.

"Hmm," he frowned at the readouts.

Instantly, my husband stopped his pacing, "What is it?"

"Aunt B's experiencing hormonal upheaval and her blood pressure is a little high, but that's not uncommon in pregnant women." Ki said. "Although I am surprised that morning sickness has come upon her so soon."

"Yeah, it's not uncommon in HUMAN pregnant women, but what about my B? She's a Werewolf, so she shouldn't be having these kinds of problems." Declan debated.

Ki turned off the scanner so he could turn to my spouse who hovered nearby.

"Maybe this pregnancy will be different." Ki shrugged. "When Aunt B carried Soph, it was different to when she carried Looch. It looks like your third daughter is going to be another unique experience for you both."

"Say what?" He looked on incredulous. "Ki, she hasn't thrown up since she turned into a Werewolf and the best you can say is 'ho hum, it's just the pregnancy'?"

The Medicine Man spoke quietly to my loud husband to diffuse the tension.

"What do you want me to say, Uncle? Dizziness and nausea are standard symptoms of pregnancy. Her body has to make adjustments to carrying a smaller life form inside the larger one."

The European Werewolf opened his mouth to demand that our Medicine Man do something, but he changed his mind. He hesitated as he looked from his wife to his eldest daughter and then back to our Healer. What he next asked almost made Ki laugh, but Declan and Looch thought it was worth a shot.

"Would sharing blood help her?" He wondered.

"To heal morning sickness? Probably not." Ki smirked. "You could stick to the tradition of dry toast or crackers, as well as plenty of water. Do you still have chamomile or peppermint tea in your pantry? Those calm an upset stomach."

"Gee Ki, you're a great help." He said sarcastically.

"Well, if there's nothing else then I'll see myself out." Our Healer said. "If Aunt B's dizziness continues or if she can't keep anything down then call me again."

Our Medicine Man picked up his medicine bundle, passed me a sympathetic smile then he left.

Looch and Soph stepped aside to let him out before they came into the bedroom.

"Is Mummy dying of morning sickness?" Soph asked interestedly.

"Sophia, for once and for all, your mother is NOT dying!" He rolled his eyes. "Now it's getting late and you two should've had your baths."

"C'mon Soph," her older sister spoke.

We watched our eldest take hold of our youngest's hand and pull her from the room. Then we saw them turn down the hallway towards for the bathroom. We listened to her take charge by turning on the taps and ordering her little sister to undress.

Declan waited until they had left before he looked back. I glanced up and caught his guilty expression. He looked like he regretted something, which was eating at his insides.

"What's wrong?" I asked.

"You said we'd have three daughters, right?" He recalled. "I bet it's because after this last one, you won't wanna get knocked up again."

"Don't be stupid." I frowned as I picked up his large hand and rested it over my stomach. "I happen to like being pregnant."

"Yeah, but you're not usually sick because of it."

"At least the other mothers in the tribe won't look on in jealousy anymore, now I'm going through what they did." I smirked.

His bright blue eyes were wide with worry and I felt his hand slip under my jumper to tenderly stroke the skin.

"Mmm, that's nice." I closed my eyes.

Declan lifted up the fabric and ducked his head to tenderly 'maul' my tummy with his hot, wet mouth. The heat between us turned my uneasy stomach into a melting one. I giggled from the fluttery feelings he brought out, as I felt him start to kiss up my belly towards my breasts when we were interrupted.

"Dad, we've run out of bubble bath!" Looch called out.

"Say what?" He sat up whilst pulling my jumper back down. "You need more bath formula? I'll get it."

I watched him leave the bedroom then I heard him open the linen closet in the hallway, where we kept our spare toiletries as well as our towels, sheets and blankets. Then I watched him pass the doorway once more as he went to supervise the kids with their bath. The sounds of the children giggling and my husband's gruff voice ordering them to stop splashing, were the last things I heard as I drifted off to sleep...

Sometimes sleeping proved to be the best remedy for my morning sickness. Declan offered to make me separate meals but I didn't like the exclusion. Instead, I ate my dinner slowly and in smaller amounts. If I felt queasy after eating, I'd simply lie down and half the time I was able to dull the nausea by rubbing my stomach whilst breathing deeply. That, or Declan would come and sit beside and gently rub my tummy for me.

The tension headaches were a different matter. I discovered that they wouldn't go away unless I combined lying down with taking painkillers. If I tried to sleep away a tension headache drug-free, I'd wake up with a migraine. The headaches made me hot, brought on dizziness and sometimes made me nauseas again. Declan grumbled about how many painkillers I took, especially when I had them every day. I tried not to, sometimes I'd tie my hair up to get it off my neck to cool down. Or, I'd stand outside on the freezing front veranda, which cooled my hot skin but the ache remained.

The horrible headaches would often occur in the afternoon. I'd be sitting in the study with Looch and Soph, helping them with their schoolwork, when I'd notice the symptoms start. At first my neck would feel rock hard and I'd do a couple of stretches to try to loosen the muscles. Then I'd notice my skin turn hot as the throbbing in my temples began. By this stage, if I hadn't taken any painkillers the headache could turn blinding.

Yesterday while we were working in the study, Declan carried in a large plate of crackers and cheese, celery sticks with peanut butter and carrot sticks with cream cheese, for our afternoon tea. He frowned when he saw me doing my neck exercises as I supervised the girls. Looch was doing fractions and Soph was learning how to write. However, as soon as afternoon tea was presented, they dropped everything to munch on the yummy food instead.

"Thanks Dad!" Our eldest sung gratefully, before jamming a cracker with cheese into her mouth.

Our youngest didn't thank her father, however. Trying to teach her manners was proving just as difficult as trying to teach her to share. Sophia happily ate away without casting her father a second glance.

"Thanks Declan," I said for the both of us.

He noticed that instead of eating I continued moving my head around.

"You wanna massage?" He offered.

He walked around the desk to come to stand behind my chair. Normally, I enjoyed his massages as his hot, large hands were just the thing to knead the knots. My skin already feeling hot and my neck being so tense meant that as soon as he started, I cried out in pain!

"Oow!" I squealed. "No Declan, no!"

"What the...?" He quickly moved away to show it was an accident. "But you love my massages, B."

"Normally I do..." I flexed my neck, "...but not with these tension headaches."

"How about I get you an icepack instead of more painkillers?" He asked unhappily.

"No, I really need some ibuprofen." I groaned, as I used the desk to stand up.

Dizzily, I stumbled out of the study and Declan followed me into the kitchen, walking closely behind as if he were afraid I'd fall.

I leaned on the fridge door for support before opening it to take out the jug of cold water. My husband opened a cabinet and handed me a glass to pour the water into then he put the jug back inside the fridge for me. I ignored his dissatisfied growl as I popped two more tablets and downed them with the H2o.

"Right," he took the glass and placed it in the sink, "now to put you to bed."

"No," I shook my head which made the dizziness worse. "I have to finish the girls' lessons."

"I'll take over while you nap."

"No, I'm on a roll with Lucia doing her fraction, she's responding to my teaching method. If you go in and teach her how to do fractions differently, it will confuse her."

Instead of arguing with his sick wife, the obstinate male lifted her up into his arms. I felt my feet leave the floor and I was taken up to our bedroom whether I liked it or not. If I hadn't been pregnant, he probably would have slung me over his shoulder like he'd done all the other times in the past.

"Declan, put me down!" I growled out. "You can't keep picking me up and carrying me whenever I refuse to do something!"

"Why not?" He chuckled. "It's worked for the last three hundred years."

My domineering husband quickly carried me up the stairs and down the hallway before I found myself planted on the bed.

"I can instantaneously phase back into the study," I said crankily.

"Don't!" He flared. "With your dizziness, it'd be like driving under the influence."

He removed my sneakers and replaced them with my fluffy moccasins. He then rearranged my pillows before gently pushing me down into a lying position. When he sat down by my side, I saw how full of concern his bright blue eyes were. Then his left hand tenderly smoothed back my hair as his right came to rest on my abdomen.

"Declan Domitian Sabre, you're not getting mushy on me, are you?" I teased.

"How about this B, you carry the baby and I'll carry you." He said softly.

"Huh?"

"Your illness as well as a dangerous delivery, was probably what your father worried would happen to you, for reproducing with me." He said guiltily.

"Declan, don't be an idiot." I rolled my eyes. "My head is too sore to beat some sense into you."

"Maybe we should try my blood on you?" He continued. "Remember when you were carrying Looch, you craved my blood more than usual?"

"Yeah, so?"

Then he lifted up my cardigan and long-sleeved t-shirt to sniff my belly before meeting my gaze again.

"Ki's right," he spoke. "This pregnancy will be different to the other two. Susanna's growing faster than Soph or Looch ever did, which is why your body is having more problems with her."

"I'm not having problems with her." I said adamantly. "I'm just going through what every pregnant woman goes through."

"You didn't with Lucia and Sophia." He repeated. "But Susanna is going to grow up stronger than both her sisters combined, which is putting your body under stress. Now I need you to listen to me, B."

"Listen to what?"

"Since she's going to grow up so strong, do you know what that means?"

"No, what does it mean?"

"We're gonna have to be careful with this particular pregnancy." He said in a serious manner. "Do you remember our argument that morning we fought over you becoming pregnant the first time?"

"Remember it?" My eyebrows rose. "I'll never forget it!"

"I could smell Looch would end up half and half. I could smell that Soph would be more like her Lokoti Werewolf mother. Now I can smell that Susanna is the most like her European Werewolf father."

This made me pause and I examined his face closely.

"But how can you smell it?" I queried.

"I can smell there's more European Werewolf DNA than Lokoti Werewolf DNA inside her." He said staunchly. "I smell it just like I can smell she's female."

Out of the blue, he cupped my face in between his hands and leaned in so our foreheads were touching.

"We gotta do this together B, there's no other way." He said emotionally. "You carry this baby and I'll carry you."

However, the heat in his hands made my tension headache worse and my head spun. I had to pull my head away as I gasped for breath. I breathed hard as I tried to fan my hot face with my hand.

"Maybe an icepack would be a good idea?" I said weakly. "That or I feel like standing on the icy front veranda again."

"It's her." Declan declared. "Her higher body temperature is affecting yours."

"But she's still just cells sorting themselves out -" I began.

"Nope, she's beyond that." He interrupted. "Remember I said she's growing faster as well as stronger? The next time Ki does a check up, I'll bet the entire Hodge Endeavor corporation that he's going to pick up her advanced growth."

Next, he raised his right wrist to his mouth, used his sharp teeth to put a gash in it then he pressed the wound against my lips.

"Declan..." I rolled my head away, "...you heard what Ki said, this isn't going to help."

"B, stop being such a princess and drink your husband's blood!" He snapped. "It's better for you than those damn drugs you keep taking."

He put his left hand behind my head and held it still as his right wrist remained against my mouth. I refused to part my lips although I couldn't move my head away. Futilely, I tried to push him off but it was like trying to push aside a cement wall.

"C'mon baby, c'mon baby, c'mon baby..." he urged, "...show me those beautiful sharp teeth and bite down."

I wouldn't take the bait but Declan wouldn't give up. He rolled his wrist to the side to part my lips then he tilted my head back to make the blood trickle inside. The hot, thick, savoury yet slightly sweet essence, slid over my tongue and its deliciousness tempted my senses. My automatic swallowing response kicked in when my mouth became full of his life-giving liquid.

"That's it." He encouraged as he held my head still. "A couple more mouthfuls should do it."

To my chagrin, the domineering male was right. After the second mouthful, my dizziness subsided. After the third, my headache cleared and after the fourth, it strengthened my upset stomach. By now, I was willingly sucking on his wound as my neck muscles relaxed then so did my shoulders. My skin still felt hot though, but from drinking the European Werewolf's blood I was warmed all over. It was a pleasurable sensation which my whole body welcomed.

I thought I'd had enough but Declan refused to remove his wrist. My right hand swung around and delivered a slap to his face, which made him fall backwards. He lay on the mattress, strangely laughing to himself.

"Man, I love my wife." He chuckled, as he moved his fingers to his bottom lip. "I've said it before and I'll say it again; you have the perfect disposition for the mate of a European Werewolf."

I sat upright and saw a small cut on his lip where my palm had landed, which split apart the skin. The sight of the damage I'd done actually turned me on. I climbed on top of him to give him a taste of his own medicine. With my crotch right over his, I felt his immediate arousal.

"If I get up and close the door, you wanna have a quickie?" He offered.

I licked his bleeding lip before momentarily moving off him, "Hurry."

*****

Fifteen minutes later, I was redressed and lying on top of the bed, watching the oncoming ice storm move over the mountain peaks.

Declan left the bedroom in rumpled clothes and he didn't feel like teaching fractions or writing, so the kids finished their schooling early. Instead, I could hear them play a board game which sounded like Monopoly, so I guess you could argue they were continuing their lessons. Looch was teaching Soph how to count her money and read the names of the properties.

Their father supervised from the kitchen as he made the Hungarian Goulash from scratch. I could smell the tomato paste and the herbs simmering away before he added the sour cream towards the end. I even detected the aroma of steamed rice to go with it. My stronger stomach rumbled in anticipation of eating the delicious dinner.

Over my tummy, I heard the low rumble of thunder but I saw little lightening. A couple of times the windows rattled from the blasts of icy wind which carried sleet. The frozen rain made a tinkering noise as it hit the glass and a couple of pieces stuck to the panes.

For some reason, I found watching the weather this afternoon fascinating. I liked seeing the branches bend in the wind, making the snow fall off. It looked like the trees were flexing to rid themselves of icicles. However, watching what would probably be the last ice storm for the year, made me feel something.

I could sense something was coming. The sleet seemed like winter's last attempt at digging its' icy claws in, yet change was in the air. The distant thunder of the oncoming storm confirmed this.

Ironically, as I laid there pondering, I overheard another conversation about nature begin downstairs.

"Dad, why is Mum pregnant?" Looch wondered.

"Because Mummy is carrying Susanna," Soph recited what we told them weeks ago.

"I know that, you idiot." She said crossly. "I smelled that Mum was pregnant before you did."

"No you didn't!" Soph refuted. "I thought Mummy smelled funny too."

"But how did Mum get pregnant?" She queried. "Does morning sickness cause pregnancy?"

There was a long pause and I guessed Declan was wondering how to explain? That, or he was kicking himself to be landed with the 'where do babies come from,' question. I turned my face into the pillow to stifle my giggling, as I imagined the look on his face.

"Er, Soph?" He called instead. "Can you please go out to the greenhouse and pull out some of the carrots? I'll put them in the Goulash."

I heard her chair move back from the table and the sound of her little feet walking over the wooden floorboards. Then I heard the backdoor open and close with her exit. With the coast clear, Looch continued.

"If I have morning sickness am I gonna get pregnant too?"

"Morning sickness is a side effect of pregnancy, Looch." He said gruffly. "Morning sickness doesn't make you pregnant."

She turned quiet as she waited to hear more and I listened to my mate take a deep breath and begin.

"You know how a boy's body is different to a girl's?"

"Yes, girls have vaginas and boys have penises." She said.

"To make babies, a man and woman use these body parts. Something called sperm comes out of the penis which fertilizes the eggs inside the woman, via the vagina. Then the baby grows inside a woman's womb." He spoke quickly, showing his unease.

There was another pause which meant she was pondering his words.

"So your sperm fertilized Mum's eggs and now Susanna is growing inside of Mum's womb?" She summed up.

"Yup," her father verified. "It's called having sex."

I wanted to see the awkward look on his face, so I got up from the bed and tiptoed out of the bedroom. Silently, I sat down at the top of the staircase, which made Looch look up in surprise. I raised my finger to my lips in a 'shh' gesture since Declan couldn't see while he was in the kitchen.

"I've heard of sex because I've heard of people having it." Looch looked from her mother to her father. "But not everyone who has it, makes babies."

"That's because they're having what's called 'safe sex' to prevent pregnancy and stop STD's." He advised.

"What's a STD?" She asked next.

"Sexually Transmitted Disease." Declan declared. "Werewolves don't get them with our regenerative ability, but for humans it's a serious health concern."

"Then why would people want to have sex if it's dangerous and if they don't want to make a baby?" She looked on, confused.

"When you're with the right person and in the right circumstance, it's a pleasurable experience." He said shortly.

"Mum?" Looch looked my way. "Is it?"

"Say what?" I heard his surprise and he came out of the kitchen to see me eavesdropping. His awkward look turned into one of annoyance. "Feel free to jump in anytime, B."

"No way!" I cracked up laughing. "This is too much fun!"

Just then the backdoor opened and closed again with Sophia's return. She was carrying four dirty carrots which her father took to wash and cut up. She shook the sleet off her clothes before sitting at the table again.

"Looch, can you put the board game away and set the table please?" Declan changed the subject.

Our eldest took the hint that the 'sex talk' was over with her little sister in the room and she moved to obey.

For the rest of the evening, I saw just how uncomfortable my mate was, as his face remained pink. Also, I noticed during dinner, Looch gazed on her parents strangely. So did Declan, as he passed me an uncomfortable look before shovelling more food into his mouth.

Sophia didn't pick up any of this as she ate in her customary fussy manner. She picked out the cooked carrot pieces from the Goulash, before putting them on her bread and butter plate. This made the European Werewolf glare at the waste of food, which to him was like a cardinal sin.

"Just what the heck are you doing now, Sophia?" He demanded.

"I don't wanna eat those," she said. "They were in dirt."

"They were washed, peeled and cut up!" He snapped.

But Soph refused to back down, "I'm not eating dirty stuff."

"You're eating the potatoes in the Goulash and they were in dirt, too." Looch spoke up.

"No they weren't!" She argued. "They were in the bottom of the fridge!"

"But how did they get in the bottom of the fridge?" Looch taunted. "Somebody pulled them out of the dirt and put them there."

This made her little sister stare at her plate in horror, as if she'd just realized she'd been eating maggots or worse. Her older sister giggled at the effect her words had as her father raised his eyes upwards. It looked as if he were asking some kind of deity for patience with his little 'princess'.

"Then I'll just eat the meat and the rice!" Soph cried out.

Looch went on, "That meat comes from cow."

"So?"

"That cow came from another cow's womb." She said coolly.

"Looch!" He growled.

Our littlest had no idea what a womb was, but from the look on her face I was guessing that to her, it was on the same level as dirt.

"Eew, I'm not eating dirty stuff or womb stuff!" She cried. "I hate you all!"

Then Sophia jumped off her chair and ran upstairs to her room wailing loudly. With her little sister gone and the food now sitting in the vacant spot, our eldest picked up the plate and used her fork to move the contents onto hers. Meanwhile, I was trying my best to smother my laughter by holding my hands over my mouth.

"Looch," her father said unhappily, "you can't deliberately put your sister off eating to steal her food."

"She was already put off," she shrugged.

Declan turned my way, "Next time YOU'RE doing the sex talk when it's Sophia's turn."

"I'll tell Soph what sex is." Looch offered.

"No!" He retorted. "You've already put her off eating, if we leave the other matter to you, it'll scar her for life!"

"Do animals have sex too?" She asked next. "When we've hunted, we've left alone pregnant prey."

“Yes, animals have sex too,” he answered.

“The same way as you and Mummy?”

“Lucia!” He put down his fork loudly. “That’s enough with the sex talk and it’s definitely NOT a dinner time conversation.”

“But Sophia has left the room,” she said unperturbed.

I removed my hands to answer her and spare my embarrassed husband the trouble.

“Humans do it one way, animals do it another and even Werewolves do it differently.” I advised. “Now if you have any further questions, I’d be happy to answer them for you, Lucia. But we’ll talk about it later, OK?”

“OK.”

She looked like she was about to return to eating when she hesitated.

“Hang on, if humans do it one way and Werewolves do it differently, then what about Walt and Wendy? Walt is a Lokoti Werewolf and Wendy is a human.”

Declan rubbed his red face with his hands, “Man, is this the opening of Pandora’s Box or what?”

I tried not to laugh again as Looch looked on peculiarly. I was beginning to see that where Soph was a dramatic and creative person with her fussiness and fashion sense; Looch was logical and analytical. She liked to have all of the facts and if something didn’t add up then she needed clarification.

“Well,” I began, “I think the basics are the same for all three, but how they reach the goal is by different methods.”

“Oh OK,” she shrugged, “thanks Mum.”

Next, I picked up another roll from the bread basket, cut it open and slathered it in butter. Declan and Looch looked on as I stood up from the table with it. Then they watched as I carried it towards the staircase.

“Now I’m gonna go and talk to our youngest and see what kind of damage control I can do there.” I announced.

*****

I managed to get Soph to eat the bread roll with lies that no dirt was involved. I told her the bread was made from wheat but I left out that wheat grew in dirt. When she asked what a womb was, I told her mothers had them to keep their babies safe and sound and she was happy with that. Hell, I even talked her into eating meat and vegetables again, by embellishing how everything was sanitized during preparation.

After all of our family’s growing pains this evening, I was feeling pretty proud of myself. I left her bedroom and was about to return to dinner, when something caught my eye. A flash of lightning lit up the guest bedroom before the window rattled loudly from another gust of wind.

I walked into the room and over to the window to look up at the angry sky. I could feel the cold seep through the glass, indicating just how icy it was. I'd bet the temperature was well into the minuses at the moment. Seeing the sleet hit the glass made me cringe at the cold outside.

The prior feelings I experienced this afternoon returned with a force that matched the weather. I could feel a change coming, this I knew for certain. Something was going to happen and it was something bad.

Just then I saw a figure... I blinked in surprise and when I glanced back the person began to dissolve before my eyes... it was Forrest standing underneath one of the trees on our property.

He was wearing a red flannel shirt, dark blue jeans and brown slippers. The branches above him swung in the wind but his long, white hair didn't move. He stood in a casual position with his hands in his pockets, looking up at our house. Then his image began to fade away and soon, I was staring at the tree trunk he'd been standing beside.

My mouth fell open in shock but since this wasn't the first time I've seen something like this, I wasn't about to doubt myself or question my sanity. I knew it was an after image, an omen. Besides, what we telepathically heard next, confirmed this.

MY FATHER HAS DIED – Caesar sent to the pack – *FORREST HAS LEFT THIS LIFE FOR THE NEXT.*

"B?" My husband called.

"I'm coming."

I went straight back into Sophia's room and she looked up from her dolls. She wasn't surprised when I grabbed her warmest boots from the closet then I knelt down to put them on her. As soon as they were done, I escorted her downstairs.

We found Declan helping Looch with her coat, his jacket was already on. He handed me mine and while I put on my coat, he helped Soph put on hers. Lastly, we grabbed our gloves, scarves and beanies and left the house.

Since the weather was so inhospitable we drove down the hill in the hover-car to the old Riverclaw house.

We weren't the only members of the pack arriving, but most of the others arrived on foot, including Walt Wisetail. Whereas he was fully dressed, a few Lokoti Werewolves arrived wearing just their jeans. They'd run here in their supernatural forms to come as soon as possible.

We all streamed through the front door which Tyson held open. There was many a nod or a sympathetic pat on the back as everyone came inside. The whole pack arrived at the same time then he shut the door on the wind and ice.

Declan carried Soph on his right arm as his left hand held my right. In my left hand, I held Looch's and she clung on whilst looking around with wide eyes. Soph didn't appear phased though, instead she looked a little sleepy. Her father held her closer as she rested her little head on his wide shoulder.

"Wolves," Tyson began, "thank you for coming so quickly."

"Where's Caesar, is he with him?" Derik guessed.

“He is,” he answered. “My grandfather never woke up from his afternoon nap and my father is with him now.”

The room became filled with low, sympathetic growls that were mournful rather than threatening.

At the same time, Declan squeezed my hand and Looch moved closer to her parents for comfort.

“But his death was recent,” I said, “it only happened in the last fifteen minutes.”

Instantly, everyone else’s heads snapped around in my direction.

Tyson asked curiously, “Did you sense this, Aunt B?”

I swallowed hard before I answered with the whole room listening, “I saw it.”

If a human blurted out that they can see dead people, there would be questions about their state of mental health. However, when the whole tribe knows you’re a Circulator and protects this secret, or even if you belong to a pack of supernatural creatures? They were willing to give you the benefit of the doubt.

“You foresaw Forrest’s death?” Walt’s eyes widened.

“I didn’t foresee it, I saw him.” I confessed. “I saw his after image as his energy left the timeline.”

There were several more growls as the other Werewolves stared in my direction.

“You’re right.” Tyson smiled sadly. “My father went to check on grandfather because he sensed something too. He still feels warm but there’s no pulse.”

Abruptly, the room filled with noise as several different people began to talk at once. One person wondered over who would be activated to take Forrest’s place as another talked about my visions never being wrong. Declan frowned at the commotion before he turned my way.

“C’mon,” he said.

The Second in the pack led his mate and young upstairs. Tyson didn’t try to stop us instead he watched us go. I think he appreciated that the relatives who knew his grandfather the longest, were saying their goodbyes first.

Declan led his family into Forrest’s bedroom where Caesar was sitting on the side of the queen-sized bed. Beside him, lying in a peaceful pose was his late father. When I saw what clothes he was wearing, I stopped short.

Forrest was wearing the same red flannel shirt, dark blue jeans and brown slippers I saw him in.

“B, what is it?” My husband queried.

“Um, he’s wearing the same clothes I saw him in, in my vision.” I said uneasily.

Looch looked up afraid but Caesar seemed unresponsive. The middle - aged Lokoti Werewolf sat next to the elderly one, in mourning. Silent tears trickled down his cheeks as he looked downcast at his late father.

My husband handed over his youngest to his wife to hold so he could approach the bed. I rocked Soph on my right arm and in my left hand I still held onto Looch. We watched their father walk up to stand beside our leader. He rested a sympathetic hand on his shoulder, before speaking softly in his deep voice.

"Your father is with your mother now and they're together again in the afterlife, before they're reborn."

Caesar exhaled heavily as he turned to look out at the cold, wet, windy night outside.

"I know Uncle... I know," he said distantly.

The Second in the pack squeezed his First's shoulder with his supernaturally strong hand, as if he were lending him his strength. Caesar sadly stared out the dark window with the bits of ice stuck to it, like he was staring into the great beyond. A heavy silence descended on the bedroom as Soph fell asleep on my shoulder and Looch tearfully looked on our dead relative.

It was at that moment that she let go of my hand, ran past her father and threw her arms around our leader's neck.

Caesar enveloped her in a hug as several sobs escaped him. Looch cried too as the younger Werewolf clutched onto the older one. Declan stepped back to let the two mourn as he returned to my side.

Carefully, he lifted his slumbering young into his arms without waking her. As he gently rocked her, he stood closely beside to allow me to lean against him. I rubbed my wet face against his large arm as I exhaled emotionally. My eyes overflowed at our loss as I gazed upon the departed lying on the bed.

It was then that the muscles in my neck turned rock hard. At first I tried to dismiss it as stress from the situation. However, when I felt the throbbing in my temples start, I knew it was the onset of another tension headache.

"Oh no, not again." I moaned as I flexed my neck.

The 'crack' it emitted was loud enough to attract my husband's attention.

"How about you and Soph go lie down in one of the spare rooms?" He suggested.

"No, I'll be fine." I lied.

Next, Tyson, Ki, Walt and Derik appeared in the doorway. I sensed they were unsure if they should enter the room lest disrupt Caesar's sorrow. But when he sensed the presence of his men, he stopped sobbing. He released Looch and looked behind at his audience when he caught sight of what I was doing.

"Aunt B," he began, "Ki tells me that you've begun to experience morning sickness and tension headaches from your pregnancy."

“I’ll be fine,” I insisted.

“I think you should take up your husband’s suggestion.” He said. “Ki, I have some paracetamol in the kitchen that Aunt B can have.”

Immediately, our Medicine Man moved to obey, which made me feel even more self-conscious than I’d felt downstairs.

I released Declan’s hand to walk up and place mine on Caesar’s shoulder.

“I know, Aunt B.” He patted it. “I appreciate you coming in this weather and in your condition, but I think you should lie down.”

Before I could disagree, his Second walked up to gently lead his wife away.

“C’mon B,” he said softly, taking hold of my hand once more as he looked down on his youngest in his other arm. “It’s time for my beautiful but tired female Werewolves, to catch up on their beauty sleep.”

Looch tried to remain behind but Caesar gave her a tearful smile before tweaking her nose.

“That means you too, Lucia.” He told her.

“But I’m not tired and I haven’t got morning sickness,” she objected.

“Then you can lie beside your mother and sister and watch over them.”

Like a dutiful soldier, our eldest who was accustomed to following her First’s orders, reluctantly obeyed.

Declan paused in the doorway to allow her to catch up as Tyson, Walt and Derik moved aside for us.

My face which was already feeling hot from the tension headache, now burned in embarrassment. I felt like this pregnancy literally made me into the weaker sex. I bristled at how the males including my husband, were treating me with kid gloves.

The European Werewolf led his family into a spare room with a double bed inside. He gently laid his youngest on one side of the bed as I lay down in the middle and Looch came to lie on the other side of me. He then picked up a crochet blanket which was sitting on a rocking chair in the corner and put it over his family.

“Here we go,” Ki walked into the room with a glass of water and tablets. “If the paracetamol and the nap don’t get rid of the headache, I’ll scan you.”

I sat up to take the medication as my mate watched with dissatisfaction. I sensed he would rather share his blood again but he had to return to his First. Then Ki took the glass and exited as Declan tucked in his family.

“I’ll ask him to scan you anyway, to check the baby’s growth.” He said quietly.

“The next baby we have, YOU can carry it.” I grumbled. “Then I can treat you like the weaker sex and put you to bed whenever I want.”

Looch giggled as she gazed up at her father who lovingly looked down on his family.

"Well then," he said in amusement, "if I get pregnant then at least we're following the prophecy that YOU don't have anymore than three children."

Declan smoothed back Looch's hair before planting a kiss on all three of our foreheads. Then he stood up, switched off the lamp and walked out of the room. He cast a last look our way before he closed the door behind. I knew he shut it to offer us peace and quiet, but with our sensitive ears we could still hear their murmuring.

"Mum?"

"Yes Looch?"

"How come you saw Forrest leaving the timeline, is it because you're a Light Person?"

"Yes."

"But Dad's a Light Person and he didn't see it."

The headache pounded painfully on the inside of my head but I forced myself to answer.

"Everyone's gifts are different, Looch. Although your father is a Circulator like I am, he can see auras and I can't. But I see things that your father can't, like my visions."

"Doesn't Dad have visions?"

"Only if he uses a mirror and concentrates on a particular timeframe."

"But Dad has warning feelings that are always right."

"Yes he does."

She was quiet for a moment then she asked, "Mum are you smarter than Dad? Because he lets you do most of the schooling and when you say you saw something, he always believes you."

For a second, my headache actually lifted as I experienced mild elation.

All this time, I was worried about how my daughters saw their parents. I was concerned that the occasional sexism could impact my young. However, Looch's observation made me hopeful that she acknowledged everyone had their strengths and weaknesses, but they used them to work together.

"We all have special abilities, Looch." I said. "Your father is strong in so many ways and he can fix things that I can't. But where your Dad can't do certain things, I can. Hopefully you'll meet somebody one day who'll fit in with you as your other half."

"Will I fight with him, like you and Dad fight?"

"Hopefully," I closed my eyes. "Sometimes it can be the best part of marriage."

I wanted to sleep off the rest of my disintegrating headache. The painkillers were coming into effect albeit slowly. My eldest saw I needed the rest so she turned quiet. I felt her curl up against my side as she tucked her face into my arm and eventually, drifted off.

*****

Speaking of visions, one formed in my unconscious mind while I was sleeping. In this dream-like state, I was a bodiless mass, watching over events in the timeline. Instead of floating over a faraway location, I hovered over the old Riverclaw home. I watched time fast forward through the history of the house.

I saw Flint Riverclaw with the help of John Wisetail build the log cabin. In a small clearing on the forest-encrusted hill, the cement foundations were laid. Then the wooden frame went up, closely followed by the stone chimney, the logs for the walls, and lastly the rooftop.

After fast forwarding through the years of his solitary lifestyle, I watched Flint bring Jessica to her new home. Then I saw the couple and their son David, go in and out of the house, as they went about their lives. Next, I saw my great grandma Clara with her small son Emanuel, move in with Flint after Jessica and David's demise. It was here I saw the extensions take place, which turned the single-story log cabin into a two-story house.

Then I saw my grandmother Arabella move in with my grandfather Emanuel as well as his mother and grandfather. Afterwards, I saw two children who were my Mum and Uncle Julian, run out of the house. Then I watched my father, Hunter Wisetail, move in during the first month of his mating with my mother, before they moved to a house of their own.

The years sped through my childhood where I watched many a family dinner take place. I would arrive with my parents as my cousins Phoenix and Phoebe would arrive with theirs; Uncle Julian and Aunt Danika. I saw an eighteen year old version of myself come to dinner with my first husband Grant then six years later, with my current husband Declan.

After Gran and Grandfather's departure to the space time continuum, I saw Phoenix's son Chiron move in. Then he passed away and his grandson Forrest took over the old family home. When Caesar's human wife died, he moved in with his father. Next, I saw Declan, Lucia and myself come to stay when our house was being renovated.

It was here that the fast forwarding through the years slowed down to what you could call, 'real time'.

My bodiless mass hovered closer as I drifted down through the roof and passed through the upstairs ceiling. I found myself looking down on my figure lying on the bed with both of my daughters sleeping on either side. Light came in through the bedroom window from a clear sky as the raging storm had raged elsewhere, allowing dawn to break.

I thought I'd wake up however, my vision didn't appear to be over because I was next pulled through the wooden floor and into the living room below. Here, I was met by the First and Second of the Lokoti Werewolf pack, sitting alone at the dining table, indicating everyone else had left. The two men were sipping coffee whilst sitting across from each other.

For some reason, I found myself eavesdropping on their conversation, as if it were important somehow.

Caesar looked up with bloodshot eyes to examine the youthful European Werewolf in human form, sitting opposite. Declan wasn't sure, but he thought he saw a brief look of jealousy flash across the aged Lokoti Werewolf's face. What he next said, confirmed this.

"You're a happy man, aren't you Uncle." Caesar stated rather than asked.

"What's that?" He arched his eyebrows. "Not right now, because your father just died."

"No, I mean in general."

He let out a sigh before answering, "I'm in hog heaven."

"It's ironic that of all the breeds of Werewolves, it's the most dangerous that finds domestic content." Caesar said with a sad smile.

He said with a bitter laugh, "Yeah, but I've had to fight for that happiness."

"Are you the happiest now than you've ever been?"

"Nope."

"No?"

"Now is the fourth time I've felt this happy." He said coolly.

The European Werewolf picked up his mug and took another mouthful of the caffeinated liquid. A full minute went by until he realized he was being watched. The Lokoti Werewolf sat patiently, waiting to hear more.

Being a typical male, Declan hated talking about his feelings. But he saw the haunted look in Caesar's eye, so he cleared his throat and began. He spoke honestly which came out with his usual bluntness.

"The first time I experienced true happiness was the morning I woke up next to B, the day after I moved in with her. Sure, she woke me up and yelled at me to get out of her bed and out of her house..." Here, both men chuckled before he continued, "...but that morning, we both realized we were in it together for the long haul."

"And the second time?"

"The second time I was this happy was when I killed Marcus, the European Werewolf who kidnapped B. I ripped out his throat then she ran up and threw her arms about me. That night we fought European Vampire and European Werewolf foe, but in that moment, I knew I'd won my mate."

My husband paused as he shifted uncomfortably in his seat at all this 'mushy stuff'. However, Caesar was leaning forward, listening intently. Declan thought it must help to take his mind off things.

"The third time I was this happy was when B turned me into a Light Person," he said. "Not only did she make me hers for all time, but that day was the beginning of our best sex yet, thanks to our auras rubbing together."

Our First let out a laugh at his Second's candour, before he went on.

"The fourth time I've felt this happy is now, when she's carrying my third child. She finally relies on me, after three centuries of threatening to run away all of the time. She's settled now and we have two beautiful daughters, as a result."

Caesar cleared his throat before he spoke, "I can see how it's taken the strongest breed of Werewolf to hold onto her. Sometimes Aunt B's behaviour is less Lokoti Werewolf and more Circulator. It's like she can't stop herself from moving around."

My mate said wryly, "Yeah, sometimes I've wondered what it'd be like to have mated with a male Lokoti Werewolf instead; sure, steady, sturdy and who never strays far from Lokoti land."

The two shared a chuckle then together they picked up their mugs and finished their coffees.

"Then again," Caesar swallowed, "European Werewolves were nomads before you came along."

"My breed were psychotic, hot-blooded, hungry killers, before I came along." He said unhappily. "But neither I nor my daughters are like that."

Caesar opened his mouth to say something else but it wavered, as if he were unsure. Declan nursed his mug as he waited to hear what his 'boss' had to say. Our First turned his coffee mug around in a circle on top of the table, like he was contemplating.

"Uncle, sometimes we sense the same psychotic, hot-blooded, hunger, inside of you." Caesar kept his voice calm. "It causes us concern of what would happen to you, if something happened to Aunt B."

"Don't go there." He said curtly.

"But I feel I must," our leader went on. "We've all felt the rage almost take control of you and a couple of times it has."

"So who doesn't get angry?" He retorted. "Who doesn't lash out occasionally? Nobody's a saint, Caesar."

He passed my husband a knowing look as he turned serious.

"When were the times you were the unhappiest, Uncle?"

"There's lots of times I've been unhappy." He said casually. "As have you or any other male whose woman was taken away."

"That's what we worry about," the Lokoti Werewolf stated. "You let your bloodlust get the better of you when you're worried about losing Aunt B."

Declan shifted uncomfortably once more as he looked up the staircase, as if he were searching for me. As he stared upwards, he talked in a low voice. What came out sounded like a confession, but a bitter and unrepentant one.

"The day I secretly watched from the woods B's Joining Ceremony to Grant Elm, I was absolutely miserable. But I couldn't look away as I imagined it was OUR Joining Ceremony. I was so angry about the racism in the pack and the tribe to pick a Lokoti Werewolf instead of a European one. The five years B was married to that bastard was worse than the time I was impaled with a silver sword. Everyone, including B's family, all approved of the way Grant was being 'nice' and 'patient' with his younger wife. But I saw the way he preened about scoring the first female Lokoti Werewolf. Those five years he was with B, my bloodlust didn't crave human flesh, it wanted to kill Grant Elm. If those humans hadn't of taken him out, I would have."

Our First's eyes narrowed at the threat to one of his pack and someone who was remembered as a hero, but he remained quiet as Declan continued.

"When B returned to me after Grant's death, it pissed me off that it had to be in secret. It pissed me off that the Lokoti Werewolves needed my help to patrol, but they didn't approve of our coupling. It pissed me off that Hunter Wisetail never trusted me with his daughter. He's probably watching us now from the space time continuum, just waiting for me to screw up. And it pisses me off that you brought all of this up Caesar and I'm still not trusted because of what I am."

The older looking Native Alaskan met the angry eyes of younger looking Caucasian sitting across. They held the other's gaze in a silent challenge. Then Declan looked down into his mug as he muttered:

"I take damn good care of my family and the only person who acknowledges this, is my wife."

Caesar spoke in an even tone but the seriousness of the message was relayed by the concise way he said it.

"Lokoti Werewolves are overprotective of their mate and young, just as you are, Uncle. However, your methods of protecting your own are uncontrolled. Your bloodlust revels in fighting for your territory which is your family. You've shown your supernatural form to the public on numerous occasions, when some of these could have been dealt with covertly. You've been filmed and photographed by the World Wide Media, which has threatened exposure of the pack and your wife. I know the lawyer called Jonathan Bourne who works for Aunt B, had to smooth things over after the two Vampire attacks which you fought very publicly. European Werewolves weren't known for tact, diplomacy or level-headed behaviour; they were known for reckless, primitive and violent altercations. It worries your First and the men in your pack when you behave like one of them."

"And you're bringing this up now after your father's death because...?"

"Death is part of the cycle of life. I miss my father, just as I miss my late wife Marie. We all worry of what would become of you Uncle, if you went through what a Lokoti Werewolf experiences when they lose a mate or family member."

"I've lost family members." He said coldly. "I lost my Mom and little brother and their progeny continue to drop like flies, thanks to time. But I cope because I have B, who's not only a Light Person but she's the light of my life. What would I be like if I lost her? Like I said, don't go there because you won't like the answer."

Caesar sighed in resignation, "That's what we worry about."

Our leader rubbed his red eyes as he slumped backwards into his chair. It was my mate who changed the subject when he caught sight of the time. He stood up with his empty coffee mug whilst looking at the clock on the wall.

"B and the kids will be waking up soon," he said. "How about I cook up some bacon and scrambled eggs for breakfast?"

Without receiving an invitation first, he helped himself to the kitchen. As he quit the table, he quit the discussion. But this wasn't just the end of their conversation, it was the end of my vision.

Abruptly, everything went black and I no longer felt like I was a bodiless mass.

Physically, I opened my eyes to find myself back in bed with the two kids. It took a minute or so to get my bearings, having a body again. The creature comforts of the warm blanket and my children lying on either side, expedited the return of reality.

Lucia stirred the same time as I did. She sat up as she rubbed the sleep from her eyes. Then I saw her sniff the air at the smell of bacon sizzling. She was just like her father, thinking with her stomach.

"Yummy, we're having bacon and eggs for breakfast!" She sang chirpily.

She threw off the blanket and bounced off the bed. Her movements were enough to wake up Soph. Grouchily, she sat up to see her older sister open the bedroom door and skip downstairs. Before she could start whinging at the disruption, I picked her up and carried her. I knew the yummy breakfast cooking would serve as a distraction.

When I was halfway down the stairs, I paused. The sight of Caesar sitting slumped in the chair, perturbed me. Why would I have a vision of their conversation in my sleep? What was so important that I had to hear? It's not like I learned anything, it only confirmed what I already knew.

My relative looked up to see me standing on the staircase.

"Good morning Aunt B, how's your head?" He greeted.

"Fine." I answered, before continuing on my way down.

Soph squirmed in my arms, indicating she wanted to be put down. As soon as I did, she ran into the kitchen after her sister. The two liked to hang around in case their father was handing out treats, like a beater or the bowl with leftover dessert mix. In this instance, I saw him hand out a slice of buttered toast to each, which they happily crunched on.

I went and sat in the chair Declan had and Caesar frowned at how tired I looked.

"Are you sure you're feeling alright?" He checked.

"I'm fine..." I yawned, "...I just dreamed a lot."

His eyes widened, "Did you have anymore visions?"

I paused for a moment as I wondered what to say?

"Um, I think I did, but I'm not sure what it means."

"Did you 'see' my father again?" He asked hopeful.

"I did." I said, as I reached out my hand and rested it over his. "I had a dream about all the Riverclaw's who've lived in this house over the years."

This touched him and I could tell how much by the way he squeezed my hand.

"Time moves on," he blinked back his tears. "But I'm sure in another three hundred years you and Uncle Dec will still be here, looking after the new Riverclaw's in this house."

"Just as we'll continue to keep the current Riverclaw's company," I smiled.

*****

Forrest's funeral was held two days later and it wasn't just Declan and I standing with Caesar to offer our support, but all of the Riverclaws. Behind them stood the members of the pack, showing their solidarity and support for their leader. Surrounding them was the rest of the tribe, as everyone came to pay their last respects.

The Lokoti congregated on the Holy Grounds before the seven Sacred Totems. In front of the relics burned the large funeral pyre and the flames reached high into the night sky. We felt the heat on our faces as the smoke stung our watering eyes.

Many of the children turned restless as they were uncomfortable watching the cremation, including one of our own. Soph kept whining about the smell of the burning body. Looch elbowed her to shut up and show some respect, but it only made her whinge louder. It wasn't until Declan bent over so she could see his eyes were glowing green in anger that she turned silent.

Tearfully, our eldest watched the flames destroy the body of her great x3 grandnephew that'd been like a grandfather to her. She stood in between her parents while holding onto their hands tightly. In my other hand I held onto Soph's but she wouldn't stop squirming. To hold her steady, my mate pulled his youngest over to his side so he was holding onto her instead. In his iron-clad grip, she had no hope of escaping and finally she stood still.

When the ceremony was over, we were approached by Tyson who invited us back to his place for refreshments.

Declan and I exchanged a long look as we could sense what the other was thinking. My mate politely declined then we watched Caesar walk away with his grandchildren. We saw he wasn't alone and if we'd suspected he needed company, we would have said yes immediately. Besides, after attending so many funerals over the last three centuries, all we wanted to do was go home.

When we did, my husband tried to improve his family's mood by spoiling us with a gourmet supper.

He opened his jars of antipasto, sun-dried tomatoes, olives and even the jar of preserved capsicums stuffed with feta, which he saved for special occasions. He served them with mini toasts and cabanossi on two large, white, square plates. We sat around the table with the delicacies sitting before us but nobody attacked them with their usual gusto.

He sat down in the chair beside mine with our daughters sitting opposite. His hand rested over mine underneath the table then he used his free one to pop some food into his mouth. Usually, he'd be accompanied by his eldest in feasting but tonight, she looked too tearful to eat.

"I remember when Forrest used to read to me," she said dismally.

"I remember when I used to read to Forrest and his little sister," he sighed.

"I remember how Forrest grew up as a vegetarian before his change." I smiled sadly.

"Do you remember his first hunt and the astonished look on his face?" He chuckled. "After he attacked that caribou, his expression said so clearly, 'did I do that?'"

I giggled at the memory as Declan gave my hand a supportive squeeze.

"Mum and Dad," Looch looked on the two of us together, "are you really the oldest people in the tribe?"

"Yup," her father answered then he put some more food into his mouth.

"But don't you feel sad as everyone dies around you?" She asked, helplessly.

He paused in his eating when he saw his daughter's pain. Then he moved over to his usual seat at the head of the table, so he could be sitting near his wife and his eldest daughter. Then in one tug, he pulled Lucia into his lap for a cuddle. I could tell she appreciated the gesture, as she curled up in his arms just like she used to when she was little.

"Sure it's sad sweetie..." he said, "...but there's still lots of things to look forward to."

"But all your family are gone!" She wailed.

"Not all," I said. "We still have the Riverclaw's, Wisetail's, Sabre's and the Elm's."

"But don't you miss your Mum and Dad?" She looked up at her father.

"My Mom died over two hundred years ago but I still think about her everyday." He admitted. "I still have memories of my Dad and he died three hundred years ago."

Next, Looch looked my way to hear what I had to say.

"My parents evolved to the space time continuum over a hundred years ago." I told her. "But I don't see it as dying, I see it as going to a holiday destination where I'll meet up with them."

Our eldest looked relieved at my words but our youngest appeared confused.

"What's a space time continuum?" Soph wondered aloud.

Declan smirked, "I'll let you answer this one, since you're the lead Circulator in this family."

Then he let go of my hand to pop some more delicacies into his mouth as he listened.

"Well, you know how our planet is in a solar system and that solar system is in a galaxy and that galaxy is in a universe, don't you?"

"Yes," she answered, "you taught me that in astronomy."

"So all of that is in space which spaceships traverse," I went on. "The space time continuum is the force that holds up all of space and time."

Looch listened perplexed and she clearly looked worried about something.

"Has Forrest gone to the Holy Hunting Grounds, or has he gone to this space time continuum where your parents are?" She asked, concerned.

I reached out my hand to smooth back her hair as she wore a haunted expression on her small face.

"The Holy Hunting Grounds and the space time continuum are the same thing, sweetie." I explained. "Souls go there to rest and they're reunited with their loved ones, before returning to the timeline to live again."

"So I'm gonna see Forrest when I go there?" She asked hopeful.

"We think so, Looch," their father said as he looked from her to Soph. "We think you'll both see Forrest again one day."

In an effort to cheer up his family Declan initiated a group hug. He moved Looch to sit on his right leg as he pulled me over to sit on his left. Then we giggled as he tickled us together whilst growling playfully.

"Ladies and Gentlemen, here's my beautiful wife and daughter." He boomed out, like an announcer. "You guys are what I look forward to in life."

Then we heard a small voice beside, "But I'm your daughter too."

We looked over to see Soph standing close by, looking a little left out.

"Damn straight you are, Sophia Clara," he grinned.

Then Declan picked her up and planted her in the middle of our huddle. His arms were so large he could hold all three of us at once. Then he delivered a kiss to all three of our cheeks.

"Who's your Daddy, huh?" He growled affectionately. "Who's your Daddy?"

Soph and Looch giggled at his signs of affection as they threw their smaller arms about his neck.

~~~~~~
~~~~~~

~ 24 ~

16th April 2374

I lay in bed at night as another horrible headache hit. The sensation immobilized me and I literally felt like I couldn't move lest my head would fall off. The tension headache turned my spine into a rusty, iron rod and the muscles into elastic bands strung so tight, they could snap at any moment. It created a highway of pain, a toll-free expressway to agony, along my central nerve system.

They also produced dark dreams where the images were fleeting but they left their burning mark, scorched into my slushy brain. Sometimes I saw a dark cavern in conjunction with screaming, voices in hideous agony. Other times I floated in darkness, a black pit of despair where no images let alone light could be seen.

I didn't like the darkness or the sensations that came with it. The tension headache turned into torture and the pit of despair frightened me. But what truly scared me, was sometimes I didn't know if I was awake or asleep?

In my delirium, I groped for some kind of escape route, a way out of this soul-destroying bleakness.

"Declan...?"

"Hmm?"

"Declan...!"

"Huh?"

"Declan...please!"

"What? Wake up B. C'mon, open your eyes."

"Declan!"

"I'm here, now open your frickin' eyes!"

The European Werewolf's hands pulled my subconscious out of the dark pit. Although he wasn't deliberately using his supernatural strength, a gentle shake from him could make a human lurch back and forth. But I never complained, in fact I appreciated it. I was wrenched to safety where instead of seeing darkness, I found myself looking up into his bright blue eyes.

I'd find myself back in bed, in the same bedroom we've had for centuries, in the same house on tribal lands which was home to heart, hearth and kin.

By this stage, my mate would be well and truly awake and looking down in concern. It was the middle of the night and my cries woke him from his slumber. He rubbed the sleep from his eyes before frowning at his wife.

"Declan..." I grabbed hold of his broad shoulders, "...I saw it again."

"You saw what?"

"The dark pit filled with screaming..." I whimpered, "...and my head is killing me!"

"Shhh," he pulled me close, "they're just dreams produced from the pregnancy, or at least I hope so."

His hot body would normally soothe me but with my tension headaches, I'd become sensitive to heat. It would turn the rusty, iron rod into a scalding one. I had to push him away as my headache would turn blinding.

"I need water! Icy cold water! With some ibuprofen!" I pleaded.

"I'll get you a drink," he promised.

Instead of feeling the mattress rise with his removal, I felt his wrist press against my lips. I'd heard his grunt of discomfort as he bit into his own flesh, before tasting his injury. Although his elixir of life was tempting, my body would be screaming for chilled fluid, not something hot and thick.

"No, Declan." I moved my head away. "I want something cold!"

"C'mon B."

"No!" I objected. "I need some cold water!"

"C'mon, c'mon, c'mon..." he'd chant, "...the bar's open and it's happy hour for pregnant female Werewolves."

Then something paranormal would happen; after the first mouthful the pain would dissipate. By my fourth mouthful, it had completely dissolved away. The rusty, iron rod would turn into a spine once more and the stretched elastic bands which were my neck muscles would loosen. I felt like a prisoner being released from a medieval torture device such as the rack. Instead of his heat making me feel dizzy, all of my body would feel a relaxed warmth. His supernatural strength coursed through my veins and made me feel stronger.

One minute I'd be experiencing the kind of agony that migraine sufferers would pass me a membership card for their club. Then the next, I'd be feeling release as well as empowerment which a supernatural constitution could provide. Thankful, I'd lap at his wound with my tongue to expedite his regeneration.

As soon as he felt his skin seal itself shut, he loosened his hold. But I'd miss the removal of his body. Both of my hands would cup his face and pull him in for an appreciative kiss, to which he'd eagerly respond.

"Mmm..." he moaned happily, "...you must be feeling better."

Rather than answering, I locked lips with him. Sometimes after sharing his blood, I'd feel his heavy body lie over mine but not tonight. This time I felt myself pushed upright against the headboard so I was sitting with my husband in between my legs. Quickly, he rid us of our sleepwear before moving onto the next stage.

Our mouths mashed against each other's as the both of us enjoyed the other's taste. Amidst the exchange of saliva, our tongues entwined and twisted about. As his mouth engulfed mine, I felt his hands run up and down the inside of my thighs.

I murmured, "Make love to me, Declan."

To which he replied, "Yes ma'am!"

Instead of gorging himself on his wife, he took his sweet time. His mouth moved down my neck as his hands continuously ran over my body. Then his lips enveloped my left breast and next my right. He continued to kiss his way down my torso when I felt his right hand begin to intimately massage my crotch. I gasped, widening my legs to ensure he had better access.

His hand which was doing the pleasuring became wet as I felt his moist mouth make its way down to my right leg. He kissed his way down my thigh, over my knee and towards my foot before my big toe was engulfed. I gasped again as he proceeded to suck on each of my toes, teasing them with his tongue.

"Oh shit!" I breathed. "I can't remember the last time you did THAT."

"Suck on your toes?" He smirked as he moved his head over to my next foot. "It was probably twenty years ago."

He lifted up my left foot before taking in all of my toes at once and playfully chewing on them. Then he kissed his way up, over my knee and up my inner thigh. Next, he helped himself to tugging my body lower on the bed, before removing his hand from my crotch and replacing it with his mouth instead.

"Mmm...!" I closed my eyes as I lay back. "Tonight feels like some kind of special occasion."

"Huh?" He paused long enough to look up.

"Your attentiveness tonight..." I opened my eyes to meet his gaze, "...it feels like a special occasion or something."

However, what he said next blew all sentimentality out of the water.

"With all of your tension headaches lately, it's literally a case of me getting lucky." He spoke bluntly. "I'm just enjoying the moment while it lasts."

I grabbed hold of his scruffy hair and forced him to look up, "Excuse me?!"

"Thanks to your morning sickness our sex life has decreased," he brushed my hand off. "Now do you mind NOT pulling my hair when I'm supposed to be pleasuring you?"

"Oh excuse me for having nausea, dizziness and tension headaches!" I cried indignantly.

Then we both paused when we realized what I blurted out, we'd heard before...from a bickering human couple in the birthing classes we went to.

Declan chuckled, "I don't think we need couples counselling yet."

Next, he lowered his head once more to finish gratifying his wife.

He parted my legs even further to push his tongue in as far as possible, making my head fall backwards in delight. He helped himself to moving my hips in a rhythmic manner as he 'mauled' my crotch, before I took over by gyrating my hips myself. This brought on the orgasm even faster.

I rolled onto my side satiated as Declan moved up behind. Gently, he pushed me onto my stomach, parted my legs again and lay over my back. He moved slowly at first, enjoying how prepared my body was. However, to keep me in the mood, his right hand moved down to massage my clit again as he rode me. The teasing of his fingers coupled with his throbbing member increased my ecstasy. His pleasuring worked a little too well, when I accidentally cried out from another oncoming orgasm!

Abruptly, his left hand flew over my mouth as he stopped to listen.

We both froze with our wide eyes turned towards the locked bedroom door. Our ears were peeled for the sounds of children stirring. Then I felt him remove his hand from my mouth.

"It's fine, they're still asleep." He said quietly. "Just try not to scream the house down."

I passed a mischievous smile over my shoulder, "Maybe you'd better keep your hand over my mouth."

I caught his lips upturn in a grin, "Or, I have a better idea."

He raised his left wrist to his mouth and put another gash in the skin before returning it to mine. I sensed what he was trying to do, keep my strength up so he could please himself as much as he liked. I didn't mind, in fact my bloodlust was more than happy to go along with what he had planned.

I think the bouts of nausea were frustrating my supernatural appetite which preferred to feed, not throw up. A Werewolf's bloodlust dictated we craved fresh kill which meant we feasted on warm flesh. But tasting blood was also enticing to us. It was like biting into the juiciest plum but sucking on it instead of tearing away the sweet tissue. Sharing blood could heal us but it was also an intimate gesture.

On this note, I was quite happy to sup on Declan's wound as we continued to gratify ourselves in ways our dark needs produced.

*****

The downside to drinking the European Werewolf's blood was taking on his appetite. Sure, it helped our sex life but the perpetual hunger resulted in phenomenal cravings. Or perhaps they were another side effect of the pregnancy? With all the abnormalities lately, it was hard to tell. But the urges felt stronger than the cravings I experienced when I was carrying Lucia.

When the headaches faded and my queasy stomach settled, I'd feel ravenously hungry! If sex didn't fill me up, I'd need food instead. But I didn't just snack, I found myself binge eating again.

If the headaches occurred in the afternoon, Declan would share his blood then I'd have a nap. On the positive side, I didn't need to take any painkillers anymore. But on the negative side, I'd eat as much as my husband. Looch and Soph would stare as I'd heap the food on my plate before eating so quickly, I barely stopped for air.

My favourite foods to gorge myself on, were mashed potato, creamy potato bake, creamy pasta dishes, rice dishes or other carb-powered food. Declan even cooked up extra as he endorsed my appetite. I sensed he felt guilty when I threw up, like he blamed himself for my morning sickness. So when I wasn't nauseas, he'd pro-actively cater to my cravings.

Last night, he cooked up a roast leg of lamb, mint peas, honey cinnamon carrots, mashed potato and a huge dish of creamy cauliflower bake.

We were all sitting at the table hungrily looking on our delicious feast. The children watched as their father carved the roast and their mother served the vegetables. Looch's mouth watered as she looked on the marinated medium-rare meat prepared to perfection. After he served up, Declan had to play mediator when the girls struck up a fight over the gravy.

As I put down the peas, I started to experience the warning signs that a headache was on its way. I didn't have one in the afternoon so now it chose to rear its ugly head. I moved my sore neck around and tried to continue, but the throbbing in my temples began.

"B, are you feeling alright?" Declan frowned. "Your aura is fading."

"Another headache," I moaned, as I rested my head in my hands.

"You didn't get one this afternoon so it's hit you now," he said unhappily. "C'mon, let's get you to bed."

He stood up and gallantly pulled out my chair for me before helping me out of my seat and towards the staircase.

"I can finish off Mum's plate for her," Looch less-than-gallantly offered.

"Nice try," her father replied. "Nobody's touching your Mom's plate except your Mom. We'll keep it warm in the oven for her."

My husband escorted his pregnant wife upstairs, down the hall and into the master bedroom. He was turning into a pro at this; lying me down, taking off my shoes then wrapping me up in the quilt. Then he sat down beside, raised his left wrist to his mouth and offered his sick mate his healing liquid.

"Declan, you can't keep sharing your blood everyday."

"B, don't get all prima donna on me," he scolded. "I'd rather do this then watch you pop paracetamol like candy."

Then he shoved his wound past my lips and watched intently as he waited for me to drink. Reluctantly, I had a couple of mouthfuls and as soon as my headache started to fade, I started to lick his broken skin closed. However, he felt what I was doing and berated me for it.

"Nah ah, a couple more mouthfuls should do it, you've hardly had any."

I passed him a glare and swallowed several more times before he removed his arm himself to use his own saliva to seal the wound shut.

"Maybe we should alternate," I tried again, "one day I use painkillers then the next, your blood."

"Nup, no deal," he said stubbornly. "Remember B, you carry this baby and I'll carry you. Ki's coming over tomorrow morning and I'll bet he'd prefer it my way, especially when we hear what he has to say about the baby."

Dissatisfied, I looked away when I felt his large, hot hand slip under my top and stroke my tummy.

"Besides, you don't drink much," he reassured. "I haven't had a head spin from sharing blood with you and whatever I do give, I'll bet my body's recouped in less than an hour."

"That's a European Werewolf for you," I said.

"You see B, that's what you get for having the good taste to shack up with me." He smirked. "European Werewolves take a lickin' and keep on tickin'."

He made me giggle and I could see it was what he was waiting for, as his smile widened.

"Declan Domitian Sabre, I love you." I sighed out.

He picked up my hands in his and moved them to his mouth to kiss.

"In unan B, in unan," he mumbled, as his lips caressed my palms.

Then I closed my eyes and when he saw I was dozing off, he stood up to leave.

I slept until 11 PM so my husband tidied up after dinner, put the kids to bed then retired too. I shared a shower with him in the ensuite before we put on our sleepwear then I returned to unconsciousness. Since I slept through dinner time, I woke up ravenously hungry at 3 AM.

Silently, I crept out of bed, careful not to disturb the slumbering giant. He's been doing so much for his family lately, I wanted him to have a full nights' rest. I tip-toed over to the bedroom door, quietly unlocked and opened it before slipping out. Declan rolled over in bed but he was still out to the world.

Doing my best to remain silent, I tip-toed along the hallway and then down the stairs.

As soon as I went into the kitchen, I opened up our large, double-door, industrial-sized, fridge/freezer. The fully stocked shelves sat there, invitingly. My mouth watered as I looked on all the cold products before my hungry eyes settled on my plate of dinner. It was covered in cling wrap, like the tray of leftover creamy cauliflower bake was, sitting beside it.

Gleefully, I grabbed the plate and sat down on the floor with it. Sitting cross-legged with the fridge door open to use the light, I quickly ate the cold food. I didn't want to turn on the main light nor use the microwave to heat it up, in case I woke up my family.

The cold didn't spoil the food, in fact it was delicious! Sometimes I felt like I hit the jackpot by landing the gourmet chef that was my husband. It probably helped that he was a Werewolf and food was his passion.

I devoured the meal with my bare hands so quickly that soon I ran out of dinner. But I'm still hungry! I couldn't believe how ravenous I was, like I was a walking, bottomless pit.

My eyes drifted upwards and I found myself staring at the huge dish of creamy cauliflower bake. My arms seemed to move by themselves as they lifted it down then so did my hands as I started picking up fistfuls of congealed, cheesy bake with large chunks of vegetable. Mmm, this tastes so good!

C'mon B, you're gonna have to stop soon. If I eat all of it, Declan's not gonna be happy. I think he cooked it up to experiment with different ways to cover the fact that vegetables grew in dirt. Soph would still have a hissy-fit if she thought her meal had any contact with the ground since she deemed it 'dirty'.

Oh shit, I can't stop. It tastes too good and it's filling me up. No, stop it B, stop...but I can't! It felt like indulging in naughty bedroom behaviour when our young were asleep. In fact, this probably was naughty because my husband and my young were unconscious and therefore unable to stop me.

"B?"

I almost jumped out of my skin when I heard his voice! Instantly, I looked up into the sleepy blue eyes of my huge mate, looming over. I was probably wearing the same guilty expression we saw Looch give, when she was caught sneaking food.

"I thought you were asleep!" I cried out. "I didn't wake you, did I?"

"I woke up because you weren't lying beside me." He rubbed the sleep from his eyes, before giving a peculiar look. "You wanna fork to eat that with?"

I remained sitting cross-legged on the floor with the huge baking dish in my lap as I shook my head. Inwardly, I felt ashamed at being sprung and I was also scared he'd try to take the food away. But to my surprise, he sat down on the floor beside and even dipped his hand into what was left.

"Mmm, it does taste good cold," he observed.

In relief, I recommenced eating and together, we soon finished off what was left. Then he reached up and pulled down the plate with the leftover meat. Roast lamb also tasted good cold and he tore off several pieces for his mate before hogging what was left on the bone.

"Mmm," we happily chewed away.

"Man, I haven't had a late night feed like this in ages," he commented.

"I've never done this before," I said embarrassed.

"Not even when you first changed into a Werewolf?" He asked in surprise and I shook my head. "When I was a kid, I was always getting into trouble for clearing out the fridge in the middle of the night."

"That's right, when we first moved in together, I think your family mentioned it."

"Before you, I thought food could cure all ills." He said. "Food is a Werewolf's best friend, it certainly brought me comfort when I couldn't be with you."

"Do you mean when I was married to Grant?"

"Yup and before that too," he explained. "Remember, I had to wait until you turned when I was twenty-one."

"So you ate?"

"Yup," he said simply. "I ate and I ate then I hunted and then I ate some more."

Appreciatively, my eyes ran over his muscled body which could make a weightlifter jealous. "You hide it well."

"Thanks to our supernatural metabolism," he shrugged it off. "It digests food fast but it also makes us constantly hungry."

The European Werewolf put down the now bare bone before looking into the fridge for more.

"So, what's next?" He offered. "There's some cheeses or some yoghurt, or some vegetables in the crisper."

"You don't mind my midnight feasting?" I asked in further surprise. "I thought you'd get angry."

He passed me a peculiar look, "Angry?"

"For eating all the food," I said guiltily.

"B, we've been married for nearly three centuries and we still have to leave the backdoor open for when I have to hunt in between full moons." He reminded. "Now we have Lucia who has to hunt with her father. I'm always hungry and I can see the same in our eldest. She's always trying to sneak more food, but we have to teach her self-control."

"Maybe I should relearn self-control," I looked downcast.

"You already exercise self-control," he said coolly, as he reached for the ricotta cheese. He opened the vegetable crisper and I watched him pull out some washed carrots and celery. He shared out the vegetables then he took the lid off the cheese which we dipped them into. As he ate, he continued, "You do a better job at teaching the girls' self-control than I do."

"Me?" I scoffed. "But you're the lawkeeper."

"I may act like a brick wall but you lead by example," he spoke in between mouthfuls. "Soph emulates your style, by studying hard and dressing like you. Looch may not be interested in fashion but she respects you as a teacher. She knows I'm just as hungry as she is, but she tries to act like her mother who doesn't think with her stomach."

"I always thought that Looch looked up to you since you're both alike."

"She looks up to me because I'm her big, strong, European Werewolf father who's teaching her how to hunt and cook. But she also looks up to her Lokoti Werewolf mother, for wisdom and self control." He announced.

I sighed in relief, "Thanks Dec, I don't feel so guilty now."

"Trust me B, I'm not gonna judge a pregnant woman's cravings. It's like for nine months, we have more in common." He smiled, before he noticed what I was holding in my hand. "Hey, are you gonna eat that other celery stick?"

"Yes!" I munched on it before he could.

He growled in annoyance and turned towards the fridge to eat something else when I stopped him. To his pleasant surprise, I moved to sit in his lap so I was straddling him. Then I picked up the ricotta cheese, dipped my finger into it and I smeared it along my collar bone.

"Come and get it," I sung in a lilting tone.

"Heh heh!" He chuckled as he licked it off. "Man, I love my wife!"

*****

Later that morning, I lay on a couch in the lounge area with my husband sitting on another. Our daughters sat at the dining table with several jars of water and sheets of paper, using water paints for their 'art class'. I thought this should keep them amused for the duration of my check up.

Ki was sitting on the side of the coffee table, waving his medical scanner over my body. We watched him concentrate it over my abdomen to scan the baby's development. Declan and I were waiting for his customary 'hmm,' which would usually precede his diagnosis. However, this morning he acted differently. I watched his dark eyes widen as he looked on the results and as if he couldn't believe what he saw, he scanned my womb again.

"Er, what was the date again that conception occurred?" He asked.

Declan said perfunctory, "The first of March."

"It couldn't have happened before then?" He lowered his scanner to look on, perplexed.

"Nope," my husband shook his head. "B was on heat from ovulating that day."

"But I understand that your..." Ki paused as he cast a look at our daughters and he used innuendoes, "...'bedroom activities' are pretty regular?"

"Yeah, so?" He shrugged.

"Perhaps conception occurred earlier?" Our Healer tried again.

"Nope!" He repeated. "I would have smelled it."

"Indeed," the Medicine Man agreed however, he seemed baffled.

"Ki, what is it?" I sat up, concerned.

"You understand that you're six weeks pregnant but according to my readouts..." he struggled out, "...the baby is showing the growth of a twelve week old foetus."

"Say what?" Declan straightened in alarm. "I smelled it was growing faster than a normal baby, but I didn't know it was THAT fast!"

"When I scanned Aunt B in her first week of pregnancy, the cells were still dividing. In five weeks, the baby has advanced in growth of eleven weeks." He said, dumbfounded.

"Hang on," I thought aloud, "this means Susanna's passed her first trimester."

"Correct." Ki confirmed then he waved the scanner over me once more. He spoke whilst looking on the readouts, "I understand why Uncle Declan's blood has been able to dispel your tension headaches and nausea. I can see a high concentration of European Werewolf DNA in your bloodstream, Aunt B. The majority of which is centred in your womb. Your body needs Uncle Declan's blood because the baby is absorbing so much of your blood sugar, vitamin and mineral reserves with its accelerated growth. His DNA is not only adding to your strength, but half of it is going straight into the baby."

Declan leaned forward in concern, "If I stopped sharing my blood with B, would it slow down the baby's growth?"

"No," he said sharply. "The baby would still be growing at an accelerated rate, if you did or didn't share blood. But because the baby is growing so fast, Aunt B's body is struggling to provide the nourishment it requires. The foetus is absorbing some of its food from its father's blood."

I swung my legs over the edge of the couch so I was sitting up properly and facing the two males in the room.

"But I can't keep drinking Declan's blood everyday," I said unhappily, "my husband can't be 'on tap' for his pregnant wife all the time."

The European Werewolf's eyes glowed green in anger, "Ki, tell my wife once and for all, that my blood is better for her than those damned painkillers!"

"Right now Aunt B, I'd agree with your bossy husband," our Medicine Man spoke calmly. "Your body needs what your husband's can provide to help with the baby."

"Remember what I said, B?" He tried to hold my gaze. "You carry the baby and I'll carry you."

The Lokoti Werewolf looked on in approval, "Sounds like a good plan to me."

"But Ki, sometimes it's twice a day that I drink his blood." I frowned. "What about Declan's body? What if it weakens him?"

The Medicine Man turned around so he was facing in my husband's direction. We watched him wave the scanner over the European Werewolf as Declan rolled his eyes. His face reddened in embarrassment at the concern for his welfare.

"I'm fine!" He snapped. "I told B that I don't even get dizzy spells. She doesn't drink that much anyways, I'd say it's half a litre at the most."

For a second time that morning we saw our Healer's eyes bulge in surprise.

"Um, I'm willing to believe what he says," he swallowed hard as he stared at the results.

"Ki, what's wrong?" I asked anxiously.

He lowered the scanner to look on my husband closely, "How have you been feeling lately, Uncle Dec?"

"Fine!" He barked impatiently. "Why, how does that stupid contraption say I feel?"

"Do you remember how I scanned you when Aunt B was carrying Lucia?" He began. "I said that your muscle density had increased by ten percent."

"Yeah, so?" Declan demanded.

"With the advent of Susanna, your muscle density has increased by an extra five percent." He announced.

"He's a hundred and fifteen percent stronger...?" I uttered out in shock.

"Right now Uncle, you are the strongest Werewolf ever recorded in existence," our Medicine Man declared.

Both Looch and Soph who must have been listening in as they painted, paused. Their paint brushes hovered over the paper as they looked impressed at their big, strong daddy. Instead of looking surprised or concerned, Declan rolled his eyes again. Feeling conscious of being the centre of attention, he stood up to pace up and down as he grumbled.

"What about the First Werewolf in the dinosaur era? Remember European Werewolves reduced in size and I bet our strength decreased too. I bet the First Werewolf was stronger than me. Right now you're comparing me to something which is extinct and I'm the last full-blooded European Werewolf in existence!"

"Sorry Uncle, but I have to correct you there." Ki said dryly.

"Say what?" He stopped in surprise.

"The foetus growing inside Aunt B shows over ninety percent composition of European Werewolf DNA." Ki stated.

Next, all eyes in the room became trained on my abdomen, including those of our two daughters.

"Is Mummy having a European Werewolf baby?" Soph asked interested.

"Does this mean Susanna's gonna be stronger than me?" Looch asked, disappointedly.

I think she preferred the idea that not only would she the eldest, but she'd be the strongest of her siblings.

Frantically, Declan rushed to my side and put his hands on my tummy.

"Is B OK? Is she in any danger? Can we still remove the baby after the first trimester if her life is in jeopardy?" He panicked.

I wouldn't hear of abortion and especially not in front of the children.

Indignantly, I pushed his hands away as I roused, "Not this again, and not in front of the kids!"

Soph asked puzzled, "Is Mummy having the baby early?"

Looch shook her head as she watched with concern as her parents discussed the fate of her littlest sister.

Ki did his best to console, "Although Aunt B is experiencing symptoms like tension headaches from the foetus' advanced growth; I can also see that the blood you've shared has enabled her body to wrap her womb in an extra layer of muscle. It's taking measures to ensure the mother remains safe, especially when the foetus kicks or moves around."

His mouth hung open in horror at the words, 'kicks' or 'moves around'. I watched his face fall, as if he no longer celebrated the new life we'd created, he mourned it. This made my heart race and anxiously I put my hands over his.

"Declan, it's OK." I tried to reassure him. "We're going to be alright. You keep sharing your blood and I won't whinge anymore when I drink it. I'll become stronger and the baby will grow with no dramas."

But my words seemed to have no effect on him as he looked away with a haunted expression. Then he noticed his daughters were watching him as well as our Medicine Man. So he'd no longer be the focus of attention he stood up, left the lounge area and then the house via the front door.

"Not this again." I complained before I stood up and followed him out.

In annoyance, I flung open the front door and found him standing at the end of the veranda. His arms were folded in front as he glared at the surrounding woods. I marched up, grabbed hold of his hair and MADE him look at me.

"Oow!" He swiped my hand off. "What's with the hair? You're always pulling my hair!"

"Because it's the only part of you that I can hurt!" I growled as I whacked him on the arm. "See, that doesn't even sting, does it?"

"No, but you look cute when you try to beat me up," he almost smiled.

"Declan Domitian Sabre..." I whacked him each time I said a word in his name, "...GET OVER IT! We're the luckiest people on this planet because we have each other and our family! You almost died of old age but I changed you and because of it, a miracle happened in the form of our children! Now if I see you look morose or act like I'm doomed one more time, I'm going to send you to the space time continuum without me! Now snap out of it!"

Finally, a silly smile appeared on his youthful face, "Hit me again."

"What?"

"Hit me again."

I raised my right hand to deliver the hardest slap I could muster, but he didn't even jolt from the impact.

"Every time you hit me, a flurry of sparks come flying off your aura like fireworks." He grinned like an idiot.

"Excuse me?"

"Hit me again." He repeated.

"No!"

"C'mon B, I've been a bad boy. You said so yourself. Now spank me." He chuckled mischievously.

"I don't believe this..." I turned away to go back inside.

I didn't get very far before his arms wrapped around my waist and he pulled me backwards. He held me firmly against him as he ducked his face to smell my hair. I must admit, I appreciated the feel of his hot body against mine when we were standing out in the cold.

He murmured in my ear, "I wish I could get one of those scientific cameras that can take pictures of people's electromagnetic fields. Then you'd see what I'm goin' on about all the time. Here's a pic of B's aura when she's angry, or when she's happy or even when she's turned on."

"Can you please be serious about this?"

He turned me around in his arms so I could see his unhappy expression.

"I was serious about this and you didn't like it."

"No, you were homicidal about this and I didn't like it." I glared back.

He moaned, "Man, you are one frustrating bird to be married to sometimes."

"You're no picnic yourself!"

He met my angry gaze with his own, "It's like you live in this dream world where because you think things will turn out well, they will. Although you see a hell of a lot more than I do, even you have to admit you don't know everything."

Declan's deadly serious attitude towards this possible threat made me pause.

"Hang on," I looked on him closely, "you're not getting a warning feeling about this pregnancy, are you?"

He answered by looking at me right in the eye, "Yes."

"But I don't have one..." I said confused, "...how can you be getting a bad feeling about this baby, if I'm not?"

"I dunno," he shrugged. "You're the experienced Circulator so you tell me."

Disconcerted, I glanced away to stare at the wet woods which were going through the spring thaw. There was still the odd patch of snow on the ground or an icicle hanging from a branch. But I could spot tiny green leaves on the deciduous trees which were coming back to life.

"B," he cupped my face between his hands. "We've got to go through this pregnancy together. You're gonna have to lean on me and let me do more for you. Otherwise I'm scared that when the ninth month rolls around... I'm gonna be a single parent."

As Declan uttered the words 'single parent' his voice broke as his eyes filled with tears. His eyes watered profusely as his broad shoulders sunk. He rubbed his wet face against mine and I felt his hot tears on my cheeks.

"Together forever B," he uttered out. "You changed me so we'd be together forever. Don't leave me in this life without you, coz I wouldn't cope. The darkness would win without your light there anymore."

His sadness turned into my sadness and I clung onto the front of his shirt as I turned tearful myself. From our empathic connection, I felt his profound fear. I experienced his hopelessness at having his reason for living, in jeopardy.

As we stood hugging and crying on the front veranda, I realized what my previous vision meant. Now I know why I saw the conversation Declan and Caesar had after Forrest's death. I could recall what my mate had said:

"I've lost family members." He said coldly. "I lost my Mom and little brother and their progeny continue to drop like flies, thanks to time. But I cope because I have B, who's not only a Light Person but she's the light of my life. What would I be like if I lost her? Like I said, don't go there because you won't like the answer."

An ominous feeling weighed down my chest. The sense of foreboding was telling me that Declan was right, he really would lose it if he lost his beloved mate. It may even mean further loss of life if his bloodlust did take control.

An emotional quantum singularity threatened to envelop my dangerous mate. When he was happy, his blue eyes would be bright and there was nothing he wouldn't do for his loved ones. However, if he felt that his source of happiness was threatened, his darkness would escape. The pervading blackness could snuff out life, as it annihilated all in its path of destruction, similar to the gravity well of a black hole.

I've always been aware of my mate's dark side but what the hell, I married it. Besides, I wasn't without faults of my own. We both have the bloodlust and we've both wrestled with our control of it. But here was the man who also wrestled me when the bloodlust did take control.

"Sorry Sabre," I pulled on his scruffy, blonde hair, "you're stuck with me."

"Say it again," he closed his watery eyes.

"You're stuck with me forever and ever."

"Say it again."

"From here into infinity."

"Say it one more time," he took a deep breath.

"Eternally and then some," I planted a soft kiss on his lips.

Declan opened his eyes and smirked, "Your nose is red and swollen."

"You damn well made me cry!"

"How about I make some toasted cheese and tomato sandwiches for lunch?" He changed the subject with a smile.

Here we go, he was returning to normal which was thinking with his stomach.

I went along, "Can I have four toasted sandwiches instead of my usual two?"

"You can have as many as you damn well want," he straightened himself.

Then he took hold of my hand and led the way inside.

We found Ki sitting at the dining table with our daughters, talking to them softly. I sensed he was trying to reassure them during the domestic drama. However, as soon as their Mummy and Daddy returned, their gazes turned our way.

Their father boomed out, "Who's hungry?"

"I am!" Lucia cried out the loudest then she hopped off her chair to follow her father into the kitchen.

I wandered over to look on what she had created for her art lesson. I found she had painted a landscape picture of our small part of the Alaska Range. She had depicted tall mountains, evergreen trees and sweeping valleys. When I looked over at Sophia's work, I saw she'd painted a woman wearing a long dress. I think it was her attempt at fashion design by painting an evening gown.

"Look at these pretty pictures!" I beamed. "We're going to have to put them on display to show the world."

I carried them both into the kitchen and used the magnets on the fridge to post the pictures on both of the double doors. Declan paused in his food preparation long enough to have a look.

"Nice," he said impressed. "Looch, did you paint the landscape?"

She nodded as her little sister came into the kitchen to point at her creation.

"I did that one, Daddy." Soph said proudly.

"Ladies and Gentlemen, we have a fashion designer in the family!" He cried out like an announcer.

I sat up on the kitchen bench to watch the family's chefs at work. Declan was slicing the tomatoes as Looch was buttering the slices of bread. Soph tugged on my jeans, implying she wanted to be picked up. I started to lean over to do so when her father beat me to it. He put down the knife and hoisted his young into the air. Then I held her in my lap and together we looked on. I could tell he appreciated having an audience, for when he opened the packet of sliced cheese, he passed us a piece each. Our eldest opened her mouth and her father popped some cheese into it, too.

Smilingly, Ki looked on our family bond together over food.

"I'll be off now, but I'll come by next week." He excused himself. "With this pregnancy Aunt B, I think we should increase your check ups to once a week."

I opened my mouth to disagree when my husband said firmly, "I agree."

Our Medicine Man 'bowed out' with the front door opening and closing with his departure.

~~~~~~

27th April 2374

The full moon rose on a Saturday night. My husband cooked dinner early so we could eat at 5 PM. Afterwards, once the dirty dishes were stacked inside the dishwasher, we organized our young for the hunt.

Declan went into Soph's room to get her ready. In the other bedroom I oversaw Looch, who pulled on an old set of black gym clothes. However, from taking down her prey fighting, there were several large tears in the front.

"You can't wear that." I frowned. "Take them off and I'll see if either your father or I can mend them later. For tonight, put on your blue gym clothes."

As she changed, I left her room and went into Soph's. I wondered what was taking them so long and I soon saw why. Inside, both my mate and my second born stood with their hands on their hips, in a stand-off.

"I want to wear my pink gym clothes!" Sophia barked.

"They're dirty and we're not doing a load of laundry just to go hunting!" He snapped back.

"I WANT to wear my PINK gym clothes!" She shouted.

"I heard you the first time and the answer is still NO!" He yelled back.

I saw with their similar tempers they could argue all night so I intervened.

"Soph, how about you wear your silver gym clothes then you can wear your glittery hair clips with it?"

My husband looked on incredulous, "Say what?"

Quickly, I thought up, "And we'll put your hair in a pony tail with your hot pink scrunchie, that'll go with the silver colour and the glitter."

She opened her mouth to yell some more, but then she agreed with a petulant, "Alright."

Declan turned to leave the room and I caught him mutter on the way out, "I don't believe this...accessorizing for a hunt?!"

He went into our bedroom to take off all his clothes and put on his 'hunting' robe.

I helped Soph dress and I did her hair in the way that I promised. Then I sent her downstairs to wait with Looch, so I too could change into my gym clothes. Inside our bedroom, I found Declan sitting on the bed.
~~~~~~

"Do you feel well enough to hunt tonight?" He checked.

"Yep," I answered as I stripped. "Actually, I'm craving fresh kill more than usual."

"OK then," he stood up and patted my tummy, "just let me do the killing and then eat with me."

"Yes Papa Bear," I sung mockingly.

"That's right Momma Bear, just you remember who has the bigger claws in this family." He tickled his wife before he darted out the door. "I'd better go supervise the baby bears downstairs."

From the sound of the commotion he was just in time too. I'd bet the whole tribe could hear their yelling. They always fought more on a full moon.

*****

Within minutes I'd put on my dark red gym clothes and trod down the stairs barefoot. In the living area stood my husband in just his robe as well as my little girls in their stretchy clothing. Soph was chasing Looch around and around their father as he snapped at them to "quit it".

"OK, it's time for the Sabre's to go hunting." He walked over to the front door and held it open for his family. "C'mon you two, scoot!"

Looch ran outside with Soph right on her heels where they continued their fight on the gravel driveway. I walked out next then Declan shut the door behind himself, leaving it unlocked. The crime rate on tribal lands was low and besides, there weren't many who were game to pilfer a house that belonged to the world's most dangerous breed of Werewolf.

As soon as he went down the veranda steps, he took off his robe, hung it over the veranda railing and underwent a second change that evening. Our daughters watched fascinated their father's transformation. I too, found the sight spectacular of a bipedal, muscled man morphing into a giant, four-legged, canine monster. Then he looked expectantly on his family with his glowing green eyes.

Looch and Soph were the next to change as their bodies also bulked up with muscle. The nails on their hands and feet grew long and sharp as did their elongated teeth. Both their eyes turned glowing green with narrow slits for pupils, thanks to their father. However, Looch's face altered further by her mouth and nose becoming conjoined in a canine appearance. Her top lip attached itself to her nostrils as her breathing came out as panting.

I was the last to shape shift as my upper body expanded into a muscled build that made me look like a female weightlifter. The nails on my feet and hands extended as did my teeth and all three sharpened. My eyes also changed as the dark blue colour glowed turquoise instead.

"Daddy! Daddy! Daddy!" Soph growled out, as she ran in front of her father.

My mate knew what she wanted was a ride. He swooped her up with his front right claw and swung her up. As soon as she landed on his hardened back, she leaned over to cling onto his thick neck.

Just as we were about to run into the woods to race after the pack, we were interrupted.

AUNT B AND UNCLE DEC, HAVE YOU LEFT YET? – Walt's thoughts pervaded our own.

WE'RE JUST ABOUT TO – I thought back.

BEFORE YOU JOIN THE PACK, CAN YOU SWING BY MY PLACE FIRST? I NEED YOUR HELP WITH SOMETHING – He asked.

WE'RE ON OUR WAY – Declan answered.

He leapt into the tree line first and ran down the forest covered hill in the direction of the Wisetail's house. Looch ran right after him with me taking the rear. Our supernatural body heat staved off the chill of the night and the rushing air barely stung.

It was barely a minute later when we three leapt out of the tree line, this time landing on Wisetail property.

Declan trotted around to the front of the house and came to a stop before the veranda. Looch and I came to stand beside with Soph still hanging onto her father's back. Through the front window, we spotted Hugh and Katrina looking at our paranormal physique with wide eyes. That was until Wendy moved them on and told them it was rude to stare.

Not that we blamed them, humans in the tribe didn't often see us in these shapes. Those that had a Werewolf in the family were more accustomed than those that didn't. The members of the pack didn't hide themselves, but our dangerous appearances wouldn't come out unless we were hunting or fighting.

Then the front door opened with Walt walking out in his jeans and in his Lokoti Werewolf body. His eyes glowed orange as his sharp, elongated teeth jutted past his lips. He gave us a nod in greeting then he stepped aside so we could see who was standing behind him.

There stood a fourteen year old Kurt as a new Lokoti Werewolf. Declan and I exchanged surprised glances since we had expected, as most of the pack had, that Samuel would change to take Forrest's place. However, it was Kurt's Lokoti Werewolf DNA which was activated instead.

Awkwardness was written all over the muscled boy's body, as Kurt seemed embarrassed over his change. His glowing red eyes remained averted, as if he couldn't meet our gazes. His younger brothers and sister peaked around the front doorway, looking from him to the European Werewolf on their driveway.

Wendy walked up and placed her hands on his shoulders to reassure him.

"It's alright, Kurt." She spoke softly. "You're not alone, you can hunt with your father and your Sabre relations."

The look on her face was grave with concern but I also saw she was trying hard to put on a brave front. I felt sorry for Kurt who looked afraid of what was happening to him. Walt put his claw-like hand on his arm and gently pulled him forwards.

"Tonight you hunt with your father and pack, son." He spoke in his thunderous Werewolf voice. "The pack has come to welcome you. Your Uncle Declan is Second and he will help guide you."

Ah, so that's why Walt asked us to come. Kurt was apprehensive about going on his first hunt so we were called in as reinforcements. With Declan's position as Second, he was to act as the representative for the pack.

I lifted Soph off his large back and as soon as I did, he walked forwards on all-fours. He was so large, his head was almost the same height as Kurt's, who was standing on the front veranda. I watched as the boy tried not to shrink backwards in fear at my husband's monstrous appearance.

WELCOME TO THE CLUB – my mate thought humorously.

Kurt's mind had yet to adjust to the will of the pack, so he didn't receive the message properly.

"Your Uncle Declan said, 'welcome to the club'." Walt voiced his thoughts instead.

Kurt let out an uneasy laugh however, he stopped himself when he heard how deep and growly it was.

It was here that Looch walked past her gigantic father and up the steps of the veranda. My tall, strong daughter who was the height of a twelve year old when she was really ten, stood before the fourteen year old Lokoti Werewolf.

"You don't look that bad," she growled out. Then she delivered a whack to his arm and the strength of her playful hit made him lurch sideways. "C'mon then, we don't have all night."

As she came back down the steps, Kurt followed her. When she broke into a run, he ran right after. Together they disappeared into the woods with Looch leading the way. Soph growled demandingly at her father who swung her up onto his back once more. Then he, Walt and I leapt out of the yard as we bolted after the children.

Wendy watched us go with her watery eyes full of worry. When her eldest changed into the same kind of creature her husband was, she tried to grin and bear it. However, as her child went through the physical and emotional pain of their first transformation, it made her stomach turn. She had to stand back and let her husband take over using his own experience.

All she could do was try to keep the house calm as Kurt's siblings acted out. Edwina overdramatically locked herself in her bedroom, effectively locking out Katrina who had to share with her. Kevin and Hugh gaped at what Kurt had become, before making growling noises and pretending they were changing too. If their older brother was going to be a Werewolf, so were they.

Kevin asked hopeful, "Mom, can I go hunting with Dad and Kurt?"

"No you can't." Wendy said briskly as she ushered everyone back inside. "The full moon is for Werewolves but bedtime is for humans."

"Aw, Mom!" Hugh whined. "When am I gonna turn into a Werewolf?"

"Hopefully never," she said under her breath before she took charge. "Kevin and Hugh, go and brush your teeth. Katrina, is Edwina still locked inside your bedroom? Then I'll get the master key so you can get ready for bed."

~~~~~~
~~~~~~

~ 25 ~

21st May 2374

The well dressed but pale looking man, hung back in case they picked up his scent. He walked on the opposite side of the busy street, remaining behind them at all times. This meant that he could keep out of direct eye line of his target and was camouflaged by the other pedestrians.

It was a busy Saturday morning in the commercial centre of Alma. The woman he was following had ushered her two daughters into two book stores as well as several clothing boutiques. Each time they exited, their hands were full of more shopping bags.

The woman was tall with long, dark, glossy hair spilling down her back. She walked with a carefree stride, whilst flicking the said hair over her broad shoulders. She had an athletic build, which hinted at her supernatural strength. Her eyes were dark blue which stood out against her white skin and black hair in a striking contrast. But what truly made her a spectacle was the bright aura surrounding her, which the humans couldn't see. It captivated as well as baffled him, as he'd never seen an aura that bright before.

On either side walked her young but they didn't glow like their mother did. He could smell they were half breeds; they were part this woman and part something else. When he first smelled it, it made him pause in surprise as he'd thought this breed extinct. But here they were, shopping for school books and clothes with their mother, reeking of their father's DNA. Hell, he could even smell that she was pregnant with another which was growing quickly inside her.

The littlest mongrel walking on the left had black hair and was as attractive as her mother. The eldest mongrel walking on the right was something else. This half breed seemed more like her father, as she was tall for her age and more muscled. She had dark blonde hair, bright blue eyes and a good sense of smell. A couple of times she looked around whilst visibly sniffing the air, as if she'd picked up his scent. When she gazed in his direction, he had to either duck through a shop door or hide behind someone else.

Their stalker could move in the speed of sound as well as slip silently between people or buildings, to go unnoticed. Like this, he continued to follow the bitch and her pups, all the way down the street until they walked around a corner a supermarket was on. He hid behind the edge of the building to watch them approach a hover-car, unlock it with a remote and put all of their shopping in the boot. Afterwards, they all hopped in then the vehicle lifted up into the air.

Casually, they cruised out of the car park, waited for a pause in traffic and then zoomed off, out of town.

It wasn't necessary to race to his hover-car to give chase as he knew where they were going...the Lokoti National Park. The dogs had kennels in the wilderness and even called it a community centre although his snobbish tastes questioned what they called 'civilization'. He couldn't step foot on tribal lands though, as he knew the dogs with their territorial behaviour, would pick up his scent.

However, he hadn't known the bitch in the pack of predominantly male mutts, had mated with his greatest foe and yet favoured prey: European Werewolves.

The European Vampire put on his sunglasses over his faded hazel eyes which objected to the bright sunlight. He took his time to stroll down the street and over to his own hover-car which was parked nearby. Once inside the tinted-window vehicle, he used the rear view mirror to reapply his sunscreen. It was warmer here than his people had anticipated when he was chosen for this mission. The UV readings broadcasted by the Alaskan Bureau of Meteorology was also higher than expected. He knew these factors would make his coven attack at night when they came.

His task was to spy on the pack of dogs and look for weaknesses in their defences. His coven initially thought of holding the dogs' human wives and children hostage, to force them to submit. However, history told that the last time this tactic was applied the pack still fought them off. So he spied on their bitch, to see if she would be useful as a prisoner. But smelling the European Werewolf DNA in her pups was like winning the jackpot.

Eventually, he started up the engine of his hover-car. Once it rose from the ground, he turned midair and cruised out of town. He found himself on the highway which led to Tok but he turned off at the exit for the Lokoti National Park. As soon as he saw the sign advising visitors they were about to enter the World Heritage Listed wilderness, he pulled over and powered down the vehicle.

His supernatural sense of smell told him that in a couple more meters, he'd be on the dog's territory and they'd pick up his scent. Not to give away his presence, he began to walk along the perimeter of the woods. He inhaled through his nose and exhaled out of his mouth as he walked, occasionally holding his breath. The scent of European Werewolf was heavy in the air, indicating he'd found the territory of this predator.

A smug smile appeared on his pale face which looked gaunt with his sickly features. He pulled out his mobile phone and started to type a text message to his coven to alert them of this wondrous news: their favoured food source still existed. Then everything happened so suddenly...

Firstly, he picked up the scent of one of the mongrels in the vicinity. Then his ears picked up the dog's silent footsteps, as it tried to sneak up on him. When he turned to run with his greater speed to his hover-car; he ran right into an awaiting fist.

Bam!

His nose emitted a 'crack' as it broke and he fell flat on his back, with blood spurting out. When he tried to jump up and run away, the tall, strong, Native Alaskan wearing a Park Ranger's uniform wouldn't let him. The dog in human form used its supernatural strength to deliver an even harder blow to his head.

BAM!

The last thing the European Vampire saw was the Native Alaskan man's dark brown eyes glow orange. Their brightness looked eerie against the man's bronzed skin and long hair which was tied back in a ponytail. The Park Ranger made sure the Vampire was unconscious before picking up the fallen phone.

"Damn it!" He growled when he saw the message had the status of 'sent'.

I'M TOO LATE – Walt thought grimly to his First and Second – *HE GOT WORD TO HIS COVEN.*

WHERE ARE YOU NOW? – Caesar asked.

I'M ON THE SOUTH SIDE OF THE BORDER, NEAR THE HIGHWAY EXITING ALMA – Walt answered.

IS THE VAMPIRE'S VEHICLE NEARBY? – Declan guessed.

YUP – Walt guessed what they were thinking – *YOU WANT ME TO GET RID OF IT?*

NO, FORENSICS COULD PICK UP YOU WERE IN THE CAR – Caesar thought – *JUST BRING THE FANG HEAD TO THE CAVES IN THE NORTH EASTERN VALLEY.*

WE'LL LET THE CAR SIT THERE OVERNIGHT THEN WE'LL REPORT IT TO THE POLICE – Declan planned – *IF WE'RE THE ONES CALLING IN AN ABANDONED VEHICLE, HOPEFULLY THEY WON'T THINK WE'RE TO BLAME FOR THE DRIVER'S DISAPPEARANCE.*

GOOD IDEA – Caesar concurred – *WALT, WE'LL MEET YOU AT THE CAVES TO INTEROGATE THE FANG HEAD. WE NEED TO FIND OUT HOW MANY ARE IN HIS COVEN SO WE CAN PREPARE A DEFENSE.*

ALRIGHTIE THEN – Walt moved to obey.

The stronger man slung the sickly one over his broad shoulder before he trudged away.

*****

The darkness turned into a dim, blurry light but it was a light nonetheless. He blinked again and then again as his eyes slowly re-focussed. His head was aching from his injuries, especially his face. It was a foreign sensation to him since he was used to being in the position of inflicting pain, not receiving it.

As he recovered his senses, he realized he was tied to a wooden chair by coarse ropes. He almost laughed at the antiquated fashion! However, as he tugged at the bonds, he found himself tied so securely there was no escaping.

He could smell his captors were all Werewolves by their overbearing pheromones. The delicious scent made his stomach rumble as his mouth watered. The idea that he was being held captive by what was seen as a delicacy amongst his kind, amused him. He could hear their gruff voices with the odd growling in between.

"It's awake."

"Where's our Second? He wanted to interrogate the prisoner."

"Declan's coming, he's just left home now."

"Why isn't he here already?"

"Sophia was having one of her tantrums," another warned. "And you know what's she's like when she gets started."

Just then a chorus of groans, moans and more growling came to his ears.

From the sound of things his captors were all male. Curiosity got the better of him and brazenly he took a long look around. What he found didn't surprise him; his kidnappers were thirteen Native Alaskan men, topless and barefoot.

The abductee found himself inside of a large cave. He examined the damp rock face with the odd stalactite hanging from the ceiling and moss on the cave walls. The cavern had minimum lighting provided by a plasma-powered lantern sitting here or there.

His kidnappers looked his way unhappily as they flexed their enlarged muscles, as if they were physically restraining themselves. Although his mouth watered at their aroma, he sensed that they wanted to destroy him. Instead of feeling afraid, he saw it as the equivalent of chickens capturing a fox. His inflated ego and sense of superiority kept his fears at bay.

The European Vampire openly examined them. He noted by their glances or nods to each other there existed some kind of hierarchy. They mentioned a 'Second', so he tried to work out who could be 'First' in this pack of dogs? Then he spotted a middle-aged man leaning against a cave wall and although he was standing alone, he observed the others kept a respectful distance. He stood casually in only a pair of jeans like he was accustomed to it and his Lokoti Werewolf eyes glowed blue.

"Am I right in thinking that you are First amongst this pack of dogs?" He asked loudly in his French accent.

Instantly, all of the Native Alaskan men who were wandering around or murmuring to each other, paused.

"I will take that as oui," the Vampire continued. "I'll also take it that you have kept me alive for a reason. I tell you now that if you plan on using me as some kind of hostage, your plan will fail. My coven knows of my location, as I've reported to them my findings. When they come to rescue me, they will destroy you."

The Lokoti Werewolves with their different coloured glowing eyes looked at their leader in alarm.

However, their First remained as cool as a cucumber. He looked down at his claw-like nails and proceeded to clean blood out from underneath one. His men took his lead and tried to carry on as normal, but the Vampire smelled their fear.

"Release me now and my coven will show mercy by killing you quickly," the fang head went on. "But if you continue to hold me, not even your human families will be spared."

Twelve of the muscled Native Alaskan men looked unsettled by his words, but the thirteenth remained calm. Next, the Vampire watched their First finish cleaning his claws then he casually looked at his watch. He was clearly waiting on somebody, was it this Second that was mentioned before?

"Hmm...interesting," the Vampire thought aloud. "It appears that it is mainly the males in your tribe that turn into one of you. Tell me, when my coven feeds on your pack, will the other males in your tribe turn? If so, my coven has found its very own Werewolf 'food synthesizer'! We feast on you and fifteen more are created then we feast on them and another fifteen are created!"

The muscled man with the glowing orange eyes walked up to him with his clawed hand raised to strike. But he stopped when his First said, "No Walt."

"Down boy," the European Vampire smirked. "Sit doggy, sit!"

"C'mon Walt," a Werewolf with glowing pink eyes, pulled him away. "Leave him for Declan. When he's finished with him, he'll be begging us to put him out of his misery."

The European Vampire's cruel laughter came out between his poisonous teeth as he sensed he'd found the Lokoti Werewolf's weakness – family.

"Ah, I see!" He smiled cunningly. "You are uncomfortable over the subject of new Werewolves created, because it means the new dogs could be family members, oui?"

Just then the cavern was filled with the unhappy snarls of all of the fathers in the pack.

"I am prepared to negotiate the terms of your surrender," the Vampire sat back in its chair. "One of the terms we offer is that we would feast on your progeny swiftly, to spare them a painful death."

All of the Lokoti Werewolves except the First advanced threateningly on the prisoner's position...

"Wolves," the First growled out in a deep, rumbling voice like thunder.

The Vampire watched the men halt in their steps whilst flexing their bulging muscles and sharp claws. Their different coloured glowing eyes flashed dangerously. The Vampire didn't have to be psychic to know that he was in grave danger by the murderous looks on their faces. However, all of this changed upon a loud male voice calling out:

"Hi honey, I'm home!"

Immediately, the tense atmosphere in the cavern lifted as all of the men's heads turned at the approach of the owner of the voice.

The fang head saw a Caucasian male with scruffy, blonde hair and bright blue eyes, walk naked into the cave. But what caught the Vampire's attention besides his tall stature and muscular build, was the man's aura. It was almost as bright as the bitch he'd been spying on and it ignited his curiosity.

This newcomer looked to be in his early twenties but the European Vampire's refined sense of smell, detected the centuries on him. Instantly, he smelled the naked man was a European Werewolf, but it baffled him how a mongrel such as this, had such a bright aura? He suspected it was part of the reason why he looked so young. Interestedly, he watched the blonde approach the First.

"Sorry I'm late," he said. "Soph was having one of her hissy-fits and B was hitting me up with 'Twenty Questions' on what we did with the fang head."

"Here," the First handed his Second a spare pair of jeans. "We though we'd let you have the honours of interrogating the intruder."

"Heh heh," the muscled man chuckled as he pulled on the clothing. "Man, I love having the reputation of being the pack's bad-ass!"

"Er, those are my spare pair that I brought along," the Werewolf with the glowing pink eyes, spoke. "Try not to get too much blood on them, Jenny will kill me if she can't get the stains out."

"You get your wife to do your washing, Ki?" The Werewolf with the glowing orange eyes, asked in a disapproving tone.

"I have no trouble with tipping a load into the machine along with the detergent and then turning it on." He replied. "But when I accidentally dyed Jenny's white blouse pink, she banished me from the laundry."

The fang head listened to the rest of the pack, including the First and Second, chuckle in sympathy.

"You're a Medicine Man who deals with potions and poultices, but you didn't think to wash your reds separate to your whites?" A Werewolf with glowing silver eyes, taunted.

"Shut up Derik!" The pink-eyed Werewolf looked away in annoyance.

There was further laughter amongst the men but the Vampire was more interested in watching the First and Second. He eyed the two men as they talked quietly and with all the rowdy behaviour from the dogs, he couldn't hear what they were saying. However, the blonde's bright aura fascinated him, he hadn't even seen psychic's with auras that bright. He pondered how the European mongrel did it, had it fed on several humans with ESP?

"Tell me, what kind of psychic did you feed on to get such an aura?" The prisoner called out. "I was under the impression that only Vampires could take on the abilities of who they fed on."

The noise in the cavern died down as the Lokoti Werewolves quieted to watch.

"You think I got an aura like this from feeding on a human?" The Second raised his eyebrows.

"Lokoti Werewolves including the pack's Second, don't hunt human," the First proclaimed.

"A 'pacifist' European Werewolf?" He scoffed. "Hardly!"

"Why am I not surprised that a fang head just doesn't get it?" The Second said.

“Don’t look down your nose at me, dog!” The Vampire snapped. “My kind hunted your kind into extinction because you’re just a rabid animal!”

“If I’m such a rabid animal then how come your kind feeds on my kind for our strength and regenerative ability?” He replied, coolly.

“Like humans milking a cow,” the fang head responded, “and they have no qualms with killing it when they want to eat steak.”

“That’s one of the best things about being a Werewolf, we eat,” the blonde responded. “We can eat a whole range of food besides fresh kill. When was the last time you ate something? Man, you must get bored of drinking blood all of the time.”

“A diet which is beneficial to our state of health,” the Vampire said smugly. “Look at some of your pack, look at how old they grow! I’ve had the same appearance for hundreds of years.”

“We may age, but we can heal as well as procreate unlike you,” the Second pointed out. "You have to feed off humans or Werewolves to heal yourself.”

“I procreate by sharing my blood with the chosen!” The Vampire rebuked.

“Oh yeah, turning a human into one of you whether they want it or not? Try having sex and watching the woman you love carry the new life inside her.”

“Your children are your weakness!” The Vampire spat out. “If my progeny is killed, I simply create more. But if your children are killed, you howl and whine.”

The European Werewolf walked over to look the European Vampire right in the eye.

“Can you even have sex? You can’t get it up without drinking blood first, can you? You smell decrepit because you are decrepit.” He taunted.

“That’s so typical of a dog to prioritize as such,” the Vampire sneered. “You would hump your master’s leg, as you’d grind against anything that moves!”

“It’s why you hunt us,” the Second said simply. “We create life and all you create is death. You’re parasites, you spread Vampirism like it’s a disease!”

“Unlike you and how your breed is created by bite, blood or birth,” the prisoner returned.

“I’ve never changed a human by bite or sharing blood,” the European Werewolf announced. “And I never will.”

“It’s because your breed would turn on their own!” The Vampire refuted. “You’re scared of changing another and having the new mongrel turn on you.”

“Don’t I know it,” the Second grumbled. “My own breed turned on me so I killed them.”

“A Vampire’s coven is family,” the prisoner said proudly. “We would never turn on our creator, instead we revere them.”

"Lokoti Werewolves don't turn on each other and they revere me as one of their Elders," the Second shrugged.

As if to demonstrate their respect, a second wooden chair was brought forward for their Second to sit on. The blonde man turned the chair around and sat on it back to front. Casually, he leaned forward and fixed his foe with a glare.

"Where did you get your aura from?" The Vampire tried again.

"Like I'd tell you," the blonde man scoffed. "But now it's my turn to ask the questions. How big is your coven and when is the attack?"

To show he wouldn't answer, the prisoner coolly looked away. Instead of turning angry at the defiance, the Second smiled. Then so did the rest of the pack and for some reason, they looked happy about something.

"I was hoping you'd be like that," the European Werewolf grinned. "I truly was."

Then his captor moved his large hand towards the Vampire's face. His thumb was sticking out and the Vampire soon felt why, as it was used it to squash his left eyeball. The prisoner's screams filled the cavern as his eye was gouged.

*****

Half an hour later, a heavily bleeding European Vampire sat still tied to the wooden chair. The European Werewolf sat across, still back to front in his chair, in a casual manner. The captor smirked at his prisoner and in return the prisoner hissed back.

To retaliate in anyway it could, the Vampire had shape shifted from human to other. Its one remaining eye had turned glowing white and one of its poisonous fangs had detracted. It was missing its other however, when the Werewolf had slowly and painfully pulled it out. The fang head was also missing his left ear from being torn off. It left a gaping, bloody hole in the side of his head.

"So, how big is your coven and when is the attack?" The European Werewolf asked again.

The European Vampire hissed back with its one remaining poisonous fang.

"You know, when adult humans lose teeth, they don't grow back. I wonder if it's the same with Vampires?" The Second looked over his shoulder to his pack.

They watched with interest as their second-in-charge held the Vampire's head still in one hand whilst he used his other to pull the second fang out.

Futilely, the Vampire struggled against both the ropes and his much stronger opponent.

The prisoner's agony was evident as his cries rebounded against the cave walls.

*****

Another thirty minutes later, the Vampire remained tied to its chair with his torturer sitting across.

The prisoner's remaining eye was black and swollen and his crooked nose was bleeding heavily. His fingers and toes had also been broken and the pain put him in torment. He couldn't heal himself without imbibing blood, which his captors knew.

"Do I get to hurt you some more, or are you going to spoil my fun by telling us what we wanna know?" The European Werewolf asked.

"If I tell you, my coven will kill me," the European Vampire spluttered out of its bloody mouth.

"Well, you're gonna die anyway," the Second shrugged casually. "You're not gonna see tomorrow."

The prisoner groaned in pain, "Then why ssshould I talk...?"

"Because if you don't, I'm just gonna keep hurting you and I know you're hurting," the blonde man smirked. "By now a Werewolf's regenerative ability would have stopped the bleeding and we'd be healed. But look at you... you can't even heal yourself! You're useless! You have to drink another's blood to recuperate."

As if to prove his point, the Werewolf forced the Vampire's mouth open once more to look at the bloodied gums where its fangs used to be.

"You see, no new teeth have grown back," his captor showed off. "I've lost teeth before on a hunt and they've grown back in twenty-four hours."

The Vampire lisped out of its aching mouth, "Then give me sssome blood and you'll sssee the power of our regeneration."

"Like hell I'd help a fang head heal itself," the Werewolf glared. "Face it buddy, you're at the bottom of the food chain NOT the top of it."

Instead of degrading the prisoner, his words made him to laugh. At first the bloodied and broken man laughed quietly to himself but then it got louder. His head rolled around as if he were in hysterics at the taunts.

"You want to play the 'who isss sssuperior' game with me, dog?" The Vampire laughed out. "We can live for five hundred yearsss and by imbibing blood, we can heal from almossst anything."

"What's the point in living for five hundred years when you can't live life to the full? We enjoy everything our world has to offer; food, family, sunshine, moonlight and hunting. We too can heal from almost anything and we don't have to rely on drinking someone else's blood to do it," the Werewolf boasted.

"Not all blood tastesss the sssame, you ssstupid mongrel," the Vampire hissed. "We too enjoy variety; animal blood, human blood and of course,

Werewolf blood. No two humans taste the same and it'sss the sssame with the different breedsss of Werewolf. Have you noticed how no one huntsss my kind asss a food sssource?"

"Yeah, because it'd be worse than being infected with HIV," he retorted. "Your blood takes away instead of gives. I bet you can't even get it up without drinking blood first. Tell me, have you even had sex since you were turned?"

There was snickering from the pack at his insult but it only made the prisoner more determined.

"Ah, but of courssse!" He cried out. "All you care about is sssex! It'sss the reason why you're mated to a female Werewolf, asss they're just bitchesss on heat! Female Werewolvesss are ssso hungry for it, they need it all the time! When I usssed to hunt femalesss of your breed, all I had to do wasss look in an alleyway behind a bar and there they were; sssurrounded by men and ssstill begging for more!"

He saw his words hit home by the look of hate on the Second's face. Indeed, the whole cavern had turned deathly still. The rest of the pack looked on in anger, as if a sister's honour had been insulted.

"You have Werewolf daughtersss asss well, oui?" The Vampire carried on recklessly. "When my kind huntsss them we'll know where to find them... flat on their backsss!"

The European Werewolf's speed let alone his strength took the wounded European Vampire by surprise. He knew what was coming but not how fast it would happen. The Second's fist lashed out so fast, his arm looked like bright a blur.

However, the crack of the European Vampire's jaw breaking was clearly audible. The prisoner's chair went flying backwards, landing hard on the rocky floor. The enraged European Werewolf didn't stop there, as he picked up the captive, chair and all, and hurled them against a distant wall.

The wooden chair smashed upon impact then it and the broken Vampire fell to the cavern floor.

The Lokoti Werewolves stood back to watch the European Werewolf unleash its bloodlust on the male who had insulted his mate's honour.

"No, not the jeans!" The pink-eyed Werewolf cried out, but it was too late.

Their Second had already begun to shape shift. The Vampire watched in part amazement and part horror, as the large, blonde man began to expand in size. The monster stood in full glory of its prey as the torn denim slipped to the floor in pieces.

"Damn it, they were a new pair too," the pink-eyed Werewolf lamented.

Before their Second could finish what he'd started, their First walked over and picked up the prisoner. The Lokoti Werewolf dangled the wounded European Vampire in the air by his fist clutching the front of his designer clothes. Meanwhile, the European Werewolf loomed behind as it hungrily licked its lips.

"As Uncle Declan said, you're going to die today," the First spoke in his thunderous voice. "As you so graciously offered in your terms, we will also give you the choice of how you die. Tell us when your coven will attack and how many there'll be and our Second will kill you quickly. If you do not, we will watch our Uncle devour you piece by piece, in a slow death."

Instead of looking afraid, the Vampire managed to give the Werewolves a defiant smile with its bleeding and broken mouth.

The First dropped him as if he were a bag of garbage then he turned and walked away.

The European Vampire's cries of horrendous agony followed him out as he headed towards the entrance of the cave. The European Werewolf did indeed eat him 'piece by piece', starting with his left foot. In one chomp, the huge jaws completely bit it off. After swallowing it, the monster started to make its way up his left leg before turning to the right foot and then munching on the right leg.

The middle-aged Lokoti Werewolf's glowing blue eyes scanned the surrounding countryside.

Pensively, he stared out at the winding river and its green valley which looked peaceful in the afternoon sun. The river was a dark blue colour, complimenting the evergreen trees and the snow-tipped mountain peaks acted as a majestic backdrop. He sighed heavily as he looked on the serene beauty which was in direct contrast to the bloodshed inside.

Soon he was joined by the tribe's Healer who was looking a little uncomfortable himself with what was happening behind them.

"What are we going to do now?" He asked his First. "Start patrolling the borders to keep an eye out for the other fang heads?"

"It's a start," the blue-eyed Werewolf frowned. "Hopefully, we can battle them deep inside the National Park, away from the community centre."

"And away from our human families," his subordinate agreed. "But Caesar, I'm worried about how many fang heads could be coming. With all the deaths announced on the World Wide News, the European covens must be large. What if we can't fight them all? Perhaps we should evacuate tribal lands."

"That's over six hundred people we'd be asking to leave," the First frowned. "Lokoti Werewolves were created to fight off invaders. We were born in battle to protect our mate, family and tribe. We'll discuss it with the Tribal Elders, but I'll bet they'd vote to stay."

"We should also include the tribe's Light Person," the pink-eyed Werewolf agreed. "Maybe Aunt B could see something in one of her visions."

"I'll talk to her tomorrow," his leader concurred before he turned around.

The two Lokoti Werewolves left behind the brightness to return to the darkness.

The European Vampire was still screaming, expressing his hideous torture of slowly being eaten alive, whereas the European Werewolf didn't even wince with guilt, as it chomped away. Its' bloodlust revelled at being released from its leash of strict self-control...

...

...darkness and pain, I've seen these things before. The caves in the north eastern valley resembled the dark pit I've been dreaming about recently. Hell, the Vampire's screams mirrored the voices I've heard cry out in anguish and torment. The dark pit of despair which I'd seen in my nightmares had come true.

I opened my eyes to find myself lying on top of my bed with my young sleeping on either side. When I put them down for an afternoon nap, I'd accidentally fallen asleep too. But I knew what I'd seen wasn't a dream, it was a vision.

As a floating, bodiless, invisible mass, I spied on the Vampire who'd been spying on us this morning. Somehow, I even heard his thoughts as he observed us. I watched the fate which befell him for encroaching on our territory. The bloodshed left me feeling cold as it made me shudder.

The pack - bar Kurt and myself - had no doubt that the fang head must die and most of them didn't flinch at the manner it was carried out.

However, it was the same reaction I saw in the European Vampire. It had stalked me and my daughters this morning the same way we stalked our prey on a hunt. When the fang head sniffed the European Werewolf DNA in my little girls, it thought it had found a rare wine to share.

Now there'd be more European Vampires who could move in the speed of sound. Declan and I had the advantage of being able to move in the speed of light, but the rest of the pack didn't. Lokoti Werewolves are stronger than European Vampires, but would that be enough against a coven of European Vampires? I didn't think it would... From experience, I knew they fought with silver swords which were lethal with their faster reflexes. They also had the advantage of poisonous fangs which could paralyze a Werewolf and kill a human.

Walt had a lucky break when he was able to jump the one this morning. Because he knew these lands like the back of his hand and the Vampire was unarmed; he was able to get the upper hand. But the sense of foreboding which was building inside my chest, knew it wouldn't happen again. My warning feelings were telling me that the dark pit of despair would soon have a chorus of voices as the tally of dead grew.

I sat upright to look about my cheerfully bright bedroom which basked in the afternoon sun. Everything appeared normal on the surface however, underneath it was anything but. Then perfectly timed, I heard the front door downstairs open and shut with the return of my husband.

I listened to him come upstairs and then down the hallway. He paused in the bedroom doorway to smile on his mate and young curled up together, on top of the bed. I stared back at his bloodied hands and mouth. They were rubbing off onto his old flannel robe, which he put on again once he reverted to human.

"Did you have any problems putting Sophia to bed?" He asked quietly. "With her tantrum after lunch, I thought I'd have to sit on her again."

"Er, no." I said vacantly as I continued to stare at his messy mouth and hands.

I could smell it was the Vampire's blood. He noticed what I was looking at, which made him self-consciously look downwards. Then he spoke as he headed into the ensuite:

"I'd better jump in the shower before I start on dinner."

I watched him pass through the bedroom then shut the door behind. Shortly after, I heard the shower turn on as my husband washed away his transgressions. I didn't sense one drop of guilt inside him, rather, I sensed he felt proud of his actions. His bloodlust was gloating that it got to torture and kill in the name of 'protecting' his loved ones.

Carefully, I slid off the bed to make sure I wouldn't disturb my daughters' sleep. Then I walked over to the ensuite door, opened it, went inside and closed it behind. I found Declan was using a small brush to clean under his nails as his wet, muscled body was covered in soap suds. When he saw me, he paused to pass a cheeky grin my way.

"Have you come to get in a quickie while the kids are asleep?" He offered.

I looked down to see how excited he was from his prior activities in the cavern. The fact that my husband was turned on by slowly eating a person alive was disturbing. Anxiously, I looked away as I began to pace up and down in the small space. Casually, he continued to clean under his nails then he stood under the stream of water to wash the rest of the suds off.

"Relax B, it's taken care of," he said.

"But it's not is it, Declan?!" I hissed. "You didn't find out how many are coming or when is the attack, did you?"

He paused a second time to look on curiously, "How the hell do you know about THAT?"

"I saw what you did this afternoon in a vision!" I shouted in a whisper, so not to wake the kids.

"You 'saw'?" He arched his eyebrows. "Then did you 'hear' what the Vampire was planning?"

"Yes I heard his threats." I shook my head in disapproval. "But it doesn't justify torture."

"Oh yes it does," he said unhappily.

Then he turned off the taps, stepped out onto the mat and proceeded to dry himself off with his huge towel.

"I know what the Vampire said about me and the girls," I said uneasily.

"And it turned into one of the last things it ever said," he said coldly.

I watched him return the towel to the heated towel rack before pulling on a pair of boxer shorts. I followed him out of the ensuite as he proceeded to dress in the bedroom. When he opened the drawers of our tallboy, the noise was enough to wake our young who sleepily sat up.

"Daddy?" Soph rubbed her eyes. "Have you been hunting?"

"Yeah you could say that," he smirked.

"Did you find the fang head?" Looch asked.

"Yes I did," he said simply.

"Did you eat it like you ate the other fang heads?" She guessed.

"Don't fang heads taste dirty?" Soph screwed up her face in distaste.

I passed my mate an unimpressed look at how our daughter's were already being taught that fang heads should automatically be eaten.

"Who wants Beef Stroganoff for dinner?" He changed the subject.

"I do!" Our girls cried out before jumping off the king-sized bed.

I watched them stream through bedroom door behind their father, acting like it was normal to go from the subject of murder to 'what's for dinner'. I sunk onto the bed as my feelings of foreboding went from bad to worse. This was wrong on so many levels and I didn't know what to do or where to begin. There was such ingrained hate and anger between the species of Vampires and breeds of Werewolves that now our daughters were becoming part of it.

*****

After dinner, I sat on the couch in the lounge area with the Internet Radio on. I had selected a classical music station to listen to, as a book sat open in my lap. However, I wasn't taking in the pictures of the Grecian temples, rather, I was pretending I was studying. In actuality, I was thinking about what happened today and what the ramifications would be.

My mate kept our young amused by making them help with dinner. Once the meal was over and the table was cleared, he played a board game with them. Their laughter periodically interrupted my thoughts, but I liked seeing them play together instead of fighting each other. I only put my book aside when it was the girls' bedtime.

Everyone congregated in Sophia's room and sat on top of her small bed. Our little ones smelled soapy from their bath and together they curled up in our laps, in their pyjamas. It was Declan's turn to read tonight since I read last night. He was an old hand at storytelling thanks to centuries of babysitting. We were reading 'The Neverending Story' to them and I must admit, with his deep voice he could make the characters Rock Biter and Falkor come alive.

When the chapter finished, we tucked in Soph and turned out her light before escorting Looch into her room. There we did the same for our eldest, with us each delivering a kiss to her forehead. Smilingly, she watched us depart from her bedroom, turning off her light as we went.

Upon returning downstairs, I sat down with my history book again. To the soft tunes of Pachelbel's Canon in D, I stared at the pictures of the ancient architecture. Subconsciously, my thumb ran along my lips, which was a habit I'd developed when I was deep in thought.

I felt that this constant war between Werewolf and Vampire should be stopped. Why couldn't we exist together peacefully? Why are they deliberately searching us out? Is the world's Werewolf population THAT low? Maybe I could work out some kind of peace treaty to ensure my daughters wouldn't be hunted for the rest of their lives...

"I didn't think you were reading."

I looked up in surprise to find my husband looming over. He stood there with his hands on his hips and a knowing look on his face. Then he sat beside on the couch which made me awkwardly slide away from him.

He frowned, "Not this again."

"What?"

"I killed my wife and children's stalker and you make me out to be the bad guy," he said unhappily.

"Declan, what are you talking about?"

"In New Orleans you carried on like I was the dingo that ate the baby, after I killed the Voodoo crazies. Now after you've 'seen' me kill the Vampire, you're acting the same way again." He said unhappily.

"No I'm not!"

"Then why did you edge away from me when I sat down?"

But I decided not to answer and I picked up my book again when he pulled it out of my hands and put it aside.

"No, we're gonna talk about this," he said firmly.

"Or fight about it, you mean." I said grumpily.

"Just as long as we don't wake the kids," he said coolly, as his eyes turned towards the staircase. "Soph was getting irritable during the board game and I don't want to set off one of her tantrums."

This made me laugh and I put my hand over my mouth to guffaw quietly.

He saw what I was doing which prompted him to ask, "What's so funny?"

"You have no qualms about torturing and then slowly eating a European Vampire alive, but you're afraid of your five year old daughter?"

"I'm not afraid, but I have a healthy respect for it." He shifted uncomfortably in his seat. "That girl's tantrums could make the meanest European Werewolf think twice about crossing paths."

He made me snicker as I envisioned either Marcus, Leo or Michelle catching sight of Sophia and then hurrying off in another direction.

"There it is, your aura is getting brighter," he observed. "Now are you going to tell me what you've been stewing over while you've been pretending to read?"

"How do you know I was pretending?"

"You did your thoughtful gesture of when your thumb caresses your lips." He said knowingly. "You only do that when you're thinking or planning something."

"We've been married for too long." I looked away, sulkily.

"Tell me about it," he said tiredly, as he put his feet up on the coffee table.

"But I've been thinking..." I began.

"Yeah?"

"...that maybe we should try to make peace with the Vampires."

"Say what?!" Declan spluttered in surprise.

Startled, he sat upright as he removed his feet from their resting position.

"I'm tired of always fighting and what if the oncoming attack could be averted?" I thought aloud.

"You've got to be kidding!"

"No, but since you killed that Vampire today, it may not induce its' coven into listening."

"It was hunting my mate and young!" He cried out indignantly.

"Sssshhh!" I shushed him as I cast a wary look towards the stairs.

"I don't believe this..." he grumbled as he stood up to walk a small distance away before turning around to look in my direction, "...you said you saw what happened today?"

"Yes."

"And did you see the text message the fang head sent to its coven?"

"Well, no."

Then he quoted the message as if he were reading it from the screen:

"I SUGGEST WE ATTACK AT NIGHT. ASIDE FROM THE EXPTECTED 14 LOKOTI DOGS AND 1 LOKOTI BITCH, THERE'S 1 EUROPEAN MONGREL WITH 2 HALF BREED PUPS. RECOMMEND LEAVING BITCH ALIVE FOR NOW AS SHE'S CARRYING A 3RD HALF BREED."

This knocked the wind out of my sails as well as the air out of my lungs. I gasped in horror at the cold and callous nature of my enemy. I was talking about peace with these fiends without knowing this small but important fact...? I can't believe I actually felt sorry for this killer this afternoon!

"Aw B," he looked on unhappily, "your aura is fading again."

Tears filled my eyes as I confessed, "I saw it, Declan."

"Now what did you see?" He asked in a weary tone.

"All those nights I woke up in pain from the tension headaches, remember the nightmares that came with them?"

Then I started to cry from the fear and helplessness pressing down on me. I wasn't sure if it was my tears that got his attention or what I was trying to say. But he came back over and dropped to his knees so he was kneeling before his wife.

"I dreamed of a dark pit with lots of voices screaming." I reminded him. "And today, I saw you in a dark cavern making a Vampire scream. But he's not the only one, Declan. There's going to be more... many, many more!"

"OK," he cupped my wet face between his hands and tried to hold my gaze. "You think you've been having visions about this? Then tell me what else you saw, B."

"That's it!" I pushed his hands away in frustration. "I saw a dark pit of despair with numerous voices screaming. It's started today with the first scream but I know there's going to be many more joining it."

Then I sat there and cried as he looked on with a helpless expression of his own.

"Are you saying what I did today could have triggered this?" He frowned. "But the Vampires already knew about us! His coven sent him to case the joint way before I sunk my teeth into him."

"I don't know, Declan..." I sniffed, "...there's something big coming and I don't know how to stop it. I wish my Mum and Gran were here! They could help me fight the Vampires like they did before."

"What am I, chopped liver?" He asked, offended.

"No, but we need more Circulators with silver swords to fight the Vampires when they come with their own!" I said fearfully. "A large coven of European Vampires armed with silver swords would easily mow down the pack of Lokoti Werewolves!"

"Not if I eat them first!" Declan said vehemently. "Not only am I stronger than the fang heads, but I'm faster than them too! If I run at them in light speed with my jaws open and ready, they've got no chance!"

"What if you run right onto a silver sword?" I pointed out. "You'll impale yourself!"

"B, listen to me." He cupped my face a second time. "I know you're scared, I can see it by your fading aura. But you need to listen to me, I know why I'm 115% stronger now. It's nature's way of enabling me to protect my mate and young."

"No it's not, it's so you'll remain stronger than your offspring." I pulled out of his grasp. "The other European Werewolves who were fathers, destroyed their young, remember?"

"Stop being so argumentative and listen to me!" He growled in frustration. "I'm stronger because my DNA is designed to help my breed survive. I was the last of my kind, remember B? The LAST. Now with Susanna growing inside you, my DNA has made me stronger still to ensure our survival. Nature is making sure neither me nor my daughters become extinct."

"If only we had more time to further your training as a Circulator," I sighed heavily. "I could have taught you how to swordfight in the speed of light."

"Swords...?" He gave a funny look. "B, I'm a European Werewolf and baby, we don't need swords!"

"So that's your tactic; tooth and claw?" I arched my eyebrows, unimpressed.

"Yes!" He straightened in indignation. "This method's worked for the last three hundred years, hasn't it?"

I groaned as I began to rub my face with my hands which showed my stress.

"C'mon B, don't be afraid." He caught my hands in his. "I can protect you and the girls."

My watery dark blue eyes met his bright blue ones which held them back in a defiant expression.

"But who's going to protect you, Declan? Or the pack for that matter?" I asked in a small voice. "I'll be fighting along side of you, but I'm scared that -"

However, I didn't get to finish my sentence from the dangerously low growl he emitted.

"There's no way in hell my pregnant wife is going anywhere near the battlefield!"

"Declan, the baby bump isn't that big -"

"Do I have to knock you unconscious again?" He warned as his eyes glowed green in anger. "My pregnant wife is NOT fighting any fang heads!"

"You don't have a choice!" I yelled back in his face. "You're gonna need my help!"

Then we both paused and turned our heads towards the staircase when we realized we had an audience.

Our two little girls were sitting at the top of the stairs, watching and listening to the ruckus. They looked scared which was evident by how Looch protectively had her arms around her little sister. Because it was so rare that the two ever showed affection for the other, it gave away their fear.

Their father's glowing eyes returned to their human colour in an effort to show his young that everything was alright.

"It's alright sweeties, you can go back to bed. Your Mommy and I will stop yelling at each other so you can get some sleep." He promised.

"Why are we going to be attacked by Vampires? I thought you killed it." Looch asked, confused.

"European Vampires live in covens," I said as I walked up the stairs to sit by them. "Occasionally, they send out one or two, but they belong to a group."

"So its' pack is gonna come and get us?" Looch's eyes widened fearfully.

"Nobody's coming to get you, I'd eat them before that happens." Declan said adamantly, as he leaned on the banister.

"Daddy ate the other Vampires," Soph smiled at his words. "Daddy eats all of the Vampires in his bigger body."

"Damn straight," her father said determinedly, "and I'm gonna keep eating anything that looks at my mate and young the wrong way."

Soph giggled in delight but Looch still looked afraid.

"Then how come you and Mum are arguing?" She wondered. "Why is Mum gonna help you fight them instead of you just eating them?"

Declan glared my way as he answered, "Your mother's not fighting."

"Oh yes she is," I seethed back before I faced my daughters to explain. "There's going to be a lot of European Vampires coming. They can move faster than Werewolves and they fight with silver swords which makes them very dangerous. So the pack will need me to fight back with my silver katana."

Looch blanched at the news as Soph's mouth fell open in surprise.

"How many fang heads are coming?" Our youngest asked, concerned.

What I said next didn't just capture my daughters' attention but it made their father's eyes widen as well.

"There'll be thirty and they'll attack at night." I said as I stared down at the polished wooden floor. "They'll approach from the north since Alma is so close to the south and they'll want to avoid the human authorities."

"Huh?" Soph asked, puzzled. "How do you know this, Mummy?"

"Shhh!" My husband shushed her as he came up the stairs to crouch in front of his wife. "What night is this B? Can you give us a date?"

Looch also realized I was 'seeing' this in a vision so she thought she should help by putting her hand over her little sister's mouth to ensure silence.

"The European Vampires won't be all from the same coven." I stared hypnotically. "The two covens have made an agreement to share the blood of the last remaining European Werewolf. They want to wound you, to keep you alive to farm your blood. If they can't take you alive, they'll kill you and then infect another human with your blood and turn them."

Then my family watched in concern as I closed my eyes and shook my head to try to end the vision.

Once upon a time, Marcus told Declan how a coven of European Vampires had killed his mate by draining her with hoses. I saw something similar happen to my mate in his huge body, chained up, with several hoses attached. His regenerative ability would recoup the blood loss before his captors drew several more litres. I saw his muscle bulk and his hardened hide begin to look sunken, as the constant blood loss slowly killed him. At first he struggled against the thick, silver chains in his once powerful body. Then he slumped to the cement floor of where ever they were keeping him. His glowing green eyes dulled and eventually emptied of life, as his body did.

"B, your aura has all but disappeared." Declan spoke. "Are you OK?"

I think I scared my daughters when I started to rub my face hard and I didn't stop. It looked like I was maddeningly trying to rub out my own features. My eyes were squeezed shut but the damn vision wouldn't stop!

"I don't want to see it anymore I don't want to see it anymore I don't want to see it anymore..." I whimpered helplessly.

"Is Mummy going crazy?" I heard Soph speak that was closely followed by an, "Oow!" which was from Looch pinching her.

"B, snap out of it!" My mate pushed down my hands to replace them with his. I relished the feel of his hot, hard palms pressing against my cheeks. "C'mon B, open your eyes and look at me."

His deep voice began to bring me back. I think I did open my eyes, but it took nearly a minute for the darkness to clear. However, when it did, it was just like waking from a nightmare and I found myself staring into his bright blue eyes.

"Declan...?" I blinked repeatedly in a dazed manner. "Declan!"

I threw my arms about his neck and held onto him for dear life. I treasured the sensation of him holding me back and squeezing me against his stronger build. I even felt his large hand stroke my hair.

"Frickin' hell woman, you'll be the death of me," he let out a rueful laugh. "One minute it's talk about my pregnant wife going into battle then the next you're the embodiment of the lights are on but nobody's home."

"Mummy has gone crazy," Soph decided which was followed by another, "Oow! Stop pinching me, Lucia!"

Then our youngest shoved our eldest away, disgruntled at the physical chastisements.

Their father laughed at the sibling rivalry and then whilst keeping one arm about their mother, he used his other to pull them in for a group hug.

I felt Looch's strong little arms encircle my waist as she affectionately rubbed her face against my back. Instead of hugging from behind, Soph pushed her way into the middle of the huddle. She's always liked to be the centre of attention.

"I love my Sabre women," Declan declared, "and nobody in this family is dying from a fang head leeching off them."

*****

After we put the girls to bed again my husband drew his wife a bath. We undressed in the bedroom then I went into the bathroom to drop a Lush Bath Bomb into the hot water. As if I was still in a daze, I stood by the side of the large bathtub, watching the 'bomb' fizzle away. A divine smell filled the air and small flower petals floated on the surface.

He climbed into the tub first so he could help his pregnant wife in second. I sunk into the perfumed water and leaned back against his wide chest. He wrapped his arms around and I felt his hands tenderly stroke my tummy.

"You know what? I just realized something." He began. "Human women get stretch marks from pregnancy, but you don't. Do you think it's because of your Werewolf regenerative ability, or because you're a Circulator?"

I shrugged back as I stared at the flower petals drifting over the water. Anytime either of us moved, the ripples would act like tidal waves and threaten to capsize them. Declan reached for a loofa and dunked it into the water causing further disruption. Then he ran it over my shoulders and down my arms as he washed his wife.

"Can you remember if your Mom or your Gran had stretch marks?" He asked.

"I didn't see their tummies but I don't think they did," I answered. "Remember how their bodies reverted to a pre-pregnant state?"

"I saw my Mom's stomach before and after Derik was born and she had stretch marks." He mused. "They didn't look bad or anything. Actually, they kinda reminded me of ripples on butter or cream."

"Do you wish my body changed permanently and I had stretch marks?"

"Nope," his answer was quick as it was finite. "As much as I love to see how your body changes during pregnancy, I love how you revert afterwards. It's like your body is the one constant in my life. Humans age and die, the seasons change, but my B will always be my B."

My hair was tied up in a knot which gave him ample access to my bare shoulders. I felt his teeth graze the surface of the skin before his mouth kissed his way up my neck. Lastly, I felt him chew on my left ear which made my eyes flutter closed.

"That's why you can't fight the fang heads," he breathed. "You're married to a murderer B, and I like killing for my wife and kids. Leave the fighting to me."

I turned around in the water so I could meet his waiting gaze, "Maybe I'm a murderer too?"

"Nope." He said strongly. "You're not afraid to fight for what you love, but you don't get a thrill from it, not like I do."

My hand ran up his wet torso and then his neck to finally linger on his lips. My fingertips caressed the surface of his mouth. The flesh felt deceptively soft and warm in his human form but in his other, it was hot, hungry and dangerous.

"How can a monster like you, make a girl like me, feel like the most loved woman in all existence?" I said softly.

He grinned, "Because we belong together like peas and a pod. You're the pea and I'm the pod. The girls are the other peas and I'm gonna keep all of you happy, healthy and above all, safe."

"So you're the tough exterior?" I smiled in amusement.

"You'd better believe it, baby." He gave a wink.

Then we leaned forwards at the same time to gently bump foreheads. I shut my eyes as I rubbed my face against his and our noses tickled the other's. He returned the affection with a lasting kiss as our eyes remained closed.

"June 1st," I said reluctantly.

"Huh?" He opened his eyes to give a peculiar look.

"June 1st is when the covens will arrive and more people will die."

~~~~~~
~~~~~~

~ 26 ~

28th May, 2374

Battle plans were made in the lead up to the fight for our survival. The pack convened several times at their First or Second's house. However, what surprised the men was how often Looch and Soph were in attendance.

The grown male Lokoti Werewolves were happy to leave their human families at home; safe and sound and ignorant of the imminent danger. The only other members of the tribe in the know were our Tribal Elders. However, since three Lokoti Werewolves in the shapes of Caesar, Ki and Phil sat on the council of nine, really it was only six members.

In the beginning, Declan and I had a preliminary meeting with our First and Medicine Man. Over a cup of coffee, they sat at our dining table to hear what I had 'seen'. As I recanted the vision, Looch and Soph sat at the top of the stairs to listen. Our Healer glanced upwards at our underage audience.

"Aunt B and Uncle Dec, shouldn't you send the girls to their rooms while we discuss this?" He asked uneasily.

"We did," my husband answered. "But as you can see, they don't feel like playing dolls or reading fairy tales right now."

Ki opened his mouth to debate that our conversation wasn't a subject for young ears, when Caesar spoke over the top of him.

"Sophia and Lucia are no strangers to death being Werewolves," he said solemnly. "They hunt with the pack and they hear our will. Although they won't be fighting with their parents, they'll know what they'll be doing."

"Parent." Declan said adamantly. "One parent will be fighting and that'll be me. B and the girls won't be anywhere near this."

I exchanged a long look with our First, before Caesar said in a solemn voice, "I'm afraid that this time you're incorrect, Uncle."

"Say what?" He looked on in astonishment. "You're gonna let my pregnant wife run around the battlefield with fang heads trying to feed on her?!"

"Aunt B, although Ki tells me the foetus is the size of a five month old; your stomach isn't protruding much." Caesar looked me up and down. "How is your movement, are you hindered in anyway?"

"I still work out in the self-defence training room at Circulate Headquarters." I promised. "I was there yesterday, giving the girls a lesson."

"Yeah, but she works out against a holographic partner!" Declan debated. "These fang heads are gonna be real."

"I'm sorry Uncle, I really am," our leader said. "But we'll be fighting thirty European Vampires with silver swords who can move in the speed of sound. Not only are we going to need a European Werewolf/Circulator that can fight in the speed of light, but we'll need another Circulator with the same ability and a silver sword of her own."

Declan growled under his breath as he stood up from the table to walk away. He stood with his back to us, as if he were holding himself back from challenging his leader. I sensed his conflict of emotions, with his bloodlust bubbling underneath the surface just waiting to escape in a loss of control.

Caesar continued, "We're already outnumbered and facing insurmountable odds. I'll be telling Walt that his fourteen year old son Kurt won't be fighting. Your little girls will also be sitting this out. This means we're down to fifteen wolves against thirty poisonous snakes. We need the tribe's Light Person to shine the way."

My husband didn't respond as he crossed his arms in front and his jaw set.

The next time we met with our First and the rest of the men, it was at the old Riverclaw home.

Soph and Looch insisted on coming to hear what their pack was planning. When we tried to take them to the Wisetail's instead to play with their cousins, our youngest threw one of her tantrums. Rather than sitting on her again, their father relented and they came with us.

When we arrived we found that Kurt had come with his father. Walt and Declan shook hands upon greeting then they went to talk to the other men. Kurt walked over to Looch and gave her a playful punch on the arm, which she returned. Then the three youngest Werewolves in the pack, sat in the lounge area as their parents converged around the dining table.

Walt brought a large aerial map of the Lokoti National Park. He spread it over the top of the dining table and pencilled in our plans. I stood in between our First and Second as they asked more questions about what I'd 'seen'.

"You said the covens would attack from the north," Caesar's eyes scanned the top perimeter of the Park. "Can you tell us whereabouts?"

"Um," I frowned as I tried to tune in to my warning feeling. "I think around here." I waved my hand over a part of the map.

"That's Gulliver's Gulch." Walt put an asterisk on where I'd indicated. "It's a narrow break in the range that runs parallel to the north eastern valley."

"Besides multiplying like cockroaches, the fang heads scurry through the cracks and into our home." Declan glared.

"It's closer to Fairbanks than the north eastern valley." Derik said warily. "I'll bet they'll fly into Alaska via Fairbanks instead of Anchorage."

"Do we have any friends at Fairbanks airport that could keep an eye out for any particularly pale visitors arriving on aircraft from Europe?" Phil wondered.

"None that are Lokoti," Caesar frowned.

"Wait," Declan turned my way, "B didn't you say that Jonathan Bourne and Hodge Endeavor are politically connected?"

"Yes?"

"What if you give the human leech your lawyer a call and see what he can do about monitoring Fairbanks airport?" He suggested.

"Excuse me," I moved away to put his plan into action.

I walked out of the house to stand on the front veranda whilst pulling my mobile phone out of my pocket.

"Hallo, Jonathan? It's B Sabre."

"B, how are you?" He greeted in his crisp English accent.

"Good, but I need you to do something for me."

"Any help I render you, helps my bank account." He said congenially. "Has your hover-car been confiscated again in another murder investigation?"

"Not today, no."

"Then how may Hodge Endeavor assist its Head Chairwoman?"

"I need someone to watch over arrivals at Fairbanks airport." I spoke frankly. "We're expecting visitors from Europe on or a day before June 1st."

"European visitors?" He paused for a moment. "Is there a particular part of Europe they're coming from?"

"We're not sure yet, which is why I'm not asking you to monitor departures from the major European cities." I said unhappily. "Just keep an eye out on the arrivals at Fairbanks airport. They'll most likely fly in on private plane and have substantial means. They'll be recognizable by pale or sickly appearances."

I heard him gulp before he said uneasily, "Oh, I see."

Now this made me pause and I wondered if I should activate the video screen on my phone so I could see his face.

"Jonathan, what's wrong?"

"Um, I was going to discuss this with you when you came to the Board Meeting next month." He began.

"Yes?"

"Do you remember Gavin Farrah?"

"No."

"He was the executive at Hodge Endeavor that we fired for corporate espionage. We also hit him with bankruptcy when he tried to blackmail the company by going to the media with information on the Circulate. We filed a gag order as his assets were seized and we continued to monitor his silence."

"Oh, him." I remembered. "Yeah and?"

"Well erm, he's missing."

"He's what?" I thought I misheard. "But I thought we'd tapped his phone and computer as well as hired private investigators to follow him."

"The European Union Police force as well as our own investigators did have him under surveillance, but um..."

"Yes?"

"In the last report they submitted, they noted that Farrah had made some new friends. He'd been invited several times to dine with an eastern European aristocrat called Count Onesti, in several five star restaurants. However, one evening he didn't come home afterwards and the police have been unable to locate him."

Suddenly, my stomach felt like it turned into cement and dropped to the floor...

"Do these new friends look pale and sickly by any chance?" I managed out.

"I'm looking at the surveillance photos now..." he mused, "...they are well dressed and are wearing a lot of make-up. Actually, their skin is rather white and they do look particularly thin. They look like those 21st Century fashion models that had eating disorders."

"Party?"

"Count Onesti doesn't like being alone, he's always seen with an entourage." He said wryly. "He's politically connected and has old money from a castle his family retained after three world wars."

Now it was my turn to gulp... it all made sense! The European Vampires were seeking us out from the information given to them by a disgruntled Hodge Endeavor employee. That's how they knew we existed and where to find us.

I bet my former Calculator, Vincent, must be sulking somewhere in the space time continuum. He programmed the Circulate Mainframe to run the multinational company as security for the Last Circulator and instead it's turned into a liability. He used to fume over losing a game of chess, so he must be having a huge temper tantrum right now.

"Has the police investigated this Count Onesti over Farrah's disappearance?" I demanded.

"They questioned him briefly, yes."

"Did they inspect Count Onesti's castle?"

"Er, no," he faltered. "As I said, the Count is also politically connected. They would need a warrant to get inside and no officer would risk offending the aristocrat whose glamorous parties entertain their supervisors and politicians."

The lawyer's cowardice made my eyes glow in anger as a growl made its way up my throat.

"Just who the hell is the more powerful here, a dusty old count or the richest company in human history?"

"Why you are...er, I mean Hodge Endeavor is." He back-pedalled.

"Then frickin' investigate the Count!" I roared. "You didn't think the Count's pale entourage is related to my request about looking out for pale, rich people flying into Fairbanks?!"

"Why yes of course..." he said nervously as I heard him scramble about his desk, "...I'll demand a warrant to inspect the Count's castle immediately. I'll also contact the Alaskan State Government. They can alert the Customs office at Fairbanks airport to hold the suspects -"

"I don't want them arrested!" I interrupted. "That'll draw more attention to us! But I want you to text message me if a private plane from Europe lands in Fairbanks, with pale, rich people on board. They'll have swords and possibly other weapons too, so that'll show up in the luggage manifest!"

"They'll be armed?" He uttered in surprise.

"Yes!"

"Do you require police protection? We can also send highly trained bodyguards to your position immediately. There are several safe houses that are at your disposal -" he prattled off.

"It's not necessary, I can protect myself!" I cut him off. "But I'm so angry about this slip up, I'll be reconsidering your future with the company, that's for sure!"

"Allow me to make this up to you." He said apologetically. "In twelve hours I'll call you with the results of the search on Count Onesti's castle, any travel plans he's made and Customs at Fairbanks Airport reporting to me directly."

Furious, I disconnected the call, threw open the front door and marched inside.

I approached the crowded dining area where all the men were standing around the table. Only Kurt and Looch were sitting in the lounge area now as Soph had grown bored and went to her father to be held. Declan was doing just that, bouncing his second born on his right arm whilst using his left hand to point out possible tactical positions on the map.

Instantly, my mate looked my way upon my approach. "Hey guys, you wanna move over and make some room for my wife?" The men obeyed by clearing a path to the table when he spoke again, "Oh oh, B's aura is burning blue with tiny sparks flying off, she's pissed about something."

Caesar frowned from across the table, "What's wrong, Aunt B?"

I spoke to my husband with the room listening in, "Do you remember the morning we first met Jonathan Bourne, he told us of an ex-employee who tried to blackmail Hodge Endeavor? He said he had information on me and the Circulate and threatened to take it to the media."

"Yeah and as I recall, I wasn't allowed to hunt him down." He said in annoyance. "So why are you bringing up this guy again?"

"Guess who's gone missing after dining in several five star restaurants with a European Vampire coven...?"

The atmosphere in the room quickly changed as it went from grave to lots of angry growling.

"That's how the European Vampires know about us!" Ki cried indignantly.

“Our existence isn’t secret anymore!” Derik fumed.

“If we win this battle, who’s to say there won’t be more?” Walt gazed in concern upon his son, the newest member of the pack.

Poor Kurt, it was a hell of a time to join the ranks. He could be facing a future of perpetually being targeted for being who he was. His very existence could put his human loved ones at risk.

“But the leech who’s your lawyer said that this guy was being monitored.” Declan remembered. "Where was he when all of this was happening?”

“Tell me about it!” I retorted. “After this war, I’m gonna fire his ass!”

“Right, that’s it,” he plonked his second born onto the table and turned away. “I’m finishing this before it gets any worse.”

We watched him walk towards the front door while taking off his flannel shirt and kicking off his shoes.

“Declan, where are you going?” I asked, confused.

“I’m gonna instantaneously phase to Europe and hunt this human down.” He barked back. “If the fang heads haven’t killed him, I will!”

Firmly, Caesar spoke to his second-in-charge, “Uncle, no.”

However, the infuriated European Werewolf disregarded this as he continued on his way out.

“UNCLE DECLAN I GAVE YOU AN ORDER!”

The roar of our First made the whole room stand to attention. Looch and Kurt sat up straighter on the lounge and Soph stared with wide eyes. Declan paused with his hand on the door handle and I felt his inner turmoil. His bloodlust was ignited but all his years as Second stayed his claws.

“We already have two covens coming for us,” Caesar said unhappily. “We need to stand strong and stand as one. You, going on a rampage on the European continent, won’t solve the problem.”

Our Medicine Man agreed, “After they get their fangs into you, they’ll still come for your young.”

I walked up and turned my tall mate around so my dark blue eyes could hold his bright blue ones.

“They’re coming for us, Declan.” I said. “The damage has already been done.”

“But B,” he looked on with a pained expression. “What if killing this human means that only these two covens know about us? If I kill this blabber mouth, then he can’t tell anyone else!”

“It’s too late,” I cupped his face to get the message across. “European Vampire covens are connected. The fang heads we fought in Scotland knew about us from the fang heads we fought in Russia. Now this Count Onesti has confirmation that we still exist. I can use the Viewing Room to see who knows what, but my warning feeling says the word has been spread.”

The European Werewolf's eyes glowed green in anger as he looked down at the floor and muttered to himself.

“I KNEW I should have killed this human as soon as I heard about him, I should've gone with my gut instincts!”

“It's not your fault -” I tried but he interrupted.

“B, the only time I get a warning feeling as a Circulator is if my mate and young are in danger. You're always dribbling on about Circulators sensing changes to the timeline. I had a knowing feeling but I didn't act on it. Now you and the girls are in jeopardy so damn it, I'm gonna go out and kill something!”

He made another move for the door so this time I grabbed hold of his arm and yanked him backwards.

“Just listen to me!” I cried out desperately. “We need to stay together! If we fight as one, we can get through this! If we remain together, we can get through anything.”

He paused a second time as his eyes dropped down to where my hand was on his muscled arm. I watched his angry expression dissolve into a pensive one. He seemed transfixed by our contact for some reason.

Then he put his hand over mine and used it to move it over to his chest. As my hand hovered over his bare skin, he closed his eyes and exhaled. I realized he was relishing the contact of our auras touching each other. When he opened his eyes again, the glowing green colour had dulled back to his human blue.

“Nice work, Aunt B,” our Medicine Man said in approval.

“If only we all had auras we could use to calm down enraged European Werewolves.” Derik chuckled.

However, Caesar didn't seem relieved to have a calmer monster in the room, he was still livid.

“Uncle Declan, you will take yourself and your family home.”

Oh oh, we were being dismissed for bad behaviour, or one of us was.

I could understand why our First was furious. As Second, Declan was supposed to pass on orders to the pack and make sure they were adhered to. It didn't bode well when the Second disobeyed instead.

Silently, my mate picked up his shirt and shoes from the floor then Soph from the table. He didn't meet the eyes of the men under his command and I noticed they too kept their gazes averted. Like this, he carried both his daughter and his clothes from the house with me walking behind him. Looch stood up without saying goodbye to Kurt and followed her family out.

We walked up the hill to our house in the warm sun. The light glistened off my husband's bare shoulders as he walked barefoot. On his left arm he carried his shirt and shoes and on his right, his second born. Periodically, she looked up into her father's face, but she didn't say anything. In fact, we were all silent.

Once we arrived home Declan put down his daughter and his clothes then he went into the kitchen. His little girls followed him as did his wife, to watch him make lunch. He washed his hands at the kitchen sink then he took the bread rolls out of the pantry. Looch washed her hands too so she could help and he gave her the task of cutting open the bread rolls. I recognized he was making a family favourite, which was bread rolls with pesto, tomato and bocconcini.

When the rolls were made and he was divvying them up onto different plates, Soph broke the silence.

"Daddy got in trouble for a temper tantrum!" She exclaimed before she asked, "But how come Caesar didn't sit on him?"

The kitchen filled with laughter as her father gave her a bashful smile.

"Because you trash your bedroom, Soph," he pointed out. "I didn't trash Caesar's house, did I?"

Then he tweaked her nose before handing out the plates of food to everyone.

*****

We took our lunch outside to sit on the veranda steps and eat. It was a beautiful day and we wanted to enjoy the sunshine and the breeze. Our garden looked luminous with the purple Jacaranda Tree and the colourful flower beds in bloom. We admired the scenery as we ate our delicious meal.

After we'd eaten, the girls left their plates on the stairs to play. They ran around on the lawn with Soph squealing to her heart's content. Occasionally, Looch would catch her and swing her around in her strong arms. After she was put down then Soph would turn around and chase her instead.

Smilingly, their parents watched with their father pulling their mother closer. I was sitting on the top step and Declan was sitting on the third, so I was higher. Happily, he hugged my legs against his chest before resting his head in my lap. Affectionately, my hands ran through his scruffy hair which I knew he liked.

"It feels surreal," he said, "like this is one of the last moments we'll have as a family before the shit hits the fan."

"The calm before the storm," I sighed in agreement.

"If I can act like a brick wall and prevent my daughters from hunting human, why can't I prevent other creatures from hunting them?" He sighed sadly.

"Daddy Declan," I repeated from a long ago conversation.

"Momma B," he kissed the top of my leg before resting on it again. "I wish as Circulators we could freeze this moment forever."

"Maybe one day we could do something like that." I mused. "Make a single day play over and over again, like a time loop."

"If I could just see my daughters grow up into strong women, I'd die content."

"Nobody's dying!" I said curtly as I gave his hair a playful tug.

"Seriously B, if it comes down to it and it's either your life or mine, I wouldn't think twice. I wouldn't even hesitate. I'd instantaneously phase to my death before you could stop me."

"Declan, stop it." I scolded. "I know the both of us will live through this battle. I've seen us in the future with our three daughters, remember?"

Then he looked up with a mischievous grin, "So I'm stuck with you?"

"Into infinity come," I repeated something else said a while ago.

"In unan, B," my husband recited. "Always and forever."

*****

When the going gets tough, the tough get cooking. Declan's frustration about the danger which was descending upon his family came out in the gourmet banquet he prepared. As he cooked up a three course dinner, I sat at the dining table with my laptop.

I could hear the girls playfully bickering whilst helping their father in the kitchen. Looch was chopping the tomato, oregano and olives for the bruschetta which their father was preparing for our entrée. Soph was grating the cheese to go on top of the lasagne which was the main course. Declan supervised the two as he did the rest, which included making a tiramisu for dessert.

When I opened the inbox of my email account, I found I had three new emails and all from the same source.

I was wondering where the Circulate Mainframe had been in all this... I clicked on the first email it had sent with the subject line:

I NEED TO ADVISE YOU OF AN UPCOMING CHANGE TO THE TIMELINE.

No shit Sherlock, why didn't you notify me before?

YOU SHOULD RECEIVE THIS COMMUNICATION ON MAY 28TH. (Yes I did). THE HODGE ENDEAVOUR EMPLOYEE GAVIN FARRAH I ADVISED WAS DISMISSED FOR CORPORATE THEFT THIRTEEN YEARS AGO WILL BE MAKING A REAPPEARANCE. (Gee, you don't say?) HE HAS DIVULGED TO A EUROPEAN VAMPIRE COVEN YOUR STATUS AS THE HEAD CHAIRWOMAN OF HODGE ENDEAVOUR AND THE CIRCULATE'S CONTROL OF THE COMPANY. (What, you mean the Vampire initially came here because he thought he was hunting Circulators and not Werewolves?) HOWEVER THE COVEN ALREADY KNEW OF YOUR STATUS AS THE LAST CIRCULATOR AND FIRST FEMALE LOKOTI WEREWOLF (That would explain why the fang head was stalking me the other day).

THE COVENS CONTRIBUTE TO A LIBRARY TO STORE THEIR HISTORY. THEY HAVE RECORDED THE SIGHTINGS OF DECLAN IN EUROPEAN WEREWOLF FORM ON THE WORLD WIDE MEDIA. WHEN TOLD OF THE CIRCULATE CONTROLLING HODGE ENDEAVOUR, THE

COVEN SENT A SCOUT TO CONFIRM THAT YOU WERE BOTH STILL ALIVE.

My stomach shrank in trepidation over the thought that it could be Declan's and my fault that the covens were coming.

TWO EUROPEAN VAMPRE COVENS WILL ARRIVE ON A PRIVATE SHUTTLECRAFT AT FAIRBANKS AIRPORT, JUNE 1ST AT 7.20 PM. THE COVENS WILL BE LED BY A 483 YEAR OLD GERMAN CALLED BARON STUTTGART AND THE 235 YEAR OLD FRENCH COUNTESS RICARD. THEY WILL INVADE VIA THE NORTH PERIMETER OF THE LOKOTI NATIONAL PARK AND COME INTO YOUR TERRITORY VIA THE NARROW GULLIVER'S GULCH. THEY WILL BE ARMED WITH SILVER SWORDS AND LASER RIFLES. YOU WILL ENGAGE THEM IN BATTLE IN THE NORTH WEST PLAINS CAMPING AREA AT 11.03 PM.

Laser rifles as well as silver swords? That's unfair! These fang heads don't plan on losing, so now what do I do? All I could do at that moment was keep reading.

BY ENGAGING YOUR ABILITY TO PHASE WHICH EFFECTS ELECTRICAL EQUIPMENT IN THE VICINITY; YOU WILL BE ABLE TO RENDER THE LASER RIFLES INOPERATIVE.

Phew! I should have thought of that. Man, it's helpful having a computer calculating a battle for you.

YOU WILL HAVE TO COMBAT BARON STUTTGART WITH YOUR SILVER KATANA. WARN DECLAN TO STAY AWAY FROM THIS VAMPIRE AS HE HAS EXPERIENCE IN WOUNDING AND CAPTURING EUROPEAN WEREWOLVES. THIS PARTICULAR VAMPIRE WOUNDED AND ALMOST CAPTURED THE EUROPEAN WEREWOLF LEO GDANSK, WHOM WAS DESTROYED BY YOUR GRANDPARENTS AFTER YOUR KIDNAPPING.

Ah yes, Leo. I remembered the large, ugly, Russian whom I had the displeasure of meeting long ago. He had only one eye with just a pit in his face where the other once was. Could this Baron Stuttgart be responsible for this? And now this Baron was coming for Declan...

I AM MONITORING JONATHAN BOURNE'S CHARGES AGAINST COUNT ONESKI WITH THE EUROPEAN UNION POLICE FORCE. ALTHOUGH HE SENT THE SCOUT, HIS COVEN WILL NOT BE INVOLVED IN THE ATTACK. HIS ROLE WAS SELLING THE INFORMATION TO BARON STUTTGART FOR A SHARE IN DECLAN'S BLOOD UPON CAPTURE.

The image of Declan in European Werewolf form, chained up and with those hoses draining him dry, made me flinch again.

THE CHARGES WILL CAUSE UNWANTED ATTENTION ON THE COUNT AND OTHER EUROPEAN VAMPIRE COVENS. THIS WILL FORCE THEM TO LAY LOW AND REDUCE HUMAN CASUALTIES IN THEIR FEEDING. IT WILL ALSO STAVE OFF ANOTHER ATTACK ON YOUR FAMILY FOR SEVERAL YEARS. I RECOMMEND THAT YOU DO NOT DISMISS JONATHAN BOURNE FOR HIS MISTAKE. INSTEAD HE WILL MAKE AN EXCELLENT PUPPET AS A PRETEND HEAD CHAIRMAN OF HODGE ENDEAVOUR.

What the...? Instead of firing his ass, the computer wants me to promote it?!

JONATHAN BOURNE IS GREEDY WHICH MAKES HIM LOYAL TO HIS HIGH SALARY. HE ENJOYS POWER AND MEDIA ATTENTION AND WOULD WILLINGLY AGREE. HOWEVER, HE AND THE BOARD WILL STILL ACKNOWLEDGE YOU AS THE REAL OWNER BY YOUR CONTROLLING SHARES. JONATHAN WILL DIVERT ENQUIRIES AWAY FROM THE CIRCULATE. THE EUROPEAN VAMPIRES WILL NOT RISK A PUBLIC WAR WITH THE MOST POWERFUL COMPANY IN HUMAN HISTORY, WHICH WILL CONTINUE TO MONITOR THEIR MOVEMENTS.

OK, so the Circulate Mainframe thinks it's covered every contingency. But what about big-mouthed Farrah, is he still alive and liable to keep blabbing? Ah, here it is...

LASTLY, I NEED TO INFORM YOU OF THE FATE OF GAVIN FARRAH. AS A REWARD FOR HIS INFORMATION, COUNT ONESKI'S COVEN TURNED HIM INTO A EUROPEAN VAMPIRE. HOWEVER HE WILL BE ACCOMPANYING BARON STUTTGART AND COUNTESS RICARD'S COVENS IN THE ATTACK, AS AN ADVISER. I RECOMMEND GIVING THE TASK OF DESTROYING FARRAH TO DECLAN, WHILE YOU FIGHT THE BARON. SHOULD YOU FEEL APPREHENSION IN ASSISTING IN THE ANNIHILATION OF THIS FORMER HUMAN, PLEASE BE ADVISED FARRAH HAS ALREADY MURDERED WITH HIS NEW DIETARY REQUIREMENTS. BY DESTROYING THIS FOE, YOU WILL BE PREVENTING FURTHER LOSS OF LIFE.

Don't worry computer, I won't feel a single twinge of guilt for letting my husband loose on this guy. He leeched off the company when he was alive, now he's officially a leech being half dead. I just hoped my battle with the Baron would be over before Declan litters the camping grounds with the fang head's mutilated corpse. I would really love to watch what the European Werewolf's jaws could do to his pale, bloated body.

The second email the Mainframe sent had been Cc'd to Jonathan Bourne. It had pictures of what Baron Stuttgart and Countess Ricard looked like. The photos looked like they'd been taken from society pages off the world wide web. The computer included several police reports of charred corpses discovered in towns or cities their covens had visited. I saw what the computer was doing, it was building Jonathan's legal defence when the fang heads went 'missing' after the battle. With the perpetrators disappearance, my lawyer could lead the police to think that they were in hiding, rather than annihilated.

Finally, I opened the third email which was sent by the Mainframe to just myself.

B, I CALCULATE THAT YOU WOULD HAVE POSSIBLY 'SEEN' THE ONCOMING ATTACK BEFORE YOU RECEIVED THESE EMAILS. I ALSO SUSPECT THAT YOU MAY BE DISAPPOINTED AT NOT BEING NOTIFIED OF THIS FUTURE INCIDENT EARLIER. AFTER THE BATTLE I NEED YOU TO COME TO THE VIEWING ROOM. I HAVE TO REPORT ON AN ONGOING SYSTEM MALFUNCTION.

Oh oh... don't tell me my smart computer is broken?

AS YOU ARE AWARE, YOUR CALCULATOR VINCENT MOHER REPORTED THAT PARTS OF YOUR LIFE ARE 'BLANKED OUT' WHICH INTERFERES WITH CALCULATING YOUR FUTURE. WHEN YOU VISITED THE VIEWING ROOM IN THE PAST, YOU HAVE SEEN THESE BLANKS APPEAR AS A WHITE SCREEN WITH DAYS, WEEKS OR OCCASSIONALLY MONTHS MISSING FROM YOUR TIMELINE. I MUST ADVISE YOU THAT THIS PROBLEM HAS NOT BEEN RECTIFIED.

HOWEVER, I HAVE CALCULATED THIS ERROR IS NOT A RESULT OF CIRCULATE SYSTEMS, BUT FROM AN EXTERNAL CAUSE. THE WHITE SCREEN IS ACTUALLY A RECORDING OF A PURE LIGHT SOURCE WHICH IS IN TEMPORAL FLUX. AFTER REVIEWING THE CIRCULATE'S EVOLUTION IN THE 'FINAL PHASE', THE ENERGY SIGNATURES OF THE DEPARTED, MATCHES THE SAME EXTERNAL LIGHT SOURCE INTERFERING WITH OUR SYSTEMS. ON THIS EVIDENCE, I POSTURE THAT THE SPACE TIME CONTINUUM COULD BE PURPOSEFULLY INTERFERING WITH YOUR TIMELINE.

And that was it... that was where the email ended. I sat and stared at the screen in shock. I guessed that the computer didn't want to say anything else via email, as it wanted to talk about this in person. It wanted me to come to the Viewing Room and see this for myself.

But why me? Why was the space time continuum picking on me? Isn't it busy upholding space, time and all existence? Why was I the only Circulator in Circulate history this was happening to? There were so many questions and I was running out of time to have all of them answered.

I closed the message and deleted it because I didn't want Declan to see, as I didn't want to worry him. I sensed there was something bigger happening here, besides the threat of thirsty fang heads. It also made me wonder what kind of change happened to time and space, when I made my husband a Circulator?

"Declan," I stood up from the table.

"Yeah?" He called back from the kitchen.

"We need to invite Caesar to dinner, there's an email he has to read about our uninvited guests."

*****

When Caesar came to dinner he brought Tyson with him. At first I wondered why but by the end of the evening I had my answer. His son followed his father's orders similar to the way a Second functions to a First. After our leader read the email, he sent Tyson outside to call Walt via mobile phone, to close the National Park to campers.

I knew we were closing the World Heritage listed wilderness to reduce the risk of human casualties. But what I didn't know is why he didn't ask Declan to do this instead? I opened my mouth to ask, when I felt my mate's hand squeeze mine under the table. I looked his way and he gave a small shake of his head to leave it alone.

After dinner, the girls went upstairs for their bath and I stacked the dirty dishes into the dishwasher. However, as I worked I tried to eavesdrop on what was taking place on the front veranda. I spied through the front windows Declan had gone outside to talk to Caesar and Tyson. The expressions on two of their faces were solemn whereas my husband's hardened into a glare.

They were outside for a good ten minutes before Caesar and Tyson left and Declan came inside.

I watched him close the front door and slowly walk into the living area. He knew I'd been watching the whole time. He stood by the dining table and waited for my approach.

I walked up whilst wiping my hands on a tea towel, "What was all that about?"

His gaze was waiting to hold my own as I sensed an emotion which could be resignation radiate inside of him.

"I'm no longer Second," he said calmly. "Tyson is."

"What...?" I gaped. "When? How? Where? Why?"

"It's because I can't function properly as second-in-command when I'm too busy worrying about my pregnant wife on the battle field."

"But – but – but it's unfair!" I cried indignantly. "You served faithfully as Second for centuries and just because of one little disagreement -"

"No, it's a long time coming," he shook his head, "at least ten years long."

I gave a funny look, "Huh?"

"The moment I knocked you up, my objectivity was thrown out the window."

"Oh great, so we're back to the wife and kids hindering you...?" I turned defensive.

"Shut up B," he chuckled. "There you go, flying off the handle in light speed, as usual."

He wrapped his arms about my waist and pulled me close, so our bodies were touching.

"That morning we first found out you were pregnant, I would've done anything to keep you safe." He spoke bluntly. "Remember when Ki threatened to call on Caesar to intervene? I would have challenged our First and the whole pack if they tried to stop me from saving you."

I remembered clearly what he was talking about as his behaviour that horrible morning still gave me goose bumps.

"Thank god you delivered Lucia and Sophia without serious injury and now we're a family complete with the 2.5 kids and I'm happy." He declared. "I'm so happy, it's almost unreal. I love my life right now. But Caesar knows this is a double edged sword, because if anything and I mean ANYTHING jeopardized my family, I'd go all out to destroy it and this makes me a risk to the pack."

He was right, his demotion did seem inevitable. I recalled the vision I had of Caesar and Declan's conversation the night that Forrest died. Our First tried to talk to his Second about his dangerous side, but was warned off with the ominous words, "Don't go there."

"Oh Declan," I sighed heavily, "oh my poor, pathetic, psycho monster."

It was at that moment we were interrupted by Sophia's ear-piercing squeal.

"Mummy!" She shrieked. "Mummy, Looch won't let me use the raspberry bubble bath!"

"We had the raspberry last night, I want the lavender!" Looch yelled next.

"Don't you just love it?" Declan smilingly shook his head. "We're gonna be fighting for our lives in a couple of days, but right now it all comes down to bubble bath."

Then he took hold of my hand and led the way upstairs to supervise the two littlest monsters in the house.

~~~~~~

30th May 2374

There was one last meeting before the battle when the pack convened at the home of their First a second time.

The youngest members of the pack insisted on coming. Kurt sat in the lounge area, colouring in at the coffee table with Looch and Soph. Occasionally, he and Looch looked up to watch as they listened in, but Soph acted oblivious.

The meeting itself was awkward at first when the news that Tyson was the new Second came out. The abrupt change in hierarchy before the fight left the fighters uneasy. I noticed as Walt gave his report, he was looking at three people instead of two. Rather than looking at his First and new Second, he often glanced at my husband, too.

"I've driven to all the different campsites and told the campers that they have to leave." He looked at the Riverclaws then his eyes darted to Declan. "I've also put up 'No Camping' signs at the main, rear and side entrances to the Park."

To demonstrate, Walt pointed out the six different roads on the aerial map of the National Park we were using to mark out our battle plans.

"What excuse are you using?" Tyson asked.

"I told them that the earthquake we experienced last month made the mountains unstable with risk of landslides." He answered, before he turned his gaze towards my husband once more. "It's too risky to use the mutant, hairless, albino grizzly excuse. The police have all the National Parks in Alaska and the west side of Canada on alert for the beast."
~~~~~~

I caught Caesar frown as he passed a sideways glance at the cause of the unwanted attention. I think Declan sensed his leader's glare, but he pretended not to see it. Instead, he busied himself by examining the mountainous area as if he were making mental notes.

"What about the different picnic areas, like the ones near the north west plains?" Derik checked.

"Those picnic areas should be safe to remain open during the day, especially if the battle is taking place at night." Walt shrugged then he accidentally looked at Declan instead of Tyson again. "If we completely close the National Park, it will draw suspicion."

"He's right," our First sighed in resignation. "The Lokoti Tribal Elders were contacted today by both the World Heritage Trust and the Alaskan State Government, offering to send Geologists to inspect the danger areas."

"What did you tell them?" Declan finally looked his way.

"We made an appointment for them to come on the 10th of June with their equipment." Phil answered for him.

"Ten days after the battle? Good thinking." Derik commended.

"The SSIT Report on the Separate Species of Vampires advises that the fang heads completely decompose into a sort of biological 'ash' seven days after their demise." I spoke. "So if Geologists come with scanners as well as seismographs to examine the earth, they won't detect any remains."

"Then they'll deem the Park safe and reopen it to the public." Walt accidentally chuckled to Declan before he looked towards Tyson. "Sorry man, it's just -"

"- going to take some getting used to, I know." Tyson said understandingly. "Last night when the Tribal Elders had a meeting, Dad said his Second was following up on the Park's closure and I thought he was talking about Uncle Declan instead of me."

The grown members of the pack laughed quietly however, I noticed they averted their eyes not only from their First but from their former Second as well.

Declan exchanged a long look with Caesar in the ill-at-ease room before he decided to speak.

"Yeah alright, so I'm not Second anymore. So what? You think I'd leave you with an idiot for a new second-in-charge?" His voice was hard but his sarcasm which we all knew and loved, captured our attention. "Tyson knows what he's doing. He knows what's at stake being a husband and father. If we screw this up, we're gonna widow the ones we love and no one wants that. If you do, you can see me outside and I'll save the fang heads the trouble. I may not be your boss anymore, but I'm still stronger than all of you put together and if I see you slacking off with your new Second? I'm gonna bitch-slap you for endangering my mate and young."

I listened to the room chuckle softly as they looked on my husband with renewed respect.

My heart swelled with pride. I was already standing by his side but now I squeezed his hand as hard as I could. I could tell he appreciated it, by the way he returned it in his stronger grip.

"You heard the European Werewolf," our First recalled our attention. "Now let's finish this meeting so we can all go home to our families."

Everyone moved forwards to get a better look at the north west plains which Walt had circled with yellow highlighter.

"When we first see the enemy, hang back until Aunt B and Uncle Declan go into phase." Caesar instructed. "The fang heads will be carrying laser rifles, so the Circulators will raise the electromagnetic field in the air, to render the electrical weapons useless."

"Uncle Declan will then attack this fang head." Tyson put down a photo of Farrah on top of the map before he put down a second of the Baron. "Meanwhile, Aunt B will engage in a sword fight with this guy."

I helped myself to taking the photo of the Countess out of his hands and putting this down too.

"I'm also going to have a go at her." I announced and when the room looked puzzled, I added on, "I don't like the mink coat she's wearing."

"I second that." Walt raised his hand. "I'm against killing animals for fashion and not for food."

"OK then," our leader's eyebrows rose, "any fang head wearing real fur and not faux fur, will be the first to perish."

There was the sound of chuckling around the table as the tribe's supernatural soldiers found relief in the humour amid dire circumstances.

"Only my wife can turn battle plans into a political statement," Declan smilingly shook his head.

The room became reenergized with new hope as we began to strategize our defence tactics against the oncoming attack.

Walt acted as scribe at first, either highlighting or putting different coloured asterisks on the map. He was so fastidious, he ended up borrowing Soph's different coloured textas to represent which Werewolf would be fighting where. He used the same colour textas as were the colour of our eyes in our Lokoti Werewolf forms. The turquoise asterisks which were me, were put in several different places as my targets changed. The light green asterisks were Declan, the orange were Walt, the blue were Caesar and so on.

Since their textas were being used, the kids ended up joining in. Kurt sat on Walt's lap at the table as Soph sat in mine and Looch stood next to Declan. Kurt and Soph helped Walt put in the different coloured asterisks as Caesar and Tyson issued their orders.

"Phil, I want you to take on fang head #23 instead of Ki fighting him." Caesar planned aloud. "I want to free up our Medicine Man as much as possible, to tend to any wounded."

"Good idea." Tyson concurred. "Ki will fight in the beginning but then he should drop back to see to the fallen."

Walt then pointed at the area on the map for Soph to use her maroon texta for the maroon-eyed Werewolf. The Tribal Elder nodded in agreement at his First's and Second's decision. In his younger days, Phil had worked at the Garage when Declan ran it. I wondered if it felt strange for them at the switch in hierarchy; now that Phil was a Tribal Elder and Declan was no longer Second, he'd have to obey Phil's orders.

"How come there aren't any red asterisks?" Kurt frowned at the map.

"Son, we talked about this." Walt said seriously. "You won't be fighting, you'll be helping your mother look after your little brothers and sisters."

"But I can fight too!" He objected. "I helped you take down that grizzly on the last hunt."

"Yeah, but fang heads are a hell of a lot faster than grizzly bears." Declan said dryly.

"And grizzlies don't carry silver swords," I added.

"But I'm faster and stronger than a grizzly," he tried again.

"Kurt Wisetail," our leader growled out. "You will obey your father and your pack!"

The teenager's head dropped in disappointment. I passed Walt a sympathetic smile. Teens were rebellious enough, but a teen with the bloodlust to boot? To add fuel to the fire, Kurt's had to take time off school while learning to control his murderous urges and had fallen behind. Walt and Wendy had a meeting with the school principal who wanted to make their son repeat the year. But an agreement was made that he'd do summer school to advance with his peers.

"As the eldest in your family, you have another important role to fill." Walt said gravely. "There's a chance that I may not come back from this fight. Because you're the eldest, it falls on your shoulders to help your mother."

"But Dad, if I'm fighting with you, I could make sure you make it out alive," his eyes watered.

"No son, you're my back up plan." Walt's eyes filled with tears, too. "No matter what happens to me, our family will have you to look after them."

*****

Walt wasn't the only Werewolf planning for his family's future. On the day of the battle, all the members of the pack told the truth to their mates and young. But what we didn't know until the battle had begun, was a human male by the surname of Creillaic was planning something for a family of his own.

On the afternoon of June the 1st, a hover-car which was packed with camping equipment, ignored the signs and powered down in the north west plain.

A ten year old boy and an eight year old girl, hopped out of the back doors and began to merrily chase each other around the vehicle.

"I don't know about this, Connor," the mother reluctantly climbed out after the father. "The signs warned of landslides."

"Stella, look where we are," the father spoke as he walked around to the boot, to pull out the camping gear. "We're in the middle of a grassy field, away from the mountain slopes. If there was a landslide which I highly doubt, we're well out of the way. Relax, we're gonna have a fun family holiday."

But his wife wasn't convinced, "This sounds like the time you organized a 'fun family holiday' in Florida and that hurricane hit."

"When are you going to stop bringing that up?" He asked crankily. "We're in Alaska, do you hear? ALASKA! It's summertime now so there's no snow. What kinda natural catastrophe do you think can happen here?"

"Oh you mean besides landslides?"

"We've planned this family holiday for months," he said stubbornly. "We need this time with each other. It's either Xenthe's music lessons, or your long shifts at the power plant, keeping us apart. Our family is in danger of becoming strangers. There ain't no sign in the world that's gonna put this off."

Then the family from Memphis began to set up their camping site complete with tents, air mattresses, sleeping bags and an esky full of food...

...

... other than this unforeseen occurrence, the rest of events in the timeline played out as expected.

At 7.43 PM I received a phone call from Jonathan Bourne, "The private shuttlecraft owned by Baron Stuttgart, has landed at Fairbanks Airport. Customs advised that as soon as their passports were stamped, they departed in several hover-cars heading south. They declared the laser rifles were for hunting which they had permits for. The silver swords they were carrying they said were for showing in an unnamed antiques fair. European Customs had already signed the authority papers before U.S. Customs could block them."

"OK," I took a deep breath. "What of the case files you were sent?"

"I forwarded them on to my contacts in the European Union Police Force and they want to interview them. The Baron's flight plan has him departing Fairbanks airport at 6.30 AM tomorrow. When he or the Countess don't show up, it'll look like they're avoiding the authorities."

"Good, now encourage your contacts to also watch Count Onesti and the three other groups you were given files on."

"Done," he promised. "I've also put together a small but elite team of lawyers in the London Head Office of Hodge Endeavor. They're compiling a list of all the unsolved murders in Europe which match the cases you gave me. They'll liaise with the Police in monitoring these groups on a full-time basis."

When I ended the call, I turned to look into Declan's waiting gaze. He'd been standing nearby, using his sensitive ears to eavesdrop. I watched his eyes narrow into a hateful glare.

"After tonight, I should wipe out the other covens," he said stubbornly. "If I attack now, we won't have to worry about them in the future."

“Then you’ll create more unwanted attention,” I said, unimpressed. “Next, we’d have three police forces looking for the mutant, albino, hairless grizzly. So the answer is no, Declan. After the tonight, we’re going to do things the human way and avoid further suspicion.”

Frustrated, he growled under his breath as he went upstairs to hurry along our young. Looch and Soph were packing their overnight bags for another sleepover at their cousins. Wendy kindly offered to care for them while their parents were busy, fighting for their safety.

Then I heard Soph squeal from her bedroom, “No Daddy, I wanna wear my Miss Piggy pyjamas tonight!”

“But they’re in the dirty laundry basket!” He argued back. “You can wear your fairy princess pyjamas instead.”

“I WANT to WEAR my PINK Miss Piggy pyjamas!” She roared in a temper.

“Your fairy princess pyjamas are PINK!” He yelled back.

“But I wanna wear my pink MISS PIGGY pyjamas!” She screamed.

I giggled as I watched my husband storm back downstairs on his way into the laundry to throw the pyjamas into the washer/dryer on the express cycle.

I bet the rest of the pack who were saying their goodbyes to their families tonight, it was a much more solemn occasion. But in a household with a European Werewolf for a father and half breed young, it was a different story. However, when I saw his small smile escape, it said that he wouldn’t have his daughters any other way...

...

... at 11.03 PM the pack silently stalked the attackers by approaching the tree line which hedged the camping grounds of the north west plain.

Our different coloured eyes glowed brightly in the night as our supernatural muscle bulk rippled with each of our movements. The European Werewolf stayed close to his Lokoti Werewolf wife in a protective manner. My protruding abdomen gave away my pregnant state, but I was ready for battle with my sheathed silver katana, strapped to my back.

We weren’t entirely sure what to expect when we first set eyes on the European Vampires. However, what we weren’t expecting to see, were them feeding on a human family. Talk about the wrong place at the wrong time!

Five fang heads had drained the father within minutes of drinking from the arteries in his neck, arms and legs. Three other leeches had also killed his daughter in similar fashion. The wounded mother was being dangled in the air, with a cold hand at her throat, before the son who was trying to play a piece of music on a keyboard. The way he kept making mistakes, gave away his terrified state, which meant he was being forced to play.

We recognized three of leeches with their glowing white eyes and two long fangs as Baron Stuttgart, Countess Ricard and Gavin Farrah. The Baron and the Countess were looming over the boy, as Farrah was holding up the wounded woman by her throat. The rest of the leeches, stood around in their haute couture clothing, hissing thirstily.

"My chihuahua can play better than this," the Countess said in a French accent.

"He's frightened of us, that's all," the Baron replied in a German accent. "Let us give him courage."

To the further horror of the wounded mother, we watched the Baron grab hold of the front of the boy's clothing and lift him to his dangerous mouth.

The leech's poisonous fangs pierced the side of the boy's neck and made him cry out in pain. Instead of draining him, the Baron moved him to one arm as he put a bloodied gash in his other. He lowered the wound to the weakened boy's mouth and forced him to drink.

He's turning a human child who looked no older than the age of ten...? The poor boy would be stuck in this childish body for all five hundred years of his existence! I couldn't think of anything worse or so cruel, as to create a European Vampire child!

I heard the low growls emanate from my mate and the members of the pack, as we all looked on in disgust... and unfortunately, so did the European Vampires. When they heard our displeasure, our battle plans were almost thrown to the wind.

They heard our growls first and spotted our glowing eyes, second. Several fang heads powered up their laser rifles and aimed them our way. Instantly, we ducked behind the trees that we'd just been crouching beside.

Gavin Farrah dropped the wounded mother and unhooked the laser rifle which hung in a holster on his back.

At the same time, the fang heads all fired our way as deadly, red hot lasers, hit the trees which protected us.

"Are you ready?" I growled out between my elongated, sharp teeth.

The European Werewolf hungrily licked his lips – *BRING IT ON!*

I went into phase first and Declan second. Our muscled bodies dissolved into beings of light, which made us look see-through and bright. We leapt out from behind the trees and ran into the grassy field in light speed.

At first the European Vampires blinked in surprise at the two bright blurs whizzing towards them. Then they momentarily looked down at their laser rifles which had mysteriously stopped working. The fang heads didn't even have time to drop their rifles and reach for their swords when we pounced.

We reformed into our biological bodies once we reached our targets. Declan pounced on Farrah, with his huge jaws locking onto the European Vampire's face. I deliberately ran into the Baron and knocked him over, which made him drop the boy.

Using his speed of sound reflexes, the Baron was quick to leap to his feet with his sword in hand. His weapon looked like a European medieval blade by how long and thick it was. I smelled the age on it, just as I smelled the silver coating it. The Baron examined the Japanese katana in my hands, which was thinner, curved and slightly shorter.

To his surprise, I used my light speed reflexes as well as my supernatural strength to swing my weapon around and cut his in half.

"Size doesn't always matter." I growled out. "My sword may be shorter, but it's stronger and sharper."

The Baron looked on the broken metal stump in his hands then he sprang into action.

I swung my sword around a second time but he was able to duck and roll away on the ground. He rolled over to Farrah's fallen form, which was now missing most of a head thanks to my mate's jaws. He unsheathed his sword as Declan raised himself from his meal and growled at the Baron.

My opponent swung his new sword at my husband, when my sword blocked it. Clang! When the Baron returned his attention to me, he swung low but I parried. Clang! He leapt to his feet and engaged me in a proper sword fight. Clang! Clang! Clang!

"I look forward to adding your sssword to my antiquesss collection," he hissed out between his poisonous fangs.

"You'll be waiting awhile then." I growled back.

Clang, clang, clang, clang, clang, clang, claaaaannngg!

The European Vampire fenced in the speed of sound as the Circulator fought back in the speed of light.

My husband leapt off the decapitated Farrah and jumped another two leeches who were looming up behind his wife. With the bigger and stronger European Werewolf leaping, jumping and mauling in light speed, he took the European Vampires by surprise. Their swords fell to the grass the same time they did.

Before the covens could attack the Circulators altogether, they had to defend themselves against the thirteen Lokoti Werewolves who ran over.

Unfortunately, the pack weren't as strong as European Werewolves nor as fast as European Vampires, but they were determined.

My kinsmen did their best to weave between the silver swords swung their way and use their claws to swipe their opponents. When they got lucky, their strong arms and long nails staggered the enemy. If the leeches faltered, they used their elongated teeth to rip out their throats. Unfortunately though, the pack were outnumbered and unarmed, so it was more like the Vampires mowing down the Werewolves. Once they wounded them with their silver swords, they dug their poisonous fangs in.

I saw three and then four Lokoti Werewolves fall, with deep cuts which were bleeding freely as well as a red smoke rising into the air, which was caused from the allergic reaction to the silver. As soon as the Werewolf hit the ground, one or two Vampires landed on top with their mouths heading straight for a major artery. The poison instantly paralysed them and all they could do was lie there as their life force was sucked right out of them.

I felt helpless rage build up inside as I watched my pack fall one by one. But I battled on against the Baron, who was using every fencing skill he had. He was trying hard to take down his opponent who was faster and stronger than him. When we both saw there were seven fallen Lokoti Werewolves being fed on, he gave an evil grin.

"I'm offended that you're not concentrating on thisss fight," he hissed.

"I'm sorry," I growled back, "let me make it up to you."

To the Baron's surprise, I disappeared in a bright flash of light to reappear in another right behind him. By the time he turned around with his sword, mine met his neck. I chopped off his poisonous head in a single blow then I rushed upon the Countess with my bloodied weapon.

She and another female fang head had wounded and were feeding upon Phil. His glowing maroon green eyes were fading as his opponents drank from his jugular and right arm. The Countess looked up in surprise the same time my sword sent her head flying into the air.

Enraged, I flung off the second female fang head with my greater strength. But before I could kneel down and check Phil's injuries, she sprang back with her silver sword ready. I instantaneously phased to the spot behind her and decapitated her before she could whirl around. That's three leeches lying in the grassy field, thanks to my katana.

I saw that Declan was doing what I was, attacking the fang heads which were feeding on our fallen.

Once we rid our members from the leeches draining them, they didn't get up. Not only had the poison paralyzed them, they had difficulty regenerating from silver-caused injuries. All they could do there was lie there in the grass and slowly bleed to death.

I spotted Ki run from wounded to wounded, sharing his blood from his open wrist. He didn't have time to give them much more than a few sips. Occasionally, he had to duck and dodge a Vampire as he ran from patient to patient. I sensed he was sharing what he could, to stop the bleeding and lessen the paralysis.

I also saw that Caesar endeavoured to act as Ki's cover. When a Vampire tried to stop our Medicine Man from treating the wounded, our First dealt with it. His muscled torso became redder as he fought on, with his blood and the red smoke streaming from his numerous cuts left by the silver swords he'd knocked from their hands.

Tyson, Derik and Walt fought by their First's side, each with wounds of their own.

Another fang head tried to sneak up on Walt while he was busy fighting and Declan leapt upon the cheater and made waste of it. Next, Tyson's opponent swiped its silver sword along his Achilles heal, which made him drop to the ground in agony. Before the fang head could feed on him, I threw my katana in the air and it landed right in its chest. Then I instantaneously phased to its position in the grass to reclaim my weapon and use it to remove its head.

Now there were six Werewolves to fourteen Vampires left as the battle between fang and claw raged on.

Sixteen European Vampires had been destroyed by either their throats ripped out or by decapitation from either my sword or Declan's jaws. Nine Lokoti Werewolves were gravely injured and unable to fight let alone move.

Rather than think of defeat, the Werewolves fought on, led by a bleeding but stubborn First. Even my husband had a couple of cuts on his body, but his greater muscle bulk offered a little more protection against the silver.

Our Medicine Man was still tending to the wounded and now he was sharing blood with Tyson. His blood worked faster on him since he was only cut and not poisoned. After a couple of mouthfuls, he helped his new Second to stand. Tyson wobbled on his wounded legs but he was adamant that he could fight some more.

The remaining opponents faced off against the other like two line-ups.

The night air turned deathly still as the only sounds that came to our sensitive ears were the Vampires hissing, or the Werewolves growling, or the wounded groaning in pain.

That was until we heard a distant cry, "Dad! Dad! I'm coming, Dad!"

Oh no, you've got to be kidding! Tonight seemed to be the night for wrong places at wrong times. Then everything happened at once as the battle went from bad to worse...

The topless and changed Kurt leapt out of the tree line and ran as fast as he could towards his father.

To distract our enemy, Declan broke formation to leap onto another two fang heads. When the leeches on either side tried to stake him with their silver swords, Derik and I attacked them. Then the rest of the fighters came together in one last offensive, in an effort to wipe the other out.

The six remaining Werewolves were fighting eight Vampires at once and unfortunately, it gave the other six their chance to attack.

The way a flock of birds all swoop in at once around a food source, all six European Vampires moved in the speed of sound, towards Kurt.

"GET AWAY FROM MY SON YOU BLOODSUCKING PERVERTS!" Walt roared in his thunderous voice, as he turned to run after them.

Caesar raced after Walt but they were too late, the leeches reached the boy first.

The fourteen year old Lokoti Werewolf was knocked onto his muscled back and pinned by six thirsty European Vampires. Within a matter of seconds, each of their fangs had pierced the major arteries of his arms, legs and neck. They drained him to the point of death as their poison paralyzed the youth.

I was half watching the attack on Kurt and the other half my opponent, who was swinging her sword madly in my direction.

Clearly, this fang head was young and didn't have much training. Out of the blue, I ducked at the same time as swinging around my left leg, which knocked her feet out from under. Then I separated her head from her body, too.

As fast as we could, Declan and I turned to run towards Kurt's position. But the flock of fang heads had killed Kurt before his father and First could stop them. Upon their approach, the six leeches fanned out, leaving the limp body on the ground.

Walt's glowing orange eyes were filled with tears as he skidded to a stop on his knees beside his son's lifeless form. Two of the Vampires made a move on him as the other four attacked our leader. Our First was impaled through the chest with a silver sword whilst running to the boy's aid.

Declan bolted on all-fours in light speed and rammed over Caesar's attackers. I ran upright in the same velocity, deliberately knocking down Walt's. I stood on one of the fang heads' arms, pinning his hand holding his sword, while using mine to decapitate his friend's head. Then I swung low and chopped off his head, as well.

The European Werewolf's infuriated roar echoed throughout the north west plain as he mauled our leader's murderers.

His claws held down three writhing fang heads at once while his large jaws snatched up the fourth. I could hear the Vampire's bones break as the Werewolf chomped apart his enemy before finishing off the other three. Their cries of agony were the last sounds we heard which signalled the end.

Silence...the removal of noise was as sudden as it was suffocating.

The abrupt end of battle filled my ears like the vacuum of space. I didn't move, I simply stood there, surrounded by the corpses of those that feasted on flesh or blood. There was no more growling or hissing or any swords clashing.

After a moment, the sound which came to my ears was sobbing. I looked down to find a mourning father nurse his fallen son. With all the strength and speed I possessed, the only thing I felt now was a profound helplessness.

Uselessly, Walt tried to share his blood with his son, but Kurt's open eyes stared vacantly into the great beyond. His body had shrunk back into its human shape as soon as his heart stopped. His normally bronzed skin looked unnaturally white though, coupled with small, bloodied holes left by the fangs.

Like my own Achilles heal had been cut, my legs gave out and I landed on the ground beside. My heart felt like it stopped for a second before it painfully beat on. Walt cried louder as he rocked Kurt's lifeless body against his chest.

Gone was the boy who helped his parents supervise his siblings. Goodbye to the ready grin and the cheeky sense of humour. So long to the sideways looks towards Looch in puppy love. Farewell to the teen who'd only begun to live a life which was supposed to be supernaturally long.

My watery eyes searched for my mate and I found him sitting loyally by our First, who lay dying.

Declan withdrew his bleeding claw which meant his attempt at healing Caesar had been unsuccessful. I saw that our First had a gaping hole through his chest where there was hardly anything left of a beating heart. There was so much red smoke rising from his injury, his flesh looked like a smouldering ruin. His breathing became shallower as his glowing eyes dulled.

Our Medicine Man helped his Second over to his father, where he dropped to his side. He looked like he was about to open his wrist as well, when my mate gave a sad shake with his monstrous head. As our former and current

Seconds sat by our First, Ki left them to say their goodbyes. Besides, he still had so much work to do, seeing to our fallen.

I was sitting beside a father who'd lost his son as my husband was sitting opposite to a son who was about to lose his father.

Tearfully, I looked away to watch our Medicine Man share more of his blood. It amazed me that this Werewolf was still walking after how much he'd donated. But I saw he didn't have a choice, as Derik joined him by opening up his wrist for another. Where many of our wounded were starting to sit up which showed they were healing, there were others that didn't.

Aside from Caesar and Kurt, I counted another two Lokoti Werewolves who didn't make it. Phil lay lifeless in the grass as did another member of the pack, Pete. The two older Werewolves had given their all for the safety of their pack and tribe and paid for it with their lives.

I felt my shoulders tremble then I realized it was my whole body that was shaking, because I was crying so hard. My chest heaved as I sobbed wretchedly. Walt continued to howl mournfully as he held his first born. Then I heard Tyson make similar noises as Caesar's glowing eyes went out.

The First of the Lokoti Werewolves deflated into his human form the same time as all the air left his lungs.

By this stage, the remaining members of the pack bar Walt and myself, had stumbled over to farewell our leader.

To send him off with full honours, the males all lifted their heads up into the air and emitted one of the loudest howls I had ever heard.

AAAAAARRRRROOOOOOOOOOOOOOOOAAAAAWRRR!

The noise travelled over the plain then the woods and it even seemed to reverberate through the mountain range.

It sparked something else as moments later we heard a distant howling in return. It came from the Lokoti Wolves living in the surrounding wilds. It was as if they too were acknowledging the passing of kin.

Respectfully, Declan 'bowed out' by walking backwards on all fours before trotting over to where his wife and friend were. He sat closely beside to allow his wife to lean against his hot, hard hide. His glowing green eyes refilled with tears, as he looked on the dead boy who'd been a playmate to his young.

Then I heard the soft cracking noises his bones made when he was shape shifting. He shrunk back to his natural body with only his supernatural eyes remaining. I knew it was so he could still see in the dark and he slung his human arm about his wife's shoulders.

"I'm so sorry Walt..." he rasped out, "...I can't imagine what you're feeling right now."

Walt didn't respond, I don't think he could. All he could do was sit there and hold his son tightly to his chest. He sat there, rocking backwards and forwards as his crying sounded like a mournful howling.

Tearfully, I looked away once more when I noticed Ki was no longer treating the Werewolves, instead he was checking on the human casualties.

He looked like he'd given up on the father and small daughter, but he seemed hopeful when he checked the mother. I watched our Medicine Man lean the woman against his bare chest to share his body heat and also so she wouldn't choke when he shared his blood. Repeatedly, he tried to put his wrist inside her mouth but she refused to drink.

"Don't you worry 'bout me..." she mumbled out, "...just you see to my son."

"I'm afraid there's nothing we can do for your boy," he said sadly. "He's been contaminated with European Vampire blood, but not enough to live. He'll die from his injuries before the transformation is complete."

"Don't gimme your blood..." she moaned, "...share it with my son instead."

This made the Healer pause as he looked pained upon the patient.

"I'm sorry but I can't heal your son." Ki said gravely. "If I did, he would turn into what attacked you."

The dying woman said defiantly, "If he dies then I die."

Again, he tried to put his bleeding wrist into her mouth but again she turned her head away.

"Heal my son!" She begged. "He's name is Xenthe and he's only ten years old. That's his dead father and sister lying over there. I have nothing left if I don't have Xenthe, so if you're gonna help me then help him first!"

All the Werewolves watched with conflicting emotions. However, there was one who decided that both mother and son would live that night. Like a flick of a switch, Walt suddenly stood up and to our surprise, marched over to the ten year old boy.

He reopened his wrist which he'd tried to feed to his dead son and shoved it into the son's mouth who still had some kind of life left.

The woman was fading fast thanks to the European Vampire venom in her system. She blinked repeatedly as she looked around in a daze. I think she'd lost her vision, as her body stopped working one organ at a time.

"Xenthe...?" She called weakly. "Where's my boy?"

"Your son will live," our Healer promised. "But he will live as a European Vampire."

Then he pressed his wrist firmly against her mouth and this time she drank.

Declan stood up first then pulled me up, second. Together, we walked over to where mother and son were being treated. We were soon joined by Derik and the survivors of the pack. I noticed how all the male Werewolves looked on the unconscious child, suspiciously.

Just then the ten year old awoke with a gasp, which made his saviour remove his wrist to look on. Now, the boy's former bright blue eyes looked faded and his skin looked pale in a sickly appearance he would have for the rest of his long life. When Walt offered his wrist once more to finish the healing process, the new European Vampire eagerly sucked on it.

"Isn't that just peachy," Declan griped. "We killed thirty fang heads tonight just to let a new born fanger survive?"

I overheard Derik and the remaining Lokoti Werewolves bar Walt, growl threateningly as they looked on the child.

Instead of feeling frightened at the creation of this new European Vampire, I felt hopeful. I even felt a little tingly, which must have been my aura brightening as I experienced one of my all-knowing feelings as a Circulator. I felt a rush of exhilaration as I recalled the vision I had on the day Lucia was born...

... I saw a teenaged girl with broad shoulders, long blonde hair and bright blue eyes, with a teenaged boy who looked as strong as her, but with a Lokoti appearance. There was another teenaged boy, who was thin and pale and his faded blue eyes turned completely white, indicating he was a European Vampire. When he did that, the other boy's eyes glowed red, showing he was a Lokoti Werewolf and the girl's eyes glowed green with narrow slits for pupils, indicating she was part European Werewolf. I guessed I was seeing a grown Lucia, but who her friends were, I didn't know. They were sitting on the steps of the front veranda, laughing together like friends sharing a joke...

...no way! This boy was the one I'd seen with my daughter when she grows into a teenager! Then the other boy was Kevin, who'd turn into a Lokoti Werewolf after Kurt's death. It all made sense now! A European Vampire befriends a half European Werewolf and a Lokoti Werewolf. They were the different elements of the supernatural combining into one!

"Declan," I spoke loudly for the pack to hear as well. "Once upon a time, the Lokoti thought my Grandfather was nuts, for sparing the life of a three year old European Werewolf. If you could be trained not to hunt human, then so can this European Vampire."

"B, have you gone nuts?!" He exclaimed. "You seriously think we can train a fang head to respect human life?!"

Walt said simply, "I'll help you train him."

Then he took his wrist from the boy's mouth and put it in his own, to use his saliva to speed up his regeneration. When he removed it, we saw he had healed. He stood up and faced both Declan and Tyson. The mourning father met the gazes of his former and current Second.

"I didn't save the boy's life tonight just to see it end." He said firmly. "I will teach him to hunt animal instead of human."

With that, Walt walked away from his pack towards his son's body.

Everyone quieted as we watched the grieving father pick up his first born and carefully rest him over his shoulder. Without another word, he carried Kurt home to his mother. This put things in perspective for many, including my husband.

After Walt disappeared into the night, we turned to look on the human woman crying out for her son. Ki waved him to come closer and we saw what was left of the Creillaic family, hug each other as they cried over their own losses. The wife had lost her husband and daughter; the son had lost his father and sister.

The Medicine Man who'd healed the woman as best as he could, moved away to let them grieve.

"The boy and his mother can stay with Jenny and I," he spoke quietly to Tyson. "Her injuries are going to take a while to heal, thanks to the Vampire's venom."

"If we're really going to adopt this boy into our pack, they're gonna need a house of their own here on tribal lands." Derik frowned.

"Aunt B, are you sure about this?" Tyson looked my way in a wary manner.

I met his gaze as I spoke earnestly, "On the day of Lucia's birth, I had a vision of her as a sixteen year old girl. She was laughing with Kevin and Xenthe. Altogether, I saw a European Vampire, a half European Werewolf and a Lokoti Werewolf, hanging out as friends."

"THIS is what you saw?" Declan's mouth fell open in surprise.

Ki's eyes widened impressed before he turned towards Tyson.

"I told your father that Aunt B had a vision the morning after Lucia's birth." He said to our Second. "But before now, she'd never said what it was about."

"Oh shit, I remember B dribbling something about changes that are meant to happen." Declan groaned. "Man, I hate it when my wife is right!"

"Is your wife ever wrong?" Ki smirked.

"Yeah, all the time!" He snapped. "Last week she nearly put coriander instead of oregano into the bolognaise, until I chased her out of the kitchen."

"But she's not wrong about what she 'sees'." Tyson frowned. "Very well, because the tribe's 'Light Person' says the boy can be trained, we'll train him."

Derik said ruefully, "It looks like our new Second is now our new First."

Next, Tyson walked over to Declan to look him in the eye.

"If I'm the new First then I'd appreciate having somebody with experience, to continue being Second."

My hand found my husband's which he returned with an appreciative squeeze before he answered.

"Yeah sure, why not," he said casually.

"Hey, I'll take a shot at it." Derik joked.

But the rest of us gave an incredulous look at the idea...

"No thanks, Derik." Ki said coolly. "If you tried to lead us, we'd end up in Canada."

This made the rest us chuckle in agreement as our Healer gave his fellow pack member a playful elbow in the ribs.

"What are we going to do with all the dead fang heads lying around?" I looked around disheartened at the new task ahead.

"The pack has played their part and now we have to see to our fallen and their families." Tyson said flatly. "The Tribal Elders have made arrangements for the aftermath."

Then we watched him take out his mobile phone from his jeans pocket and text message the words - SEND IN THE CLEAN UP CREW.

"Who's the clean up crew?" I wondered aloud.

"That would be Jay Shallow Water and the other Lokoti who work for that construction company, 'Grand Schemes'." Derik explained.

"Hey, Jay and that company did our renovations." I remembered.

"Having access to earth-moving machinery comes in handy when mass graves become a necessity." Ki said with a heavy sigh.

I looked Declan's way in curiosity, as if something like this has happened before?

"When we destroyed those North American Vampires, Jay and a couple of the guys helped us dig the mass grave in the woods." He said. "They borrowed a couple of machines from a building site."

"Oh," I looked away perturbed.

As a member of the pack, I should have known this. But since I was excluded from that battle, I guess the information was left out like I was. I tried not to get angry as I knelt down in the grass and wiped the blood off my sword. I reasoned at least I wasn't excluded from this fight, otherwise it would have been a blood bath.

Ki addressed our new First, "If I may be permitted to leave, I have patients to see to."

"Go," he nodded.

The Medicine Man returned to the crying mother and son to gently separate the two. Carefully, he picked up the mother as the son stood up to follow. I watched the little boy trail after him as Ki began the trek back to tribal lands.

The rest of the pack followed suit. I watched Tyson return to his fallen father, pick him up and sling him over his back. Derik and Neil followed suit, by picking up and carrying the late Phil and Pete.

"C'mon B, let's get the girls and take them home," my husband squeezed my hand. "I don't think Wendy will feel up to babysitting tonight."

"Oh shit!" I stopped still in horror. "Poor Wendy...! Poor, poor Wendy!"

"So let's get the girls so the family can mourn in peace," he said sadly.

In a bright flash of light, Declan instantaneously phased us out of the north west plain and onto the Wisetail's driveway.

It was the worst timing in the world again, for as soon as our bare feet felt the gravel drive underneath, our ears were hit with the most frightful screaming.

Walt had beaten us home and brought his son to his wife and family.

Declan hid his nakedness by remaining on the dark driveway as I tiptoed into the house to retrieve my children.

I found Soph and Looch were sitting on a couch with their eyes filled with tears. I felt rotten as I made my way around the weeping family, all sitting around Kurt's body lying on the floor. I took hold of my daughters' hands and led them out of the house.

I tried not to look at Walt who was holding his hysterical wife, as he nor his children were able to acknowledge us amidst their grief.

Wendy's screams turned shrill over the state her first born came home in. Under the living room lights, Kurt's bite marks and pallor looked even more hideous. Edwina, Kevin, Katrina and Hugh sat sobbing around their older brother, who was lying lifeless and far from peaceful.

Outside, Declan picked up Looch as I carried Soph in my arms and then the parents instantaneously phased their living children home.

*****

~ 27 ~

I sat on the side of the bed and cried as my hurt and helplessness was released in the form of hot tears and soft whining.

If only I could howl properly! I'd climb up onto the roof and howl my lungs out. Oh, I'd howl so thunderously that all of time and space could hear!

"B?"

My dressed husband stood in the doorway, looking on in concern.

"Go away!" I barked out. "Go put the kids to bed or something."

"I have, three times now," he said softly. "But they won't stay down."

As if to prove his point, I saw their small faces peak out from behind him. They looked scared at how their world was crumbling so; two of their relations were murdered tonight and their Mummy was 'losing it'.

My whining turned high pitched as I squashed my hands against my wet face, as if to block everything out.

"C'mon B," he came to kneel before me.

He used his larger hands to hold my head and meet my tearful gaze with his own. I sensed he was mourning too. But I also felt he was trying to impart some of his strength onto his wife.

"Why...?" I uttered out. "Why can't I be a Circulator like my Gran? She and the Circulate were able to dispel nuclear bomb blasts in the beginning of World War Three! She could guide my mother through visions from the space time continuum! She could create time warps in non-corporeal form! So why the fuck couldn't I save a fourteen year old boy...?"

"B, don't do this," he pleaded.

"Why Declan, why?!" I shouted. "Why am I so fucking useless I can't even save Wendy and Walt's eldest child?!"

"STOP IT!" He yelled, as he gripped onto my shoulders. "You're still a mother so drop the 'melt down' bullshit and frickin' get on with it!"

The European Werewolf was so loud, he made the bedroom windows rattle.

Our daughters who were standing in the bedroom doorway, looked taken aback. They'd seen their mother and father fight dozens of times, but they'd never heard him roar like that before. Usually, he only raised his voice when Soph's tantrums were getting out of control and he had to exert his influence.

Then their Mummy broke down into another set of sobbing which made their Daddy watch wretchedly.

"Oh Declan..." I rasped out of my aching chest, "...I wish I could howl like you or another male Werewolf can."

He blinked in surprise before his expression turned into a hopeful one.

"You want me to howl for you, B?" He asked eagerly. "You want me to howl for Kurt?"

My head moved by its own accord as it jerked up and down.

"Then I'll howl for you," he said determinedly.

He tugged me to my feet then pulled me towards one of the bedroom windows.

I don't know if he'd sensed what I was thinking or we'd been married for too long? But he pushed up the glass and climbed out onto a section of the roof. Once he was outside, he reached through the opening and helped me out after him.

Excitedly, our little girls ran after us, especially since they've never climbed the roof before. We made sure they made it out safely and then my big, strong mate led the way up to the crest. Declan held mine and Lucia's hands in his own, as I tugged along Sophia for the ride.

The view from the roof was impressive. Since we lived on top of the hill, you could sing we were the 'Kings of the Castle'. From the roof of our two story house, we could see over the tree tops of the forest which sloped away from us. We could even spot the lights of the houses here on tribal lands.

Papa Werewolf, Mama Werewolf and the two baby Werewolves' eyes glowed so we could see in the night. Looch proceeded to point out the river to Soph, as the girls enjoyed the new vantage point. Declan held firmly onto my hand, showing there was no way he would let me fall.

Next, my husband raised his head into the air as he closed his eyes and opened his mouth.

AAAAAARRRRROOOOOOOOOOOOOOOOAAAAAWRRRR!

I swear, I could feel the power vibrate out of his chest and through the rest of his body. The noise carried down the hill and travelled over tribal lands and into the surrounding National Park. We probably woke the neighbours, but those who had a Werewolf in the family were no doubt awake.

Just then Declan and I were surprised by a second howl:

AAAAAARRRRROOOOOOOOOOOOOOOOAAAAAWRRRR!

We turned to see Looch's little head was tilted upwards and her eyes were closed. Her mouth hung open and she already looked like a natural for her first howl. When she opened her eyes again, she noticed all of us staring.

Awkwardly, she cleared her throat and said, "What?"

Soph wanted to try too, so she squeezed her eyes shut, opened her mouth wide and spluttered out:

"AaaarrooooOOOOooooohh!" (cough cough).

We cracked up laughing at our youngest whose face turned pink in embarrassment.

"Don't worry Soph, your mother sucks at howling too," her father consoled.

I crouched down and sat on top of the roof as our daughters followed suit with their father sitting last. We could no longer see the lights down in the valley below but the starlight above, more than made up for it. All four of us looked upwards as we gazed into the great beyond.

"Mummy, where is the space time continuum?" Looch asked enquiringly.

"It's far away, so far that not even astronomers can see it." I answered. "Human scientists postulate what's at the end of the universe, or even how it will end. They colonize planets with breathable atmospheres, or look for signs of life to know we're not alone. But we haven't even left the Milky Way yet, with space travel. The space time continuum is at the end of the universe, it exists on the edge of existence. It is existence, as it upholds time and space."

Soph asked curiously, "Then why do people go there when they die?"

"Well, you know how I told you about the Big Bang, the Big Crunch and how there's another Big Bang...?"

"Yes?"

"For a human or a werewolf's soul, or their energy signature, it's the same." I explained. "Just as the universe is born and dies and then is reborn, so are people."

She asked next, "Don't vampires' souls go there too?"

"Fang heads don't have souls," her father growled out.

I elbowed him in the ribs to be more careful about letting his prejudice slip in front of the children, before I answered.

"I don't know Soph, maybe."

"Why wouldn't a vampire have a soul?" Looch pondered with her analytical mind. "They're alive, aren't they?"

"Barely," her father muttered.

I answered, "They still breathe and have a heart beat, but most of their body has been necrotized. It's why they have to feed on blood to regulate many of their body functions which are no longer working."

"Sucks to be a Vampire!" Soph pronounced.

Declan and I exchanged a long look before I turned back to our daughters.

"Girls, we have to tell you about something that happened tonight."

"You mean besides Kurt dying?" Looch asked emotionally, as her eyes refilled with tears.

"Caesar died too," Soph reminded.

Sympathetically, Declan rubbed Looch's back as I rested my arm about Soph's shoulders.

"Our pack weren't the only ones who suffered casualties." I said. "When we arrived, we found the fang heads feeding on a human family who were camping there."

“But I thought Walt closed the camping grounds,” Soph interjected.

“He did, but these are humans we’re talking about.” Declan scoffed. “They’re not exactly the brightest of species on this planet.”

Our daughters snickered at their father’s sarcasm before I continued.

“Just as our pack will have four new members to train, the tribe will have a new family moving in.”

“What new family?” Looch listened.

Their father said gruffly, “Your mother had a ‘vision’ that we should adopt a frickin’ fang head.”

“Huh...?” Our eldest’s mouth fell open in surprise.

I explained, “Tonight, a ten year old boy lost his little sister and father, as his mother suffered serious injuries. One of the European Vampires who attacked, forced his blood upon the boy. Walt saved his life but now we need to train him to hunt animal and not human.”

Soph gave a funny look, “Why doesn’t Daddy just kill him?”

“My thoughts exactly,” he looked away in annoyance.

“But if he lost his father and sister tonight, and his mother’s sick...” Looch thought aloud, “...he really does need our help.”

“You’re right, Lucia.” I smiled proudly. “This boy and his mother need our compassion and understanding right now.”

“But he’s a fang head and he tastes dirty!” Soph said indignantly.

“Not dirty, just stale,” her father tried to explain. “My mother’s recipe for lasagne tastes better than Vampire flesh.”

“Declan!” I elbowed him a second time. “You’re not helping with the lesson of 'goodwill to all mankind'!”

“What ‘mankind’, we’re Shape Shifters!” He retorted.

“Exactly!” I fired up. “Werewolves and Vampires are both Shape Shifters, which means we’re related! Once, you were human as was I and so were they, so therefore all mankind!”

Sophia’s eyes bulged, “We’re related to fang heads?!”

Lucia giggled back, “Yeah Soph, you’re related to a dirty Vampire.”

Her reaction was immediate, “I’m NOT related to a DIRTY fang head!”

She stood up to stomp away when she nearly slipped off the roof! Luckily, her father used his light speed reflexes to jump up and grab hold. However, we saw the signs of one of her famous tantrums setting in.

“I’m NOT related to a DIRTY fang head!” She raged as she writhed in her father’s arms. “I’m not! I’m not!”

Declan sighed wearily, “I’m gonna try putting her to bed again.”

Rather than carry down the kicking and screaming child in his arms, he instantaneously phased off the roof and into her bedroom.

Unperturbed, Looch conversed as normal, “What’s the boy’s name?”

"Xenthe."

"And he's my age?"

"Uh huh."

"What's he like?"

"Um, I think he's into music."

"He's not gonna be like Kurt," her eyes watered once more. "Kurt was a cool older brother and he was my best friend."

"No, nobody will ever be like Kurt." I hugged her to my side. "He was a unique little boy and one that can never be copied."

Then we were interrupted by the high-pitch squealing of her little sister. Sophia was working herself into such a state, putting her to bed would be difficult. As if to confirm this, we heard the sound of something breaking. I bet Declan was going to have to sit on her again...

"And your sister is a unique little girl as well," I said wryly.

Looch tittered as she hugged her mother back before looking up at the starry sky again.

*****

When it was time to come inside I instantaneously phased the both of us back.

In a bright flash of light we disappeared off the roof and reappeared in another, inside the master bedroom.

I escorted Looch to bed and on our way we looked in on Soph, to find her father sitting on her back. Her face was red and wet from angry tears, but she seemed to be asleep! Declan was reading from the Macquarie Dictionary of all things and beside them lay a broken lamp, another casualty of her temper.

"Autonomics; the science, study, or practice of developing a number of self-governing systems, as within a large business organization." He droned on until he saw us standing there. "Is she asleep? Please say she is, as I'm about to lose it myself."

Relief washed over his face when we nodded back. Carefully, he moved off his daughter's back and put aside the book. Then he gently lifted his five year old into his arms and put her down again on the mattress. We watched as he tucked her in and left her room, shutting the door behind him.

"Right, let's put you to bed so your parents can get some shut-eye," he said to our eldest.

Willingly, Looch allowed herself to be led into her room and over to her bed. I leaned on the doorframe and watched her father tuck her in before delivering a kiss to her forehead. I blew her a kiss goodnight then Declan turned off her bedside lamp and departed, closing her door too.

My husband tiredly turned to his wife, "Now put me to bed, Mrs. Sabre."

I took hold of his hand and pulled him into our bedroom and for privacy I shut the door behind us.

Inside, we automatically undressed to share a shower before retiring. When I pulled off my stretchy gym clothes that I'd fought in, I noticed the bits of blood splatter on the fabric. Curious, I looked his way to examine his cuts, to find he had completely healed.

"Declan," I stared in amazement, "you've regenerated."

He paused just as he'd dropped his boxers into the laundry basket, "Huh?"

I came over to his position and ran my hands over his skin to feel the new tissue and I also noticed how hard his muscles felt.

"That's weird!" I gazed up into his face. "You're cuts are completely healed. Usually, it takes our kind longer to heal from silver inflicted injuries."

"Yeah, I think it's from eating the fang heads' flesh," he shrugged it off. "Like you said tonight, we're both Shape Shifters. I could feel my stomach churn over the Vampire's flesh and use it."

"Amazing..." I breathed, "...your European Werewolf metabolism absorbed the European Vampire flesh and used the other Shape Shifter's cells to regenerate your damaged ones."

"Gees B, when you turn all scientific on me, it makes me hot," he grinned.

"Anything makes you hot." I poked him in the side.

"I'm just hot period," he used his high body temperature as a pun.

Then he pulled me closer the same time as he ducked his head to kiss along my right shoulder.

"Not tonight, I'm tired and so much has happened." I said emotionally, as I backed away. "Really, I'm not in the mood."

His arms encircled my waist and pulled me to him a second time. He gently bumped his forehead against mine and held my gaze with his. I could feel his hot breath on my face and tenderly his lips met mine.

"It's exactly why I need you tonight, B."

I hesitated, as I felt my husband's emotional and physical needs. But right at that moment I wasn't feeling sexy, even if we were standing closely together, naked. Sex was the last thing on my mind after our losses tonight, but it made my mate crave comfort of this kind.

Declan sat down on the bed then carefully pulled me over him. I straddled him and when he moved his hand to my crotch to massage it, I pushed it away. I took him inside and moved mechanically, but he didn't like the, 'let's get this over with' attitude. He changed our positions by rolling us onto our sides.

After hooking my right leg over his waist, he returned his hand to my crotch to massage it with the same speed as his pushing. I gasped as I felt a rush of wetness from his actions, which was my body's way of saying, 'now we're talking!' He felt this, as his eyes remained on my face to watch for further reactions to his technique.

My eyes drifted closed as the escalating pleasure took over. I felt his sharp teeth graze my jaw line as his mouth moved towards my ear. He chewed on it at first before murmuring his instructions into it:

"Dig your nails into my back."

As if they acted by their own accord, my claws detracted.

"Yes..." he breathed before uttering out, "...harder."

I felt them pierce his skin and the sensation of his blood getting under my nails. He groaned quietly but his massage and rhythm remained steady. His finger continued to tease and tantalize my sensitive, protruding tissue.

The pleasure soon turned into rapture as I neared the slippery slopes of the sought after orgasm. I felt the ripples of my abdominal muscles balloon into ecstasy which made me try to hold onto the exquisite delight for as long as possible. I thrust my hips against his as my claws dug into his muscles.

"Aaargh!" He grunted in pain.

"Oh shit!" Instantly, I retracted my claws. "Are you OK?"

"Frickin' hell woman, don't stop now!" He complained.

Then I noticed he hadn't stopped moving. Quickly, I grabbed onto his back and held onto it tightly once more, which helped him to come. I watched his eyes close and his mouth fall open as my crotch felt wetter. Then we simply lay there like that, with my leg over his waist which his hand came to rest on top of.

Still, I was concerned over the damage I'd done and I raised my head to look over his shoulder and inspect his wounds.

There were bloodied holes in his back where my claws had gouged him, but they weren't bleeding much. In fact, when I ran my finger over one of them, it wiped the blood off to reveal new tissue underneath. My eyes widened as I stared in disbelief.

"Declan, you're healing faster than ever tonight!"

"Am I?" He asked disinterested, as he kept his eyes closed.

"I was scared I almost killed you." I said, guiltily.

"Ha!" He smirked. "Dream on."

"Declan?"

"B?"

"Are you feeling alright?" I wondered. "You fought so hard tonight but you still seem to have so much energy and your regeneration is faster than Speedy Gonzales."

Finally, he opened his eyes to look into my concerned ones and he gave a grin.

"I'm a little tired." He said casually. "In fact, I'm sure after another round I'd go straight to sleep."

"ANOTHER ROUND?!"

"Shhh!" He hushed his wife. "If you wake up Sophia, you're the one who's sending her back to sleep."

Then the husband pulled his wife closer and at first we simply held each other. We relished the feel of our naked bodies pressed together, how supple the other's skin felt or even how warm. Next, his hands ran up and down my sides and then over my rounded belly before moving up to cup my enlarged breasts.

Declan ducked his scruffy blonde head to scrape his sharp teeth over my nipples. It sent shivers down my spine as I felt his hot, wet tongue next lick the stinging flesh. I moaned as he tried to take my entire right breast inside his mouth. I found myself pushed onto my back as he grew more amorous.

My mouth fell open in both pleasure and pain, as he ravenously left bites and licks over different parts of my body. His right hand returned to my crotch which added to my delight. But when he bit deeply into my left shoulder, I almost cried out. Quickly, he licked away the bloodied teeth marks, turning the wound numb while simultaneously healing it.

His face hovered over mine and I saw his eyes were glowing green and his teeth were longer and sharper. Also, I noticed there was blood in the corners of his mouth, showing both his lust and bloodlust were ignited. He moved his hand away from my clit to slowly rub his member against it instead, before pushing deep inside. He fell into a strong, steady rhythm, while holding himself over my baby bulge.

"Bite me B," he growled softly, "have me while I have you."

I looked on with uncertainty, worried that it might further stir the beast within.

"C'mon baby, be a good pregnant wife and bite your husband."

Momentarily, he stopped moving so he could lift up my head to his right shoulder. His maple syrup scent was strong in his sweat, which I found enticing. The same time he started moving again, my elongated teeth punctured his skin and embedded themselves in his muscle tissue. He groaned and pushed harder, which pumped his blood straight into my mouth. I didn't stop drinking until he collapsed onto the bed beside, in happy exhaustion.

Instead of lying on top of his wife like he used to, he lay closely beside. Since Declan's become stronger, he's also felt heavier. If I wasn't with child, he'd act as my blanket by sleeping over me. But because I was, he'd spoon me instead. He gave my belly another affectionate caress then he pulled me into his arms a third time that night.

We fell asleep like that, on our sides facing the other. Whenever I rolled over in my sleep, he'd move up against me again. Like wolves in the wild sleeping together to share warmth, the European Werewolf husband remained close to his Lokoti Werewolf wife. In fact, it would have taken more than two covens of European Vampires to separate the stubborn male from his mate.

~~~~~~
~~~~~~

5th June 2374

The funerals for Caesar, Kurt, Phil and Pete were held on the 3rd of June. In conjunction with the four pyres for our fallen, two more were included for Connor and Bridie Creillaic, the father and daughter. With six pyres set alight, this turned into the largest funeral that Declan and I had ever attended.

The whole tribe came to show their respects on the Holy Grounds, a grassy glade by the river with seven totem poles.

On the front of the totems were the carved animal spirits held sacred to our people and on the back, inscribed in old Lokoti and then English, were the names of all who'd passed. As a gesture of welcoming the outsiders into the tribe, Connor and Bridie Creillaic were also inscribed. Whereas each member had a picture of an animal guide inscribed next to their names to indicate their family lineage, two fangs were carved next to Connor and Bridie's names. It was a reference to Xenthe's new supernatural status and would become the family's emblem from now on.

Ki and Jenny brought Stella and Xenthe to the funeral to say their goodbyes. Stella was sitting in a wheelchair because she was still recovering from her injuries. Dutifully, Xenthe stood beside her, holding tightly onto her hand.

The ten year old boy's pallor and faded eyes attracted many a glance, as I overheard some members of the tribe whisper about him.

It annoyed me at how everybody stared at the new European Vampire, like the poor kid didn't have enough on his plate. Not only was his father and sister slaughtered in front of him, but his mother was still sick from the Vampire's venom. I'm sure he was also struggling with his new dietary requirements.

"I overheard Ki tell Walt that the little fang head has to hunt at least once a week." Derik whispered to wife, Uma. "Werewolves only have to hunt on a full moon."

Together, they glared at the boy in distrust until I hissed at the two.

"Not all Werewolves only hunt on a full moon, just ask my husband and eldest daughter." I berated them. "So stop staring at the poor boy like he's going to turn into a serial killer!"

Derik's eyes widened at his telling off and guiltily he looked away.

Walt overheard them too and he glared at him for not falling in line. It was understood by the pack that they'd at least try to train the boy. He looked pained towards Xenthe and Stella, as if he wanted to go over to show his support but if he did, Wendy would fall over. He was literally holding his wife up, as their son's body burned on one of the funeral pyres.

Then his second son Kevin, who was standing on the other side of his mother, saw what was going on.

He looked from his father to the boy his age. With a determined expression on his face, he squared off his small shoulders and marched towards them. Since he had to walk around the front of the crowd to reach them, all eyes of the tribe were on him.

The Lokoti boy stuck out his hand towards the European Vampire.

"Hi, I'm Kevin Wisetail. The European Vampires who killed your father and little sister, also killed my older brother. You wanna be friends?"

The pale boy looked on the youth standing before him, before his faded eyes swung around the crowd. He saw that the whole tribe was watching. He guessed this offer of friendship was also an offer of support amidst suspicion. He took hold of Kevin's warmer hand in his cooler one and shook on it.

"I'm Xenthe Creillaic, we can be friends if you like."

Then Kevin politely shook Stella's hand and came to stand beside her son.

Our eldest who'd just watched what occurred, followed suit.

"Lucia Grace, get back here!" Declan shouted in a whisper but it was too late, she was already half way there.

When he made a move to bring her back, I put a restraining hand on his arm.

"No Declan, let her do this."

She came to stand before the pale boy with the faded blue eyes. Looch was the same age as he and Kevin, but clearly looked taller and stronger. It made Xenthe's eyes widen and sniff her warily, like his new instincts were warning him against her.

The European Werewolf saw the European Vampire examine his daughter and he made a move to pull her back to safety.

"No, it's OK." I held him back. "Just watch and see."

She said boldly, "I'm Lucia Sabre and I'm half Lokoti Werewolf and half European Werewolf. I hear you're a European Vampire and you're going to hunt with us from now on. That makes us friends too."

Xenthe's eyes widened in hope, "Do you drink blood too?"

"No, I'm a flesh eater, but we both have the bloodlust." She said brazenly. "You crave fresh blood and I crave fresh kill."

"So when we hunt together, you'll eat flesh while I drink blood?"

"Yep, we may even share the same kill," she shrugged. "Usually, I share my prey with my parents and little sister. But when Kurt turned, sometimes I shared with him and his father, too."

"So I won't be alone when I hunt?" Xenthe looked relieved.

"No, you're in my pack and we all hunt together." She declared. "Sometimes when the bloodlust gets bad, I hunt in between full moons with my Dad. When Kurt first turned, he and his father hunted with us until he got his bloodlust under control. So you can hunt with us, if you like?"

"And you and your Mom are part of the tribe now," Kevin added on.

"You hear that, Momma?" Xenthe turned to his mother, in excitement. "I'm not gonna be alone! There are kids like me that have the bloodlust too!"

The woman in the wheelchair smiled tearfully and patted her son's hand which had never let go of hers.

Then Looch came to stand beside Kevin and three stood together in solidarity.

Again, my mate made a move to retrieve her, but again I pulled him back.

"It's alright Declan, this is meant to happen." I reassured. "They're meant to become best friends, relying on their similarities so they don't feel excluded."

"But B, I swore to myself I'd never let a fang head near you or the girls."

In the yellow glow of the funeral pyres, I cupped his face and our blue eyes met and held.

"I've got a good feeling about this Dec," I said strongly, "this is our future revealing itself to our present."

He knew better than to question one of my all-knowing feelings. Instead, he picked up his second born and bounced her on his right arm as his left arm circled my waist to hold me against his side. With his arms around his family, he looked on in mistrust at his breed's greatest foe, fraternizing with his offspring.

*****

Since the funeral was held the same day as Looch's birthday, we had a belated birthday party for her the following day.

Her Wisetail cousins came over for the small gathering at our house although Walt stayed home with Wendy.

The funeral had done little to lessen the parents' loss. Wendy was inconsolable and her behaviour was either hysterical or depressed. Walt was on annual leave to take care of his wife and kids. But even the supernaturally strong Lokoti Werewolf was looking dishevelled during this difficult period.

When Declan and I went over to pick up the kids, he also handed over a large Tupperware container with tuna bake inside.

"Here, there should be enough to feed your family for a couple of nights."

"Thanks Uncle." Walt took it and went to go put it inside their fridge.

As I helped the kids get ready by grabbing what they needed to play with, such as toys or a soccer ball; my mate followed their father into the kitchen. Their mother wasn't downstairs though, Wendy was resting in the main bedroom. I'd heard that Ki had prescribed her a herbal sleeping draught.

"How are you both?" Declan asked quietly.

"As much as you'd expect when you lose a child," Walt said shortly, then he relented. "Sorry, I didn't mean -"

"Shut up Walt, don't you dare apologise," Declan said firmly. "But we're gonna keep asking those questions, or bring over food, or help out with babysitting, until the day you answer, 'we're fine thanks'."

Walt's eyes watered as he looked on his big, strong Second in gratitude. In return, Declan gave him a pat on the arm. Then he returned to the living area to help me supervise the children into getting ready.

At first Edwina, Kevin, Katrina and Hugh were reluctant to leave their mourning parents. I think they thought if they stayed, they could help somehow. But Walt gave each of his children a hug and sent them to their cousins' house.

As we walked up the hill, their childish laughter, taunts and playing began to resurface. It was like watching the Wisetail children come to life again. I can't imagine what it must be like to lose a sibling, since I was an only child. Declan would have a better understanding, as he lost his little brother to old age.

On the front lawn, Looch, Kevin, Katrina and Hugh started up a soccer game. Meanwhile, Edwina and Soph played with their dolls on a rug in the shade of our huge, blooming Jacaranda Tree. Declan and I watched over the children from the kitchen window, as we prepared Looch's birthday lunch.

The gourmet chef that was my husband was preparing another three course feast. To start with, we were having a platter with antipasto, cheeses and preserved meats like salami and cabanossi. For the main, he made his mother's recipe for fettuccine carbonara as well as garlic bread. Lastly for dessert, we would serve Looch's birthday cake which in this instance, was Black Forrest.

The cake was baked, the cream was whipped, there were chocolate shavings and two bowls of different types of cherries; tinned and glace. All that needed to be done was to put it altogether. This was my job, while Declan made the pasta dish. I enjoyed smearing the sweetened cream on with a spatula then adding the cherries and chocolate shavings.

"There we go," I stepped back to admire my work. "All that's missing are the birthday candles."

"Not bad," he looked over from the stove. "We'll put the candles on before we serve."

I walked over to the sink and stared out the kitchen window at the children's soccer game in the sunshine.

"It's such a lovely day outside," I commented.

"It is," he agreed. "We haven't used our fold up chairs and tables in a while. Why don't we set up under the Jacaranda Tree and eat in the garden?"

"Good idea." I agreed. "But we'll need to make sure the table is definitely in the shade for one of our guests."

"Huh?" He gave a funny look and before he could ask, he saw why.

Ki's hover-car powered down on our gravel driveway. He climbed out first, followed by Jenny and Xenthe. Then the Medicine Man and the boy helped the fourth person out, which was his mother. Stella didn't come with a wheelchair this time, instead she used her son's shoulder to lean on.

Looch, Kevin, Katrina and Hugh momentarily forgot about their soccer game as they ran up to greet their new friend.

"You invited a frickin' fang head to your daughter's birthday party?!" Declan fumed.

I ignored his protest and left the house to welcome our guests.

"Hi, you must be Stella and Xenthe." I smiled warmly, as I walked down the drive. "My name is B Sabre, thanks for coming."

"Thanks for invitin' us to your little un's party." Stella shook my hand. "I'm just sorry we're arrivin' empty handed."

"Don't be silly." I waved it off, before I looked down at the pale little boy. "Hi Xenthe, how are you?"

"I'm alright, Ki took me hunting last night so I won't crave anyone." He looked uncomfortable and I wondered why? But then I saw what he was looking at, which was Declan coming down the drive while glaring at the poor kid.

"This big, unfriendly giant is my husband, Declan Sabre." I introduced when he reached my side.

"Gees B, don't build me up in front of our guests, will you," he rolled his eyes.

"Look at this big, strong, hunk of blonde." Stella laughed off the tension in the air. "I'm glad I'm not gonna be the only blonde in the tribe. We blondes have to stick together, especially when the blonde jokes start flyin' around the room."

The Southerner's frank speech and cheeky sense of humour instantly won over the European Werewolf.

"You can come over more often," he laughingly shook her hand. "Now what can we get you to drink?"

"A bourbon thanks, but if you're outta spirits then a beer would be fine."

"Er, the Sabre's also being Werewolves, don't drink alcohol either." Ki said.

"You too, huh?" She looked on Declan closely. "Say, you wouldn't have been that creature that looked part 'Lassie' and part 'Incredible Hulk' I saw at the battle, would you?"

"That'd be me," he smiled. "'The Incredible Hulk' used to be my brother's nickname for me."

"I'll bet and let me guess, we'd better not make you angry either." She played along.

Fifteen minutes later, the adults were all sitting down on the fold up chairs we'd put out, under the tree. Declan and I had also set up the long, fold up table, covered with a red tablecloth. Stella rested her soda on it as the rest of us did.

"Xenthe, c'mere boy!" She called. "Let's put some more sunscreen onto that pale face o'yours."

The little boy whose sickly complexion was starting to look a little red from sunburn, obediently ran to his mother. We watched her pull a tube of sunscreen out of her handbag and begin to rub it over her son's exposed skin. I guessed by the way he stood there as she lathered him down, he was already adjusting to his strengths and weaknesses.

"Look at you, little man," she tutted. "You burn as easily as salt poured onto a snail."

"At least he's not exploding into flames." Declan muttered, but we overheard.

"Ha!" She laughed out loud. "Nope, he don't turn into dust from sunlight nor does he shrink from the sight of crosses."

To illustrate, she pulled out the gold crucifix which hung around his neck to show us, before tucking it back underneath his shirt.

"Off you go and mind your fangs," she gave him a pat on the backside.

We watched him run back to the soccer game where he showed off his new speed of sound reflexes, by expertly getting the ball away from Kevin. However, Looch used her greater strength by blocking him then scoring a goal in a single kick. Kevin, Katrina and Hugh whooped and cheered as they jumped up and down excitedly at their supernatural skills.

Stella uttered out tearfully, "That was Connor's crucifix, he got it on his confirmation when he was Xenthe's age. I took it off his body before they burned it at the funeral, I'm sure he'd want his son to have it."

Our table turned quiet as we looked on the widow who was trying hard to remain upbeat and strong for her remaining child, but the sorrow was still there.

"Then you're Catholic?" Declan pulled out the gold crucifix from under his white t-shirt. "This used to be my mother's."

"Are y'all Catholic too?" She brightened.

"I was christened Catholic, but never confirmed. My parents were, but my father was murdered by the monster who turned me. When the Lokoti took us in, we couldn't really practice the faith. In those days there weren't any Catholic Churches for us to go to in Alma, like there is today. Occasionally, Mom read to us from the bible and we celebrated Christmas and Easter with B's family, who were some of the few families in the tribe that celebrated those holidays."

"Sounds like what happened to us, happened to you." Stella looked on him as a source of hope. "And how did your mother cope with the move to Alaska? Maybe I could meet her for a cup of coffee and a good ole gossip."

"Er, that could be difficult since she's been dead for over two centuries." He let out an uneasy laugh.

"Excuse me...?" She blinked in disbelief. "Just how old are y'all? You've got the baby face of a college student!"

Declan put his hand over mine, "I was born right after World War Three and B came three years later."

Stella stared in shock at our appearances of a couple in their twenties.

"So you're the older man in this relationship?" She looked disappointed. "Here I was, about to toast the woman for landing herself a young bit o'fun!"

The adults sitting at the table all laughed at her taunt at how I looked older even if I was younger than my mate.

"You're calling Aunt B a 'cougar'? Now that IS funny!" Jenny teased. "Now she knows how the rest of us feel, who are married to a Lokoti Werewolf."

She was referring to the fact that she looked like a woman in her late forties whereas Ki looked like a man in his early thirties. Their children were grown and had moved out of home and into new ones with their respective partners. Declan and I had attended their Housewarmings with the kids.

"But you don't look a day over nineteen, when we first became mates." Ki smiled warmly on his wife.

"It's a good thing that Werewolves make such loyal partners." Jenny tweaked her husband's nose.

"It's a good thing that you're mated to a Lokoti Werewolf." Declan pointed out. "The other breeds aren't exactly known for their loyalty."

"What's that?" Stella looked quizzically his way.

"The other breeds of Werewolf like the North American and the European weren't known to be loyal. I'm the last pure blood European Werewolf but I was raised the Lokoti way. Before me, my breed were monsters who were constantly on the hunt. But thanks to the Lokoti Werewolves, I was taught loyalty as well as to hunt animal and not human." Declan educated.

"I see," she turned thoughtful. "Just as I was cursing the heavens above for camping in the wrong place at the wrong time; I see that Xenthe and I have landed in the right place and the right time. At least he wasn't abducted by that coven and he's being taught how to hunt and not turn into a murderer."

I looked Ki's way, "How was Xenthe's first hunt?"

"I've taken him twice now since his change." He told the table. "The first time he was apprehensive about drinking animal blood, but the second time he dove right in. I think the bloodlust forced him not to be picky. However, we also discovered something interesting about the European Vampire last night."

"Oh yeah and what's that?" Declan listened warily.

"Xenthe drank a glass of milk." Stella said proudly, as we stared in surprise. "Not only does my little Vampire drink blood, but he can also drink milk."

The pack's Second looked on our Medicine Man to explain, "Ki?"

“Think about it for a moment,” he mused, “milk was created to nurture our young and it has carbohydrates, vitamins, minerals and protein. Xenthe can drink fresh milk but it must be plain with no additives.”

“Why, what happens if he drinks flavoured or treated milk?” Declan wondered.

“Treated or processed milk can’t sustain him and the additives can make him sick.” He frowned.

The table full of parents all looked on Stella in sympathy to see how she was adjusting to her son’s supernatural state.

“Y’all stop frettin’,” she lightly scolded. “My boy has food allergies, that’s all! I’m sure there must be other things out there that he can have and I’m gonna find them.”

“Hang on, can milk really sustain him, or does it just act as a placebo between hunts?” I checked.

Declan smirked, “There’s my wife the professor and that enquiring mind of hers.”

“Milk doesn’t placate his bloodlust and it can’t sustain his supernatural lifespan.” Ki explained to the table. “But its properties do help in some small way, like the calcium strengthening his fangs for example. More importantly, milk acts as an excellent placebo for when he’s out in public or at social gatherings. While everyone around him eats or drinks, he can join in with a glass of milk.”

And drink milk he did... after another hour of children playing and adults talking, I helped Declan serve up. Everybody bar one ate what was on offer with gusto. As our guests thanked my husband for his wonderful culinary skills, Xenthe sat quietly in his seat holding onto his glass.

He watched with interest as his mother and new friends ate in delight. His faded blue eyes scanned the antipasto, cheeses and preserved meat, as we gobbled down the entrée. He licked his lips as we ate the fettuccine carbonara and I caught the jealousy in his eyes when we brought out the Black Forrest Cake.

“Happy Birthday to you... Happy Birthday to you... Happy Birthday dear Lucia... Happy Birthday to you!”

Her father sang the loudest as Looch sat in my lap and I sat in Declan’s.

Ki snapped several shots of us sitting altogether as such. This family photo was turning into a tradition for birthdays, with the proud Papa Bear holding his mate and young in his large arms. Soph even clambered up to pose with us and Declan could still hold all of us at once, in his strong embrace.

To make sure everyone felt included on this special day, I took my digital camera back from Ki to take a couple more pictures.

I took one of Xenthe sitting on his mother’s lap, with the pale Vampire son posing with his pale human mother. Stella’s pallor came from the fact that she was still healing, but the upside was it made her and her son look more alike. She laughed at this remark and made me promise to email her a copy.

Also, I took a pic of Ki and Jenny sitting together, with the Lokoti Werewolf husband lifting up a giggling human wife to sit in his lap too.

Lastly, I took a couple of the Wisetail kids, as I knew their parents would also appreciate copies. I got a snap of the four all sitting beside each other at the table, then another of Hugh sitting in Edwina's lap and Katrina sitting in Kevin's. I also managed to take a couple of cute pics of Hugh and Soph guzzling down the cake, with the cream and grated chocolate all around their mouths.

All in all, I think the party was a success even with a sense of loss hanging in the air.

At 5 PM our guests called it a day and we saw off Xenthe, Stella, Jenny and Ki. We escorted the four back to Ki's hover-car and watched the vehicle take off. Then as a family, we walked the Wisetail kids home, which was half way down the hill.

The six kids walked in front, all laughing, jostling and play fighting with each other. Declan and I walked behind, overseeing our small herd. My husband held my hand in his then he used his free one to give my stomach an affectionate caress. This made me smile, I liked how he was already including baby number three in our family.

However, as soon as we arrived at the Wisetail's house, it was as if a dark cloud appeared over everyone's mood.

"Sssshhh!" Walt put up his hands to hush their laughter. "I just put your mother down for another nap."

This wiped the grins off the children's faces, which Declan and I noted.

"Walt," my mate stepped up to him for a quiet word, "how is she?"

"Not good." Walt looked worn out. "Has Ki gone home?"

"Yes he has," he nodded.

"Good, coz I'm gonna call and ask him to take another look at Wendy," the weary husband ran his hand through his long, dark hair. "The sleeping draught is losing its potency and sometimes -"

"Yeah?" Declan prompted as we listened in.

"- sometimes she starts screaming and I don't know what to do." He said miserably. "It's like she can't get the image of Kurt's body outta her head."

This made my husband snap to and instantly he turned to the rest of the room.

"OK kids, change of plan," he clapped his hands together to capture the children's attention. "We're gonna do pizzas and a sleepover at our house tonight. Now run upstairs and get your pyjamas and toothbrushes."

Edwina, Kevin, Katrina and Hugh all looked guiltily on their father, as if they didn't want to abandon him.

"It's OK kids, I want you to go and have a good time." Walt reassured. "Just behave yourselves when you're guests in another person's home."

However, the four didn't move and several of their eyes watered with emotion.

“C’mon then,” Looch grabbed hold of Kev’s arm. “We’ll put your toothbrushes and spare clothes in your school bags.”

Then the five children led by my eldest, made their way upstairs.

“Just be quiet when you’re getting your things.” Walt shouted in a whisper.

This made them pause to look back, before they tiptoed the rest of the way. Declan picked up Soph in his arms, to stop her from making any noise. She was already tired and grumpy after the big day we’d had.

“Would it help if the kids stayed with us for more than one night?” I offered.

“Thanks Aunt B and Uncle Dec.” He said humbly. “But when Wendy’s lucid, she asks after them. If we can just give her something to stop the waking nightmares, she could draw strength from having the kids around her.”

“Walt,” my husband began, “you’re a Lokoti Werewolf and I thought you guys were not only empathic, but you could use your will over your mates from time to time.”

Puzzled, Soph looked on the two men before glancing my way. I rolled my eyes at their lack of subtlety before I pulled her out of Declan’s arms. I didn’t like her listening to the men’s discussion on how to control their wives.

“I am using my will on Wendy, it’s the only thing that stops the screaming.” He confessed. “But we can only pass on basic commands, like the small bursts of telepathy within our pack. It’s not mind control and even if it were, I certainly wouldn’t turn Wendy into a ‘Stepford Wife’.”

For some reason, Declan appeared confused as he looked from his friend to his wife.

“But B uses her will over me all the time,” he stated.

“No I don’t!” I retorted.

“Yes you do.”

“Oh yeah, like when?” I demanded.

“Like today and every other day!” He snapped back. “You stopped me from destroying that little fang head that came to lunch today.”

Walt looked on in amusement, “Erm Uncle, the pack can’t sense your Lokoti Werewolf wife using her will on you. I’m sure she can sense your emotions, but she’s never exercised her will as such.”

“Say what?” He stared in surprise.

“I’m sure she’s not above using her aura from time to time.” Walt smirked. “We’ve ALL seen the way you react to her light.”

“Yeah well it’s still cheating, isn’t it?” He blushed. “If it’s not her Lokoti Werewolf will, then it’s her aura as a Circulator.”

I shook my head at our second born, “Your Daddy is an idiot.”

Soph squealed with laughter when Walt’s smile vanished and he held up his hands for silence once more.

~~~~~~

10th June 2374

The full moon following the battle was an important one for several reasons. Four new Lokoti Werewolves were created and I followed the Circulate Mainframe's instructions on 'activating' Jonathan Bourne. I invited the lawyer to our house and in reparations for his incompetence, he flew from London to Fairbanks in one of the company's private shuttlecraft.

Promptly, at 6 PM he reported in with our door chime sounding his arrival. The girls were sitting at the dining table colouring in, while their father was in the kitchen, putting leftovers from our early dinner into several Tupperware containers. Declan wasn't ecstatic that I'd invited Jonathan over, especially before a hunt. I think he would've heard what my mate called out.

"B, the human leech your lawyer is here!"

I walked out of the study and passed Declan a glare to behave, before walking over to the front door and opening it.

"Good evening, B." He greeted, wearing another haute couture suit and holding his expensive leather briefcase.

"Jonathan, please come in." I stepped aside.

He came to stand in the middle of our living area and held up his briefcase.

"I've brought my laptop to show you the work we've done on monitoring those groups of people that we talked about." He said.

"Good, but I invited you here to talk about another matter."

He looked on enquiringly, "Oh?"

"Um, how do we do this..." I looked around as I wondered if we should be standing or sitting, "...what if we sit down on the lounges?"

"It sounds like you want to impart bad news," his face fell. "B, if you've brought me here to fire me then I'd rather be standing."

"I'm not going to fire you, although I was tempted to after your mishap." I said coolly. "Instead, I've asked you here for a promotion."

"A promotion?" He brightened. "You want me to lead the Legal Department in the London Head Office?"

"No."

"Then where am I being promoted to?" He wore a puzzled expression. "Not some small divisional office on an off-world colony, I hope."

"I want you to be the next Head Chairman on the Board of Directors of Hodge Endeavor."

His eyes bulged, "You want to make me the leader of the entire company?"
~~~~~~

“I’ll still be the real owner, especially since I’m the majority shareholder.” I smirked. “But for the sake of publicity, I want the media to think that you’re the Head Chairman.”

Jonathan’s face broke into a broad grin like he’d just won the lottery.

“So it’ll draw unwanted attention away from you? That’s an understandable request, especially how you prefer to keep out of the limelight. Thank you for this offer B and I won’t let you down!” He rushed out.

Then Declan came out of the kitchen to give him a dirty look, “Before your huge head gets any bigger, you’re gonna have to hear the reason why.”

“Oh?” He looked from me to my husband and back again. “And what reason would that be?”

“Those groups of people I have you keeping a close eye on are covens of European Vampires.” I announced.

“Excuse me?” He blinked as if he’d misheard. “I’m sorry, I didn’t quite catch that.”

I continued, “European Vampires are responsible for a large percentage of the murders in the UK and the European continent. There are other several species of Vampires inhabiting Earth and we can provide police reports which fit their MO.”

“Wait a moment...” he disagreed, “...the victims’ bodies are usually found burned to a crisp from a laser rifle. Humans shoot humans everyday with such weapons, in either robberies, crimes of passion or other violent altercations.”

Declan walked over to the human in the house to frown down upon him.

“If you fed on people by digging your fangs into their major arteries, you’d be leaving your DNA on the body.” He spoke plainly. “So what would you do about it?”

Jonathan’s eyes widen, “So they burn the victims to destroy any evidence they’d be leaving behind?”

“If the body is burned afterwards, it can also cover the fact that they’ve been drained first.” My mate educated. “The fang heads have been hunting for thousands of years, they know how to cover their tracks. They don’t want to risk exposure which would threaten their feeding.”

“What you’re suggesting is a world-wide conspiracy.” He shook his head. “If this is true, the police would have recognized a pattern.”

“Like you said, humans kill humans everyday.” I said dryly. “The police think they’re investigating normal homicides, not paranormal ones.”

The lawyer still looked sceptical, so I indicated the briefcase in his hands.

“Let me guess what’s in the work you brought over, especially about Count Onesti. The photos of the Count and the Count’s father and maybe even his grandfather, all look similar. Maybe the hairstyles change, or maybe they dye their hair? But the family resemblance is uncanny.” I sung knowingly.

His eyes narrowed suspiciously at how I could've possibly known this?

"Yes, I downloaded the photos of his ancestry when I was personally investigating him and they are indeed similar. But that doesn't make the Count a Vampire, family resemblance is a genetic trait. I look the most like my grandfather than my father, but that doesn't mean I'm a Vampire." He scoffed.

"Nah, you're just a human leech instead of a supernatural one." Declan folded his arms in front, as he gave a dissatisfied look.

I continued, "Jonathan, not all of the murders were carried out by Vampires, but sometimes it was committed by a Werewolf."

The lawyer must have reached the end of his patience, for he threw back his head and laughed!

"A Werewolf? Of course!" He played along. "Of course there are Werewolves, just as there are Vampires! They're the ones that are to blame for this world."

"I wouldn't go that far," my husband sneered. "We didn't start three world wars, nor contaminate our natural resources with nuclear fall out."

"'We'?" Our legal expert caught what he said. "Are you saying that you're a Werewolf or a Vampire?"

This made our youngest pipe up from the table, "I'm NOT a dirty fang head!"

Then our eldest added, "I'm half European and half Lokoti Werewolf, but my new friend Xenthe is a European Vampire."

Jonathan Bourne looked from the little girls colouring in at the table, to their parents and in particular, their big, strong father and warily he took a step back. I think he thought we'd all gone mad. I even caught him look from us to the front door, as if he were judging his chances of making it out of here alive.

"The difference with Werewolves hunting human instead of Vampires, is they don't leave behind a body behind, they're flesh eaters. In this instance, they'd be to blame for the missing person's reports, rather than the burnt bodies." I told him.

"In the world there are four different breeds of Werewolves." Declan declared. "They are European, Asian, North American and Lokoti. Two of these breeds no longer hunt human whereas the other two do."

The lawyer took another step back from the people he thought were not just insane, but possibly dangerous. "Then who do and who don't?"

"I'm the last European Werewolf and B is the first female Lokoti Werewolf." He answered. "Neither I nor my wife or daughters, hunt human."

"Well, I'm delighted to hear that." Jonathan tried to carry on as normal. "But I came today at your request, to show how the investigations on those groups of people are going. We're liaising with the European Union Police Force, just as you ordered. I'm afraid I have to leave now to make my flight home."

We watched the lawyer back away from us until he reached the front door.

"C'mon Jonathan, connect the dots." I rolled my eyes. "Vampires hunt Werewolves just as they hunt human. In the past, we've been attacked by the creatures your files are on. The two times you know about were in the supermarket car park. The police investigated a large, mutant, hairless, albino grizzly running to my rescue, remember? Our hover-car was confiscated twice in the murder investigations which I called you about."

This caught his attention and he stopped to swing his eyes my husband's way.

"My European Werewolf form looks like a large, mutant, hairless, albino grizzly to some." Declan shrugged. "I dunno why, but then again humans are weird."

We saw him look down at the briefcase he was holding as he seemed to be contemplating something.

"Forensics said that the bodies of the suspects that attacked B in the supermarket car park had several genetic defects. Their blood work and cellular structure showed unexplainable abnormalities. But before a full autopsy could be carried out, the bodies abruptly decomposed. The rate astounded the doctors, for within a week of death all that was left of the headless corpses was a biological 'ash'." He said with uncertainty.

"Bingo!" Declan smirked. "Fang heads aren't immortal, they're living beings that breathe and have a pulse. But because half of their bodies are necrotized, when they completely die there's not much left."

"And what happens when Werewolves die?" He wondered aloud.

"We're completely alive so we don't turn to ash." Declan said proudly. "We slowly decompose just as humans do."

I explained, "If a Werewolf dies in their supernatural form, their bodies return to their human state. The aversion to this rule is the Asian Werewolf, who remains in their Werewolf form. It's because they look the most like wolves when they turn."

Just then Declan turned to our daughters, "Girls, go upstairs and put on your hunting clothes."

Immediately, they moved to obey, leaving behind their work and a puzzled human.

"Their hunting clothes?" Jonathan queried.

"It is a full moon tonight," my husband pointed out.

To our guest's surprise, Declan started to undress by first taking off his wedding ring and crucifix, before removing his clothes.

"Perhaps I should leave..." the human backed away again.

"Relax Jonathan, we didn't ask you here to fire or eat you." I said wryly.

The European Werewolf next kicked off his shoes and removed the rest of his garments, with an embarrassed human looking on.

“Come outside,” he ordered our employee.

“Er, why?” Jonathan asked uneasy.

“Because if I change inside, my claws will scratch the wooden floorboards and we had them re-polished recently.” He said perfunctory.

Then the naked man led the way with his wife on his heels and the visitor reluctantly trailing behind.

I took off my shoes and socks and left them on the front veranda. I was wearing maternity jeans with a stretchy t-shirt, so I didn't think my clothes would tear. The three of us came to stand on the gravel drive.

The lawyer stared in shock as my husband began to expand in size. His bones made soft cracking noises as his height almost doubled and his width tripled. Within a minute my husband changed into a large canine-like creature. Then Declan fell forwards, so he was standing on all fours, which put him at the same height as our guest. His glowing green eyes with the narrow slits for pupils, glared into the human's natural green ones.

The high-profile lawyer who was accustomed to finding loop holes in the law, managed out, “You don't look like large, mutant, hairless, albino grizzly.”

Declan rolled his eyes as he looked away and I spoke for him, “He said, ‘tell me something I don't know’.”

“He can't talk in his Werewolf body?” Jonathan observed.

“Not verbally, but telepathically.” I answered. “Lokoti and Asian Werewolves are pack animals, so we can send short bursts of mental communication to each other. However, European and North American Werewolves being solitary creatures, can't talk with their minds. Since Declan was raised by the Lokoti Werewolf pack, our will converted his thoughts to hear ours.”

To the human's further surprise, I too began to change. My dark blue eyes glowed turquoise with my pupils disappearing. My stretchy t-shirt expanded from my supernatural muscle bulk. He looked down at my nails which grew into long, sharp claws. My breathing turned into panting, which came out between my elongated, sharp teeth, which jutted past my lips.

In my deep, rumbling, Werewolf voice, I said, “Some Lokoti Werewolves can talk verbally in their changed forms, while some can't.”

The outsider's face remained a mask of surprise when our front door was thrown open by my daughters running outside, in their stretchy gym clothes. As they ran, they too expanded into their supernaturally strong bodies. Jonathan blinked at Looch's canine-like face as her mouth and nose became one. He gaped at how their eyes glowed green like their father's, with the same narrow slits for pupils.

He stood still like he was stuck to the spot, as he watched Soph chase Looch around their gigantic father. When Soph pounced on Looch's muscled back, Declan separated them. His sharp teeth caught the back of her gym clothes and he lifted her off to stand her on his other side.

"She started it!" Soph roared in her deep, rumbling voice. "She said all I'm good for is hunting rabbits and shrews!"

Looch laughed which sounded like a loud panting, while pointing her claw-like hand at her. But she stopped when their father emitted a dangerously low growl, to order them to behave. The human looked incredulous at the family of monsters and how we weren't acting afraid of the biggest one standing on all-fours, before him.

Nervously, the human cleared his throat, "Erm, on the topic of hunting, if you don't eat human then what do you eat?"

"Large animals in the National Park," I answered. "Like brown bear, black bear, moose, caribou, dall sheep and occasionally deer or mountain lion, who stray into our territory."

"But never human?" He double checked.

I spoke to him directly, "Investigate us, I don't mind but do it quietly. Research any and all missing person's reports or murders in Alaska, but you won't find evidence that we were responsible. Not unless the victims were Vampires and even then the fang heads were the ones who attacked first."

He opened his mouth to reply when he shut it again because I wasn't looking at him anymore. In fact, he noticed all four of the Werewolves before him seemed preoccupied with something. What he didn't know was that the whole pack was interrupted by Walt's distress.

CAN EVERYONE MEET AT MY HOUSE BEFORE THE HUNT? WENDY NEEDS TO BE PERSUADED THAT KEVIN'S NOT IN DANGER.

Oh oh, it sounds like Wendy was having a fit of hysterics over her second son's change.

"You'd better come with us," I growled to the human.

*****

While the Werewolves took a shortcut by running through the forest, the human drove himself to the next house down the hill in his luxury hover-car. He pulled into the driveway shortly after we'd arrived. He found he wasn't alone, as several more people showed up the same time as he did, but they didn't come in vehicles.

Slowly, he climbed out of the driver's side to look on a small congregation of topless Native Alaskan men. At first, they stood there with their backs to him, but when they turned to look in his direction, it made him pause. All of their eyes glowed a different colour, as their elongated teeth protruded from their mouths. He noticed that they too had claws on the ends of their hands and feet, as well as supernaturally inflated muscles.

He swallowed hard then after reminding himself that they don't eat human, he walked amongst them. He found his employers up the front of the crowd, looking on a distressed human woman who was clinging onto a young male Lokoti Werewolf. The boy had tears streaming from his glowing red eyes as his mother cried over him. A Werewolf with orange eyes, whom he guessed was the father, was trying to calm the woman.

"Wendy, please." He growled softly. "Kevin's not in any danger, we're just going to take him hunting in the National Park."

"No!" She shouted tearfully. "You've taken one son away from me, I won't let you take another!"

"Sweetheart, Kevin needs to hunt or the bloodlust will give him terrible stomach pains."

"I don't care about your bloodlust!" She bawled. "The bloodlust was responsible for Kurt's death, when those bloodsuckers murdered my eldest!"

The lawyer blanched when he heard what befell a child, by the people he was nearly fired for not watching properly.

"I too lost a family member," our First stepped up. "The pack mourns our fallen just as you do."

"Your father was old but my son wasn't yet out of his teens!" She rebuked. "There's no way in hell, I'm gonna let my second son become one of you! I'll take him to a gene therapy clinic! I'll have them eradicate his Lokoti Werewolf genes like they were cancer!"

"Erm, those gene therapy clinics are to treat pregnant women carrying foetuses with genetic defects." Jonathan spoke up. "The other kind of treatment you're proposing, would be an impossible let alone a painful process."

"Who's this guy?" Derik gave the human a peculiar look.

"He's Aunt B's lawyer from Hodge Endeavor." Ki answered, as Xenthe stood beside, listening in.

"I don't care!" She sobbed. "I don't want Kevin to become one of you! Go and activate somebody else!"

"Wendy," our First spoke in his deep, rumbling voice. "We have no control over who turns and who doesn't."

"If you can't control your supernatural genes then I'll resort to science instead!" She threatened. "I'll take him to that clinic in Anchorage tomorrow! Either by chemo or radiotherapy, I'll kill every Lokoti Werewolf cell in his body!"

Worried, Walt tried to reach for his son but his wife yanked him backwards.

Suddenly, a loud roar from the front of the small crowd drew everyone's attention.

"STOP THIS!"

All of the heads including the lawyer's, snapped around in the direction the deafening noise came from.

Determinedly, I walked up the wooden steps towards the emotional woman on the front veranda.

"Look at what you're doing!" I raised my thunderous voice. "You're frightening your ten year old son!"

Guiltily, Wendy clung to the boy as her tears wetted his muscled torso.

"Look at me, Wendy." I demanded. "LOOK AT ME!"

My roar was loud enough to make the Wisetail's windows rattle.

"Kevin has no more choice in becoming one of us than we did, when we first changed. Now we all miss Kurt, your family, friends and pack alike. We all see how much you're suffering from the loss of your child. But it's no excuse to terrorize his little brother with threats of painful and useless medical procedures! The worst thing a new Lokoti Werewolf can face is hostility at their change and your reaction isn't helping your son. What he needs is acceptance, tolerance and support. To borrow the words of my husband, 'you're still a mother so drop the 'melt down' bullshit and frickin' get on with it!'"

I wasn't sure if it was working or not, but I was trying to impart my will onto her. I've never done this before, but it was like thinking really hard in a person's direction. It was difficult trying to mentally communicate with a non-telepathic person. My glowing turquoise eyes held her dark brown ones as she stared back, hypnotically.

"He needs to be trained how to cope with his new condition. Not only can the pack take him hunting and teach him to crave animal and not human, but they can teach him to defend himself. We can't protect our children from everything that can and will go wrong, but we can at least teach them to be prepared." I finished.

Everybody, including Walt, watched and waited with baited breath. Our sighs of relief were clearly audible when Wendy's arms slipped from Kevin. Sobbing, she sunk to the floor as her husband knelt beside her. He embraced his mate and held her tightly against his bare chest.

I knelt before Kevin as my turquoise eyes met his tearful red ones and I tried to give him a brave smile with my elongated teeth.

I told him, "You have red eyes, like Kurt had. But did you know that the colour of our eyes is carried down the family line? Your Wisetail ancestors like my father had glowing red eyes and my Grandpa had glowing orange eyes. My turquoise eyes come from my great, great grandfather Flint Riverclaw."

Kevin opened his mouth to reply, but all that came out was a peculiar growling which meant he couldn't talk in Werewolf form.

I tried not to laugh, "Don't worry, not all Werewolves can talk. My husband can't and it's the only peace and quiet I get."

The pack snickered at my joke as my mate emitted a dissatisfied snarl.

Tyson stepped up to lay his hand on the boy's shoulder, "Welcome, little wolf."

Since he couldn't speak, he nodded respectfully to his First.

Then Looch and Xenthe approached their friend. The three examined each other's differences; Xenthe with his white eyes, Looch with her green ones and Kevin's red eyes. Next, the Vampire held out his hands to see whose nails were longer, which Looch and Kevin's were. So he showed off his longer teeth in the form of his fangs and the other two gave him the thumbs up.

"Wendy, look around you," our new First addressed her. "Samuel Riverclaw has also changed, as has Andrew Evergreen and Joshua Lightfoot."

Walt loosened his hold on his wife so she could look on the newest members of the pack.

The other three new Lokoti Werewolves were in their early twenties. Joshua Lightfoot was Ki's son and our Medicine Man looked on him proudly. Whereas his father had glowing pink eyes, Joshua's glowing eyes were lilac coloured.

The European Werewolf pawed at the ground impatiently - *CAN WE HUNT NOW?*

"I agree, I'm starved!" Derik put up his clawed hand.

Tyson looked on Walt who remained crouched by his wife's side.

"I'll stay with Wendy, if you could take Kevin on his first hunt." He growled out.

"No Walt." I spoke up a second time. "I'll stay with Wendy so you can take him."

Everyone watched as I shrunk back into human form with my protruding stomach looking more pronounced in this shape.

"Please take care of Kevin," his mother pleaded. "He has the kindest of hearts, he's not a killer."

"Of course I will, sweetheart." Walt pulled her in for one last hug.

To allow them privacy, I went back down the veranda steps and over to my mate. Jonathan watched as I approached the huge European Werewolf in my smaller body. He couldn't hear our thoughts, all he saw were our actions.

WANT ME TO BRING YOU BACK SOMETHING? – My mate offered.

YES PLEASE – I nodded back.

Then he delivered an affectionate lick to my cheek before he turned away to supervise Soph.

Tyson roared out, "Wolves, tonight we hunt caribou!"

It was literally a case of blink and you'll miss it, as the First then the Second in the pack, leapt into the tree line of the surrounding woods.

Right behind them ran the rest of the Werewolves with the children amongst them. Walt ran last, as he raced after his son who was running with his friends. The entire pack bar one had disappeared within a matter of seconds.

I went up the veranda stairs to put a supportive arm about Wendy and I motioned to Jonathan to follow.

"He's just a ten year old boy..." she anxiously wrung her hands, "...what if more Vampires show up?"

"It'll be a few years yet before another fang head is game to step foot on our land." I promised. "Wendy, I'd like you to meet my lawyer, Jonathan Bourne. I gave him a promotion tonight and he and the huge corporation Hodge Endeavor, are going to help the police keep an eye on the Vampires."

"Oh," she looked on the well-dressed man and self-consciously she wiped her wet face then stuck out her hand. "I'm pleased to meet you."

"And you," he shook on it. "It's been quite the night for introductions."

"You're telling me!" She exhaled loudly. "Jonathan, do you have children?"

"I have two, who live with my ex-wife in the south of France," he admitted.

"For your sake, I hope they don't turn into Werewolves," she said.

"It could be worse, at least Kevin didn't turn into a Vampire." I said wryly. "He won't have to worry about food allergies, or the inability to heal without imbibing blood first. He'll continue to grow and live an almost normal life, but for hunting every full moon."

"You're referring to the Vampire boy that the pack is training?" She guessed. "You know, the one that Walt saved."

I opened the front door for her and Jonathan before walking in after them.

"Wendy, next week I'm gonna invite you over for morning tea." I thought aloud. "There's an interesting woman that I want you to meet, her name is Stella Creillaic."

~~~~~~
~~~~~~

~ 28 ~

21st September 2374

I can't say I was that surprised about the extreme manner of Susanna's birth. Maybe on a subconscious level I was even expecting it? It would make sense, if one thought of a set of scales.

Lucia was born exactly half and half, so the scales were even. But Sophia physically resembled the most like her Lokoti Werewolf mother. So fate made Susanna physically resemble the most like her European Werewolf father.

But it was the manner of her arrival that caused concern. You couldn't really blame her, she didn't mean to cause any harm. One could argue that she was only doing what was natural – or supernatural – for her nature.

The 3rd of September seemed like a typical Tuesday morning in the Sabre household. Declan had beaten me downstairs and taken the kids with him. As he cooked up a hot breakfast for his growing family, he made Looch and Soph help, to keep them out of trouble.

The girls were arguing as usual and I heard Declan raise his voice, ordering them to behave. I heard how he tried to distract them by giving them tasks to do. Soph was made to stir the pancake mix while Looch set the table.

I listened to their banter as I finished pulling my hair back into a ponytail. Then I waddled out of my bedroom and down the stairs, gripping the banister as I went. I couldn't see the steps over my gargantuan tummy.

Susanna's growth at six months was cause for concern, she was already the size of a nine month old. At my last check up, Ki advised that she would have to be induced early, to prevent trauma at giving birth to a huge baby. It was that or a caesarean, which he said he could perform in an emergency.

"Mummy!" Soph and Looch cried out at the same time as I entered the kitchen.

"Watch out, wide load comin' through." Declan joked.

Upon my arrival, he handed me a glass of freshly-squeezed orange juice along with a kiss on the cheek.

"What's for breakfast?" I asked cheerfully.

"Pancakes!" Soph held up a spoonful of pancake mix she was stirring.

"With sausages and scrambled eggs," Looch added on.

I watched as she opened a cupboard to fetch the bread and butter plates to put on the table.

I looked around for a task to do, "Is there anything I can do to help?"

All three sung out, "No!"

"You go and rest, Mummy." Soph pointed the batter-covered spoon my way.

"Yeah Mum, take a load off." Looch patted me on the tummy, on her way to the table.

"Your PA called while you were in the bathroom." Declan recited as he cooked over the stove. "She said your lecture for this Wednesday may have to be cancelled, as there's something wrong with the venue or whatever."

"What? That's weird." I paused. "The lecture is at UCLA. What, does the University only have ONE lecture theatre? Couldn't they put me in another?"

"I dunno, so don't shoot the messenger." He replied, as he simultaneously fried up the sausages in one pan while stirring the scrambled eggs in another. "Personally, I'm glad it's cancelled. You tire pretty easily now with this latest rug rat you're carrying. I'd be happy if you stayed home and napped the day away."

"Daddy, the mix is ready!" Soph carried over the bowl.

"Thanks sweetie," he was quick to take it off her.

I watched him place it onto the bench beside the stove. Then I watched him pour a little bit of the mixture into a third pan he had ready. Altogether, he was cooking up three things at once.

"Well, aren't you Superdad." I smiled in amusement. "Able to take phone messages while minding two kids and still cook three things at once."

"Damn straight," he gloated. "I'm Super Dad and Super Husband."

"Are you sure about that?" I asked playfully.

"Does my wife have any complaints?"

"Nope," I grinned like an idiot.

"I should hope not!" He chuckled, before patting my large tummy. "If I was doing something wrong, you wouldn't have been impregnated three times now."

It was then we realized we had an audience when Sophia chimed in from behind us.

"Daddy, what's 'impregnate'?"

Looch giggled as she finished setting the table and she came back into the kitchen to watch.

"Er..." the parents squirmed before her Dad asked diplomatically, "...well, you know what the word pregnant means, don't you?"

"Yeah, Mummy is pregnant because Susanna is inside of her." She recited what we'd told her.

"So 'impregnate' means to become pregnant." Declan said simply, as he returned his attention to the stove.

But Soph wouldn't be so easily dissuaded, "Then how come it matters if you do something wrong or not, if Mummy becomes pregnant?"

Her father, mother and sister cracked up laughing which she didn't like. Her face hardened in anger as it reddened in embarrassment. It looked like one of her tantrums were coming, so her sister thought she should help.

"Dad impregnated Mum, so that's why Mum is pregnant with Susanna." She volunteered.

"Shut up, Lucia!" Her sister fired up. "You're lying! Daddy can't put Susanna inside of Mummy! Susanna's too big!"

"She wasn't at the time," Declan muttered, as he stirred the scrambled eggs.

It was either perfectly timed or perhaps horrifically timed, that our little family moment was shattered. This warm reality instantly switched to a cold surreality within a matter of seconds...

...I remember turning away from Declan to speak to Sophia directly, to offer her reassurance that this was boring 'adult stuff' and therefore uninteresting to her. I was holding my half-drunk glass of OJ in my hand, with the taste still in my mouth. Then time seemed to slow down to an excruciatingly slow pace...

...I was in the midst of turning my upper body, when the most hideous tearing sensation filled my abdomen. It made me lower my eyes to see, as Declan also looked down at my tummy, as if he heard the tearing noise. My stomach which was already bulging, abruptly expanded to twice its size!

Simultaneously, the skin on my abdomen stretched and bloodied tear marks appeared, while inside I felt more tissue get torn apart.

Agonizing blotches of pain erupted inside of me, as I literally felt several of my organs get squashed! Coupled with the tearing, I swear I felt a kind of squishing as well as a sloshing sensation. It felt as if my squashed organs had blood squelching out of them.

It was then that everything turned surreal...I was standing still, but my balance began to waver. It was like I couldn't see or hear properly, as if everything seemed far away. Vaguely, I heard Declan start to yell, but it took a moment to work out what he was saying.

"B...? B! Oh shit, she's expanded inside of you! She's changed into her Werewolf body inside of your body! Oh shit! Oh no B, no...!"

I think I heard Sophia and Lucia cry out for their Mummy, as their eyes filled with frightened tears.

It was then that my knees gave out and I started to sink to the floor, whilst still clutching onto the glass of orange juice. By this stage the glass was trembling in my hand, spilling juice all over the place. As I came to kneel on the kitchen tiles, I looked down at the orange liquid when I also saw red spots of blood.

"Lucia!" Her father yelled. "Pick up your sister! Go to the Wisetail's! Go! Run to the Wisetail's and stay there!"

In the corner of my eye, I saw my ten year old daughter pick up her five year old sister and bolt out of the house. I heard the front door open and close and her footsteps disappear down the gravel drive. Then my husband took over my field of vision as he crouched down on the floor before me.

I came to realize I was slumped against the bottom cabinet doors, clutching onto the handle of a cupboard in one hand and still hanging onto that juice with the other. Declan removed the glass from my hand before he cupped my face, to make me look on him. I saw his eyes were watering and he looked scared, but for some reason I couldn't hear him properly. His mouth was moving, but I only caught every second or third word he said.

But the both of our eyes were diverted when my extra large stomach began to move! With her amniotic sack torn, Susanna in her Werewolf form began to struggle inside. I sensed she was in as great distress as I was, even if she was the one who had inadvertently caused it.

Declan pulled up my t-shirt and pushed down the top of my maternity jeans. I heard him gasp when we both saw the bloodied stretch marks over my hideously huge stomach. This, coupled with Susanna moving around underneath, it was as if an alien could pop out at any minute!

The really strange thing about all of this was my brain seemed to have shut down. I think that's why I couldn't see or hear or think properly. It was like the extreme and horrific torture of having your insides crushed; had switched off my senses, so I couldn't register anything properly. Perhaps it was to protect my sanity from the unbelievable amount of agony? But there sure was a lot of blood, the legs of my jeans felt wet because of it.

"...Ki is on his way, but he was in Fairbanks when I called him. He'll be here in half an hour. But Walt and Tyson are coming. Stay with me, B! C'mon just drink my blood and you'll get through this! Drink my blood and you can make it until Ki comes..."

Declan's voice started to register and it occurred to me that he'd been talking this whole time. My eyes darted away from my bloodied clothes, to see his bloodied wrist hovering in front of my face. He pressed it against my lips, but I didn't feel it. It was as if all of me had turned numb. The only things I were aware of was my hand holding onto the cupboard handle, my clothes were wet with blood and that Susanna was writhing inside of me.

I sensed her turmoil as she struggled. She was in danger since the placenta that was responsible for her food and oxygen was torn. She could die! This single thought overtook my brain and it triggered me to act.

"...Declan...?"

"B?" He instantly moved his wrist away to hear me speak.

"...cut her out, Declan..."

"Huh?"

"...cut Susanna out, she's in trouble..."

"She's the least of my worries, B! Let's worry about you right now."

"...cut her out Declan, cut Susanna out of me..."

"Just drink my blood! Ki will be here in half an hour! He's gunning down the highway in his hover-car now."

"...cut her out Declan, cut her out of me now..."

"Just hold on, B! Drink my blood and build up your strength and hold on. My blood will help you."

"...cut her out of me, Declan..."

"B, you don't know what you're saying! Ki isn't here yet but he's on his way. Just drink my blood and build up your strength so we can wait for him."

"...Declan, please...!" My wide eyes met his tearful ones. "Cut her out of me! Now! Cut her out of me."

Then he heard me whimper the same time as my torn stomach lurched this way and that, with Susanna's strong movements.

Slowly, his hand reached up to the cutlery draw and he pulled out a sharp, stainless steel knife. He looked murderously on my stomach, which made my heart race. I realized he was going to follow through with my request but not to save the baby, but to save his beloved B instead.

As quick as lightening, my hand sprung up and grabbed the front of his shirt.

I spoke in desperation, "It's not her fault! It's not! She didn't deliberately harm me!"

A low, threatening growl came out between his bared teeth, as he looked on my stomach in pure hatred.

"Declan!" I gasped. "Save the baby and you'll save your mate!"

And that was it...that was where the last of my strength ended.

My hand dropped from his shirt the same time as my other hand holding onto the cupboard did. My head drooped forwards as my vision clouded over. My heart rate slowed as my pulse felt fainter and fainter.

"B...? B!" Distantly, I heard Declan's sobbing. "Stay with me, B! Stay with me! Noooo! B!! B!!"

Another moment passed as he hesitated. I think his hand holding the knife was shaking badly too. With my fuzzy vision, I saw a flash of steel, as my crying husband stuck his wife with the blade.

With one hand holding up my bleeding baby bulge, his other ran the said blade across the front of my hips. Then I heard the clang of the bloodied knife hit the tiled floor when he dropped it. Using both of his hands, he reached forward and they disappeared inside my stomach. I watched them find what they were looking for, grab hold and give a strong tug.

I felt Susanna's hefty weight leave my body, as a bloodied, folded up creature dropped onto the already bloodied floor. I heard a small growling noise, as the creature unfolded itself. I made out a small snout, over rows of tiny razor-sharp teeth, along with four tiny claws. Quickly and a little carelessly, Declan discarded the last remains of the amniotic sack from her. Then Susanna opened her glowing green eyes and looked up at her father and saviour.

Declan left her lying curled up on the tiled floor as he reached for me. My clouded vision changed again as I felt a new sensation. I felt my back was against something hard and my eyes were fixated on a bright light. Then I realized that I was lying on the kitchen floor and that the bright light was the ceiling light.

My husband's distraught face blocked it as it loomed over mine. His hot tears trickled down his cheeks and landed on my face. I felt something part my lips and next, a familiar, warm, liquid pool inside my mouth. I realized Declan was feeding me his blood.

I started to feel cold but I didn't have the strength to shiver. With the absence of Susanna's weight, my body also missed her excessive heat. There was a strange background noise in the back of my mind, which sounded like static. Now, looking back, I realized that the static which was interfering with my perception was pain; excruciating, agonizing, unbelievable pain.

"Stay with me stay with me stay with me stay with me stay with me stay with me stay with me stay with me stay with me."

Declan's chanting was the last thing I heard as my eyes drifted shut and everything went dark...

...

...light, a bright, cold, sterile light. It wasn't warm or encompassing like in the stories of near-death experiences. It wasn't as welcoming as I remembered when I visited the space time continuum, after I was shot in the head. It was just a bright, cold, sterile fluorescent light attached to a cold, sterile, white ceiling.

I was able to move my hands and I felt myself lying on a padded surface. I didn't have much strength and I was still feeling light headed, but I managed to roll my head sideways. I found myself lying in a small, sterile, white room with a couple of computers nearby. On screen were my vital signs, such as my heart rate, blood pressure, temperature and whatever else.

Where am I? This place no only looked sterile and felt sterile, it smelled sterile. I think – I think – I think this may be a hospital room that I was in?

I'm in an actual hospital?! I've never been to hospital before, except to visit sick humans. Werewolves couldn't risk being scanned by doctors or nurses, or our supernatural natures would be discovered. So what am I doing in a place like this?

I was able raise my head for a moment, to see myself lying on a white mattress with a thin, white, gauze-like sheet resting over my naked body. I saw an IV connected to my wrist, as well as several other tubes attached to my abdomen, which was wrapped up in rounds of medical tape. However, my stomach was back to its normal size, so maybe Declan's blood did the trick?

Speak of the devil, I saw him standing in the room. His back was turned with his arms folded in front, as he stood by a window. He was staring outside, at what I know not. His clothes had dried blood on them, which from the smell of it, I think it was mine.

I think he heard me move and when he turned around, I saw his face was pale and wet, which made his red eyes and nose stand out.

"B? No, don't move!"

Giddily, I tried to sit up but he was quick to come to my side and hold me still. Puzzled, I looked up into his tearful eyes. I had so many questions that needed answers, especially why I was here?

"You've had two operations," he began. "You're scheduled for a third this afternoon, which will be your last. But you can't move, as they had to artificially inflate your repaired organs. That's why there are tubes sticking into your stomach."

I opened my mouth to ask him how Susanna was, but my mouth and throat were so dry, nothing came out.

"Shhh..." he leaned in to place several soft kisses on my forehead, "...it's alright B, everything's gonna be OK."

So I communicated with him via another method.

SUSANNA? – I asked with my mind - *WHERE IS SHE?*

"Back on tribal lands with Ki," he said stiffly. "The Lightfoot's are looking after her while girls are staying with the Wisetail's."

WHERE AM I?

"The Hodge Endeavor Hospital in Anchorage," he said.

BUT ISN'T THAT RISKY?

"Funny you should say that," he scoffed. "But when I weighed my options and the other choice was a dead wife? I thought I'd take a gamble."

Declan looked worn out, emotionally and physically, so I didn't take his bad attitude personally. Next, he emitted a heavy sigh as if he were inwardly chastising himself. Then he sat on the side of my bed so he could be close, as his hand stroked my hair.

He continued, "Don't worry, your buddy Jonathan Bourne is overseeing everything. As I understand it, everyone's been paid to keep their traps shut and just do their jobs. Besides, if anyone does end up blabbing, I'll take care of them myself."

WHY DIDN'T KI TREAT ME?

"Because your insides were soup!" He snapped. "Ki didn't have the right medical equipment to treat your obliterated organs! He said we didn't have a choice but to bring you here. So I called Jonathan Bourne to organize the hospital staff's confidentiality before I instantaneously phased you here."

BUT WHAT ABOUT YOUR BLOOD, COULDN'T IT HEAL ME?

"My blood kept you alive," he muttered unhappily. "I gave you as much as I could in the kitchen, then Ki shared his during your first operation. Tyson stepped up to share his blood during your second op. The doctors wanted to give you artificial blood, but Ki stopped them. No wonder humans don't have half our strength with their artificial food and their artificial blood!"

WHAT ABOUT SUSANNA, IS SHE OK?

I watched his whole demeanour turn cold, "She's alive and let's leave it at that."

I didn't like his attitude towards our newborn and if I'd the strength, I would've shuddered. I've seen this iciness in his eyes before, usually when he deemed someone had to die. It was the same expression he wore when he interrogated the European Vampire in the cave, or he killed the European Werewolves in St Petersburg, or even with the Voodoo Witch Doctors in New Orleans.

DECLAN, IT'S NOT HER FAULT – I began but he cut me off.

"Not her fault?" He laughed in an incredulous manner. "It's NOT her fault?! B, do you know what this third op is for? To rebuild your intestines, bowel and bladder! Thanks to our youngest, there's a chance you may have to use colostomy bags for the rest of your mortal existence!"

Oh oh...my heart raced in fear at his attitude towards our newborn. He blamed Susanna for harming her mother just as he blamed himself for putting her there. His past feelings of self-hatred exploded into our present. Declan almost wiped his species out all but one – himself – when they made an attack on his mate. Today, I saw the same cold, hard, resolution written on his face again.

The computer showing my heart beat began to beep, showing a sharp rise in my heart rate. This caught his attention, as he looked from the monitor to his frightened wife.

"Look B, don't get overexcited." He sighed wearily. "Right now, I need you to rest and take it easy."

PLEASE DON'T BLAME THE BABY FOR THIS – I pleaded – *PROMISE ME YOU WON'T DO ANYTHING STUPID.*

"Oh you mean besides knock up my wife a third time and push our luck too far, by having a child that's the most like me?" He said bitterly.

DECLAN PLEASE – I began to falter – *DON'T MAKE ME FEEL AFRAID OF WHAT WILL HAPPEN IF I FALL ASLEEP!*

"Close your eyes and get some rest." He continued to stroke my hair. "I'm gonna share my blood with you again during your last operation. So the next time you open your eyes, hopefully you'll be fully regenerated."

DECLAN... PLEASE PROMISE ME!

"Go to sleep, B." He leaned in to tenderly run his lips over my forehead in several soft kisses. "It's bedtime for all female Werewolves in the room."

Damn him to hell, he knows I'm too weak to fight him on this! So what does he do? He encourages my clouded mind to slip back into unconsciousness. Futilely, I struggled in the darkness as I groped around for some kind of switch to turn my consciousness back on again...

...

...ah ha, there it is! The blackness turned into a kind of greyness, as a dim light slowly filled my mind. I was still feeling groggy, which must have been the drugs in my system. It was an effort to even open my eyelids.

"Aunt B, can you hear me? If you can hear me, squeeze my hand." Ki's voice sounded close by.

I rolled my head towards the source of the noise as I blinked and blinked again. A blurry figure sitting by the side of my bed slowly came into focus. To my relief, I saw it was indeed our Medicine Man. I stared up into his tired face, which broke into a grin when he realized I was lucid.

"Welcome back to the land of the living," he greeted in good humour.

"D – D – Declan?" I managed out.

He nodded in a particular direction and weakly I turned my head to see my husband still in his bloodied clothes, slumbering away in a chair nearby.

I croaked out, "Have I had the third operation?"

"Yes and it was a resounding success." He reassured. "When the surgeons opened you up a third time, low and behold they found their patient is healing much faster than expected. Your artificially inflated organs had regenerated and they put in synthetic parts for those that were damaged beyond repair."

"Susanna..." my voice cracked, "...where's she?"

Ki filled a cup with water from a jug that was sitting on the bedside table and he slowly fed it to his patient.

"She's staying with Jenny and I while Looch and Soph are with the Wisetail's."

"How many days have I been out?" I wondered.

"You've been here at the hospital for five days now." He advised. When he saw me look in Declan's direction he added on, "Look at the old fool. He hasn't left your side since the accident. He almost bled himself dry by sharing his blood with you twice. I think it's pure will power that's holding him up, as he's determined to play bodyguard for you."

"Take him home and put him to bed."

"Yes, that would be the correct course of action, wouldn't it? But the problem is your husband is the able-bodied Circulator at the moment, so it's up to him whether we go to and fro. He's been instantaneously phasing you, me and even Tyson, between the hospital and tribal lands. Not even our new First is game to try to order his Second to get some rest, especially after the growling he gave Jonathan Bourne."

"Hmm?" I looked on, quizzically.

"When your husband called your lawyer to organize your treatment, quote unquote; 'trust me if she dies, so does the company when I disband it, pull it apart and sell it off piece by piece! If B lives then so do your cushy jobs!'"

"Really?" I almost laughed, but my abdomen hurt too much.

He went on, "Thanks to that phone call, the hospital's best and brightest were ready and waiting when we instantaneously phased you here. Jonathan Bourne even flew in from London and is staying in Anchorage's finest hotel, as he monitors your recovery and the confidentiality of the hospital staff."

I believed that too, I knew the lawyer had grown quite accustomed to his comfortable living. The idea of taking away his livelihood certainly would have frightened him into acting on Declan's demands. To protect his bank balance he had to protect his employer. Also, I don't think he wanted to step down as the Head Chairman of one of the most powerful companies on Earth.

I took a deep breath and released it, before raising my head to look down at myself. The thin, white, gauze-like sheet was replaced by a grey hospital gown. There was still an IV attached to my wrist, but the tubes sticking into my stomach had gone.

"Have I healed?" I queried.

"Mostly," he promised. "The majority of your organs were repaired and your regenerative ability is working overtime, to heal you completely. But we're going to have to take small steps on your road to recovery."

"What do you mean?" I asked, worriedly.

"Today we'll start you on fluids," he implied the cup of water in his hand. "In about a week's time, we'll let you have soups. In a month's time if your new digestive system is coping, you can try eating soft food."

"A month?" I echoed in horror.

"Aunt B, not even 24th Century medicine can work miracles." He said wryly. "You had to be given artificial intestines, bladder and bowel. Not to alarm you since you're now on the road to recovery, but five days ago when we first brought you in here, I warned your husband to prepare for the worst."

"Say what?" My mouth fell open. "That's not supposed to ALARM me?!"

Just then we were interrupted by a third person entering the conversation when Declan said grouchily:

"He's got a pathetic bedside manner for a Healer, hasn't he?"

I watched him yawn as he sat upright from his slouched position while opening his sleepy eyes.

"Then what happened?" I fretted. "Tell me everything."

Ki recanted, "When I arrived at your house and found you on the kitchen floor, Uncle Dec was sharing his blood with you. It's what kept you alive. Tyson and Walt were there, they were looking after Susanna. Walt cleaned her up and Tyson wrapped her in a blanket. I took one look at you and told your husband that this was past my expertise, you required intensive care. Uncle Dec immediately called Jonathan Bourne and threatened him into preparing a hospital for us. I held onto Declan's arm as he carried you and he instantaneously phased the three of us into the operating room. There was a medical staff waiting for you and instantly they went to work. When I took your husband outside to the Waiting Room, I promised I'd stay in the operating theatre, to offer my advice on treating Werewolves. As they operated and I observed, my blood was given to you intravenously."

Declan stood up from the chair and he moved so slowly, I saw exhaustion was written all over him. Wearily, he shuffled over to our position and came to collapse on the other side of my bed. His eyes looked bloodshot which stood out against his pallor.

"I stood and watched through the window while they worked on you," he said.

"Mine, Tyson's and Declan's blood was given to you intravenously during the three operations." Ki went on. "The first operation stabilized you. The second operation began the repair work. Now with the third op completed, you're not just a female Lokoti Werewolf or Circulator anymore, but you can also be called the 'Bionic Woman'. You have artificial parts for the organs which were damaged beyond repair."

"Like my intestines, bladder and bowel." I said unhappily.

Ki said awkwardly, "And there are other parts of you that didn't regenerate but the doctors couldn't give you artificial parts for those."

"And that is...?" I asked anxiously.

"Your womb was a mess," he spoke frankly. "Basically your reproductive organs like your ovaries and fallopian tubes no longer exist. I'm afraid you won't be able to become pregnant again."

My stomach shrank at this piece of news as I stared up at the ceiling while my eyes filled with tears.

I said quietly, "So that's how the timeline stops me from reproducing after baby number three."

Then I closed my eyes and took several laboured breaths as I tried not to cry. I'm barren again. After ten wonderful years of feeling like a fertile woman and creating life, it's been taken away from me a second time.

"Hey, c'mon now," my husband squeezed my hand. "Now is NOT the time to be cursing over the little things. You're alive B, you hear me? You're ALIVE! Five days ago, I was scared I'd lost you."

"But I'm barren again, Declan!" I let out a loud sob. "I can't have anymore of your children!"

"Hey..." he leaned over to hold me carefully, "...right now, after all the trouble this reproducing business has caused? It's a blessing, trust me!"

"But I don't even have ovaries anymore! I'm a hen that doesn't produce any eggs! I'm not even a proper woman!" I cried.

"Hey, stop that!" He growled out. "We always knew we were going to have three daughters, like you saw in your vision. You only just made it out alive with this last pregnancy. So if you even think about whining again about being unable to conceive, I'm gonna go out and break something!"

Tearfully, I let out a laugh as he bent his head to rub my wet face with his.

"You and Susanna are both well." Ki pointed out. "Considering your circumstances, I'd say you're both very lucky to be alive. Don't forget even female European Werewolves have died the same way you almost did."

Upon hearing Susanna's name, Declan turned his face away but not before I saw the look of cold hatred he tried to hide.

"Ki, what's Susanna like?" I asked, interested.

"She's the most different kind of baby we've ever had to care for, but she's healthy."

"Is she still in her European Werewolf body?" I guessed.

"She is, which makes putting a diaper on her rather a challenge," he chuckled. "But she's stronger in her Werewolf form. If a human baby was born three months premature, it may have to go into a humidicrib. But not your daughter, she's sleeping soundly in our old cot we brought down from the attic and we're feeding her formula."

"Really?" I brightened. "She's doing well then?"

"Susanna will be as right as rain," he promised. "I'm not sure when she'll shrink back into her human body, but for now it's safest for her to remain in Werewolf form."

"I should be with her," I tried to get up, but I was stopped via two ways.

Firstly, pain hit me with the force of a bowling ball landing on my stomach. Secondly, both Ki and Declan put out their hands to gently push me back down onto the bed. I gasped at the amount of agony that the small action created.

"Frickin' hell B," my mate swore in annoyance. "Give your repaired organs time to heal, why don't you?"

"Right now, Susanna is doing better than you are." Ki said sternly. "You need to remain in hospital under observation, to ensure your body doesn't reject your artificial implants. Maybe in another week you'll be released, but you'll be bed bound for a fortnight with strict instructions of no strenuous activity."

"So this means no home schooling, no lecturing, no researching and completely leaving the kids to me." Declan glared.

"But won't Susanna need to be breastfed?" I wondered aloud.

Again, Declan looked away in irritation at the mention of her name whereas Ki looked serious.

"No, your breasts aren't lactating properly, Aunt B." He advised. "After the trauma your body's been through, it's best to leave Susanna on formula."

Then my husband addressed our Medicine Man, "Maybe Susanna should stay with you and Jenny until B is all better?"

"Do you mean for the next month?" He sounded surprised. "Er, I could check with Jenny to see if that's OK -"

But I interrupted, "No Declan, Susanna comes home when I come home!"

"B, you're not well enough to take care of yourself let alone a newborn!" He argued back. "My main concern is getting you back on your feet!"

"Is that really your concern?" I asked knowingly. "Or do you still blame our newborn for me ending up like this?"

"Of course it's her fault that you're like this!" He rebuked.

"So she's struck out of the house, is that it?" My eyes narrowed. "Declan you can't blame a newborn -"

"A newborn European Werewolf?" He cut in. "If this kid is already out to kill her mother, what else is she going to be capable of?"

"Uncle Declan," our Healer spoke up, "the last couple of days I've been watching Susanna closely. She hasn't made any threatening overtures towards Jenny or myself. In fact, she growls affectionately when we hold her and she even keeps her claws to herself."

"Awww...really?" I melted upon hearing his description of my daughter. "What does she look like, Ki?"

"She looks just like Uncle Declan does in European Werewolf form, even down to the same colour of her hide." He smiled. "I think she'll have his blonde hair when she reverts to human form."

"Ooooh I can't wait to see her!" I grabbed hold of my husband's arm.

"Yeah, isn't she just peachy?" Declan muttered, as he looked away in dissatisfaction.

Ki cast a wary look over my dangerous mate, "Maybe Susanna should stay with Jenny and I, until Aunt B is well enough to look after her."

Before I could disagree, my husband said coolly, "I think that's a good idea."

"What? Wait a minute here! No!" I objected loudly, before flinching at the pain my exertion caused. I took a deep breath before I spoke in a calmer manner, "Susanna belongs at home with her family."

"Normally, I'd agree with you Aunt B but in this case..." our Medicine Man looked uncomfortable, "...it might be a good idea for Susanna to stay with us until you're on your feet again. Of course I'll bring her over for visits."

"That's not necessary," my mate said coldly.

Immediately, my hand whacked him on his larger arm, which probably caused me more pain than him.

The two men saw me flinch again as any kind of movement set off sparks of agony in my abdominal area.

"B, you should be taking it easy," my husband berated. "Beating up your husband is called a 'strenuous activity', which our Medicine Man is advising against right now."

"Declan please stop this..." I dissolved into another set of tears, "...please don't blame Susanna for what happened to me."

"Shhh," he leaned over to place a kiss on the end of my nose, "it's time for all female Werewolves in the room to go back to sleep."

Awkwardly, Ki stood up from his chair by the bed to walk a little way away. I saw the frown on his face as he looked from the couple in the room, to the window. He was contemplating something, although I know not what.

"Catch some Zzz's B and so will I." Declan pulled his chair closer to my bed. Then he sat back into the seat whilst putting his feet up on the end of my bed. "How about everybody just catches some Zzz's?"

Our Medicine Man turned back around, "Before you get too comfortable Uncle, I'll ask that you take me home."

"There's always one, isn't there?" He grumbled, as he reluctantly clambered back to his feet.

"Go home and shower and change." I ordered. "You look like crap."

"Thanks B," he snickered at my bluntness.

"And Ki, you'll look after Susanna, won't you?" I called to him. "I mean, you won't let anything happen to her, will you?"

Although our Healer didn't look at my husband, he understood my meaning.

"Susanna will remain safe until the day I bring her home to you," he said solemnly.

"Oh yeah, you guys are real subtle," my mate rolled his eyes.

I watched Declan cross over to Ki's side and as soon as his hand touched the other man's arm, they disappeared in a bright flash of light. He instantaneously phased our Medicine Man back to tribal lands before you could say the words, 'instantaneously phase'. With their departure, a pervading sense of fear and helplessness overtook me, as I lay incapacitated on the hospital bed.

The majority of my mind was scoffing, 'nah, Declan wouldn't hurt his children' however, there was a minority of concerns whispering, 'careful'. I knew he'd never harm Looch or Soph, but then again they didn't resemble pure-blooded European Werewolves.

My husband's opinion of Susanna was the same he had of Leo, Michelle and Marcus. In his eyes, the three had been a menace to society as well as to his mate, which he felt responsible to remove. To ensure Susanna's safety, I'd have to change Declan's views of her... but how? I remained awake over the next twenty minutes as I stewed over this.

That was until I was interrupted by a bright flash of light, from my mate instantaneously phasing back into the hospital room. He smelled soapy from having a shower and was wearing clean clothes. He was also holding onto a Tupperware container full of leftover lasagne he'd taken out of the freezer. Casually, he sat in the seat beside my bed, put his feet up and proceeded to eat his heated-up meal with a fork.

He noticed I was watching him and felt obliged to apologise, "I would offer you some, but apparently you can't eat solids for the next month."

"I'm not hungry." I looked up at the ceiling. "You should be eating that at home."

"Hey, I showered and changed just as you requested," he said coolly.

"I wanted you to stay home and eat and get some rest."

"I'll stay home and rest when you can stay home and rest." He replied between mouthfuls.

"How are Looch and Soph?" I asked next. "Have you seen them?"

"They're fine I guess." He shrugged. "Wendy and Walt are looking after them, so of course they're gonna be OK."

"But you haven't seen them?" I asked, concerned.

"B, look around you." He said in annoyance. "You're a Werewolf in a 24th Century hospital, where the medical staff are aware of your supernatural state. On top of that, you're in a strange city with leeches like Jonathan Bourne secretly hoping you'll die, so he can get his hands on Hodge Endeavor. When I showered, changed and heated up some dinner, it was the first time I'd been home since I brought you here."

I let out a weary sigh at his continued scepticism, "If Jonathan Bourne couldn't be trusted, the Mainframe would have fired him by now."

"No B," he said pointedly, "I made Jonathan Bourne help us by threatening to fire him."

The pain in my abdomen was building up to the point of agony. My eyes filled with tears again as my breathing became laboured. My husband noticed my torment with his keen Werewolf senses, which made him sit upright in alarm.

"Are you in pain?" He guessed. "I'll go and get a doctor."

Declan jumped to his feet and bolted out of the automatic door to my room, as he went on a mission of 'fetch'.

*****

To everyone's surprise and especially for the hospital staff, I had a fourth operation. My body not only rejected the artificial intestines, bladder and bowel, but grew new ones. The doctors were left scratching their heads in befuddlement at the power of our regeneration.

This time it was Walt who was the willing blood donor. He sat by my side in the operating theatre in his Werewolf form, so he wouldn't pass out from blood loss. The topless, muscled, Native Alaskan man was connected to the unconscious woman on the operating table, intravenously. The long, plastic tube fed his life-giving liquid via needles in our arms. When the operation was over, Walt put his injured arm in his mouth. His elongated teeth and claws made the hospital staff nervous, but it didn't stop their amazement when he removed his arm and the hole the thick needle had left, had healed over.

On the tenth day of my stay, the hospital's top doctor came to give his medical verdict before discharging his patient.

I was sitting upright in bed with Declan sitting beside, holding my hand. Ki stood on the other side of the bed along with Jonathan Bourne. The four of us were watching a holographic, 3-D representation, of an ultrasound of my body. The physician narrated what we were seeing and although he must have given hundreds of diagnosis in the past, it had never been to a patient like myself.

"As you can see you've almost completely healed," he had to swallow his disbelief. "Your body has repaired almost all of the damaged tissue and you've healed in less time than I've ever thought possible."

"It's a combination of Aunt B's regenerative ability as well as our own, when we shared our blood with her." Ki said simply to the outsider.

"And can all Werewolves do this?" The doctor enquired.

"Most breeds can," he said smoothly.

"Er, do you mean there's more than one breed of Werewolf?"

"Humans differ physiologically and so do we," our Healer replied.

"Good point," the doctor looked impressed.

Then my lawyer said staunchly, "The supernatural differences of my clients compared to the others of their kind, are on a need to know basis. Since my employer is on the mend, you don't need to know anymore than that."

However, the physician wasn't dissuaded, "You know, this makes fascinating evidence that not only does the supernatural exist, but are such amazing healers. If we examined your regenerative capabilities, it could be beneficial for all mankind."

"You want to spread my genes around?" Declan growled out, allowing his blue eyes to glow green. "You want to turn more humans into creatures like me?"

The doctor took a step back, "Oh er, perhaps not."

"You will not carry out any research, nor publicize any findings of my client's nature." Jonathan went into prosecution mode. "Need I remind you of the legally binding 'patient confidentiality', as well as the additional confidentiality agreement I had you sign before the patient was admitted? If I even see in a small tabloid website about supernatural creatures existing in Alaska, you and the rest of your staff will be sued for breaking the Gag Order."

The doctor cleared his throat which showed his unease as our Healer looked on sympathetically.

"I'm sure the physician was just curious as he's always looking for a way to further medicine to help all mankind." Ki said understandingly.

However, as I stared at the holographic 3D picture of my innards, my mind was elsewhere.

"Hang on," I pointed at the lower area of my body, "have my ovaries grown back too?"

"Excuse me?" The doctor turned back my way. "Erm no, they haven't. Your reproductive organs are the only part of your body that hasn't regenerated."

"But why?" I whined.

Declan rolled his glowing green eyes, "Come off it, B!"

"I think I have an answer to this," Ki put up his hand. "Your body is deliberately not regenerating your reproductive organs, to stop this from happening again. Just as a male Lokoti Werewolf's semen levels drop to stop them from impregnating their mates, your body isn't going to produce any more eggs."

"It makes sense," my husband shrugged.

"Your bodies can actually shut down your reproductive organs, instead of getting a vasectomy or something as such?" The doctor asked, amazed.

“This information is irrelevant to treating my client’s injuries.” Jonathan interjected.

But Ki answered, “If a male Lokoti Werewolf senses that having further children will endanger their mate, their bodies will stop reproducing.”

The human wondered aloud, “Then why don’t you go off and impregnate another woman who can give you more children?”

“Other breeds of Werewolves may be like that, but not the Lokoti Werewolf.” Ki’s voice hardened.

“Then what would happen if you ended up with a sterile female who can’t reproduce?” He gave a peculiar look.

“Just as our bodies can stop reproduction, our semen is also potent in fertilizing the female who may have reproductive difficulties.” Ki explained. “If there is some kind of ovary to work with, a union between a Lokoti Werewolf and mate has hardly ever been a childless one.”

“Except now I don’t have an ovary to work with.” I said dismally.

“Would you quit whining?” Declan retorted. “Besides, our union isn’t childless! We’ve got two kids waiting for us at home.”

“Three kids!” I said sharply.

“Yeah right...three,” he looked away in hatred once more.

Then I turned to the Medicine Man, “My union with Grant was childless.”

“You just had to bring up THAT guy again, didn’t you?” Declan stood up from the bed.

“I did say ‘hardly ever’, Aunt B,” he gently corrected. “Yours, Grant’s and Declan’s situation is a unique one. Your union with another Lokoti Werewolf may not have produced offspring, but you remain the first Lokoti Werewolf in history that’s taken a second mate.”

“Hey!” The European Werewolf roared. “I was B’s FIRST mate! We were involved BEFORE she married Grant!”

Ki held up his hands in surrender, “I never said otherwise, Uncle.”

“Good because Grant was her second mate, not me!” He fired up.

The doctor watched our bickering disconcerted, before he turned to our Medicine Man.

“I don’t think it’s safe to discharge the patient in this kind of hostile environment.” He said seriously. “She needs complete rest without agitation.”

Ki promised him, “Trust me, this is a quiet day for them.”

My husband glared at the human doctor as he marched over to swoop up his wife into his arms.

Impatiently, he snapped, “Ki are you coming or do you wanna hitch-hike back to tribal lands?”

I wrapped my arms about my mate’s strong neck as our Medicine Man left the doctor’s position to come to ours instead.

"You could hitch-hike you know." I said wryly. "With your long, shiny, dark hair, I'm sure you'd be the belle of the ball to many a lonely trucker."

Although Declan snickered at my joke, Ki looked mortified. He marched over to our position and slapped his hand on my mate's large shoulder. He gave us both an indignant look.

"Just take me home, you terrible two!"

The able-bodied Circulator said, "Please stow your hand luggage securely and place your tray tables in their upright position. You will notice the 'seat belt' sign is on which means you must remain in your seats, until the sign is switched off. It's a comfortable 17° Celsius on Lokoti Tribal Lands today. Thank you for travelling 'Air Declan' and we hope that you enjoy your flight."

Before our shocked witnesses, the three of us disappeared in a bright flash of light, as we instantaneously phased home.

The doctor and lawyer shivered as the temperature in the room dropped and the hairs on the back of their necks stood on end.

"I didn't know Werewolves could teleport," the physician said confused.

"Werewolves can't," the lawyer answered.

"So they're not just Werewolves then?"

"Like I said Dr. Musgrave, you don't need to know anything further in treating my client." Jonathan said coolly. "Now that my employer is on the mend, you can dismiss any further thoughts on the matter."

"They didn't even sign the release forms," the doctor grumbled under his breath, as he turned off the holographic projection.

"I have the authority to sign those," the lawyer volunteered. "Your bonuses will be paid at the end of the week. I suggest you and your medical team simply enjoy the extra credits which will be paid on top of your usual salaries."

Then the lawyer followed the physician out of the room as the man in the more expensive clothing oversaw everything.

*****

~ 29 ~

Instantaneously phasing between destinations may look like two bright flashes of light, departing from one place and arriving in another; but to the travellers it was only one. In a blinding flash of brilliance and a brief feeling like you were floating; the hospital room disappeared and our master bedroom reappeared. Just like that, we were back home on Lokoti Tribal Lands.

Immediately, Ki let go of Declan's shoulder and stepped back. My husband carried me over to our king-sized bed and carefully laid me out. He acted quickly, pulling down the covers then tugging them back up to tuck me in. He even fluffed up the pillows before gently pushing me back into their softness.

As if to make sure his patient survived this unusual mode of transport, Ki took out his medical scanner from his 'medicine bundle' he'd been carrying. He waved it over the injured woman once before checking the readouts. My mate looked on expectantly as our Medicine Man announced the results.

"All good," he declared. "Her vital organs and secondary systems remain repaired." This made Declan pass a peculiar look his way, which made Ki give a bashful grin. "Sorry, with all those computers inside the technologically advanced hospital, I forgot myself."

"Get out of my house," my husband said.

"OK," he raised his eyebrows.

Hastily, he packed up his things and prepared to leave.

"Wait!" I called out. "What about Susanna?"

"Not now, B!" My mate growled. "Let's get you back on your feet, first."

But Ki promised, "I'll bring your daughter over tomorrow morning for a visit."

"No, I wanna see her now!" I demanded.

"NOT NOW B!" The European Werewolf roared, making his wife and Medicine Man jump in fright. Then he dropped his voice, "First things first, let's get you a hundred percent better then you can concentrate on being a mother again."

I looked away from my mate who was walking on the crazy side of the fence and over to our Healer.

"I'll bring your daughter to you tomorrow morning," he repeated.

After casting one last wary look at my husband, he gave me a nod and departed from the house.

My eyes welled with helpless tears as I watched him go. As soon as he'd left, my husband sat on the side of the bed to soothingly smooth back my hair. His large hand brushed back any stray hairs from my face as he gazed concerned at his wife in the hospital gown.

"How about you have a nap while I prepare a soup for lunch." He recommended. "What do you feel like, pumpkin, chicken or tomato?"

However, I didn't answer, as I sat there and tearfully glared at him instead.

"We haven't had cream of chicken in a while." He continued, as if nothing were amiss. "But I'm sorry baby, I can't let you have any toast or a bread roll to go with it, not until you can have solids again."

Food was the last thing on my mind as I fretted over my little girls being anywhere but here.

My overbearing husband leaned over his sick wife to deliver several soft kisses to the top of her head whilst murmuring, "Together forever B, I won't lose you again." Then he stood up and left the bedroom as he went downstairs.

I laid there and listened to him bang around the kitchen as he prepared the soup from scratch. Meanwhile, I gazed up at the bedroom ceiling, as internally I tossed and turned over what to do? Declan was solely fixated on his wife which pushed his kids to the side. He even blamed one of them for putting me in this state. His obsessive love for his mate was splitting apart our family.

Besides the sterile smell coming from the hospital gown, the familiar scents of home did make me feel a bit better. The delicious aroma of lunch being cooked also lulled me into false sense of security. All of this combined with my soft, warm bed, made me slip into an uneasy sleep...

....

....I'm not sure if it was my subconscious transposing elements of my life into horrific images, but what I saw disturbed me.

In my dream, I could move with ease and I stood up from the bed. I could hear a baby crying so I went to answer it. I left my bedroom and opened the nursery door. Inside, I found my husband in his huge European Werewolf form.

He stood with his back to the doorway as he loomed over the cot. At first this didn't concern me, I simply thought he tended to our child before I did. But what came next sent shivers down my spine.

"Declan, is Susanna OK?" I checked.

When he turned around, there was fresh blood dripping from his razor sharp jaws. Then I looked into the cot and I saw more blood staining the torn and empty baby clothes...

...

...I woke with a start to find it was night time and the bedroom was dimly lit with only Declan's bedside lamp on.

"Hey, you're awake."

I turned my head to see my husband in human form, sitting on his side of the bed, reading a book. But the sight of him didn't soothe, not after the nightmare I had. In fact, I would've preferred to wake up alone.

"You had a good rest," he put aside his reading, "you were out for eight hours."

I rolled away from him and came to stare out the bedroom doorway and into the nursery which was across the hallway.

I saw the back of the cot which sat in the middle of the room with the tall boy along the wall. I couldn't see the rocking chair or baby change table though, they were hidden by the wall. My eyes filled with fresh tears as I looked on the empty room. It felt unnatural with just the two of us in this large, quiet house.

"I've already eaten but I'll bring you up a bowl," he said chirpily.

I felt the bed rise as he got up then I watched the back of his tall frame disappear through the bedroom doorway.

In a couple of minutes he returned with a bowl of cream of chicken soup. He sat on my side of the bed and patiently fed me with a spoon. I wasn't hungry though and Declan noticed my reluctance.

"C'mon B, you need to build your strength," he gently chastised.

I looked away again and he noticed my gaze fall on the nursery across.

"The sooner you get better, the sooner Looch and Soph can come home." He cajoled.

"And Susanna," I said.

The spoon hung midair which gave away his disturbed state. I looked closely on him but he wouldn't meet my gaze. After a moment, he drew himself together and recommenced feeding his wife.

"Just eat the soup."

But when he moved the spoon to my mouth, I moved my head away.

I challenged, "How long is this going to go on for, Declan?"

"Well, if you don't eat then your recuperation will be pretty slow!" He snapped.

"How long are you going to hate Susanna for what happened?"

"I dunno, let's see..." he pretended to think, "...how long do Circulators live in biological form, wasn't it for a thousand years? So there you go."

He tried again to feed me some soup but I moved my head away once more.

"We can't raise our daughters in a house full of hate." I said seriously.

"And we can't have the mother starving herself either." He said coolly. "Now eat or I'll hold you still and pour the soup down your throat!"

My eyes watered at his coldness towards our newborn, which he saw. He let out a frustrated sigh as he lowered the bowl for a moment. Then his face softened as he looked on his weepy wife.

"We've got chocolate custard for dessert." He tried to tempt me. "Tyson came over with a box of liquids for you when you were asleep."

My response to this was to sob softly as my tears spilled down my cheeks.

"C'mon B, please." His voice broke. "I made the soup extra special, just the way you like it. I put a little corn in it, which you prefer and you know I don't."

I asked emotionally, "Why don't you like corn in chicken soup?"

"Because it tastes like the chicken and corn soup you get in Chinese restaurants." He complained. "I don't hate the chicken and corn soup when we order Chinese, but I don't want corn in my cream of chicken soup. It detracts from the other herbs."

I met his gaze, "Susanna isn't going to detract from our family, she's going to add to it."

"OK! Alright!" He cried out exasperated. "If I pretend I'm happy over my youngest nearly killing her mother, will you eat the frickin' soup?!"

Loudly, he started to scrape the sides of the bowl with the spoon before he shoved the utensil into my mouth, whether I was ready or not.

"For three hundred years of marriage I fought off European Werewolves, European Vampires, South American Vampires, North American Vampires and Voodoo Witch Doctors. Just as I think my wife's safe, she's nearly taken out by my spawn!" He muttered unhappily, as he continued to shovel the soup.

Suddenly, I surprised him when I grabbed the bowl and flung it towards the bedroom door!

The crockery cracked upon landing on the wooden floor, as the soup was smeared in a large circle with several droplets leading back to the bed.

I expected him to yell or growl in anger, but my husband simply sat there and stared at it instead.

"Damn, I'm gonna have to clean that up." He said flatly then after another moment, his face broke into a grin. "You want me to bring up the saucepan, so you can throw the leftovers around too?"

I blinked at his blasé behaviour until I realized what he had, I'd just done the exact same thing as I did the night Declan and I became a couple. During that fight, I'd thrown around bowls of stew. Only then it was me who had to clean up the mess, the morning after.

A loud laugh escaped which pulled on my sore stomach muscles and made me flinch. As soon as he saw this, he raised his wrist to his mouth and I saw his teeth extend. But I reached out and stopped him from biting himself.

"No Declan, I don't want you to."

"What if giving you more blood helps you heal faster?" He asked hopeful.

"I've had your blood two times now and that of three other Werewolves already. I think it's up to time to heal me now." I sighed. He looked away discouraged and I sensed he hated feeling so helpless or even guilty, like he was to blame for my condition. So I changed the subject, "Wasn't it funny how that old fight came up again."

"It was the night I made you mine." He spoke with feeling. "Your aura had all but vanished but I made you glow again. I was the one who brought you back to life but then we had to hide our love."

His words made my cry again as I grabbed hold of his broad shoulders and pulled him closer.

"I love you, you hard-headed, stupid, violent, psychopathic monster." I rasped out. "So please don't make me afraid to leave you alone with our children."

"And I love you, you moody, stubborn-as-a-horse's-ass, brilliant girl who glows as bright as the sun when she's happy." He returned. "And I'd jump you if you weren't so broken."

We emitted a loud laugh and when I looked into his bright blue eyes, I saw they were tearful too.

"I'll make a deal with you," he straightened. "If you eat just one bowl of soup, I'll ask Walt to bring the girls home tomorrow."

"Looch, Soph and Sues?" I brightened.

"He's got Looch and Soph but remember Ki's minding Susanna." He pointed out. "We'll bring our eldest girls home first."

My heart hurt as I wanted all of my daughters home, where they belong. Then Declan stood up from the bed and stepping over the spill, he left the room. He wasn't gone for long before he returned with a second bowl and a new spoon.

"Here we go," he returned to my side and recommenced feeding his wife.

After a couple of mouthfuls, I queried, "I thought you said you put corn in it."

"I did put corn in it."

"I can vaguely taste the corn but where are the corn kernels?" I wondered.

"I blended the soup," he answered. "You're not supposed to have solids so I had to eradicate anything chunky. The chicken pieces and corn kernels have officially been obliterated."

His consideration made me smile, "Declan, you do make a good carer."

"You mean when my sperm isn't creating spawn that tries to kill you?" He said unhappily.

And we're back to that.

Disheartened, I looked away as my husband prepared another spoonful.

"Here comes the choo-choo train." He sung, as if he were feeding one of our daughters.

*****

The next morning I got my wish when I had all three daughters under one roof.

Firstly, Walt came over with our first and second born. I overheard Declan greet them at the front door, as I remained in bed. The girls cried out, "Daddy!" then there was a second of silence, which probably meant they were hugging.

Looch asked, "Is Mummy OK? Where is she?"

"She's upstairs in bed," her father replied.

Then I heard the footfall of a ten and five year old, racing up the stairs and down the hallway. Soon, I was looking on their familiar faces as they stood in the bedroom doorway. They hesitated for a minute, I think out of concern at my appearance, before they leapt on top of the bed to swamp me with cuddles and kisses.

"Mummy! Mummy! Mummy!"

"Here are my little monsters!" I turned tearful, as I held them both back tightly.

But when Soph crawled into my lap, she accidentally pressed down on my abdomen which made me flinch in agony.

"Woah woah woah!" Declan cried out as he and Walt walked into the room. "Gently girls, gently."

He lifted up his second born and bounced her on his arm instead as Looch carefully came to sit by my side, wary not to inflict any further pain.

"It's good to see you conscious, Aunt B." Walt joked, as he quickly bent over to plant a kiss on my cheek.

"How are you and your family?" I enquired.

"We're well, thanks." He gave a nod. "How are you feeling?"

"A little stiff and sore," I admitted. "But glad to be home."

"That's understandable after everything you went through." He nodded along.

Just then we heard someone call from downstairs, "Knock, knock!"

It was Ki's voice and he helped himself into the house. I sat upright in excitement as I couldn't wait to see who he brought with him. Declan frowned as he left the bedroom, carrying Soph with him. I overheard him greet Ki at the top of the stairs.

"This is it!" I gushed. "This is where we get to see your little sister."

"Who, Susanna?" My eldest giggled. "We've seen Susanna plenty of times, when Walt took us to visit her."

My mate walked in first, still carrying our second born on his right arm. In fact his frown was so deeply ingrained, I thought he was going to get new wrinkles. He didn't look happy, whereas Soph swung her legs cheerfully.

"Susanna's here!" She cried out.

Then our Medicine Man walked in carrying a large baby wrapped in a blanket.

Susanna was huge! She looked the size of a two year old, so no wonder my abdomen tore as it did. Peeking out from the blanket was her small, stubby snout as well as one of her little claws.

Eagerly, I held out my eager arms and Ki delivered my newborn into them.

"Oh my gosh...!" I started to cry. "This is Susanna Ling Sabre."

I laid her in my lap so I could take off the blanket and behold my third daughter.

Her eyes were closed which reminded me of how newborn puppies kept their eyes shut. She really did look like Declan in European Werewolf form, only a much smaller version. The colour of her hide was the same as his too, indicating she'd have blonde hair in human form. Since she was the size of a two year old, she had a toddler's disposable nappy on.

"She's so cute!" I cried over her. "Look at this beautiful little girl!"

Soph squirmed to be put down and as soon as Declan did, she climbed up onto the bed to sit with her mother and sisters.

"She looks like a puppy, Mummy." She giggled at her younger sister.

"Nope, she's cuter than a puppy." Looch smiled. "Mum, watch this."

I watched my ten year old lean over the newborn Werewolf and growl softly to her. To our delight, the baby growled back. Then Soph growled to her, which the baby returned. After a minute of this, my newborn opened her glowing green eyes with the narrow slits for pupils, and gazed up at her mother.

"Hallo Susanna," I held one of her little claws which tightened about my fingers. "Hallo Susanna, I'm your Mummy."

Then I watched my littlest Werewolf's snout move up and down as she sniffed me, to smell who I was. Afterwards, she started to cry, but it didn't sound like a human baby's cry. It sounded like a series of whimpering and yelping noises, like a puppy makes.

"Aw, come here baby." I picked her up from my lap and held her closely against my chest. As soon as I did, her yelping stopped and I felt her little claws cling to me tightly. This made me cry harder, "She's knows I'm her mother! She really does know that I'm her mother!"

Tearfully, I looked up to share this moment with my husband, but to my surprise he was gone.

Awkwardly, Walt and Ki stood there with the father of my children noticeably missing.

"Um, I think Uncle Dec went downstairs to make coffees." Walt came up with an excuse. "I'll just go and see if he needs a hand."

He turned and left as my tearful eyes met Ki's sympathetic ones. He came and sat on the end of the bed to watch our interaction. He also thought he'd use this chance to tell me more about my daughter.

"We're feeding her formula but with her large appetite, she has three bottles per feed. Because she's so big, we buy her nappies for ages 18-24 months. But she sleeps a lot, which is expected for a newborn. When she's awake, she's a very switched on baby. If she does open her eyes, it's like she's examining you. She sniffs her surroundings a lot too, as if she's getting her bearings."

Soph and Looch ran their hands affectionately up and down Susanna's hardened hide.

"Mum, can I hold her?" My eldest requested.

"Sit back against the bed head." I instructed

Once she obeyed, I handed over her littlest sister. Looch easily took hold of the heavy baby with her supernatural strength. She even gently rocked her side to side as she examined Sues' features.

"Hallo Susanna." She cooed down at her. "I'm your oldest sister."

Ki asked, "Aunt B, where's your camera?"

"On the top shelf in the wardrobe," I pointed at it.

Next, our Medicine Man took several snaps of the Susanna with her sisters and mother. The first pic was of Looch holding Sues then the second was with Soph holding her. Lastly, he took a shot of me holding her again with my other two daughters sitting on either side.

"Where's Daddy?" Soph peered out the bedroom door. "We should get a picture of him holding Susanna too."

"I'll go see if I can find him." Ki volunteered, as he put down the camera and left the room.

He was gone for ten minutes before he returned with the two other men. Walt looked worried and Declan looked angry. My husband stood by the bedroom door like he didn't want to come near the bed that his newborn was on. You didn't have to be an empath to feel the hostility radiate from him. I felt my eyes renew with tears and this time they weren't happy ones.

"Aunt B, I have to go now so I'll take Susanna with me and bring her back tomorrow for another visit." Ki announced.

Protectively, I clung onto my newborn and growled dangerously when he came forwards to collect her.

"No!" I said fiercely. "Susanna stays here!"

"No B, let him take her," Declan disputed. "You're still healing."

"NO!" I roared. "Susanna belongs with her family!"

Then our first born thought she should take up the responsibility of helping to care for her younger siblings, "I can help Mum look after Susanna."

Her father's face reddened in anger, "B what's it going to take to get through your thick head that you almost died eleven days ago?!"

His furious words frightened our little girls who turned tearful. I kept a protective arm around Susanna as I used my other to pull my two older daughters closer. Altogether I was holding the three girls at once, as I glared up at their father.

"The Sabre women stay together." I said defiantly. "And if the Sabre man can't deal with it, he can leave."

The other two Lokoti Werewolves in the room saw how their female went on the attack mode. They realized my protective instincts were well and truly ignited. So they rallied around their kin by showing their support.

"If Susanna is staying, she'll need her formula and diapers." Ki kept his tone neutral. "I'll just run home and get them."

Warily, our Healer passed the fuming European Werewolf in the doorway as he went on his mission of fetch.

Then Walt sat on the end of the bed to show his support for the mother and her children.

"Wendy made a beef and vegetable soup for you, which I put in your kitchen." Walt told me. "She also included a baby chew toy for Susanna."

Declan saw how his men had sided with his wife and in a fury, he spun on his heel and stormed off downstairs.

Concerned, I exchanged glances with Walt, while Soph looked at Looch in confusion.

"Why is Daddy so angry?" She asked. "I haven't had a tantrum or broken anything."

"You're not the one he's angry with, Soph." Her sister said ruefully.

Then Looch reached out to stroke Sues' hardened hide once more.

*****

An hour later Ki returned with the baby products and to my surprise, Tyson and Samuel arrived with him.

The three Lokoti Werewolves carried the boxes of formula, diapers and other baby products into the nursery. Walt stood up from the bed and left the room to greet his brothers-in-arms. I watched the three talk quietly in the other room, with our First casting a concerned look my way.

I was sitting upright in bed, rocking Sues in my arms. But I listened in to their conversation with my sensitive ears. It appears I wasn't the only one concerned over my husband's attitude towards his third born.

"Right," Tyson spoke in a normal voice. "Walt, would you like to make the cot? Ki, could you put away the diapers and take the formula down to the kitchen? And Samuel, you can come with me and welcome Aunt B and the baby home."

The Lokoti Werewolves went about with their tasks as our First came into my bedroom with his son.

"Look, it's the living dead." Samuel joked before he planted a kiss on my cheek. "Boy, you had us worried, Aunt B."

"I'm relieved to see both mother and infant are well." Tyson kissed the top of my head next. He looked down on the newborn wrapped in her blanket, sleeping peacefully. "May I?"

I loosened my grip and Tyson like an experienced father, expertly picked her up and held her closely without even waking her.

"I feel like I'm the proud Uncle instead of the other way around." He grinned.

"Can I hold her after you, Dad?" Samuel asked.

I watched the older Lokoti Werewolf hand over the babe to the youngest Lokoti Werewolf in the room.

Gently, Samuel rocked my newborn in his arms as he stared down at her sleeping form. "Man, they sure are cute at this age."

"They are indeed." Tyson smiled on. "Son, tell Aunt B the news."

"What news?" I wondered.

"I proposed to Jo and she said yes." Samuel beamed. "Our Housewarming is next month and we'll move into the old Riverclaw house."

"That's great news!" I beamed. "A new Riverclaw family in the old Riverclaw home, I know Caesar would be pleased."

"In twelve months time this could be us, visiting Samuel's first born," our First chuckled proudly.

"Aw, c'mon, Dad." He blushed. "Jo may not instantly fall pregnant."

But it made the adults in the room crack up laughing at his modesty. Looch giggled too, as it was a well-known fact that a marriage with a Lokoti Werewolf, resulted in a family straight away. However, Soph looked even more confused.

"Do you mean Samuel might do something wrong and Jo will be impregnated?" She pondered.

This resulted in more laughter as the perspective groom's face further reddened.

Then the room quieted at the appearance of my sombre mate standing in the doorway. He looked on unhappily at how everyone was carrying on without him. I sensed he was embarrassed at how his First and other members of the pack came to show their support for Susanna. I also felt his turmoil, as he hated feeling separated from his wife and kids.

"I was just about to prepare the soup that Walt brought over," he said stiffly. "Is it safe to assume you'll be staying for lunch?"

Tyson said evenly, "Yes we will."

Declan looked at Looch, "Can you set the table for our guests?" Obediently, she hopped off the bed and disappeared downstairs. Then he looked on his wife, "If you can sit up in bed, you should be able to sit at the table. When lunch is ready, I'll carry you down."

He spun on his heel and stalked off downstairs to the kitchen. He'd looked on Looch and Soph sitting on the bed, but he hardly cast a glance at Sues. My chest tightened with disappointment at his distant behaviour.

Next, Walt and Ki reappeared after finishing their tasks; the formula was stacked neatly in our pantry and the cot was made. Two tasks that Declan should have done but didn't. I blinked back my tears as I didn't want to cry openly in front of my First.

Ki offered, "Before we go downstairs for lunch, would you like to feed Susanna?"

"Yes please." I nodded along, gratefully.

Then he set about the task of readying the bottles of formula for the baby, another task her father should have done.

*****

Our Medicine Man was right, Susanna's appetite wasn't appeased until she finished her third bottle of formula. The rubber nipples already looked chewed from her razor sharp teeth. She made happy slurping noises as she fed before she belched up a hefty European Werewolf style burp.

When I'd finished feeding her Ki put her in the cot inside the nursery. I watched longingly as he tucked her in. I wished I was strong enough to care for her and it felt frustrating watching other people do it for me.

When lunch was ready, my husband strode into the bedroom and prepared his wife. He put my slippers on then he helped me with my robe. Easily, he lifted me up into his arms then carried me down to the stairs.

Gently, he placed me in my seat at the table as our children and guests sat around us. A steaming bowl of soup waited at my place with a large basket of bread rolls sitting in the middle of the table. I looked on a little enviously as everyone but me, broke open their rolls and slathered them with butter.

I noticed how our First sat at one end of the table with our Second at the other. Tyson and Declan picked up their spoons first then the rest of the table commenced eating. I watched how Samuel and Looch didn't reach for their cutlery, instead they dipped bits of their bread into the broth.

"Mmm, good soup Walt," our First congratulated. "Be sure to pass our thanks on to Wendy."

"Um, I'll do that," Walt looked uncertain for some reason. "But I don't think this is the soup I brought."

"It is, but I had to blend it because B can't have chunky meat or vegetables." Declan smirked. "As I reheated it, I added some extra herbs."

"Oh, but I better not tell Wendy that," her husband snickered.

I piped up, "Thank Wendy for kindly cooking for us though."

"Will do," he nodded as he heartily ate his meal.

I sipped on the soup slowly to ensure I didn't aggravate my sore stomach, whereas everyone else ate with gusto. The bread basket soon emptied as the adults at the table helped themselves to seconds. I wished I could have had a freshly baked bread roll with my soup too. This being sick business sucks, I can't care for my newborn and I can't eat the foods I wanted to.

Curiously, Looch enquired, "How long is Susanna gonna be in her Werewolf form?"

I caught Declan's spoon pause midair at the subject of conversation then avoiding eye-contact, he carried on eating.

"I'm not sure," Ki thought out loud. "I think she'll remain in her European Werewolf body for a while. You see, she was born premature and when human babies are born early, they have to be kept inside a humidicrib. But in her stronger body, she doesn't have to. So it's safer for her to remain as such for a little while longer."

"What's a humidicrib?" Soph wondered.

"It's a specially designed crib that regulates the atmosphere for a newborn." He educated. "It's see-through though, so you can see the baby inside."

"Is Susanna gonna remain in Werewolf form for the rest of her life?" Soph asked next.

Declan almost choked on his food when he heard that and he coughed loudly.

His displeasure didn't escape the grown Lokoti Werewolves at the table and I exchanged glances with Tyson.

Ki answered, "We don't think so, Soph."

Looch laughed, "It'd be funny if she did though."

Soph giggled with her, "Then we'd have a puppy instead of a sister."

But their playful banter was cut short when their father growled at them.

"That's enough you two! Now eat your lunch."

I saw the way Tyson, Samuel, Ki and Walt all looked at each other. Not only did Declan's hatred of his newborn bother them, but so did his short temper. Lokoti Werewolves were extremely protective over their mates and their young, so the European Werewolf's behaviour left them unsettled.

I shared their concern as I regarded my mate with narrow eyes. I couldn't share my children with a father I was wary of leaving them alone with. If it came down to it, if I had to choose between my husband and my children, there'd be no competition. My own protective instincts would choose my kids any day of the week and twice on Sundays.

*****

Once lunch was over, Declan carried me upstairs and put me back to bed before returning downstairs to clean up.

The girls came to sit beside their mother with Looch carrying a book for me to read to them called 'The Princess Bride' by William Goldman.

Walt, Ki and Samuel went home however Tyson remained behind. I suspected our First was going to have a serious discussion with his Second. It wasn't hard to guess what the subject would be. But their talk didn't go for long, ten minutes later, I heard the front door open and close with his departure.

As soon as he left, my husband stormed into the bedroom, interrupting my reading.

"Girls, go outside and play!" He barked out.

"But we're only halfway through the chapter!" Soph complained.

"I need to talk to your mother," he said gruffly.

Looch took hold of her sister's hand and pulled her off the bed then out of the room. On her way out, she looked back at her mother, as if she was concerned for my welfare. This further angered her father and he slammed the bedroom door shut behind them!

I was about to berate him to watch his temper when he started to pace up and down in the bedroom.

"I don't believe this..." he growled under his breath, "...our First just asked me if I can be trusted with our newborn and now my daughters are looking like they don't trust their father either!"

"Well, what did you expect?" I asked curtly, as I put aside the book. "Your behaviour hasn't been very fatherly the past couple of days."

"Oh excuse me for cleaning up their mother from the kitchen floor eleven days ago!" He ranted. "B, you didn't see your stomach, it was hideous! You were bleeding and broken and I had to frickin' cut the foetus out of you!"

Declan paced faster and faster as he ranted during this tirade.

"The kitchen floor was completely covered in your blood!" He continued. "It would have taken Walt hours to mop up that much mess."

"Walt mopped up the blood?" I asked in surprise.

"Who else would have, the cleaning fairy?" Declan snapped. "I think he did it when he came over to get some clothes for the girls."

"We really should get the Wisetail's a gift hamper or something to thank them for all their help." I said, feeling abashed by their generosity.

"A gift hamper?" He asked incredulous. "A GIFT HAMPER?! Is that the only thing you can come up with after hearing about the state the baby left you in?!"

My heart hardened against his rage as my eyes narrowed.

"Why am I the only one who's reacting as they should, to the little monster who almost killed her mother?!" He shouted. "That baby European Werewolf could have clawed its way out of you, if I hadn't of cut it out!"

"Don't be ridiculous, she was suffocating which is why I told you to save her," I rebuked.

"You saw what happened to the other women who carried European Werewolf young, their wombs exploded and so did yours!" He yelled tearfully. "You swore to me that your pregnancies would be safe! If I'd known you were lying, I wouldn't have touched you with a six foot pole! I'd have rather ripped off my testicles than put a beast inside of your body!"

Right at that moment we heard our newborn begin to cry, as her father's shouting had woken her. She made whimpering and yelping sounds and I sensed she was afraid. She wasn't in the cot she'd become accustomed to at Ki's place and this new house she was in was full of hatred, which was what I wanted to avoid.

Instead of tending to his newborn Declan just stood there. His face was cold and hard and he looked completely indifferent to her cries. When I saw he wasn't going to look after her, I thought I should. I swung my legs out of bed which triggered an agonizing spasm in my abdomen.

"Don't be stupid B," he rolled his eyes. "You can't go to her, hell you can't even walk and guess whose fault is that?!"

Then through the closed door, I heard the footsteps of my older daughters, answering her distress. A momentary quietness came from the nursery, which indicated Looch had picked Sues up. Then the baby started crying again and I sensed she wanted her mother instead.

"It's OK little baby, it's OK." Soph tried to soothe. "Where do we get the bottles from to feed her?"

"They're in the kitchen but we have to make the formula first and I don't know how to." Looch said helplessly.

OK, that's enough!

I flung off the bedcovers and heaved myself to my feet. When Declan tried to stop me, I shoved his hands away. I wobbled over to the door on my unsteady legs and threw it open.

Slowly and painfully, I made my way across the hallway and into the nursery. My daughters looked upon my appearance in obvious relief and Looch eagerly handed my newborn to me. I started to walk around in circles as I rocked her in my arms. The tighter I held her, the less Susanna cried and after a couple of minutes, her whimpering subsided.

"Does she need more formula?" Soph asked.

"No, she's scared that's all." I placed a kiss on the end of her snout. "But there's nothing to be scared about, because we love our baby girl."

"Dad was pretty loud, we could hear his yelling outside in the garden." Looch said anxiously. "He must be really angry with Susanna."

As soon as she said that, hers and her little sister's heads whipped around to the doorway where their big, strong, scary father, was standing.

The hardness in my heart spread throughout my body as I hardened all over. The same time as I underwent my emotional transformation, I underwent a physical one, too. My human body expanded with muscle as my dark blue eyes burned their glowing turquoise colour. Although I changed into my Lokoti Werewolf form to protect my daughters, changing into my stronger body also decreased the pain I was in.

"Get out!" I bit out in my thunderous voice. "Not just out of the room, but out of the house!"

"Huh?" Declan's eyes widened in surprise.

"You heard me." I spoke in a low voice. "Get out and don't come back."

"What?" He blinked.

"Get your things together and get out of this house."

"B?"

I emitted one of the most threatening growls in my supernatural career as a Werewolf, "I mean it!"

My little girls stared on in shock as did their father from the doorway.

"You don't mean that," he shook his head.

"I told you this house wouldn't turn into one of hate and I'm gonna raise all of my little girls with love." I said strongly. "You're not welcome here."

Finally, my words hit home as I saw his face fall, "B...?"

"Your mother would be ashamed of you!" I thundered out. "She could raise a European Werewolf, but you can't? Get out of my house, you hypocrite!"

Declan paled as his normally bright blue eyes watered with emotion. We watched him start to tremble as he sniffled loudly. His tearful eyes left mine to settle on the baby in my arms. I watched his hurt turn into hatred, which was directed at what he saw as the cause.

I turned around and carefully lowered my baby into my eldest's arms. "Go and sit in the rocking chair and sing to your sister."

Instantly, Looch obeyed as she sat down on the furniture and started singing to her the songs she was sang to, when she was younger. Soph came to stand beside and joined in. When I saw all three of my daughters were safe, I turned on the threat in the room which was their father.

I marched out of the nursery and back into the main bedroom. I grabbed an old cardboard box which was sitting on top of the wardrobe. Declan watched as I tipped out the bits and pieces, before I carried it over to the tallboy.

"Great and we're back to you running away again," he moaned.

"I'M not leaving, YOU are!" I snarled.

He stood by and watched as my clawed hands grabbed a pile of his underwear, a heap of his t-shirts and a couple of his jeans and carelessly, I tossed them into the box. It wasn't big enough for all of his things but I didn't care. I carried the overflowing box out of the bedroom and down the stairs.

He trailed after to see what I was doing with his things and he blanched when he saw me open the front door and plant the box on the veranda.

I held the door open and growled out a second time, "Get out!"

"B, c'mon now..." he shook his head, "...it's not funny anymore."

"Get out."

"You really shouldn't kid around like this in front of our daughters, it might give them the wrong idea."

"GET OUT!!" I roared so loudly, I made the windows rattle.

Like he was stuck to the spot, my husband simply stood there dumbfounded and hurting. I saw a second set of tears course down his face as he looked from me to the open doorway. His face was ashen but I didn't care, I carried on for the good of my family.

"You don't mean that," he shook his head in a maddening way. "You're just hurting at the moment."

"I warned you Declan Sabre." I proclaimed. "I warned you and I pleaded with you and I gave you several chances."

"When?"

"I pleaded with you when Looch was born, I cajoled you when Soph was born and I begged you when Sues was born." I said bitterly. "But now I see you're just like all the other male European Werewolves, you're not father material."

"B!" He cried out in pain like I'd just stabbed him in the heart. "Please don't do this!"

"You once accused me of choosing the baby over you and guess what, you made me do this!" I boomed out. "You made me choose our children's welfare over a father who could hurt them!"

"No B, no!" He sunk to his knees. "Don't do this, please don't do this!"

"Get out!" I barked.

"I'm sorry!" He collapsed to his knees. "I'm sorry B, I'm so sorry!"

"Get out or I'll call on the pack to throw you out!" I threatened.

"Noooo...!" He howled like he was in pain.

Of course he was faster and stronger than the Lokoti Werewolves, but he knew what calling on them would mean, that there was no going back. If the pack became involved then so would the Tribal Elders. They could call a dissolution to our marriage. The idea frightened Declan so much, he crawled over to where I was standing to look up beseechingly.

"I'm sorry B, I'm so sorry..." he tried to take hold of my hands, "...I'll do better I promise."

"Don't apologise to me, say sorry to our daughters who you frightened...! Say sorry to our youngest whom you refused to answer when she cried...! Say sorry to our newborn whom you hate...! Say sorry to our baby whom you refused to care for...!" I ranted back at him.

"I'm sorry B, I'm sorry." He cried into my swollen belly as he clung to his mate. "Don't throw me out! Together forever B, remember? Together forever!"

My heart which was empathically bonded to my mate felt like it was splitting into two, but for my children I carried on.

"I can't raise my three daughters with a father who separates them by hating one." I growled out.

"No you can't." He shook his head. "It's wrong, I see that now."

"Do you?!" I demanded.

Apologetically, Declan looked up into my glowing turquoise eyes.

"You love the monster who's our baby, just like you love the monster who's your husband..." he rasped out, "...and I promise I'll do a better job in raising all three of our daughters with you."

For a long moment, I looked down to examine my husband's face as he openly cried.

"I'm sorry B, I'm so sorry." He repeated over and over again. "You don't have to worry what I'll be like with the children, you don't, I promise."

"Do you know how disappointed I am with you right now, Declan? Our First had to speak to you about your behaviour! I had to threaten to throw you out of the house to protect my children!"

"I'm sorry I'm sorry I'm sorry I'm sorry..." he chanted whilst clinging to me, "...I'm sorry I'm sorry I'm sorry I'm sorry I'm sorry!"

I was torn in two, just like my heart was. My protective instincts didn't trust this turn around but my aching heart was willing to give him the benefit of the doubt. My big, strong husband had crawled on his knees for forgiveness and was still on his knees, begging. I hated hurting him but I feared more of what kind of damage he could do, if he stayed.

Upstairs, I heard more crying from our children. Sues was yelping and whimpering, Looch was tearfully trying to soothe her in a broken voice. Even Soph sounded scared as her voice cracked as she kept trying to sing.

"Mum, come here!" Looch cried out frightened. "Sues is sick!"

What the...?

My eyes bulged in fear and even Declan snapped to. Quickly, he stood up, grabbed my hand and instantaneously phased us upstairs. We reformed into our biological beings inside the nursery, before our children.

There, we found Looch was desperately trying to hold onto our youngest, who was not only crying but convulsing!

"I didn't do anything, I was rocking her and singing to her, just as you said!" She panicked.

"Give her to me," their father said curtly.

Declan took control by pulling his large newborn from her arms. Then we watched him lay Sues on the floor, which made her spasms worse. When I tried to pick her up, he pushed my hands away.

"No B, I think I know what's wrong, we need to give her space." He said. "If we hold her, it'll make it worse."

"Make what worse?" I growled out. "I'll call Ki."

"Just wait!" He flashed an annoyed look my way.

All four pair of eyes were on the convulsing newborn European Werewolf. Then the familiar sounds of bones cracking came to our sensitive ears. We all looked at their European Werewolf father, but it wasn't him that was changing. When our eyes returned to the newborn, we saw her muscles were decreasing, her hardened hide was turning into soft skin and her short, stubby snout was flattening out. Her four little claws turned into two human hands and feet.

Susanna literally shrunk before our very eyes to the size of a human baby. The toddler's nappy now looked gigantic on her and slipped off. Then the baby cried even louder and I sensed she was in pain from her transformation. I also sensed that she felt cold without her muscle bulk.

"Shhhh...I know it hurts baby," her father picked her up.

As he nursed her in his left arm, he raised his right wrist to his mouth. We watched him extend his teeth and put a gash in it, which he lowered to his baby's mouth. Immediately, she began to suckle on it as her crying subsided. Her father held the small, naked newborn close to him, to share his body heat as well as his blood, and she emitted an appreciative gurgle.

Looch, Soph and I all sat there stunned at the transformation we'd just witnessed.

Declan cooed down at her as he fed her his blood to ease her pain. The baby continued to drink as her human blue eyes met her father's. The top of her head had soft, blonde curls and other than her nails looking a little long, she appeared completely human.

"Expanding into a European Werewolf then decreasing back into human form hurts like hell." He said, as he looked on his littlest with new understanding. "For the first couple of months as she gets used to the transition, she's gonna look like she's convulsing. When I underwent my first change, my Mom thought I was having a seizure! It hurt so much, I howled for an hour afterwards. It was your mother's grandfather who shared his blood with me to lessen the pain."

We sat there and watched transfixed as Declan removed his wrist from Sues' mouth and momentarily put it in his own to kick-start his healing. Then he moved her to his shoulder and rubbed her back which made her burp. Lastly, he stood up with his daughter, walked over to the wardrobe and hunted around for something. We watched him pull out one of the smaller disposable nappies we had as leftovers from when Soph was a baby. Casually, he carried his naked newborn to the change table to put it on and also dressed her in one of Soph's old jumpsuits.

My husband seemed like a new man...or the old one I fell in love with. Gone was the scary, hateful presence in the house but back was the father who was both physically and emotionally strong for his family. He dressed his third born like an old pro and afterwards, he held her in his left arm again.

When he turned back around, he found his wife and kids were still sitting on the floor, looking on baffled.

"So B, would you like to reintroduce yourself to our youngest Sabre?" He offered.

I was still in my Lokoti Werewolf body, I had to be as I needed my supernatural muscle to move around. I got up from the floor and sat in the rocking chair. He carried over our newborn and gently placed her in my arms. Then he knelt on the floor before the both of us as our other daughters crowded around to see.

The beautiful blue eyed, blonde haired, babe with the perfect pink lips and smooth white skin, stared up at the Lokoti Werewolf who was her mother. Mindful of my claws, I caressed her skin and growled softly to her. My human baby emitted a smile and replied with a gurgle.

Soph said jealously, "I liked her better when she was a puppy."

"Ha ha, sucked in." Looch taunted. "You're not the cutest anymore."

"Yes I am!" She fired up but her father silenced her.

"Quit it!" He growled warningly. Then his bright blue eyes met my glowing turquoise ones. "I'm sorry B, I really am."

I nursed my human baby in my muscled arms as I examined his face once more. Declan appeared apologetic and even a little embarrassed. He moved in closer to the monstrous mother holding his child.

"I'll never behave like that again," he said firmly. "You're right, my mother would've been ashamed of my behaviour."

I reached out and rested my clawed hand on his wide chest as my other arm held the baby.

"There's to be no more self-loathing." I rumbled out. "And there's to be no more hate, because it spills out onto your children."

"No," his eyes watered one last time. "No more hate."

"No more anger, no more hate, and no more self-loathing." I repeated.

"From here into infinity come," he pledged.

Then he leaned forwards to gently bump his forehead against mine. The two of us hugged for a minute, before he made the girls giggle by swamping them into his arms and turning it into a group hug. The four of us locked arms as the youngest member laid in the middle of our family circle.

Sues' bright blue eyes looked from Mama Werewolf, Papa Werewolf to the two younger Werewolves, as her expression looked like a combination of surprise and amusement. It looked like she was thinking, "What kind of crazy family have I been born into now?" Declan laughed the loudest when I said this then he planted grateful kisses on all four of the Sabre women's heads.

~~~~~~
~~~~~~

~ 30 ~

Over the next five years we found that although our youngest physically resembled her father the most, her personality was something else.

Susanna may have been as big and strong as a pure-blooded, female European Werewolf, but she quickly proved to be a gentle giant. Her heart must have been as big as her muscled chest with her never ending kindness. She worshipped her sisters, let alone her parents, and there was nothing she wouldn't do for them.

She was the exact opposite of Sophia. While our middle daughter had the mentality of a predator, with her cunning and foul temper; Susanna was both loving and loved life. Then our eldest in the shape of Lucia, seemed to sit in the middle of the scale, as she presided over her siblings. She could show both love and a frightening temper, if her patience was pushed too far.

Our eldest continued to follow in her father's footsteps with her eating, cooking and hunting. Sophia followed her mother or society, by studying hard and following fashion trends. Then Susanna would admire her pretty middle sister who unfortunately was so self-obsessed, she wouldn't give her the time of day. Looch would see Susanna's tears and would try to think of a way to spend time with someone ten years her junior. Declan or I would walk past and find the two sitting together at the dining table, with Looch doing her homework and Susanna colouring in beside her.

When Soph deigned to 'spend time' with Susanna, she would ask her little sister to tidy her room or do her other chores. On more than one occasion, my husband and I would find our littlest doing either gardening or cleaning tasks which we'd set for Sophia. Either her mother, father or eldest sister would interrupt and our littlest would always look up in surprise, at having being stopped. A couple of times she would even beg to keep going, to earn Sophia's affections.

Declan would scoop up his youngest in his arms, "C'mon Sues, you don't have to weed the garden beds anymore, that's Sophia's job."

"But I like weeding, Daddy," she said chirpily.

"Yeah I'm sure you do." He'd say unhappily. "I'm sure you like any old thing that Soph gets you to do for her, huh?"

Then he would carry his little girl inside the house and his deep voice would boom out, "SOPHIA!"

Looch and I would exchange a knowing look as we could guess what was wrong.

Soph would come down the stairs from her bedroom while blowing on her freshly polished nails. "Yes Daddy?"

"Don't 'yes Daddy' me like you don't know what's wrong," her father snapped. "If I catch you palming off your chores onto your little sister one more time, I'm going to give her your pocket money instead. Then what will you use to buy your make-up and accessories?"

This made her mouth fall open in horror, "But she asked me if she could do the weeding!"

"Yeah, Susanna asked if she could work alongside you to spend time with you. It doesn't mean that you can walk off and leave her doing it alone. Now I mean it, if I catch your little sister doing one more of your jobs, I'm transferring the credit onto her credit card instead." He seethed.

Our daughter snuck an evil look in her little sister's direction in silent blame for her telling off, although it was her fault.

"Quit it, Soph." I said coolly as I walked over to Declan's side to affectionately ruffle Sues' hair. "You're in the wrong and you know it."

"Now go outside and finish the weeding," her father ordered.

She cried out indignant, "But I just did my nails!"

"Ha ha, sucked in!" Looch laughed at her.

Susanna looked on her prettiest sister with the painted nails in adoration, before she piped up, "I'll finish the weeding."

"No Sues," I shook my head.

"But I wanna do the weeding, really I do!"

"If Soph wants her pocket money put on her credit card this weekend then she has to earn it." I explained.

"C'mon Sues, you can talk to Daddy while he starts making dinner." He carried her into the kitchen with him.

Soph's eyes narrowed as she watched her sister disappear with her father, "Can I talk to Daddy while he's cooking and Susanna does the weeding?"

Quickly, I walked after them before I lost the last of my patience. I overheard Declan's dissatisfied growl under his breath at how his middle daughter was turning out. Looch shook her head at Soph who was proving to be as vapid as she was beautiful.

"You're such a vain little show pony," she said before she too joined us.

"At least people wanna look at me Lucia, which is more than I can say for you and Susanna with how big you are!" Soph fired off before she stormed out of the house.

In the kitchen, I sat up on the bench beside Sues as Declan was slicing up raw steak on a chopping board nearby. Looch had just opened the fridge to pull out the mushrooms to cut up for her father, when Soph's shrill voice rang out with her parting taunt. Her angry words were water off a duck's back with our eldest however, it upset our youngest.

"Why am I so big, Mummy?" Sues looked over her muscled body.

Even in human form, our five year old looked as big as an eight year old.

"Because you're half European Werewolf, sweetie," I put my arm around her.

"So is Soph, so how come she's not as big as we are?"

"You mean she's not as muscled." Declan paused in his food preparation. "You and Looch aren't fat, you're muscled. So the good thing is you're much stronger than Sophia is."

But Sues didn't look happy about this as she examined herself again.

"Soph looks the most like a Lokoti Werewolf, like what Mum is, but even Lokoti Werewolves look bigger than humans." Looch explained as she sliced the mushrooms on another chopping board. "So Soph is still gonna look bigger than the other girls in her class."

"Oh?" Sues listened with interest.

"Soph looks athletic but we look like bodybuilders," she finished on a rueful note.

"What's a bodybuilder?" Sues queried.

"Humans who for the hell of it, make themselves bigger and stronger by eating certain foods and lifting weights," their father scoffed.

"Why?" Sues gave a funny look.

"Because some humans fantasize about being as big and strong as we are. Werewolves are muscled because we're hunters and the bloodlust makes us fighters. Some humans make themselves muscled for sports or fighting. While humans work hard to enlarge their physique, you two have naturally got your supernatural strength from your good looking father."

This made the two erupt into giggles as I passed my mate a smile on his handling of the matter.

Human children grew up with questions about their differences and it was doubly so with our little Werewolves. To combat their insecurities, Declan and I adopted a 'free speech' policy where everything was discussed openly. Sure, the sex questions which occasionally popped up could still make their father's face flush however, we'd rather know what our children were thinking or doing than if they hid it from us.

With hunting, another unique quality to Susanna's personality was the unusual way her bloodlust displayed itself. Normally on the night of a full moon, a Werewolf's bloodlust demanded to feast on fresh kill. Our youngest was no stranger to eating flesh, as she happily gobbled down the bits and pieces her father brought back from a hunt. But what surprised us, was her aversion to violence even with her bloodlust peaking.

When she was four years old, we took her on her first hunt with the pack. Unlike her older sisters whom began by riding on their father's back, Susanna ran alongside. She was already half of Declan's gigantic size in European Werewolf form, so she was too big to carry. She was so excited about being included that she was jumping everywhere on her four claws, like she could have been a giant bunny rabbit. When she tried to jump on me to lick my face, her father gently clasped the back of her neck in his huge jaws and lifted her away.

Susanna could easily keep up with the pack and I sensed her exhilaration at running with the grown ups. She almost made me laugh, seeing her run on all-fours with her tongue hanging out of her mouth. She reminded me of the way a dog looks, when they happily stick their head out of a hover-car window.

Joyfully, she ran between her parents before dropping back to run with her older sisters. Both Looch and Soph ran upright on two legs like their Lokoti Werewolf mother, wearing gym clothes which could handle their muscle bulk. Then there was Sues who was galloped along on all-fours, like their European Werewolf father.

The pack chased after a small herd of caribou. We smelled there were two males and five females, which meant there was enough for everyone. Declan readied to tackle the strongest male, which he'd kill alone and then share the flesh with his family. I dropped back to give him space as my daughters also slowed to a stop.

We watched their father combat his prey with our glowing eyes enabling us to see in the night as clear as day. The male caribou tried to run his antlers through my mate, but his hardened hide and muscle bulk protected him from injury. Then his jaws ripped apart his foe's throat and the male caribou's decapitated head fell to the ground before its large body did.

Just as his mate and young advanced to share his kill, his family were distracted by a missing member. We heard first then saw second, Susanna's pathetic yelps as she bolted off home! I sensed she was horrified at seeing where her fresh kill came from. Now you see her, now you don't.

Declan panted out his surprise as he did a double take. His youngest who physically resembled him, was running away instead of towards the bloodshed. She even emitted a couple of sympathetic whines for the caribou.

Xenthe who shared his prey with Kevin, Walt, Ki and Joshua, looked up in surprise from his drinking. This made the other four Lokoti Werewolves pause, as the rest of the pack did. Tyson and Samuel exchanged a look of amusement as I ran after my youngest.

I called over my shoulder in my thunderous Werewolf voice, "I got it!"

Susanna ran all the way home where I found her behind the greenhouse. It was as if she was trying to hide her huge, hulking, hairless form but her large silhouette was easily seen through the glass walls. She was crouched on the ground with hot tears pouring out of her glowing green eyes. Like this, I heard her soft howling as she cried over the loss of life she'd witnessed tonight.

"Susie sweetie," I growled out as I sat down beside her monstrous head, "you know fresh kill comes from animals in the National Park."

BUT I DIDN'T KNOW DADDY KILLED THEM LIKE THAT – she thought as her hardened hide shuddered.

"It was a quick death," I tried.

NO IT WASN'T, DADDY FOUGHT IT AND THEN HE KILLED IT – she rebuked.

I emitted a heavy sigh which sounded like a long pant. I didn't know what to say because she was right. Her father had to take down his kill fighting, to appease his bloodlust. I wondered how to explain it to my youngest who was turning out to be the first pacifist European Werewolf?

My claw-like hand affectionately stroked her short, stubby snout before scratching behind her left ear. She loved it when I did that and although she was upset, she moved her head closer for me to scratch behind her right ear, too. I finished with a tickle under her chin.

"Sues, you know how you feel restless when it's a full moon?" I rumbled out. "So does Daddy and the way he manages it, is to take down his food fighting."

WHY? – she wondered.

"Because Daddy is a full-blooded European Werewolf and that's what European Werewolves do."

WHY? – she asked again.

"Because European Werewolves used to be man-eaters but your father has learned to hunt animal instead. But when he hunts, he has to take the animal down fighting otherwise there's no challenge. When there's no challenge, his bloodlust isn't happy." I explained.

EUROPEAN WEREWOLVES HUNT PEOPLE?! – Susanna sat upright with a start – *BUT YOU AND DADDY SAY I'M THE MOST LIKE A EUROPEAN WEREWOLF AND I DON'T WANNA EAT PEOPLE!*

This made me smile softly on my youngest, which was probably negated by my elongated teeth.

"No, you're way more special, Sues."

Then I wrapped my muscled arms around her bulky body and hugged her with all my might.

I'M SORRY MUMMY THAT I'M NOT A VERY GOOD WEREWOLF – she thought dismally.

When she pulled away, I saw another hot tear roll down her snout. This made me pause as I experienced a case of déjà vu. I remembered saying something similar to my Lokoti Werewolf father when I was learning how to hunt.

I held her huge head in between my two claw-like hands so my glowing turquoise eyes could meet her glowing green ones.

"I said that to my father when he took me on my first hunt too. I felt so bad that I hurt a grizzly, I turned and ran away. But do you know what my father said to me?"

Sues shook her beastly head as she listened intently.

"My father said he was damn proud to have me, his daughter, as the tribe's first female Lokoti Werewolf. And you know what Sues? I'm prouder still to have you, my youngest, as the nicest and kindest Werewolf in all the world."

My four year old's response to that was knocking me backwards to repeatedly lick my face. It was her way of showering me with kisses. I laughed as I engaged her in a play fight, by rolling over and pulling her with me. I tackled her to the ground but since she was nearly as strong as me, she pinned me instead. This didn't last long when I freed one of my arms and tickled her, which made her jump away whilst panting louder as her way of laughter.

Two hours later when my husband and older daughters came home, they found Sues and I in the garden. We were still in our supernatural forms and playing Frisbee. Not only could we see the spinning toy with our glowing eyes, but the garden was lit up by the light of the full moon.

Gleefully, Susanna was leaping into the air to catch it in her mouth before she'd give a flick of her head to throw it back. Her coordination in her bulky body was a bit of a challenge though, as I'd have to run in light speed after her returns. The Frisbee flew off in all directions except mine.

Declan's jaws were covered in blood especially since he'd carried home a hind leg for his mate and youngest to share. The bleeding body part left trickles of blood going down his thick neck. He sat upright on his hind legs on the gravel driveway as our other daughters continued inside to shower and change. They too had blood around their mouths and under their claw-like nails.

DADDY! – Susanna saw the treat and ran right for it.

SHARE IT WITH YOUR MOTHER – he ordered.

Obediently, she skidded to a stop on the gravel driveway before she moved to sit on her hind legs too.

I walked over and picked up the hind leg, breaking it into two with my supernatural strength. I handed to Sues the hind quarter which she carefully took with her dangerous mouth and I started on the lower leg. Declan watched his family feast, occasionally licking his lips at the sight of his muscled mate in her tight gym clothes, become covered in blood.

I sat cross legged on the gravel driveway in between the two large forms of my mate and young. Susanna's head was above mine and Declan's head was above hers. She ate her offering much faster than I did thanks to her larger jaws. Inheriting her father's greater strength and appetite, she even scoffed down the bones once all the meat had been torn off. I heard the bone-tingling crunching noises as she munched away on them.

Since I couldn't eat bone, once I'd eaten off all the flesh I gave her the rest. Crunch, crunch, crunch! It was crushed to smithereens and when the food was all gone, she delivered an appreciative lick to the side of my face.

OK, TIME FOR YOUR BATH AND THEN BED – Her father thought.

AW, DO I HAVE TO? – she rose to all-fours – *CAN'T WE PLAY FRISBEE A LITTLE LONGER?*

Declan and I exchanged glances as we knew where her abundance in energy was coming from - her bloodlust. It wasn't completely purged by hunting, so we knew it was going to be a bit of a challenge putting her down for the night.

CHANGE PLEASE AND GO INSIDE – Declan ordered.

Sues emitted a reluctant whine before we watched her start to shrink. Her hardened hide turned into soft skin once more as her muscle bulk reduced.

I heard the soft cracking noises her bones made, as her four legged shape turned into a two legged one. Her snout retreated into a round face and her eyes watered from the pain her transformation put her body under. This made me reach out and pull her close for a sympathetic hug.

"Mummy, when is it gonna stop hurting?" She asked tearfully.

IT DOESN'T – Her father thought grimly – *BUT YOU GET USED TO IT.*

Then I took hold of her hand and led my naked little girl inside, with her father shrinking into his human body after us. He pulled on his old, tatty, blood-stained bathrobe to hide his nakedness, before following us inside.

As our eldest girls used the main bathroom to shower then put on their pyjamas, we let Sues use our ensuite. She shared a quick shower with me as her father politely waited in the master bedroom. Then I dressed her as he washed the blood off his muscled body. I put her into a pair of her favourite blue 'Gonzo' pyjamas and when her father was dressed, we put her to bed.

We tucked in then kissed goodnight our four, nine and fourteen year old daughters in their respective bedrooms. It was nearly 4 AM when their bedside lamps were turned off and they settled down to sleep. The parents were about to switch off their lamps in the main bedroom, when their mother hesitated.

"What are we going to do about Sues?" I asked concerned.

Declan was just about to turn off his light, when he left it on for he knew a PD&M coming up - Parent's Deep and Meaningful.

"Everybody screws up their first hunt." He shrugged it off. "She just needs practice that's all."

"I right royally stuffed up my first hunt." I said brazenly. "What were you like?"

"Huh?

"What were you like on your first hunt?" I pressed.

"I dunno, I was three years old!" He complained. But by my demanding gaze he saw I wasn't going to let it drop. He let out a huff, "I got...carried away."

"What do you mean, 'carried away'?"

"I shredded the moose a little too well with my claws." He said uncomfortably. "There was minced moose all over the forest."

This made me crack up laughing to his chagrin.

"Yeah, so?" He turned defensive. "Like I said, everyone screws up on their first hunt."

"Soph was funny on hers." I giggled. "She tried to attack that wolverine and landed face first in the snow!"

"Yeah that was pretty funny." He chuckled along. "Then she chased it for a kilometre and kept falling over in the slush."

Accidentally, we laughed too loudly when we heard our second born call out from her bedroom, "We can hear you!"

Then we heard Looch and Sues giggle from their bedrooms too. My husband switched off his bedside lamp and lay down with his wife in his arms. I snuggled against his hot chest and we both sighed contentedly.

"But what are we gonna do about Sues' bloodlust?" I murmured in the darkness. "I mean, she must have it since she enjoys eating fresh kill, even if the manner of how it's killed, disturbs her."

"Hmm, the way she's hyperactive on a full moon is another indication."

"So what are we gonna do to help her hunt?" I whispered.

His eyes met mine and he gave an evil grin, "I've an idea."

The following full moon, our pack chased down a herd of Dall sheep up the high slopes in our small part of the majestic Alaska Range.

Again, Sues excitedly ran alongside her father in their supernatural forms. But when she saw him close in on a ram, she dropped back. Instead of attacking the large, male Dall sheep himself, Declan dropped back too. This made the male make grunting noises as it readied its horns for ramming, thinking it was frightening off the predators.

LOOK AT IT SUES, THAT RAM IS MEAN – Declan thought her way – *HE SAID AFTER HE TRIES TO KNOCK YOU OVER, HE WAS GONNA HAVE A GO AT GONZO!*

Her glowing green eyes widened in alarm at the idea of her favourite Muppet being in danger. Never mind the episodes of the Muppet Show we showed her were over 300 years old. Her four year old brain only saw black and white, the Muppets were real and the ram was mean. She bared her razor sharp teeth and emitted a dangerous growl. When the ram pawed at the ground with its hoof, Sues did the same with her front left claw.

Smack BANG!

The large, male Dall sheep tried to ram over my four year old European Werewolf, who met her foe head on. Next, it tumbled down the steep mountain slope, half conscious from running into the equivalent of a brick wall. Looch caught the free food rolling towards her and raised it into the air with a loud roar. She snapped the ram's neck and dropped it to the ground.

Soph clambered up for a share as did Xenthe and Kevin. But Looch kept them back and pointed her claw-like hand Sues' way to show it was her fresh kill so she got to have the first bite. The older children looked on my youngest impressed and I think I saw a blush come over her hardened hide.

Declan gave her a nudge with his head – *OFF YOU GO AND ENJOY YOUR MEAL.*

Her Lokoti Werewolf mother stood beside her European Werewolf father, to watch the kids feast. Xenthe's fangs pierced the sheep's jugular and he drank thirstily while the others began to tear strips of flesh from the animal. Looch guided her little sister's jaws towards the ram's heart which was like a delicacy among our kind.

"You're a cunning bastard, you know that?" I growled out.

Declan panted out a laugh before leaving an affectionate lick on my cheek.

ALL THE BETTER TO FEED BABY WEREWOLF, MY DEAR – he thought then he bolted off to feed himself.

*****

Raising three little Werewolves kept us busy and there were good days as well as bad. We could tell when it was nearing a full moon as our children fought the most around this period. Even Sues' angelic nature had its limits when the moon grew round and bright.

One afternoon we found Soph trying to tackle Looch with Sues trying to tackle Soph, as the three fought over the remote for the Internet TV. The altercation knocked over our coffee table and overturned a couch. I let my bigger and stronger husband pull them apart as his roar put them in their place.

"Settle down NOW!" He boomed out as his blue eyes flashed glowing green. "What the hell is going on here?!"

Automatically, he looked to our eldest to explain the ruckus.

"Er, I wanted to watch the music channel," she began.

"But 'The Bold and The Beautiful; The Next Generation' is on!" Soph shouted. "I ALWAYS watch that program this time in the afternoon!"

Next, Declan looked at our youngest who simply shrugged back, "Soph was pulling Looch's hair again which isn't nice."

"Say what?" He blinked. "So as these two were getting into it, you tried to pull Soph off Looch?"

Sues ducked her head as she nodded back as her answer.

"Right," her father took the remote off his first born and put it into the hand of his second born. "Soph's program is on so if you want music, then listen to your music system in your bedroom. You can take your littlest sister with you."

"But she's watching reruns of episodes she's already seen before!" Looch whined. "It's a live concert that I want to watch."

"Huh?" Their father paused then he looked on Soph. "Are you watching reruns you've already seen?"

"Well um, yes but -" she faltered and her father grabbed the remote and gave it back to Looch. This made her scream, "I HATE YOU LUCIA AND I HOPE ON A HUNT A GRIZZLY KILLS YOU!"

Declan flinched at the high-pitched noise as her shrillness still caused discomfort to his ears. Tearfully, she ran upstairs to her bedroom as Looch gloatingly sat down on the remaining couch which was still standing. Sues climbed up beside her and when Looch put an arm about her, she snuggled into her sister's side.

"Not so fast, girls," he said gruffly. "Clean up the mess you made."

The two made a move to obey as their father started to walk away.

"Why do we only have one Internet TV in the house, anyways?" Looch grumbled under her breath.

Her father turned around to lecture, "Because we don't want our little Werewolves turning into one of those human kids who sit in front of the Internet TV all day. They're either watching porn, or violent shows or playing those war games on the interactive channels. Our family only needs one Internet TV so we can watch nice programs altogether."

Looch and I tried not to laugh at the fact that her European Werewolf father who took his family hunting, was perturbed about violence on Internet TV.

"What's porn?" Sues wondered.

"Yucky adult stuff that you really don't want to know about." He said dismissively. "Now, who wants chocolate crackles I made for afternoon tea?"

*****

When we were out and about on tribal lands we didn't have to hide our supernatural differences, but our trips into Alma were a different story.

When Looch was 13 years old, her parents finally approved her attending public school. She was confident she could control the bloodlust and Declan and I knew we couldn't lock our little girls away from the world forever. So that September our whole family took Looch to her first day of school.

Jonathan Bourne paved the way by contacting the Alaskan State Government Board of Education. Looch had to sit several exams to show her learning was on par with the other children her age. When the Government tried to poke its nose further into our family to find out why we were home schooling, my lawyer cleverly hit back with we were protecting our cultural heritage.

I think the fact that the Head Chairman on the board of Hodge Endeavor showing particular interest in this student also helped. After the exams, Looch didn't have to go on any waiting lists and she was placed in the same classes as Kevin, as we requested. On her first day, the school principal even showed up to personally escort Looch to her first class.

Declan carried Sues on his right arm as I held onto Soph's hand but Looch, as if to prove her independence, walked ahead of her family. With her height and strong appearance, we doubted she would be physically bullied. But this also worked as a downside as she looked different to her classmates. She was a full head higher than the boys in her year with only Kevin as the exception, thanks to his own supernatural state.

Through the window of the classroom door, my husband and I watched the kids stare at our eldest as she walked over to the seat next to Kevin's. But there were a couple of other Lokoti kids in the class who smiled warmly to her. My free hand sought out my mate's and he squeezed it back.

“I’m scared for her, Declan.” I murmured quietly, so the principal wouldn’t hear. “We had it lucky, going to a small community school after the war. Big schools can be dangerous places, either damaging a child’s personality with bullying, or drugs or sex or whatever else.”

“She’ll be fine,” he kissed the top of my head. “She has Kevin and the other Lokoti who go to this school. She’s a strong girl, not just physically but emotionally. She knows her own mind and she knows what’s right or wrong.”

When we turned to leave, I noticed Soph was reluctant to go home. Curiously, she peered through the window at her sister sitting with the other students. I even caught her examining the latest fashion the girls were wearing.

Our eight year old enquired, “When can I go to school, Mummy?”

“When you can control your temper,” her father answered.

We ended up seeing the same school principal again two years later when Soph was ten. Only Looch wasn’t at her school anymore, she’d started High School. This time we were bringing Soph for her first day.

Our middle daughter practiced hard to keep a reign on her temper tantrums. From the age of nine her father didn’t have to sit on her anymore. Slowly, she stopped trashing her room, although she could still say some nasty things.

The week before she attended public school, Soph demanded she have a whole new wardrobe. She paid particular attention to the latest styles she saw on Internet TV so she knew what she was shopping for. Whereas Looch was happy with casual dress which meant wearing jeans everyday; Soph insisted on having several different outfits and accessorizing them.

Declan volunteered to stay home with Sues unsurprisingly. I knew my mate liked shopping the same amount he liked European Vampires – zilch. So I took Soph shopping for new clothes in Fairbanks, but I drew the line at ten new outfits. When she tried to weasel her way to more, I threatened she couldn’t have any. It’s not that I couldn’t afford it, but I didn’t want to spoil her. She already shops more than any other girl in the tribe, as her credit card constantly sat on empty. As soon as she received her pocket money, she’d spend it.

“But Mum...!” Soph whined. “I NEED more clothes!”

“No you don’t.” I said coolly as I paid on my credit card at the register. “You can mix and match the outfits after wearing them a couple of times.”

She stomped her foot, “But it’s not going to get me through a whole term!”

“Then save your pocket money to buy more.” I gave a pointed look.

So here we were, taking our second born to her first day at school. Again Declan carried Sues on his right arm as his left hung about my waist. We watched our 10 year old confidently walk into the classroom and take her seat.

Soph was tall with broad shoulders, but she wasn’t as muscled as her eldest or youngest sisters. She flicked her long, dark, glossy hair and pretended she didn’t see the curiosity in the boy’s eyes or the jealousy in the girl’s. We could tell by her false modesty that she knew her efforts in embellishing her beauty was working.

"I'm not looking forward to her High School years," her father muttered.

I snickered at how he was worried about protecting his daughters from supernatural as well as natural threats, now including teenaged boys.

As we walked down the school corridor towards the exit, our youngest looked around at the different classrooms.

"When am I going to go to school too?" She wondered.

"Aw, c'mon Sues," her father pretended to look hurt. "You're not gonna leave me all alone, are you? We're at least gonna get a couple more years with you at home, aren't we?"

"Poor Daddy," she hugged him tightly. "Of course you've still got me."

As he hugged her back, he passed me a wary look which I returned.

Our youngest didn't crave human flesh nor did she have horrific tantrums. But coming up to her fifth birthday, her muscle bulk in human form was so great, she looked like a mini weightlifter. We worried how her differences were more pronounced than her sisters', as she'd grow up to be stronger than the two combined.

Whenever we took her into Alma, people stared and our sensitive ears heard the words, "weird", "too big", "freaky", "steroids".

In summer, if Declan was just wearing a t-shirt and jeans, his muscled body was as obvious as Susanna's. Strangers took my husband for a weightlifter and thought we were training Susanna for the same thing. A couple of times when we said her age, people would argue back that she wasn't, as she was too tall, too big, too developed.

Declan made lunch as usual after we'd taken Soph to her first day of school. After we'd eaten, I sat on the veranda steps to watch my littlest play. I sensed she was lonely without her sisters or Wisetail cousins to join her, since they were in school. So she climbed the Jacaranda Tree and very skilfully too. She dug her claws into the bark and used her muscle to swing herself up.

The front door opened and my mate carried out two cups of coffee. As soon as he sat down he handed me one then he turned to watch the same thing. Susanna realized she had an audience and waved to us from the top branch. We waved back then sat forwards in concern, when we saw her lose her balance and topple out of the tree!

Bam! Her muscled little body hit the grassy ground hard. If she'd been human we would've leapt to our feet, frightened about broken bones. But since she wasn't, she laughed as she picked herself up.

"That was a good fall, Sues," her father called out and we put down our coffees to applaud. "Now what's your encore?"

"Huh?" She looked on confused.

"He means what can you do to top the fall?" I called out.

"Oh..." she looked stumped, "...I don't know."

Declan gave a mischievous grin, "I know."

We watched him take another gulp of the caffeinated liquid then he stood up to undress.

Sues giggled excitedly as she could guess what was coming and she too removed her clothes. Her father changed into their European Werewolf forms first, with her a close second. Then the two monsters standing on all-fours on the gravel drive, looked my way.

ARE YOU COMING OR WHAT? – he telepathically taunted.

I remained sitting on the step, "But I don't wanna turn and I'm not wearing stretchy clothes."

PLEASE, MUMMY? – Sues jumped up and down – *PRETTY PLEASE?*

"You go on, I was going to do some research this afternoon anyways."

COME HERE YOU WUSS – Declan came closer – *CLIMB UP ONTO MY BACK BUT LIKE IT OR NOT, YOU'RE COMING WITH US.*

"Oh really?" I smirked. "When you put it like that, how can I say no?"

I had one last mouthful of coffee before I stood up. The European Werewolf lowered himself to the ground so I could climb up. Slowly, he raised himself onto all-fours again and waited as he felt me wrap my legs about his wide waist and grab hold of his bulky shoulders. The smaller European Werewolf which was my young, half hopped up to see if I was on properly and when she came back down, she gave her father a nod.

NOW IF ALL WHINING WIVES WOULD HOLD ON TIGHTLY – he joked – *WE'LL GO FOR A FUN RUN.*

"Bite me!" I laughed back.

LATER – He licked his lips.

In a single leap, the garden disappeared and I found ourselves running through the forest.

Her father led the way down the hill and through the woods with our smaller daughter keeping pace. By the whiz of the passing tree trunks, I guessed we were running at 300km/h which was European Werewolf speed. Declan could run faster being a Circulator, but we didn't want to lose our youngest.

I loved going for rides on his back when he was in his supernatural form. I felt safe as houses as I trusted him implicitly. After running for over fifteen minutes, he began to scramble up a steep, rocky, mountain side. When he felt me nearly slip off, his right claw caught me while his left dug into the rock face. He returned me to his back before climbing up a cliff which had a drop of over a hundred meters.

Sues easily climbed up after us and came to sit beside on an overlook. The wind was icy up here, but leaning against my husband's hot, hardened hide staved off the chill. My youngest moved closer to share her body heat as well.

The three of us were looking over an impressive view of the Alaska Range. We stared at the dark blue rivers snaking their way around the snow-tipped mountains, with the tree tops below looking like a green, uneven carpet.

We were higher than the birds sitting up here, with only a bald eagle gliding past.

SURE YOU MIGHT FEEL LONELY STUDYING AT HOME SUES – her father thought her way – *BUT HOW MANY HUMANS CAN DO WHAT YOU JUST DID, BY CLIMBING WITHOUT ROPE OR OTHER EQUIPMENT?*

She shrugged her bulky shoulders and stared longingly out at the view. I sensed she saw our point, her differences had advantages as well as drawbacks. However, I also sensed she didn't like that secrecy and exclusion were part of the downside. She wanted to be part of the world just as she craved its company.

AND NOW FOR THE ENCORE – he raised himself onto all-fours.

Abruptly, Declan leapt off the rocky overlook and into the air... Sues and my mouths fell open, as we watched her father sail downwards. He fell over a hundred meters to land deftly and uninjured on the steep, rocky ground below.

SUES, COME ON DOWN! – he prompted.

"No Declan, it's too high -" I began but my youngest quite happily leapt off the ledge, after her father. "Sues!"

My littlest landed on all-fours but not as skilfully as her father though. When it looked like she was about to tumble down the rocky slope, her father used his light speed reflexes to catch her. He locked his jaws onto her right shoulder and returned her to her four claws. Once he was sure she'd found her footing, he let go and she gave him an appreciative lick to the side of his snout.

THAT WAS COOL! – she thought excitedly – *CAN WE DO THAT AGAIN?*

My mate laughed proudly at his 'tough as nails' daughter, which came out as a round of fast panting. My youngest joined him, with her panting coming out faster. Then the two European Werewolves looked up at me, still standing there a hundred meters above.

There was no way my smaller Lokoti Werewolf body could land unharmed, so I simply instantaneously phased to their sides instead.

"Shut up!" I said grouchily, as I started to make my way down the rest of the steep slope.

But I didn't get very far when a large claw wrapped about my waist and swung me up onto a hardened hide. As soon as he ascertained his wife was holding on, my husband bolted back home. The rocky slope turned into wood once more, as he and Sues showed off by leaping over log and bush alike.

NOW THAT'S WHAT I CALL A PHYSICAL EDUCATION LESSON – he joked.

*****

Sues wasn't the only kid in the tribe whose supernatural differences alienated her, Xenthe was another example. But with the case of the tribe's only European Vampire, his story was sadder. While the humans in Alma stared at my little girl's height and muscled form, they also stared at the boy's pallor, sickly appearance and stunted growth. He too had to be home schooled by his parent, as his craving for fresh blood was too great a temptation.

After the battle with the two European Vampire covens, the Creillaic and Wisetail families struggled on. Wendy's mourning had good days and bad, where unfortunately the bad outnumbered the good. Walt used up his four weeks annual leave to stay home with his grieving wife and children but then he needed more time off, especially after Kevin's change.

I contacted Jonathan Bourne and ordered Hodge Endeavor to set up a living assistance to be paid into the Creillaic's and the Wisetail's bank accounts. As the families were healing, I didn't want them worrying about how to put food on the table or pay the bills which didn't stop, although it felt like their lives did.

Jonathan also allocated a lawyer within the company to see to Stella's and Xenthe's move to Alaska. She oversaw the sale of their home in Memphis which Stella then put the funds towards buying a house on tribal lands. Then the lawyer hired an expensive removals company to pack up and transport their furniture, belongings and hover-car to Alaska.

Ki and Stella found that not only Xenthe could drink milk, but he could also drink particular fruit or vegetable juices. Orange and tomato juice were too acidic but he could stomach apple, pear or grape. Or he could tolerate carrot, spinach, celery or broccoli juice. However, these only served as placebos for what the Vampire really craved - fresh blood.

Occasionally, Declan still had to hunt in between full moons as did Lucia. When Kevin was a new Lokoti Werewolf so did he, as he was trained to curb his craving for human to animal. When Walt took Kevin out to hunt, he would take Xenthe with them. Although the Vampire craved blood everyday, hunting once a week sustained his health and taught him self control.

Our families saw how Lucia, Kevin and Xenthe's bloodlust bonded them together in best friendship. They hunted together, played together and did their homework together. When Looch started going to school with Kevin, Stella saved some of Xenthe's studies to coincide with his friends' homework. Then the three would all sit together and help each other with Math or what else.

My European Werewolf mate still hated the idea of his young mingling with his sworn enemy; a European Vampire. But he kept his mouth shut as he saw how the friendship helped the children as it did the parents. The Sabre, Wisetail and Creillaic families would often get together for lunches or dinners, with the Lightfoot's and Riverclaw's joining in for special occasions like birthdays.

For Xenthe's 11th Birthday Party, everyone convened at the Creillaic's house. We all brought a dish to share as well as drinks. Stella had baked a birthday cake for the festivities, which was more symbolic since Xenthe couldn't eat it. The little Vampire watched jealously as his party guests ate the chocolate dessert and he had to make do with a fruit and vegetable juice instead.

I felt bad for the little boy, I swear his sadness made his complexion look paler. He didn't enjoy the party his mother put on for him. Stella tried very hard to make her supernatural son still feel part of the natural world and usually with her cheerful demeanour, it worked. But not today...

His two best friends who were growing when he wasn't, stood on his left side as his mother stood on his right. Everyone sang loudly, "Happy Birthday dear Xenthe, Happy Birthday to you!" Then Stella handed her son the knife to cut the cake.

"Blow out the candles and make a wish o' son of mine," she kissed his chalky white cheek.

The eleven year old who still looked like he was ten, stared dismally at the decorated dessert. So he wouldn't cause a scene, he blew out the candles but handed the cutlery back. It was clear he didn't want to cut the cake he couldn't partake in.

"You do it, since I can't eat it," he said sullenly.

Everyone watched how the sad little boy stood up from the table and left the room. With his departure, people paused in the festivities from guilt. But Stella tried to make a joke of it.

"He knows how much of a terrible cook I am and feels bad that you're being made to eat it."

We watched her follow her son out of the room to console him, as did Kevin and Looch. I too went after and found the small group in Xenthe's bedroom. Xenthe was sitting in a sulk on his bed, with Kevin and Looch on either side of him. His mother knelt on the floor before him and gave him her brightest smile.

"I'm not growing up and I'm not as big and strong as a Werewolf, so what good am I...?" He asked, dismally.

"Yeah but you're way faster than Looch and I." Kevin said optimistically.

"Big deal," he moped.

"Actually, it could be a very big deal." I walked into the bedroom. "European Vampires are some of the best fencers in the world."

"Huh?" He gave a peculiar look.

"I could teach you." I offered. "I'm teaching my little girls self-defence and I could teach you armed and unarmed combat."

"Really?" He brightened.

"You could learn to fence and with your speed of sound reflexes, you'd be brilliant at it." I promised.

"Yeah!" He sat up straighter in excitement. "Then I could fight off any fang heads who tries to hurt my Momma again!"

"And with your speed and how you can move silently, you could be like a Ninja!" Kevin cried out exuberantly.

"That'd be pretty cool." Looch laughed along with the boys.

Then the mothers left the kids to plan on becoming some of the tribe's most dangerous warriors.

“Thanks a bunch, B,” she patted me on the arm. “That boy needs some light in his dark life right now.”

But there was a nagging feeling inside me that I could do more to help. I couldn’t explain it, but it was like one of my all-knowing feelings I’d get. I sensed fate had something in store for the good fang head in this world. It wasn’t until I went to bed that night, when one of my visions revealed to me what it was.

As I slept soundly in my husband’s warm embrace, I dreamed I was floating through outer space. I saw black holes, supernovas, and galaxies merging. As I floated through these surreal images, the sight of Earth spinning on its axis as it gravitated around the sun came into view. Next, I zoomed in on North America but instead of finding myself in Alaska, I found myself in the city of New York.

Hover-cars zipped over the busy city streets, occasionally landing to drop off or pick up. Humans walked in and out of the city’s subway stations which hover-trains glided through the underground tunnels. One subway station was in front of some kind of large theatre, where formally dressed people went inside.

I drifted inside the building where I saw on stage an orchestra set up with a grand piano at the front. A pale, thin man wearing a tuxedo played it superbly, with the other instruments accompanying his classical piece. When the music ended, the pale, thin man with faded blue eyes stood up as did the audience to applaud enthusiastically. The pianist made several bows, before blowing a kiss to someone sitting in the balcony area.

He honoured a beautiful, tall woman who had broad shoulders and dark hair tied up in an elegant style. She was wearing an expensive, strapless evening dress with diamonds hanging from her ears and neck. Her dark brown eyes sparkled as she looked on the pale, thin pianist with love.

I knew the pianist and the attractive woman, as they were a grown up versions of the European Vampire and female Lokoti Werewolf, I was raising now.

When I jolted awake, I accidentally woke my mate. Sleepily, he rubbed his eyes as I sat upright and looked at the time. It was only 5.43 AM but I knew what had to be done and I climbed out of bed. I had a future to organize...

“B?” He mumbled out. “Why are you getting dressed? It’s not even six o’clock!”

“It’s time.” I said simply then he watched as I picked up my mobile phone and rang our Medicine Man. “Ki, it’s B. Yes I know what time it is. No it’s not an emergency as such, but I need your help as I help Xenthe.”

Just as my husband watched my departure puzzled, it was the same expression on Stella’s face when she answered the door in her pyjamas.

Then she, her son and our Healer all sat in the Creillaic’s lounge room as they listened to my idea.

“Stella, I’m not sure if you know this about Circulators, but not only can we phase through time, but in phase we can also alter our physical ages.”

"I'm sorry," she blinked, still half asleep, "but what's this got to do with my boy?"

"I could put Xenthe in phase and alter his age." I went on. "I could make your son grow up this way."

The small eleven year old's eyes widened in hope.

"But I believe there could be medical drawbacks to this, which I was telling Aunt B on our way here." Ki said seriously. "If she ages your European Vampire son by a year, then she'd be detracting his life span by the equivalent time."

His mother frowned in confusion, "So you're saying that if this Circulator ages my boy by a year, he'll have one less year to live?"

"Yes."

"No deal." Stella protectively put her arm about her son's shoulders. "We're doing well as we are, aren't we Xenthe?"

"No we're not!" He flung it off. "Mom, I don't wanna spend 500 years looking like a frickin' ten year old!"

"And I'm not about to let you lose a minute of your life, either!" She retorted.

"But Mom, think about it," he turned around on the couch to face her. "I'm supposed to live for 500 years. What's the big deal if I lose a year here and there? If Aunt B ages me until I look like a grown up then that's something like ten years I'll lose. Who cares! I don't wanna be a freak all my long life! You're gonna die before I turn a hundred and then what? I'll still look like a freaky ten year old kid but with no mother!"

"It would be more like twenty years Xenthe would lose." Ki corrected. "Not only in the next ten years will he be aging naturally, but supernaturally as Aunt B alters his very DNA."

"No way in hell!" She riled up. "I'm not lettin' my lil' boy lose twenty years of his life!"

"Mom, who cares if I live until I'm 480 years old?!" Xenthe snapped back. "I'm already gonna outlive Kevin and Looch, as they'll only live 200 or 300 years. Like I said, you're gonna die from old age and leave me before I turn 100 years old anyways."

The mother looked tearfully on son who stubbornly glared back.

"I DON'T wanna be the only kid in the tribe let alone the world, who never grows up." He said adamantly. "Peter Pan can have that honour, not me!"

Frightened, Stella turned my way with a haunted look in her eyes.

"B, I've lost my husband and my daughter. My lil' boy is the only thing I've got left. Promise me if you do this, I won't lose him too?"

"You won't." I shook my head. "I was thinking that today I'll age him by a year, so he'll look like an eleven year old. Then every six months I'll age him by six months, so his growth spurts won't be too obvious."

Her teary eyes swung back her son's way who looked excited about the idea.

"Please Mom, plleeaaassee...?" He whined. "I may be a freak but I don't wanna look like one."

"You're not a freak!" She scolded. "You're a special little boy who's gifted academically as well as musically."

"Mom, c'mon." He took hold of her hand. "You ain't gonna lose a ten year old boy but you're gonna gain an eleven year old son."

There was a long moment of silence as the human mother looked on her European Vampire son.

"Oh alright then!" She huffed. "Change my baby boy into a man if you must!"

Xenthe threw his small arms about her neck and gave her a hug.

"So, how do we do this?" Ki looked my way.

"Stand up please, Xenthe." I instructed.

The little boy obeyed and together we stood in the middle of the lounge room, facing the other. The human mother and Lokoti Werewolf watched in curiosity. I put my hands on his small shoulders and then to Stella's amazement, I went into phase first then put the little boy into phase with me.

At first we looked like two bright, see-through versions of ourselves, like ghosts. I'd converted our biological bodies into light waves and now I had to concentrate harder. Xenthe's light waves increased in brightness as I altered his particles. Stella gasped as she watched her ghost-like son's height increase by a couple of centimetres before I took us out of phase. When we reformed into our solid shapes once more, his pyjamas looked smaller on him.

"Wow...!" He gushed. "That felt all warm and tingly, like I was floating in mid air!"

But no sooner than the words left his lips, he crumpled to the floor in pain. The poor boy howled in agony as he curled up in a foetal position. In alarm, Stella knelt by his side and tried to help him.

"It's growing pains." Ki told her. "Remember the kind of cramps in your arms or legs you had when you were a little? Now times it by fifty in a half necrotized body whose sole principal is never changing."

"He's not dying, is he?" Stella panicked.

"Not at all," our Medicine Man rolled up his sleeve. "His heart beat and blood pressure aren't faltering. In fact, they're a little stronger right now from the energy Aunt B infused him with."

Then the Lokoti Werewolf bit into his wrist and lowered the wound to the European Vampire's lips. As soon as Xenthe started to drink, his cries lessened as his body began to relax. We could clearly see his pain relief.

"He isn't gonna feel this kinda agony every time you age him, is he?" She asked warily.

"Unfortunately, yes." Ki said matter-of-factly. "Growing pains can't be escaped, when one's body grows up naturally or supernaturally."

*****

Now that Xenthe was growing up his mood greatly improved. He didn't feel so isolated and it also motivated him to concentrate harder on controlling his bloodlust. Instead of just Ki or Stella experimenting with different juices, he'd help himself to the juicing machine and make his own concoctions.

One day when we all sat down to a lunch Declan had prepared, Xenthe poured himself a mysterious green drink from his thermos.

"What's that?" Soph gave a funny look.

"Carrot juice with broccoli, spinach, as well as a dash of Spirulina powder." He answered. "Spirulina is one of nature's wonder foods, as it's high in vitamins and minerals."

"It is indeed." Ki smiled proudly. "Well done Xenthe, you've certainly been doing your homework. I sometimes prescribe Spirulina to some of my patients instead of multivitamins."

"Eew, it looks gross!" Soph turned up her nose.

Looch showed her support by picking up the drink and sniffing it, "Smells just like vegetable juice to me."

"Taste it," he offered.

So she did and looked pleasantly surprised afterwards, "It's not bad, it's kinda like a combination of seaweed and vegetable juice."

Kevin joined his best friends by picking up the glass to sniff it and taste, too.

"OK everybody," Declan interrupted. "Let's not deprive the Vampire of his lunch and get on with ours."

Stella gave her son's hair an affectionate ruffle before she recommenced eating.

With Xenthe's steady diet of animal blood once a week then either milk or juice every other day, his pallor improved slightly. His skin still looked as white as chalk but his features weren't so gaunt. What little organs left in his body that worked, appreciated the vitamins and minerals in the juice or milk. Then his European Vampire DNA thrived on fresh animal blood. However, if someone injured themselves when he was around and their blood became exposed, he would quickly leave to resist temptation.

One day a Lokoti kid fell off his hover-board while performing tricks outside the General Store and his jeans were torn as his knees bled. Xenthe's fangs extended as his faded blue eyes turned completely white. He looked like he was about to pounce on the injured human, when suddenly he spun around and ran off. He bolted out of the community centre and straight into the woods.

Kevin and Looch ran after him to make sure he was alright, to find him squatting behind a tree, feeding on Snowshoe Hare he'd caught.

The twelve year old looked up embarrassed, with the dead and drained small, furry animal in his trembling hands.

But Kevin said exactly the right thing, "Man you're fast! I've never been able to catch one of those little bastards. What do they taste like?"

"Er, like rabbit I guess." Xenthe passed the dead animal his way.

Next, Kevin expanded into his Lokoti Werewolf body to use his claws and teeth to finish off the animal. However, he politely tore off a hind leg to pass to Looch. She extended her teeth and nails to eat the offering.

"Mmm, I like sharing my prey with you, Xenthe." She spoke with her mouthful. "At least when you drain the body first, there's less blood to clean off."

The European Vampire let out a laugh in relief for having two Werewolves as his best friends.

But it wasn't until Xenthe was fifteen that he was permitted by the pack as well as the Tribal Elders, to attend public school with Kevin and Looch.

The Elders which included two members of the pack, convened in the meeting hall to discuss this and I was invited for my input. Declan stayed home with the kids and kept my dinner warm in the oven, since the meeting was in the evening. Normally, the Council of Tribal Elders met on Sunday mornings, but if a topic arose that couldn't wait, they'd come together midweek to discuss it.

I walked into the large, decorated, wooden building where many of our tribe's festivities took place. Inside, I found a ring of fold up chairs where everyone was sitting, near the stage area. I took the seat next to Tyson as Ki sat on the other side of him. Naturally, the two Lokoti Werewolves were on the council being First of the pack as well as the tribe's Medicine Man.

"Aunt B," the elderly Feather nodded in acknowledgement, "thank you for coming."

"No problem." I sat back and crossed my legs. "We're here to talk about Xenthe attending school, right?"

"Among other things," Bobby smirked.

"Well, what do you think, Aunt B?" Tyson cut to the chase. "Is it safe to let a fifteen year old European Vampire attend public school with the humans?"

"I think so." I shrugged. "I don't have one of my warning feelings about it."

Ki said to the assembled council, "Aunt B's visions haven't been wrong yet."

"No they haven't." Tyson agreed. "The pack often draws on her counsel."

Feather looked around at the other Elders on the council, which were Bobby, Sun, Grace, Steve and Wind.

"We're in agreement," Sun smiled widely.

Next, Feather looked on the two Werewolves on the council, "Tyson and Ki?"

"We're in agreement," Ki nodded, "about trusting the Vampire's control over his bloodlust and the other matter."

"What other matter?" I wondered.

"What we also wanted to discuss tonight was you, Aunt B." Wind announced.

"Me?" I sat upright in surprise. "Er, has my bloodlust come under speculation lately?"

The eight members laughed at my reaction and how nervous I seemed.

Bobby began, "As you can see with the current Council of Tribal Elders, we're missing a member."

"Yeah," I sighed sadly, "Phil died in battle and you haven't found a replacement for him yet."

"As you know and especially by living in this tribe for over three centuries, usually we have three Lokoti Werewolves on the council." Steve reminded.

"Yup, that sounds familiar." I nodded along.

"We would like you to be the third Lokoti Werewolf to sit on the council." Sun smiled warmly.

"Huh?" I uttered in shock. "Me? Are you kidding?"

"Nope," Grace shook her head. "As you also know, the Lokoti Tribal Elders have a council of nine members. Three are Lokoti Werewolves, three are Seers and the other three are humans."

"Uh huh..." I looked around the circle, "...so you thought you'd kill two birds with one stone, by selecting a member who's both Seer and Lokoti Werewolf?"

"Bingo." Wind confirmed. "I'm a Seer and so is Grace, but there aren't any other humans in the tribe with this gift."

"Since your visions are never wrong, how can we overlook you?" Steve chuckled. "We need a third Werewolf and it's a bonus that you're also a Seer."

"What if I'm not wise or impartial?" I warned. "You want me to help guide this tribe and make judgements? I get in trouble by my husband for not looking up from my academic work and noticing life!"

This made the council members chuckle again at my husband's well-known temper.

Ki said sympathetically, "When is someone NOT in trouble with that cranky old European Werewolf?"

I tittered back, "Good point."

"Or he just likes having his 'Light Person' for a wife's complete attention so he can bask in your aura." Tyson said knowingly.

"You got that right." I rolled my eyes.

"Aunt B," the elderly Feather turned serious, "we're not expecting you to turn into a wise old prophet overnight. We're not asking you to just be the third Werewolf on the council, but we respect that you speak up when you see something's wrong. Your grandmother was the 'Light Person' who prepared the tribe for World War Three. Your mother was the 'Light Person' who protected our people after the War. We know your counsel in the past has helped the pack and many others over the years. We want to add your foresight to ours."

"Oh." I fidgeted nervously. "Um, are you sure you want me? I mean, I won't mind if you ask somebody else but just borrow me from time to time."

"Why can't we borrow you now?" Steve smiled patiently.

"And yes, we're sure about this." Bobby snickered.

"Also being a History Professor, you'll be able to help us teach the tribe's younger generations about our cultural history." Grace added on.

"Just say yes, Aunt B." Tyson jokingly ordered. "Then if your husband tries to boss you around being Second in the pack? You can boss him around outside of pack matters, because you'll be his Tribal Elder."

His suggestion got the reaction everyone was hoping for when I cried out ecstatically, "Yes!"

Everyone laughed again since Declan and I were famous for not only being the longest married couple in the tribe, but the most argumentative.

"So what now?" I enquired. "Do I need to do anything, to become a Tribal Elder?"

"Damn it, I left my hot coals at home that we make our new members walk across." Ki teased.

"I knew I should have brought my lasso to make our new member jump through hoops." Bobby joked.

"Do you mean if we're going to make you sit in a Sweat Lodge to go on a hallucinogenic journey, to contact our spirit guides? Or smoke a Peace Pipe? Not tonight, no." Wind giggled.

"But it will be your turn to bring coffee and cake to the next meeting this Sunday morning." Grace said. "We take turns with bringing refreshments to help our concentration, especially when we have a lot to discuss."

Then all of the Tribal Elders stood up and collected their coats or handbags.

"What, that's it?" I watched them get ready to leave.

"We get together every Sunday at 10 AM in the Meeting Hall." Sun announced. "Tonight was just a 'quickie' to discuss Xenthe and you."

Already, Ki was walking towards one of the exits, "It's dinner time and I'm starved!"

"Me too!" Tyson walked beside him. "Tania's made Chicken and Vegetable Stir Fry in Oyster Sauce."

"I'm glad to hear that she's following my recommendation about adding more greens to your meals." Ki patted him on the back.

"Following...? We've eaten steamed greens almost every night for the past month!" Tyson complained. "Soon, the tribe isn't gonna have to worry about the Vampire losing control of its bloodlust, it'll be me!"

As I walked out with the elderly women, I asked, "Tribal Elders also keep a record of the tribe's events over the years, don't we?"

"The Tribal Elders make sure records are kept, but we don't keep them." Sun explained. "The tribe's record keeper does that. But we'll go through everything at your first meeting as an Elder this Sunday."

"Cool." I smiled.

The elderly humans laughed at my youthful mode of discourse even though I was older than they were.

When I arrived home, I found my little girls sitting at the table. Looch was doing her homework, Soph was sketching fashion designs and Sues was drawing with crayons. In the kitchen, Declan had just finished stacking dinner's mess into the dishwasher and he smiled warmly upon my return.

"So how did the meeting with the Tribal Elders go?" He asked. "Are they gonna let the little fang head attend school again?"

I sat up on top of the bench which was my favourite place to sit when I was talking to my husband in his favoured domain, which was the kitchen.

"Yup," I confirmed then I looked over to Looch. "Next week, Xenthe will be catching the school bus with you and Kevin."

She looked up excitedly from her class assignment, "Really? Cool!"

"I'll give it to the little fanger, he's got a good handle on his bloodlust." He reluctantly admitted. "It's just a pity the rest of the world's Vampires can't do what a fifteen year old one can."

"Daddy..." Sues turned around in her seat to ask, "...what if we tried to train the world's Vampires to hunt animal and not human?"

"Ha!" Her father scoffed. "That's a hell of a lot of fang heads, Sues."

"Why are there more Vampires than Werewolves in the world?" Soph asked next.

"Well, one reason is because there aren't many female Werewolves born these days." He answered. "The other is because some Vampires hunt Werewolves, almost to extinction."

"Like when they came to attack us?" Looch asked, warily.

"But your devilishly handsome Daddy ate the ones who came to eat us." He joked to lighten the room again. "Chomp, chomp, chomp!"

Sues and Looch erupted into giggles but Soph rolled her eyes.

My husband shut the dishwasher door and turned to his wife, "Would you like your dinner now?"

"Sure." I agreed and I watched him take my plate out of the oven. "Declan?"

"B?" He didn't look my way as he opened the fridge next.

"Something else happened tonight," I began.

"Oh yeah?" He listened as he cut open my baked potato to put on a dollop of sour cream.

"Um, you know how I'm over three hundred years old and I'm a Lokoti Werewolf as well as a Light Person and my visions haven't been wrong?"

He still didn't look my way as he picked up the gravy boat to pour Dianne sauce over my rare steak. "Uh huh."

"Well, since there's only two Lokoti Werewolves on the council at the moment as well as only two Seers, the council has asked me to become a Tribal Elder."

This got his attention and finally he forgot about the food to turn around and give an incredulous look.

"The Lokoti Tribal Elders have asked you to join the council?" He asked. "You're going to be the ninth member as the third Lokoti Werewolf and third Seer?"

"Uh huh." I answered then I flinched as I expected some kind of sarcastic retort.

A huge grin broke out on his face, "My baby B is finally a Tribal Elder?"

"Huh?" I stared in surprise.

Next, he walked up and lifted me up from the bench and into his arms.

"My beautiful 'Light Person' is gonna light the way for the tribe?" He held me closely. "My gorgeous girl is gonna be a Tribal Elder so the whole tribe will listen to your visions? What the hell took the Elders so long to ask you?!"

"Declan, I was expecting some kind of smartass retort like, 'now we're in trouble'!" I laughed aloud.

"Hey kids," their father called, "your Dad is Second in the pack and now you're Mom is a Tribal Elder!"

Their reaction was immediate as they leapt up from the table to run into the kitchen.

"Yaaaayyy!"

My husband lowered me to the ground so I could be swamped by three sets of smaller arms. Laughingly, I hugged my kids back before Declan hugged the whole lot of us together. The girls squealed at getting squashed, but they didn't let go either.

"Does this mean we'll have more money for shopping?" Soph asked hopeful.

"Frickin' hell, Soph!" Looch cried out exasperated. "You and your shopping!"

"But Mummy's gonna be the youngest Tribal Elder." Sues said confused.

"Actually Sues," her father picked her up, "you're mother is gonna be the oldest person on the council."

Our littlest looked puzzled upon his youthful features before examining mine.

"But Aunt Feather looks really old and her hair is all white!" She argued.

"Appearances aren't everything." Looch pulled her into her arms next. "I mean look at you, you're five years old but people think you're nine or something."

"Oh yeah," she realized, which made us all chuckle.

"OK kids," their father clapped his hands together to recapture their attention, "your mother's dinner is going cold."

Instantly, our little Werewolves moved out of the way. Just as their bloodlust demanded fresh kill which meant the flesh had to be warm, the same went with our dinner. My husband carried over my hot plate to the table where I sat down and ate. I was soon joined by my daughters as they returned to their tasks at the table and then their father, as he carried over a cup of coffee.

The parents sat side by side, as one ate and the other drank and together they smiled on their children's work.

*****

I never told Declan about Xenthe and Sophia becoming a couple, because I sensed he was still holding himself back from pulverizing the teenaged Vampire just for being around his mate and young. I don't think he disliked Xenthe personally, but his DNA wanted to annihilate what it saw was his breed's greatest enemy. So if I told my husband that his second born may 'shack up' with someone as such, I wouldn't need a vision to know what would happen next.

Besides, whenever I saw Soph and Xenthe at social gatherings, I could see it would be some time yet that a romance would blossom. The European Vampire didn't seem partial to the mostly Lokoti Werewolf. With Sophia, she treated him with the indifference of her older sister's friend and nothing more. They did have a lot in common though, such as academic work and creativity. Soph didn't play an instrument but often we'd hear music playing on her Internet Radio while she sketched her fashion designs.

What I also came to realize was Xenthe could behave masterfully by hiding his true nature when he ventured off tribal lands or even his feelings in day to day life. It was over the years in the forms of small gifts or other offerings towards the prettiest of my daughters, his feelings became known. But he was skilled at keeping it from my mate, as he too didn't need a vision to know what Declan's reaction would be.

After several lengthy PD&M's in bed while the kids were asleep, Declan and I decided to surprise Looch on her 16th Birthday with a hover-car. It was second-hand but ran reliably. Our eldest was thrilled that she could drive herself to and from school now on, as well as give Kevin and Xenthe lifts.

The former 'grease monkey' which was my husband, spent many an afternoon teaching our first born the basics of mechanics. He taught her how to check the engine or other parts of the vehicle if it wouldn't start or if it broke down. Looch was an eager student too, her analytical mind was curious to see how the motor worked. Also with her independence, she'd rather fix the hover-car herself than call on someone else.

For Soph's 11th Birthday, we granted her wish by taking her on a shopping expedition in Anchorage to buy her more clothes. Then it ended up just being me who took her, as Declan and Looch came up with the excuse that it was father and daughter mechanic day. My eldest preferred to get dirty in the garage than go clothes shopping. Sues was going to come with us, until another fight with Soph before we left the house resulted in our youngest running into her bedroom in tears.

"What did you say to her now?" Her father asked wearily.

"She wanted to wear my pink blouse but I said no coz she'd stretch it since she's fatter than me." Soph said coolly.

"She's not fatter, she's just more muscled!" He repeated his old saying. Then he carried his crying youngest downstairs with him. "C'mon Sues, you're spared the mundane task of clothes shopping. You can spend the day with us in the garage. Hell, I'll even make pizza for lunch. You love pizza, right?"

"Yes Daddy," she wiped her wet face on his t-shirt.

For Sues' 6th Birthday, we held a large party for her in the garden. Since she had to study at home while her sisters and cousins went to school, we made her birthday a huge social event. Not only did the Wisetail's and Creillaic's came over, but so did the Riverclaw's, the Lightfoot's, the Elm's, the Sabre's and the Shallow Water's.

Everyone brought a dish and a bottle of soda to share, as well as presents. I could tell Sues felt so humbled by everybody's kindness that half the time she couldn't speak, she giggled instead. Declan and I hosted the children's party games such as Pass the Parcel or Musical Chairs. Not only did the younger kids play, but the older ones joined in, like Looch, Kevin and Xenthe.

The humans enjoyed watching the half European Werewolf, the Lokoti Werewolf and the European Vampire, use their supernatural abilities on each other for Musical Chairs. When it was just down to two, the European Vampire easily won one with his greater speed. Since Looch was that little bit faster than Kevin being part European Werewolf, she scored the second chair. To much laughter, Kevin used his supernatural strength to pick up Xenthe, chair and all, and tried to tip him off!

"No deal Kevin, you're out." Declan laughed.

We also bought a piñata for the younger children to take turns hitting when blindfolded. Whereas the human youngsters had difficulty breaking it open, with Sues' strength one whack was all it took to make the lollies fall out. Gleefully, she shared them out with the other children and even ran over to a couple of the adults to give them some too.

"That little girl has a heart of gold." Wendy smiled, after Sues gave her and her husband some lollies before running off to deliver more.

“She must get it exclusively from her mother.” Walt teased.

“Shut up Walt,” my husband pretended to be offended. “This is the last time that I’m feeding you.”

We three laughed at the European Werewolf as I happily leaned into his side. Contentedly, he rested his arm about my shoulders before looking down into my face. His bright blue eyes met and held my dark blue ones.

“Did I tell you how pretty you look today, Mrs. Sabre?” He said softly.

“In unan, Mr. Sabre.” I replied. “Always and forever.”

Wendy watched us before enquiring, “In unan, I’ve heard you guys say that a couple of times now but what does it mean?”

“It’s Lokoti for ‘I love you’.” He announced.

“‘In unan’ means ‘in my heart’ in the old language,” I added on. “So if somebody’s in your heart -”

“- then you love them.” Declan finished for me.

“My gosh, you guys are soppy,” she taunted.

“Soppy? Did you just say, soppy?” He riled up. “Wendy, I’m a European Werewolf and trust me, we ain’t soppy! That’s it, I’m not feeding you again either.”

The Wisetail’s laughed as I planted a kiss on his reddening cheek.

Just then the garden darkened as a large, grey cloud covered up the sun. A chilly wind followed it which made Wendy stand closer to Walt to share his body heat. He put his arm about his mate as we watched our young, run around screaming in the midst of some kind of game or other.

Nobody seemed to mind the momentary absence of sunlight, as everybody happily carried on. But I took this as a sign because an all-knowing feeling made my stomach tighten. I looked up at the clouds to see how long it would take to pass, before the sun could peek through. I needed to see if this sign was a warning or just an indication of something to come? Within a minute sunshine reappeared on the other side.

I let out a sigh of relief, as I didn’t take the sign as something ominous. As I stared up into the sky, I saw how quickly more clouds were moving across the sky with the sun being blotted out a couple more times. I knew something big was coming and by the speed of the wind, it would happen soon.

It was a couple of days later when everybody found out that I was right again.

~~~~~~
~~~~~~

SSIT Report on The Separate Species of Vampires

INTRODUCTION

Of all the legends of Shape Shifters in the world, Vampires have one of the longest and most varied history.

When the Supernatural Scientific Investigative Team began to look into Vampire legends of Eastern Europe, the first species discovered was the European Vampire. Then as the investigation deepened, more and more legends, superstitions and stories based on historical and/or cultural fact of this type of Shape Shifter became known. It became apparent that Vampires differ just as humans around the globe do. However, a common factor arose which indicated Vampires are Shape Shifters - in their transition from human to 'other'.

In the case of the different breeds of Werewolves, their Shape Shifter DNA could be linked to a genetic forefather, 'The First Werewolf', which was a hot-blooded predator located in the Mesozoic Age. As discussed in the introduction of the SSIT Report on the Different Breeds of Werewolves, the 'First Werewolf' had similar physical characteristics to its prehistoric cousins such as the Raptor. However the true origins of Vampire DNA are much harder to track, due to the range of cultural differences such as 'the cause' of becoming a Vampire.

Vampire DNA changes the living body to a state of near death; or scientifically put, Vampires enter a kind of biological 'stasis' which shuts down many of their normal functions. This permanent paralysis of organs may heighten certain physical abilities, but it will also decrease others to the point of necrotizing flesh. Some Vampires change from a human appearance to their other form at will, when engaged in hunting or combat. With other species, undergo a complete transformation that it's sometimes difficult to look human once more.

Interestingly, some Vampires share similar physical traits as Werewolves. Another commonality is the 'bloodlust', which is the overpowering need to drink fresh blood or eat fresh kill. Then of course, there is the allergy to silver, which is apparent in all Shape Shifters.

Many species of Vampire are also allergic to garlic. This is because the unique combination of vitamins, minerals and other chemicals found in this organic product, results in a side effect of thinning the blood. Vampires encounter great difficulty regulating their blood, since many of their internal organs that normally do this in a human body, are either no longer functioning or functioning properly. Due to this, imbibing garlic or any kind of drug or plant, which affects the thickening or the thinning of blood, is detrimental to a species whose health is solely based on the principle of never changing. However, if a Vampire is poisoned by garlic or another plant or drug, they can regenerate by drinking blood.

By imbibing the life force of their chosen prey, it became apparent that they take on many of their victims physical traits. What needs further investigating by SSIT, is that if a European Vampire should feed on a human with ESP; they also develop this paranormal ability. Werewolves as well as Vampires can differentiate a psychic from a non-psychic human, by their differing bio-electromagnetic field, which is also called their aura. It is by honing in on the human with the aura, they hunt psychics for their uncanny talent.

The Vampire's urge to feed on fresh blood or other biological matter is similar to the Werewolf's bloodlust. If a Werewolf should eat 'bad meat' i.e., flesh from a corpse which decomposition had begun, or even if the human is ill; this can affect the health of the creature. It's the same if a human ate meat which was infected by debilitating bacteria such as Salmonella. On this premise, Vampires must feed on fresh blood from a healthy being as it can and does affect their health and therefore their longevity.

Much of the Western world term Vampires as the 'undead', although doubtful to apply in the natural world, one can relegate this term loosely to particular Vampire species. Where some Vampire's organs undergo a change to become stronger, others became damaged and ergo useless. However, Vampires still have a heart rate, pulse and therefore breathe, which enables their bodily movements by transporting the blood to their muscles. But in the change to Vampire, the medical drawbacks are numerous, which in turn is responsible for their need to feed on fresh blood.

Another superstition about Vampires, which needs to be quashed is the notion that they are immortal. This is scientifically impossible due to the fact that not even the universe is immortal. With differing scientific groups such as NASA or otherwise, proving with their work in astronomy or physics on matter, anti-matter, dark matter, atoms and molecules, with The Big Bang as well as The Big Crunch, very little let alone biological matter can be deemed to be 'eternal'.

Many species of Vampire have a supernaturally long existence due to a successful feeding pattern. But what became obvious was that for many, if their feeding pattern was not successful then neither was the longevity of the subject. This can be said for any biological creature in the natural world. If the living conditions are plentiful in providing for the life form, then the life form will flourish. However, if food or other necessary elements to survive are not available, then the life form may either change to adapt to their environmental conditions or perish.

Vampires maintain an ambient body temperature, depending on their environmental conditions. This means that they do not sweat from hot weather nor do they suffer from hypothermia. With this said, Vampires still encounter physical injury from frost bite. Because of this, Vampires are very wary of what they experience as they must be careful not to damage their flesh even if they do not always feel pain.

By their bodies existing in a semi-stasis, they may not age; however, another drawback to this is they encounter a great deal of difficulty in healing from physical injury. Vampires may heal themselves after physical harm by drinking either human or Werewolf blood, with the latter their preferred choice. Because of this, particular species such as the European Vampire, have extensively hunted Werewolves - primarily the European Werewolf. When they drink from this other supernatural creature, they take on their physical attributes such as their greater strength and their powerful regenerative ability for up to seven days.

With this said, the same is applied to Vampires drinking human blood. By drinking from a healthy human then the Vampire is able to replenish its protein, vitamins, minerals, sugar-level, white cell count, red cell count and anti-bodies. However, should the Vampire drink blood from a decomposing body or a human with an illness, this can severely weaken them and in some cases lead to their demise.

Another myth in popular culture of Vampires being allergic to sunlight needs to be re-examined. Since they must be continually hydrated by drinking fresh blood, they are photosensitive to bright light and in particular Ultraviolet rays. Humans encounter sunburn every day and from this exposure, they heal by their skin cells reproducing to replace the damaged ones. But because Vampires do not age, their skin is also in stasis and unable to repair itself. They will not turn to dust from exposure to sunlight, but they cannot heal from sunburn unless they drink blood.

By examining the separate species of Vampire, SSIT barely scratched the surface of this global phenomenon. The subjects in this report, shows just how polymorphic this supernatural creature can be. Each species which was investigated, differed physically by appearance, dietary requirements, longevity and living conditions. Another important note was the different causes of how humans or even other biological life forms could be turned into a 'Vampire'. Due to this, the true origin of 'Vampire' cannot be traced to one pure source.

On a humorous note, from a brush over the subject of Vampirism in Wikipedia, there are people in the Balkans who believe and even documented that they have Vampire Pumpkins and/or Watermelons. The symptoms are trembling, growling and 'blood' appearing on the epidermis of the fruit or vegetable. Apparently there are two ways this fruit and vegetable can become a Vampire. The first - if the fruit or vegetable is left outside on the night of a full moon and the second - if the fruit or vegetable is kept more than 10 days after Christmas (1). The first leans towards Werewolf legends with those affected by the lunar cycle. The second reason crosses into the subject of religion and how Vampires can sometimes be called 'The Damned'.

Religious implications on Vampires are minimal. Religion does not have any scientific effect on this species of Shape Shifter. In this scientist's view, religion is folklore itself and is generally used to either inspire false hope or try to explain the unexplainable; however, my partner on SSIT Elisha Worthall, agrees to disagree on this matter with her ever-present crucifix worn around her neck. Holy water and crucifixes to do not work to ward off the Vampires that SSIT investigated. On this note, Vampires can certainly attack human religious figures as well as freely enter a church, and set foot on sacred or consecrated ground. When SSIT investigated European Vampires for instance, we interviewed many members of the community in different Eastern European countries. We encountered several stories of how humans had escaped a Vampire attack by the use of crucifixes as well as by running into a church.

When we asked the witnesses to show us the crucifixes, we found that they were in jewellery form and made of silver. Then we asked to see the church which the subjects had found safety in, to find the buildings had unkempt cemeteries surrounding them. As the up-keep on the said cemetery was not immaculate, this caused the grass to grow long and flowering weeds to appear. Two of these weeds were not in fact weeds, but upon closer examination there were smatterings of flowering garlic stalks as well as 'Wolf's Bane', Arnica Montana that in certain locations in Europe grows abundantly. 'Wolf's Bane' can be used for human medicinal purposes but if used incorrectly, it can cause severe gastroenteritis and even internal bleeding of the intestinal tract (2). These symptoms can be deadly to Vampires and even injure a Werewolf. With this evidence in mind, SSIT concluded that the European Vampires broke off their pursuits, due to the fact silver or because of the flora which was present, when the humans sought sanctuary.

From examining the differing legends of Vampire, the idea that they can also change into animals such as a bat or a wolf, can be allocated to their cellular structure being members of the Shape Shifter 'family'. However, on this note, when investigating the European Vampire, North American Vampire, South American Vampire and West African Vampire, SSIT did not find any evidence that these Vampires could shift their shapes in such a way. The Vampires that SSIT investigated and gathered factual data and biological evidence, always retained a humanoid form. SSIT did another investigation on Human/Animal Shape Shifters from Africa, India, Asia and the Americas, on beings who were able to completely transform into native animals of similar size.

The example of the 'Vampire Pumpkin or Watermelon', of how a fruit or vegetable may have characteristics of a supernatural creature, goes to show how sometimes the term 'Vampire' can be used to define in psychoanalytical terms the 'other'. This is generally feared as it hovers on the boundaries of the known and the unknown universe. Indeed by investigating the global legends of the Vampire, SSIT encountered stories of when a human was simply born different i.e. were albino or had red hair and this was even called Vampire by some cultures. By allowing fear to breed by simply not being able to understand something, easily results in stories to tell children when you tuck them into bed at night. It is through investigation and collecting facts that the truth can be taught instead.

EUROPEAN VAMPIRE

~Physical Characteristics~

WARNING – This species of Vampire has poisonous fangs which can kill humans.

When a European Vampire changes from human to their supernatural form, their eyes turn completely white and their upper canine teeth become long and sharp like the fangs on a snake. This species of Vampire has venom that is secreted by the fangs which can kill humans and paralyse Werewolves. The nails on the European Vampire's hands can become longer and sharper, although not as strong as claws on other supernatural beings. This means they can pierce human tissue; however, they may break on harder substances like clothing such as denim or leather.

The strength of a European Vampire is ten times that of a human. They have supernaturally fast reflexes, which can be measured at the same rate as the speed of sound. However, they are unable to maintain this speed by running long distances, but are able to use this by jumping heights equivalent to four story buildings.

This species' lifespan is one of the longest in the supernatural world, up to 500 years old. It was told when interviewing one European Vampire subject that there was a member of his species surpassing his 600th birthday, although our investigators were unable to contact, meet and examine this individual. It was explained that he was able to obtain his great age from successfully hunting to prolong his strength and regenerative ability. However, if a European Vampire cannot feed on fresh blood at least once a week, then their metabolic system, strength and life expectancy fails.

They also have an excellent sense of smell. This species can smell a Werewolf within a 100 km radius and track it with a 99.9% success rate. They advise it is by the potent pheromones the Werewolf releases. Although European Vampires are severely allergic to silver, they often use silver coated weapons when hunting their favoured source of nourishment.

European Vampires appear to exist precariously on a double-edged sword, as their supernatural state can bring many benefits but just as many downfalls. As their bodies enter a form of biological stasis, they do not age and can maintain the same appearance for all of their existence. To some, this can be a vain benefit; however, the medical repercussions are plentiful. As mentioned previously, Vampires do breathe and they have a heartbeat which in turn moves the blood around their bodies to ensure motor function. However, from the almost suspended state their bodies exist in, their heart beat dramatically decreases, which means European Vampires encounter difficulty with strenuous physical activity. On this note, this species is required to spend a significant portion of their time slumbering to conserve their energy.

The idea of Vampires turning to dust from a stake to the heart; may be attributed to a European Vampire's rapid decomposition when it can be clinically called dead. As their bodies were partially shut down from the moment they were turned, their rate of decay is rapid with a drying effect. Even their skeletons are broken down to basic components in minimal time with only a biological 'ash' left. The full rate of decomposition occurs in seven days, which means an autopsy on this species must happen immediately from the time of death. This was noted when SSIT attempted to study a decapitated body. This mode of murder was a common one, to ensure the Vampire could not regenerate by imbibing blood.

~History~

The history of the European Vampire is long and they can be found in ancient texts spanning across several European and Middle Eastern countries. Tales of gods, demons and monsters who drank blood, creep out of ancient mythology and into local lore today. The bloodlust then as it does now, comes in differing shapes and sizes by its feeding and/or hunting pattern. Logically speaking, it's not surprising to see how European Vampires have evolved just as humans have, since they are a life form too, albeit a supernatural one.

The medieval ages and then the Witch Hunts witnessed two of the greatest upheavals for European Vampires. This parasitic hunter commonly preyed upon the rich to pay their way through the ages. Not only did hunting the wealthy fill their purses; however, the rich were considered safer to drink, with greater hygiene and less sickness than the poorer classes. But during the unrest, European Vampires had to hide their supernatural profiles to avoid being destroyed by religious authorities.

During the medieval times in the mountainous areas of Eastern Europe, there were many battles with European Werewolves. The wars were caused from the Vampires hunting the Werewolves to excess, with the volatile beasts rebelling. The battles became so public that it caught the attention of both the Roman and the Orthodox Churches, who were the predominant authorities. As the number of human victims caught in the crossfire continued to grow, church-empowered Knights, Sheriffs and other Noblemen became involved. Since there were too many witnesses, the Vampires slipped into secrecy and continued to hunt on the sly.

It was during the Witch Hunts that European Vampires began to prey upon humans with ESP. At first they were entranced by their auras which were caused by their different bio-electromagnetic fields. However, as soon as Vampires learned that the humans had telepathic, telekinetic, pyrokinetic gifts or who could 'see' into the past or future; they were put on the menu. Not only did Witches have to hide from Church Inquisitors, they also had to defend themselves against Vampires who mercilessly hunted them. The Witches then created protective 'spell bags' made from silver charms, garlic and 'Wolf's Bane' to keep the predators away, which also ended up keeping the wolves at bay. Werewolves are not allergic to garlic but 'Wolf's Bane' can make them ill, and then there is their severe allergy to silver.

By feeding on those with ESP, European Vampires were able to absorb many of their psychic abilities. Symbiogenesis theory is applied to microscopic organisms which imbibe other cells through ingestion which then becomes part of the larger cell's working machinery (3). Normally this isn't seen in animals as large as mammals, but Vampires are an example of this behaviour. It's conjectured that this is how the fable of Vampires charming their victims eventuated. By adapting their new psychic prowess to their hunting pattern, they were able to seduce their victims into either being led back to the European Vampire's coven to be fed on; or hypnotize them into blindly following their will for other purposes.

~Reproduction/Mating Habits~

European Vampires cannot reproduce by sexual means due to the fact that their reproductive organs are shut down during the transformation into Vampire. Sperm production in males ceases as do the ovaries in a female; therefore this species reproduce by infecting others with their blood.

When a European Vampire changes a human, the transformation can take anywhere between 1 - 7 days, depending on the amount of Vampire blood that was transferred. If the change was done deliberately, the transformation usually takes 24 hours and the new need to feed on blood is immediate once completed.

However, there have been instances in the past where a human may inadvertently be turned into a European Vampire by accidental contamination. This can occur if Vampire blood infects a cut or another injury on the human, similar to contamination by HIV. When this happens, the transformation can take up to 7 days, with the mutation a slow and painful process. With this example, often the human may not realize until it's too late and the majority of their bodily functions have been either necrotized or transformed.

On this note, when the European Vampire or its' coven discover what's happened, usually the accidental Vampire is destroyed. This species are exceptionally choosy whom they change due to the fact that they don't live alone. When a European Vampire transforms a human, it's to create a companion in their usually youthful form. A candidate is chosen by appearance, intelligence, wealth or other attributes. Then they are inducted where in most instances it could be the entire coven which share blood to transform them.

SOUTH AMERICAN VAMPIRE

~Physical Characteristics~

When a South American Vampire changes from human to other, their eyes turn completely red with their black pupils disappearing. All of their teeth become pointed and sharp and look similar to a piranha. This species of Vampire does not produce venom, however they rely on their teeth, nails and speed. The nails on the South American Vampire's hands become long and sharp like small knives and are the strongest nails of all the species SSIT encountered.

The strength of a South American Vampire is ten times that of a human. Like their European cousins, they have supernaturally fast reflexes, which can be measured at the same rate as the speed of sound. However, South American

Vampires are able to maintain this speed by running long distances, but they cannot jump the same heights a European Vampire can.

This species longevity may reach 400 years if they are successful in hunting. If they cannot feed on fresh blood at least once every 5 days, then their metabolic system, strength and life expectancy fails. Using their ability to take extremely long breaths, they can successfully hunt underwater. By utilizing their multiple sharp teeth, they aren't averse to masticating the flesh of their victims to squeeze out more blood. It is because of this that many humans who are dragged from rivers such as the Amazon, are accounted to have been the victims of a piranha attack instead.

South American Vampires are extremely sensitive to the cold, and are the most susceptible to frost bite. Only once did SSIT hear of an instance where three South American Vampires ventured into a cold habitat, when they came to hunt the Lokoti Werewolves in Alaska. It was said this occurred during the summer, with the long hours of daylight which warmed temperatures. Instead, this species prefer the hot jungles or other regions where it does not snow, in South America.

On this note, it's not uncommon to find South American Vampires in Mexico either. Those who reside in this country often prey upon animals to avoid detection and therefore destruction by humans. Domestic live stock, such as goats are chosen for their accessibility and then the El Chupacabra aka 'the Mexican Goat Sucker', is blamed instead.

~History~

With the invasion and subsequent destruction of the Aztecs, Mayan, Incan and other South American cultures by the Spanish Conquistadores; it is difficult to trace the history of the South American Vampire past this period. Therefore, SSIT could not create an accurate timeline, tracking the evolution or distribution of this supernatural creature before the 15th Century. Therefore, the history of this species will begin at the end of the Aztec reign.

What happened to the Aztecs by the Spanish Conquistadores is a horrific chapter of history. Coupled with stories of how the Aztecs lived, fought and performed their religious ceremonies; the bloodied tales unsurprisingly lead us towards the South American Vampire's feeding pattern. A common practice of the Aztecs was to maim their opponent in battle, capture them and later use them in rituals. Aztec Priests would cut open the human sacrifices and pull out their organs, which would become apart of the ceremony and even, part of the ceremonial costume such as wearing the intestines around the neck (4). With this practice, it's little wonder that some of these Priests were South American Vampires.

After the decimation of the Aztecs, three South American Vampires migrated north. SSIT was told by local historians that when the Spanish put an end to the human sacrificial ceremonies, the three Aztec Priests decided to depart for new hunting grounds. The small coven travelled up through the United States, feeding on several Native American Tribes along the way, before reaching Canada where they heard of the Lokoti Werewolves.

The coven hunted for the Lokoti Tribe in the vast Alaska Range. The Tribal Elders shared their oral history with SSIT of when the South American Vampires attacked. It was a bloody battle with high casualties, with the South American Vampires ultimately destroyed by the stronger Lokoti Werewolves. However, the coven managed to kill several humans and members of the pack with their greater speed and knife-like nails, before they met their demise.

During the Spanish invasion, this species retreated from the cities to hide and hunt in the jungles or remote areas. By slipping into obscurity, they were able to continue to feed on human, albeit in significantly lesser numbers. Today, local authorities continue to account the victims as dying in 'animal attacks'. However, local Shaman in the smaller towns, pass on the history of the South American Vampire to younger generations in an effort to warn them.

~Reproduction/Mating Habits~

South American Vampires cannot sexually reproduce but instead create more of their kind by sharing their blood with the chosen.

If there's an accidental turning of a human who becomes infected, then the new Vampire is destroyed. This species are territorial and either lives alone or in small covens up to three Vampires but no more, as they do not like to share their hunting grounds. They prefer not to mingle with other covens like European Vampires do, and disagreements are 'settled' using their teeth and nails.

Whereas European Vampires prefer to live in towns and cities, South American Vampires are the exact opposite. They are by no means treated as 'the poor relation' but instead they receive the treatment of 'steer clear'. They may not be seen as 'refined' as their European cousins since they prefer the outdoors to hunt, they're not interested in intellect, nor are they choosy over who they feed on. However, they are extremely selective on whom they turn, and it's not uncommon for their kind to become dissatisfied with a new Vampire and killing/feeding on them instead.

NORTH AMERICAN VAMPIRE

~Physical Characteristics~

WARNING – This species of Vampire has poisonous fangs which can paralyse humans.

When they change from human to Vampire, their eyes glow and appear red on the outside of their irises, with yellow in the middle. Also, their foreheads become pronounced giving this species along with their glowing reddish eyes, a more 'demonic' appearance. Their upper canine teeth become long and sharp like the fangs on a snake. The venom is secreted by the fangs, which can paralyse humans for up to 3 days – if they survive an attack. The nails on the Vampire's hands become longer and sharper.

The strength of a North American Vampire is fifteen times that of a human and they are the strongest of the species investigated by SSIT. They have lightening fast reflexes, although they are not as fast as European or South American Vampires. They can run up to speeds of 360 km/h in short bursts and cannot jump as high as their European 'cousins'.

Their longevity is 300 years and it's believed their life span is shorter than the other species because of their faster metabolic rate, which attributes to their greater strength. South American Vampires need to hunt every third day to survive. However, after drinking from another Vampire or a Werewolf, 7 days can pass before they have to hunt again. It's not uncommon that this species will hunt their own kind, or cannibalize their own coven.

North American Vampires can perform strenuous physical activity with ease. With their bloodlust, they relish killing their victims in as a violent way as possible. Unlike the European variety that use cunning and covert tactics when hunting; they prefer a 'smash and grab' approach. Often, news reports of highway car-jacking with the vehicles destroyed and the owners missing can be attributed to their destructive nature.

~History~

The North American Vampire is an excellent example how polymorphic Vampire DNA can be; as this species is the result of a cross-contamination between the European and South American Vampire. This mongrel owes its history as well as its physical characteristics to its genetic 'forefathers'. But due to their nomadic culture, it's hard to pinpoint exactly how this genetic transference took place.

What SSIT has been able to conclude though, is this species did not exist prior to the 15th Century. With the advent of Christopher Columbus 'discovering' America and the subsequent invasion by European settlers, amidst this cross-cultural foray, was a coven of European Vampires. It's believed they came to the 'new world' to find fresh hunting grounds. Sometime during this period, their blood was mixed with a South American Vampire's, which incubated in a human and henceforth created the first North American Vampire.

Using elements of human history, as well as information obtained from an interview with a European Vampire; SSIT attempted to make a juxtaposition how this cross-contamination occurred.

The coven of European Vampires settled in the state which is now called Texas. Then, parts of this land were laid claim upon by Mexico. The territorial South American Vampires, who lived there, would have seen this geography as their hunting grounds. The South American Vampires would have fought the European Vampires and in this violent altercation, an unlucky human witness was pulled into the battle. The subsequent contamination by both Vampires occurred during the bloodshed.

To reconfirm, this is only conjecture however, several facts lend credence to this theory. Firstly, was the interview with the European Vampire subject who confirmed the story of a coven which departed for the 'Colonies', but only two survivors came back. They were granted sanctuary on their return because they sold an important piece of information; the existence of South American Vampires. With this knowledge, the 'Colonies' which eventually became the United States of America, was avoided by the European covens for over two centuries. It was not until the borders defining California, Texas and Mexico developed that European Vampires came to this country again.

When they did, they were shocked to discover the existence of the North American Vampire. Then to their horror, their refined sense of smell confirmed it was part of their DNA which had created them. Several European Vampire covens attempted to wipe out the 'accidental vampire'; however, with the North American Vampire's strength, the annihilation was unsuccessful.

~Reproduction/Mating Habits~

North American Vampires reproduce by sharing their blood with the chosen. However, they are the most violent of all of the species and prefer to hunt using brute force alone. Because of this, they are predominantly a male culture with very few covens containing a female.

When their kind attacks a woman, it's not in sexual assault as their sexual organs are no longer functioning. However, male North American Vampires derive sadistic pleasure from brutalizing their weaker victims. With this said, they often conflict with European Vampires where females are treated as equals, since their abilities match their male counterparts. If a male North American Vampire should try to feed on a female European Vampire; her coven will declare war and the majority of these battles are won by the Europeans due to their greater cunning, speed and use of silver swords.

Since North American Vampires are disorganized in their attacks, it's a frequent occurrence their human victims accidentally turn into more of their kind. When this happens, the new Vampire may begin a coven of their own. On a sadder note, there are other cases where the new Vampire may be so repelled by the experience, or if their loved ones were slaughtered; that they decide against becoming the monsters that made them. Then they painfully ignore their new bloodlust and starve to death after only three days.

WEST AFRICAN VAMPIRE

~Physical Characteristics~

As mentioned in the Introduction, most Vampires appear human but change form when fighting or feeding. However, there are a few species which may only attain a human appearance by feeding on this mammal. The West African Vampire is an example of this.

They are biologically a 'blank slate', that is to say they have a rare mutation of the albino gene, which has no skin pigmentation, hair or eye colouring. They literally are a translucent white because their bodies are missing the basic hormones which regulate their colouring. They have the unnerving appearance of a native to the continent of Africa, but with white afro hair, white eyes with small black pupils and a white, sometimes translucent skin.

This species is always male and as such, their feeding is concentrated on human males. The West African Vampire's choice of meal is not born from luxury; rather it is out of necessity. Not only do they drink the blood of the victim, but they take other fluids from the human body including from the pituitary gland. By ingesting the victim's blood, hormones and other bodily fluids, the West African Vampire adopts the colouring of its victim and sometimes other physical characteristics. This species is the most like a Shape Shifter, as its appearance can alter depending on the appearance of its meal.

On this note, West African Vampires choose human males to feed on because if it fed on a female and imbibed a large amount of oestrogen; it would greatly effect its shift in shape. Although SSIT cannot confirm if this could actually cause the male West African Vampire to change into a female, scientifically we can project it would be worse than a transsexual undergoing medical treatment to change gender.

West African Vampires do not have fangs or sharp elongated teeth, and its strength is five times that of a human being. Instead, this species uses the flora or fauna in its native area, such as specific plants or venom that has a paralysing effect, to make poisoned darts and stun their victims. When their prey has been neutralized, the West African Vampire then carries the human male to their hide-out/home to slowly drain them. The feeding is a drawn out process as they use many of the victim's bodily fluids to replenish its own. This is while the human is alive, paralysed and in subsequent agony throughout the entire time.

Their longevity is one of the shortest of the Vampire species, reaching 200 years old. Of course, this age can only be reached from successfully hunting to prolong its strength and regeneration. However, if a West African Vampire cannot feed at least once a month, then their metabolic system, strength and life expectancy fails.

~History~

One of the parts of the human body that the West African Vampire feeds on is the pituitary gland, which is responsible for growth hormones, prolactins and melanotrophins (5) to name a few. Since this is located in the brain, West African Vampires use tools such as straws carved out of wood or metal, to reach the gland. Because of this, they are often mistaken for another brain-feeding supernatural creature - the Zombie.

SSIT was investigating legends of the Zombie in Africa when we accidentally stumbled upon this unique species of Vampire. At first there were arguments within SSIT if this creature was in fact a Vampire, because its feeding was not just to exist on blood, but other bodily fluids. Also it could do something no other Vampire in the world can; it can procreate via sexual means. With these facts standing out, we postulated if the being was a Vampire? Or was it another kind of Shape Shifter? Or was it a new category of Zombie?

Some kinds of Zombie eat brain matter for the unique combination of chemicals and high concentrations of glucose. After further studying the West

African Vampire, it became apparent it did not eat the brain matter but drank from one part of the brain; the pituitary gland. As Elisha Worthall continued to secretly observe this species, she noted a pattern. The colouring of the West African Vampire changed the more it fed, from white to dark.

After our subject fed on an obese human male, Elisha Worthall noted that its physical form was heavier. This lasted for approximately one month before the creature had to feed again. After drinking its' next victim and absorbing their blood and other bodily fluids, its skin colouring and weight changed again. It became obvious that we were dealing with a Shape Shifter and not a Zombie. Once we confirmed this Shape Shifter's longevity relied on this feeding pattern, we officially categorized the life form as the West African Vampire.

This species has an undistinguished past, as it relies on living quietly in society to hide its supernatural status. Should their Vampiric nature be discovered, then it could cost their lives when their feeding is disrupted. In the past of living in huts in villages to today of houses in the suburbs; this species has mastered the role of the 'inconspicuous neighbour'. They are permanently situated on the western side of the continent and use their natural habitat to their advantage. They would not consider leaving the geography which provides them with the tools they need, because if they miss a monthly meal; they are threatened with not just starvation but by their unusual white colour returning. This would attract unwanted attention and make hunting much more difficult.

~Reproduction/Mating Habits~

West African Vampires lead double lives as outwardly they can appear completely normal. They can consume food, preferably in soup form, and they can marry and procreate with a human female. When they reproduce, they create one child which is always a son. Upon reaching puberty, the sons learn how to hunt from their father. In most cases, the wives are oblivious to their husbands and sons' supernatural status. However, should the wife find out and threaten exposure, she is eliminated.

When the son ‘turns’ during adolescence, their colouring begins to fade and illnesses such as blood disorders set in. To stop their skin, hair and eye colour from turning albino, the father takes the son hunting as soon as possible. The older West African Vampire trains the younger in an eating pattern they will need to sustain for the rest of its existence. During puberty, the child also learns how to hide their new dietary requirements from society.

Scientifically, you could relate the West African Vampire’s inability to sustain natural colouring or bodily functions, to the other species’ necrotized flesh or organs. Just as another Vampire encounters difficulty with sunburn, so does this species with their albino colouring. Whereas the other species drink blood to heal the damaged skin cells, the West African Vampire imbibes the hormones necessary to darken their skin to provide better protection. However, their kind like all the species profiled in this report, rely on the humans they consume to function in their day-to-day lives.

CONCLUSION

The West African Vampire was the most interesting species SSIT examined. They appear to embody not just Vampiric tendencies, but also incorporate elements of other supernatural creatures. This life form shares similarities with not only Zombies but with Egyptian Mummies.

When examining objectively the process of Mummification, this ritual can be seen as a human's attempt at longer life. Vampire bodies exist in a semi-stasis, which is the result of the necrotizing of the flesh or other organs. The Ancient Egyptian mummification process entails several of the deceased's organs such as the brain and heart, to be extracted as the body is dried with salt, to preserve the flesh. The extracted organs are not discarded but are kept close to the Mummy in Canopic jars, so the dead may use them in the 'After Life' (6).

One could speculate that the embalming ritual was the Ancient Egyptian's primitive attempt at Vampirism; the flesh is preserved with the no longer functioning organs removed. Depicted in Hollywood movies, it is the Mummy itself enacting the horrible deeds of taking the organs from the living to replace its own, so it may live once more. Although this is clearly fiction, it's remarkable how these relate to the West African Vampire. This species feeds not only on blood, but it also takes fluids from other parts of the body.

The Ancient Egyptian curse entails that if a tomb robber or archaeologist (which sometimes can be one and the same) unearths a Mummy or their burial treasure; certain death can come to the disturber. Historically, it is also interesting to note the run of 'bad luck' which has fallen on different members of archaeological digs. For example, the infamous unearthing of Tutankhamen.

One may argue that it was a set of circumstances which when lumped together, is simply called coincidence. But all of the cases that SSIT have investigated on supernatural topics such as phantom lights, haunted houses, Ley Lines, Stone Circles, ESP as well as the Bermuda Triangle; what's proven is sometimes a series of natural events combine to create a supernatural event. Aside from the stories of misfortune on the Tutankhamen dig, it's interesting to note that many Egyptians show a sizeable respect in leaving the ancients to rest in peace; which is the same wariness as Koreans may feel towards the mine fields that separate the North and South of their countries. Why tempt fate which may seal your own?

The cross-cultural similarities between Vampirism and other facets of the supernatural are so alike that the borders between them can be blurred. When one looks in hindsight at the fact European Vampires are not the strongest in the supernatural world, so their hunting pattern is traditionally nocturnal. This is not just for the fact that their skin has difficulty healing from sunburn, but because their food source aka humans, are usually slumbering during night-time. European Vampires use their agility by slipping unseen into the bedrooms, which saves the Vampire from physical exertion if they hunted them when they were awake. If the Vampire was unlucky, their feeding may be interrupted by another human walking in. The witness finds the Vampire lying on top so it will have a better angle to place their mouths on the jugular and hence; they're thought to be the Incubus or Succubus who are also called sex demons.

The different kinds of Asian Vampire also prefer to hunt at night. Since there were several subdivisions of this species, SSIT could not include them all in this report. Instead, we launched a separate investigation into this group. Just as Asia is divided into many cultural entities and languages, so too were its Vampires. To briefly mention, a common characteristic of some subspecies, was a hunting pattern which made them similar to the West African Vampire. Whereas the West African Vampire is all-male and hunted male-kind; many subspecies of Asian Vampires were all-female and hunted female-kind, including pregnant women or newborns.

Whilst we can analyse a Vampire's physiology and why it takes from others, the explanation of how Vampire DNA was first created, still eludes us. What caused this biological enigma on a world wide scale? How did the bloodlust develop in creatures whose supernatural longevity depends on the natural world? As a Vampire Bat must drink ten times its weight to survive; its paranormal cousins follow similar behaviour and feed on human.

FOOTNOTES

(1) http://en.wikipedia.org/wiki/Vampire_watermelon

(2) http://en.wikipedia.org/wiki/Arnica_montana

(3) Bormanis, Andre. Star Trek Science Logs. Pocket Books. New York. 1998. p. 82

(4) Burchell, David. Lecture Notes from History 1: The World Encircled 1450 - 1750. Faculty of Humanities and Social Sciences. University of Western Sydney, Nepean Campus. 1996

(5) http://en.wikipedia.org/wiki/Pituitary_gland

(6) Chisholm, Jane and Millard, Anne and Jackson, Ian. The Usborne Book Of The Ancient World. The Usborne Publishing Ltd. London. 1991. p. 18

~ The Circulate Series ~
By K.R. Smith

~ Book One: Circulate ~
Elisha Baker learns something new about herself when she attends the haunted international boarding school, Hamilton's College.

~ Book Two: Circulating ~
Elisha and her friends graduate from Hamilton's and the Circulate; to begin University and SSIT – Supernatural Scientific Investigative Team.

~ Book Three: Circulation ~
Armed with degrees, Elisha and her friends continue with SSIT. However adult life isn't as straightforward as they imagined, especially when an investigation into past lives interferes with a present romance.

~ Book Four: Progeny ~
Alexandrina and twin brother Bastian, grew up without a mother and a distant father. But it's to Jarrod's chagrin that his daughter mirrors his late wife, with the fact that she too is a Circulator.

~ Book Five: Ardor & Redolence ~
Arabella joins her grandmother on a SSIT case and meets Emanuel Riverclaw. Eventually they marry and create twins Julian and Jessica; a son who will become a Lokoti Werewolf like his father and a daughter who is a Circulator like her mother.

~ Book Six: Scent ~
At first the Last Circulator can't stand the tribe's most dangerous Werewolf, then Bianca and Declan's fiery arguments turn into something else.

~ Book Seven: Sororate ~
Claws come out in the marriage of the tribe's first female Lokoti Werewolf and the world's last European Werewolf; who spend their tumultuous years together traveling the world and through time.

~ Book Eight: Small Fry ~
Declan swore he wouldn't create anymore European Werewolves like himself, so his wife's new condition has his already hot blood boiling.

~ Book Nine: Alma ~
The new girl in Alma High School called Mali Roanne, suspects there's more than meets the eye with her Lokoti friends. However Mali is hiding a supernatural secret of her own.

~ Book Ten: Heterogeneous ~
In a space age, the different breeds of Werewolves are confined to Earth because of the influence of its one moon. But there's no such holds on the separate species of Vampires or even Human/ Animal Shape Shifters.

~ Book Eleven: Cohesion ~
Parents become grandparents when their children marry and procreate; with all of the different elements of the supernatural combining into one unusual family.

~ Book Twelve: Full Circle ~
The end is nigh, with answers as to why the futuristic Circulate technology never advanced past the 25th Century; because humankind doesn't.

To find out more on the series or the author please visit:

http://onaya3.blogspot.com/

http://www.facebook.com/Circulate.Series.KRSmith

~ References ~

Smith, K.R. SSIT Reports on the Different Breeds of Werewolf, Separate Species of Vampire and Human/Animal Shape Shifters By Elisha Worthall and Dr. Xavier Bell. K.R. Smith. Sydney. 2011

Heacox, Kim. In Denali, A Photographic Essay Of Denali National Park & Preserve Alaska. Companion Press. Santa Barbara. 2001

Alaska, A Scenic Wonderland. Arctic Circle Enterprises Inc. Terrell Publishing Co. Anchorage. 1995

Alaskan Wildlife. Arctic Circle Enterprises Inc. Terrell Publishing Co. Anchorage. 1995

The Macquarie Dictionary and Thesaurus New Budget Edition. Herron Publications. West End, QLD. 1991

Cooke, Kaz. Up The Duff, The Real Guide To Pregnancy. Penguin Books. Camberwell, Victoria. 1999

http://www.betterhealth.vic.gov.au/bhcv2/bhcarticles.nsf/pages/Milk_the_facts_and_fallacies

http://www.australianspirulina.com.au/spirulina/spirulina.html

http://www.babycenter.com/404_will-my-babys-eyes-stay-this-color_10009.bc

https://www.breastfeeding.asn.au/bf-info/your-baby-arrives/choosing-maternity-bra

http://en.wikipedia.org/wiki/Child_development_stages

http://en.wikipedia.org/wiki/Pregnancy

http://www.absak.com/library/average-annual-insolation-alaska

http://www.chugachschools.com/community_information/community_pages/fairbanks.html

www.ingramcontent.com/pod-product-compliance
Lightning Source LLC
Chambersburg PA
CBHW022014120726
47902CB00012B/22

* 9 7 8 0 6 4 6 9 3 2 8 5 9 *